PORNO

Irvine Welsh is the author of six previous works of
fiction, most recently *Glue*. He lives in London.

Porno

IRVINE WELSH

JONATHAN CAPE
LONDON

Published by Jonathan Cape 2002

2 4 6 8 10 9 7 5 3

Copyright © Irvine Welsh 2002

Irvine Welsh has asserted his right under the Copyright, Designs
and Patents Act 1988 to be identified as the author of this work

First published in Great Britain in 2002 by
Jonathan Cape
Random House, 20 Vauxhall Bridge Road,
London SW1V 2SA

Random House Australia (Pty) Limited
20 Alfred Street, Milsons Point, Sydney,
New South Wales 2061, Australia

Random House New Zealand Limited
18 Poland Road, Glenfield,
Auckland 10, New Zealand

Random House South Africa (Pty) Limited
Endulini, 5A Jubilee Road, Parktown 2193, South Africa

The Random House Group Limited Reg. No. 954009
www.randomhouse.co.uk

A CIP catalogue record for this book
is available from the British Library

ISBN 0 224 06181 X (Paperback)
ISBN 0 224 06296 4 (Hardback)

Papers used by Random House are natural,
recyclable products made from wood grown in sustainable forests;
the manufacturing processes conform to the environmental
regulations of the country of origin

Typeset by Palimpsest Book Production Limited
Polmont, Stirlingshire
Printed and bound in Great Britain by
Clays Ltd, St Ives plc

For:
Johny Brown
Janet Hay
Stan Keiltyka
John McCartney
Helen McCartney
Paul Reekie
Rosie Savin
Franck Sauzee

And remembering:
John Boyle

Contents

'Without cruelty there is no festival . . .'
— Nietzsche
Genealogy of Morals, Essay 2, Section 6

1

Stag

1

Scam # 18,732

Croxy, sweating from exertion rather than from drug abuse for once in his life, struggles up the stairs with the last box of records as I collapse on the bed, gaping through a numb depression at the cream woodchip walls. *This* is my new home. One poky room, fourteen foot by twelve, with an attached hallway, kitchen and bathroom. The room contains a built-in wardrobe with no doors, my bed, and just about space for two chairs and a table. I couldn't sit in here: prison would be better. I'd fucking well go back up to Edinburgh and swap Frank Begbie his cell for this frozen hovel.

In this confined space the stench of old fags from Croxy is suffocating. I've gone three weeks without a cigarette, but I've passive-smoked about thirty a day just from being in his proximity. — Thirsty work, eh, Simon? You coming down the Pepys for one? he asks, his enthusiasm seeming like a gloat, a calculated sneer at one Simon David Williamson's reduced circumstances.

On one level it would be sheer fucking folly to go down Mare Street, to the Pepys, so that they can all snicker, 'Back in Hackney, Simon?' but, aye, company is what's wanted. Ears must be bent. Steam has to be let off. Also, Croxy needs an airing. Trying to give up fags in his company is like trying to come off gear in a squat full of junkies.

— You're lucky to get this place, Croxy tells me, as he helps me unload the boxes. Lucky my fuckin arse. I lie down on the bed and the whole joint shakes as the express train to Liverpool Street hurtles through Hackney Downs station, which is about one foot outside the kitchen window.

Staying put in my state of mind is even less of an option than going out, so we're cagily descending the threadbare stairs, the carpet so worn that it's as hazardous as the side of a glacier. Outside, sleet falls and there's a dull aura of festive hangover everywhere, as we make our way towards Mare Street and the town hall. Croxy, with absolutely no sense of irony, is telling me that 'Hackney's a better manor than Islington, any roads. Islington's been facked for years.'

You can be a crustie for too long. He should be designing websites in Clerkenwell or Soho, rather than organising squats and parties in Hackney. I put the cunt wise to the ways of the world, not because it'll do him any good, but simply to stop nonsense like that filtering into the culture unchallenged. — No, it's a step backwards, I say, blowing on my hands, my fingers as pink as uncooked pork sausages. — For a twenty-five-year-old crustie, Hackney's fine. For an upwardly mobile thirty-six-year-old entrepreneur, I point at myself, it has to be Izzy. How can you give a class bit of fanny in a Soho bar an E8 address? What do you say when she asks, 'Where's the nearest Tube?'

— The overland's orlroight, he says, pointing up to the railway bridge beneath the turgid sky. A 38 bus chugs past, spewing its toxic carbon. These fucking London Transport cunts, they whinge on in their expensive pamphlets about the damage the car causes to the environment as they blooter in your respiratory system at will.

— It's no fucking awright, I snap, — it's shite. This place'll be the last part of north London ever to get the Tube. Even fuckin Bermondsey's got it now, for fuck sake. They can build it out tae that stupid fuckin circus tent, which nae cunt wants tae go tae, and they cannae do it here, that's well fucked.

Croxy's narrow face twitches in a sort of smile and he looks at me through those big, hollowed-out eyes. — You're throwing a right farkin moody today, aintcha, he tells me.

And it's true. So I do what I always do, drown my sorrows in drink, tell them all in the pub – Bernie, Mona, Billy, Candy, Stevie and Dee – that Hackney is just a temporary switch, don't expect to see me back on this manor full-time. No siree. Bigger plans, matey. And yes, I'm visiting the toilet frequently, but it's invariably to ingest rather than excrete.

Even as I'm shovelling it up my hooter, I realise the sad truth. Coke bores me, it bores us all. We're jaded cunts, in a scene we hate, a city we hate, pretending that we're at the centre of the universe, trashing ourselves with crap drugs to stave off the feeling that real life is happening somewhere else, aware that all we're doing is feeding that paranoia and disenchantment, yet somehow we're too apathetic to stop. Cause, sadly, there's nothing else of interest to stop for. On that note, rumours abound that Breeny's got a shitload of ching and a fair bit seems to be flying around already.

Suddenly it's tomorrow and we're in a flat somewhere hitting the pipe and Stevie's going on about how much it cost to purchase this load he's washing up and grudging crumpled notes come out as the stink of ammonia fills the air. Whenever that horrible pipe hits and blisters my lips, I feel sick and defeated until the toke sends me into another corner of the room: cold, iced, content, full of myself, talking shite, hatching plans to rule the world.

Then I'm out into the street. I didn't know that I was back in Islington, wandering around, until I saw the girl struggling with the map at the Green, trying to open it through her mittens, and reacted with a sleazy 'Lost, baby?' But the weeping tones of my voice, pregnant with emotion, expectation, and even loss, staggered me. I reeled back as much from the shock of this as from the hit of the purple tin I was holding. What the fuck was this? Who put this in his hand? How the fuck did I get here? Where are they all? There was a few moans and departures and I walked out into the cold rain and now . . .

The girl went as stiff as the stick of fleshy Blackpool rock in my troosers and snapped: — Fuck off . . . I'm not your baby . . .

— Sorry, doll, I brashly apologise.

— I'm not a doll either, she informs me.

— That depends on your standpoint, sweetheart. Try looking at it from my angle, I hear myself saying, like it's somebody else, and I see myself through her eyes: a smelly, dirty, purple-tinned jakey. But I've a job to do, birds to see, even a bit of money in the bank, better clothes than this stained and smelly fleece, this old woolly hat and gloves, so what the fuck's going on here, Simon?

— Piss off, creep! she says, turning away.

— I suppose we just got off oan the wrong foot. Never mind, the only way is up, eh?

— Fuck off, she shouts back over her shoulder.

Chicks, they can be a bit negative. I'm cursing my lack of knowledge with women. I've known a few, but my knob's always got in the way, come between me, them and something deeper.

I start to think back, attempting to recolonise my warped and overheated mind, stretching it out and breaking it down into units of perspective. It came to me that I'd actually been home, I'd got back to the new pad depressed that morning, having blown the last of the coke and started sweating and jerking off to a newspaper picture of Hillary Clinton in a power suit running for Senator of New York. I was giving her the old line about never mind those Jews, she was still a beautiful-looking woman and Monica wasn't in her league. Why, Bill needs his head looked at. Then we made love. After, as Hillary slept contentedly, I went next door to where Monica was waiting. Leith met Beverly Hills in a tasteful fuck of post-alienation. Then I got Hillary and Monica to get it on together while I watched. They'd resisted at first, but, obviously, I'd talked them round. Sitting back on that threadbare chair Croxy gave me, I relaxed to enjoy the show with a Havana cigar, well, a slim panatella.

A police car wails down Upper Street in a hunt for a slow civilian to maim as I shudder back into reality.

The bland but sordid nature of the fantasy causes me a bit of distress, but that's only because, I rationalise, that the comedown's making those ugly thoughts – that should be fleeting – stick around, clogging up the works, forcing you to engage with them. It's put me right off cocaine – not that I'll be able to afford any again for a while. Which is of no relevance at all when you're on it.

I'm on autopilot, but becoming slowly aware that I'm heading downhill from the Angel towards King's Cross now, inherently a sign of desperation if ever there was one. I hit the bookies in Pentonville Road to see if I can see any faces, but there's nobody I recognise. The scum turnover is high these days with vigilant polis everywhere around the Cross. They zoom about like powerboats through a swamp of sewage, only dispersing and displacing but never treating or erad- icating the toxic waste.

Then I see Tanya come in, looking skagged. Her shrunken face is ash white but her eyes burn in recognition. — Darlin . . . she puts her arms round me. There's a skinny wee guy in tow with her, who I realise is actually a bird. — This is Val, she says, in the archetypal nasal whine of the London skag-bag. — Haven't seen you down here in ages.

6

I wonder why. — Aye, I'm back in Hackney. Temporary, likes. Been hittin the pipe a bit this weekend, I explain, as a squad of crackpot niggers jerk in: tense, rangy and hostile. I wonder if any cunt bets in this place. I don't like the vibe so we exit, that weird, anaemic-looking Val cow and one of the black cunts sniping something at each other, and head to King's Cross station. Tanya whinges something about cigarettes and, aye, I'm trying to stop but no way, needs fuckin must n all and I'm checking my pocket for slummy. I buy some fags, lighting up down the Underground. This fat, puffy, officious white cunt in one of those new light-blue, gay-stormtrooper London Transport uniforms tells me to put the snout out. He points to a plaque on the wall which commemorates the scores of people who died in a fire caused by some doss cunt's throwaway tab. — Are you stupid? Don't you care about that?

Who the hell does this clown think he's talking to? — No, I don't fucking well care, the cunts deserved it. You take that fucking risk when you travel, I snap at him.

— I lost a good friend in that fire, you bastard! This irate tosser screams.

— He'd be a wanker if he had a scumbag like you as a mate, I shout, but at the same time I extinguish the snout as we pile down the escalator onto the line. Tanya's laughing and this Val bird's hysterical, she's doing her fucking nut.

We tube it up to Camden and Bernie's pad. — You girls shouldn't be hanging around King's Cross, I smile, knowing exactly why they are, — and certainly not with fuckin niggers, I tell them. — All they want tae dae is get a nice white bird and pimp her oot.

The Val lassie smiles at that, but Tanya gets all wide. — How can you say that? We're going to Bernie's. He's one of your best mates and he's black.

— Of course he is. I'm no talking about *me*, that's my brothers, my people. Practically all my mates here are black. I'm talking about *you*. They don't want tae pimp *me* oot. Mind you, fuckin Bernie would if he could get away wi it.

The wee Val boy-lady giggles again in a strangely fetching way as Tanya pouts sourly.

We get up to Bernie's flat, me forgetting for a second which block

7

on this miserable estate it's in, as it's very unusual to get here in the daylight hours. We disturb a solitary jakey, crashed out in his own piss at the bend in the stair. — Morning, I shout in brisk cheer, and the jake makes a noise between a groan and a growl. — That's easy for you to say, I quip, and the lassies smile at that.

Bernie's still up, just back from Stevie's himself. He's as wired as fuck, a gold and black mass of chains, teeth and soveys. I smell ammonia and sure enough he's got a pipe on the go in the kitchen and he gives me a hit. I take a long, hard suck, his large eyes full of manic encouragement as his lighter burns the rocks. As I hold and slowly exhale, I feel that dirty, smoky burn in my chest and a weakness in my legs, but I grip the edge of the worktop and enjoy the cool, frazzled high. I look at every crumb of bread, every drop of water in the aluminium sink in compulsive detail, which should sicken but doesn't, as the freeze bangs me, taking my psyche into a cold place in the room. Bernie's wasted no time, he's got another set rocked up in his dirty old spoon and he's laying a bed of ash on the foil and putting the rocks down as gently and tenderly as a parent might lower an infant into a cot. I hold the lighter in place and marvel at the controlled violence of his sucking. Bernie once told me he practised holding his breath underwater in the bath in order to increase his lung capacity. I look at the spoon, the paraphernalia, and think with a detached concern about how it all seems too reminiscent of my skag days. But fuck that; I'm older and wiser and skag's skag and crack's crack.

We're talking shite, ranting into each other's faces which are just inches apart, as we hold on to the worktops, like a couple of *Star Trek*'s top boys on the bridge when the enemy beams rock the ship.

Bernie's on about women, hoors who have fucked him around, ruined the poor cunt's life, and I'm doing the same. Then we go on to the cunts (masculine) who've fucked us over, and how they'll get theirs. Bernie and I have a mutual dislike of a guy called Clayton who used to be a friend of sorts but who's now burning every fucker down. Clayton's always a good target for us if there's a lull in the conversation. If adversaries like that didn't exist, you'd need to invent them, to give life some drama, some structure, some meaning. —

He grows sicker by the day, Bernie says, a strange pseudo-sincere concern in his voice, — sicker by the day, he repeats, tapping his head.

— Aye . . . that Carmel, is he still riding her? I ask. Always wanted to give her one.

— No, man, no, she fucked off to where she came from, Nottingham or some shit like thaa . . . he says in that drawl which lurches from Jamaica to north London, whistle-stopping at Brooklyn. Then he bares those choppers and says: — That's you, Scotsman, you see a new girl around on the street, you want to know what she's about, who her boyfriend is. Even when you have the nice wife and the child and the money. You can't help yourself.

— It's just being public-spirited. I try to maintain an interest in the community, that's all, I smile, looking next door where the lassies are sitting on the couch.

— The community . . . Bernie laughs and repeats, — it is good to maintain interest in the community . . .

And he's back at the washing-up again. — Keep on rocking in the free world, I chortle, heading next door.

As I head through, I note that Tanya's scratching at her arms through her top, obviously going into smack withdrawal, and as if by some ghostly transmission my own eye starts to shiver. I fancy a fuck to sweat out some of the toxins, but I don't like fucking junkies cause they don't move. Fuck knows what that boy-bird Val's on but I grab her arm and half drag her through to the toilet.

— What ya doin? she asks, offering neither compliance nor resistance.

— Gittin a blow job offay ye, I tell her, with a wink, and she looks at me with no fear, then just a little smile. I can tell that she wants to please me so much cause she's that kind of lassie. The damaged kind, who always just wants to please but never, ever will. Her role in life's theatre: a face to stop some fucked-up cunt's fist.

So in we go and I whip it out and the wood comes up. She's onto her fuckin knees and I'm holding that greasy head to my crotch and she's sucking and it's like . . . nothing really. It's awright, but I hate the way her beady eyes rise up to take stock of me, to ascertain

9

whether or not I'm enjoying this, which seems a totally fucking ridiculous concept now. Most of all though, I wish I'd brought my beer through here with me.

I look down on that grey skull, the perishing eyes flicking up at me and most of all those big teeth, stuck in gums which have receded back due tae drug ingestion, malnutrition and non-existent dental care. I feel like Bruce Campbell in some out-take of *The Evil Dead 3, Army of Darkness*, where he's getting gammed by a Deadite. Bruce would just smash that brittle skull to powder, and I've got to get out before I'm tempted to do the same and before my softening dick is torn to shreds on that rank bed of rotting teeth.

I hear the front door go and, to my excited horror, one of the voices is unmistakably Croxy's, he's back for another round. Possibly Breeny as well. I think about that beer and I can't stand the thought of some cunt just casually picking it up and drinking it. It's the idea that it would mean absolutely nothing to them as well, whereas to me, right now, it's everything. If it's who I think it is, my beer is fuckin well gone if I don't make a move. I push this Val away and fire through, stuffing it in and zipping up as I go.

It's still there. The gear's left me already and I'm crack-hungry again. I slump down into the couch. It *is* Croxy, looking fucked, and Breeny, looking fresh, but wondering how he's missed out on a session, and they've actually brought some more beer up. Funny, but this doesn't produce any elation. It just makes *that* particular beer I cherished seem tepid, stagnant and undrinkable.

But there are more!

So more beers are drunk, more foolhardy deals are concocted and more rocks appear, Croxy knocking up a pipe out of an old placky lemonade bottle to compliment Bernie's activities, and pretty soon we're all fucked up again. This Val lassie's stumbled back in, looking like a refugee that's just been turfed out a fucking camp. Which, I suppose, is exactly what she is. She signals over to Tanya and she gets up and they head off without saying a word.

I'm aware that an argument between Bernie and Breeny is getting increasingly heated. We're out of ammonia and have had to move on to bicarb to wash up, which requires greater skill and Breeny's giving Bernie a hard time about his wasting of gear. —You're messin up, ya fughin prick, he says, his mouth half full of semi-broken yellow and black teeth.

Bernie says something back and I'm thinking about how I have to work later and should get some shut-eye. As I head down the hallway and open the door, I hear shouting and the unmistakable sound of glass breaking. I consider going back for about one second but decide that my presence would only complicate an already messy situation. I slip quietly out the front door and close it behind me, shutting out the screams and threats. Then I'm out and off down the road.

When I get back to the Hackney shithouse, which I must now call home, I'm sweating, shaking and cursing my stupidity and weakness as the Great Eastern from Liverpool Street to Norwich rumbles the building again.

2

'. . . the attachments . . .'

Colin gets up and out of the bed. By the bay window he takes shape in a silhouette. My eyes fall upon his hanging cock. It's almost guilty-looking, caught as it is in a triangle of moonlight as he opens the blinds. — I can't understand it. He turns and I register his apologetic gallows grin as the light washes his tight dark curls to silver. It also shows me the bags under his eyes, and the unsightly sack of flesh hanging beneath his chin.

On Colin: a middle-aged fuck of whom we must now add declining sexual prowess to reducing social and intellectual interest. It's time now. God, is it time.

I stretch in the bed, feeling the coolness in my legs, and twist to flush out the last spasm of my frustration. Turning away from him, I bring my knees up to my chest.

— I know it may seem like a cliché, but this genuinely has never happened to me before. It's like . . . this year the bastards have given me four extra hours of seminar groups and two extra hours of lecturing. Last night I was up all night marking papers. Miranda's giving me a hard time, and the kids are so fucking demanding . . . there's no time to be *me*. There's no time to be Colin Addison. Who cares anyway? Who the fuck cares about Colin Addison?

I can vaguely hear this whining lament to erections lost as I begin to stumble down the ladder of consciousness into sleep.

— Nikki? Can you hear me?

— Mmm . . .

— What I'm thinking is that we need to normalise our relationship. And this isn't just a spur-of-the-moment thing. Miranda and I: it's run its course. Oh, I know what you're going to say, and yes, there have been other girls, other students, for sure there have, he says, now letting a satisfied air slip into his tone. The male ego may seem fragile, but it doesn't, in my experience, take too long to repair itself, — . . . but they've all been teenagers and it's just been a bit of daft fun. The thing is, you're more mature, you're twenty-five, there's not *that* much of an age difference between us, and it's different with you. It's not just a . . . I mean, this is a real relationship, Nikki, and I want it to be, well, *real*. You know what I'm saying? Nikki? Nikki!

Having joined the assembly line of Colin Addison's student shags, I suppose I ought to be pleased to be elevated to the status of bona fide lover. But somehow, no.

— Nikki!

— What? I groan, turning around in bed and sitting up, pulling my hair from my face. — What are you going on about? If you can't shag me, at least let me get some sleep. I've got a class in the morning and I've got to work at that fucking sauna again tomorrow night.

Colin's now sitting on the edge of the bed, breathing slowly. As I watch his shoulders move up and down, he seems to me like a peculiar wounded animal in the dark, unsure of whether to counter-attack or beat a retreat. — I don't like you working there, he exhales in those petulant, possessive tones that have become so *him* recently.

And now I'm thinking, this is it, this is my time. The weeks of deference finally building up into that couldn't-give-a-toss critical mass, where you know you're finally empowered enough to just tell them to fuck off. — That sauna probably represents my best chance of getting properly fucked right now, I coolly explain.

The cold silence in the air and the stillness of Colin's dark contour tells me that I've hit the spot and finally got through. Then he suddenly moves, jerky and tense, over to the armchair where his clothes sit. He starts scrambling into them. There's a thud of a foot on something in the dark, a chair leg or maybe the edge of the bed, and it's followed by a cat's spit of a 'fuck'. He *is* in haste to depart as he normally showers first, for Miranda, but this time no fluids have been spilt so he may be okay. At least he's had the decency not to put on the light, for which I'm grateful. As he tugs himself into his jeans, I admire his arse, probably for the last time. Impotence is bad and clinginess is awful, but the two in tandem simply can't be tolerated. The idea of becoming a nurse to this old fool is repulsive. Pity about that arse, I'll miss it. I always did like a good, firm arse on a man.

— There's no reasoning with you when you're like this. I'll call you later, he puffs, pulling on his jersey.

— Don't bother, I say icily, pulling up the quilt to cover my tits. I think about why I feel the need to do this as he's sucked them, had his cock between them, fondled, groped, mashed and eaten them with my blessing and in some cases instigation. Why then is such a casual glance in semi-darkness so violating? The answer has to be that my essence is telling me that we are history, Colin and I. Yes, it *is* that time.

— What?

— I said don't bother. Calling me later. Don't fucking well bother, I tell him, and I'm wishing I had a cigarette. I feel like asking him for one but it somehow seems inappropriate.

He turns round to face me and I can see that silly moustache which I always begged him to shave off and his mouth under it, again illuminated by a glimmer of silver light through the blind, with his eyes above concealed in darkness. The mouth is telling me:
— Right, fuck you then! You're a silly wee lassie, Nikki, an arrogant little cow. You think you're it at the moment, girl, but you're going to have big fucking problems in your life if you don't grow up and join the rest of the human race.

There's a battle going on in my soul between outrage and humour, with neither prepared to concede supremacy to the other. In this dissonant state it's all I can do to cough out: — Like you? Don't make me laugh . . .

But Colin's off and the bedroom door slams, followed by the front door. My body starts to unravel in relief till I irksomely remember that it needs to be double-locked. Lauren is very security-conscious and in any case she'll be far from amused as our row must have interrupted her sleep. The varnished floorboards in the hallway are cold under my bare feet and I'm happy to turn the mortise and head back to the bedroom. I think about going to the window to see if I can see Colin emerging from stair door into empty street, but I think we've both made our positions clear and that the link

14

is now severed. That word seems particularly satisfactory. I'm thinking, in a playful way, of course, about his penis in that state, sent through the post to Miranda. And her not recognising it. They're all the same really, unless of course you're a big, sloppy, slack old cow. If your walls have any power, you can fuck round anything, well, almost anything. It's not the penises that are the problem, it's the attachments; they come in varying sizes alright, varying sizes and degrees of annoyance.

Lauren comes through in her sky-blue dressing gown, her eyes blinking with sleep, hair tousled, as she rubs her glasses and pulls them on. — Is everything okay? I heard shouting . . .

— Just the sounds of an impotent menopausal man bellowing piteously into the night. I thought it would be sweet music to your feminist ears, I smile cheerfully.

Approaching me slowly, she extends her arms and wraps them round me. What a fundamentally lovely woman she is; always prepared to read me more sympathetically than I deserve. She believes that I use humour to hide hurt, sarcasm to deflect vulnerability, and she's always looking searchingly and earnestly at me as if to find the real Nikki behind the façade. Lauren thinks I'm like her but, for all her affectations, I'm a colder cow that she'll ever be. In spite of the strident politics she's adopted, she's a sweet kid, smelling wonderful, lavender-soapy and fresh. — I'm sorry . . . I know I told you that you were mad having an affair with a lecturer, but I only said it cause I knew you'd get hurt . . .

I'm shaking, physically shaking in her arms and she's going: — There, there . . . it's okay . . . it's awright . . . but she doesn't realise I'm shaking with *laughter* at her assumption that I care. I raise my head a little and laugh, which I regret instantly as she *is* a sweetheart and now I've humiliated her a bit. Sometimes cruelty comes by instinct. One can't be proud, but one can strive to be aware.

I rub the back of her slim neck placatingly, but I still can't stop laughing. — Ha ha ha ha . . . you've called it wrong, honey. He's the one who's been chucked, he's the one who's hurt. 'Having an affair with a lecturer . . .' ha ha ha . . . you sound just like him.

— Well, how else could you put it? He *is* married. Youse are having an affair . . .

15

I shake my head slowly. — I'm not having an affair? I'm shagging him. Or rather I was. But no more. The histrionics you heard was the sound of him *not* shagging me any more?

Lauren gives a happy, but slightly guilty, little smile. The girl's too decent, too well mannered, to overtly wallow in the misfortunes of others, even those she dislikes. And it was one of Colin's least endearing features that he didn't like her, saw only the superficial image she wanted him to see. But that's him, he's not astute at all.

I pull back my duvet. — Now come under here and give me a proper cuddle, I say.

Lauren looks at me, averting her eyes from my naked body. — Stop it, Nikki, she says bashfully.

— I only want a cuddle, I pout, and move towards her. She senses that there's her thick dressing gown between our naked flesh and that she's not going to be raped and she gives me a stiff reluctant hug, but I won't let go and I pull the duvet over us.

— Och, Nikki, she says, but soon I can feel her settle and I drift off into a beautiful sleep with the smell of lavender in my nostrils.

In the morning I wake up to a space in the bed and can hear busy kitchen sounds. Lauren. Every woman should have a sweet young wife. I rise, wrapping my dressing gown around me and head to the kitchen. Coffee hisses and spits from the filter into the pot. I can hear her in the shower now. Back through in our front room, the red flickering light on the answer machine tells me to check the messages.

I either overestimated or underestimated Colin. He's left quite a few messages on the machine.

Beep.

— Nikki, call me. This is stupid.

— Well, hello, stupid, I say in the direction of the phone, — this is Nikki.

He gives good phone, Colin does, but only in the comedic sense.

Beep.

— Nikki, I'm sorry. I lost my head. I really care about you, honest I do. That was the whole point I was trying to make. Come up to my office tomorrow. C'mon, Nik.

Beep.

— Nikki, let's not end it like this. Let me take you for lunch at the staff club. You liked it there. C'mon. Call me at the office.

Age makes most girls into women, but men never really stop being boys. That's what I envy about them, their ability to wallow in silliness and immaturity, which is something I always strive to imitate. It can be tiresome though, if you are constantly on the receiving end of it.

3

Scam # 18,733

It's the last shit-arse section of Soho; narrow and sleazy with the reek of cheap perfume, fried food, alcohol and kerbside rubbish from split black bin liners. Rasping banks of neon slowly, almost defiantly, crackle to listless life through a twilight of frail drizzle, proffering those ancient and barren pledges.

And you only occasionally glimpsed the agents of these sublime pleasures, the square-jawed, shaven-headed, suited and coated wideos in the doorways, or the worn crack hoors hanging in a stair whose faces flashed sick naked-lightbulb-yellow at weary punters, nervous tourists and drunken, sneering youths.

For me though, this is the closest to home I've ever felt. Swaggering past the brawny chappie of my acquaintance at the drinking-club door, his expensive overcoat flapping in the wind, this to me is a sign that I've come a long way from when I worked with sauna rejects in Leith, pimping out smackhead lassies who fucked for fixes.

And Henry the Bus was nodding. — Alroight, Si mate, and I'm smiling and trying not to let my nostrils flare that slight involuntary way they always did when I'm confronted with brainless, ten-a-penny muscle — cause you needed them and these boys always knew when they were being patronised. So my coupon crinkles into a wincing smile. — Awright, Henry? I'm a bit dazed right now, mate. Sticking my cock in all the wrong faces.

Henry nods grimly, and we rap away for a bit, as I watch his cold eyes set in that troglodyte head occasionally flick over my shoulder in concern at something happening behind me. Firing a gaze raptorish enough to put out small fires before they grow into bigger ones.

— Is Colville in today?

— Nah, thank fuck, Henry tells me. Safe ground that one; we

both hate our boss with a passion. I'm thinking of Matt Colville's wife as I go in and say ta-ta to Henry. While the cat's away . . . I should get Tanya down here to start punting. I bell her on the mobby but surprise, surprise, hers has been disconnected, the voice tells me. It's hard to maintain both smack and crack habits and remember to keep up mobile-phone payments. It spells minor opportunity lost and I feel my soul frost over slightly as it tends to do when I'm indirectly inconvenienced by the careless actions of others.

But minus Colville, and with Dewry in the office, I'm the man. And Marco and Lenny are on today, both good, keen grafters, which means that my role is purely social. I sit mainly on the right side of the bar, and hold court, only getting up to serve and show attentive respect if a face, footballer, villain or a very sexy lady (every one of them) enters the establishment. At the end of my shift I stop off at Randolph's shop and pick up a load of gay pornography, which will be an anonymous gift to an old buddy of mine. Then I head for a beer in a nondescript café-bar. I always like to get the fuck away from the club when I finish, the social equivalent of having a good bath. This bar fits the bill, an Ikea-bland monument to our lack of imagination. It's Soho, but it could be anywhere that has no character any more.

I'm a bit run-down and therefore surprised that I seem to have pulled quite easily. I thought that the timing was way off. I was even starting to feel stupid and weak once again. Weak to end up destroyed with Croxy, as if the use of the cunt's van and gaff and muscle to help me move entitles him to poison me with chemicals. He's useless, they all are fuckin useless. That fuckin dippit little hoor Tanya, hanging around King's Cross when I set it up for her to go to the club and pull some punters with proper cash. Weak. And the older you get, the more of an expensive luxury that type of weakness becomes.

But enough of the self-loathing, cause I got through the shift okay and now I'm in a Soho bar with an enthusiastic and pretty lassie in a suit called Rachel, who works in advertising and has just done an important presentation and is a bit pished cause it went well and who says 'oh gosh' a lot. I caught her eye up at the bar, the pleasantries and smiles were subsequently exchanged and I've separated her from her drunken pack. Of course, my own place in

Islington is being renovated and I'm forced to stay at a friend's crummy bedsit. Thank God for that Armani suit, worth every penny. And when I suggest hers at Camden, she says: — Oh gosh, my flat-mate's having some people round.

So now I'm having to eat humble pie and cough out the E8 address to the minicab boy. At least he's got the fuckin decency to take us out there. The black-cab wankers won't, or if they do they look at you like they're fuckin social workers – all for the privilege of taking twenty quid out off your pocket for five or six poxy miles. Even this Arab or Turk tosser's on about fifteen snaps.

Sly sideways glances at this Rachel woman, discreetly stolen in between conversational lulls, indicate that her expectations are lowering with every set of traffic lights we pass. She's pretty gabby though, and with the weekend hangover's ferocity, I'm finding it hard to maintain concentration. Also, when you've pulled and you know you're in, there's that feeling of anti-climax. You've got her back so you're on a ride, there's no fucking shiting around, but then the ritual becomes so depressing. You start making the small talk, then move onto the Benny Hill stuff. And now the hardest thing to do is to listen, but it's also the most important. It's important because I can see that she needs to pretend more than I do that all this has a social veneer and is (at least potentially) more than just a shag, more than just animal lust. But for my part I feel like saying, shut the fuck up and git those keks off, we're never going to see each other again, and if our paths do cross we'll cover up our embarrassment with stoicism and feigned indifference, while I'll be thinking, hatefully, of the noises you make while you're getting fucked and the regret on your face the next day. How it's only the negatives that stand out, that are in any way memorable.

But this won't do, because we're up the stairs and into the gaff, me apologising for the 'upheaval', and sorry that all I have to offer is brandy, and as she drones on, I'm replying, — Yes, Rachel, Edinburgh originally, as I get the drinks for us. I'm delighted to find a set of real brandy glasses unpacked.

— Oh, it's so lovely up there. I was up there for the festival a couple of years ago. We had a great time, she informs me as she looks through some of the boxes of records.

That should have been a crass and hateful statement for schemie ears, but it sounds so agreeable as I teasingly chuck the brandy around in a glass. I'm admiring her grace, the umblemished skin, and that full toothy smile as she says: — . . . Barry White . . . Prince . . . you've got great taste in music . . . there's loads of soul and garage stuff here . . .

And it's not just the glow from the brandy because as she picks up her glass from the stained coffee table I feel the imaginary zip in my belly starting to open up, and I think NOW. Now is the time to fall in love. Just open that fuckin zip up and let the entrails of love engulf you both in a messy rapture, as this raging bull and mad cow get on board the love boat. Look stupidly into each other's eyes; talk shite, get fat. But no. I do what I always do and use sex as a means of undermining love by grabbing her, enjoying her theatrical appearances-sake shock, and we're snogging, then undressing, frigging, licking, teasing and fucking.

Prior to this though, I've ascertained that her salary, position in the organisation and social background are not as impressive as I first envisaged. She's a fuck, that's all. You sometimes have to fight hard not to get to know somebody.

After a bit of kip we're at it again in the morning. As soon as I'm hard I'm back up her and we're shaking and pumping away as the 7.21 express to Norwich thrashes through Hackney Downs station, almost like it's going to sweep us up to East Anglia with it and she's going: — Oh my God . . . Simon . . . Si-mehnnnn . . .

Rachel falls asleep and I get up, leaving a note, which informs her that I have an early start and that I'll give her a bell. I go over to the café across the road and sip at some tea, waiting for her to come downstairs. I get a bit dewy-eyed when I think of her pretty face. I fantasise about going back up those stairs, maybe with some flowers, opening my heart, pledging undying love, making her life special, being that prince on the white charger. It's as much a male fantasy as a female one. But that's all it is. A sickening feeling of loss hangs over me. It's easy to love, or for that matter hate, somebody in their absence, somebody we don't really know and I'm an expert at that. That hardest problem is the other bit.

Then, like the polis on a stake-out, I see her leave by my stair door. Her movements are tense and jerky, as she struggles to orientate herself, looking like a chick who's fallen out of a nest; ugly, gawky and graceless, a different girl from the gorgeous alcohol-assisted fuck who shared my bed, and briefly my life, last night. I turn away to the sports pages of the *Sun*. — I think England should have a Scottish manager, I shout over at Ivan the Turkish proprietor. — Ronnie fuckin Corbett or somebody like that.

— Ronnie Corbett, Ivan repeats with a smile.

— A Jambo cunt, I tell him, raising the hot, sugared tea to my lips.

When I get back up the stairs, Rachel's left some of her scent behind in this squalid box, which is welcome, and a note, which is less so.

Simon,
Sorry I missed you this morning. I'd like to see you again.
Give me a call.
Rachel. X

Aw. It's always nice to leave somebody when they say they'd like to see you again, because there will inevitably come a time when you leave them because they *don't* want to see you again. So much more pleasant all round. I crumple the note up and stick it in the bin.

I can't really place Rachel on my matrix. When I started off in London in a Forest Gate squat, I was determined I'd work my way west: Essex Girls to North London Jewesses, ending up with Sloane Rangers. They know the score though. While the first ones want to exchange sex for the trinkets of life, the middle ones will swap neuroses, and the last will bang you till the cows come home but the ring on the finger's not for you, it's promised to Chinless Chuckie. These fucking feudal inbred rich-peasant cunts always have arranged marriages. So I gave up scanning *Debrett's*, and checked back into Hampstead.

Now Tanya, who doesn't even hit first base on my classification, calls me on the red mobile to say she's coming over. I consider that skull-white face, which has seen as much sun in recent years as Nosferatu, lips big and blistered as if she's had bad implants, her jerky

22

frame and bug-eyed stare. Crack hoors; where the fuck do they fit in?

I stick a copy of the Great Eastern Railway timetable on my headboard and by the time she gets here, everything's in place. She confesses to me that that shit-broker Matt Colville threw her out the bar the other night. Her big eyes crave smack, not cock. I'm telling her that she's an ungrateful slag, that I've set everything up for her, and that she'd rather have her arse panelled in by some scab-baws for a bag or a rock in some shitey hovel in King's Cross than ply her trade in a nice entertainment-industry establishment in Soho.

— I try so hard for you, but it's no good, I spit, wondering how many times she's heard that one before from parents, social workers, care officers. She takes my rant, crumbling on the settee, her arms around herself, looking at me like her jawbone's become detached from her skull and is just hanging loosely in the skin.

— But ee frew me aht, she moans, — Colville. Ee bleedin well frew me aht.

— No wonder, look at ye. You look like a fuckin Weedgie. This is London, you've got to have some fuckin standards. Am I the only person that believes in standards . . . ?

— Sorry, Simon . . .

— It's okay, doll, I sing, and pull her up from the couch, and take her in my arms marvelling at her lightness. — I'm a bit grumpy today because it's been a funny old week. Come and lie down beside me . . . I pull her on to the bed and look at the clock on the locker: 12.15. I'm touching her, watching her lips go into spasm, then the clothes are strewn and I'm on her and in her. Her face is fucking mangled in discomfort and I'm thinking, where's that fuckin train?

12.21.

That fuckin train, fuckin Anglian Railways or whatever you call the privatised shit . . . 12.22, the fuckin cunts . . . should be due here by now . . . — You're fuckin gorgeous, babes, you are fucking dyna-mite, I lie in encouragement.

— Eughhh . . . she's wheezing.

Fuck me, if that's all she puts into it she should go to work filling burgers cause she's got nae future in the industry.

I grit my teeth and hold on another five miserable minutes till

23

12.27 when the bastard finally slices through the station shaking the gaff to bits and she starts screaming undying love.

— Strong finish, I explain to her. I'm trying to do a Terry Venables-coaching thing; stick to basics, remind them what they're good at. Positive encouragement, no shouting or losing the rag. — But we need mair commitment. I'm telling you this for your own good.

— Thanks, Simon, she smiles, exposing that crownless chipped tooth.

— Now I'll have to chase you, as I've business.

Her face drops a bit again, but she hauls her clothes on, almost in one miserable action. I hand her a tenner for fares and fags and she says her goodbyes and files out.

When she's gone, I gather up the load of gay porn I picked up yesterday in Soho. I stick it in a padded envelope and address it:

FRANCIS BEGBIE
PRISONER NO: 6892BK
HMP SAUGHTON
SAUGHTON MAINS
EDINBURGH
SCOTLAND

I always take a wee stock for my old pal Begbie, which I post every time I go back to Scotland, so that he sees the local postmark on it when he receives it. I wonder who the fuck he blames for sending it, probably everyone in the Lothian region. It's all part of my little war against my home city.

Liberally applying the Gibbs SR, I brush the scabby dregs of Tanya from my mouth and jump in the shower, scrubbing from my genitals the remnants of that diseased pot I've been stirring. And wouldn't you know it, the phone goes and my weakness is that I can never, ever let it ring, and the answer machine is not switched on. I wrap a towel round myself and pick it up.

— Hiya, Simon son . . .

It takes a second or two to register the owner of the voice. It's my Aunt Paula up in Edinburgh.

24

4

'. . . badly executed handjobs . . .'

E very time I change my course I feel more of a failure. But for
me academic courses are like men; even the most fascinating
only seem to hold the interest for so long. Now Christmas is over
and I'm a single woman again. But changing course doesn't make
you feel as bad as when you change educational institutions or towns.
And I content myself with the fact that I've now been at Edinburgh
University for one whole year, well, almost. It was Lauren who
convinced me to change from literature to film and media studies.
The new literature is film, she said, quoting from some stupid magazine. Of course, I told her that where people learn about narrative
now is not the book, but it's not the film either, it's the video game.
Split narrative. If we really wanted to be hip, radical and cutting
edge, we'd be down Johnny's Amusements on the South Side, jostling
with anaemic truants for space on the machines.

I have to stick to one module of literature, however, and I elected
to keep with Scottish literature, as I'm English, and contrariness is
always reason enough to do anything.

McClymont is lecturing to the smattering of patriots and wannabe
Scots (God, I was one myself last year on account of some great-
grandmother I never knew who went to Kilmarnock or Dumbarton
for her holidays . . . We move on, quickly, hopefully . . .). You can
almost hear the soundtrack of pipes playing in the background, as
he spouts his nationalist propaganda. Why do I stick with this?
Lauren's idea again, it's easy grades, she reckons.

The gum in my mouth tastes metallic and the effort of chewing
it is hurting my jaw. I take it out and stick it under the desk. I'm
really hungry. I made two hundred quid last night, on badly executed
handjobs. Masturbating men under towels. Those fat, red faces gazing
at you with intent as you look through them pulling different

expressions for what you think they want: cold, cruel bitch; doe-eyed, open-mouthed little girl; anything. It's all so remote, so detached, it reminds me of when my brother and I used to wank the dog, Monty, and watch him try to bring himself off against the couch.

I'm thinking about how unnatural it would be to be good at handjobs, thinking about men's cocks, and soon McClymont is finishing up. Lauren has pages of notes on the Scottish diaspora. Ross, the 'American Scat' in front of us is probably hard as a rock in his Levi's as he scribbles, filling pages with tales of English cruelty and injustice. We snap shut our folder rings in concert and rise. As I leave, McClymont catches my eye. That owl-like face. Stupid. I don't know what the ornithologists say, but the real bad-birdie experts – the falconers, the hawk handlers – all of them will tell you that the owl is not wise, it's the thickest out of all the birds of prey.

— Miss Fuller-Smith, can I speak to you for a minute? he says starchily.

I turn to him and push the hair from my face and tuck it behind my ear. A lot of men can't help responding when you do that: virgin offerings. That act of pulling away the bridal veil, of opening up. McClymont is a cynical, wizened alcoholic therefore perfectly programmed to respond. I stand a bit too close to him. It's always a good idea to do that to fundamentally shy but predatory men. Worked a treat with Colin. Worked too fucking well.

The permanently startled dark eyes under the glasses ignite further. That thinning, electric-shock hair seems to rise half an inch. The ridiculous shoulder-padded suit fills as he involuntarily puffs out. — I'm afraid I still haven't received your second-term essay, he says, a slight leer in his voice.

— That's because I haven't done it. I've had to work at nights? I smile.

McClymont, who is either too experienced (as he would have you believe) or his hormones are too depleted to have his cool blown for too long, nods sombrely. — Next Monday, Miss Fuller-Smith.

— Nikki, please, I grin, tossing my head sideways.

— Next Monday, McClymont humphs and starts to tidy up: his

26

bony, knotted hands stiffly tugging at his papers and cramming them into his case.

To win at anything requires persistence. I persist. — I really, really, really enjoyed the lecture? I beam at him.

He raises his head and gives a sly grin. — Good, he says curtly.

I flush with this small victory as Lauren and I head for the refectory. — This film studies seminar group? What's the talent like?

Lauren frowns darkly as she considers the potential hassles ahead, all the possible visitors to the flat; the ones who may be untidy, the ones who may ponce, the potentially unruly. — There's one or two that's okay. I usually sit next to this guy Rab. He's a bit older, maybe about thirty, but he's awright.

— Shaggable? I ask.

— Nikki, you're terrible, she says shaking her head.

— I'm a free agent! I protest, as we down our coffees and make our way to the class.

The tutor is an intense guy with long hands. His spindly frame and round shoulders twist him into a posture so perfect for gazing at his navel. When he talks it's in a soft, low southern Irish accent. The class is underway and we watch a short Russian film with an unpronounceable title on video. It's nonsense. Halfway through it, a guy in a blue jacket with an Italian label comes in, and nods a curt apology at the tutor. He smiles at Lauren and raises his eyebrows, and slumps into the seat next to her.

I glance at him and he does back at me, very briefly.

After the lecture, Lauren introduces him as Rab. He's friendly, but not gushing, which I quite like. About five ten, not overweight, light-brown hair, brown eyes. We go down to the union for a drink and talk about the course. This Rab's not the sort of guy who immediately stands out in a crowd, which is strange because he's quite handsome. It's a very conventional handsome, however, the type you fuck between serious boyfriends. After a beer he heads to the toilet. — He's got a nice arse, I tell her. — You fancy him?

Lauren shakes her head in a dismissive pout. — He's got a girl-friend and she's expecting a kid.

— I didn't ask for his CV, I tell her, — I just asked you if you fancied him.

Lauren nudges me quite sharply with her elbow and calls me daft. She's a puritanical girl in a lot of ways, and seems a bit out of time, as in old-fashioned. I love the almost translucent skin she has, the hair scraped back and her glasses are really sexy, as are the precise dainty movements of her hands. She's a slender, graceful and self-contained nineteen-year-old, and I sometimes wonder if she's ever had a serious boyfriend. By which I suppose I mean, I wonder if she's ever been fucked. Of course, I'm far too fond of her to tell that I know that she's adopted those feminist politics because she's basically a small-town prude who needs a good shagging.

She habitually goes with this Rab lad for a drink, to talk film and moan about the course. Well, now this is a *ménage à trois*. Rab's got that world-weary, I've-done-it-all-before aspect to him. I think he likes Lauren's maturity and intelligence. I wonder if he fancies her, because she likes him, you can tell a mile away. Well, if it's maturity he wants, I'm almost twenty-five.

Rab returns and sets up a round of drinks. He tells me that he works in his brother's bar as a means of raising extra cash. I tell him that I do sauna work some afternoons and evenings. He's intrigued at this, as most people are. Cocking his head to the side, he gives me a searching look, which totally changes his face. — Ye dinnae . . . well, eh, you know . . .

Lauren puckers her thin little mouth in distaste.

— Sleep with my clients? No, I just bash them, I explain, making a chopping motion with my hands. — Obviously, some will proposition you, but it's outside the agency's official terms and conditions, I lie, spouting the party line. — I did . . . I pause for a second. They both look so open-mouthed in anticipation, I feel like a granny reading a bedtime story to a couple of innocent waifs, and I'm nearly at the bit where the big bad wolf is about to make an appearance. . . . — I did give one sweet old guy a handjob one time, after he started going on about missing his dead wife. I didn't want to take two hundred quid from him, but he insisted. Then he said that he saw I was a nice girl and apologised profusely for putting me in this position. He was so sweet.

— How could you, Nikki? Lauren bleats.

— It's okay for you, love, you're Scottish, you get your fees paid, I tell her. Lauren knows that there's little she can say about that, which suits me fine. The brutal truth is that I give loads of handjobs, but it's not something you'd do for anything other than money.

5

Scam # 18,734

I was prepared for Colville, thanks to Tanya's notice of the cunt's behaviour. He had been wanting to get rid of me for a long time and now the wanker had the chance. Of course, I wasn't going down without a fight, and for the past year I'd been well acquainted with the insides of Chez Colville at Holloway.

He'd wait until the end of my shift, of course. It had been a quiet night. Then Henry and Ghengis had come in with a few boys and they were all pretty pished. There had been some row with another mob and they were all chuffed in victory, swapping stories and the like. There was talk that Aberdeen and Tottenham had teamed up. — Wouldnae like to be in that company, who the fuck would pay for the drinks? The fuckin barman probably, I laugh, and some of the boys join in. I'm holding court, pouring quite a few nips on the house, because I feel my reign here is coming to an end.

In a way it's sad, it's been a second home, a way in, a place to meet the kind of people I always seem to meet, but it is limited. It's time to move on. You never win by working in places like this, you've got to own one. From the corner of my vision, Lynsey appears and winks at me, as she prepares to take the stage.

Aye, it's all plastic, chrome and pristine fittings but you can still smell the stale fags and spunk in the gadges' flannels, the lassies' cheap perfume and the watered-down beer and the sick desperation amid the bonhomie.

Lynsey's got the right idea though, far too sussed ever to be a victim hanging around in a place like this after her fuck-by date. She's careful never to show the punters the contempt that a smart, educated young woman like her must feel for them, and, I suppose, for me, although we all love to entertain the notion that we're different, that we have our own unique take on all this tack, our own special redeeming irony. She *is* different though, and she's got the right idea. She's done a few stag vids, got her own website, to get her name known, and now she just packs them in, at this lap-dancing lark. Not a pimp boyfriend in sight and her engaged smile turns into detached ice whenever you overstep the mark. She's playing nobody else's game but her own and therefore she's no good to me.

Pity. Watching her up there, doing that athletic pelvic thrust which would send a crack-shag hoor like Tanya into intensive care, I trace those sunbed thighs up to that silver mini as studiously as any paying punter and I'm thinking that a search for one of Lynsey's vids has to be on the cards.

Sure enough, at the end of the shift Dewry comes up to me with that school-sneak idiot grin on his face. — Colville wants to see you in his office, the repugnant bastard nearly fucking sings.

I know what this is all about, and entering the office, I sit in the chair opposite him without being asked. Colville's slitty eyes dart around in that wan, mendacious face, looking at me like I'm pond life. He slides an envelope across the table. There's a stain on the lapel of that stupid grey jacket he wears. No wonder she . . .

— Your P45 and backpay, he explains, in that cringing voice of his. — As you're still two weeks short of your 104 weeks' tenure we don't have to pay you compensation for your dismissal. You'll find it's all above board. It's the law, he grins.

I look earnestly at him. — Why, Matt? I ask, feigning injury, — We go back a long way!

Nope, the stare isnae working; Matty-boy's face remains impassive as he slides back in the chair and shakes his head slowly. — I've warned you about your timekeeping. I need a head barman who's going to be here. More importantly, I've also warned you about that fucking little whore friend of yours coming in here and propositioning my customers. She even tried it on with one of the Old Bill the other week, he nods again in disgust, and I hear a little snicker from Dewry, who's enjoying this as much as Colville.

— They've got cocks as well, or so I've been told, I smile at him. Once again I catch a faint chuckle from behind me.

Colville sits forward, his coupon set in serious mode. This is his show and he doesn't want it upstaged. — Don't be fucking smart,

Williamson. I know you think that you're it, but you're just another ten-a-penny Jock scumbag from Hackney as far as I'm concerned.

— Islington, I say quickly. That last bit hurt.

— Whatever. I expect a head barman to do my business here, not to use this place as a front for his own sordid little activities. All sorts of rubbish are hanging around here now; whores, petty criminals, football thugs, porn merchants, drug dealers, and you know what? It's all been in the last two years, since *you* started here.

— It's a fucking lap-dancing club, a fuckin strip club. Of course you're going to get some dodgy characters around. We're in a sleazy business! I protest angrily. — I've brought some loyal paying customers down here! People who spend!

— Just fucking go, he points to the door.

— So that's it, I'm sacked?

Matt Colville's smile grows even wider. — Yeah, and as unprofessional as it is of me to admit it, I'm enjoying this.

I hear another snigger from Dewry behind me. It's time. I raise my eyes and look directly into his. — Well, I suppose now's the time to come clean. I've been shagging your wife regularly for about eight months.

— Whaa . . . Colville looks at me, and I sense Dewry freeze in shock behind me, then he makes a hasty exit, coughing some kind of excuse. Colville's stunned into speechlessness for a second or two, but after a tremor, a slight, wary smile creases his thin lips. Then he shakes his head in a contemptuous loathing. — You're really quite a sad case, Williamson.

— I've done awright as well, I say, ignoring him. — Check the statements on her Visa card. Hotels, designer clathes, the lot. I finger the Versace shirt. — No oan the money you pey, pal.

There's another spasm of fear in his eyes, but it's replaced by scornful anger. — You sad bastard. You really expect me to get wound up by your nonsense? It's pathe . . .

I stand up, and as I do, I pull out the Polaroids from my inside jacket pocket and throw them onto the desk. — Maybe you'll get wound up by this. I was keeping them for a rainy day. Worth a thousand words, eh, I wink, turning and departing with dignified haste out his office and across the bar. A wave of anxiety powers me to a trot when I get into the street, but nobody's followed me and I'm laughing loudly through Soho's backstreets.

As I walk up Charing Cross Road, there's a bit of a comedown as it hits me that I've lost my most regular source of income. I try to balance this with the loss of the hassle, making a pros and cons list, thinking of the opportunities and threats presented by the new situ. I head back across to Liverpool Street on the Central Line and take the overland to Hackney Downs. We halt at the Downs and I get out, looking over the wall at the platform into my own back window. I can practically touch the manky glass. There's so much grime, grease and dirt on it, it's impossible to see inside. Those Great Eastern Rail cunts should fucking well pay to have it cleaned, it's their shitey diesel trains that fuck it up. On my way out of the station I take a new GER timetable, fresh out today.

Back in the gaff I look out from the front window of this bedsit that estate agents love to call a studio flat. That's the English for you: ridiculously pompous to the last. Who else would be grandiosely deluded enough to call a scheme an estate? I'm huntin, fishin, shootin Simon David Williamson from Leith's Banana Flats Estate. Looking down, I spy a young mum with a pushchair outside the chemist. The bags under her eyes tell me that she could have been a model, for Samsonite, that is. They also tell me that I've come five hundred miles south to live in fuckin Great Junction Street. Suddenly, the building shakes and rattles as an express train roars past the back window towards Norwich. I check the clock: 6.40, or 18.40 as those rail wankers call it. On time.

Whenever you can, you fuckin well invest. That's what I was trying to tell Bernie the other day, even though I was too wired to get it across properly. That's the key; that's what marks out the winners from the losers, distinguishes the real business heads from the mouthy barrow-boy-made-good twat, who bores the arse of you in the papers and on the telly, telling you how they've always been a ducker and diver and all that shite. You always hear the so-called success stories trumpeted in the media, but in the real world we know that they're the tip of the iceberg, because we see the failures as well. Stuck in a bar next tae some arsehole giein it the big one about how if it wasn't for those cunts, that slag, these arseholes, they could've been in clover, blaming everybody else but themselves for buying into the lie that you simply blag your way to the top. Bernie had better watch, cause he's starting to sound exactly like one of those wankers. Cause that shit only lasts for so long, then you have to look at your pile and invest it (if you're lucky enough to have one) before you spunk the fucker away. Then it's back tae the whingein old pub bore of what-could've-been, or worse, the crack pipe or the old purple tin.

I need something to invest, and now I've got to go and see Amanda, that cold cow who has loads and loads to invest, and who still fucking well sucks me dry.

Aunt Paula's proposition, which I almost laughed at down the phone – nearly just started sniggering in the poor old doll's ear – well, it just gets better all the time.

Duty calls though, and I'm up through a tortuous route of bus and train to Mandy-I-came-and-you-did-all-the-taking's place in Highgate, picking up the laddie and giving her the forty quid per week that just vanishes into that hole in the boy's face. For, make no mistake, the kid is fat. The last time I took him up to Scotland to see my mother, she said in that Eyetie-Scots accent: 'He's-ah jist-ah like-ah you at that age.' Just like me at that age; a fat kid who bruises easily and is porky – porky prey to the thin, mean serpents of the playground and the street. Thank fuck for puberty and hormones and their deliverance from fat hell. Maybe my ambivalence towards him is due to the fact that the poor wee bastard does remind me of a younger, less cool self. But I can't believe I was ever like that. It's more likely to have come from his fat Jew bastard of a grandfather: on her side, of course.

Now we're trudging around the West End, en route to Hamley's to choose his Christmas present. Of course, the gig has long passed; now we're into January-sales-greed frenzy. I gave him vouchers on the basis that the concept of freedom of choice should be learned as soon as possible. Amanda has kept them back, insisting that I accompany him as he makes his selection. We've not been walking that much since alighting at Oxford Circus, although it's nippy, but the wee cunt complains, hangs back, rubs at his legs. A vid-game slug, he'd rather be at home indoors on the PlayStation. Even at this festive time of year, I'm as much of an imposition to him as he is to me. As we go in, I continue my pusillanimous attempts at conversation, hoping that there'll be some fanny around the shops to leer at.

That's the problem with winter: the lassies are too wrapped up. You don't know what you're getting until you get it back home and open it up, then it's too late to take it back. Christmas. I check the white phone for messages first. I always give out that number to women I haven't shagged. Then the red mobile, for the second-hand goods and the green one for business. Nothing.

The shops and the crowds and carrying lots of rubbish around soon begins to get me down. As for the kid . . . there's no connection. I try. Not a great deal, but as much as is within my capacity. It's a shift to put in, for us both, I expect. At the end of it, I'm bloated and greasy on junk food and totally skint, and for what? Parental duty? Social interaction?

Is this doing anybody any good?

I look at the fanny and recall bitterly a few weeks ago when I took Ben (the name was her idea) to Madame Tussaud's. All I could do was think of her all full of herself cause she's getting fucked by the selfish yuppie cunt of her dreams, saying it was great for them that I had Ben, they could just ennnjoooyyy being alone together for a bit. Paying forty quid a week and taking him out soas that she can fucking well bang in peace. I should have a tattoo on my forehead: M-U-G.

When I get him home, I have to admit that Mand's looking a lot better. This last year is the first time I'd seen her in shape since Ben was born. I thought she'd just sprint to gross fatness, like other members of her fuckin family, but no, she looks well tidy. If she'd worked out and dieted like that when we were an item, I might not have found it necessary to humiliate her. I'm an ambitious man and no chappie with any self-esteem likes to be seen with a fat cunt on his arm.

But fat cunts do have their uses: as aunties. As kind, plump aunties. Aunt Paula was always my favourite auntie. Granted, there was little opposition. Poor old Paula, she inherited a pub, but she was daft enough to marry a wideo who almost drank her out of house and

35

home before she kicked him into touch. It's almost reassuring that even such strong, wilful cows as Paula can have their blind spots. Keeps the likes of me in business. Now she was offering me the pub for twenty grand.

The first major problem was that I didn't have that kind of money. The second was that the pub was back in Leith.

6

'. . . naughty secrets . . .'

You see the flint in Rab's eyes, a quality that hints at something else. He measures his words like the old boys measure nips in those tight-arsed local pubs. Rab's mentally circling Lauren, cause she's tensed up like an alley cat, ready to spit or hiss, so he's playing it carefully. She's wanting to justify the anxiety she feels about him being here when she thinks it should be just us, girls together, or maybe even just them. But I live with her so I know that Rab's getting the brunt of her PMT. As true sisters do, we've synchronised our menstruation, and she's waiting to find a reason to turn her anxiety into dislike.

Poor Rab, he's got two mad cows in tow. I'm feeling that heady, heavy way and I've a spot coming through on my chin. Lauren and I are a bit uptight because there's a new girl moving into the flat tomorrow. Her name's Dianne and she seems okay, a master's student in psychology. Just as long as she doesn't try to get into our heads. We had half agreed to get home and tidy the place up for her arrival, but two drinks tell me it's not going to happen. The union's getting crowded but there's not a lot of serious drinking going on, we're all nursing our tipples. Roger behind the bar is smoking a fag in a leisurely manner. Two guys playing pool look at me, one nudges the other and he smiles over. Ten-a-penny, but I actively consider flirting a little with them, if only because I don't like the way our conversation's heading.

— I suppose if I was a lassie, I'd be a feminist n aw, Rab concedes, defusing one of Lauren's shrill, wilting attacks. There are quite a few carpet-munchers in the union tonight, and their presence seems to bring out the worst in Lauren, encouraging her to be more right-on. The fact is that most of them won't even be out when they return to their home towns for the break. The chest-beating goes on here, in this safe environment, this lab for the real world.

Lamenting the lack of atmosphere, we decide to move on to a Cowgate pub. It's a mild evening outside, although when we head down into the dark bowels of the city, the sun's almost completely blocked out and only the sliver of clear blue sky above testifies to the beauty of the day. We head into a bar which was considered *the* place, although that may have been a couple of weeks ago now. This is a mistake, as my lover, or my ex-lover, Colin Addison, MA (Hons), MPhil, PhD, is in.

Colin's wearing a fleece, which makes him look like one of his students and I'm feeling quite powerful about that because it's the kind of thing he never wore before he was with me. Of course, it looks a bit silly on him. We've just got our drinks and sat down when he comes over to me. — We need to talk, he says.

— I disagree, I tell him, looking at the stain of lipstick on my glass.

— We can't leave it like this. I want an explanation. I deserve at least that.

I shake my head and screw up my face. *I deserve at least that.* What a tosser. This is both boring *and* mildly embarrassing, two states of emotion which should surely be distinct. — Go away, will you?

Colin's all puffed up and he's pointing the finger at me, jabbing it in the air to punctuate his outraged words. — You've got a lot of growing up to do, you fucking little bitch, if you think you can just tre . . .

— Look, you'd better just go, mate, Rab stands up. You can see Colin's eyes flash in brief recognition, thinking that it's just a student and he has the university senate and expulsion as a threat if Rab tries to get rough. Mind you, he should be more worried as to what the senate would do *him*: screwing, or trying to screw, a student. It seems that, since I chucked him, Colin's stuck on this theme of me needing to grow up. Whatever happened to that mature relationship we used to enjoy back in those halcyon days of, well, last week?

I'm about to let fly with this, when Lauren decides to intervene as well. Her face is pinched and harsh and I see a tougher side to her that she undermines slightly by saying: — We're having a private drink, which causes me to giggle a little, drunkenly and stupidly, as I think of a private drink in a public house.

I don't need their help though. When it comes to slapping Colin down, I'm in a league of my own — Look, I'm *really* heartily sick of you, Colin. I'm sick of your soft, alcoholic middle-aged dick. I'm sick of taking the blame cause you can't get it up. I'm sick of your self-pity because life's passed you by. I've sucked out all I can from you. Now I choose to discard the sapless shell that's left. I'm in company at the moment, so do us all a favour and just fuck off out my face. Please?

— You fucking bitch . . . he says again, his face crimson like a stain as he looks round self-consciously.

— Yeeww fucking bitch . . . I imitate his whine. — Can you not do a bit better than that?

Rab starts to say something, but I speak over him, addressing Colin directly again. — You're simply not elevating the standard of debate? Even at this table? Just go, please.

— Nikki . . . I . . . he begins placatingly, again looking to see if there are any of his students present, — . . . all I want to do is talk. If it's over, fine. It's just that I don't see the point of leaving things like this.

— Don't fucking bleat, replace me with someone else, someone naive enough to be impressed. If you can last through to next freshers' week. I'm afraid I just don't hate myself enough to go out with you.

— Cow, he snaps, then: — Fucking cunt! And he exits with haste. As the door slams heavily behind him, I'm flushing a bit for a second or two, but it soon passes and we're all having a bit of laugh. The barmaid looks over at me and I shrug.

— You're shameless, Nikki, Lauren gasps.

— You're right, Lauren, I say looking straight at Rab, — having an affair with lecturers . . . it's not fun. It's the second one I've had. The first time was with an English literature professor when I was in London. He was a funny sort alright, what might be termed exceptionally weird.

— Oh, don't . . . Lauren starts. She's heard this before.

But no, I'm telling the Miles story and embarrasing the fuck out of her. — He was a real literary man. Like Bloom in *Ulysses*, he liked the tang of urine in the kidney. He used to buy fresh kidneys and have me pee into a little bowl. He would then put the kidneys in this bowl of my piss, leaving them to soak overnight in it before cooking them in the morning for his breakfast. He was a very civilised pervert. He used to take me shopping in boutiques. Loved to pick my clothes for me. Especially if there was a young, trendy, female assistant attending to me. He said he liked the idea of one young woman dressing another, but in a commercial environment. His erection was always visible and sometimes he used to come in his pants.

Lauren looks lovely when she's angry, rising to a marvellous incandescence, which adds to her. Her face grows slightly ruddy, her eyes glaze. That's probably why people like to see her angry, it's the closest they get to seeing what she'd look like getting fucked.

Rab's laughing, raising his eyebrows and Lauren's face is furrowed. — Don't you think Lauren's beautiful, Rab? I ask him.

Lauren is not happy with that. Her face colours a little more and her eyes water slightly. — Fuck off, Nikki, stop messing aboot, she says. — You're making a fool of yourself. Stop trying to embarrass me and embarrass Rab.

But Rab isn't bothered at all, because he then freaks us both out a bit, Lauren evidently so, but me much more than I let on. Putting one arm round Lauren and one round me, he in turn kisses us gently on the side of our faces. I see Lauren stiffen and blush fully-fledged, and I feel a randy flush and an intrusive bracing all at once. — You're both beautiful, he says with diplomacy, or is it feeling? Whatever it is, it's unerring, showing me a coolness, depth and power of expression in him I simply hadn't bargained for. Then it's gone. As his arms slide away, he adds coolly: — See, if I didnae have the likes of youse here, I'd've jacked in this course. We're talking about fuckin analysing films like bastard critics when we've never held a camera in our hands. Nor have any of the cunts that teach us. All we're being taught is how to whinge at or arselick people who've got the bottle to get off their holes and do things. That's all arts degrees do, turn out another clutch of parasitic drones.

I feel despondency setting in. Intentionally or not, this boy is a fucking tease. He gave us a glimpse of something beautiful, and now he's sent us right back to studentland.

— If you say that, Lauren's retorting testily, though relieved that Rab's affectionate display has gone no further, — that means you agree with that whole Thatcherite paradigm of running down the arts and just making everything vocational. If you kill off the idea of knowledge for its own sake, then that just kills off any critical analysis of what's happening in soci . . .

— Naw . . . naw . . . Rab protests, — what I mean is . . .

And so they go on, battling away like this, sparring and telling themselves that they don't fundamentally disagree when there's a chasm between their positions, or alternatively, arguing savagely over minor, pedantic differences in emphasis. In other words, they're being total fucking students.

I hate those kind of arguments, especially between a man and woman, particularly when one of them has just upped the stakes in that way. I feel like screaming in their faces: STOP LOOKING FOR REASONS NOT TO FUCK EACH OTHER.

The bar starts to become that more acceptable soft-focus way after a few drinks, where things seem to slow down and people are happy enough just to be in each other's company and it's good to talk shit. And now I decide that I quite fancy Rab. It's not been an instant thing, it's been a kind of slow build-up. There's something clean and Caledonian about him, noble and Celtic. An almost puri-tanical stoicism that you don't really find with men his age in England, certainly not in Reading. But they do go on, those Scots: arguing, discussing and debating in a way that only the leisured and metro-politan media classes in England tend to do. — Fuck all these silly arguments, I tell them grandly. — I told you both a naughty secret earlier. Don't you have any naughty secrets, Lauren?

— No, she says, her face colouring again, her head bowing. And I see Rab raise his eyebrows as if urging me to leave it and it's like he has some kind of empathy with Lauren's pain which I wish I had.

— What about you then, Rab?

He grins and shakes his head. You see mischief in his eyes for the first time. — Naw, my mate Terry, he's the man for them.

— Terry, eh. I'd like to meet him. Have you met him, Lauren?

— No, she says curtly, still tense but thawing a little.

Rab raises his eyebrows again, as if to suggest that it might not be a good idea, which sort of intrigues me a little bit. Yes, I think it might be nice to meet this Terry and I like the way that Rab thinks that it might not. — So what does he get up to? I quiz.

— Well, Rab begins cautiously, — he's got this shag club. They make stag videos and all that kind of thing. I mean, it's no my scene, but that's Terry.

— Tell me more!

— Well, Terry used to go back tae this pub for a lock-in. There would be some lassies he knew and maybe a tourist or two. One night they all got a wee bit drunk and frisky and started going for it, you know. It became a regular thing. One time it got recorded on the security camera, he said it was an accident, Rab spins his eyes doubtfully, — but it got them started in the amateur-video thing. They make their fuck films and show clips of them on the Net, then send them off on mail order or swap them with other people who do the same. They put on a show, usually for the old boys in the pub for a fiver a head. Eh . . . every Thursday night.

Lauren's looking pretty disgusted with this, and you can tell Rab is going down in her estimation, which is something he's very much aware of. However, I'm finding it all very inspiring. And it's Thursday tomorrow. — Will they be screening tomorrow? I enquire.

— Aye, probably.

— Can we come along?

Rab isn't too sure about this. — Well, eh . . . I'd have to vouch for youse. It's a private sort ay do. Terry's eh . . . he might try tae get yis tae take part, so if we do go, just ignore everything he says. He's full of shite.

I sweep my hair back, exclaiming grandly: — I might be up for that! Lauren as well, I add. — Fucking is a good way of getting to know people.

Lauren gives me a look that could down a charging bull. — I'm not going to watch pornographic films in a grotty pub with dirty old men, far less take part in them.

— C'mon. It'll be fun.

— No, it won't. It'll be filthy, disgusting and sad. Obviously, we've got differing concepts of fun, she ripostes vehemently.

I know she's edgy and I don't want to fall out with her, but I've a point to make here. I shake my head. — We're supposed to be studying film? Studying culture? Rab's telling us that there's a whole underground film-making culture happening under our very noses. We have to go for it. For educational reasons. And, we have a chance of getting laid as well!

— Keep yir voice doon! You're drunk! She squeals at me, looking furtively around the pub.

Rab's laughing at Lauren's discomfort, or maybe it's a way to hide his own. — You like tae shock, don't you, he says to me.

— Only myself, I tell him. — What about you, do you ever take part?

— Eh, naw, it's no really my thing, he stresses again, but in an almost guilty way.

Now I'm thinking about this Terry guy who *does* like to take part, wondering what he's like. Wishing Rab and Lauren were a little bit more adventurous and considering what great fun a threesome might be.

7

Scam # 18,735

I'm back (finally) in my home city. A journey by rail, which once took four and a half hours, now takes seven. Progress my arse. Modernisation my hole. And the prices get higher in direct correlation with the journey time getting fucking longer. I stick my package addressed to Begbie into the postbox at the station. Chug on that one, head boy. I taxi down to the foot of the Walk, that grand old thoroughfare looking much the same as ever. The Walk's like a very expensive old Axminster carpet. It might be a bit dark and faded, but it's still got enough quality about it to absorb society's inevitable crumbs. Alighting at Paula's gaff, I pay the comedian of a taxi driver his rip-off fee and meander past the burst entryphone, up the pish-smelling stair.

Paula gives me a hug, lets me into the gaff and sits me down in her cosy front room with tea and digestives. She's on good form, I'll say that for her, although she still looks like a road traffic accident on pianny legs. We're not stopping here long though, nor are we going to Paula's bar, the famous Port Sunshine Tavern. Too much of a busman's holiday for her. No, we head into the Spey Lounge for one and I'm at once elated and disappointed to note the absence of kent faces.

Paula toys with her drink, and can't help letting a self-satisfied smile mould her big slack face. — Aye, ah've spent too much time in thon place. Ah've goat ma ain life now, son, she tells me. — Ye see, ah've met this felly.

I'm staring into Paula's eyes, and I know that my eyebrow is involuntarily arching, Leslie Phillips-style, but I'm powerless to stop it. However, I scarcely need to provide her with even the flimsiest cue to cut to the chase. Paula always was a bit of a man-eater. One of my most harrowing teenage memories was slow-dancing with her

44

at my sister's wedding, her hand clasped over my arse, as Bryan Ferry sang 'Slave to Love'.

— Eh's Spanish, a lovely felly, his ain place oot in Alicante. Ah've been oot tae see it. Eh wants ays oot thaire wi him. Gittin oot intae the sun, gittin this auld lum swept properly, she squeezes her thighs together and unrolls her bottom lip like a red carpet, — that's whit it's aw aboot, Simon. They say tae ays, aw thum aroond here, she snorts, including at least the entire port of Leith in her derision, — 'Paula, yir livin in fool's paradise, it'll never last.' Dinnae git me wrong, ah've nae illusions, if it doesnae last it doesnae last. What dis last? Any paradise seems awright tae me right now, she says, knocking back the last of her drink and taking the slice of lemon in her mouth, chomping it between those false gnashers and sucking out every last drop from it, before spitting it, mangled, back into the empty glass.

It doesn't take a lot of imagination to see that sorry shaving of lemon as a terrified Spaniard's cock.

Paula's anticipated all objections, not that I would be enough of a killjoy to try and raise any. Her belief in me is touching: my lies of London leisure-industry success have impressed. She wants me to take over the Port Sunshine. The problem of her wanting twenty grand for the hovel is resolved surprisingly easily as she suggests that I pay it off as the bar earns. Until then, she'll be my sleeping partner.

The place is a potential gold mine, just waiting for a makeover job. You can feel the gentrification creeping up from the Shore and forcing house prices up and I can hear the tills ringing as I give the Port Sunshine a tart-up from Jakey Central to New Leith café society. It's got the lot, the big function room at the back, and the old bar up the stairs, long since shut and used as storage.

I need to apply for a licence, so as soon as I leave Paula, I'm up to the City Chambers to get the forms. Afterwards, I treat myself to a cappuccino (done surprisingly well for Scotland) and an oatmeal biscuit, in the patisserie round the corner. I examine the council paperwork and, thinking of the Hackney bedsit, start work on the documentation. Leith is on the up. It'll be on the Tube line before Hackney.

Later, I head up to my parents' house on the South Side. My

45

mother is delighted to see me, grabbing me in a rib-cracking embrace and breaking into a sob. — Look, Davie, she says to the old boy, who can barely tear himself from the telly, — my laddie is-a back! Oh, son, I love ye!

— C'mon, Ma . . . Mama, I say, mildly embarrassed.

— Wait till Carlotta sees you! And Louisa!

— Thing is, I have tae go back soon . . .

— Aw, son, son, son . . . no . . .

— Aye but, the thing is, Ma, I'll be back up soon. For good!

My mother bursts into tears. — Davie! Dae ye hear-a that? I'm going to have my laddie back!

— Aye, Paula's said I could take over the Port Sunshine.

My old man swivels round in the chair and raises a doubtful eye.

— What's up-a with your face! my mother says.

— The Port Sunshine? Widnae be seen died in thair. Fill ay hoors n comic singers, my father scoffs. The old bastard looks tired, sitting there with his weather-beaten tan. It's as if he's now admitted to himself that he can no longer fuck my mother about or she'll throw the semi-jakey out on his arse and he's now too enfeebled to find another daft cow to run after him, particularly one that makes pasta like her.

Conceding to her wishes for a family get-together, I decide to stay an extra night. My wee sister Carlotta comes in and squeals excitedly, planting a heavy kiss on each cheek, and calls Louisa on the mobile. I sit there with a sister on either side, fussing all over me, as the old man grunts and raises a bitter eye. Every so often my mother pulls Carlotta or Louisa from the couch and shouts: — Up-a the now. I want tae get-a proper hug ay that-a laddie of mine. Ah widnae believe it, ma wee laddie back here! For good as well!

Content with the way things are going, I head downhill to Sun City. I'm bouncing down the Walk, breathing in the sea air as scummy Edinburgh makes way to my beautiful home port. Then I go down to the bar with Paula behind it, and instantly suffer a massive comedown. The bar itself is shambolic enough: old red floor tiles, formica-topped tables, nicotine-tanned walls and ceiling, but it's the punters that get me. It's like a crowd of zombies in a George A. Romero movie, decaying away under the harsh strip lighting, which magnifies the multitude of sins. I've seen crack dens on estates in Hackney and Islington which are like fucking palaces compared to this shithouse.

Leith? I spent so many years trying to get out of here. How could I set foot in this place again? Now that the old girl's moved to the South Side, there is absolutely no need. I'm up at the bar drinking a Scotch, watching Paula and her pal Morag, who's a total Paula clone, serve up meals to these whining toothless old cunts like it's a soup kitchen. On the other side of the bar incongruously loud dance music blares from the jukebox and several skeletal young men sniff and twitch and stare. Already I find myself anxious to get away from the pub, Paula and Leith. The London train is calling.

I make my excuses and I'm walking further down into the new Leith: the Royal Yacht Britannia, the Scottish Office, renovated docks, wine bars, restaurants, yuppie pads. This is the future, and it's only two blocks away. The next year, the year after maybe, just one block away. Then bingo!

All I need to do is to swallow my pride and sit pretty for a bit. In the meantime, there will be some top scamming going on; the natives are far too much like backwoodsmen to be able to keep up to pace with a metropolitan swashbuckler like Simon David Williamson.

8

'. . . just the solitary lens . . .'

Rab seems nervous. He's picking the skin around his fingers. When I challenge him he says something about giving up smoking, muttering about a baby being on the way. It's his first ever hint to me, apart from this mysterious Terry guy, about a life outside the student world. It's strange to think that some people actually do have them; whole, self-contained arenas, broken off into little compartments. Like me. And now we're going right into at least a part of his hidden world.

Our taxi clicks and lurches its way from one set of lights to the next, the meter rolling by as relentlessly as a Scottish summer. It halts outside this small pub, but although the sinal yellow light spills out onto the grey-blue pavement and you can hear smoked throats bellowing laughter, we don't go in. No, we're down a piss-and-gravel side lane and to a black-painted back door on which Rab beats out a tattoo. Di-di, di-di-di, di-di-di-di, di-di.

You hear the noise of somebody cascading down a set of stairs. Then silence.

— S'Rab, he slurs, rapping again, another football rhythm.

A bolt slides, a chain rattles and a frizzy-topped head pops out from behind the door like a jack-in-the-box. A pair of hungry, slitty eyes briefly acknowledge Rab, then scan my body with such a casual intensity that I almost want to scream for the police. Then any sense of threat or discomfort evaporates in the heat of a white-hot smile, which seems to reach out to my own face like a sculptor's fingers, moulding it into its own image. The grin is amazing, turning his face from that of a belligerent, hostile fool to some kind of feral genius with the secrets of the world at his disposal. The head twists one way, then the other, scanning the alley for any further activity.

— This is Nikki, Rab explains.

— Come in, come in, the guy nods.

Rab shoots me a quick 'are you sure' look and explains: — This is Terry, as I answer him by way of stepping over the door.

— Juice Terry, this big, curly-haired guy smiles, stepping aside to let me go up the narrow staircase first. He follows in silence, so that he can look at my bum, I expect. I take my time, showing him that I won't be fazed by this. Let *him* be fazed.

— You've got an amazing arse, Nikki, I'll tell ye that for nowt, he says with cheerful enthusiasm. I'm starting to really like him already. That's my weakness; too easily impressed by the wrong type of person. They always said that; parents, teachers, coaches, even peers.

— Thank you, Terry, I say coolly, turning as I get to the top of the stair. His eyes are glowing and I look straight at him, holding the gaze. That grin expands further and he nods to the door and I open it and step in.

Sometimes the otherness of a place really hits you. When the summer fades and the term starts and everything is blue, grey and purple. The cleansing air in your lungs, the purity of it, then turning to cold until you huddle together for warmth in the dimly lit bars away from the bland could-be-anywhere Witherspoons/Falcon and Firkin/All Bar One/O'Neill's-land that's the corporate, colonised social hub of every urban centre of the UK. Go a bit out though, and you find the real places. Usually just a brisk walk, maybe a few stops on the bus, it never takes too long. This is one of those places, so overwhelmingly like stepping back into another age that its tawdriness dazzles. I head to the toilet in order to take stock. The Ladies is like a small coffin standing up Egyptian-style, barely big enough to sit down in, with a broken toilet, no bog paper, chipped tiles, a wash-hand basin with no hot water and a cracked mirror above it. I look into it, cheered that the spot I feared erupting seems to have gone into remission. There's a blotch on my cheek but it's fading. Red wine. Avoid red wine. That shouldn't be difficult in here. I apply some eyeliner and more of that purple-red lipstick, and quickly brush my hair. Then I take a deep breath and walk out, ready for this new world.

A lot of eyes are on me; eyes I was vaguely aware of but had blanked out on my way to the toilet. One hard-looking girl with black hair, cut short, has an overtly hostile gaze. I see Terry raise his eyes in my peripheral vision and he signals to a woman behind the bar. The place is half empty but I'm keeping Terry in my sights.

— Get them in then, Birrell ya cunt, he says to Rab, but not averting his eyes from me. — So, Nikki, you're at college wi Rab. That must be . . . Terry gropes for a word, seems to select then spit one out, then another, before concluding, — Naw, some things are jist better no thinkin aboot.

I laugh at his performance. He's fun. There's no need to burst his balls straight away, that can be done later on. — Yeah, I'm at uni. We're on the same film studies course.

— Ah'll show ye some film tae study awright! C'mon, sit beside me, he says, pointing at a seat in the corner, like an eager primary-age pupil anxious to show off what he's done at school. — They goat any mair like you up at that college? he asks, though it seems as if it's for Rab's benefit. I've already found that Terry and myself both enjoy making Rab feel uncomfortable. Something shared.

We sit in a corner near two youngish women, a couple and the barmaid.

Terry is wearing an old Paul and Shark black zipper fleece over a V-necked T-shirt. He has a pair of Levi's and some Adidas trainers. On his finger he has a gold ring and a chain hangs from his neck. — So you're the famous Terry then, I enquire, hoping to get a reaction.

— Aye, Terry says matter-of-factly, as if this éclat is both widely known and uncontentious, — Juice Terry, he repeats. — We're just aboot tae show the yin we did the other night thaire.

A gang of old guys and not so old guys come in and sit down, many of them on seats pulled out and lined up under the screen. It has the atmosphere of a football match. There's acknowledgement and jokes and drinks, and that hostile-looking girl is collecting money from them. Terry shouts to this stocky, vaguely threatening presence: — Gina, goan draw they curtains, hen.

She looks quite sourly at him, goes to say something and thinks better of it.

The show starts up, and the picture was obviously shot on a cheap digital video; one camera, no edit, just the solitary lens pulling out and in. It's from a tripod cause the image is steady, but it's a one-take of people shagging, rather than any real attempt to craft a film. The quality of picture's okay, you can tell that Terry is shagging that Gina across the very bar that they're serving the drinks from.

— Aye, ah've loast a bit ay weight this last year, he whispers to me, evidently quite pleased about it, patting his sides to show what must be his now-diminished love handles. I turn to look, but I can hardly keep my eyes from the screen, as a young girl, — Melanie, Terry whispers, comes into the picture. He nods to the bar and I recognise her now as the same girl that was standing there earlier. She looks different, really sexy on the screen. Now Gina is performing cunnilingus on her. Somebody makes a comment and there's a bit of laughter and the Melanie girl smiles in coy embarrassment, but it's followed by silencing shushes. There's barely any sound quality now, I can just about make out a few gasps and comments and Terry faintly saying things like 'come on', 'yes' and 'that's the game, doll'. On the picture a blonde girl comes in and he's frigging her and she's sucking him off. Then he bends her over a couch and starts fucking her from behind. Her face looks right into the camera and her large breasts dangle. Then we see Terry's head over her shoulder, looking right into the lens, winking at us, and saying something which sounds like 'spice of life'. — Ursula, Swedish lassie, he explains to me in a stage whisper, — or is it Danish . . . anywey, au pair girl, hings aroond the Grassmarket. Game as fuck, he explains. As the other players enter the fray, Terry's occasional commentary flits into my head: — . . . Craig . . . good mate ay mine. Top shagger. No exactly well-hung, bit a total sex case. Kin eh find wid but . . . Ronnie . . . could pump fir Scotland that boy . . .

The show ends up in a free-for-all and the camera work deteriorates. At times all you can see is a pink blur. Then it pulls out and in the background you see the Gina girl chopping out some lines of coke, as if bored by the sex. It badly needs editing and I'm tempted to share this thought with Terry, but he senses the audience's growing boredom and switches it off from the handset. — That's aboot us, folks, he smiles.

After the show, I'm having a chat at the bar with Rab, asking him how long this has been going on for. He's about to reply, when Terry sidles up to me and asks: — What did ye think ay that then?

— Amateurs, I reply, more loudly and pompously in drink than I intended, as I whisk my hair back. My blood chills a little, because I think that Gina girl heard me and I caught a cold, razor glint in her eye.

— N you could dae better? he asks, his eyes hooding and brows arching.

I look him steadily in the eye. — Yeah, I tell him.

He rolls his eyes and eagerly scribbles a number down on a beer mat. — Any time, doll. Any time, he says softly.

— I'll hold you to that, I say, to the distaste of Rab.

I notice for the first time the two other guys in the film, Craig and Ronnie. Craig is a thin, nervous-looking, chain-smoker with a modish mop of light-brown hair, Ronnie a relaxed guy with thin fair hair and the same idiot grin that he wears on the screen, although he seems podgier in the flesh.

Shortly afterwards, the Scandinavian girl, Ursula, comes in, and Terry introduces us. Her initial glance at me is polar, though she greets me with over-the-top warmth. Ursula doesn't look as good in the flesh as she does on screen; her features are slightly pudgy, troll-like even. She offers to get me a drink and the party looks like it's going to continue but I make my apologies and head home. Something interesting might be about to happen but that look in Terry's eye tells me that it's wrong to play all my cards at once. He'll wait. They all will. And besides, I've an essay to finish.

When I get back home I find that Lauren's still up, and she's with Dianne, who's moved her stuff in. Lauren seems to be really in the huff with me for going out, for not being here to help, or to welcome Dianne or whatever. The fact is, though, that she's pissed off with me for going along to this stag-video show, but you can also tell that she's desperate to ask me about it.

— Hi, Dianne! Sorry, I had to go out, I tell her.

Dianne doesn't seem to mind. She's a very cool, pretty woman, who must be ages with me; she has thick, luxuriant, black shoulder-length hair, in which she wears a blue band. Her eyes are busy and full of life and she has quite thin, rather sly lips which pull open to expose large, white teeth, completely changing her expression. She's wearing a blue sweatshirt, blue jeans and trainers. — Anywhere fun? she asks in a local accent.

— I went to a stag-video show in a pub, I tell her.

I watch Lauren redden with embarrassment, and when she says, — That's a little more information than we needed, Nikki, it sounds pathetic, like an adolescent trying to be grown up but only making herself seem more childlike in the process.

— Any good? Dianne asks, and to Lauren's horror, totally unfazed.

— Not bad. It was Lauren's friend I went along with, I tell her.

— No he's not! He's your friend as well! she says too loudly, then realising this, trails off. — It's just a guy on the course.

— That's very interesting, Dianne says, — because I'm doing research for my MPhil in psychology on workers in the sex industry. You know, prostitutes, lap dancers, strippers, call-centre operators, massage-parlour people, escort girls, all that stuff.

— How's it going?

— It's hard to find people who want to talk about it, she tells me.

I smile at her. — I just might be able to help you there.

— Brilliant, she says and we make an arrangement to have a natter about my work in the sauna, the next shift of which starts tomorrow evening. I go to my room, half drunk, and try to read my essay for McClymont on the word processor. After a couple of pages my eyes nip and I laugh at the stupid sentence: 'It is impossible to escape the contention that migratory Scots enriched every society they came into contact with.' This is for McClymont's benefit. Of course, I won't mention their role in slavery, racism or the formation of the Ku Klux Klan. After a while my eyes grow heavy and I feel myself drifting back onto my bed and easing slowly into a hot, nomadic trek and then I'm somewhere else . . .

. . . *he's holding onto me . . . that smell . . . and her face in the background, her twisted and eager smiles as he bends me round the bar like I'm made of rubber . . . that voice, commanding, urging . . . and I see the faces of Mum and Dad and my brother Will in the crowd and I'm trying to shout . . . please stop this . . . please . . . but it's like they can't see me and I'm being groped and tickled . . .*

It was a bruising, unsatisfactory, alcoholic sleep. I sit up and my head pounds, and an urge to vomit grips me, then passes, leaving me with a thumping heart and a toxic sweat on my face and under my armpits.

The computer was left on dozing, and as I brush the mouse, the power surge kicks McClymont's essay back onto the screen, like it was issuing a challenge. I have to get it in. Noting that Dianne and Lauren have gone, I make a quick coffee, then read the essay, tinker a bit, check the word count, put it through the spell check and click 'Print'. I need to get this essay in at the uni by noon; as it raps out the three thousand required words I head to the bathroom and shower away yesterday's alcohol, sweat and grimy cigarette smoke, giving my hair a good wash.

I apply moisturiser to my face, a little make-up, and throw on my clothes, taking the stuff for my shift at the sauna out with me in a holdall. I'm heading across the Meadows at speed, only occasionally aware of the cold, stiff wind as it bends back the essay paper I'm trying to read. I realise that the American word-processing-package spell check has corrected in American English: 'z's' everywhere and 'u's' thrown away, something that inordinately irritates McClymont and will probably negate the gains made by the sychophantic comments. If this is a pass, then it's a bare one.

I hand it in to the departmental secretary's office at 11.47 a.m. and after a coffee and a sandwich I head for the library where I spend the afternoon reading film texts before getting down to the sauna round teatime.

The sauna is on a dirty, narrow, gloomy main road which serves traffic coming into town. The smell of the hops from the nearby brewery is seedy if you've been drinking, like the dregs of last night thrown back in your face. The grime from the buses and lorries blackens most of the shopfronts permanently and the 'Miss Argentina Latin Sauna and Massage Parlour' is no exception. Inside, however, everything is pristine. — Mind n wipe up, Bobby Keats, the proprietor, always tells us with great urgency. There are more cleaning fluids than massage oils and we're all urged to use them as liberally.

The laundry bill for the fresh towels alone must be astronomical.

There's a permanent, synthetic scent in the air. Yet the soaps, mouthwashes, lotions, oils, talcs and fragrances, unsparingly applied to cover the trail of stale cum and sweat, oddly just seem to complement the rank atmosphere outside.

We have to look and act like air hostesses. In keeping with the theme of the sauna, Bobby employs girls he considers have Latin looks. Professionalism is the name of the game. My first client is a small, grey-haired man called Alfred. After I give him a deep aromatherapy massage using copious amounts of lavender oil on his tight, knotted back, he nervously asks for 'extras' and I offer him a 'special massage'.

I get a hold of his penis under the towel and begin to stroke him slowly, conscious of my poor wanking skills. I only hold down this job because Bobby fancies me. I'm thinking back to de Sade's writings where the young kidnapped girls are trained in the art of male masturbation by old men. But I think about my own experiences, and I've only ever wanked off my first two boyfriends, Jon and Richard, whom I didn't fuck. Since then I associated wanking a boy with not fucking him, and it sort of slipped off my sexual menu before it properly went on.

Sometimes clients do complain and I get the odd threat of dismissal. After a while though, I discovered Bobby was all mouth and no trousers on this issue. He regularly invites me out to various events: parties, casinos, big football games, cinema premieres, boxing matches, the races, the dog track or simply 'a drink' or 'a bite to eat' at a 'smart restaurant run by a good friend'. I always make an excuse or politely decline.

Fortunately, Alfred is too ecstatic to even notice, let alone complain. Any sexual contact is enough to send him off and he spurts his load in no time, paying me with gratitude. Many of the other girls, who do blow jobs and full sex, they don't make as much as me, a bad wanker, I know that for a fact. My pal Jayne, who's been here a lot longer than I have, smugly says that I'll go all the way before long. I rap back 'no chance' but there's some days when I feel that she's right, that it's inevitable, just a matter of time.

When I finish my shift, I check the message service on my mobile.

Lauren tells me that they're out drinking so I bell her back and meet them in a Cowgate pub. Along with Lauren is Dianne and also Lynda and Coral, two girls from the uni. The Bacardi Breezers flow and pretty soon we're all quite pissed again. At closing time Dianne, Lauren and I head back to our Tollcross flat. — Are you seeing anybody, Dianne? I ask as we walk up towards Chambers Street.

— No, I'm finishing my dissertation before I get into that, she says quite primly, and Lauren's nodding in approbation only to be cut to the quick when Dianne adds, — then I'll be shagging anything that's got a cock, because celibacy's fuckin well killing me! I snigger, and she throws her head back in laughter. — Cocks! Big cocks, small cocks, thick cocks, thin cocks. Circumcised, uncircumcised! White, black, yellow, red. When I hand that dissertation in it'll be a new dawn and heralded by COCK-A-DOODLE-DOO! She cups her hands and crows into the night air outside the museum as Lauren wilts and I laugh. I'm going to enjoy living with this girl.

I feel rough in the morning and I'm a bit narky and nippy in the lectures, short with this guy Dave, who's clumsily trying to chat me up. There's no Lauren to be seen, she must've been drunker than I thought. I catch up with Rab, holding court in the Square with that Dave and another guy, Chris. We walk across George Square towards the library, Rab's profile edged in a burst of sunlight.

— I'm not going to the library, I'm going home for a bit, I tell him.

He looks slightly hurt. Abandoned, even. — Right . . . he goes.

— I'm going up to mine for a blow. You coming? I offer. I know that Dianne said she'd be out all day, and I'm hoping Lauren's not in either.

— Aye, awright, he says. Rab's a bit of a hash-head.

We're up in the flat and I've skinned up and put on a Macy Gray CD. Rab's got the telly on with the sound turned down. Seems he needs as many reference points as possible. There's a session tonight in a Grassmarket pub as it's Chris's birthday. Rab doesn't really like drinking with the other students too much. He's social and affable enough with them, but you can tell he thinks they're wankers. I agree. I want, not so much into Rab's keks, but into his world. I know that he's seen and done a lot more than he lets on about. It fascinates me to think of there being this zone he inhabits that I know so little about. People like Juice Terry open up another, strange place. — Is everybody going straight out after the workshop? I ask him. The workshop's a joke, our one concession on the course to real film-making. And it's optional. But I don't want to get Rab started on that.

— Aye, according to Dave, he tells me, taking a long toke and keeping it in his lungs for an implausible amount of time.

— I'd better change, I announce and I go through to the bedroom and take off my jeans. I look at myself in the mirror then decide to head out to the kitchen. Then I come into the lounge and I'm standing behind him. His hair is sticking up a bit, or at least a tuft of it is. It's been bothering me all day. After we've made love, after I've earned the right to such intimacy, I'll wet it and smooth it down. I sit down on the couch next to him wearing just my red sleeveless top and white cotton knickers. He's watching the television. Cricket with the sound turned down. — I'll just get a toke first, I tell him, sweeping my hair back.

Rab's still looking at the soundless fucking cricket.

— That mate of yours, that Terry, he's a monster, I laugh. It sounds a bit forced.

Rab shrugs. He seems to do that a lot. Shrugs it off. What is he shrugging off? Embarrassment? Discomfort? Now he's handing me the joint, trying not to stare at my legs, at my white cotton pants, but he seems to be managing. He fucking well seems to be managing to be so fucking cool about it all. It's not as if he's gay; he's got a girlfriend and he's ignoring me . . .

I feel my voice getting a notch higher, a touch desperate. — You think we're sluts, don't you, the likes of me and Terry? Like me going along to get into it? You know I didn't do anything, well, not this time anyway, I giggle.

— Naw . . . ah mean, it's up tae you, Rab says. — Ah telt ye what he was intae. Ah telt ye he'd want tae get ye involved. It's up tae you whether you go along and what ye dae.

— But you disapprove, just like Lauren. She's been avoiding me, you know, I say, taking another toke.

— I know Terry. He's been my mate for donkey's years. I ken

57

what eh's like, aye, but if I'd disapproved I wouldnae have got ye tae meet him, Rab says matter-of-factly, displaying a casual maturity which is making me feel young and silly.

— You know it's just fucking, just a laugh though. I could never be into him, I explain, feeling all the more stupid and weak for doing so.

— That's you . . . he starts, then stops, and turns to me, his head still back hard against the couch. — Ah mean, it's up tae you who you shag.

I'm looking him right in the eye as I put the joint in the ashtray. — I wish it was, I tell him.

But Rab remains silent, turning his face away and looking straight at the screen. The fucking stupid cricket on the telly. Scots are supposed to hate cricket, I always considered that one of their great virtues.

He's not getting off that easy. — I said I wish it was.

— What dae ye mean? He says, and there's a slight quaver in his voice.

I nudge his leg with mine. — I'm sitting here in a pair of knickers and I want you to take them off me and fuck me.

I feel him tensing under my touch. He looks at me, then, in a sudden violent movement pulls me to him and he's snogging me but it's stiff and harsh and hateful, all anger and no passion and it dissipates and then he pulls away.

I look away, out the window. I can see some people in the flat opposite having a conversation. Of course. I stand up and pull the blinds. — Is it the blinds?

— It's no the blinds, he snaps. — I've got a girlfriend. She's having our kid. He goes silent for a bit, then adds: — That might no mean nowt tae you but it doesnae mean nowt tae me.

I feel a surge of anger, feel like saying, yes, you're fucking correct. It does mean 'nowt' to me. Less than nothing. — I want to fuck you, that's all. I don't want to marry you. If you'd rather watch the cricket, that's fine.

Rab says nothing, but there's a tension in his face and his eyes glint a little bit. I get up, experiencing the pain of rejection, feeling it right in the core of my self.

— It's no that ah dinnae fancy ye, Nikki, he says. — Fuckin hell, I'd be mad no tae. It's just . . .

— I'm going to get changed, I tell him sharply, and head into the bedroom. I hear the door, it must be Lauren.

9

Scam # 18,736

The hallway smells of cats' pish as I go to retrieve the morning post at the foot of the door, but the good news cheers me somewhat. It's official! I'm legit. At long fucking last, Simon David Williamson, local businessman, is returning to his Leith roots, courtesy of Edinburgh Council. I always said that Leith was the place to be, and SDW can play a significant part in the regeneration of the Port area.

I can see the *Evening News* now: Williamson, one of the dynamic new breed of Edinburgh entrepreneurs talks to the *News*'s very own John Gibson, a fellow Leither.

JG: Simon, what is it about Leith that makes people like yourself and Terence Conran, archetypal London success stories, want to invest so heavily in the area?

SDW: Well, John, funnily enough, I was speaking to Terry about this at a charity lunch recently and we both came to the same conclusion: Leith is on the way up, and we want to be part of the success story. It's especially poignant for me, being a local boy. My aim is to keep the Port Sunshine as a traditional pub, but be poised to upgrade it to a restaurant when the area finally takes off. It won't happen overnight, but I see my actions as an act of faith in Leith. It's no hyperbole to state: I love the old port. I like to think that Leith's been good to me and I've been good to her.

JG: So this is the way forward for Leith?

SDW: John, Leith's been a grand old lady far too long. Yes, we love her, as she's warm and maternal; a heavy, soft bosom to curl into on those cold, dark winter nights. But I want to reinvent her as a sexy, hot young bitch and pimp that dirty wee hoor oot for aw she's fuckin worth. In a word: business. I want Leith to be about business. Whenever people hear the word 'Leith', I want them to think, 'business'. Port of Leith, Port of Business.

I scrutinise the letter from Councillor Tom Mason, the chair of the licensing board for the city council.

City of Edinburgh
Licensing Committee

17 January

Dear Mr Williamson,

I am pleased to inform you that your application for a licence to sell alcoholic beverages for the premises at 56 Murray Street, Edinburgh EH6 7ED, known as the Port Sunshine Arms has been granted. This licence is conditional on acceptance of the terms and conditions detailed in the enclosed contract.

Please sign both copies of this contract and return it to us by Monday, 8 February.

Yours sincerely

Cllr T.J. Mason
Chair, Licensing Committee

Tom and I should get together soon, a round of golf at Gleneagles wish Sean perhapsh, when heash nexsht in town. We may stall and linger a while on the nineteenth, where I'll bend Tom's ear about my plansh for a shecond café-bar, further up the Walk. Perhaps Sean might also be persuaded to make an investment in helping to drag his city out of the fucking mediocrity it's been steeped in for decades.

Yesh, Shimon, there'sh definite inveshtment potential there. But fursht we musht rid ourshelves of the underclash that comprishes the current clientele of thish pub.

Exshachtly, Shean. Theesh people have no playsh in the new Leesh.

61

10

Counselling

It's like when the Avril lassie says tae us what brings ye doon, and ah think, well, Hibs and rain likesay. Then ah think, well, naw, cause when Hibs are daein well ah'm still doon sometimes so it disnae always match up. Obviously but, I'd rather see the cats in emerald green daein the biz, likes. But it's an excuse really, well, maybe no rain, cause rain eywis gies me the blues. When ah wis younger pittin oan a tune used tae help, but that's a no-go now cause maist ay the auld vinyl's gone, man, it's been sold off tae the second-hand record shops, that trek up the Walk tae Vinyl Villains, the proceeds used tae score broon and cook it up and stick it intae ma veins. Even Zappa's gone, man, that's Frank Zappa, no Zappa ma pet cat likesay. I'm tryin so hard tae keep away fae the broon, but ah like ma speed n thir's loads ay base gaun roond here right now n see when yir oan a comedoon wi it, ye really crave a nice bit ay broon tae take the edge offay it, likes.

The Avril chick here at the group reckons that every cat present needs a project, man, something tae stop the boredom, tae gie they listless lives a bit ay structure n direction. Cannae really spraff against the concept, man; wi aw need it, it simply hus tae be hud. — The next time you come, I want you to think of something you can do, she sais, drummin the pen oaf that set ay pearly-white front teeth.

Whoah, man, they gnashers pure pit bad thoughts intae ma heid, but ah shouldnae be thinkin that wey aboot Avs, cause she's a nice lassie, likes.

It's good though tae be thinkin aboot somethin sortay upbeat cause the thoughts recently huv been pure dark spooky black, likes. The thing is, what ah've been thinkin mair n mair aboot is, like, leavin this toon for good, as that Vic Godard cat said aboot the Johnny Thunders boy. It's an obsession now, man, especially whin the blues kick in. It first came tae ays when ah wis in the nick, readin this book. Ah've never really been a cat ay letters, but ah wis readin this *Crime and Punishment* book by that Russian gadgie.

Thing is but, man, it defo took ays a while tae get intae it but. It's like aw they Russian punters seemed tae huv two names, so it wis likesay, dead confusin. Funny, cause ower here, since way back tae the poll tax, loads ay gadges dinnae huv *any* names, at least no officially, so it aw sort ay evens itself oot.

There's me stuck in a cell wi thon auld bit ay deid tree but, and eventually ah really dug it. Thing wis, it sort ay got me thinkin ay a scam, likes. A fiddle tae sort oot aw the problems, the ones ah've caused by likesay, just being me, ah suppose. Aye, the modern world hus a kind ay natural selection and it's no really the sort ay gig where ah fit in. Cats like me have become extinct. Cannae adapt, so cannae survive. Sortay like the sabre-toothed tiger. The funny thing but, is that ah never really dug how that species became extinct, when less hard cats survived. Ah mean likesay, in a heid-tae-heid tussle n that, ye'd huv tae pit yir dough on the sabre-toothed gadgie tae pagger any common-or-gairdin other cat, even just an ordinary tiger. Answers oan a postcaird, man, answers right oan the dotted line.

Thing is, as ye git aulder, this character-deficiency gig becomes mair sapping. Thir wis a time ah used tae say tae aw the teachers, bosses, dole punters, poll-tax guys, magistrates, when they telt me ah was deficient: 'Hi, cool it, gadge, ah'm jist me, jist intae a different sort ay gig fae youse but, ken?' Now though, ah've goat tae concede thit mibee they cats had it sussed. Ye take a healthier slapping the aulder ye git. The blows hit hame mair. It's like yon Mike Tyson boy at the boxing, ken? Every time ye git it thegither tae make a comeback, thir's jist a wee bit mair missin. So ye fuck up again. Yip, ah'm jist no a gadge cut oot fir modern life n that's aw thir is tae it, man. Sometimes the gig goes smooth, then ah jist pure panic n it's back tae the auld weys. What kin ah dae?

Loadsay us have faults, man. Mine is gear, gear and gear. It's just likes a shame that one person hus tae pey so many times ower for the one fault. Of course, ah've goat chorin n aw, but if ah kicked the collies seriously, then the chorin might stop, or at least slow doon a bit.

The counsellin gig is somethin that ah dinnae really think is daein me much good. Ah mean, every time ah talk wi these dudes ah still feel the pull ay the junk, man. It never goes. We can likesay, rationalise it and look at it, but as soon as ye leave the room, yir thinkin aboot scorin. One time ah left a meeting and ah wis walkin in a haze and before ah knew where ah wis, ah wis bangin oan Seeker's door. Ah just sortay jolted into consciousness, and there ah wis, jist sortay rappin on that blue door. Ah fairly nashed doon that road before any cat answered it.

Ah do look forward tae the group though. It's just likesay, good, tae have a nice person tae listen tae ye. N that Avril is a nice lassie, likes. And she's no that posh n aw. Ye wonder if she's been through it aw herself, or whether it's aw jist college stuff. No thit ah'm knockin college stuff, cause if ah'd goat masel an education ah might no be in this mess ah'm in now. But every gadge and gadgette has to, or will go through something big n bad in their life; it's a terminal illness which thir's nae escape fae. None at aw, man.

The cats here range fae the feral hostile tae too timid and shy tae even purr. One lassie, Judy her name is, she's a weird yin. Pure says nowt for ages but see, when she starts, she cannae stop spraffin. N it's sortay likesay, pure personal n aw, things that ah could never talk aboot in public.

Like now, man. Ah'm findin it awfay embarrassin n ah want tae pit ma hands up in front ay ma face like ma wee laddie does when he goes aw shy. — And ah wis a virgin and after we'd made love eh gave me a shot ay smack tae bang up. That wis ma first time . . . the Judy chick says, aw serious.

— Sounds like a cunt tae me, Joey Parke goes. Wee Parkie, ma best mate here, but some boy. Nae brakes, man, even worse thin moi. Good at steyin oaf it, bit cannae allow ehsel jist one tiny slip which wi aw huv fae time tae time. Ah mean, one wee gless ay wine wi ehs burd ower a nice candlelit dinner fir two, in fact, jist one *wee sip* oot ay the gless ay wine, n two weeks later yi'll find um in some crack den pure rockin n rollin.

The Judy lassie's well upset at the wee man but. — You don't know him! You don't know what a lovely person he is! Don't you say anything about him!

Judy isnae a bad-lookin lassie n aw, but ye kin see thit the drugs have hagged her oot before her time. We use the powder tae pit a witchy hex oan ye, doll. Sorry.

No like Avril, the chick runnin the show. She's a thin lassie wi shining blonde-white hair cut in a bob and eyes sortay intense but no wired, like, kind ay energised but untroubled, if ye get ma drift. N Avs disnae like the raised voices. Conflict, this lassie always says, can be dealt with positively. And it's right n aw when ye think aboot it, but ah suppose only fir some cats, like. Ah mean, ye couldnae huv guys like Franco Begbie or Nelly Hunter or Alec Doyle or Lexo Setterington or some ay the boys ah met in the nick like Chizzie the Beast, or Hammy or Cracked Craigy sayin, 'Hey, man, let's just deal with this conflict issue positively.' Wudnae work, man, just would not work. Nae offence tae they sort ay boys but they've aw goat thir ain weys, likes. Avs though, she's cool enough tae handle the likes ay Joey n Judy. — I think we should take a break here, she says. — How do the others feel about that?

Judy nods sadly, and wee Joey Parke shrugs. One chunky gadgette, Monica she's called, says nothing, just sucks her hair and bites her finger. Sortay they big ham-shank type airms, ken, no that it's anything tae be ashamed ay or nowt like that. Ah smile at Avs n say: — That's sound by me. Could handle a coffee n snout, like. The caffeine injection, man, com-pul-sor-ee, or what?

Avs returns the smile and ah get a wee flutter in ma chest, cause it's barry havin a lassie smile at ye. N this feelin ay bliss disnae really last, as ah realise that it's a long time since ah made ma Alison smile like thon.

11

'. . . ugly . . .'

—You fucking horror show, I sneer at my image in the mirror. I'm looking at my naked body and then at the model in the magazine, holding it up trying to scale it to my size in my mind's eye, comparing the shape and curves. There's no way mine is as perfect as hers. My breasts are too small. I will never be in the magazine, cause I'm not magazine material, I don't look like her.

I'M NOTHING FUCKING LIKE HER.

The most horrible thing a man can say to me is that I've got a great body. Because I don't want a good, great, lovely, beautiful body. I want a body good enough to be in the magazines and if I had one I would be in them and I'm not cause I don't. My mascara's running with my tears, and why am I crying? Cause I'm going nowhere, that's why.

I'M NOT IN THE MAGAZINES.

And they tell me I've a great body cause they want to shag me, cause they're aroused by me. But if one of the girls in that magazine wanted to fuck them, they wouldn't even look at me. So here I am, and I know what I'm doing, I *know* I'm constantly fighting off negative images of perfection showered on me by a media I'm totally obsessed with. And I know that the more men are turned on by me, the more I have to compare myself to others.

I rip the page out of the magazine and screw it into a ball.

I should be in the library studying or working on my essay instead of spending half my time in W.H. Smith's skimming that rack shame-lessly: *Elle, Cosmo, New Woman, Vanity Fair,* looking at them all; the men's as well, *GQ, Loaded, Maxim,* gaping at all those bodies; obdu-rately scanning the airbrushed perfection of them all, until one of them, just one, induces a hateful self-loathing that I'll never be like that, never look like that. Oh yeah, knowing, on a cognitive, intellectual level that those images are compositions, they're made up, airbrushed, the one good picture a result of the photographer using make-up on the model, lots of sympathetic lighting and shooting rolls and rolls of film. And knowing that the model, actress, pop starlet is a fucked-up neurotic bitch just like me, who shits and dribbles in her pants, erupts in pus-filled spots under stress, has chronic halitosis as she's thrown up the contents of her guts so many times, has no septum from the coke she's snorted to keep going, and has a dark, stagnant monthly discharge dripping from her. Yes. But knowing intellectually is not enough, because 'real' isn't 'fact' any more. Real knowledge is emotional and in *feeling* and real feelings are engendered by the airbrushed image, the slogan and the soundbite.

I'M NOT A LOSER.

A quarter of a century almost gone, the best quarter, and I've done nothing, nothing, nothing . . .

I'M NOT A FUCKING LOSER.

I am beautiful Nicola Fuller-Smith who any man in his right mind would want to sleep with because my beauty would complement the highest image of his self he could have.

And now I'm thinking about Rab, about that disc of almost amberish-brown in his eye, and how when he smiles I want him, and he does not fucking want me, who does he think he is, he should be pleased that a gorgeous girl younger than him wants . . . no, an UGLY UGLY UGLY GIRL, A FUCKING REPULSIVE WHORE . . .

The door. I pull my dressing gown around me and head through to my essay, abandoned on the table in the front room, as the keys turn in the lock.

It's Lauren.

Little, stupid, slight, beautiful Lauren, who is SIX YEARS younger than me and behind her silly clothes and daft specs she's a fucking little fresh-meat goddess and she doesn't even realise it, nor do most of the equally blind and stupid men around her.

Those six years. What old, ugly Nicola Fuller-Smith here would give for even one or two of those six years that she, silly little Lauren Fuckall, will just waste away without ever even realising that she had them.

Oh-Oh-O-L-D, keep the fuck away from me.

— Hi, Nikki, she says enthusiastically. — I found a great text in the library and . . . she looks at me for the first time. — What's up with you?

— Can't get into this fucking essay for McClymont, I tell her. She can see that my book and papers are in exactly the same spot they've been in for the last week or so. She can also see the magazines on the table.

— There's a great new film website, some brilliant reviews, really analytical without being up themselves, if you know what I mean . . . she babbles, but she knows I'm not interested.

— Seen Dianne? I ask.

Lauren looks sniffily at me. — She was in the library when I last saw her, working on that dissertation. She's very focused, she purrs admiringly. So now she's got a new big sister and I'm stuck with a couple of swots. She starts to speak, falters, and then goes ahead anyway. — So what's the big problem with McClymont's essay? You used to be able to knock them off in no time.

So I'm telling her exactly what the problem is. — The big problem is not one of understanding or intellect. It's direction; I'm doing shit I don't want to do. The only way it'll happen for me is to be there, on the cover of the magazines, I tell her, slamming the *Elle* down on the coffee table, knocking some skins and tobacco on to the floor. — And that won't happen doing an essay on seventeenth-century Scottish immigration for McClymont.

— But it's self-defeating, Lauren slurs. — Just suppose you were on the magazine cov . . .

She's saying that so off-handedly and all I'm thinking is: when when when when when? — Do you really think I could be? But she's not answering me, not responding with what I want and need to know. Instead, she's telling me shit that will never cause me anything but pain, misery and boredom, because she's making me face the truths that we need at all costs to avoid in order to survive in this world . . . — you'd feel good for a bit, then next week you'd be older and a younger lassie would be on it. How would you feel then?

As I look at her, an insect coldness running through me, I want to scream:

I'M NOT IN MAGAZINES. I'M NOT ON TELEVISION. I NEVER WILL BE UNTIL I'M A FAT FUCKING LOSER BEING HUMILIATED BY SOME FAT LOSER HUSBAND ON REALITY TV, FOR THE GAWPING AMUSEMENT OF OTHER FAT LOSERS JUST LIKE ME. IS THAT YOUR 'FEMINISM'? IS THAT IT? CAUSE THAT'S THE FUCKING BEST-CASE SCENARIO FOR ME AND COUNTLESS OTHERS UNLESS WE TAKE REAL CONTROL.

But instead I compose myself and tell her: — I would feel great because at least I would have been there. At least I would have achieved something. That's what it's all about. I want to be up there. I want to act, sing and dance. Me. I want them to see that I lived. Nikki Fuller-Smith fucking well lived.

Lauren's looking at me with great concern, like a mother does to a kid who says 'I don't feel like going to school today . . .' — But you do live . . .

But I'm ranting now, spouting stupid nonsense, yet of the type within which the real truth must always lie. — And after doing stag films, I want to do real porn, then I want to produce or direct. To be the one in control. Me. A woman. And I'll tell you this right now, the only industry in the world where you have that control to any meaningful extent is pornography.

— Bullshit, Lauren shakes her head.

— No bullshit, I tell her firmly. What does she know about pornography? She's watched none, she's never studied the production of it, never been a sex worker, never even visited a pornographic website. — You don't understand, I tell her.

Picking up the skins and baccy, Lauren puts them back on the table. — You're sounding like somebody else. Probably that mate of Rab's, she pouts.

— Don't be stupid. And if it's Terry you're on about, I haven't even shagged him yet, I tell her, feeling bad at disclosing this.

— Yet being the operative word.

— I don't know if I will. I don't even fancy him, I snap testily. I talk too much. Lauren knows everything about me, almost everything about me, and I know nothing about her. She does have secrets, and I hope for her sake that they're interesting ones. Looking sorrowfully at me, the tone of her voice changes. — I don't know why you feel so bad about yourself, Nikki. You're the best-looking girl . . . woman I've ever met.

— Huh, try telling that to the guy I've just made a fool of myself over, I spit, but I'm starting to feel great inside. My response to flattery: I sneer, but I feel that nauseating lift in the muscles in my face, involuntary, controlling me, and then the rush in my stomach which spreads to the extremities of my arms and legs. I'm a sucker for it.

— Who was that, Lauren nearly squeaks, worried, touching the frames of her glasses.

— Oh, just a guy, you know how it is, I smile knowing too fucking well that she doesn't and she's about to say something else when we hear Dianne's key turn in the lock.

12

Czars and Huns

The group has become the soup, man. It's now the main nourishment ay the social kind that the boy Murphy gits. Lying in the kip wi Ali, feeling her recoil when ah touch her, it's bad, man, pure bad. Mind you, ah suppose she's jist gittin her ain back, fir aw the times ah've lain thaire, too junked tae make love, jist starin at the ceilin, or twisted up intae a foetal baw, saturatin the kip wi sweat as the horror ay withdrawal stepped forward. Now it's usually me lyin like a surfboard in the bed; wired head racin, no really able tae go tae sleep until she's taken the wee boy oot tae school.

Been leadin different lives they past few weeks, man. When did it aw start? Monny's perty? Funny, it eywis begins as a wee session, then spills intae a week, then ye realise that yir lives are pure, like, same space, but parallel universes for, like, yonks. So it's the group for me, makin an effort, likes, for Ali n the wee man's sakes, ken?

Eftir coffee Avril gits us thegither again. Ah dinnae really like this room, it's in an auld school buildin, n it's goat they uncomfy kind ay dole seats: rid plastic mouldings wi the black frames. Ye huv tae be straight tae sit in thum; it jist widnae be possible if yir twitchy oan drugs or sick. Avs is up at the big whiteboard which stands oan three aluminium legs. She writes wi a blue Magic Marker:

DREAMS

Then she says that dreams are important, it's likes we gie up oan thum too soon. When ye think aboot it: aye. But that astronaut gig; that first gadges oan Mars thing that me and ma auld mate Rents used tae talk aboot bein whin wi wir sprogs: it wis never really a serious runner, man. Inner space wis a better deal: less ay aw thon trainin required.

Rents but. He wis some boy. Sorted me oot awright.

Avril tells us that we should be prepared tae indulge oor fantasies mair. Joey Parke comes back wi something like: — We'll git locked up if we dae that. Fuck sakes! Eh turns tae me. — Indulge oor fantasies, eh, Spud! Ah laughs n the Monica lassie, her that bites the knuckles oan her hand, digs in a wee bit harder.

So then Avs is askin us in the group what sort ay job we'd like, in an ideal world, likes, if we could dae absolutely anything. Thing is, ah wis a wee bit bombed. Ah'm no usually like that in the group, it's jist thit ah hud a bit ay a shock at hame the other day n couldnae stoap thinkin aboot it. Ah pure needed some gear. But oot ay respect ah'd mixed it wi some charlie intae a speedbomb soas ah widnae be seen no tae be participating, sortay for the sake ay the group, likesay. Now though, nae cat's talkin so it's like ah'm pitching in tae say that ah'd like tae huv become an agent.

— Like a footballer's agent? They're very well paid, Avril says.

Joey Parke shakes ehs heid. — Parasites. Thir takin money oot the game.

— Naw, naw, naw, ah explain. — Ah wis thinkin mair as an agent for aw they blonde burds thit they huv oan the telly; the likes ay Ulrika Jonsson, Zoë Ball, Denise Van Outen, Gail Porter n aw that. Then ah think aboot it n say: — But it's the likes ay Sick Boy n that, that's an auld mate ay mine, they would git in thaire first. That's the kind ay job that they gie tae these cats, nae offence tae the boy, likes.

Sick Boy. Some cat.

Avril listens aw sort ay patient, likes, but ye tell she's no that impressed. Parkie goes oan aboot wantin tae dae the job ay Drug Czar. This gets a few ay them slaggin oaf that job n the boy thit's daein it, and well, that's oot ay order as far as ah see it.

So ah leaps tae the cat's defence, likes. — Naw, man, ah think it's a great idea, cause some ay the quality ay the gear these days is pure crap. It's aboot time the government were daein something aboot that instead ay just throwin people in jail aw the time. Moi's opinion, ma petite chats, moi's opinion.

A boy called Alfie pits oan this daft grin, then turns ehs face away. Then ah sees Parkie's laughin and shakin ehs heid. Eh goes: — Naw,

Spud, yuv goat the wrong end ay the stick, man. That boy's meant tae *stoap* ye fae takin drugs.

That gits me thinkin, n ah starts feelin sorry fir the dude, cause there's a gadgie that's goat ehs work cut oot. Ah mean, ah ken how difficult it is tae stoap masel fae takin drugs, nivir mind every other cat. What a thankless task for the poor boy. Ah dinnae see but, how they huv tae gie that joab tae a Russian boy when there's plenty punters in Scotland could dae it.

So thir gaun oan n oan aboot this. The weird thing aboot this group is thit we spend mair time talkin aboot drugs than we dae oan them. Sometimes whin yir straight, it really makes ye want thum, sortay pits ye in mind ay thum whin ye wirnae thinkin aboot thum, ken? But the Russian Drug Czar boy's pit me in mind again ay thon Dostoevsky book n that insurance policy ay mine. We goat it when the pramkicker came along, n ah wis clean n daein the slabbyin. Then they stoaped the slabbyin, man, peyed us aw oaf. But when ah did that hoose n goat sent doon, ah mind ay this boy in Perth gien me that Russian dude's book *Crime and Punishment*. Thir's eywis a copy circulatin roond in the nick, but ah never bothered before, no bein much ay a reader, likes. Liked this yin but, n it fair goat me thinkin aboot yon policy.

In the book, the gadge kills the auld money-lendin wifie that everybody hates. Now if ah wis tae top masel it wid pure be suicide, n they dinnae pey oot for that. But what if ah wis tae git killed, murdered likes, by some other party? Aye, the insurance thing hus tae be done; fir Ali and the wee gadge. It's the wey forward. Ah'm pure chronic, man, so when ye think aboot it, it makes sense tae leave the gig. Ah love those kittens tae death, but let's face it, man, ah am one big liability. Cannae make money, cannae keep straight, cannae stoap bringing grief back hame tae the bosom of. Ah am killing that chick slowly, man, she'll soon be back oan the gear herself, then wee Andy'll git taken away. Naw, ah'm no huvin that. So it's the insurance, man. Split. Leave the gig, makin sure the Ali-cat and Andy-cat are provided for. It's like that *Family Fortunes* thing whaire they ask the gadges what they want, likesay £20,000 insurance bread or a fucked-up, penniless, unskilled, junkie wi a ragin habit which will jist not go away. No much ay a contest for the sane of mind, man. So it's time tae go, bit it hus tae be done jist right.

The big, bad shock ah wis oan aboot came yesterday when ah wis lookin aroond the gaff for her purse n some dosh, n ah found a diary by mistake. Well, ah jist couldnae help masel, man, hud tae huv a wee nose. Ah mean, ah ken it wis wrong n that, dead wrong, but cause wi hudnae been speakin ah jist hud tae git intae her state ay mind. Big mistake but, man, ignorance wis pure bliss. What sort ay goat ays wis what she wrote: it wis like she was talkin tae wee Andy.

I don't know where he is, your daddy. He's let us down again, pal, and I'm the one again who's got to be strong. Your dad can mess up, but I can't. Just because somebody has to be strong and I'm just a wee bit better at it than your weak, stupid daddy. I wish he was a real bastard, because that would make it easier. It makes it hard that he's the nicest man you'll ever meet, and don't let anybody tell you different. But I can't be his ma and your ma as well. I can't cause I'm not strong enough. If I was strong enough I would, even though I know he'd be taking me for a mug. I'd still do it though, if I was strong enough. But I'm not and I have to put you first. Just because you're that wee.

It hit ays hard, man. Read it once, twice, and it must be said, found masel sheddin one or two tears, no just for me, but for the catgirl authoress. Aw that love goin tae the wrong place. Ah mind when ah wis younger ah wis just crazy, crazy, crazy aboot that lassie, but ah thought, this is a wee bit oot ay yir reach, man. A top-six SPL chick isnae gaunnae hook up wi an East of Scotland League journeyman. But the Junk Cup kin be a great leveller and there's the luck ay the draw tae consider. Aye, one time we were walkin hame thegither eftir a session, totally fucked, when it jist sortay happened. Ah think aboot what eight years wi me has done tae her. Naw, ah've got tae let her go, and leave the gig, and gie her a good pey-oaf.

It's got tae be done, man.

So it's after the counsellin do, ah'm shamblin up the Walk, tryin tae get intae a stride pattern before the old cramps and sweats commence and ah start spazin oot. Ah'm trying tae cheer maself up by thinkin aboot blondes and books and ah'm contemplatin that intelligent blonde lassie, the one wi the deep voice that's meant tae be the thinkin man's chug. Ye'd be able tae talk Russian novels awright wi her, too right. Oan that very subject, thir's a wee bookshop opened up and ah cross ower tae huv a quick look inside. Problem is thit the timin's a wee bit oaf n this nippy motor nearly hits ays, horn blarin as it tears past me doon the street. Ah git a jolt ay fear like yir skeleton jumps oot ay yir body n does a wee jig before hoppin back in.

Ah'm safe, safe, safe but. The shoap's got that fusty auld smell thit auld bookshoaps've goat, bit thir's new stuff here n aw. Thir's an auld fat boy wi silver hair n glesses n eh's pure keepin ehs mincers oan the boy Murphy here. Ah'm huvin a wee browse but, n ah spys yin oan Leith's history. It's aw auld stuff but, though mind you, ah suppose that's what history's meant tae be aboot! Ah look at its last section oan contemporary Leith, n it's aw *Royal Yacht Britannias* n aw that stuff, nowt aboot the YLT even. Some cat should write the *real* history ay the famous auld port, talk tae the punters that were aroond; like the auld cats that worked the docks, yards n bonds, drank in the boozers, hung oot wi the Teds, the YLT, the CCS, right through tae the present, aw the wee gadges wi the sovies oan thir fingers, they hip-hop rappy kids like ma wee mate Curtis wi the stammer.

Ah pits the books back, n ah heads back oot intae the street n continues up taewards fair Edina. Then, acroass the road, at the cashpoint oan the corner, ah see a boy who looks familiar, and it's Cousin Dode, a Glesgey felly likes. Ah'm straight ower, this time watchin fir traffic.

— Dode . . .

— Awright there, Spud, eh sais, ehs eyes flickerin in a sort ay disapproval, then suddenly lightin up. — S'pose yir wahntin a bung?

Jist like that, the Weedgie boy said it, man, n ah couldnae believe it! Withoot ays askin, jist like that! God bless those Glasgow Hun cats. Great boy, Dode. Sortay stocky wee boy wi greyish hair whae goes oan aboot how great Glesgey is, but well, obviously, the boy lives through here but, man. — Eh, ah dunno when ah'll be able tae square ye up, catboy . . .

— Hi! This is me yir talkin tae! Dode points tae ehsel, and we're over the road intae the Old Salt.

— Just been in n chenged ma pin number. They let ye dae that in ma bank, Dode explains, — personal like, so thit yi'll remember it easier. Bet your bank disnae let you dae that, eh sais, aw superior.

Ah'm sortay thinkin aboot this. — Eh, ah never really bother wi banks, man. Once when they sent ays oan this scheme, daein the slabbyin, likes, they made ays git an account. Ah goes, no, catboy, ah'm no a bank sortay gadge really, jist gie me cash, but they jist goes tae ays: sorry, man, pure modern gig, likes, ken?

Dode nods n goes tae speak, but ah press on cause ye cannae let Weedgies start, man, cause as cool as those cats are, once they git intae this 'awright, big man, how's it gaun, by the way' stuff, well, those cats could spraff for Scotland. If ye selected a talk team tae represent the country it's an absolute cert at least eight or nine fae the eleven would be Weedgies. So ah goes oan: — Well, they let me get intae the bank for a bit. But they kicked ays oot whin the green gages stoaped. The East Fife's goat an account, well, she's really the Lemon Curd but ah call her the East cause it's sortay likes ay common law, man, ken?

— Yir some boey, Spud, Cousin Dode smiles, putting a hand oan ma shoodir. — *Interdum stultus bene loquitur*, eh, mate.

Dode's quite a bright cunt for a soapdodger, likes, kens loads ay Latin n that. — Too true, Cousin Dode . . . eh, what does it mean, but?

— It means that ye, eh, talk a lot ay sense, Spud, eh sais.

Well, that's eywis nice tae hear, sortay welcome words soothin tae the auld ego n that, so that's me well chuffed. Also, that twenty bar the good Cuz slipped intae ma mit is appreciated n aw, it maist certainly is.

13

Whores of Amsterdam Pt 1

The DJ's good; you can tell by the number of trainspotters jostling around the box to watch him, and how relaxed he is in the face of the almost pensive-looking audience who're just waiting for something to happen, little knowing, most of them, that it already is.

Sure enough, he slips in *that* tune and they explode, shocked at the ferocity of their reaction, suddenly realising that he's been toying with them, tweaking them for a good half-hour. As the cheer goes up he gives a canny, sly smile which sparks across the dance floor.

Across the floor of *my* club, here on the Herengracht, 'the gentleman's canal' in old Amsterdam. I sip my vodka and Coke from my vantage point in the shadows at the back of the house, aware that I should be looking after this guy, extending the hand of friendship and hospitality like I do to all my guest DJs, even the ones who I think are arseholes. But Martin can look after this boy, I'm keeping out the road as he's from my home town and known to me. I've nothing against people from my home town, I just don't like running into them over here.

I see Katrin, her back to me, wearing that short, dark-blue dress, tight to her thin body which tapers up to her neck, the shock of razor-cut blonde hair sprouting from her head: she's standing with Miz and some shaggable porno teen he's picked up. I can't tell what kind of mood Katrin's in, I hope she's taken a pill. I put my arm around her waist but my spirits dip as I feel her tense at my contact. Nonetheless, I make the effort. — Good night, eh? I shout in her ear.

She turns her head to me and says in a gloomy German voice: — I want to go home . . .

Miz catches my eye and flashes me a look of understanding.

I move away from them, over to the office, and see Martin in there with Sian and this Brummie lassie who's started hanging around with them. They're doing lines of coke, which are chopped up, spread across the pine desk. He holds up a rolled fifty-guilder note to me as I contemplate the urging, eager saucer eyes of the girls. — Nah, ah'm alright, I tell him.

Martin, nodding at the lassies, throws a wrap on the desk, and pulls me into the small ante-room where we keep the photocopier and the clandestine conversations. — You okay?

— Aye . . . It's just Katrin . . . you know how things are.

Martin's face crinkles under his greying brown hair, and his big teeth flash in wired alert. — You know my advice, mate . . .

— Aye . . .

— Sorry, Mark, but she's a miserable cow and she's making you the same way, he tells me yet again, then he points to the door of the office. — You should be having the time of your life. Drinks, chicks, drugs. I mean, look at Miz out there, he shakes his head. — He's older than either of us. You only get one life, mate.

Martin and I are partners in the club, the same in so many ways, but the difference is that I can never be as flighty as him. When I get together with somebody, I believe in sticking it out. Even when there's nothing left to stick out. But he means well, and I let him bend my ear for a bit, before heading back to the floor.

And I find myself looking for Katrin, straying down to the front of the house. For some reason I glance up, and the DJ, the Edinburgh guy, catches my eye for a brief second and we give each other a thin-lipped smile of acknowledgement, and something uneasy rises in my chest. Then I turn away and catch sight of Katrin by the bar.

14

Scam # 18,737

All those people who have no place in the new Leith are here on my first day at the helm. A load of dirty auld mingers and these wee tartan techno and hip-hop cunts wi the sovies on every fuckin finger. One of the cheeky little bastards even calls me Sick Boy! Well, the only drugs that'll be dealt here will carry the Simon Williamson seal of approval, you insolent wee fuckers. Especially as yesterday I had the good fortune to run into an auld associate called Seeker, and now my pockets are fairly bulging with pills and wraps of ching.

And auld Morag will have to go; a fat wifie with retro National Health frames is too old-skool Leith for the type of regime the Williamson boy plans to institute. Too seventies, Mo. Style police: nee naw nee naw nee naw . . . She's serving one of the wee cunts now, or trying too. — F-f-f-four p-p-p-pints ay l-l-l . . . the boy says tae the sniggers of his mates, his face twisting in impersonation of a stroke victim as Morag stands in open-mouthed embarrassment.

Changes may have to be made. Alex McLeish?

Well, I think that's right, Simon. When I arrived here the club was in a shambles. Straight away I saw the potential, but we had to clear away some of the dead wood before we were ripe for investment.

That's the process, Alex.

Morag specialises in the catering side of the enterprise. We do meals here, three-course fuckers for something like ninety-nine pence a head for the pensioners. It irks me at what this is *not* doing to the profit margins: if I'd wanted to serve socialised food I'd have gone into meals on wheels. Aye, those bar lunches are fucking scandalously cheap: I'm subbing those auld parasites to stay alive.

One auld bear shuffles up tae me, somewhat menacing blue eyes set in yellow and red crystalline skin, so jaunty for such an ancient bastard. The cunt smells so badly of pish you'd think he'd been in a golden showers video. Maybe those auld fuckers are into the water sports at that centre they go to. — Fish or shepherd's pie, fish or shepherd's pie . . . he rasps, — did ye batter yir fish the day?

— Naw, ah jist gie'd it a slap and telt it tae behave itself, I quip with a smile and a wink.

My attempts at playing jocular mine host are obviously doomed to failure in this fucking sad arcade of rancid old losers. He looks at me, his auld wee Scots terrier face aw screwed up in belligerence. — Is that breadcrumbs or batter?

— Batter, I inform the vexatious auld fuck in tired resignation.

— Ah like it best done wi breadcrumbs, he goes, that mumpy face twisted into a circusy girn as he looks over intae the corner. — N Tam n Alec n Mabel n Ginty'll tell ye same, right? Eh shouts across, soliciting some enthusiastic nods from similar human remains.

— I humbly apologise, I say, biting my tongue, trying to retain a mood of superficial bonhomie.

— The batter, is it crispy? Ah mean, it's no that mushy wey, is it? I am making a supreme fucking effort here, the wide auld cunt. — As crisp as a new twenty-pound note, I tell him.

— Huh, it's been a long time since *ah* hud a new twenty-pound note, the old ratbag moans. — The peas, ur they mushy or gairden?

— Nae peas if thir no gairdin peas! this famine-victim wifie called Mabel shouts over.

The captain's wife was Mabel, by Christ, and she was able . . . tae gie the crew, their daily screw . . . upon the kitchen table.

Mushy or gairdin. Now there's a consideration for a man of enterprise. If Matt Colville could see me now, for him to witness this humiliation would be worth about five fucks at his wife. The burning issues of the day, right enough. Mushy or gairdin. I don't know. I don't care. I feel like shouting back: the only stale pees in here are in your fuckin scabby auld knickers, hen.

I turn to Morag the Toerag and let her sort it all out. A queue of sorts is building at the bar. *Oh fuck.* There's one recognisable figure standing there, shaking and shivering, and I'm resolutely cleaning the glasses, trying to avoid his big, lamplight eyes, but those searchlights of need are trained relentlessly on me. I know how lassies feel when they say 'he was undressing me with his eyes' because in this case I can say 'he was debiting my bank account with his eyes'.

Eventually, I can't *not* look. — Spud, I smile. — Long time no see. How goes it? It's been a few year.

— Fine, eh . . . awright, he stammers. Mr Murphy is a more wizened, depleted version of how I remember him, if that's possible. In fact, he looks like a recently deceased scrawny tomcat which has been dug up from its back-garden resting place by an urban fox. His eyes have that doolally mix of a man who's done too many uppers and downers for the different constituent parts of his brain to ever agree again as to what time of the day it is. He's a fucking ragged, rancid shell of a human being, propelled by drugs from one scabby flat or grotty pub to a subsequent similar den of corruption in search of his next toxic ingestion.

— Excellent. And how's Ali? I ask, wondering if she's still shacked up with him. I occasionally think about her. In a strange way I felt that we'd somehow end up together, once we'd got all our fucking-up out the way. She was always my woman, but I suppose I feel like that about all of them. But her and him being together; it isn't right, not right at all.

If she's any sense she'll have kicked him into touch years ago, not that I'm to be granted the courtesy of an answer. It's not even 'So what are you doing up here working behind a bar in Leith, Simon?' His crooked, selfish frame can't even impart that rudimentary level of curiosity, far less a genuine fucking greeting. — Look, ye ken what ah'm gaunnae ask ye, catboy, he coughs out.

— Not until you do, I smile, as patronisingly and frostily as I can manage, which I think, particularly in this case, is quite a fucking bit.

Murphy has the cheek to shoot *me* back an expression of hurt betrayal: a so-this-is-how-it's-gaunnae-be look. Then he inhales deeply, a strange, slow sound as the air struggles to push out his puny, scrawny lungs rendered so inefficient by what? bronchitis, pneumonia, tuberculosis, cigarettes, crack cocaine, Aids? — Ah widnae ask ye but ah'm really sick. Ah'm sick like nowt oan earth.

I look him over, and decide that he's not wrong. Then I hold the cleaned glass up to the light. I curtly inform him, while checking it for stains: — Half a mile up the road there. On the other side of the street.

— What? he goes, open-mouthed, fairground-goldfish style, framed as he is in the yellow lights of the pub.

— Edinburgh Council Department of Social Work, I inform him. — This, on the other hand, is a public house. I think you may have come to the wrong place. Here we're only licensed to sell intoxicating liquor. I convey him this information with all due officiousness, picking up another glass.

I almost regretted my words as Spud looked incredulously at me for a second, let the hurt sink in and then skulked out in a broken silence. Fortunately, the rush of shame was instantly replaced by a surge of pride and relief as yet another lame duck hobbled out of my life.

Aye, we went back a long way, but those were different times.

A wee crowd come in, then to my horror I see some Scottish Office suits poke their heads round the door and wrinkle their noses before beating a hasty retreat. Potential newcomers with wallets driven out by dogged old scumbags with pennies and young cunts who seem to be consuming every drug to great excess – except, that is, the alcohol I try to make my living from by selling in this bar. It's going to be a long first shift. I get on with it in mounting despondency, thinking of old Paula's warm fools' paradise.

At long last, I spy a friendly face coming into the pub, under a rash of curly hair cut shorter than I'm used to, and belonging on a much slimmer model than I could have believed. The last time I saw this man, I was convinced that he was heading for Fat Hell. It's like he saw the signs and found the slip road for the bypass in time, and is now back on the Svelte Heaven motorway. It's none other than the best-known former aerated waters' salesman this fine city has ever produced, 'Juice' Terry Lawson, from Saughton's Chosen Few. Terry's a bit off his manor down here, but he's a welcome face nonetheless. He greets me heartily and I note that his clothes have also changed for the better; expensive-looking leather jacket, Queen's Park FC-style black-and-white hooped Lacoste top, although the effect is somewhat spoiled by what looks like Calvin Klein jeans and Timberland shoes. I make a mental note to have a word. I buy him a drink and we chat about days gone by. Terry's telling me what he's been up to and I have to say it sounds interesting . . . — as game as fuck, the lassies. Ye widnae believe it; viddy the scenes n pit oan a show. We've started tae shift some through mail order in the grotmags. At first they wir rough, but wir gittin better, takin it forward like, cause a mate's aw pally wi this community group in Niddrie that huv goat this proper editin suite for digital vid. That's jist the start; one ay the boys wants tae design a website, then get the credit-card details and let the cunts download what they want ontae it. Fuck aw that business shite, it's porn that made the Internet.

— Sounds excellent, I nod, refreshing his glass. — You're way up with play here, Terry mate.

— Aye, and ah star in thum masel. You ken me, ah eywis liked a bird, n ah wis ey intae makin a bob or two withoot daein too much graft. Plenty new young talent up for it n aw, it's the spice ay life, he grins with great enthusiasm.

— It's ideal for ye, Terry, I consider, thinking it was probably only a matter or time before Terry, even in his own cruddy way, got into the industry.

Terry gets in another and then I decide that Mo can manage and so move to the more comfortable side of the bar, securing two large brandy and Cokes for us first. Terry's soon giving it the big one about it being great that I'm back up here, and with my connections in the industry we should try to start up something together. Of course, I can feel the bite coming in from about fifty yards away. — Ye see but, mate, his eyes widen, — the thing is, ah think we might be gittin bombed oot the other gaff, so ah could be lookin for a wee stay-back here.

This could prove interesting. I'm thinking about that big room upstairs. It has a bar, but now it's put to no use at all. — No harm in sucking it and seeing, eh, Terry, I smile.

— Eh, what aboot a wee trial run the night? he asks tentatively.

I consider this for a heartbeat, then nod slowly. — No time like the present, I smile.

Terry slaps my shoulder. — Sick Boy, it's fuckin well barry tae huv you up here. You're a welcome burst ay positive energy, mate. Thir's too many mumpy cunts in this city whae bring ye doon, thi'll dae nowt, then thi'll fuckin turn roond n moan when some other cunt hus a go. No you but, mate, you're up fir it! And he dances with a little twist out onto the floor of the bar and snaps on his mobile and starts calling.

Come closing time, I'm trying very hard to get the wee cunts who gather round the jukey out the door. — WILL YOU FINISH YOUR DRINKS PLEASE, LADIES AND GENTS! I screech across the bar, sending some old fuckers shuffling into the night. Terry's still gassing on the mobby. It's those young cunts but. That nosy wee cackbag, Philip they call him, a bad little bastard that, a fistful of sovies on him, he's clocked on that we're up to something. And that boy Curtis, his stammering, gormless-looking mate, I saw Murphy talking to him as he went out. Birds of a feather, right enough.

I open the side door and nod to them. As they make to leave, the Philip laddie asks me: — Is thir no a stey-back, Sick Boy, his narrow, slitty wee eyes burning and gold tooth glinting. — It's jist thit ah heard ye talkin tae that Juice Terry boy aboot it, he grins, aw cocky and pushy.

— Naw, it's a fuckin Freemasons' meeting, mate, I tell him, pushing his skinny frame out into the street, as his daft pal shuffles out behind him, the rest following suit.

— Thoat we'd git a stey-back, another insolent young pup smiles.

I ignore the tube but wink at a cute wee bird who follows him. She looks blankly in response before smiling slightly as she heads out. A bit too young for me though. I nod back in to Mo, who switches off the jukey, as I shut the door and repair to the bar to pour another couple of brandies for Terry and myself. A few minutes later there's a bang, which I ignore, then the fitba standard di-di, di-di-di, di-di-di-di, di-di.

Terry's snapped the mobby shut. — That's oor crew, he says.

I open the door and there's a boy I vaguely recognise and the hackles rise slightly as I'm sure he's an old Hibs boy, but, mind you, just about everybody from twenty-five tae thirty-five years old in Edinburgh is an old Hibs boy. There's another couple ay faces I half know but can't put a name to. Far more impressive are the lassies: three real dolls, a chunkier, dirty-looking bird, and a cute wee specky girl who looks really out of place here. One of the dolls is particularly enticing. Light-brown hair, almost oriental eyes with well-manicured, thinly plucked eyebrows, and a small mouth but with very full lips. Fuck me, her body ripples fitly under those expensive-looking clothes. Doll *Numero Duo* is a bit younger and though not quite so elegantly togged is a million light years from unshaggable. The third is a fuckable blonde. The two wee cunts, Philip and Curtis, are still there, hanging about, clocking the company, as do I, especially the spectacularly curved Doll *Numero Uno* with that long, brown hair and sultry, arrogant grace. That one in particular seems way past Terry's class. — What sort ay Freemason is she then? that cheeky wee Philip toss goes.

— Lodge sixty-nine, I whisper back at them, shutting the door in their faces once again, as Terry welcomes everybody with great gusto.

I turn to face my new guests. — Right, folks, we need to go upstairs, so if you just go through the door on your left, I explain. — Mo, I'll leave you to lock up behind ye, doll.

Morag raises her eyes briefly, trying to work out what's going on, then goes to the office and grabs her coat. I follow the crowd upstairs. Aye, this could be interesting.

15

Whores of Amsterdam Pt 2

Katrin was my girlfriend, a German lassie from Hanover. I met her one night in Luxury, my club, about five years ago. I don't remember the details very well. My memory's fucked, too many drugs. I stopped the smack when I settled in Amsterdam. But even Es and cocaine, over the years they blow holes in your brain, rob you of your memories, your past. Which is fair enough, convenient even.

I'd slowly learned to respect these drugs, using them more sparingly. You could be indiscriminate in your teens and twenties, as you had little conception of your own mortality. Of course, that wasn't to say that you'd necessarily survive this period. But in your thirties it was another matter. Suddenly, you knew you were going to die at some point, and you could feel in the hangovers and comedowns the extent to which drugs assisted this process; depleting spiritual, mental and physical resources, fuelling ennui as often as excitement. It became a mathematical problem where you played with the variables: units of drugs consumed, age, constitution and desire to get fucked up. Some people just opted out. A few kept right on to the end of the road, settling for life as one big suicide-attempt-by-instalment. I decided to maintain the same kind of life, going out, having it, but under controlled conditions. Then after one bad week, I sacked the lot, joined a gym and took up karate.

This morning I had to get out of the apartment. The atmosphere with Katrin is tense. Rows I can handle, but the silences eat away at me and her barbed comments sting like a boxer's jab. So I picked up my sports bag and headed to where I always head when I feel like this.

Now my arms are in the pulley levers and fully extended across my chest. I inhale long and deep, spreading them wide into a rigid cross. Today I've increased the weight and I feel the burn in my muscles, once so puny, now chunks of rock . . . red orgasm spots dance in front of my eyes . . . *and nineteen* . . . blood surges and roars in my ears . . . my lungs explode like a tyre blow-out in the motorway fast lane . . . *and twenty* . . .

. . . and thirty later I stop and feel the sweat from my forehead stinging my eyes and run my tongue around my lips to taste the salt. Then I repeat the performance, giving another piece of apparatus the same treatment. Then the treadmill gets thirty minutes, moving up from 10 kph to 14 kph speed.

In the changing room I pull off my old grey sweatshirt and shorts and pants and get under the shower, starting hot, then warm then bringing it down to cold, to fuckin freezing and I'm standing there, feeling my system charging up inside and I step out and almost collapse as my breath goes into a spasm, but then it's great, I'm whole again and warm, relaxed and alert as I slowly dress.

I see a couple of other guys who come here regularly. We never converse, only nod, in a stern approval at each other's presence. Men who are far too busy, too focused, to waste time on small talk. Men with a mission. Irreplaceable men; unique and at the centre of things.

Or so we like to think.

16

'. . . never mind Adam Smith's pin factory . . .'

It's been a busy day at the sauna. I gave a couple of massages which ended in handjobs but I told this creepy Arthur Scargill-looka-like guy to get fucked (politely) when he asked me to suck his cock.

Bobby pulls me up, standing before me in that Pringle jersey stretched implausibly over his large gut. — Listen, Nikki, yir popular here, wi the pun . . . clients n that. Thing is, yuv goat tae dae a wee bit mair sometimes. Ah mean, that guy ye hud that run-in wi, that wis Gordon Johnson. Eh's a well-known man in this city, a special client if ye like, he explains as I'm transfixed by the hair spilling from his nostrils, and that incongruously camp way he holds a ciga-rette in his hand.

— What are you saying to me, Bobby?

— Ah'd hate tae lose ye, hen, but if ye dinnae dae the biz, yir nae good tae me.

I feel a sick flush and I take the towels and stick them in the large laundry basket.

— Ye hear me?

I look back at him. — I hear you.

— Good.

I get my coat with Jayne, and we head up town. I'm thinking about how much I need the job, and how far I'll go to keep it. That's the thing with sex work, it always comes down to the most basic of formulas. If you really want to see how capitalism operates, never mind Adam Smith's pin factory, this is the place to study. Jayne wants to buy a new pair of shoes in a shop up Waverley Market but I have to go and meet the others in the pub up the South Side.

They're all present, and I'm surprised that Lauren's with Rab. This is a big shock. I thought that she'd welcome a night in with Dianne, would have wanted to take the opportunity to sit up drinking wine and having a midnight feast of fridge snacks with her new favourite big sister. I thought that I was relegated to the role of the kooky, embarrassing, promiscuous auntie in her life. I get the feeling that Lauren's here as she's taken it on herself to 'save' me from a life of debauchery. How boring. The guy in the pub said there was no chance of a stay-back, so Terry's gone ahead to scout this place. Then he calls us up on the mobile and we head down in a couple of taxis. I'm startled that Lauren's elected to join us, but she's been assured by Rab that he kept his clothes on and that shagging wasn't compulsory.

The new venue is an even more sleazy-looking bar in Leith. As we go in, again through a side door, a group of bad-skinned youths are leaving, and they make some comments. Lauren bristles angrily. Inside the pub, we get introduced to this sunbed-tanned man with his hair Brylcreemed back. With his dark, slanted brows and his wicked, twisting mouth, he looks a bit like a slightly crueller Steven Seagal. He takes us up the stairs to another room, which has a bar running the length of one wall and several tables and chairs. It smells dank and fusty, like it's not been used for a while. — This angel is Nikki, Terry says, running his hands up and down my back. When I stop and look at him, he protests: — Just checkin fir they wings, doll, cannae believe thit thir no thaire . . . then he turns to Lauren and says: — . . . N this wee honey here is Lauren. My auld pal Simon, Terry says, banging the Steven Seagal guy heartily on the back. He also introduces this Simon to Rab, Gina, Mel, Ursula, Craig and Ronnie.

The Simon guy unbolts the shutters on the bar and, in turn, offers us all his hand. His grip is strong and warm and he looks so painfully sincere that it just has to be an act. I've never seen anything like it before. — Thanks a lot for coming down, he says. — It's great to see you. I'm drinking malt whisky. It's a vice of mine. I'd be delighted if you'd all join me, he says, pouring out some Glenmorangie into glasses. — Apologies for the mess of this place, he explains, — I've only recently taken over and this room was used to store . . . well, I'd better not go into what it was used to store, he chuckles at Terry who responds with a knowing grin, — but I've had a clear-out.

— Not for me, thanks, Lauren says.

— C'mon, doll, huv a wee swally, Terry urges.

— Terry, Simon says seriously, — it's not the fucking army. Unless they've altered the English language the word 'no' generally means 'no'. Regarding Lauren, he asks gravely, — Is there anything else I can get you? Then he slaps his hands together and pushes them into his chest, his elbows pointing outwards. His eyes are open; intent and balefully sincere.

— Nothing, thanks, Lauren says stiffly, holding her ground, but I'm sure there's a slight smile playing round her lips.

The drinks are flowing and soon we're all engrossed in chat. Gina's still a bit unsure about me, although she must be getting used to my presence as the rancorous stares have abated somewhat. The rest are friendly, Melanie in particular. She's been telling me about her young son, and a horror story about the debts left to her by this guy she was with. We start listening to a conversation Simon (or 'Sick Boy' as Terry often refers to him, which he reacts to like someone's run their fingernails down a blackboard) is having with Rab. They're getting drunk on the whisky and are talking about making a porn movie.

— If you need a producer, I'm your boy. I worked in the industry in London, this Simon chap explains. — Videos, lap-dancing clubs. There's money to be made.

Rab's nodding along in agreement, to Lauren's increased distress. She's changed her mind about the drink and she's knocking back double vodkas and taking turns on the joints of skunk that are being passed around. — Yeah, porn always looks better on video, Rab asserts, — well, hard-core porn anyway. You lose the arty veil. It's like video records and film films.

— Yeah, says Simon. — I'd love to make a proper porn film. An old-school one, on film, an erotic tease, but with extended hard-core fuck scenes filmed on video inserted into it. That *Human Traffic* movie, they used digital video, super 16 and 32 mil, as far as I know.

Rab is intoxicated with the whisky and the idea. — Aye, you can do anything in edit, when you grade the film. But what ye want is no just a grainy wank-boy's cheapo vid, but a proper porno-graphic movie with a great script, a decent budget and really sound production values. One that'll enter into the canon of great films of the genre.

Lauren looks harshly at Rab, her face cast in outrage. — Great films of the genre! What great films! It's all exploitative fuckin trash, appealing to the basest instincts in . . . she looks round and faces Terry's lascivious gaze, — . . . people.

Terry shakes his head and says something about the Spice Girls, or it could be that, cause I'm a bit pissed and this skunk is deadly. People seem to be spinning by me and it's only through a wrenching effort of will that I can pull them into focus.

Rab's standing his ground with Lauren, his voice booming: — There are great films in the pornographic genre. *Deep Throat*, *The Devil in Miss Jones* . . . some of the Russ Meyer stuff, these are classic movies and they're more innovative and feminist than arty shit like . . . like . . . *The Piano!*

That last comment was below the belt, and even through my haze I see that Lauren actually looks physically wounded by it. She almost buckles and I worry for a split second that she's going to faint. — You can't call . . . you can't call that cheap, sleazy junk . . . you can't . . . she looks at Rab, almost pleading, — . . . you just can't . . .

— Fuck talking movies, let's make movies, Rab sneers. Lauren is looking at this whiskied-up guy like he's turned into a monster that's betrayed her. — I've done nothing for two years but listen tae hot air, he adds. — My girlfriend's having a kid. What have I done? I want tae dae something!

I find myself nodding through a fog, wanting to shout, 'Yes!', but I'm beaten to the punch by Terry, who roars: — That's the fuckin spirit, Birrell, and thumps Rab on the back, — Yuv goat tae huv a go! Then he looks around at us all and says grandly: — The question isnae why should we dae it, but *what else* would we fuckin well dae?

As Craig nods tensely and Ursula and Ronnie grin, Simon sings in affirmation: — Too right, Terry! Pointing at his friend he contends: — This man is a fucking genius. Always has been, always will be. End of, he sings to us. Then he turns to Terry and says, in genuine reverence: — Godlike, Tel, godlike.

He's drunk of course, we all are. But I'm not just feeling intoxicated by the alcohol and the spliff; it's the talk, the company, the idea of the film. I love it, I want to be part of it, and I don't care what anybody thinks. A flash of elation rises and settles as it dawns on me: this is the *real* reason I ended up in Edinburgh. This is the karma, this is the fate. — I want to be a porn star. I want to have men masturbating to images of me, all over the world, men whom I don't know even exist! I hiss, right in poor Lauren's face, and dissolve into a stoned, witch-like cackle.

— But you're making yourself a commodity, an object, you can't, Nikki, you can't! she shrieks.

— Not true, Simon says to her. — Straight actors are bigger whores than porn stars, he insists. — Just letting somebody use your body, or the images of it you create, that's fuck all. It's when you let them use your emotions; that's real hooring. You can never, ever prostitute those! he says in impressive grandiloquence.

Lauren seems as if she's going to start screaming, as if she's trying to catch her breath. She puts her hand to her chest as her face crinkles in discomfort. — No, no, because . . .

— Calm doon, Lauren, for fuck sakes. It's jist a bit too much skunk and whisky here, Rab says, gripping her arm lightly. — We're making a movie. So it's porno, it's no big deal. The thing is doing it, showing the world that we can.

I'm looking at her and telling her: — It's me that's controlling the production of the image of myself. The tart they imagine and construct in their mind, the role that I play on screen, that person will be my creation and will bear no resemblance to the real me, I tell her.

— You can't . . . she gasps almost tearfully.

— Yes, I can.

— But . . .

— Lauren, you're so priggish, and your views are antiquated.

Aggravated and choleric, she rises unsteadily, propelling herself to the window, clasping the edge of the sill and looking out onto the street. There's a few raised eyebrows at her abrupt move but most of us are too into the drink and the talk to notice or bother. Rab goes to her and starts talking to her. He's nodding to her in a placatory manner and then he comes over and says to me: — I'm going to get her home in a taxi. You want to come?

— No, I'll hang out here for a bit, I say, looking at Terry and Simon and bartering wry grins.

— She's upset and pretty fucked on that skunk and somebody should sit with her in case she throws a whitey, Rab says.

Terry slaps Rab's back again, this time hard enough for us all to sense the punitive force lurking in the camaraderie. — For fuck sakes, Birrell, slip thon dozy wee hoor a length and get her thawed oot.

Rab looks at Terry with cold steel in his eyes. — Ah've goat tae get hame tae Charlene.

Terry shrugs as if to say, it's your loss. — Looks like it's doon tae me again then, he smiles. — Sex therapist Lawson. Purely as professional caseload, likes. Tell ye what, Rab, you tuck her up in bed n ah'll be doon later, he laughs.

Rab looks at me a bit longer but I'm not going home to sit and self-justify to that closet lesbo frigid little moraliser. I want a piece of the action. All my life I've been looking for it, and it's my quarter-century this year, how long have I got before my looks have gone? People go on about Madonna, but she's the exception to the rule. It's the Britneys, the Steps, the Billies, the Atomic Kittens and the S-Club Sevens that count and they're all fucking babies compared to me. I want it now, need it now, because there is no tomorrow. If you're a woman and you have looks, you are in possession of the only finite resource worth having, the only one you'll ever have, that's what it screams to you in magazines, on telly, on the cinema screen. EVERY FUCKING WHERE: BEAUTY EQUALS YOUTH, DO IT NOW! — Let Dianne sit up with her, I tell Rab. Then I turn to the others. — I want a fucking piece of the action, I shout.

— You are fuckin sound! Terry hugs me in a genuine, delirious joy. My head's spinning now as Simon goes downstairs with a tense-looking Rab and a shaky Lauren to let them out.

Craig's setting up the camera, a simple DVC on a tripod, as Terry and Mel start snogging. Ursula's fallen to her knees at Ronnie's feet and she's unbuttoning his flies. As Simon comes up the stairs, I'm thinking that I should do something now, but as I stand up, something rises in my chest and I start heaving. I feel somebody, I think it's Gina, helping me to the toilet, but the room's spinning and I hear laughter and groans and Terry saying: — Lightweight, and I want to sort myself out but I can hear Gina shouting: — Fuck off, Terry, she's no well, and I'm shaking and shivering and the last thing I hear is Simon's voice making a loud toast: — To success, folks. It's gaunnae happen. It *will* happen! We've got the team, we'll get the cash. One just simply can't see any possible spectres at the feast!

17

OOTSIDE

Nivir fuckin well slept last night. Didnae fuckin well want tae. Jist sat up lookin at they waws, thinkin: the morn, ah'm fuckin ootay here. Kept that cunt Donald up aw night wi ma tales. Last chance the cunt'll huv tae hear anybody talkin sense cause thill probably pit some fuckin dippit cunt in the cell wi um. Nae fuckin conversation. Ah telt the cunt, enjoy it while ye kin, ya cunt, cause thill pit some fuckin sad cunt in here wi ye n that'll be you, bored tae fuck.

— Aye, Franco, eh jist goes. Ah tell um the fuckin loat: aboot aw the birds ah'll be ridin n aw they wide cunts thit'll be fuckin well gittin it. Ah'll be fuckin cool aboot it n aw but, cause ah'm no comin back in here, that's a fuckin dead cert, bit thill be some cunts thit'll be huvin sleepless nights whin they find oot thit ah'm back oan the fuckin scene.

Funny thing wis, ah thoat thit the night wid drag, bit nup, it jist fuckin well flew past. Hud tae slap that cunt Donald awake a couple ay times whin the rude fucker drifted oaf. Cunt wis lucky thit ah wis chuffed tae be gaun oot or eh'd've goat a fuckin loat worse thin jist a fuckin slap ah kin fuckin well tell ye. Tired or no fuckin tired, manners nivir cost nae cunt fuckin nowt. No huvin thum bit, well, that's cost quite a few cunts, ah kin fuckin well tell ye.

Screw comes in wi the fuckin breakfasts. Ah goes: — Ye kin take mine away. Ah'll be in the café ower the road in two ooirs' time.

— Thoat ye might want something, Frank, eh goes.

Ah jist look at the cunt. — Naw, ah want fuck all.

The screw cunt, McKecknie, jist shrugs n fucks oaf leavin jist one breakfast fir Donald.

— Aw, Franco, man, Donald goes, — ye should've said thit ye wanted it soas thit ah could've hud thum baith!

95

— Shut it, ya fat cunt, ah sais, — ye need tae fuckin well lose weight anywey.

Funny thing wis bit, see, as soon as the cunt started eatin, ah gits as hungry as fuck. — Gie's a fuckin bit ay that sausage then, ya cunt, ah goes.

Cunt fuckin well looks at ays like eh wisnae gaunnae fuckin gies it. Muh last fuckin day n aw. Ah jist springs ower n grabs it oot ay the cunt's tray n starts noshin it back.

— Aw, Franco, man! Moan tae fuck!

— Shut the fuck up, ya cunt, ah goes, pittin the other sausage n then the egg oantae the roll. — If ye cannae fuckin well dae anything wi a fuckin good hert, then some cunt's gaunnae come along n make ye fuckin well dae it.

That's the wey it goes, in here as well as ootside. Ye cooperate: fine; ye dinnae: burst mooth. Now the cunt's sittin wi a face like a well-skelped erse.

Ah tell the soor-faced cunt a few tales tae cheer um up a bit, aboot aw the shaggin n bevvyin thit's gaunnae be done doon in Sunny Leith, cause the poor bastard's gaunnae ken aw aboot it whin ah'm away. Eh's no goat what it takes tae git by in prison; two fuckin suicide attempts that cunt's hud in here, n that's jist since eh's been sharin a cell wi me, so fuck knows whit eh wis like before.

McIlhone, the screw thit's littin ays oot, comes along fir ays. Ah say cheerio tae Donald, n McIlhone slams the door shut on the poor wee cunt. It's the last time ah'll hear that fuckin sound. Eh hands ays ma gear and takes ays oot through one door, then another. Ma hert's beatin like fuck and ah kin see the ootside doon a hallway, through two doors, wi the visitors bit in between. We go intae the hall where the waitin room n reception are. Ah take a deep breath as an auld wifie opens the door tae git in, littin aw that fresh air come through. Ah sign fir ma gear n walk through that fuckin door. McIlhone's wi ays every step ay the wey, as if ah'm gaunnae try n sneak past the cunt tae git back intae the fuckin nick. Eh goes: — There ye go, Franco. That's you.

Ah jist looks straight ahead.

— We'll keep the cell warm fir ye. See ye soon.

The screws eywis say that n the cons eywis shrug n go, ah'll no be back, n the screws sneer n gie ye a look thit says, aye, ye fuckin well will, ya daft cunt.

Bit no me. Ah've rehearsed this yin. N ah wis hopin thit it wis that cunt McIlhone thit wis littin ays oot. Ah turns tae the cunt n says softly, soas thit nae cunt else kin hear: — Ah'm oan the ootside now. Same place as your missus. Mibee ah'll be back in here eftir ah've cut her fuckin heid oaf, eh. 12 Beecham Crescent. Two bairns n aw, eh.

Ah see the cunt's face go a bit rid n ehs eyes start tae water. Eh goes tae speak, bit they rubber lips ay his are gaun aw fuckin spazzy.

Ah jist turns n goes.

Ootside.

2
Porno

18

POOFS' PORN

One fuckin thing ah'm gaunnae dae is tae find the fuckin sick cunt that kept sendin ays that fuckin filthy poofs' porn whin ah wis inside. Added six months oantae muh fuckin sentence whin ah battered this wide wee cunt thit laughed whin ah sais: 'Lexo n me's partners.'

Ah wis taking aboot the fuckin shoap wi hud.

So that's muh first fuckin port ay call. Somethin's up, cause that big cunt stoaped comin intae the fuckin nick tae see ays ages ago. Jist like that. Nae fuckin explanation. So ah gits a bus tae Leith, bit whin ah gits doon ah sees thit the fuckin shoap isnae even thaire! Ah mean, it's *thaire*, bit it's aw fuckin changed. Intae some fuckin daft café.

Ah sees him but, sittin behind a counter readin the fuckin paper. Cannae miss yon big cunt, the fuckin size ay um. The place is fuckin empty; an auld wifie n two dippit cunts eatin a breakfast. Lexo, servin food in a café like a big fuckin lassie. Eh looks up n clocks ays, nearly daein a fuckin double take. — Awright, Frank!

— Aye, ah goes. Ah looks aroond at this dump, aw wee tables n sortay Chinky writin oan the waws n daft fuckin dragons n that. — What's aw this?

— Made it intae a café. Nae dosh in used furniture. At nights it turns intae a Thai café. Popular wi the new Leith trendies n the student population, eh grins, aw fill ay ehsel.

Fuckin tie café? What the fuck is this cunt oan aboot? — Eh?

— Muh girlfriend, Tina, she runs it really. She's goat an HNC in caterin. Reckoned the place wid dae better as a café.

— So you've done no bad, ah sortay accuses the cunt, lookin around, littin um see thit ah'm no fuckin chuffed.

Ye kin see the cunt's ready tae pit ehs cairds oan the fuckin table.

Ehs voice goes aw even n low, as eh nods fir ays tae come through the back. Now ehs lookin ays in the eye. — Aye, hud tae sort masel oot. Nae mair dealin. Too much fuckin heat fae the bizzies. This is Tina's now, he sais again, then goes: — Of course, you'll be taken care ay, mate.

Ah'm still lookin at um, leanin back against the waw, then glancin through tae the kitchen. Ah kin feel um tensin up a bit, as if ehs worried thit ah'll jist fuckin well kick oaf right now. Thon big cunt fancies ehsel, but hands the size ay shovels mean fuck all whin thir's a chib in yir gut. Aye, ye kin see ehs eyes gaun tae the kitchen, jist whaire mine went n aw. So ah pits the big cunt right in the fuckin picture. — Nivir been tae see ays for a bit in the jail, eh no, ah goes.

Eh jist looks at ays wi that wee fuckin smile thit eh's goat. Ye kin feel thit the cunt's goat nae fuckin time fir ays really, underneath it aw eh's jist wantin tae stomp ays aw the fuckin wey doon Leith Walk.

Lit um fuckin well try it. — N ah'll fuckin well tell ye somethin else, half ay the auld shoap wis fuckin mine so that makes it thit half ay this is fuckin mine, ahm sayin tae the cunt, lookin oot at the café, scannin muh new fuckin investment.

N ye kin see thit the cunt's blood's fuckin bubblin but eh's still giein ays aw the shite ay the day. — Ah cannae really see ye servin tea n rolls, Frank, but we'll come tae some arrangement. Ah'll see ye awright, ma auld mucker, ye ken that.

— Aye, ah goes, — ah'm fuckin well needin sorted oot fir some cash right now, ah tells the big cunt.

— Nae bother at aw, buddy boy, eh goes, n ehs countin oot some twenties.

Ma heid's buzzin, ah dinnae ken whether um comin or gaun here. Ehs handin ower some dough, bit at the same time comin oot wi shite. — Listen, Franco, ah hear that Larry Wylie's still knockin aboot wi Donny Laing, eh sais.

Muh heid shoots up n ah meets ehs eyes. — Aye?

— Aye. Wis it no you thit goat thaime crewed up thegither? Lexo goes aw that fuckin smiley innocent wey then gies ays this sort ay severe stare n nod, like eh's tryin tae say thit thir takin the fuckin pish.

N ah'm tryin tae work oot in muh fuckin heid what eh fuckin means, n what the fuckin score is, n whae's takin the fuckin pish oot ay whae n eh goes: — N you'll never guess whae's got the Port Sunshine now. That auld pal ay yours. Sick Boy, they used tae call the cunt.

Now ah've goat a proper fuckin migraine startin, like one ay the yins ah used tae git inside the fuckin jail . . . ah feel like muh heid's gaunnae fuckin explode. It's aw fuckin changed roond here . . . Lexo wi a café . . . Sick Boy wi a pub . . . Larry Wylie workin fir Donny . . . ah've goat tae git oot ay here intae the air, git time tae fuckin well think . . .

N this big cunt's gaun oan. — Ah'm gaunnae go tae the bank this affie, Frank, git ye a proper wad tae see ye through. Till wi kin sort oot something mair long-term like. Ye steyin at yir ma's, aye?

— Aye . . . ah goes, heid thumpin, no really kennin where ah'm fuckin gaun, — ah suppose . . .

— Well, I'll nip roond the night. We'll get a proper blether. Right? eh goes, n ah'm jist nodding like a daft cunt, ma fuckin temples throbbin as this auld cunt comes in n wants a bacon roll n a cup ay tea, n now this bird in an overall comes in behind um n Lexo nods tae her n she serves the auld bastard. Lexo's goat a pen n a notepad n eh's writin doon a fuckin number. Eh waves one ay they newfangled phones, nae cables like, in muh face. — That's ma mobile number, Frank.

— Aye . . . ah goes, — ivray cunt's goat one ay thaim now. Ah'll fuckin well need yin. Git ays yin, ah goes.

— Ah'll see what ah kin dae, Frank. — Anywey, eh sais, looking ower tae this lassie, — ah'll let ye git oan.

— Aye . . . see ye later, ah goes, gled tae walk oot intae the fuckin fresh air. The smell ay grease in thair wis giein ays the fuckin boak. Ah still cannae believe the wey it's aw changed, oor furniture shoap. Ah goes tae a chemist next door n the lassie gies ays these Nurofen Plus pills. Ah takes two wi a boatil ay water n goes up the Walk fir a bit. Thir fuckin barry n aw, cause eftir aboot twenty minutes the heidache's away. Ah mean, it's weird cause ah kin still fuckin feel it, it's jist thit it isnae that sair anymair. Ah double back tae look intae the café n see that Lexo cunt arguin wi ehs bird, no sae fuckin fill ay ehsel now. Aye, half that fuckin shoap's mine, n if ehs peyin ays oaf, eh'd better make it worth ma fuckin while.

Aye, ah kin see the cunt, sittin doon now at a table in the windae, fuckin well schemin away. Well, ah fuckin well am n aw, ya big cunt. Ah strides up the Walk, scannin the fuckin coupons oan the passers-by, tryin tae find some cunt ah recognise. What huv wi goat here but? Two dirty cunts wi dreadlocks, white boys n aw, walkin past like they fuckin belong here, then a poncey cunt wi a wee dug comes oot ay a shoap n gits intae this smart fuckin motor. Who ur they fuckin cunts? They urnae Leith. Whaire's aw the real gadges now? Ah looks intae ma book n stoaps oaf at a call boax n dials Larry Wylie's number. It looks like it's fir one ay they smart fuckin portable phones. Lexo better get ays one ay thaime . . .

— Franco, Larry goes, aw cool, like the wide cunt jist expected ays tae phone. — Ye phonin fae the jail?

— Naw, ah'm phonin fae the fuckin Walk, ah tells um.

Then eh goes silent for a bit, n ah hear um ask: — When did ye git oot?

— Never mind that. Whaire ur ye?

— Working up in Wester Hailes, Frank, Larry goes.

Ah starts tae think aboot this. Cannae face the auld lady yit, huv her nippin ma fuckin heid. — Right, ah'll meet ye in half an ooir at the Hailes Hotel. Ah'll jist fire up in a fast black right now.

— Eh . . . ah'm workin fir Donny, Frank. Eh might . . .

— It wis me thit fuckin well goat ye workin wi Donny in the first fuckin place, ah tells the cunt. — Ah'll see ye in the Hailes in an ooir, jist gaunnae dump muh fuckin stuff it muh ma's, then fuckin well shoot up in a fast black.

— Eh, right. See ye then.

Ah slams the phone doon, thinkin, that fuckin toss'll be right oan tae Donny Laing, aw fuckin thrilled tae be the bearer ay bad fuckin news. Aye, ah ken that cunt awright. So ah gits doon tae muh ma's n she's greetin n makin a big fuckin fuss aboot how good it is tae huv me back n aw that shite.

— Aye, ah goes. She's pit oan loads ay weight. Ye notice it mair here, in her ain hoose, thin ye did oan prison visits.

— N ah'll need tae tell oor Elspeth n Joe.

— Aye. Nae scran oan the go?

She pits her hands oan her hips. — Yi'll be starvin right enough, son. Ah'd make ye some soup, but it's ma bingo in a bit, n well, a usually meet Maisie and Daphne at the Persevere fir a wee drink first . . . hur voice drops . . . — bit ye kin go tae the chippy. Yi'll probably be lookin forward tae gittin a proper fish supper again!

— Aye, ah goes. Ah'm thinkin, at least ah kin fuckin eat it oan the wey tae see Larry.

So ah heads oot, gits the fish supper n flags doon a fast black. The cunt gies ays a wide look like eh's no that chuffed aboot ays eatin in the back ay ehs fuckin cab, bit ah stares the cunt doon n eh fuckin well shites it.

So ah'm intae the Hailes n Larry sets up the drinks. Eh's wi a couple ay boys, whae eh gies the nod tae n they melt away intae the fuckin corner. So ah'm crackin oan wi Larry, catchin up. Larry's a good fuckin mate, dinnae care what any cunt says aboot um. At least the cunt came tae see ays in the fuckin jail. Bit the cunt kin be a sneaky fucker n ah wanted tae see what him n fuckin Donny wir up tae, fuckin surein ah did. Goat tae watch ah no git too pished but, wi Lexo's wad burnin a fuckin hole in this poakit here. Larry's look tells ays thit mibee they fuckin threads uv goat oan ur a bit oot ay date. That cunt likes a fuckin peeve, but eh wants tae sort oot some business first.

Wi downs oor drinks n heads doon that auld track thit runs through the scheme, the yin thit they went oan aboot bein the new fuckin Princes Street whin it wis built. Now it's jist a concrete path thit leads fae the shoapin centre doon tae the flats, wi two banks ay gress oan either side. Build a new Princes Street in a scheme? That'll be the fuckin day.

Larry's as fuckin shifty as ever. Eh's lookin at they wee lassies thit ur skippin ootside ay the block ay flats. — Must mind tae come doon here in a few years' time, eh smiles.

The wee lassies ur singing: — *Mystic Meg said tae me, whae ma boyfriend's gaunnae be* . . . n that fuckin Larry sais tae ehsel: — W-Y-L-I-E, spellin oot ehs ain name.

— Get tae fuck, ya dirty cunt, ah goes.

— Jist jokin, Frank, eh smiles.

— Ah dinnae like that kind ay fuckin jokin, ah tells um. The cunt hud better be fuckin well jokin. Larry eywis acts cheerful enough, but eh's a fuckin ruthless cunt under it aw. At least until ehs cock gits in the fuckin road. Fell oot wi the Doyles whin eh goat one ay the sisters up the stick. That's how eh wis gled tae git in wi me n Donny. Eh's tellin ays aboot the lassie wir gaunnae be seein. — This Brian Ledgerwood cunt, eh went awol. Completely fuckin vanished, eh. Left ehs burd n bairn wi the debts. Gamblin debts, like.

— That's oot ay order, ah goes.

— Aye, sais Larry, — feel sorry for the wee burd. Fuckin tidy n aw. Business but, eh. What kin ye dae? Mind you, they tell me she's no shy. Melanie, eh sais aw that fuckin fond, smarmy wey. — That Terry Lawson's meant tae be knobbin it. Mind ay that cunt?

— Aye . . . ah goes, bit ah'm strugglin tae pit a face tae the name as Larry raps oan the door.

This Melanie lassie comes tae the door, n she looks a fuckin ride awright. Larry was well fuckin impressed. She stood thair, her hair damp, like she'd just fuckin washed it, n it was aw curling in long ringlets oantae her fuckin shoodirs. She's goat oan this fuckin green V-neck sweater and jeans n it wis likes she'd jist fuckin pilled thum oan tae answer the door. She wisnae wearin a bra n ye kin tell Larry's clocked that n ehs probably wonderin if she's wearin fuckin knickers n aw. — Look, ah've telt ye. Brian's debts huv goat nowt tae dae wi me.

— Can ah come in soas we kin talk aboot this? eh goes. Ah'm thinkin now, aye, ah mind ay Terry Lawson, him n me goat done thegither ages ago, jist wee laddies, like. The fitba.

This Melanie folds her airms. — Nowt tae talk aboot. Yi'll need tae see Brian.

— We would if we kent whaire eh wis, Larry goes, pittin oan that fuckin smile.

— Ah dinnae ken whaire eh is, she tells um.

Jist then another young lassie, about the same age, quite wee, wi black hair, comes along, pushing a bairn in a go-kart. She sees us n stoaps. — What's wrong, Mel? she asks.

— The debt collectors huv come tae git the money Bri owes thum, she goes.

This wee lassie wi the black hair turns tae me. — Bri left her wi these debts n took some ay her money. She's no seen um, that's the truth. It's nowt tae dae wi her.

So ah jist shrugs n starts tellin the wee burd thit *ah'm* no a fuckin debt collector, ah'm jist here wi Larry cause uh ran intae um in the street. Ah notices this wee yellow bruise under her eye. Ah'm askin hur what they fuckin well call her, n she's gaun Kate, n wir jist fuckin bletherin away as Larry's comin oot wi ehs fuckin spiel tae other yin. — This is the rules ay the game, doll. Yuv been telt before. The contract states that, just like the community charge, it's the household, rather than the individual that incurs a loan debt.

This Melanie's shitein it, bit shi's tryin no tae fuckin show it. That Kate lassie looks at me aw pleadin, like she wants ays tae stoap um. That Melanie's wee toddler's come oot n ehs droaped this toy n she bends doon tae pick it up n catches that clarty cunt lookin at her erse. Credit tae hur but, she's starin aw hard at the cunt.

— Hi, hi! What's that look fir? Larry goes. — Ah'm oan your side, doll.

— Aye. That'll be right, she goes, but ye kin hear the fuckin fear in her voice.

This wee Kate's still lookin at ays, n ah'm thinkin, ah could fair go fir this fuckin piece right enough, been that fuckin long . . . n that Larry, eh's a fuckin bully n the cunt's startin tae git oan muh tits. — Look, ah goes, this isnae the wey tae settle this, Larry.

— It's tough, ah ken, Larry sais, aw soothingly, lowering ehs fuckin voice, like eh's spotting the opportunity. — Listen . . . ah'm no promisin nowt, but ah'll huv a word wi the man, see if he kin gie ye a wee bit mair time, eh smiles.

This Melanie looks at the cunt and forces oot a tight smile and a grudgin thanks. — Ah ken it's no you, yir jist daein yir joab . . .

Larry huds the gaze a second, then goes: — But listen the now, ah'm wonderin if we could go fir a wee drink n discuss this in a mair civilised wey, like the night?

— No thanks, she says tae him.

Ah steams right in. — What aboot you, Kate? Git a sitter fir the bairn!

— Cannae, she smiles, — ah'm skint.

Ah jist winks n goes: — N ah'm auld-fashioned. Ah dinnae like a lassie tae pey fir anythin. Eight o'clock awright?

— Well, aye . . . but . . .

— Whaire dae ye stey?

— Jist doonstairs, the hoose below this yin.

— Ah'll pick ye up at eight, ah goes. Then ah turns tae Larry. — Right, c'moan . . . n ah grabs um n pills um away.

Wir gaun doon the stairs n eh's fuckin moanin. — Fuck sakes, Franco, she would've fuckin come oot if ye hudnae uv dragged ays away!

Ah tells um straight. — The lassie's no fuckin well interested in you, ya mingin cunt. What aboot me but, wi that wee Kate!

— Aye, they burds are easy meat, thir eywis skint n thill go fir a boy wi a wad.

— Aye, bit they didnae fuckin well go fir you, ya cunt, ah tells um. The cunt's no too pleased but thir's nowt eh kin fuckin well say. Ye kin see thit the stiff cock's run-doon n the cunt's fuckin shitein ehsel as tae what ehs gaunnae tell Donny.

That's *his* fuckin problem. Oot ay the nick fir jist a few fuckin ooirs n ah'm oan muh fuckin hole awready. Wi a tidy young burd n aw! The fuckin world record, ya cunt, ah'll be makin up fir loast time right enough!

19

Mates

S ick Boy's sniffin away, that cat's beak is streaming mair than mine, ken. It's like a brook, man, the wey it runs, meanderin doon ontae his top lip. Every so often eh pills out a Kleenex but it does nae good, the cat's conk is still like a brook. N what else dae brooks dae? They babble, man, they jist pure babble, ken. Which disnae bother me, well, normally it disnae, but it does now cause Ali's listenin tae aw ehs crap. Pure hingin oan every word, ken. It wis her idea tae come intae the Port Sunshine n see him, no likesay mine. Mibee ah wis daft comin in here the other day, n mibee ah wis a bit short wi the cat, but the nerves wir pure shredded n he's been thaire enough tae ken and show some sympathy tae an auld mucker, surely. But naw, that boy has ey been aboot ehsel. Eh's that full ay ehself it's surprising thit thir's room fir any ching, likes. Now eh's blabbin on aboot movies n the industry n aw that cack. The thing is though, that cause she's impressed n cause thir's history thaire, ah feel . . .

. . . Jealous . . . Useless . . . Both, man, both.

And the Sick Boy felly doesnae really change much, man; no, no, no, the cat most certainly does not, cause eh's gaun oan aboot ehs favourite subject again, him, him, him, and aw ehs big schemes and plans.

We get a bit ay peace when the bar gets crowded and the perr old girl, strugglin tae cope oan her ain shouts: — Simon! Eftir ignorin her twice, eh finally gets up and goes ower tae lend a reluctant hand. Alison goes tae me when eh hits the bar: — It's great tae see Simon again, and she starts gaun oan aboot the auld crowd, aboot Kelly and Mark and Tommy, poor Tommy, man.

— Aye, Ali, ah really miss Tommy, ah tell her, and ah pure want tae talk aboot Tommy cause it's sometimes like the boy's just forgotten aboot, n that's no right. See, sometimes when ah try tae talk aboot him, people go aw stroppy and accuse ays ay bein sortay morbid but it isnae like that, ah jist want tae remember the boy, ken?

Ali's been tae the hairdresser's the day and hud her hair cut shorter but wi the fringe still long. Preferred it the wey it wis if the truth be telt, man, but ah dinnae want tae say nowt. Wi lassies, if yir jaykit's awready oan the shaky, shaky peg, making a point like can likesay tip the scales, for defo. — Aye, she says, lighting up a fag, — Tommy was a lovely guy. Then she turns tae me, and exhales and there is frost in my baby's eyes. — But eh wis a smackheid.

So ah jist sit there, man, no able tae say Scottish Fitba Association, ken. Ah should huv said that Tommy wisnae that much ay a smackheid really, jist unlucky, cause the rest ay us, in fact aw ay us, pure yazed mair, but ah cannae cause now *he's* back ower beside us, likes, wi some mair drinks, and it's aw him again. Aw Sick Boy.

It's jist playin ower n ower in ma heid again: LONDON . . . MOVIES . . . THE INDUSTRY. . . LEISURE . . . BUSINESS OPPORTUNITIES . . .

And ah jist cannae resist it, man, sitting here aw fucked, listening tae this shite, n a bit ay pure nastiness comes ower me and ah jist say: — So it, eh, didnae work oot fir ye in London, likesay? Sick Boy straightens up, ehs spine coke-rigid, n sits and looks at me like ah jist telt um ehs Italian ma sucks polismen's cocks. Oh aye, there's real hate in the cat's eyes, but eh's saying nowt, jist sortay starin aw coldly, ken.

It makes ays nervous, n ah sortay huv tae talk again. — Naw, man, it's jist that ah thoat wi you bein back here n that, likesay . . .

A tightness comes ower ehs face. Sick Boy n me: we used tae wind each other up, but we were close. Now we jist wind each other up. — Let's get one thing straight, Spu . . . Daniel. I came back here for opportunity: to make movies, to run a bar . . . this, eh sweeps ehs hand around in that dismissive wey, — this is just the start.

— Ah dinnae really call a grotty pub in Leith n showin some stag-porno stuff big-time opportunity, man.

— Don't *you* fuckin start. He shakes ehs heid. — You're a fuckin loser, mate. Look at ye! He turns tae Ali. — Look at him! Sorry, Ali, but it has tae be said.

Ali's lookin aw gravely at him. — Simon, we're all meant tae be friends.

Now this gadge is daein what eh does best, shiftin blame, justifyin ehsel and pittin other people doon at the same time. — Look, Ali, ah come back here and all I get is negative energy from losers, he tells us, — and I just can't operate in that way any more. Everything I say, I get cold water poured on it. Friends? I expect encouragement from so-called friends, he sniffs. Then eh sortay points at ays aw accusin. — Did he tell you that he came in here the other day? The first time I'd seen him in yonks?

Ali's likesay shakin her heid and lookin right at ays.

— Ah wis gaunnae . . . ah try tae explain, but that Sick Cat talks ower me.

— What did I get? No even a 'hiya, Simon, how are ye, long time no see', ehs sais tae her, actin aw hurt. — Naw, no him. Straight away eh tries tae pit the bite intae me, no even a 'hello, how are you' first!

Alison sweeps her fringe back and looks at ays. — Is that right, Danny?

Well, then it's just like one ay they horrible scenes when yir Donaldo'd and sick and ye can sortay see it happening before it does. It's like that, man. Like ah jist *see* masel standin up, aw shaky n jerky like in one ay they early black-n-white films shot at funny speed n whaire the frames are aw badly spliced thegither. Ah sortay see ma mooth flappin open n ma finger pointin at um aboot a second before it does. Then, aye, ah'm up oan ma feet pointin at the radge, n telling him: — You were never a mate, never a *real* mate like Rents wis!

The Sick Felly's face twists intae a sneer and ehs boatum jaw shoots oot, sortay like the drawer ay the till at Kwik Save. — What the fuck are ye talkin aboot! That cunt ripped us off!

— He never ripped me off! Ah shout back, pointin at masel.

Sick Boy goes quiet, a real deathly quiet, man, but the cat's stare never left ays. Aw naw, ah've done it now. Blabbed. N Alison's lookin at ehs n aw. The pair ay thum, man, two sets ay big eyes, aw screamin betrayal.

— So, he says harshly, — you were in on it with him, eh looks at Ali, whae lowers her heid n stares at the flair. Ali's great at keepin secrets but she's bad at lyin.

Ah dinnae want his accusin lamps oan her, so ah spill the beans. — Nup, ah kent nowt aboot it, n that's oan Ali n Andy's life.

The Sick Cat's stare is as intense as ever, but eh kens thit ah'm no lyin. Eh kens thit thir's mair but.

Ah cough it oot, ma nails scrapin oan the soggy beer mat. — But later oan ah goat some money, sent through the post. Jist ma share, nae mair. Sick Boy's big eyes ur still screwin intae me, and ah ken right now that even tryin tae lie wid be useless cause this cat would jist ken. — It had a London postmark, and it came aboot three weeks eftir ah goat back up here. Thir was nae note. Ah've never seen or heard fae um since, but ah kent it wis him that sent the cash, it couldnae huv been anybody else, ah telt um. Then ah goes, a bit boastful likes: — Mark sorted me oot!

— The full share? eh asks, ehs eyes bulgin oot.

— Every penny, man, ah tell um wi a bit ay glee, then ah sit back doon in the seat cause ah'm fucked. Ali looks accusingly at ays, and ah kin only shrug, and hur heid droaps again.

Ye kin see Sick Boy's dome's pure spinnin. Ah'm thinkin that the inside ay that cat's nut must be like one ay they things wi aw the baws that they yaze fir the lottery or the Scottish Cup draw. Eh looks really hurt, no jist pretend hurt, but then eh suddenly smiles, ehs grin imitatin the logo oan the gadge's blue Lacoste shirt. — Aye? Well, a lot of fuckin good it did ye n aw. Ye really sorted yirself oot, eh. Really invested the money well.

Ali raises hur heid, looks at me. — That money, when ye goat that stuff for the bairn . . . that was aw fae Mark Renton?

Ah say nowt.

Looking at ehs gless ay whisky, Sick Boy picks it up and drains it, then starts tappin the empty gless oan the table. — Aye, that's right, jist sit thair in a fucking stupor, eh sneers at ays. — You dinnae dae anything, you never will dae anything, eh's tellin me.

And ah cannae help it, ah just blurt it oot; ah tell him that ah do, that ah'm writing a history ay Leith.

Sick Boy starts sniggering. — That should be fucking riveting, eh bellows acroass the bar, and a few heids turn roond.

Now Ali's lookin at me like I'm daft n aw. — What are ye talkin aboot, Danny? she asks. Ah've jist goat tae git away, oot ay here. Ah stand up n head oaf. — Negative energy, eh, ah'll mind ay that yin, likesay. Right, see yis.

Sick Boy raises ehs brows but Ali follays me tae the door and we go ootside. — Where are ye goin? she asks, wrapping her airms roond herself.

— Ah've goat ma meeting, ah tell her. It's nippy, and she's cauld, shivering, even though she's goat that navy-blue cardigan oan.

— Danny . . . she starts, rubbing the zipper oan ma jaykit between her finger and thumb, — ah'm gaunnae go back in thaire n talk tae Simon.

Ah jist look at her in pure disbelief.

— Eh's upset, Danny. If eh says anything aboot that money n it gits back tae the likes ay Second Prize . . . she hesitates fir a wee bit, — . . . or Frank Begbie . . .

— Aw aye, go n see Simon. We cannae huv him upset, kin we, likesay? ah snap, but fuck aye, that still registers. It wis me, Rents, Sick Boy, Second Prize n Begbie aw in London, n Rents pure ripped us off. Bit eh peyed me back. Eh obviously nivir peyed Sick Boy back, bit ah dinnae ken aboot the others. Probably no Begbie, cause he went mental, killed that boy Donnelly n goat sent doon, even though Donnelly wis a bad bam as well, it's goat tae be said.

— You'd better no be late, she sais, kissin ma foreheid, then she turns and she's gone back through the door.

She's gone.

So that wis what done it, likesay, ah wis aw charged up wi excitement n worry but whin ah went along tae the meeting ah jist told them aw aboot it, this history ay Leith. The thing is, man, that that Avril lassie, she was jist so happy, ken, jist so fuckin happy. It made it worthwhile, likes, just tae see the smile oan the chick's face. So now ah've done it, ah've blabbed n pure created this expectation ay masel as a man ay letters. A dude movin oan up, a distinguished local historian, a mover, a shaker.

But it isnae me, likes. That boy oan the telly, the one that goes oan aboot ancient civilisations n aw that, ye cannae really see him gaun: Hey, man, ah'd better watch this gadge fae Leith, this new kid oan the block. If ah dinnae mind masel, this radge'll be prowling roond aw ma Pyramids, giein it big licks aboot aw they Egyptian dudes. Nah, ah dinnae think so somehow.

Ah've goat tae make a stab at it but, ken, goat tae try, mibee prove tae Ali that ah'm mair than she thinks. Mibee prove it tae aw ay them.

When ah first met Alison she was a weird and wonderful kind ay lassie, wi that great sortay tanned skin, the long, dark wavy hair n the big white set ay pearly choppers. She wis ey a bit ay an intense chick but, it was like sometimes there wis an invisible vampire attached tae her neck, jist drainin the energy oot ay her.

Never really took that much notice ay me, likes. She wis eywis intae him. Then ah mind one day she jist smiled at me and ma hert blew tae smithereens in ma chist. Whin we goat thegither ah thoat it wis jist wasters stuff, man, and that once we cleaned up, she'd want tae move on. But then came the bairn n she jist sortay stayed. That's probably it, man, the wee yin, maist likely the only reason she's stuck aroond sae long.

But now she's back tae being that vampire-sucked Ali, and guess whae the vampire is? It's me, man. Me.

Eftir the gig at the group ah wonder if Ali'll still be doon the road at the Port Sunshine. Naw bit, ah cannae handle seein that Sick Boy again right now. Instead, ah turns the other wey n heads up intae toon where ah runs intae Cousin Dode, comin oot the Old Salt, n wi goes up tae his flat in Montgomery Street fir a blaw. Quite a cool wee pad tae; a bit oan the titchy side, the rooms like, a wee tenement rather thin one ay the big yins. Eh's goat it aw done up nice n aw, man, except fir the big Huns picture, the Souness era, framed oan the waw above the fireplace. Thir's a nice leather couch which ah pure collapse right intae.

Ah quite like Cousin Dode, even if eh does sortay go oan a bit, n eftir a couple joints n a beer ah'm tellin um aboot ma women problems.

— Never mind, mate, *Omnia vincit amor*, love conquers all. If yis love each other, it'll work oot, if yis dinnae, it's time tae move oan. End aff, Dode says.

Ah'm tellin um thit it's no that easy. — See, it's likes thir's a boy that used tae be a good mate, n him n her wir like an item, n now eh's back in toon, back oan the scene, like, man, ken? The guy wis a bit fill ay ehsel, so ah said a few things, telt um something ah shouldnae huv, ken?

— *Veritas odium parit*, Dode says in a sortay sage wey. — The truth begets hatred, eh adds fir ma benefit.

It's pure crazy me tryin tae dae a book n ah cannae write ma name, n there's that Cousin Dode boy whae's like some kind ay a Latin scholar n eh's a Weedgie n aw. Ye nivir think that Weedgies huv schools, but they must, n they must be better thin oors. So ah goes tae the good Cousin: — How is that you ken so much aboot things, Dode, likesay Latin n that?

Eh explains it aw tae me as ah skins up another joint. — Ah'm a self-educated lad ay pairts, Spud. You come fae a different tradition, fae us Proddies, like. Ah'm no sayin that you cannae be the same as me, ye kin. It just takes mair work fir the likes of you cause it isnae in yir culture. See, Spud, we're firmly in the Knoxian tradition ay Scottish Protestant working-class education. That's how ah'm an engineer tae trade.

Dinnae quite follow follow the cat here. — But ye work as a security guard, ken?

Dode shakes ehs heid aw dismissively like that's jist a wee detail. — Temporary thing but; till ah get back oot tae the Middle East n land another contract. Ye see, this security stuff, it keeps me busy. Ah'm no tryin tae be offensive tae you, pal, ah kin say this tae you, cause you've goat potential. But ye see, it's a case ay the devil makin work. *Otia dant vitia.* That's the difference between an enterprising Proddy and a feckless Pape. We'll work at onything tae keep wur haund in, tae keep wur discipline, until the next big thing comes along. Nae way will ah jist sit back here spunkin away aw that Oman money.

Ah'm sortay wonderin how much that cat's got stuffed away in that Clydesdale Bank basket ay his.

20

Scam # 18,738

It was good to see the lovely Alison again, even if the altercation with that fucked-up junky tattie-picking loser she's in tow with has upset me. Got pretty nippy as well, the skinny, skaggy wee cunt. Should have fucking well slung him out into the street along with the other rubbish for the binmen to pick up and incinerate.

Things either get better, or they deteriorate, and I'm thinking about Spud, thinking that the worst is now over. But no, it does get much fucking worse. *He* comes in.

— Sick Boy! A fuckin publican! You, runnin a pub in Leith. Kent ye widnae be able tae keep away fae the fuckin place!

The man is wearing an unfashionable brown bomber jacket, old Nike trainers, a pair of Levi's and what looks like a disturbingly ancient range Paul and Shark striped shirt. Of course, the total effect screams 'Jailbird'. There's maybe a little fleck of silver at the temples and a couple of extra Mars bars on the coupon, but the cunt looks in excellent condition. Hardly a day older, it's as if he's been to a fucking health farm rather than a prison. Probably doing weights twenty-four seven. Even the touch of silver looks unreal, like some film-set make-up artist has stuck it there for the purposes of ageing him. I am literally fucking speechless.

— Never thoat ah'd see the fuckin day! Telt ye ye'd fuckin well be back, ya cunt! he says again, showing me that his obsession with boring repetition is as intact as ever, possibly even developed, incubating as it did for so long in that hothouse of a slammer. Imagine sharing a cell with that! I'd take my fucking chances on the beasts' wing first.

My jaws lock together and grind slowly. And it isnae just the charlie I had before Murph the Smurf came in. I force a smile and find my tongue. — Franco. How's tricks?

In true form of old, the cunt never responds to a question when he's got several of his own. — Whair ye fuckin steyin?

— Roond the corner, I mumble vaguely.

He fixes me with that paint-stripping look for a second, but that's all the information the cunt is getting. Then his eyes go to the font, then back to me.

— Lager, Franco? I grimace.

— Thoat ye'd nivir fuckin ask, ya cunt, he says, turning to another fuckin loser next to him. I don't know this particular psycho. — Cunt kin afford tae run a pub, eh kin afford tae stand ehs auld mate Franco a fuckin peeve. The strokes me n this cunt used tae fuckin well pill, eh, Sick Boy?

— Aye . . . I force a grin, raising the glass to the tap, trying to calculate how many free drinks he'll bum per week and what this'll do to the already breadline-profit levels that this hovel just about delivers. I'm chatting away with Franco, casually throwing in info and names that'll fuck his sick head. You can see the wheels turning, him getting more and more distressed. Names and half-formed schemes are jostling to get into the right lane, like motorway traffic confronted by an oncoming emergency filter. Of course, I leave out one particular moniker. It dawns on me that I'm both perturbed and strangely excited at Franco's re-emergence, trying to concoct in my head a crude balance sheet of opportunity and threat. I'm attempting to remain studiously neutral, listening to his bullshit in a grim, mordant silence. There will be many souls much less ambivalent about Begbie's return.

This other wide cunt's glinting at me. He looks a slightly thinner, less healthy version of Franco; a body pumped up by prison steel, yes, but then honed down by drugs and alcohol. His eyes are wild, psychotic slits that bat-dance in your soul looking for good things to crush or bad elements to identify with. Shorn hair peppers a craggy skull you could punch all day and just break your fingers on. — So you're Sick Boy then, ur ye?

I just look at him as I'm pouring the beer. My expression is that hopefully insincere, urging way where a silent 'and?' is left hanging in the air, and in this battle of wills I want this moron to say more. But I'm losing control, all I'm getting is a rapscallion's smile back while the coke rush is running down and I think about that wrap in my jacket pocket hanging up in the office.

Thankfully, he breaks the impasse. — The name's Larry, mate. Larry Wylie, he tells me in a busy, sizing-up way. I shake a proffered hand with some reluctance. I can see the licence already heading down the tubes with bams like this hanging around here. — Heard we hud oor knobs poking aboot in the same place, he says, an evil, measuring grin splitting his snidey puss.

What the fuck is this cunt on about?

The Larry character must be picking up on my bemusement as he puts me in the picture. — Louise, he tells me. — Louise Malcolmson. She wis tellin me thit ye tried tae pit her oot on the game, ya dirty cunt.

Hmm. A blast from the past, that yin. — Aye? I nod, looking at the tap and then him. I hate bar work. I don't have the patience to pull pints. It's as well that those scapegrace wank-boys haven't asked for Guinness. Yes, that face of his is familiar after all, belonging to one of those vaguely malign presences in the corner of some gaff you visit to score from or chill out in.

— Cheers, mate, he smiles. — Ah ken, cause ah tried n aw.

Begbie looks from me to this Larry and back to me again. — Dirty cunts, he says, with real disgust. And suddenly an old fear comes over me for the first time since he came into the place. We're aulder, and I've not seen the cunt for ages, but Franco is still Franco. You look at the lamebrain and know that he's never going to move on; the marriage and domesticity option simply isnae one for that twat. For the Little Beggar Boy it's death or life imprisonment and taking as many doon with him en route. Yes, the man still simply beggars belief.

In mild protest Larry turns up his palms in appeal. — That's me but, Franco, he smiles, then he's looking back towards me. — That's the wey it goes, eh, mate. Once ah've shafted a bird every which wey but loose, the only thing tae dae is tae try n git some ay that Bacardi money back n git her pimped oot. The boy here'll tell ye, eh, mate?

This cunt thinks I'm the same as him. Not so. Me: Simon David Williamson, businessman, entrepreneur. You: thick, schemie thug,

118

going nowhere. I nod, but keep my smile to myself, as this fucker has the look of somebody it wouldn't do to antagonise. A great buddy for Franco, cut from the same cloth. They should just *get married now*, cause they'll never find anybody else more suitable. Like Begbie, he's nae rocket scientist but he's got hyena street cunning skooshing out of every pore and knows when he's being conde-scended to from a hundred yards away. So I look at Franco and nod over at the leisurewear- and sovie-bedecked wee toerags sitting at the table by the jukey. — What's the form thaire, Franco?

His hungry eyes dart over to the young team, instantly sucking the oxygen out of the air. — These wee cunts use this doss. Loat ay dealin goes oan. Some wide cunts come in here, he explains. But anybody gits wide wi you, you lit me ken. Some ay us dinnae forget oor mates, he adds snootily.

Mates, my fucking arse.

I'm thinking about Spud, subbed on the sly by that carrot-heided thief Renton. Bastards. *I wonder if François knows all about this cosy wee arrangement, Mister Murphy?* Oh Danny boy, the pipes, the pipes could soon very well indeed be calling. Calling fucking loud. Yes, I can almost hear them now. And the tune that they are playing is sounding very much to me like the funeral lament for one wee Leith junky. Oh aye, that is most certainly one for later.

Right now, it makes no sense to play more of my hand to this radge than is necessary. — Appreciated, Frank. Ah'm a bit oot ay the Leith scene, ken, wi spending a lot ay time in London n that, I explain, as I clock another of that posse of young cunts entering. I get their attention before Morag, who's reading a Mills and Boon, rises creakingly to her feet. — Fuckin customers. We'll git a proper blether later oan, eh, I half tell, half implore the Beggar Boy.

— Right, Franco says, and he and this Larry character sit down in the corner by the fruit machine.

The young cunts order and down a few beers at the bar. I can hear all their talk, of gittin sorted oot, of phoning such-and-such and so-and-so. I note Franco and Larry leave, which makes the wee radges' mood a bit lighter and their voices louder. That cunt Begbie disnae even bring the empty fucking glasses up to the bar. Does he think I'm here to wait on a fucking pleb like him?

I go to get the glasses, thinking about the sweeties I got from Seeker which are now secreted upstairs in the cashbox in the office drawer. Obviously, I'll keep the charlie to myself. As I stack the tumblers like a fuckin skivvy, I approach the lippiest of the wee cunts, that Philip guy. — Awright, mate?

— Aye, he says suspiciously. His taller, thicker mate, Bill Hicks, what's his name, Curtis, the one that seems tae be the butt of aw the jokes, approaches. Like the rest he's got a load of gold sovies on his hands. I focus on the big streak of pish. — Cool sovies, chaps, I remark.

The thickoid boy goes: — Aye, ah've goat fi-fi-five, n ah want three m-m-mair, soas ah kin huv yin oan every fi-fi-fi-fi-fi . . .

He's standing open-mouthed and blinking, trying to get it out and I feel like going back over to the bar and cleaning some glasses or playing 'Bohemian Rhapsody' on the jukebox before he finally spits it out.

— . . . fi-finger, likes.

— That must help ye whin yir headin up the Walk. Keep they knuckles fae gittin chapped, scrapin against yon pavement, I smile.

The dippit halfwit looks open-mouthed at me. — Eh . . . aye . . . he says, completely bemused, as his mates start laughing like drains.

— Look at thaime but, the Philip radge boasts, showing me a full set. That's as close as I want to get to them. This wee cunt is as cocky as fuck, and there's a glint of the bad bastard in his eyes. He stands uncomfortably close to me, so that the visor of his baseball cap is almost sticking in my face. He's clad in that expensive but tasteless leisurewear favoured by so many of those wee hip-hop twats.

Ah nod at him tae move a bit over intae the corner by the jukey.

— Hope youse urnae dealin pills, I tell this cretin in a whisper.

— Naw, he says, with a belligerent shake of his napper.

I drop my voice. — So ye lookin for some?

— You jokin? eh goes, mooth tightening and eyes narrowing.

— Nup.

— Well . . . aye . . .

— Ah've got doves, a fiver a time.

— Sound.

The wee cunt gets his money together and I dish him out twenty doves. After that, it's like a fuckin fair. I have to bell Seeker to send more down. Of course, he doesn't grace the bar with his presence, dispatching a ferret-like courier in his place. I shift 140, with an hour left before closing time. Then the wee cunts fuck off clubbing leaving the pub empty apart from a couple of wheezing auld jakeys in the corner with their dominoes. I count six pills from my poke, and put them into a plastic bag.

I look across at Morag, who's been washing the glasses and is back reading her Mills and Boon. — Mo, ye want tae keep an eye oan things for half an hour? Ah've jist got tae nip oot.

— Aye, nae bother, son, the obliging auld boiler grunts, lifting her head slightly from the great romance.

I saunter round to Leith Police Station. Thinking of that grand old phrase, the Leith police dismisseth us, I approach a short, fat, unstylish cop on the desk. The rancid smell of BO peels off him, like a nippy striker from a cumbersome central defender. This boy looks like he's rotting away, flakes of eczematous skin quiver on his neck, held in place only by an oily, toxic sweat. Yes, it's good to see a *proper* policeman. Grudgingly, Kebab Copper asks me what he can do for me.

I slap the six pills on the desk.

There's a focused energy now about those small, deep-set eyes.
— What's this? Where did you get these?

— I've just taken over the licence at the Port Sunshine. There's a lot of young guys drink in there. Well, I don't mind that, they're the ones that spend the money. But I saw a couple of them acting suspicious so I followed them into the toilet. They were in the same cubicle. I pushed the door in, the lock on it's broken, which I need to fix, as I say, I've just taken the bar over. So anyway, I took those pills off them and barred them.

— I see . . . I see . . . Kebab Cop says, looking from the pills to me, and back again.

— Now I don't know much about that sort ay thing myself, but it might be those fantasy tablets that you read about in the papers.
— Ecstasy . . .

This boy knows his Ecstasy from his eczema, which is just as well.
— Whatever, I say, all businessman-and-taxpayer impatient. — The

point is, I don't want to bar them permanently if they're innocent, but there's no way that anybody is dealing drugs in my pub. What I'd like you to do is to test them and tell me if they are illegal drugs. If so, I'll be straight on the phone to you if those scumbags ever set foot in my bar again.

Kebab Copper seems impressed at my vigilance, yet at the same time, put out by the bother it's going to cause him. It's like the two forces are pushing him in opposite directions, and he's wobbling on the spot, trying to work out which fucking way he'll leap, and shedding more skin in the process. — Right, sir, if you just leave your details with us, we'll send this down to our lab for testing. It looks like Ecstasy tablets to me. Unfortunately, most of the young ones are on them nowadays.

I shake my head grimly, feeling like a senior detective on *The Bill*. — Not in my pub they're not, officer.

— The Port Sunshine did have a bit of a reputation for that, the polisman explains.

— That probably explains why I got it for the price I did. Well, our drug-dealing friends are going to find out that this reputation is about to change! I tell him. The cop tries to look encouraging, but I might have overplayed it a bit, to the extent that he now thinks that I'm one of those 'have-a-go heroes', a vigilante, who'll just cause him more long-run hassle.

— Mmm, he says, — any problems though, sir, you get straight back to us. That's what we're here for.

I nod in stern appreciation and head back to the pub.

When I get back, Juice Terry's propped up against the bar, regaling auld Mo with some tale and she's cackling dangerously close to pant-pishing levels. Her big bray fairly ricochets around the walls, making me think for a second about checking the building insurance.

The Juice chappie is well in the pink alright. He sidles up close tae me. — Sick Boy, eh, Si, ah'm jist thinkin, ye should come wi us tae the Dam for Rab's stag at the weekend. Check oot the goods for sale in the red-light district.

No fuckin way. — I'd love tae, Terry, but I can't leave this place, I tell him, as I shout the last orders to the deadmeat in the corner. Not one of the old fuckers wants another beer, they just file out into the night like the ghosts they'll soon become.

I'm not into going to Amsterdam with a posse of radges. Rule one: socially surround yourself with fanny, avoiding groups of 'mates' at all costs. After I lock up the bar, Terry badgers me to come with him to this club in town that his DJ sidekick, that N-Sign boy, is playing at. Well, N-Sign's quite well known and must be loaded, so after we shut up I'm happy to tag along. We get into a taxi, and then walk past the queuing masses at a Cowgate shithouse, straight through, Terry nodding and winking to the security boys. One of them, Dexy, is an old acquaintance, and I chew the shit with him for a bit.

It being Edinburgh and not elitist London, there's no VIP bar, so we have to slum it with the fucking plebs. The N-Sign boy's at the bar and there's quite a few of the young cunts and wee birds making a fuss of him. He nods to Terry and myself and we go through to the office of the club with some other boys, where lines are being racked up. There are also a few welcome cases of beer. Terry's done all the intros, and I vaguely know the N-Sign boy anyway, an old mate of the Juice fella's from way back. The others come from Longstone, or Broomhouse or Stenhouse or somewhere like that. Somewhere predominantly Jambo. It's funny, I don't really care that much about Hibs these days, but my distaste of Hearts never wanes for a second.

Terry's telling them all about the night we had. — We huv this big session back at Sick Boy's. Thir wis this fuckin student burd, at college wi Rab Birrell, he purses his lips and turns to me, — what wis she like?

The looseness of his tongue, particularly when on cocaine, does cause concern, but the gusto of his performance is infectious. — Tidy, I acknowledge.

— They couldnae handle the skunk but. First, the wee specky yin hus a whitey, then the really shaggable yin, that Nikki, she passes oot n aw. This dirty cunt takes hur hame tae his hoose n rides hur, he says, nodding at me.

I shake my head. — Did I fuck ride her. Gina took her tae the bogs then we got her back tae mine and put her tae bed. I was a perfect gent, on my best behaviour, well, with Nikki anyway. I did shag Gina back at hers.

— Aye, then ah bet ye went back n rode that Nikki n aw, ya cunt!

— Nooo . . . I had tae get up early for a delivery so I was straight back tae the pub in the morning. When I went tae the flat Nikki was away. Even if she'd been there, I would've been a model gentleman.

— Ye expect me tae believe that?

— That's the wey it wis, Tel, I smile. — There's some lassies you need tae play the long-ball game wi. I'm not interested in poking a puking corpse.

— Aye, it wis a fuckin waste, Terry curses, — cause this wee yin wanted it awright, he says to this N-Sign boy, or Carl, as he calls him. — Here, Carl, you should git yirsel doon tae the pub, bring some ay that fanny fae yir club along n aw. Wi eywis need fresh blood, Terry teases.

This DJ boy's okay though. We're getting a bit mashed sharing a wrap and he says something to me which makes my heart race even faster than this off-the-rock line I've just done. — I was out in the Dam the other week. I saw that boy who runs this club oot there. Used tae be a mate ay yours. Renton. Youse fell oot, they telt me. Did ye ever get back in touch?

What is he saying here?

Renton? RENTON? FUCKING RENTON!

I'm thinking to myself, well, maybe I fucking well *could* do with getting over to the Dam. Check out the porn scene. Why not? A bit of R&R. And I could also get some fucking cash that's owed me!

Renton.

— Aye, we're aw sweet now, I lie. — What's his club called again? I casually remark.

— Luxury, this Carl N-Sign Ewart guy says innocently as my heart pounds in my chest.

— Aye, I agree, — that's the one. Luxury.

I'll show that fucking treacherous ginger-heided cunt luxury.

21

Whores of Amsterdam Pt 3

The canal's got a green hue today; can't work out if it's the reflection of the trees on the surface of the water, or some effluent spillage. The fat, bearded cunt in the houseboat below is sitting, his top off, contentedly smoking a pipe. A good ad for the baccy. In London, he'd be a worried man, shiteing his keks that somebody else would be trying to get what he's got. Here though, he couldn't give a toss. Someway along the line the British went from being the cunts who had it sussed out to being the biggest wankers in Europe.

I turn into the room, and Katrin's in a short, blue, imitation-silk gown, sitting on the brown leather sofa, filing her nails. Her bottom lip rolls tightly down, her brow set in a concentrated frown. I used to be able to sit and watch her do things like that for hours. Appreciate her just being there. Now we irritate each other. To me now, it's fuckin stupid. — You got that seven hundred guilders fir the rent then?

Katrin idly gestures to the table. — In my purse, she tells me, before standing up and discarding her robe with a slightly stagey flourish and going to the shower room. I hesitate, watching her very thin, white nakedness depart, strangely both arousing and slightly creepy.

I look at her purse lying there on the big oak table. The gleaming eye of its clasp winking at me, like a dare. There's something about going through a woman's purse. In my junk days, I screwed hooses, shops and did people over to get what I needed, but the strongest taboo, the one that hurt the most tae brek, wis my ma's purse. It's easier tae stick yir fingers in a strange woman's fanny than in a familiar one's purse.

Still, a roof over the head is certainly required, and I snap it open and skim off the notes. I can hear Katrin singing in the shower, or trying to. Germans cannae sing a fuckin note, like the Dutch, in fact like all Europeans. What she *can* do is do my head in. Aye, merciless needling, appalling rows, stormy sulks; Katrin can do those with panache. But her strongest card is the bitter interventions that occassionally punctuate her stony silences. Our wee flat overlooking the canal has developed an atmosphere highly conducive to paranoia.

Martin's right. It's time to move on.

22

BIG FUCKIN FLATS

Ye look at they fuckin trees here, they yins thit are strugglin in the shadows cast by the big fuckin flats. Undernourished, that's what they are, that's the fuckin word, like the bairns, like they fuckin auld cunts, that fuckin cowed and apologetic wey, shitin it as they pass a group ay young cunts ootside the shoppin centre.

Bit ah'm fuckin gaun past thair now n ah'm fuckin lookin at the young cunts n ye kin hear thir voices startin tae fuckin well droap cause aye, ah'm lookin at thaim awright. Bit a shark disnae bother chasin fuckin minnows cause that's no gaunnae fuckin well satisfy. Aye but they wee cunts are smellin fear awright n thir lookin shocked cause it's thir fuckin ain.

Some cunt's fuckin gittin it . . . muh heid is fuckin nippin . . . even the fuckin Nurofen's no workin right . . .

So ahm thinkin aboot whin it started, this moarnin, right early doors, before ah went tae muh fuckin ma's. It aw started at Kate's, me n hur in bed. She looked that fuckin barry whin ah woke up wi hur. Ah'd made the fuckin excuses wi the last two times, sais tae hur thit ah wis pished. Bit now, eftir aw this time, she wis fuckin lookin at ays, like thir wis somethin fuckin wrong wi me. Like ah wis one ay they sick cunts in that stuff thit that fuckin bastard sent ays in the nick.

Bit it's burds ah like, burds ah fuckin well want. Aw ah fuckin did wis wank masel oaf thinkin aboot burds whin ah wis inside, now thit ah'm oot n ah've goat a bird ah like, ah cannae even . . .

THAT CUNT THIT WIS FUCKIN SENDIN AYS THAT FUCKIN STUFF

Ah'm no a fuckin sick queer buftie . . .

AH CANNAE FUCKIN WELL GIT IT UP.

N see if she'd jist said that, said, 'What the fuck's up wi ye?' ah widnae huv bothered like. But she fuckin well goes, 'Is it me? Dae ye no fancy ays?' So ah jist tells ur the fuckin loat, aboot the jail, n aboot how the first thing ah wanted whin ah goat oot wis´ a fuckin ride, n how ah cannae fuckin git it up now.

N she jist cuddled intae muh side, me aw fuckin tense, n she wis tellin ays again aboot that cunt she wis wi, the boy thit used tae batter hur, thit gied her that eye she hud whin ah first met hur. N ah'm thinkin, ah need tae fuckin git oot ay here, cause muh heid is fuckin well nippin. So ah telt her ah wis gaun tae muh ma's.

Ma fuckin breathin's gaun aw yon wey as ah go intae the shoapin centre. Ah feel like a fuckin prisoner here; trapped by the fuckin need tae jist huv some cunt. It's like a fuckin addiction . . .

It's mibee jist bein here, oot here, ootside. It's like ah fuckin well dinnae belong, dinnae fit in. Muh ma, muh brar Joe, muh sister Elspeth. Muh mates: Lexo, Larry, Sick Boy, Malky. Aw aye, thir aw fuckin well pleased tae see ye, but it's like the cunts only fuckin tolerate yir presence for a while. Then they fuckin go. Aw aye, thir aw fuckin nice aboot it, but thuv aw goat things tae dae, eywis fuckin things tae dae. N what is it thit they huv tae fuckin well dae? Everything except what we used tae fuckin well dae thegithir, that's fuckin what. *We'll get a proper blether later on.* And it makes ays fuckin rage inside, makes ays feel that fuckin addiction aw the stronger, that need tae jist hurt some cunt. *When the fuck is later oan?*

N Lexo. What the fuck wis that cunt up tae, wi that bird and ehs fuckin Chinky restaurant-cum-café. A fuckin Chinky in Leith! Thir's tons ay fuckin Chinkies in Leith! A tie restaurant, eh fuckin well goes. Well, nae cunt in Leith's gaunnae come oot fir a meal n wear a tie tae a fuckin Chinky, especially no when it's a fuckin scabby wee café durin the fuckin day.

Aye, Lexo, doon at muh ma's hoose, stuffing that envelope intae ma fuckin hand. Two grand. Buying ehs oaf. And aye, ah'd taken it cause ah fuckin well needed the money, bit Lexo's thinkin through his fuckin erse if he thought thit him n that wee slag eh was wi wis elbawin ays oot, just like that. Lexo'll fuckin get it.

Bit thir's one cunt, one fuckin face thit burns in ma heid brighter thin any ay thum.

Renton.

Renton hud been muh mate. Muh best mate. Fae school. And eh'd taken the fuckin pish. It's aw been Renton's fault. Aw this fuckin rage. N it's nivir gaunnae stoap until ah kin git that cunt back. It's his fuckin fault ah goat the fuckin jail. That Donnelly goat wide, bit ah widnae huv done um sae bad if ah hudnae been fuckin crazy about bein ripped oaf. Ah left um in that fuckin car park in a pool ay ehs ain blood, dyin, n stuck muh sherpened screwdriver in ehs hand. Then ah went hame n plunged masel twice, once in the fuckin gut, once in the ribs, yazin another screwdriver. Then ah bandaged masel n staggered up tae the A&E. That goat ays manslaughter instead ay murder. If ah hudnae hud form n goat done for two GBH charges inside, ah'd huv been oot years ago. It's a fuckin joke, n it's aw doon tae that fuckin thievin cunt Renton.

Aye, ah hud tae git oot, tae git away fae Kate, cause ah couldnae be fuckin held responsible fir whit ah might huv done otherwise. Ehr ex-boyfriend was a cunt, eh battered hur, n that was oot ay order. Thir's some cows thit deserve a fuckin punchin, lassies whae wirnae satisfied till some cunt shut their mooths wi a fist. No Kate but, she isnae like that, it was a liberty treating a lassie like her that wey. Bit muh heid wis thrashin, it's like ah wis ready tae fuckin go, so ah goat the fuck oot.

Bit then, doon at muh ma's, ah wis gaun through some fuckin auld stuff; a couple ay auld holdalls worth ay fuckin personal posses-sions. Found an auld fuckin picture; me n that cunt Renton in Liverpool at the fuckin Grand National. Ah fuckin well held it that long ah thought ah could see that cunt's smile grow as eh fuckin well looked at ays. Aye, ah could see that fuckin grin become broader and aye, ah could see they fuckin cartoon asses' ears coming oot ay the toap ay ma fuckin heid. Tae trust a cunt like that . . .

The guts really started manufacturin fuckin acid, the heid wis buzzing, n it wis like muh boady wis gaun intae fuckin spasms. Ah kent thit ah could jist keep fuckin well starin at that picture, jist fuckin well kill masel daein that, just keep that stare oan that picture until ah blew every fuckin gasket. Aye, the blood boiling up and popping in ma fuckin veins under the pressure and me bein stretched away; blood streaming fae muh ears n muh nostrils. Ah held it but, tae prove thit ah wis stronger thin that cunt, then ah nearly passed oot before ah flung it away, n jist sat oan the couch, fuckin breathin aw that heavy wey, muh hert beatin like fuck.

Muh ma came intae the room, saw ays aw that fuckin agitated wey. She goes: — What's wrong, son?

Ah jist says nowt.

Then she goes: — When ur ye gaun roond tae June's, tae see the bairns?

— In a bit, ah goes. — Business tae sort oot first.

Ah heard hur talkin away in the background, jist fuckin well blabbering away tae hersel, that wey where she disnae fuckin really want or expect ye tae say nowt back, like she's singing a fuckin song or something. Thir's some new names gittin bandied aboot, as if ah should ken whae the fuck she's talkin aboot.

So now ah'm back up tae Wester Hailes n ah'm takin Kate oot. So wir up the toon in a taxi. Ah slips her some notes tae pay the boy whin wi gits ootside this club, cause ah recognises an auld fitba mate Mark, working oan the door, n ah goes up tae huv a word.

So ah'm fuckin bletherin tae Mark in the street n ah looks back n sees her squarin up n the taxi pillin away. Then this cunt comes up tae her n goes: — Is that you oot hoorin, ya dirty fuckin slag, he fuckin hisses at ur, like a fuckin viper, pittin ehs hand up as she cowers away.

— Dinnae, Davie, she pleads in this sortay high fuckin shriek n ye kin see wi that big satisfied look oan ehs face eh's heard that noise fae hur before. Ah kent right away whae it wis. Mark the bouncer fuckin steps forward, but ah stoap um. Then ah walks aw slow up tae the cunt, cause ah'm fuckin savourin every step ay this fuckin journey. The cunt's goat Kate by the wrist now, and eh sees ays stridin casually up tae thum.

— What you fuckin wantin? You fahkin well wantin some n aw, ya cunt! You fuckin well . . . eh fuckin screams at ays, but ehs gittin mair n mair desperate. Right away eh kens thit thit noise jist bothers amateurs and ah kin see the fight sinking oot ay the cunt awready. Right away this cunt kens eh's fucked; ehs bottle had gone long before ah'd goat tae within five strides ay um! The thick veins through that fuckin paper-thin neck, the throat spotting up, like a fuckin rash. N me, ah'm jist that fuckin relaxed.

Gied the cunt the slow smile n the fuckin stare, lit um cook nicely fir a second or two before pittin the fucker oot ay ehs misery n breakin ehs beak wi a flick ay the heid. A punch knocks um over, ontae the cobblestanes, n fir Kate's sake, n cause thir's that many cunts around, ah jist blootered um three times in the heid, face n small ay the back. Ah bend doon n whispers tae the shitein cunt:
— The next time ah see you, ye fuckin well die.

Eh lits oot somethin between a fuckin plea and a whimper.

Ah tells Kate thit that boy'll nivir bother her again. Wi nivir steyed long in the club but, cause ah wanted tae git hame early. Wi gits intae bed n ah fuckin well rides her ragged aw night. She tells ays she'd seen nowt like it before! Ah'm lying in bed wi her, ma thoats racin then gridlockin, n ah see her barry face n ah'm thinking: this lassie might jist fuckin well save ays.

23

Scam # 18,739

We are at the hub of a great load of shite: me and him, Simon and Mark, Sick Boy and Rent Boy, here in Amsterdam. Away from it all. I got the location of Luxury from N-Sign and he and I, along with Terry, Rab Birrell and his brother, the ex-boxer, separated from the rest of them very quickly. Some old football faces with us are pretty dodgy. Lexo, for example, is an old mate of Begbie's; makes things interesting indeed. Terry is the main one I'll stick with, as a man so single-minded about women as he is, is always good to have in tow. His chat-up methods are relatively unsophisticated, but he's relentless and he gets results.

We come across Renton's club and I ask the boy at the door if he's around. Hearing that he left about half an hour ago, I look disappointed, and the guy, with a cockney accent, says that he'll be trawling around the clubs, and to try Trance Buddah. He said it in that exasperatedly affectionate manner which is like, 'Good old Mark, you know how he is.' *I know orlroight, yew farking wenkah, but you obviously don't.* So evidently the cunt can still be plausible, still pull the wool over people's eyes. But that sums up the naffness of Renton: run a club night and then piss off to somebody else's.

Shite. I steer the crew back along to the red-light district. The Juice man grumbles: — What's wrong wi that place then, Sicky?

That corkscrew-heided tossbag, not content with calling me 'Sick Boy' instead of Simon, in front of strangers, has upped the stakes further and abbreviated it to Sicky, which is even more cringe-inducing. I keep silent about my distaste for this, hoping it will pass. Show the likes of Lawson weakness and he'll exploit it unmercifully; it's almost what I love most about the man.

Renton. Here in Amsterdam. I'm wondering what the fuck he's like now. What modifications he's made to himself over the years.

You have tae try tae work out who is and isnae you. That's our quest in life. There's what you leave behind when you come away, and what you always take with ye. And I'm E'd up, trying to work out what it is that *I* take with me, wherever I go, whatever state I get into. We get into this Trance Buddah place in the red-light district. It's a standard dance floor, chill-out space and bar club comprising locals, tourists and Brit ex-pats. I have my Renton agenda of course, but Terry and I are on instinctive minge alert and separate ourselves from the mob. Ewart gets stopped by these two birds and he's turning on the charm, and Big Birrell, the boxer, and Rab are hanging around him. I buy a couple of pills from this Dutch guy who promises that they're the business. Fuck it. I'm not in the mood to do charlie, I'll be in the fucking bogs all night. I want to get off with a Dutch bird, the good skin and all that, but Terry's got in conversation with these two English lassies and I buy them a drink and we're sitting beside them in a quiet corner. The music's getting on my tits; it's that Dutch fairground school-disco techno and it's doing my nut in. Another reason to hate Renton: having to endure this pish.

I'm with this lassie Catherine from Rochdale (dirty-blonde shoulder-length hair, strangely arresting mole on chin), and she's telling me that techno's no her thing, it's too heavy for her liking. When she's talking, I'm looking at her dark made-up eyes and I'm thinking 'Rochdale' and my thoughts go roughly, very roughly, like this: Gracie Fields from Rochdale singing 'Sally, Salleee, pride of our alley', and me fucking Catherine in an alleyway. Then, sticking to the Rochdale theme, Mike Harding singing 'The Rochdale Cowboy' and I'm thinking of Catherine as the Rochdale Cowgirl, wondering about her in the reverse cowgirl position, the classic porn shot invented to display genital penetration for the camera. What I'm saying out loud, though, is: — So, Catherine, Rochdale, eh. Juice Terry, who's got this lassie, who I think is a mate of Catherine's, tucked into his side, registers this comment and flashes me a tele- pathic look which is like he's completely read my thoughts and aye, these pills are not bad.

I'm happy to chill out here, as I can't dance to monotonous techno. Like running the London Marathon, that shit. Boom-boom- boom. Where's the funk, where's the soul? Where's the fucking clathes? Jambo music. These spazzy Dutch and holiday types seem tae be mad for it though; each to their own. One boy's off it, doing a strange wee step routine with two lassies and another guy, and there's something about this cunt. I kent the boy. He has a daft hat on, which is going over his eyes, but I recognise the way he moves about: engrossed in the DJ's mix, but occasionally looking at the floor to throw his arms in the air in recognition at some fucker in the club. It's the detached energy, the languid movements totally at odds wi the bristling commitment. No matter how involved he seems, there's a part of the bastard always on the outside, taking everything in.

There's fuck all gets past that cunt.

It was a guy I'd talked a lot of shite with in the past. Like we were gaunnae be something different. Like he wisnae a skagheid fae the Fort who'd dropped oot ay the uni and I wisnae a snidey cunt spraffing away intae the heid of any poor wee bitch who'd had a bad childhood and who was daft enough to swallow both a sorry tale and a sweaty cock.

It wis ma old mate Mark.

It wis Rents.

It was the cunt who'd ripped me off, the cunt who *owed me*.

And I can't, no, won't, take my eyes off him. Sitting here in the shadows, in a little alcove with my party, Catherine, Terry and what's the other lassie called? whatever, I'm just watching him on the dance floor. After a while, I notice that he's preparing to go with some people. And I'm out after him, tugging on Catherine's hand and she's going on about her mate and I silence her with a kiss, looking over at Renton's back receding, turning to tip Terry a libidinous nod, his carnal smile making me feel sorry for the girl he's with and her ring-piece. As we go out to pick up the coats, I snog with Catherine for a bit and realise that, although young, and with a pretty face, she's a fucking hefty piece. The black clothes should have been a giveaway, but those oil-drum thighs . . .

Not to worry.

We're outside and I can see Rents is further down the street, he and a skinny short-haired blonde bird with another couple. Boy-girl, boy-girl, as Danny Kaye says in *White Christmas*. How cosy. How civilised, as the Islington middle classes mindlessly parrot. You give the cunts a glass of wine and switch the fire on, and they say: 'This is civilised.' They cut some fuckin pieces of ciabatta with a knife, and they go: 'Isn't this civilised?'

And you want to go: no, you daft cunt, no it's fuckin well not, because civilisation extends beyond pouring wine and cutting bread and what you're *really* talking about is simply leisure and relaxation.

Now Catherine's at it, as we're following Renton's posse over the cobblestoned canal roads. She's telling me it's so ci-vi-lah-sed over here, and she's curling into my side. Civilise ays, bambino, civilise this wild Caledonian-Italiano laddie from Leith. Catherine's eyes may be on the sodium street lamps reflecting off the wet stones and the still canal waters, but mine are on the thief, just the thief and if I had a third eye in the centre of my head, it too would be on the thief.

I can almost hear him, and I wonder what he's saying. Over here the Rent Boy is free to indulge all his pretensions, without any Begbie figure coming up and saying: 'Aye, a fuckin junky fae the Fort.' Cutting him down to size: to small, small pieces. Yes, I can almost empathise with the thief, see the need he had to do this, to avoid swimming in that pool of negative energy until your arms ache and you just go down like the rest of the sad fuckers. But to do it to me, to *me*, and to sort out that useless loser Murphy, well, it destroys any fucking argument.

Catherine's babblings become a strange soundtrack to my thoughts, which are growing darker by the minute. It's as if somebody had put the score from *The Sound of Music* on top of a print of *Taxi Driver*.

They cross this narrow bridge down a canal street and head down the road, it's called the Brouwersgracht, and they get in the stair at 178. The lights go on in the second-floor flat and I steer Catherine over the bridge to get a perspective from the other side of the canal. She's still going on about 'li-bi-ril-ah-zay-shin', and 'ow it breeds a different attitude'. My eyes are on them, I see them dancing in the window, in the warm, and here's me outside, in the biting cold air, and I think, why don't I just go up and ring the bell and freak the cunt out? But no, because I'm savouring this stalking now, that's why. That feeling of power that I know where he is, but he doesn't have a clue about me. Never act in haste, act in thought and deliberation. And, most importantly, when I come face to face with that cunt I won't be on good Es, I'll be on industrial-strength cocaine.

He needs sorting out; that'll happen. I know where the thief lives: 178 Brouwersgracht. But Catherine needs the SDW experience first.

— You look so beautiful, Catherine, I tell her, suddenly, straight out of nowhere, interrupting her thoughts.

She's taken aback by this. — Don't . . . she says shyly.

— I want to make love to you, I tell her, warmly, but with what I think is deep profundity.

Catherine's eyes have become black, shimmering pools of beautiful love that you want, crave, so desperately, to drown in. — You're so sweet, Simon, she laughs. — You know, I thought for a moment that you was bored with me, it were like you weren't listening to me.

— No, it was the pill, the way you look . . . it just made me feel . . . you know . . . like I was sort of trancing out a bit. But all the time I heard your voice, felt your warmth in my side and my heart was fluttering like it was a butterfly in a breeze of warm, fresh, spring air . . . it sounds pretentious, I know . . .

— No, no, it sounds lovely . . .

— . . . I just wanted to hold on to the moment, because it was so perfect, but then I thought, no, that's so greedy, Simon. Share it. Share it with the girl who made it happen . . .

— You're so lovely . . .

I squeeze her hand and lead her back to her hotel, first checking out that it was a more expensive one than mine.

You're fuckin well gettin it, fat girl.

In the morning, my first thoughts are of extrication. As one gets older it becomes almost as important an art form as seduction itself. Gone are the bitter, tense days of pulling on your clothes and wanting to, or actually, physically running away. Catherine's by my side, sleeping like an elephant that's been brought down by a Safari dart gun. She's a crasher. It's good to have a lassie who sleeps soundly. Frees up so many extra hours in the day for you to be you. I pen a note.

Catherine,
Last night was wonderful for me. Can we meet tonight at Stone's Café at nine?
Please be there!
Love, Simon XXXXX
PS: You looked so beautiful in your sleep, I just didn't have the heart to wake you up.

I head back to the hotel. There's no sign of Terry, but Rab Birrell's up with a few of his mates. I sort of like this Birrell guy. He's too cool to ask where I've been. When you've been surrounded by snickering morons half your life you grow to appreciate the quality of quiet discretion in a man.

I get some rolls and cheese and ham and coffee from the breakfast buffet and join them. — And how are the chaps? Good and well?

— Aye, Rab says, as does his big mate Lexo Setterington. I have to watch what I say around that cunt as he's a mate of Begbie's. A bit more upstairs than that fucking lunatic though. Knows the score, the way things are going. A Thai café, in fucking Leith!

It's good to know, though, that there's no love lost between those so-called bosom buddies. — Left me in the lurch wi bills to pay and assets ay a few hundred quid's worth ay auld junk n mawkit furniture. Ah should fuckin kill the arrogant cunt . . . he laughs.

I keep my own counsel here, responding with a non-committed, — Mmm . . . because this cunt is as bad in his own way as Begbie.

— Thing aboot Franco, eh never forgets, Lexo says. — Go against the cunt n ye huv tae huv um put tae sleep for good. Or else eh'd just keep on coming back. Things is, the radge'll get his anyway, if ye just leave him tae his ain devices long enough. Somebody'll get fed up wi um and do Begbie for fuck all, savin some cunt a traceable couple ay grand, he grins. I realise that Lexo's been out all night and is still pretty drunk, because he grabs my shoulder heavily and whispers, alcohol-breathed into my ear: — Naw. Ye need tae be ruthless enough no tae indulge your ain taste for violence just for the sake ay it. Leave that tae losers like Begbie. He lets go of me, smiling, still staring carefully into my eyes. Once again, I try to make the right noises in reply, to which he responds by saying: — Of course, ye kin huv the odd wee tickle now n then . . .

With that, the conversation drifts off along the predictably depressing lines of the relative merits of the Feyernoord and Utrecht mobs. Billy Birrell, Rab's boxing brother and N-Sign Ewart have apparently bagged off and are not up for the thug excursion. Sensible. I can't stay here listening to bams on cocaine ranting about who they're going to kill; I can get that back in Leith any time. I throw back the coffee and head out into the street.

Eventually, I find a bike shop and hire a black boneshaker and pedal past the thief's flat. There's a café with huge windows opposite his pad on the other side of the canal, which I noticed last night. I chain up the bike and sit in the window of this large, airy bar with brown floorboards and yellow walls, sipping coffee *verkerd*. The trees block the view of his window, but I can see the front-stair door, and I can watch all his comings and goings.

I've stolen, robbed, choried everything that isn't tied down, and so have most of my mates here and in London. That doesn't make us thieves in my book. A thief is someone who steals from his or her own. I wouldnae do that, Terry wouldnae. Even fucking scruffy Murphy wouldnae . . . well . . . that's not quite true. There's Coventry City to consider. But the point is that Renton is getting paid back with interest.

24

Whores of Amsterdam Pt 4

There's me come out the shower and I'm standing there watching Katrin watching the world. She's got the huge glass doors which dominate our front room wide open and she's leaning on the railing looking out across the canal. I can see where her line ay vision's going, following that narrow street opposite us which runs right down, cutting across several other Jordaan canals. I'm moving up quietly behind her, not wanting to disturb her, almost mesmerised by her stillness. Over her shoulder I see a lone cyclist receding doon the road, his figure bobbing as he bounces ower a speed bump. There's something familiar about him, maybe he passes this way a lot. I see the top beams of the buildings, the ones they leave sticking out for the purpose of swinging furniture into the narrow dwellings; they jut out at each other like two lines of rifle-packing armies in a stand-off.

That chilled air must be cooling her bare legs. What does she want? Whatever it is, it can't go on like this. I feel the sun's rays in my face, on our faces, and I think that maybe this is how it should be.

We try to talk, but finding the words is like digging for water in a desert. To casually get back to humanity after dragging our relationship along the path of death takes longer and longer every time. Now our only communion are the rows we have about nothing. I kiss the back of her thin neck, in hurtful guilt and compassion, in a tender rage. There's no reaction. I move away and go into the bedroom to get dressed.

When I come back she's in exactly the same spot. I tell her I'm going out for a bit and meet the same silence. I head down the street to the Herengracht, following it to the Leidseplein and stroll through the Vondelpark, nerves jangling for some reason, although

I've not had any drugs. Nonetheless, I feel quite para. Martin always says the logic in doing drugs is that if you're totally straight, some weeks you're still gaunnae feel fucked up and paranoid; at least if you do drink and drugs you have a reason to feel that way, rather than just sitting around convincing yourself that you might be mentally ill. The paranoia is nothing like as heavy in chilled Amsterdam as it is in Edinburgh, but I still feel like every fucker's watching me, like I'm being stalked by some mad cunt.

After a bit I head up to the club, opening the office. Checking e-mails on a Sunday, because you can't bear to sit in the same room as your girlfriend: life surely doesnae get much sadder than that. I'm as well being in London.

I start doing some other things; dealing with paperwork, bills, correspondence, making phone calls and all that shite. Then I get a shock, a big, big fucking shock. I'm just sitting there, looking at the cashbook, through some bank statements from the ABN-AMRO. I still have trouble with Dutch on the page. No matter how good your verbal gets, the visual recognition in print can floor you. To ken, to know. Dutch-Jock. Just say loch.

Rekening nummer.

Reckoning.

There's a tap on the door and I anxiously check to make sure that Martin's not left any wraps of coke out, lying under the stacks of paper, but no, they'll all be in the safe that sits behind me. I get up and open the door, thinking that it's probably Nils or Martin, when this cunt pushes me inside. The thought hits me in a second, tensing up my body: I'M BEING FUCKIN WELL ROBBED HERE . . . before it evaporates and I see a figure standing in front of me, familiar and alien all at the same time.

It takes a second for the realisation to entirely strike home. It's like my brain can't quite process the sense data my eyes are sending it.

Cause standing right in front of me is Sick Boy. Simon David Williamson.

Sick Boy.

— Rents, he says in cold accusation.

— Si . . . Simon . . . what the fuck . . . I don't bel . . .

— Renton. We've business. I want my money, he barks, his eyes bulging like a Jack Russell terrier's baws when it sees a bitch on heat, scanning the office. — Where's my fuckin money?

I just stand there looking at him, zombiefied, not quite knowing what the fuck to say. All I can think is that he's gained weight but it strangely looks okay on him.

— My fuckin money, Renton, he steps towards me and snarls in ma face, and I can feel the heat and slaver from him.

— Sick . . . eh, Simon, ah'll . . . I'll gie ye it, I tell him. It seems to be all I can say.

— Five fuckin grand, Renton, he says, and he grabs a hold of my T-shirt at the chest.

— Eh? I ask, a bit scoobied, looking down at his hand on my chest like it's dug shite.

In response, he deigns to loosen the grip a little bit. — I've worked it out. Interest, plus compensation for the mental stress caused to me.

I shrug doubtfully at this, in some half-arsed defiance. It was such a big deal at the time, but now it seems a small thing, just a pair of twats mixed up in a bit of daft junky business. It hits me how, after a few years of looking over my shoulder, I've become complacent, blasé even, about the whole deal. It's only on the odd sneaky family visit to Scotland that the paranoia resurfaces, and it's only really Begbie I worry about. As far as I know he's still doing a sentence for manslaughter. I only briefly considered at the time how the whole business affected Sick Boy. The strange thing was, I intended to compensate him and Second Prize, and, I suppose, even Begbie, like I did Spud, but, somehow, I just never got round to it. Nope, I never thought about how it impacted on him, but I sense that he's going to tell me.

Sick Boy lets go of me and peels away, spinning round the office, slapping his own forehead, pacing up and down. — I had tae contend wi Begbie eftir it! He thought I wis in it wi ye! I lost a fucking tooth, he spits, halting suddenly and pointing in accusation tae a gold-toothed gap in his ivory mouth.

— What happened tae Begbie . . . Spud . . . Secon . . . ?

Sick Boy snaps savagely back at me, rocking on his heels: — Never mind those cunts! This is *me* we're talking about! Me! He thrashes his own chest with a clenched fist. Then his eyes widen and his voice drops to a soft whine. — I was supposed tae be yir best mate. Why, Mark? he pleads. — Why?

I have tae smile at his performance. I can't help it, the cunt hasn't changed a bit, but this riles the fuck out of him and he jumps on me and we go crashing to the floor, him on top of me. — DON'T FUCKING LAUGH AT ME, RENTON! he screams in my face.

That was fuckin sair. I've hurt my back and I struggle to get my breath with this fat cunt on top of me. He *has* put on weight and I'm pinned under him. Sick Boy's eyes are full of fury and he pulls back his fist. The thought of Sick Boy beating me to a pulp for the money seems faintly ridiculous. Not impossible, but ludicrous. He was never into violence. But people change. Sometimes they get more desperate when they get older, especially if they feel that their ship hasn't come in. And this might not be the Sick Boy I knew. Eight, nine years, is a long time. A taste for violence must be like a taste for anything else: some people can acquire it later on in life. I have myself, in a controlled way, through four years of karate training.

But even without that I always thought that I could take Sick Boy. I mind of giving him a doing at school, at the back of Fyfe's goods yard by the Water of Leith. It wasnae a real fight, just handbag stuff between two non-fighters, but I stuck it out longer and was more vicious. I won that battle, but he won the war, as usual, emotionally blackmailing me about it for years after. Used the best-mate routine: turned those big lamps on me and made me feel like a drunken wife-beater. Now with my shotokan karate skills I know I could immobilise him easily. But it's me who's doing nothing, and I'm thinking, what a paralysing force guilt can be, and how righteous indignation is such an energiser. I just want to get out of this without having to hurt him.

Now he's ready to punch my face in, and I'm thinking about this and I'm laughing. Sick Boy is too.

— What are you laughin at? he sais, obviously annoyed, but still grinning in spite of it.

I'm looking up at his face. He's a bit more jowly, but still in good

nick really. Well togged out as well. — You've gained weight, I tell
him.

— So have you, he says with an insulted pout, all hurt. — You
mair than me.

— Mine is muscle. I never took you for a fat cunt, I smile.

He looks down at his stomach and sucks in his gut. — Mine's
fuckin muscle too, he says.

I'm hoping now that he sees how fuckin ridiculous all this is.
And it is. We can sort this out, come to some kind of arrangement.
I'm still shocked, but not surprised, and in a strange way it's good
to see him. I always felt that we'd meet up again. — Simon, let's get
up. We both know that you're no gaunnae hit me, I tell him.

He looks at me, grins and makes a fist again and I see stars as it
crashes into my face.

25

The Edinburgh Rooms

The Edinburgh Rooms at the Central Library, man, they're like fill ay stuff aboot, well, Edinburgh. Ah mean, that stands tae reason, as it should be, likes. Ah mean, ye widnae expect tae find things aboot the likes ay Hamburg or eh . . . Boston in the Edinburgh Rooms. Thing is but, thir's stuff aboot Leith here n aw, loads n loads ay stuff, stuff which by rights should be in the Leith Public Library doon in Ferry Road, man. Fair dos, ah mean, Leith is classed as a part ay Edinburgh by the council gadges, if no by a lot ay cats doon in the old Port. But oan the other hand, ah mind ay the time whin thir wis leaflets aboot aw that decentralisation the council's meant tae believe in. So why the need for a Leith cat like me tae trek aw the wey up tae Edina, jist tae git stuff oan Leith? Why this great long march up tae George IV Bridge instead ay jist a nippy wee hop next door tae Ferry Road, ken?

Mind you, it's a nice wee walk in this biscuit-ersed March sun. The high street's a wee bit nippy but. No been up here since the festival n ah miss aw they cool chicks smilin at ye n giein ye leaflets fir thir shows. It's pure radge but, they wey they sortay make a state-ment intae a question. They go: 'We've a show in the festival?' 'It's up the Pleasance?' 'The review was brilliant?' N ye feel like sayin, hud oan a second, cool kitten-cat, cause if ye want tae dae that, n make a statement intae a question, aw ye need tae dae is tae add 'ken' oan the end. Ken?

But of course, ah ey took the leaflets anywey, cause it's no fir the likes ay me tae say anythin tae posh lassies thit uv been tae college n that, studyin hot thespian action likesay, ken?

That's always been ma problem but, man, confidence. The big dilemma has been that drug-free too often equals confidence-free, man. Right now the confidence isnae low, but it's, what's the word thit cats yaze? Precarious, man, precarious. N the first thing ah noticed whin ah goat up here wis this pub acroas the road fae the Central Library called Scruffy Murphy's. One ay they Irish theme pubs that are nowt like what real pubs in Ireland are like, ken. Thir jist for business cats, yuppies and rich students. Lookin at it made ays go aw tense n ashamed inside but. In a just world these cats that run that bar should pay the likes ay me compensation for emotional damage incurred, man. Ah mean, that wis aw ah goat whin ah wis at the school, it wis 'Scruffy Murphy, Scruffy Murphy'. Jist cause ay the auld Erin name and the poor threads due tae the adverse economic circumstances and the poverty that was endemic in the Murphy households at Tennent Strasser and Prince Regent Strasser. So it's like the oppo ay good, man, the pure oppo ay good.

Jist, likesay, seein yon pub sign, it fair put ays at a maximum disadvantage even before the off, ken? So ah'm downcast when ah git intae the library, thinkin tae masel, 'How kin Scruffbag Murphy here ever write a book?' and walking intae the place wis jist weird, weird, weird. W–E–I–R–D oan baith sides, man. Aye, ah goes through the big wooden doors n suddenly ma hert wis gaun: bang bang bang. It felt tae ays like ah wis breakin in, man, like some cat hud rammed a load ay amyl nitrate up muh beak. Ah felt aw faint, ken, like ah wis gaunnae pass oot or something, jist crumple tae the deck oan the spot. Thir's that feelin, like whin yir in a swimmin pool under the water, or up in a plane, aw that sort ay muffled noise in yir ears. So ah wis shaky, man, jist pure shaky. Then when the security cat in the uniform comes ower, ah jist sortay pure panics. Ah'm thinkin thit ah'm gubbed here; aw naw, man, ah'm huckled here awready and ah've no even done nowt, wisnae even gaunnae dae nowt, jist look at some books, likesay . . .

— Can I help you? the boy asks.

So ah'm thinking: ah've done nowt wrong, ah'm jist in the place. Ah've no even done nowt, nup, nowt. But ah'm sortay sayin: — Eh . . . eh . . . eh . . . ah jist wondered likes . . . if it wis awright likes, if ah could . . . eh . . . jist have a wee look in the eh, room wi aw the stuff oan Edinburgh . . . tae see the books n that likes.

N ah could jist sortay tell thit this boy kens what ah am: tea leaf, junky, schemie, ghetto child, third-generation bog-wog, gyppo; ah jist sortay ken, man, cause this boy's a Jambo Mason, a rotary-club gadge, ah mean ye kin jist tell, the uniform n that . . . the polished buttons, man . . .

— Downstairs, the boy sais, n eh just like, lets ays go in. Jist like that! The boy lits ays go in! The Edinburgh Rooms. Central Library. George IV Bridge likes!

Barry!

So ah goes doon the big marble staircase n there's the sign, 'The Edinburgh Rooms'. So now here's me feelin aw chuffed, man, like a total scholar. But, see whin ah gits in, it's huge, man, huge, n thir's a load ay people sitting reading at they wee desks, like thir back in primary school. It's as quiet as Falkirk n it's like thir aw looking at me, man. What it is that those cats see? A junky whae's mibee gaunnae nick some books tae sell tae get gear.

So ah'm thinkin, naw, naw, naw, man, stey cool. Innocent until proven. Jist dae what Avs at the group says n try n chill oot oan the self-sabotage vibe. Count tae five whin the stress comes oan. One, two, three . . . what's that big wifie wi the glesses lookin at . . . ? four, five. N it wis better, man, cause they wir pure lookin away eftir that, ken?

No that there's much worth nickin in thair. Ah mean, some ay they books might be valuable tae a collector, but it isnae the sort ay goods ye could shift doon the Vine Bar, aw they auld ledgers, is that what they call thum, man, ledgers, n aw that microfilm n that sort ay stuff, ken?

Anywey, ah'm daein the wee hunt through they books n thir sayin that Leith and Edinburgh merged in 1920, eftir a sort ay referendum. It would be like that 'Yes for devolution' vote, for the Parliament n that, when the people spoke and that was that. Ah mind ay seeing the *Scotsman* and they dudes there were saying 'naw, man, vote no', but cats just went 'sorry, man, we cannae dig what you gadges say in your paper so let's have a big yes'. Democracy, man, democracy. Ye cannae make a cat go for Felix when there's Whiskas on offer.

The thing is that the Leithers rejected the merger by a four-tae-one majority. Four tae one, man, but the gig still took place! Ah sort ay half mind that every old punter used to talk aboot that when we were pram-kickers. Now those auld cats are six foot under, so who'll let everybody ken what they did against the people, against democracy, way back then, man? Send for the boy Murphy! Aye, aw those felines past in the Stephen King Pet Semetary, sleep at ease, cause here ah come! So that seems like a good place for ays tae start, 1920: the great betrayal, man.

Aye, it's aw startin tae come thegither in my heid. The problem is that what ah forgot wis thit tae write a book, ye need things like a pen and paper. So ah nash next door tae Bauermeister's n chore a notepad n pen. Ah'm pure buzzin n ah cannae wait tae git back tae that desk ah wis sittin at n git intae some serious note-takin. That's it, man, a history ay Leith fae the merger tae the present. Start oaf in 1920, n maybe go back a bit, then forward again, like aw they fitba-player biographies.

Ken?

Like, Chapter One: 'I couldnae believe it when I lifted that European Cup intae the sky, man. That Alex Ferguson cat bounced right up and said tae me, "Hi, man, that likesay makes you immortal, ken?" No that I could mind that much aboot the winning goal, or the match, as I'd been in a crack den right through the night until aboot half an hour tae go before the kick-off when I got the taxi tae the groond . . .' Ye ken how the script goes, man.

Then the next chapter is: 'But the story really begins a long way fae the San Siro Stadium in Milan. In fact we have tae go back tae a humble tenement in Rat Street, The Gorbals, Glasgow, where I made my debut as the seventeenth son of Jimmy and Senga McWeedgie. It was a close-knit community and I wanted for nothing . . . blah blah blah . . .' Ye ken the score.

So that's it, start there and work back. Ah'm smokin, gadgie, pure smokin!

Then ah sees thit thuv goat the papers fae that time, the *Scotsman* n the *Evening News* n aw that. Now even though these were written by aw they rich Tory cats, they might still have a bit in them, likesay local news n that, thit's useful tae me. Thing is, it's aw microfilm thir oan, n ah need tae fill in a slip tae git thum. Then yuv goat this big, big machine, like an auld kind ay telly n yuv goat tae sort ay pit thum through it, ken? Well, ah'm no happy aboot aw this, likes.

A library, man, it's pure jist meant tae be aboot books n that, n naebody said nowt tae me aboot machines n that, likes.

So ah get they microfilm things offay the boy, ah'm aw ready tae go, cat, go, but whin ah see that big telly thing ah'm jist gaun, naw, naw, naw, cause ah'm likesay no that technical n ah'm aw sortay worried that ah'll brek it. Ah would ask one ay the staff but ah ken thit thi'll jist think thit ah'm thick n that, ken?

Naw, ah cannae work that, no way, naw, so ah jist leave the stuff thair oan the desk n ah go oot the door, up the staircase, just so gled tae get oot ay thair wi ma hert gaun thump, thump, thump. But when ah am oot, ah kin hear aw the voices in ma heid; aw laughin, sayin ah'm nothing, nowt, zilch n ah see that Scruffy Murphy's sign and it hurts, man, it hurts that much that ah pure need tae git rid ay the pain. So ah head doon tae Seeker's place, where ah ken thit ah'll git somethin, somethin ah ken willnae make me feel like Scruffy Murphy.

26

'. . . sex monsters . . .'

He took me back to his place that night and put me to bed. I woke up, fully clothed, under the duvet cover. A brief paranoid dance started in my head when I thought about the fool I'd made of myself, then the sort of things Terry could have got up to with that video camera. But I just sense and feel that nothing happened, because Gina looked after me. Gina and Simon. When I got up the flat was empty. It was a small tenement dwelling with the lounge dominated by a leather suite and sealed wooden floor with expensive-looking rugs. The wallpaper is a cascade of ghastly orange lilies. Above the fireplace is a print of a nude woman with Freud's profile superimposed onto it, with the caption, 'What's on man's mind'. I'm surprised by how immaculately tidy the place is.

I went through to a small, fitted kitchen where I found a note on one of the work surfaces.

N,
You came over a bit the worse for wear so Gina and I got you back here. I'm round at hers, then straight to work. Help yourself to tea, coffee, toast, cereal, eggs and the like. Give's a bell on 07779 441 007 (mobile) and we'll hook up some time.
All the best,
Simon Williamson

I called him to say thanks, but we didn't hook up as he was heading to Amsterdam with Rab and Terry. I wanted to get in touch with Gina to thank her but nobody seems to know her number.

So now I'm missing my new boys: Rab, Terry and, yes, Simon too. Especially Simon. I almost wish I'd gone to Amsterdam with them. I'm still having fun with my girls though, as Lauren's lightened up in the absence of the corrupting sex monsters from Leith, and Dianne, while pretty busy with her dissertation, is game for a laugh and a drink.

On the subject of sex monsters: on Tuesday afternoon we met one, a real one. It was a surprisingly mild day and the three of us were sitting outside the Pear Tree, having a lager, when this sleazy creep approached us and sat down at our table. — Good afternoon, girls, he said, sitting his pint on the end of the bench. That's the problem with the Pear Tree, the beer garden fills up quickly and the benches are long, so you often end up with somebody you don't want to sit next to. — You don't mind me sitting here, do you, he asked, harsh and arrogant. He had a hard, ferret-like face, thin, blondy-ginger hair and wore a sleeveless vest top, showing heavily tattooed arms. It wasn't just that his skin was deathly white in the spell of this mild weather; he had, to my mind, what Rab once referred to, pointing out an acquaintance of his in the bar, as 'the stink of the jail about him'.

— It's a free country, Dianne said lazily, giving him a cursory glance and turning back to me. — I'm up to about eight thousand words now.

— That's great, how many is it you need again?

— Twenty thou. If I get the sections mapped out I'll be fine. I just don't want to bang up the words and then find that I have to chop most of them out cause I've gone off on a tangent. I need to get the structure right, she explained, raising her glass and taking a gulp.

We heard a croaky voice next to us. — Youse students then?

I turned around wearily, being in the closest proximity to the guy. — Yeah, I told him. Lauren, sitting opposite was reddening, her face pinching. Dianne drummed on the table in impatience.

— What's it yis are studying well, the guy asked in a rasping tone, his eyes bleary and his face heavy and loose with alcohol.

— We all do, like, different things? I told him, hoping that this would satisfy him.

It didn't, of course. He picked up straight away on my accent. — Whaire dae you come fae then? he asked pointing at me.

— Reading.

The guy snorted, then smiled at me and turned to the others. I started to feel really uncomfortable. — What aboot youse two, youse English n aw?

— Nope, said Dianne. Lauren remained silent.

— Ah'm Chizzie, by the way, he said, extending his large, sweaty hand.

I shook it reluctantly, unnerved by the strength of grip, and Lauren did too, but Dianne turned her nose up.

— Oh, it's like that, is it? this Chizzie character said. — Never mind, he smiled, two oot ay three isnae bad, eh, girls? Ah'm in luck the day, in the company ay such lovely ladies.

— You're no in our company, Dianne told him. — *We're* in our company.

She might as well have said nothing for the way this creep reacted. He was off on his own trip and his mouth twisted lecherously as he looked us over. — Youse aw got boyfriends then? Bet yis huv. Bet youse huv aw goat fellys, eh?

— I don't think that's any of your business, Lauren said, her voice firm but small and high. I looked at this bully and at her, their difference in size, and I started to feel angry.

— Oh, that means that ye dinnae!

Dianne turned around and looked him straight in the eye. — Disnae matter whether we do or dinnae. If we've got a million cocks dancing on the end of a string, you can rest assured that yours won't be one of them. And even if there's a chronic shortage, don't expect a phone call from us.

There was a bit of menace flashing in this guy's eyes. He was a nutter. I thought: Dianne should shut up here. — You could git yirsel intae trouble wi a mooth like that, hen, he said, then added softly, — big trouble.

— Fuck off, Dianne snapped at him. — Just get the fuck out our faces and sit somewhere else, will ye!

The guy stared at her, at the side of her pretty, poised face, with his big, leering, stupid, ugly alcoholic head. — A bunch ay fuckin lesbos, he slurred. I would have told him the same as Dianne if it had been somebody like Colin, but this guy looked a dangerous, disturbed headcase. I could tell that Lauren was really frightened of him, and I suppose I was too.

Dianne wasn't, because she stood up, and she was right over him.
— Right, you, fuck off, now, ah'm tellin ye! Gaun, git!

He stood up, but she faced him down, her eyes blazing, and for a moment I thought he was going to hit her, but some guys at another table shouted something and a girl from the bar collecting glasses was across and asking what the problem was.

The guy broke into a cold smile. — Nae problem, he said, picking up his pint, downing it and moving away. — Fuckin dykes! he shouted back at us.

— Naw, we're nymphomaniacs, and we're totally desperate for it, but even we've goat fucking standards! Dianne shouted back. — AS LONG AS THERE'S STRAY DUGS IN THE STREETS AND PIGS OAN THE FARMS WE DINNAE NEED YOUR DIRTY SCABBY NONCEY WEE COCK, SON! GIT USED TAE IT!

The nutter twisted round swiftly and looked absolutely incandescent with rage, then turned and walked away, humiliated by the laughter which rang from the tables around us.

I sat in awestruck admiration of Dianne's performance. Lauren was still trembling, almost in tears. — He was a maniac, he was a rapist, why do they have to be like that, why do men have to be like that?

— He just needed shagged, the sad bastard, Dianne said, lighting up a cigarette, — but as I said, not this girl. Honestly, some people should have a wank before they venture outdoors, she grinned, hugging Lauren supportively. — Don't worry about that toss, hen, she said. — I'm going up tae get the drinks in.

We got pissed, and headed home. I have to admit I was a bit nervous on the journey, just in case we ran into that nutcase again. I think Lauren was as well, but I reckon Dianne would have welcomed it. It was later that night, after Lauren had crashed out, that I let her do the first interview with me, which she tape-recorded. — Aggressive men like the one we met today, she said, — have you encountered many of them? You know, at the sauna?

— The sauna's a very safe place to work? I told her. — There's, like, no nonsense there. I mean, I . . . I shrugged and decided to go for the truth, — . . . I limit myself to handjobs. I'd never work the streets. The clients at the sauna have money. If you don't want to do what they want, they'll find somebody else who will. Of course, there's the odd one who can become obsessed, they want to show their power over you and won't take no for an answer . . .

Dianne sucked the tip of her pen, and pulled her small reading glasses down onto her nose. — What do you do then?

And I told her, the first person I've ever told, about what had happened that time last year. It was both disturbing and cathartic to disclose. — One guy waited for me, started following me home. Never did anything, just started following me. When he came back to the sauna, he always asked for me. Said we were meant to be together and all that sort of scary stuff. I told Bobby, who threw him out and banned him. He still kept following me around outside. That's why I started going out with Colin, I suppose, the deterrence factor, I told her, realising that I'm explaining it to myself for the first time. — Surprisingly, it worked. He saw I had a boyfriend so he left me alone.

I had a long lie-in the following day, did some work and shopping, then cooked a casserole for the girls. Later, I called home. My mother picked up the phone and whispered mouse-like greetings I could hardly make out, before I heard a click, the sound of the upstairs line being picked up. — Princess! A voice boomed, and another click indicated that Mum had hung up. — How's chilly Jockoland?

— Quite warm actually, Dad. Could you put Mum back on for a minute?

— No! I most certainly could not! She's in the kitchen being a dutiful wife and cooking my dinner, ha ha ha . . . you know what she's like, he chirped, — happy in her kingdom. Anyway, how is this very, very expensive college course of yours going? Still on for a first, ha ha ha!

— Yeah, it's okay.

— When are you coming home to see us then, will you get down here for Easter?

— No, I'm working shifts up here in the restaurant. I might make it one weekend . . . I'm sorry the course is expensive, but I'm enjoying it and doing well.

— Ha ha ha . . . I don't grudge the expense, sweetie-pie, anything for you, you know that. When you're a famous film producer or director in Hollywood, you can pay me back. Or get me a part in a film, as Michelle Pfeiffer's love interest, now that would be up my street. So what else have you been up to?

Wanking off old guys in a sauna . . .

— Just the usual.

— Boozing all my hard-earned cash away, I'll bet! I know you students!

— Well, maybe a little. How's Will?

My father's voice grew a bit distant and impatient. — Fine, fine, I *think*. I just wish . . .

— Yes?

— I just wish that he had some normal friends, instead of the lost causes he seems to collect. That pansy boy he's hanging about with now; I told him that he'll get tarred by the same brush if he's not careful . . .

The ritual of the weekly phone call to my dad, and I initiated it. It shows how desperate I am for company. Lauren's gone home to Stirling for a long weekend. Dianne's still in the library most of the time, working night and day on her dissertation. Last night she took me to her family home in some part of the city I didn't know, and we had a drink with her mum and dad who are really chilled, cool people. We even smoked some grass.

So today I'm hanging around the uni out of boredom, waiting in some anticipation for the boys coming back from Amsterdam. Chris tells me that he's putting on a drama production for the festival and he asks me if I'd like to get involved. But I know what he really means. He's nice enough but I've fucked so many guys like him in the past; the sex is fine for a month, rapidly growing dull unless it becomes a gateway to something else; what: status, economic gain, love, intrigue, S&M, orgies? So I tell him, that I'm not interested, too busy. Busy hanging around with these strange local guys, some of them knocking on a bit now. Rab, the bastard who rejected me. Simon, who seems to want the world, and who apparently fancies that it's only a matter of time before he gets it. And Juice Terry, happy as things are. And why not? He's shagging everything and has enough cash to throw around on drinks. This makes him a formidable power as he's already living out a dream he's been preparing

154

for all his life. No need to make it less sordid, or to go more upmarket, no, all he wants to do is just fuck, drink and bullshit.

Terry was so often in the old port of Leith, I'd joke to Dianne and Lauren that he was like Mr Price in *Mansfield Park*, 'once in the dock-yard, he began to reckon on some happy intercourse with Fanny'. This was something we'd got into after I realised that Terry continually referred to every woman as 'Fanny'. So around the flat we started calling each other Fanny and began quoting passages from the book.

Now I'm alone, filing my nails and the phone rings. I thought it might be my mum, calling for a chat while Dad's at work, but I'm surprised, though not unpleasantly, to find that it's Rab in Amsterdam. At first, I think he more than misses me, he regrets not shagging me when he had the chance. Since he's got into all this stag stuff, his hormones have raced and he laments not having got his piece of the action. As do I, but I will. Now he wants to be Terry or Simon, for a few weeks, hours, minutes, before his kid comes along or before he ties the knot.

I play it cool, asking about Simon and Terry.

There's a chilly silence for a couple of beats before he speaks.
— Never really seen that much ay them. Terry's whoring aw the time during the day, and cruising lassies in the clubs at night. I think Sick Boy's probably daein the same. That and trying tae pull scams. Eh keeps gaun oan aboot contacts in the industry n aw that, n it does your nut in after a bit.

Sick Boy: vain, selfish and cruel. And that's his good side. But I think that it was Wilde who said that women appreciated down-right cruelty more than anything else and at times I'm inclined to believe it. I think Rab does too.

— That Sick Boy, he's a fascination to me. Lauren was right, she said that he gets into your head without you noticing, I say wist-fully, not forgetting that I'm talking to Rab on the phone, but trying to make out that I am forgetting.

— So ye like him, he says, and in what I think is quite a petty and spiteful way.

I feel my jaw tighten. There's nothing worse than a man who won't fuck you when he has the chance and then goes all funny when you consider fucking somebody else. — I didn't say I liked him. I said he fascinates me.

— He's scum. He's a pimp. Terry's just an idiot, but Sick Boy's a scheming cunt, Rab coughs with a real bitterness I've never heard from him before. It's only then that I realise that he's a bit drunk or stoned or both.

This is strange. They used to get on well. — You're working with him on a movie, remember.

— How could I forget, he sniffs.

Rab seems to have turned into Colin: possessive, controlling, disapproving and hostile, *and he hasn't even fucked me yet.* Why do I seem to have this effect on men, to bring out the worst in them? Well, I'm not taking this. — And you're having your little boys' stag night together in Amsterdam. Find a whore, Rab, enter into the spirit of it if you want laid before you get married. You've had your chance here.

Rab's silenced for a bit, then he says: — You're mental, trying to effect nonchalance, but you can tell by the tone of his voice that he knows he's behaved inappropriately, been undignified, and for somebody as proud as him, that's a terrible thing. He's fooling nobody, he wants me, but you are just too fucking late, Mr Birrell.

— Aye, he says, breaking the silence, — you're in a funny mood the day. Anyway, the real reason I called was to speak to Lauren. Is she there?

Something crashes in my chest. Lauren. What? — No, I feel my voice waver, she's gone to Stirling. Why do you want her?

— Aw, that's awright, I'll call her at her mum's. I said to her I'd check if my old man had this software which converts the stuff she's got on the Apple Mac she uses at home to Windows. Anyway, he's got it and he's happy to install it for her. It's just that she said it was quite urgent, cause she had stuff on the Mac she needed . . . Nikki?

— I'm here. Enjoy the rest of your stag, Rab.

— Cheers, see ye, he says, hanging up.

I can see why Terry gets really wound up by him. At first I couldn't, but now I can.

27

TENSION IN THE HEID

Muh heid is fuckin nippin. This fuckin migraine. Too much thinkin, that's ma problem, no thit some ay the thick cunts roond here wid understand that. Too much gaun oan in ma heid. That's what comes ay huvin fuckin brains; makes ye fuckin well think too much, think aboot aw the fuckin wide cunts thit need tae git thir fuckin faces burst. N thir's loads ay thum n aw. Crappin bastards, thir ey laughin at ye behind yir back, aw aye: ah ken n ah kin tell. They think thit ye dinnae see, bit ye fuckin well see awright. You ken. Ye eywis fuckin well ken, surein ye fuckin dae.

Ah need some fuckin Nurofen. Ah hope Kate gits back fae her ma's wi that greetin-faced bairn ay hers soon, cause a ride eywis helps, cuts oot aw the fuckin tension in the heid. Aye, whin ye shoot yir duff it's like gittin yir fuckin brain massaged. Ah cannae understand aw they cunts thit say, 'No the now, ah've goat a heidache,' like in they fuckin films n that. See, tae me, that's whin ye *need* a fuckin ride. If every cunt had a ride whin they hud a heidache, thir widnae be as much fuckin trouble in the world.

Thir's noise at the door; that'll be her now.

Bit hud oan a fuckin minute. Naw it's fuckin well no her.

Some cunt's tryin tae fuckin well brek in here . . . cause ay me sittin wi the light oaf cause ay ma heid nippin. That's thaime thinkin thit nae cunt's in! Well, some cunt's fuckin well in awright!

Game oan!

Ah roll oaf the fuckin couch oantae the deck, like one ay they Bruce Willis or Schwarzenegger type ay cunts, n crawl along the flair, standin up against the waw behind the livin-room door. If they ken whit thir daein thi'll fuckin well come ben here first, instead ay gaun up the stairs. The door flies open, the cunts huv fuckin well forced it. Thir in now. Ah dinnae ken how many, no a loat by the sound ay it. But it disnae matter how fuckin many come in, cause thir willnae be any fuckin well gaun oot.

Barry . . . this is fuckin barry . . . Ah stands behind the door, waitin oan the cunts. This wee fucker steps in, cairryin this baseball bat, the fuckin wee bastard. A big disappointment tae me. Ah shuts the door behind um. — Lookin for something then, cunt?

The wee cunt turns roond n starts waving the bat in front ay ays, but eh's fuckin well shat it right away. — Oot ma road! Lit ays oot! eh shouts. Ah recognise that wee cunt! Fae the pub, fae Sick Boy's pub! He kens me n aw, n eh's eyes go wider. — Ah didnae ken it wis your place, man, ah'm just gaunnae go . . .

Fuckin right the wee cunt didnae ken. — C'moan then, ah smile at um. Ah points tae the door. — Thaire it is. Whit ye fuckin waitin fir!

— Oot the wey . . . ah'm no wantin any bother . . .

Ah stoap smiling. — Yuv fuckin well goat it whether yir fuckin well wantin it or no, ah tell um. — So gie's that fuckin bat now. Dinnae make ays take it oaf ye. Fir yir ain sake, dinnae make ays dae that.

The wee cunt's standing fuckin tremblin, n ehs eyes start fillin wi water. Fuckin wee poof. Eh lowers the bat n ah grabs ehs wrist n takes it offay um, then ah grab ehs throat wi ma other hand. — Whit did ye no fuckin well leather ays fir, ya radge? Eh? Fuckin shitin wee cunt!

— Ah didnae . . . ah didnae ken thit . . .

Ah lits um go tae git the bat wi baith hands. — This is what ye fuckin should've done, n ah lamps the wee cunt wi it.

Eh pits ehs airms up and the bat cracks intae the wee cunt's wrist n eh lits oot this scream like a dug gittin run ower, n ah'm fuckin leatherin right intae um wi it, thinkin aboot what eh'd huv done if Kate n the fuckin bairn wir here.

Ah stoap whin ah see that thir's blood oan Kate's fuckin cairpit. The wee cunt's lyin aw fuckin well curled up n screamin like a fuckin bairn. — SHUT UP! ah fuckin shout at um. They waws are paper-thin n some cunt'll be oan tae the fuckin polis.

Ah find an auld dishcloth n pit it ower the cunt's heid whaire it's split n pit ehs basebaw cap back oan um, that'll stoap the fuckin

Roy Hudd fir a bit. Then ah git the cunt tae turn oot ehs poakits n gie um stuff fae the kitchen tae clean the cairpit wi. Thir's nowt here, jist some fuckin change, a set ay hoose keys n a wee bag ay pills.

— They Es?

— Aye . . . eh's fuckin well scrubbin away, lookin roond aw worried.

— Nae fuckin ching?

— . . . Naw . . .

Ah check the fuckin locks oan the door. Thuv been forced oot wi him shoodirin it, but the wid husnae fuckin split, which is just as well fir that wee cunt. Ah pit them back in. It's as flimsy as fuck but, n it's gaunnae need replaced.

Ah goes back tae whaire the wee cunt's still scrubbin. — They blood stains better fuckin well come oot. If ah'm gittin fuckin gyp fae hur fir huvin blood on hur cairpit, ah'll make it worth ma while n show yis fuckin blood awright.

— Aye . . . aye . . . thir comin oot . . . eh goes.

Ah finds oot thit the cunt's called Philip Muir n eh's fae Lochend. Ah'm lookin at the cairpit. Eh's no made a bad joab. — Right, you're comin wi me fir a bit, ah tells um.

The wee cunt's too feart tae say anything n wi gits tae the fuckin van. Ah opens the front passenger seat n eh gits in. Ah strolls roond tae ma seat n climbs in, kennin that eh's shitein it too much tae make a dash for it. — You navigate, pal, you ken whaire wir gaun.

— Eh . . .

— Wir gaun tae your hoose.

Ah sticks oan the radio n wi drives doon tae Lochend. This van's fucked, oan its last fuckin legs. Thir's that barry auld Slade song oan, 'Mama Weer Aw Crazee Now', n ah starts singing along tae it. — Slade's fuckin barry, ah tells the wee cunt.

We pills up ootside the fuckin gaff. — Yir ma n dad's?

— Aye.

— Nae cunt in?

— Naw . . . bit thill be back soon.

— Wi better fuckin nash then, c'moan.

So wi git inside n ah'm checkin oot the gear. Thir's a barry telly, flat-screen job, n it's goat a video, one ay they new types wi the compact disc, but wi fuckin pictures like, a fuckin VDU or whativir the fuck the cunts call it. Thir's a new stereo n aw, one ay the yins wi the tons ay fuckin speakers. — Right, cunty baws, start fuckin well loadin up, ah tells the wee fucker.

The boy's still shitein ehsel n ah'm watchin oot fir nosey cunts in the street. Any cunt blabs aboot this, n it's doon tae him, eh kens that. Wi git intae the van n take the gear back tae Kate's. The barry thing is thit thir's a Rod Stewart CD wi aw the hits oan it. Ah fuckin poakited that right away.

Whin wi comes back, she's ben the hoose wi the bairn. — Frank . . . the lock . . . she's pointin doon at they screws, back oan the fuckin flair again. — Ah jist put ma key in n they fell right through . . . she sees the wee cunt, standin behind me. He's shitein it again cause ay that fuckin lock, n eh fuckin well should be.

— Awright, ah goes, n wi head oot n come back in wi an end ay the telly each.

She's goat the bairn up in her airms. — The lock . . . Frank, what's gaun oan? What's aw this? She's lookin at the set.

— This wee mate ay mine here, ah tells her, explainin the story ah'd worked oot, oan the wey back in the motor. — Eh's a right wee fuckin good Samaritan, eh, pal? Came intae some gear, so ah sais bring it doon here. It's better thin your auld stuff.

— But the lock . . .

— Aye, ah've fuckin well telt ye aboot that but, Kate. Mind ah sais: that lock needs fixed. Ah'll git ma mate Stevo oan tae it, he's a locksmith, he'll sort it aw oot. Look at this but! New fuckin DVD n aw! Huv tae trade in aw they auld videos now.

— It's awfay nice, she sais. — Thanks, Frank . . .

— It's no me thit ye should be thankin, it's Philip here, eh, pal.

Kate looks at the shitein wee cunt. Eh's goat some fuckin eye oan um now. — Thanks, Philip . . . but what happened to your face n aw that?

Ah cuts in. — It's a long fuckin story, ah tells hur. — What it is, is thit Philip here owes ays a few favours, so whin eh goat a new stereo n telly fir ehs pad, eh phoned ays up n goes, you kin take the auld stuff if ye like. So ah fuckin well thinks, this is jist gaunnae

160

be a load ay fuckin junk, ken, but the wee cunt sais it's jist eighteen months auld!

— Ye sure, Philip? It looks awfay dear . . .

— Ye ken they young cunts, it's goat tae be the fuckin fashion wi thum. That's like the fuckin Stone Age tae they cunts! Aye, Philip thoat ay me first, but some other wide bastard thought he wis due it, tried tae pit the fuckin bite intae the wee cunt here. So, ah picks up the baseball bat, — wi went doon n hud a wee word wi the cunt, pit um right, eh, Philip?

The wee cunt gies a daft grin.

Kate's gittin the telly plugged in n set up. — It's a great picture! She's like a fuckin wee lassie at Christmas. — Look at that, she sais tae the bairn, — *Bob the Builder*! Can we fix it! Yes we can!

— Nowt but the best, hen.

The wee cunt says fuck all, eh's lucky tae be alive. Ah'm thinkin thit ah might huv uses fir a daft wee muppet like that. Ah takes um ootside. — Right, ye kin go now, but yuv tae meet ehs doon the Café del Sol bottom ay Leith Walk at eleven the morn's mornin.

— What fir? Eh asks, looking aw feart again.

— A joab. Wee cunts like you git intae too much fuckin bother if they urnae workin. The devil makes fuckin work fir idle hands, eh. Mind, Leith, eleven o'clock. If ah'm late, ask fir Lexo. N keep oot ay bother, cause yir fuckin workin fir me now. Mind, the café the morn.

The wee radge's stoaped shakin but eh still looks fuckin scoobied. — Dae ah git wages?

— Aye. Ye git tae stey alive. That's yir fuckin wages, ah whisper tae um. — Tell ye what but, ah goes, seein that eh's goat sovies oan jist aboot every finger, — nice rings but, mate. Take thum oaf.

— Aw, man, no muh sovies, please, man . . .

— Oaf, ah goes.

The wee cunt starts pillin at thum. — They willnae come oaf . . .

Ah pills oot ma blade. — Right, ah'll git the cunts oaf fir ye, ah tells um.

Funny, but they came oaf awright eftir that.

The wee cunt hands thum ower, aw sad, n ah poakits thum, keepin one back n giein um it. — Ye did awright the day. Keep daein awright, ye git thaim back in payment. Git wide or fuck up, ye die. The café the morn, ah tell um, n go back in n shut the door.

Ah bell Stevo oan the mobby, tellin the cunt it's an emergency.

Kate goes: — That stereo's brilliant, Frank! Ah cannae believe it! It was so good ay the laddie.

— Aye, eh's a good wee cunt. Eh's gaunnae be workin wi me. Yuv goat tae watch oot fir wee cunts. If thuv no goat something tae dae, they git intae bother. Ah should ken, ah tell her.

— That's good ay ye, helpin the wee boy oot. You're a big softy really, aren't ye?

Ah feel aw funny whin she says that, sortay nice, but at the same time ah'm thinkin, nae wonder that last boy she wis wi wis quick wi ehs hands if she talks like thon. It's good thit she's happy but. — It's like that political cunt goes, yuv goat tae fuckin well help ivray other cunt if yuv goat a fuckin business. Ken whit ah mean? Fling yir jackit oan, lit's go oot. A bevvy n ah Chinky but, eh.

— The bairn . . .

— Droap the fuckin bairn oaf it yir ma's. C'moan, nash. Ah've been fuckin well graftin aw day. Bevvy n a fuckin Chinky then. Entitled tae a fuckin beer tae relax. You drop her at yir ma's n ah'll jist wait for Stevo tae come n fix the door. It'll no take um any time at aw n if it does ah'll leave um the spare keys n eh kin stick thum through the letter boax whin ehs done. Ah'll meet ye at yir ma's in a bit, eh.

Kate gits hersel made up n changed n loads the bairn back intae the pushchair.

Ah sticks the auld telly in the lobby n connects the boax tae the new yin tae watch that *Inside Scottish Fitba* oan Sky. Funny, the heidaches away n ah nivir even needed a fuckin ride.

28

Scam # 18,740

It's very strange how things work out. Begbie, Spud and now Renton, all back in my life, all back on the main stage in the compelling drama that is Simon David Williamson. To call the first two pathetic losers is a chronic insult to that breed everywhere. Renton though: running a club in the Dam. I would never have thought that he had the staying power.

Of course, the thieving bastard is far from amused with me. I told him I wasn't letting the onanistic fuck out of my sight until he came up with the cash, which is now in my wallet. We're in a pavement café on Prinsengracht and he's gently touching his swollen nose. — Ah can't believe you punched me, he whines. — You always said that violence wis for losers.

I sit there and slowly shake my head at the cunt. I feel like punching him again. — I never had a friend rip off my money before, I tell him, — and I also don't know how you have the audacity, the sheer fucking gall, to try and fucking well guilt-trip me. Not only did you fucking well rip me off, I spit in a low growl, and I feel the outrage grow as I slam the table, raising my voice and getting a funny look from two fat Americans next to us, — you fuckin compensated Spud! That junky cunt never even told me for fuckin years! Even then it only slipped out when he was fucked!

Renton raises the espresso to his lips. Blows, takes a sip. — I said sorry. I did regret it, if it's any comfort tae ye. I thought about sorting ye out, and I did mean tae, but ye ken how it is with cash, it just gets frittered away. I suppose I thought you'd forget about it . . .

I glare at him. Who the fuck does this cretin think he's talking to? What planet is the cunt on? Planet Leith, in the nineteen fucking eighties, I'll wager.

— . . . well, maybe no forget about it, but you know . . . Then he shrugs. — it *was* a bit fuckin selfish. I just had tae git the fuck away, Simon, fae Leith, fae aw that junky shite.

— And I didn't, I suppose? Aw aye, you were fucking well selfish alright, chum, I smack the table again. — A bit selfish, he says. Understatement of the fucking century.

I hear the Americans say something in what sounds like Scandinavian, then realise that they're actually Swedes or Danes. Funny, they looked a bit too fat and stupid in those starchy clathes tae be anything other than middle-aged Shermans.

Renton pulls down his baseball cap to get the glint out of his eyes. Looks a bit tired. Once a druggy . . . unless you're Simon David Williamson, and by virtue of being so, instantly transcend all that crap. — I sort ay thought that I'd sub Spud first, he says, playing with the coffee cup. — I thought Sick B . . . Simon's a ducker n diver, an entrepreneurial type. He'll be okay, he'll ey land oan ehs feet.

I say nothing, but turn my head away ostentatiously and watch a boat go down the canal. One crustie cunt in the boat sees us, peeps a horn and waves up. — Hey, Mark! How are you?

— Fine, Ricardo, enjoyin the sun, mate, Rents shouts and waves back.

The fucking Rent Boy, a pillar of the cloggie community. Forgets that I've watched him junk-sick, squeaking with need; ripping into a stolen wallet like a starving predator devouring a small but unsatisfying mammal.

Now he's telling me his story, which I'm finding interesting, although I'm trying to feign indifference. — I first came here because it wis the only place ah kent . . . he starts. I roll my eyes and he says: — . . . well, apart from London and Essex, where we worked on the cross-Channel ferries. But that was how I got into the idea of coming here, like we used to after our shift on the boats, mind?

— Aye . . . I nod in hazy recall. I don't know if the place has changed. It's hard to remember what the fuck it was like before, with all the drugs we took.

— Funny, part of me thought that it would be easy for you to find me here. I thought that somebody over on holidays would run into me, I thought it'd be the first place you'd fuckin well look, he smiles.

I curse my own stupidity. None of us thought about Amsterdam. Fuck knows why. I always thought that either an acquaintance, or even myself, would run into him in London, or maybe Glasgow. — It was the first place we thought of, I lie, — and we were over a few times. You just got lucky, I tell him, — until now.

— So I suppose you'll be letting the others know about me, he says.

— Like fuck, I snarl in contempt. — Do you think I care about the likes of Begbie? That thick cunt can get his own loot back; that psychopath has nothing to do with me.

Renton considers this for a bit, then carries on with his tale. — Funny, when I got here first, I stayed in a hotel down the canal there, he says, pointing down Prinsengracht. Then I found a room down in the Pjip, which is sort of Amsterdam's Brixton, he explains, — south of touristville. Got clean, started hanging out with some punters. This guy Martin I got pally with, he'd been attached to a sound system back in Nottingham. We started putting on club nights and parties, just for a laugh. We were both into house and it was all techno here. We wanted to make inroads into that European orthodoxy. Luxury, we called it. Our nights became quite popular; then this boy Nils asked us to do a monthly at his small club, then fortnightly, then weekly. Then we had to move to bigger premises.

Renton's aware that he's starting to sound a bit smug and semi-apologises. — I mean, I make a good living, but we're always just two or three bad nights away from disaster. We don't give a fuck though: when it's over, it's over. I don't want to do a club just for the sake of it.

— So what it boils down to, I feel the contempt rise in my chest, — is that you're rolling in it and you hold out on your pals. A few measly fuckin grand.

Renton protests in a feeble manner that only accentuates his guilt. — I told you how it was. I'd drawn a kind of mental line under my life back hame. And ah'm no rolling in it, once we pay off everybody after a club night, we split it two ways. Never even had a company account till a couple of years ago. Only got it when we got bumped one night. I was walking around with thousands of pounds in my pockets every Saturday. But aye, I live well. Got the flat up here in the Brouwersgracht, he says, now definitely sounding fucking full of himself.

Whatever happened to restlessness? It would be fucking boring to do a club night for so long. — So, you've been running the same club for eight years, I accuse.

— It's no really the same club, it's changed a lot. Now we do big festivals like Dance Valley and the Queen's Day here, and the Love Parade in Berlin. We go all over Europe and the States, Ibiza, the Miami dance festival. Martin's the public face of Luxury, for the dance-music press and that, I keep in the background . . . for obvious reasons.

— Aye, like me, Begbie, Second Prize and Spu . . . oh, of course not Spud, no, you sorted that cunt out, didn't you, I accuse again. I still can't believe that he sorted out Murphy and not me.

— How is Spud? asks Agent Orange.

I nod a little while, like I'm sizing him up, letting a sheen of satisfied contempt gloss over my coupon. — Fucked, I tell him. — Oh, he was clean until your wad arrived. Then he blew the whole fucking lot on junk. Now he's going the way of Tommy, Matty and all that crowd, I tell him with a flourish.

Suck the guilt out of that one, traitor-face.

Rents's pallid skin still fails to flush but his eyes soften a little. — Is he positive?

— Aye, I tell him, — and you certainly played a big part in it. Well done, I toast him.

— Ye sure?

I've no idea as to the state of scruff-boy's immune system. If he's not HIV, he fucking well deserves to be. — I'm about as positive as he is.

Rents thinks about this for a while, then says: — Too bad.

I can't resist it, so I tell him, laying it on thick: — Ali as well. They were thegither, y'know. Goat a wee laddie that wey n aw. The British taxpayer should thank you, I quip, — eliminating drains on society.

Renton looks a bit shaken at that one. White lies, of course, though no, it certainly wouldn't surprise me if Murphy was full-blown, the state of that cunt. This, though, is just a mere down payment on the suffering the Rent Boy is going to get. He's composed himself a bit, and now he's even trying to effect a pathetic casualness. — How depressing. It's good to be over here, he smiles, looking around at the sloping narrow buildings, like staggering drunks holding each other up. — Fuck Leith. Let's go over to the red-light district for a few beers, he suggests.

We head over and have a good day out on the piss. We're settling back outside a café and I can tell that my fibs have hit home with Rents, even if the beer has made him more gung-ho again. — I'm trying to get by and fuck up as few people as possible in the process, he says grandly as we watch a group of rowdy young English lads bounce past us.

That'll be the fuckin day.

— Yes, I admit, it is hard. They *are* our greatest resource, I say and he looks at me in earnest confusion, so I expand. — Us being the men of ambition, aka the only people who count now.

Renton's about to protest, but thinks better of it, laughs and slaps me on the back and I realise that, perversely, somewhere along the line we've almost become friends of a sort again.

That night I opt to kip on Renton's couch, rather than go back to the madness of the hotel. Apparently Rab's old cashie mates wanted to swedge every cunt yesterday evening; it was like they suddenly realised that it was getting close to going-home time and they had just been smoking dope and shagging, and hadn't remembered to batter anybody. There are plans to go down to Utrecht today to have a row with some daft cloggies. Fuck that, I'm staying here with Renton.

Renton lives with this German bird Katrin, a surly, skinny Nazi lassie with no tits, in fact the sort Renton always seems to go for. Boyish. Always thought he was a closet fag but didn't have the bottle to go all the way, so he shags lassies that look like young boys. Probably up the arse, affording the satisfactory tightness for the smaller-dicked man. This Katrin bird though, she's possibly worth one. Possibly. Skinny, titless, erseless birds are usually pretty dirty, it's compensation for not having much of the padding that we chaps so enjoy. This ice-cold wee Teutonic cow hardly spoke a word, not even reacting to my attempts at flirty politeness. How the fuck could magnifico Italia ever have thrown its hand in with these pseudo-Saxon cunts in the Second World Swedge? But aye, I'd possibly give her one, if only to annoy Rents. It's funny, him just sitting there, looking fit, almost European. He's still slim really, but not disgustingly so. There's a bit of flesh on that old ginger skull face. His hair's a bit thinner and slightly receding; baldness is a curse for a lot of ginger mingers.

The best way forward is to start stringing the cunt along, letting him put some trust in me. Then he gets it. And I know who from. Because it's not about the money, it's about the betrayal. So I warm to this theme as we're getting ready to go out for another beer. — As far as Begbie's concerned, you were a hero in Leith ripping that cunt off, I tell him. Of course, this is a bare-faced lie. Begbie's a bastard, but nobody likes a rip-off merchant.

But Renton knows this. He's not stupid, in fact that's the problem, the red-headed Judas fucker is anything but stupid. The hoods of his eyes still drop in that cynical way of old when he doesn't believe or agree with what he's hearing. — I'm no sure about that, he says. — Begbie had a lot of nutty mates. The sort of boys who'd do any cunt for fun. I've given them a reason.

Too true, thiefy-boy. I wonder how big Lexo Setterington, Begbie's former 'partner', domiciled in my hotel, not half a mile from here, would react if he knew that Rents was in town. Might he be inclined to administer some justice on his mucker's behalf? Yep, he was bad-mouthing Begbie, but that, of course, means nothing to bams like him. At best he'd certainly be on the blower to his buddy François, who would be right over on the next flight. Oh aye, that big wide cunt's got a mischievous air about him. He would absolutely delight in telling the Beggar Boy that he knows Rent's address.

Tempting, but no. *I* want to be the man who delivers *that* particular piece of good news. Renton's got a club, a flat, a girlfriend. He'll be going nowhere in a hurry, particularly if he believes himself to be safe here. — That's as maybe, I say gruffly, then, changing tone, add, — but you should come back to Edinburgh, see the folks, I tell him, remembering that I've hardly seen mine since I've been back.

Renton shrugs. — I have done a few times. On the quiet, like.

— I never fuckin knew . . . I say, peeved that the cunt could slip in and out without me knowing anything about it.

The rid-heided cunt laughs loudly at that one. — I didn't think you'd want to see me.

— Oh, I'd've wanted tae see you awright, I assure the bastard.

— That's what I meant, he says, then he adds, raising his eyes hopefully, — I heard Begbie's still inside.

— Aye. He'll be in for a few years yet, I prevaricate in the most expressionless manner I can muster. And I fancy that I did alright as well.

— I might just come over then, Renton smiles.

Good. Let the cunt take his chances. I'm starting to enjoy myself now.

Later on I arrange for Terry and Rab to meet us, half thinking that Renton could come in useful with his music and Amsterdam contacts. When I tell him what we're up to, he seems quite interested. So it's me, Rab, Terry, Billy and Rents having a beer, blow and blether in the Hill Street Blues Café on the Warmoestraat. Terry and Billy vaguely remember Rents from way back; Clouds disco, the fitba, the lot. Terry still gives him a look like he's no too sure though. Too right: no cunt trusts a fraudster who does their own, and sure as fuck, he'll get it.

Rab Birrell, who (sensibly) opted out of the Utrecht trip, reasoning that burst mooths, broken noses and black eyes do not good wedding pictures make, is explaining something to us at the café. Rab seems to be a bit narked with Terry and me for some reason, probably because we've left him with his fitba mates most of the time, and I think they wanted an old boys' reunion while Rab fancied something more chilled. He knows a lot though this Birrell boy, and he's advanced a proposition, which Terry's doubtful about. — Still dinnae see how we need tae film it ower here but, he says to Rab.

Rab's looking at me, all tense and serious. — You're forgetting aboot the polis. This type of movie . . . he hestitates and gets a slight beamer as Terry purses his lips and bends his wrists, — . . . awright, Terry, this type ay film, that we're trying tae make is illegal under the OPA.

— Awright, Mister fuckin Student cunt, Juice Terry cuts in, — tell us what the OPA is.

Rab coughs and looks at Billy, then Rents, as if in some kind of appeal for support. — It's the Obscene Publications Act, the piece ay legislation that governs what we're trying tae dae.

Renton says nothing, he's got that unscrutable look on his face. Renton. Who is he? What is he? He's a traitor, a grass, a cunt, a scab, a selfish egotist, he's everything that anyone who is working class needs to be to get on in the new global capitalist order. And I envy him. I genuinely fucking envy the bastard because he really doesn't give a toss about anybody but himself. I'm trying to be like him but impulse, wild, passionate, Italian-Jock impulse, burns too strongly in me. I look at him sitting there, watching everything carefully from the edge of the scene, and I feel my hands grip the chair arms in rage as my knuckles go white.

— Aye, we've really got tae watch the polis, Rab concludes nervously.

I look at him and shake my head fiercely. — There's ways and means ay getting roond the polis. You forget one thing: coppers are just crooks who're late developers.

Rab looks doubtful at this. Renton cuts in. — Sick Boy . . . eh, Simon's correct. People learn crime because they grow up in a culture ay crime. Most cops start off as anti-crime, so it takes them longer tae catch up. But because they get extensive immersion in that culture ay crime, through their work, they soon get up tae speed. These days, the best place for a villain is on the force. Find out what works and what disnae.

You can see Birrell getting aw hot at this, it's as if he's found a kindred spirit. Terry's right about that cunt. He'll fuckin well debate whether or no the moon's made ay green cheese if you let him. So I cut in before him and Rents start going off on one. — Ah'm no wanting a fucking debate here. All I will say is leave the polis tae me. That's well in hand. I'm expecting a wee result any day now. In fact, I'll get on the blower to them right now.

So I exit the bar and try to get a signal on the green mobile. This is meant to work in Europe, but *does it fuck* work in Europe. I'm tempted to throw the toy for small minds into the canal. Instead,

170

I pocket it and go over to the tabac and buy a phonecard and bell home from a call box. I feel a sweetly twisted, sexual urge flush over me for no reason, so I call Interflora and send a dozen red roses to Nikki, and the same to her wee specky mate Lauren, even more aroused at the thought of how she would cope with it. — No message, I tell the woman on the line.

Then I call Leith's finest. — Hello. My name's Simon Williamson, I'm the proprietor of the Port Sunshine. I want to get the test results on the confiscated pills, I explain, pulling from my pocket a slip of paper Kebab Cop gave me. — My reference number is zero seven six two . . .

After a long wait, there's an apologetic voice on the other end. — I'm sorry, sir, the lab has a bit of a backlog . . .

— Fine, I snap, impatient, unsatisfied taxpayer-style, putting the phone down. When I get back the first thing I'm going to do is to write to the Chief Constable and complain like fuck about this.

29

'. . . a dozen roses . . .'

Lauren and I get a shock delivery; a dozen roses each, blood red, on dark-green stalks, sent to us anonymously, with just our names on the card. Lauren's totally freaked out, she thinks it's somebody from college. We're a bit hung-over, we went out drinking last night as she had come back from the bosom of her family in Stirling.

Dianne comes through and she's impressed with our bouquets.
— You lucky girls, she said, putting on a fake cry-baby face and moaning: — Where's mine! Where's my fuckin prince!

My co-recipient has a pinched face and bared teeth as she examines the flowers as if there's an explosive device concealed in them.
— The shop must know who sent them! I'm going to phone up and find out, Lauren bleats. — This is harassment!

— Get away, Dianne says, — that jakey in the Pear Tree last week, now that was harassment. This is romance! Think yourself lucky, hen.

It fills the rest of the day with an intrigue, which gets me through a couple of boring lectures, before I get home and changed again for my sauna shift. I want to swap a shift with Jayne and she's agreed, but I can't find Bobby to confirm this. No doubt he's in one of the steam rooms, sweating away with his cronies. It's Thursday night, which for some reason is gangster night. There's as much gold as sweat dripping from the numerous solid, slightly overweight bodies. It's funny, but Monday to Wednesday nights tend to be businessmen, Friday's mainly lads treating themselves, and Saturday it's footballers, but tonight it's the criminal element.

At the end of my shift I notice I'm out of towels and I head into the massage room next door. Jayne is pummelling a huge pile of flesh on the table, it's lobster pink from steam-room excess rendered a lime green by the lights in the pine floor. Jayne's face is bottom-lit and I can see the smile in her mouth but not her eyes as I nod

over to the stack of white towels, always virgin white, before grabbing a few and retreating as the wobbling mass groans under a chopping assault. As I exit I hear what sounds like, 'Harder . . . dinnae
be feart tae go harder . . . *never* be feart tae go harder . . .' I'm mildly
put out as I realise that it's a guy who normally asks for me. Not
to worry. I eventually see Bobby and make the shift switch. Bobby's
with a guy called Jimmy, a client whose full name I don't know and
who asks if I've ever thought about doing some escort work. I look
doubtful, but he says: — No, it's just that you'd be excellent for a
colleague of mine. It's good money, and you get wined and dined
. . . he smiles.

— It's the afters that worry me, I grin back, — the sixty-nined
part of it.

Jimmy shakes his head briskly. — No, it's nothing like that. This
guy just likes company, that's all, just likes to go out with a beautiful girl on his arm. That's the deal. Anything you negotiate separately . . . well, that's between you two. He's a politician, from overseas.

— Why are you asking me?

He gives a hearty, dental-filling-exposing laugh. — Well, one,
you're his type, and two, you're always well turned out, clothes-wise.
I'll bet you're the sort of lassie who's got a few knockout dresses in
her wardrobe, he says, shifting into a donkey-like grin. — Think
about it.

— Okay, I will, I tell him, and head home, without a drink for
the first time in a while. I go to my room and do a few intensive
stretching, bending and breathing exercises. Then I go to bed and
get the best night's sleep I've had in months.

I rise in the morning in some eagerness, unusually beating both Lauren
and Dianne into the shower, before spending an age deciding what
to wear. Why the excitement? Well, I'm off to Leith, and I'm more
than pleased that the boys are back. It's strange, but there definitely
was something missing over the last few days. When I get down to
the pub, I realise what it is. Sick Boy, or Simon, as I should call him,
in the short time following his departure to Amsterdam, has gone
from being a distraction for me to the main dish. I half thought that
I was anticipating Rab, but when I saw Simon wearing polished black

shoes, black pants and a green sweatshirt, I just thought: hold on, something's up here. He sported a few days' growth and that severe slicked-back Steven Seagal hair had gone, replaced by a bouncy, almost fluffy cut which softened him. His eyes sparkled and danced over every member of the assembled company, seeming to linger on me.

He looked so gorgeous I instantly had doubts about my own appearance. After the long debate with myself, I had settled on some white cotton slacks, black-and-white trainers and a short blue jacket which, when I buttoned the bottom tags in, accentuated my cleavage in the lighter blue V-neck top.

I'm looking at Rab and now all I see is a conventionally hand-some man, but one devoid of any charisma. That quality, in contrast, just leaks out of Simon. The way he rests his elbow on the long, stained bar and his chin on the joint of his hand and wrist, then idly lets his fingers rub the growth on his neck. I'm thinking, I want my fingers doing what his are.

Something's been going on. Simon is lording it over everyone, Terry's amused and Rab seems pensive. His wedding's a couple of months away, but he decided to get the stag in early in case they drugged him and put him on a goods train to Warsaw or some-where like that. I'm keeping my eye on Simon, but he doesn't give me any indication that he's the roses man.

Melanie arrives a bit late and sits beside me. I catch Simon glancing tetchily at his watch. Rab and him seem to be arguing constantly about the film. There's another name that keeps cropping up now, this mysterious character called Rents from Amsterdam.

Simon's throwing his hands up at Rab in a gesture of mock surrender. — Okay, okay, the movie has to be shot in Amsterdam, for legal purposes, or rather, look as if it's been shot in the Dam. Surely, though, we can do the interiors in the pub, he argues. — I mean, all we need are a few external establishing shots of trams and canals and shit. Nobody's going to know.

— Aye, I suppose, Rab concedes, sounding constipated with concern.

— Good, now let's put that one to bed, Simon says pompously, then looks right at me, and I feel my chest open and my bowels shrink in response to his lighthouse-like smile. I pull a tight grin back. Simon idly rubs his stubble again. I decide that I want to shave him with an open razor, soap him up and watch all the emotions in his big, dark eyes as I drag the blade slowly across his face . . .

My thoughts are breaking up as it's hard not to concentrate solely on Simon, but now he's saying: — Terry, you were meant to be writing the script, how's it coming along?

All I'm thinking of is how I'd like to fuck you, Mr Simon Sick Boy Williamson, to enclose myself around you and squeeze every fucking drop of you into me, to use you, spend you and exhaust you so that you'll never want any other woman ever again . . .

— Fuckin brilliant, but I've no written anything doon. It's aw in here, Terry grins widely, tapping his head and smiling at me, as if it's me that asked the question, as if the others aren't even in the room. Terry. The sort of guy who's not really that fanciable, but you'd shag, just because he's so enthusiastic about things. Maybe *he's* the phantom florist. — Terry, sex is in your head, we know that. What we need is it in a script.

— Ah ken what yir sayin, gorgeous, he smiles, running his hand through his curly hair, — but ah'm no really yin for writin things doon. What ah might dae is talk intae a tape n somebody kin type it oot, he adds, looking hopefully at me.

— So what you're saying is that you've done fuck all, Rab challenges, looking round at everybody.

I glance at Melanie who shrugs, unconcerned. Ronnie grins, Ursula's eating a Pot Noodle and Craig's looking like he has a stomach ulcer. Then Terry sheepishly produces a couple of sheets of A4. I would describe the handwriting as not so much spidery as scorpion-like.

— What did ye say that ye hud done nowt for but? Rab asks, taking the papers and scanning them.

— Writin's no ma thing, Birrell, Terry shrugs, but he's quite embarrassed. Rab's shaking his head as he passes them over to me.

I read a bit and it's so hilariously inept that I have to share it. — Terry, this is nonsense! Listen to this: 'The boy fucks the bird up the arse. The bird licks the other bird out.' It's awful!

Terry's shoulders bunch up and once again he rubs a hand through that curly mop.

— A tad minimalist, Mr Lawson, Rab snorts, as he takes back the papers from me and waves them in his face. — This is shite, Terry. It's no a script. There's nae story here. It's just shaggin, he laughs, passing them to Simon, who studies them impassively.

— That's what we want, Birrell; it's a porn film, Terry says defensively.

Rab screws his face up and sits back in the chair. — Aye, that's what aw the jakeys want, the ones you show yir stag clippings tae. Ah thoat we were meant tae be daein a real film here. Ah mean, it's no even written like a film script, he flicks his hand through the air.

— It might no seem like that now, Birrell, but ye git the actors tae bring it tae life . . . like that Jason King boy oan the telly used tae dae, Terry says, suddenly inspired. — Loads ay innuendo n aw that. The Swingin Sixties stuff's big now, gie it that kind ay feel.

During this exchange, the others, looking bored and distracted, have said absolutely nothing. Simon sets Terry's papers down on the table in front of him, reclines in his chair and starts tapping his fingers on the armrest. — As someone with experience in the industry, let me intervene, he says in that grandiose manner of his where you don't know whether he's being pompous or ironic. — Rab, why don't you take Terry's script and weave a storyline into it.

— Fuckin needs it, Rab says.

— Aye, well, it's no meant tae be a college dissertation, Birrell, Terry asserts loudly.

— Right, says Simon, yawning and stretching like a cat, his eyes glinting in the weak light, — I think you need a bit of help here, Terry. Turning to the rest of us, he proposes: — I think the best move would be if Rab and Nikki could take Terry's basic ideas and put them into a script format. Very basic, just break it down into scenes, locations . . . what am I telling you this for, you're the students of film, you've seen a screenplay, he smiles at us both so lavishly that I fancy even Rab's flattered.

But it's not Rab who I want to work with, Simon, it's *you*.

Terry cuts in at this point. — We're, eh no wantin too many . . . nae offence, but eh, students involved. What aboot if me n you

176

worked oan it, Nikki? he says hopefully, then adding: — Ah mean, we could try oot some ay the positions n that. Make sure that it aw actually worked.

— Oh, I think we'll be alright on the night, Terry, I tell him hastily. I look over to Simon, thinking that *we* could try out some of the positions, but he's saying something in Mel's ear and she's grinning. If only he'd look this way.

— I think it would be easier for me and Nikki to dae it, with us seeing each other anyway, at the university n that, Rab says, looking at me.

I really would rather it was Simon and I'm tempted to play games, but I nod in agreement, because I'm thinking: *did* Rab send the flowers after all? But why Lauren? — Okay, I say softly, — that makes sense.

Terry's a bit huffy at this, and looks away over towards the bar.

— That's fine. As long as it's got our pornographic narrative in sequence; blow jobs, straight, girl-on-girl, anal and cum shots, Simon expounds, adding, — also plenty of bondage and as many inventive set pieces as you can dream up.

Terry brightens up a bit, re-engaging as Simon gets down to the brass tacks of sex. — The big problem we have is anal. Simon turns to Mel and me. — Or rather, the big problem you lassies have.

His cold look, accompanied by that word, makes my innards freeze. — I don't do that, I tell him.

Mel's shaking her head as well and speaks up for the first time today. — No way will ah dae that. She catches Terry looking at her, and she goes a bit bashful and kicks his foot. — No oan the camera but, Terry!

Simon's face is screwed up. — Mmm . . . we need to talk about this. You see, I think it's essential these days. I mean, personally, it doesn't really do much for me, but the thing is, we live in an anal society.

Rab rolls his eyes and Terry nods in emphatic support.

— I mean, think about it, Simon waxes on, — you have rednecks in hick towns, telling us aliens have come all the way from another galaxy just to stick a probe up their sweaty arseholes . . . modern porn, the Zanes, the Blacks, it's got all that triple-penetration circus

177

stuff in it now. Look at Ben Dover's videos. Fit young birds always get it up the arse these days.

— Fuckin brilliant videos, Terry adds sagely.

Simon nods in impatient compliance. — The point is that in the old days if a bird got fucked up the arse in a video, it was odds-on that she was a stretch-marked old boiler, dripping with cellulite and fit for the knacker's yard. Now that's all changed. For any young lassie serious about being a porn star, taking it up the shitter is almost obligatory.

— Not for me, I say quietly, and only Simon's heard this but he chooses not to acknowledge it. So I amplify my voice and my concerns. — A lot of women don't do anal. Some only do girl-on-girl. We're not making a mucky men's porn movie. I thought we were going to try and be innovative with non-sexist dialogues and themes. What happened to that? Was it all destroyed by one sniggering, smutty little boys' weekend in Amsterdam?

— No. We are being innovative, Simon insists, — but we have to cover all bases and that includes anal. It's not real, Nikki, it's only acting.

No, it *is* real. It *has* to be real. Getting fucked is getting fucked, and it's one of the few things left in our lives that is real, that is unconstructed.

— Aye, Rab says, unwittingly being Simon's stooge, — we have to remember that it's the performance of sex, not real sex, and it's just freak-show stuff. I mean, who really has triple penetration in their sex life?

— Jist you n yir poofy mates fae the college, Terry says.

Rab ignores him and continues, anxious that he's not being misconstrued. — Let's get a real story, with real people, acting like they're having real sex. The anal stuff's a red herring, if the girls dinnae want tae dae it, then that's cool.

— No, Simon shakes his head. — Ye see, Rab, it's due to the way we feel about our arseholes. We now believe, as a species, if our soul is located anywhere in our bodies, it's up our arses. That's where it all goes. It makes sense. That's why we're obsessed with anal jokes, anal sex, anal hobbies . . . the arsehole − not the brain, not space − is the last frontier. *That's* what makes us revolutionaries.

But I don't want to do it, so I raise my eyebrows and look at Mel and Ursula for support. — I'm telling you again, I don't like it. I've tried it once before. I find it sore, remote, cold and uncomfortable. I like to fuck, not to sit back gasping like a circus freak tensed up and waiting to see how much of a guy I can take up my arsehole.

— Mibee ye jist need broken in. Some birds that are experienced in it really go for it, Terry says.

— I don't want a fucking arsehole like the Channel Tunnel, Terry. I'm not being a party-pooper, Terry gives me a big wink, — it's just not my thing. I've nothing against it, I just don't want to *do* it.

— Wi me, ah'm no that bothered aboot daein it, it's jist thit ah dinnae want people kennin aboot it, Melanie says. — Ah mean, some things ye dinnae want tae show everybody. Ye need some privacy.

— I'm no-that-sortay-a-girl type ay thing, Terry laughs.

— Well, Terry, it's awright fir you, it's different for lassies.

— It shouldnae be, no in this age ay feminism n that. Then he turns to Rab. — Or post-feminism, ah should say. See, Birrell, ah do listen tae yir shite sometimes.

— Glad to hear it.

Simon claps his hands together. — Think Baccarra. Nobody likes a chick who sings 'Sorry I'm a Lady' in this business. We want to hear 'Yes Sir I Can Boogie'.

— Fair enough, Simon, I smile, — but we need a certain song.

He pulls open his wallet. — This is the song, he tells me, exposing a wad of notes. Then he grabs a film poster. — And this. We're at the front line of everything here. Let's think about it. I mean, where did all this anal obsession come from?

— Oh yes, it's perfect for the type of society we live in, self-absorbed, going right up our own arses, I remark.

— No, sweetheart, it all came from porn. These cunts are the real pioneers. Pornography sneezes and popular culture catches cold. People want sex, violence, food, pets, DIY and humiliation. Let's give them the fuckin lot. Look at humiliation television, look at the papers and the mags, look at the class system, the jealousy, the bitterness that oozes out of our culture: in Britain we want to see people get fucked, he says, looking briefly like an alien in *Close Encounters* caught, as he is, in a shaft of sunlight which slips out into a gap between the tenements opposite. — Anyway, let's continue this discussion later.

Terry looks slyly and says: — Tell ye what though, ye'd better cast Gina. She'll have nae qualms aboot getting rode up the rectum.

— No way, Terry, she's okay for stag, but she's not got proper movie-star quality. Leave the casting to me. The other day I ran into this boy I know from way back, Mikey Forrester, he runs a sauna. There's some lassies working for him that are tidy. The casting will be nae problem. We dinnae need Gina, Simon says, seeming to shiver as he mentions her name.

Terry shrugs. — Well, that's up tae you, mate, but she says tae tell ye thit she's gaunnae batter yir cunt in if she cannae be in the film, he informs Simon with a gleeful smirk.

Melanie nods and confirms this. — Aye, ah widnae mess wi her, cause she's fuckin hard as fuck. She'll dae it n aw.

Simon, Sick Boy, slaps his own forehead in exasperation. — Magnificent. I'm being stalked by a fucking boiler and my leading ladies don't want to do anal. Well, you can just tell the Bride of Begbie to fuck off.

— You tell her, Terry grins.

As the meeting breaks up, I hang about and say to Simon: — The recruitment thing . . . I can maybe help. Ask a few friends if they're interested. Girls who are in the know, so to speak.

Simon nods slowly.

— I have to go, but I'll call you later, I say as I see Rab looking on as he waits for me and I'm sure that there's a spark of jealousy in his eye.

30

Packages

Ah blootered it a wee bit oan the gear again, some stuff ah'd goat fae Seeker. Ali said tae me if yir ever fucked up, dinnae come back here, ah'm no huvin that roond Andy. Which is fair enough likes, so ah didnae. Maist ay the week wis a series ay couches; Monny's, ma ma's n perr Parkie's, which isnae really oan wi him tryin hard tae turn things roond ehsel. Poor cat disnae need me twitchin n shiverin in ehs coupon. That's the worse thing now, jist one wee relapse n ye pey so much. Ye really feel withdrawal now, even eftir jist the odd wee bang. It's like the auld system minds ay everything you've done in the past n goes, 'Sorry, gadgie, but take this.'

So ah creep hame fir the first time in days. Andy'll be at the school n ah'm hopin Ali's oot. Aye, the gaff's empty, so ah sit doon in that big, battered armchair n pit oan ma Alabama 3 tape, singin along. Ah see ma mate Zappa the cat, the one boy whae never judges ays. Ah'm lookin at some stuff ah went and goat the other day fae Leith library n ah've taken some notes. Ah went in, jist tae git ootay the rain, but ah ended up note-takin oan the history. Ah wis thinkin that Leith's motto is persevere, n ah've goat tae dae jist that. Ah switch oan the telly, wi the sound doon, n gie they plants a bit ay a water, hopin thit Zappa's no been diggin oot the big yucca gadgie again.

But it's destined tae be a mad, bad day. Cause the door goes n when ah answer it ah'm jist totally gobsmacked, man. It's the feral cat himself, standing thaire in front ay ays. Ah'm thinkin when did eh git oot, then ma hert sinks in ma chist cavity n it's uh-aw, what the fuck has Sick Boy been sayin. Ah kin barely speak fir a bit, then eh smiles at ays n ah finds ma tongue. — Franco, eh, good tae see ye, man. When did ye git oot?

— Been oot fir two fuckin weeks, eh goes, walkin past ays right intae the flat, n ah'm checkin that they segged heels urnae scrappin the varnish oan the wooden flair. Ali wid dae her nut, cause the landlord's one stroppy gadge. — Didnae waste any fuckin time, sorted oot wi a bird within ooirs. Shaggin fir fuckin Scotland, ya cunt, eh tells me. — What the fuck are you up tae? eh goes, then ehs face goes aw sour. — Yir no oan fuckin smack, ur ye?

Well, when ye see the eye ay that tiger starin at ye, man, it's best no tae bullshit *too* much.

— Eh, no really, man, but it's eh, sortay one day at a time, sweet Jesus, ken? No touched it in ages, likes.

— Better fuckin no be, cause ah've hud ma fill ay junkies. Wantin a line ay coke?

— Eh . . . eh . . . ah didnae ken what tae say, man. Mind you, ah nivir ken.

Begbie takes that as an aye, and pills oot a wrap. Eh spills oot a good measure, n even though ah'm no a cokeheid, ah think thit ah've goat tae dae it oot ay pure protocol, man. It's jist goat tae be observed but, eh. N one wee line willnae hurt.

Franco starts choppin. — They tell ays thit ye wir in Perth fir a bit, eh says. — Fuckin shitey nick. Missed ye, ya daft cunt, eh goes, wi a wee smile, which ah sort ay take as meanin that the cat missed ays as likesay *me*, rather thin missed ays *in the nick*.

So what can ye say? — Eh, ah missed you n aw, Franco man, but yir lookin well, fit n that, it's goat tae be said, man.

Eh pats a rocky wall ay a stomach. — Aye, ah worked hard in the nick, no like some. It's peyin dividends now but, fuckin suren it is, eh goes doon oan a huge line. — Ah've goat a young burd, wir oot at Wester Hailes, but wir gittin a flat in Lorne Street. Fuck steyin oot thair. But shi's tidy n aw, eh sais, tracin oot the shape ay an hourgless kitten wi ehs hands. — Aye, she's goat a bairn but, likes. She wis wi some cunt whae goat wide so ah burst the cunt's fuckin mooth right open. Cunt wis fuckin lucky that wis aw eh fuckin well goat. Ah wis steyin at muh ma's but fuck that, aw she fuckin does is go oan aboot oor Elspeth and this cunt she's fuckin well gaun oot wi, Franco goes, well chinged n spittin oot syllables like an AK-47 assault rifle, man.

Ah hits the gear n snorts back. Ah stands up, rubbin ma nose. — Aye . . . how's the bairns?

— Went tae see thum the other day, eh. Thir awright, but that June cunt gits oan ma fuckin nerves, eh. What the fuck did ah ivir git in wi that fir? Wisnae even a fuckin decent poke in it, ah must've needed ma fuckin heid examined, eh.

— Ye goat the, eh, jail oot the system yet?

The Begbie cat's wired oan this ching n eh looks at ays like ehs gaunnae take ma fuckin heid oaf. — What the fuck's that meant tae mean? Eh?

— Eh, it jist took ays a long time tae git back intae the swing ay things n ah wis only in fir five minutes compared tae you, man, ah tell um. But the Beggar Boy is in fill flight and eh's talkin aboot prison now and it's very, very disturbing man, cause ah'm sortay thinkin aboot the Rent Boy, n the cash ah goat back, n blabbin like that tae Sick Boy, n what if eh's gaunnae tell Beggars?

Franco's choppin up mair cocaine n ah'm jist reelin fae the first. Eh goes oan for a bit aboot aw the twisted cunts in the jail, then eh jist stares at me wi they bad, bad lamps n goes: — Hi, Spud, see whin ah wis in the jail . . . ah goat a package.

Renton must've sorted him oot n aw! — Aye, man. Ah goat yin tae! It wis fae Mark . . .

Begbie bangs tae a halt and stares right intae ma soul, man. — You goat a fuckin package fae Renton, addressed tae you?

Ah'm buzzin n ah dinnae ken what tae say so ah jist blurt it oot. — Well, eh, thing is, Franco, ah dinnae ken for sure that it wis fae Rent Boy, likes. Ah mean, it jist came through the door, anonymous, likesay. But eh, ah jist thought it wid be him, likes.

Totally ragin, Franco slams a fist intae the palm ay his hand n starts pacin up n doon. The warnin bells ur pure ringin now, man. How's eh like this if ehs been sorted oot fir cash? — That's right, Spud! That's what ah fuckin well thought! Only that fuckin sick thievin junky cunt wid send packages wi fuckin poofs' porn, wi fuckin buftie boys shaggin each other, n address it tae us! Eh's rubbin oor fuckin faces in it, Spud! CUNT! Franco roars, n slams the table, knockin ower a gless ashtray, which thankfully disnae brek.

Gay porn . . . what the fuck . . . — Aye, that would be the Rent

Boy's crack, likesay, ah say, tryin tae work this oot, gled ah didnae blab aboot the poppy.

— Every one ay they sick cunts ah did in the jail, ah used tae imagine it wis fuckin Renton, this bad feral cat spits. Then eh racks up another two lines. Snortin one back, eh goes: — Ah saw Sick Boy, in ehs fuckin new pub, the fuckin Port Sunshine! Aye, that cunt really fuckin made it big, eh. Course, ye cannae fuckin well tell him nowt, eh's heid's fill ay the next big fuckin scam.

— Don't ah ken it, man, ah nod, droapin doon oantay yon line, even though ma hert's still thrashin n ah'm still sweatin fae the first yin.

— Aye, n ah saw Second Prize up at Scrubbers Close, wi aw they homeless cunts.

— Heard the cat wis oaf the Christopher Reeve, likes, ah gasp, as the gear hits ehs like a train.

Begbie throws ehsel back in ma airmchair. — Aye, eh wis until ah fuckin well talked some sense intae the cunt. Dragged um ower tae the EH1 in the Mile. Widnae take a fuckin drink so ah slipped a couple ay voddies intae the cunt's fuckin lemonade, eh says, in a sortay slow, mirthless cackle. — That's him right back oan it now, eh goes. — Needs some fuckin enjoyment. Singing hymns tae fuckin jakeys aw day, readin the fuckin Bible? Fuck yon shite, so that wis me daein ma fuckin good Samaritan act n savin the cunt fae a life ay fuckin boredom. They fuckin well brainwash ye, they cunts up at that fuckin mission. Ah'll gie they cunts fuckin Christianity . . .

Ah'm thinkin aboot this, n how Second Prize hud done really well tae git things back oan track. — But the doaktirs said thit eh wisnae meant tae drink, Franco, ah runs ma finger ower ma throat n makes a chokin noise, — or it's kaput.

— Eh came oot wi aw that fuckin shite wi me n aw; 'the doaktir this, the doaktir that', but ah jist telt the cunt straight, it's the fuckin quality ay life thit counts. Better one year bein able tae fuckin go fir it, instead ay fifty as a miserable cunt. Fuck gittin like aw they auld cunts in the Port Sunshine. Telt um tae git ehsel a fuckin liver transplant. Slate wiped fuckin clean.

So ah hus tae pit up wi aw this for ages, man, and ah'm relieved when the Beggar Boy goes cause aw that violence stuff ay his kin be a bit ay a drag tae listen tae. Ye eywis worry thit yir heid's noddin whin it should be shakin, n aw that sort ay thing. Even though ah'm buzzin oan this charlie, ah hud ma hoarses n gie the cat time tae git away, then ah head oot intae the drizzle, settin the hoof-pad controls fir the Central Library at George IV Bridge. Persevere.

Ma heid's still flyin a bit by the time ah gits up tae the Edinburgh Rooms, n ah watch a lassie gittin that microfiche oan. — Eh . . . excuse me, could you gie's a hand wi this? Never done it before, likes, ah goes pointin tae a free machine.

She only looks at me for a second then goes: — Sure, n shows ays how tae load it. Thing is, it wis that simple man, ah felt a total dipstick. But ah'm away! Soon ah'm readin aboot the great betrayal ay 1920 when Leith wis sucked intae Edinburgh against the people's will. That was when aw the problems pure started, man! Four-tae-one against, man, four-tae-one against.

Whin ah head back doon the toon, towards the fair port, the weather's changed n it's startin tae rain really heavy. Ah've nae cash fir the bus fare so it's a collar-up and big-strides job. In St James's Centre some youthful cats are hingin aroond n muh pal Curtis is one ay them. — Awright, buddy? Ah goes, the coke rush now quite run doon.

— Awright, Sp-Sp-Spud, eh goes. The wee gadge is jist a bit nervous wi that stutter but if ye stey cool n dinnae pit um under nae presh, the boy soon gits in the right rhythm n the auld communication jist flows like a stream, man. Wi spraff away fir a bit before ah take oaf n head through John Lewis's n oot tae Picardy Place, hittin the Walk n keepin intae the side tae try n git some shelter fae the rain.

Crossing the Pilrig border into no-sae-Sunny Leith, ah see Sick Boy in the street, and eh seems in a better mood. Ah thought eh'd blank me, but naw, man, the cat sortay apologies, or comes as close as eh gits tae apologising. — Spud. Lit's eh . . . forget aboot the other day, man, eh says.

Eh obviously nivir grassed ays tae Franco, even though the Generalissimo's been in ehs pub, so ah feel better aboot the gadge. — Aye, ah'm likesay sorry aboot that, Simon. Thanks for, eh, no mentioning it tae Franco, likes.

— Fuck that cunt, he says, shaking his heid. — I'm afraid I've far too much to think about to worry aboot the likes of him. Then he beckons ays intae the pub, the Shrub Bar. — Let's get a beer till that fuckin rain goes off, eh says.

— Sound, but . . . eh, yi'll huv tae sub ays though, mate, ah'm skint, ah tell um, comin clean.

Sick Boy exhales powerfully, but goes in anywey, so ah follay. The first gadge ah see in thair is that Cousin Dode cat, standing at the bar and wi sort ay gits lumbered wi him. Dode's giein it the Weedgie-in-Edinburgh thing: better fitba teams, better transport system, pubs, clubs, cheaper taxis, warmer people, aw the usual Weedgie stuff, man. N eh's probably right n aw, but the cat *is* in Edinburgh.

When eh goes tae the bog, Sick Boy looks aw harshly at ehs back n says: — Who the fuck is that twat?

So ah'm telling um aw aboot the Cousin Felly, and ah'm sayin that ah wished ah kent Dode's pin number cause see if ah did, ah'd huv dipped the cunt's poakits for ehs caird, cause he's goat big dosh in that account. — Aye, eh keeps gaun oan aboot how ye can choose yir ain yin in that Clydesdale Bank.

When Dode came back we gits another one in and sits doon. But then something pure radge happens! The gadge takes ehs jayket off, n Sick Boy and me jist look at each other. It's pure thaire, man, right in front ay us! Ye could see Dode's lion tattoo wi 'Aye Ready' on one airm, and his King Billy oan the hoarse oan the other. Aye, n jist below the hoarse oan a scroll wis that PIN number, tattooed so thit eh wid never forget it: 1690.

31

'. . . one buttock cut off . . .'

It's quite a little factory, our Tollcross flat. Joints of hash and cups of coffee are constantly on the go. Rab and I are up working on the script. Dianne's close by us, into her dissertation notes, enjoying our giggles as we batter away side by side on the word processor. Taking the occasional glance at the screen, she proffers purrs of approval and the odd worthy suggestion. In the corner, Lauren, also working on an assignment, is trying to shame us into joining her in the coursework. Obviously intrigued, she, however, refuses to look at our script. Rab and I keep winding her up by whispering things like 'blow job' and 'up the arse' and giggling, while Lauren's tinting red, muttering 'Fellini' or 'Powell and Pressburger'. Dianne eventually gives up and gathers her stuff. — I'm off, I can't stand it, she says.

Lauren looks over at us testily. — Are they disturbing you as well?

— No, Dianne says ruefully, — it's just that every time I take a peek I get all horny. If you hear motor sounds and gasping noises coming from my room you'll know what I'm doing.

Lauren pouts miserably, chewing on her bottom lip. If it's bothering her that much why doesn't she go to *her* room too? By the time we've finished a rough draft of about sixty pages and printed it out, her curiosity has got the better of her and she comes over. She looks at the title then pushes the page-down button, reading in mounting disbelief and distaste. — This is horrible . . . it's disgusting . . . it's obscene . . . and not even in a cool way. There's no merit in it at all. It's trash! I can't believe you could write such degrading, exploitative filth . . . she bubbles. — And you're planning to do these things with people, strangers, you're going to let them do these things to you!

I almost feel obliged to tell her, everything except anal, but instead

187

I come over all haughty, retorting with a quote I've memorised for such an occasion. — I would be glad to know which is worst: to be ravished a hundred times by pirates, to have one buttock cut off, to run the gauntlet among the Bulgarians, to be whipped and hanged at an auto-da-fé, to be dissected, to be chained to an oar in a galley; and in short, to experience all the miseries through which every one of us hath passed, I look at Rab and he joins in concert, — or to remain here doing nothing?

Lauren's shaking her head. — What rubbish are you talking now?

Rab chips in. — That's Voltaire, oot ay *Candide*, he explains. — Surprised you didnae ken that, Lauren, he says to our girl, who shakes nervously and lights up a cigarette. — What was it Candide said back? Rab raises one finger at me and again we declare together: — This is a grand question!

Lauren's still writhing in the seat, looking angry, as if we're wilfully taking the piss out of her, but we're just vibing on the script.

— Nice flooirs, Rab says, as if trying to lighten the mood, looking over at my roses. — I saw another set of fresh ones in the bucket. He smiles cheekily. — What's the story there?

Lauren shoots him a look, but I sense the innocuousness of the remark, which immediately makes me think that it *was* Sick . . . Simon. We can certainly eliminate Rab from our line of enquiry.

We sit up until the shops open, going over the draft, making amendments. If Rab and I were tired and nervous about taking it down to Leith and showing it to the others, we left the flat highly encouraged by Lauren's remarks. We went to a printer's and got several copies xeroxed off and bound. As we settle into a café for breakfast, it only really hit me, through our elation at finishing and our fatigue, just how upset Lauren was. In a sudden surge of guilt, I ask: — Do you think we should go back up and see how she is?

— Naw, it'll just make things worse. Gie her some time, Rab considers.

And that suits me; I certainly don't want to go back. Because I'm enjoying myself here with Rab. Enjoying the strong black coffees, the orange juice, the bagels, enjoying the fact that we're sitting here with a script on the table. A film script *we've done,* rejoicing that we've achieved *something*, Rab and I, we just sat down and did it. And I feel a great intimacy with him, and I think that I maybe want us to have more moments like this. But now it isn't just a sex thing, like my mounting obsession with Simon, in fact it feels strangely asexual in a way. Not just fucking, but moments like this. It makes me think though. — Do you think your girlfriend would approve if she knew you'd been up all night writing porno with another woman?

Rab sees it for what it is. He emotionally stands back from me, shrugging off the question and pouring more coffee from the cafetière. There's a silence for a bit, then he goes to say something, thinks better of it, and we square up and leave the café and jump on a Leith-bound bus.

I see him in my mind's eye on the way down to Leith, then we get to the pub and he's there. Simon Williamson. The others are arriving, shuffling in. Ursula, in a tracksuit which would look horrible on a British girl but is somehow cool on her. Craig and Ronnie, the Siamese twins, and my face lights up as I see Gina for the first time since she helped me. I go over and put my hand on her shoulder. — Thanks so much for helping me that time, I croon.

— Ye goat sick oan ma toap, she says gruffly, and I'm briefly startled but her aggression is superficial and she smiles. — Jist a wee whitey. Happens tae us aw.

Then Melanie's in, all open and friendly, hugging me like we're long-lost pals. My spirits rise as we present them each with a copy. — Remember, I explain, — this is just a very rough draft. All feedback gratefully received.

At least the title gets them. They all snigger when they read on the title page:

SEVEN RIDES FOR SEVEN BROTHERS

I quickly explain the plot. — The story is roughly this: seven lads are on an oil rig. One of them, Joe, has a bet with another, Tommy, which states that each one of the seven 'brothers' needs to get laid while on weekend shore leave. But not only do they have to get fucked, they have to have satisfied their own well-known sexual predilections. Unfortunately, there are two of them who want to do other things, of a cultural and sporting nature, and a third is a hopeless virgin. So the odds are stacked in Tommy's favour. But Joe has allies; Melinda and Suzy, who run a high-class brothel, and who contrive to find the seven rides who'll sort out those pesky brothers once and for all.

Simon nods enthusiastically, slapping his hand against his thigh. — This sounds good. This sounds very fucking good indeed.

While the others read, Rab and I elect to go downstairs and have a drink in the locked, empty pub. We have a half-hour of small talk about the script and the university before we head back up. When we open the door, they're sitting in stunned silence. I think, oh no, but then realise that they're looking in awe at us.

Suddenly Melanie's big laugh sucks the air out the room. She throws the manuscript on the desk, unable to control herself. — This is jist too fuckin mad, she smirks at me, her hand going to her mouth. — Youse are radge.

Then Terry cuts in, looking at Rab. — Aye, it's awright, but listen, Birrell, this isnae a fuckin college project. Yuv goat tae be able tae stroke yir fuckin knob n come, no yir fuckin chin n come. This is the real world, mate.

Rab looks impatiently back at him. — Read the fuckin thing, Lawson. It's seven brothers oan the rigs, fir fuck sakes, they come oaf thir shift n need tae meet they seven birds.

Simon looks at Terry in a hostile manner, then he turns to us glassy-eyed and seems genuinely emotional. — This is a work of fuckin genius, folks, he says, standing up and grabbing Rab's shoulder and then kissing my cheek before leaning across the bar and filling up some huge JD's from the optics. — You've got the fuckin lot here. I loved the bondage and spanking scenes. So fruity!

— Yeah, I explain, totally elated, but trying to maintain some sort of cool in the face of his comments as the grimy tiredness of our all-nighter kicks in, — British market, y'know. It's a very British fetish? Its cultural origins are, like, in the public-school and nanny-state culture?

Rab nods enthusiastically. — It also shows our soft-porn heritage and the repressive nature of our censorship culture, he says, our pretension now suddenly growing. — How Lauren could say there was no art in it really just beggars belief.

— Nivir mind the art, Birrell, ah liked the bit aboot the boy thit wis obsessed wi blow jobs, Terry winks, letting his bottom lip caress his top one.

Simon's nodding slowly, and in grim content, with an executioner's enthusiasm says: — Now we've got tae cast this.

— Ah want tae play aw the brothers, Terry says. — Ye kin dae that wi effects n editing now. Jist a couple ay different wigs, some costumes, like glesses n that . . .

We all laugh, but it has an incredulous edge as we know that Terry's deadly serious. Simon shakes his head. — Naw, we all need to get parts in this – or any boy whae kin find wid on camera can, that is.

— There'll be nae problems here, Terry says patting his crotch satisfyingly. Then he turns to Rab. — Notice you're keepin quiet, Birrell! No fancy a wee part, wee bein the operative word?

— Fuck off, Terry, Rab says with a mannered smile, — it's big enough, although half a dozen twelve-inchers would still rattle in your fuckin gob.

— You can dream, Birrell, Terry scoffs.

— Children, please, Simon says grandly. — It might have escaped your attention, but there's ladies present. Just because we're making a pornogra . . . eh, adult-entertainment film, it doesn't mean that we personally need to be coarse. Keep the gutter in your head, not round this table.

We're flushed with our accomplishment, Rab and I. As we prepare to head off to get up to the uni to check on our assignment results, Simon comes up to me and whispers in my ear. — All my life you've been a mirage, now you're real.

He *did* send the flowers.

We're on the bus heading up the town and Rab's going on about the movie and films in general, but my mind's elsewhere. I can't see or hear him any more, all I can think about is Simon. *All my life you've been a mirage, now you're real.*

I'm real to him. But our life's not real. This is not real life. This is entertainment. When I get to the university I see that McClymont has given me a fifty-five. It's not great but it's a pass. There are some semi-illigible notes.

A good effort, rendered less effective by irritating habit of adopting the American bastardised spelling of our language. 'Colour' is not spelt 'color'. Nonetheless, you make some good points, but don't neglect the influence of Scots immigrants in science and medicine – it wasn't all politics, philosophy, education, engineering and building.

A pass. Now I can forget about that part of the course and that creepy old bastard for ever.

32

Scam # 18,741

I look out over the back green where a wifie's hanging out her washing. Heavy, murky clouds are racing across the tops of the tenements blotting out the lovely pale-blue sky. The wifie looks up and, with a despondent, furrowed brow, realises that it's going to piss down and kicks her basket in frustration.

The film was easy to cast; Craig and Ursula will do the bondage scenes, Terry as key shagger will do Mel up the shitter. Ronnie will be the boxer who gets off watching Nikki and Melanie getting it on (and he won't be the only one), and I'll be man who wants the orgy. I'll get Mikey Forrester to do the blow-job scene with one of his daft wee hoors. All we need is one more brother for the straight-sex scene, and I might see if Rab's up for that one, or Renton even, while I need a younger stud for the cherry-popping virgin part.

The problem for this movie, to do it the way we want to, is money. I'm determined that this won't be a ham-and-egg operation. I'll show them all that they were wrong to dismiss SDW as a force, as a player in the industry. But it can't be done on the cheap, cause that's what they expect. I haven't got access to the kind of money those spoiled cunts spunk away on nothing. But Spud and his daft soap-star pal have given me an idea, and I've been doing some sounding out. It could come to fruition. Of course, as well as his paltry scheme I have a far more elaborate plan in mind, which must, of neccesity, exclude Daniel Murphy.

Alex McLeish?

It's all about depth of pool, Simon, and I'm an admirer of the outfit you've got together, especially this girl Nikki. Very talented. The boy Murphy on the other hand, well, he has done a job when he's come in, but I don't think he has the professionalism to be a member of the squad.

Thanks, Alex. My view entirely: Murphy is purely a stop-gap

signing. And I'm taking a tip from the man himself, and scouring the Continent for some new signings, under the Bosman rule. Of course, it may be difficult to entice old-crowd favourite Mark Renton back to Leith. But I begin my scouting mission closer to home. There's been a few messages left at the pub from a certain Paul Keramalandous of the Links Agency, a yuppie advertising firm down in Queen Charlotte Street who are said to epitomise the 'new Leith'. The messages state that Keramalandous is interested in the Leith Business Against Drugs Forum. I feel both that tightness in frame and salivation in mouth that tells that I'm on the scent of something and return his call. It's a fruitful conversation; the guy tells me that other businesses have been in touch, and he's suggesting a date next week for an inaugural meeting at the Assembly Rooms. He asks me if I've anybody in mind whom I'd like to 'bring to the table'. I'm thinking about my poverty of legitimate contacts here. Who the fuck could I bring along? Lexo, with his greasy-spoon-cum-Thai-café? Mikey Forrester with his sauna and scabby hoors? No way. This is my scam, and my scam only. I intimate to Paul that it might be better to keep things tight, myself, himself and a few of the names he mentions to me.

— Makes perfect sense, he whistles coolly down the blower, — at least till we get up and running. Don't want to get into the too-many-cooks scenario.

I make the appropriate noises, hang up and put the potential date, to be confirmed, into my diary. I'm confident that I'll have this toss eating the contents of my arse with subservient gratitude in no time. Buoyed by this success, I decide to pitch for the big one and go for Ginger Minger.

I begin my charm offensive by calling Renton up again and telling him about this scam, or at least as much as I want him to know. As I talk on the phone, it's difficult coping with his silence, which at one point becomes excruciating. I want to see that face, those sly, calculating eyes, the way they can quickly morph into Aled Jones-choirboy efforts when he thinks he's being rumbled. — So what do you reckon?

He seems pretty impressed. — It has possibilities, he says with what seems guarded enthusiasm.

— Too right, they'll go for it.

— Aye, Weedgies are pretty predictable, Rents considers. — I mean, every other cunt in both the UK and the Republic of Ireland has hoped for decades that those six counties would just disappear, while those wankers still do this pantomime imitation of the worst possible twats over there.

— Yes, I agree, they've no originality at all, especially the Huns. They name their mob after West Ham's, they copy Millwall's song. It's a safe bet, though, that most of them are in the Royal Bank of Scotland, but there must be a few at the Clydesdale.

— What exactly are you planning here?

— As I said, I just need a couple of offshore accounts. Come over and join me, Mark, I urge. Then I swallow hard. — I need you. You owe me. Are you in?

There's only a slight bit of hesitancy. — Aye. Can you come back over sometime? Soas that we can go over things and sort out the details, like.

— I can get back on Friday, I tell him, trying not to sound too keen.

— See you then, he says.

You'll fucking well see me awright, Renton, you thieving fucking bastard.

Just after I put the phone down, my green mobile goes off – the one I give only to guys – and it's Franco. — Goat masel a mobby, eh, he tells me. — Fuckin barry. Wir huvin a fuckin caird school the night, Malky McCarron, Larry n that. Nelly's back up fae Manchester n aw, ya cunt.

— Bummer, ah'm working, I say in false disappointment, relieved to be out off that psycho's rotary club they call Begbie's card schools. Having my money extorted from me by drunken bams isn't my idea of a good night's entertainment.

But it's very interesting that Begbie called just after I talked to Renton. I think it means that they were meant to be together.

33

Washing Up

Ali's only been roond once, wi the bairn, n we never really hud a chance tae talk. Nonetheless, ah'm surprisingly bouncy, bouncy, bouncy, man, cause the research is gaun well n ah'm oaf the collies. Ali wis pretty . . . eh . . . sceptical, man, cause it's a well-worn path she's been doon, but fair play tae her, ah think she's tryin tae gie ays the benefit ay the doubt. Another good thing is that me n Sick Boy ur sortay likesay mates again. Ah'm seein um later oan cause thir's a wee scam wir workin.

Ah've been at ma wee sister Roisin's gaff, whae, tae be as frank as our Mr Begbie, isnae really the kind ay lassie that ah've ever hit it off wi. She's ten years younger thin me, upwardly mobile, n she's never really approved ay the traditional clan Murphy lifestyle, likes. Her boyfriend is a pretty cool catboy though, and eh's away working in Spain so eh's left ays ehs season ticket for Easter Road. Never really been tae a game in ages man, but the greens are daein it fir disco. That Alex McLeish reminds me a bit ay Rents n also that cat in *NYPD Blue*, what wis it they called that gadge again? Robinson Crusoe? Naw, bit something like it. Mind you, that could just be the fur colourin. But now we've goat the French boy at the back n the wee black cat in the middle. So ah might take in the home game versus Dunfermline, combat the boredom, man, always the biggest killer. Boredom and anxiety. Wi the first we hunt fir speed. Then wi git aw anxious n that's where the auld Salisbury Crag comes intae its ain.

It's a frosty deal fi wee sis though, right enough, man. Ah mean, we once hud the nine-month tenancy oan the same womb n aw that, but ah suppose when we each gave that up we stepped oot intae different times, man, different eras. So havin stuck the ticket-book intae ma tail, ah take ma leave ay Rosh's hoose.

Oan the wey doon ah hears aw this shoutin n screamin in the stairwell. When ah gits doon tae the next landin ah sees thit it's June, Franco's ex, wi the two wee Begbie brats, n one ay thum's screamin and the bigger one's gittin battered by June, whae seems tae have lost it, man, big time before bedtime. — AH SAW YE HIT UM! DINNAE FUCKIN DENY IT! WHAT HUV AH FUCKIN TELT YE, SEAN!

The Begbie brat's just standin takin the shots, buckling like a wobbly puppet, but no really botherin ehs erse. This wee cat's like a hip-hop, body-poppin feral, jerkin tae absorb the impact ay the blows. The smaller cat looks deid feart and eh's pure silent now.

— Whae hey! ah shout. — Awright, June!

— Spud, she says, and she suddenly starts greetin, and shakin her heid, it's like she jist sortay pure breks doon, ken.

This is, likesay, a freaky situ tae land in. Ah mean, ah didnae even ken she lived in this stair. — Eh . . . ye awright . . . ah goes n ah grab the bags ay shoppin, seein thit the handle's split oan one.

— Aye . . . thanks, Spud, it's this pair, she sobs, noddin at the young gadges.

— That's laddies fir ye, eh, ah smile. The younger yin gies me a scared wee smile back, but the older kitten fae the Begbie litter is lookin at ays in a wey that is awfay spooky, even in such a young cat. Aye, the Son ay Franco, that yin, fir defo, one hus tae say!

June gits the keys in the lock and opens up. The bairns charge in, the big yin shoutin somethin aboot Sky Sports. June watches them go, a two-man demolition squad. Then she turns tae ays n goes: — Ah'd ask ye in fir a cuppa, Spud, but the place is a mess.

That's no aw that's a mess, man. The June lassie looks likesay dug-rough-ruff-ruff. The wey she says it, it's like she needs somebody tae talk tae. Ah ken ah've arranged tae meet the Sick Felly n Cousin Dode in the pub, but ah could dae wi a bit ay a chat masel. N ah git nowt fae Ali n nowt fae wee Rosh upstairs, whae couldnae really wait tae see the back ay ays. — Cannae be worse than oor gaff, ah tell her. N June looks at ays, like she's sortay considerin this, then thinkin that it sounds fair dos.

When ah git intae the hoose, it's a mess ay clathes n kids' toys. Thir's a pile ay dishes in the sink that look like they've been thaire fir years.

Ah kin barely find room oan the worktoap tae pit the bags on.

June's shakin n ah offer her a fag and light it for her. She pits oan the kettle n cannae find any clean cups. She tries tae rinse one, tries tae squeeze oot some Squeezy in at it, but aw that comes oot is a fart sound. She goes tae one ay the bags and gits a fresh bottle, but she cannae git the toap off wi her shakin hands. She bursts intae tears, no jist sobbin, proper wailin this time. — Ah'm sorry, it's ma nerves, everything's gone wrong here . . . look at the place. It's the bairns . . . thir such a handful . . . ah git nae support, ah mean Frank's back oot but eh's only been doon once tae see thum, never even took them oot! Oot ay jail fir ten minutes n wearin fancy new shirts n clathes n jewellery . . . they sovereign rings . . . ah cannae cope, Spud . . . ah cannae cope . . .

Ah look at the pile ay dishes. — Tell ye what, ah'll gie ye a hand wi thaime, let's just blitz the kitchen here. It'll make ye feel better, man, when they aw go, cause that's it, when ye feel like shite, like drained ay yir energy, n ye see a big pile ay washin in the sink; that is the worst, man, the ultimate worst, it's like aw the energy jist sortay goes doon the plughole, man, jist doon. So a problem shared is a problem halved n aw that, June, man.

— Naw, it's okay . . .

— Hey! C'moan! Ah stick oan an apron. — Lit's blitz, man, lit's blitz!

June's protestin as ah fire intae the dishes, but it's half-hearted, n she picks up a bit when wi start making headway, and in nae time at aw, it's gone, man, the problem is gone and everything is clear and possible again. Jist clear the heid and do it, man, just dae it. Ken? Like me wi the writin, man, jist git in thaire n dae it!

That's me done good, man, simple practical good. Ah'm buzzin, man, buzzin like ah'm on the strongest speed known tae man. It's goat tae be said thit the June lassie is in better mental shape thin whin ah found her, man, too right.

But when I get tae the pub I'm late for Sick Boy and the gadge is mibee one or two miles away fae the amusement arcade. Cousin Dode's bending ehs ear and eh looks at me and raises ehs watch tae ma face.

34

Scam # 18,742

I'm in this grot-hole pub on the Walk waiting on a fucked-up junky to rescue me from this boring Weedgie with the prematurely greying hair, the heavy-set features and eyes of a perpetually shocked belligerence normally only seen on the goats at Gorgie Farm. Welcome back to Scotland, right enough. This Cousin Dode fucker, this pseudo-Saxon, north European, philistine, lard-buttocked, fucking Hun nonentity; this troglodyte mutant from a west-coast slum has the audacity to try and quote Latin; *Latin*, at *me*, a Renaissance man of Mediterranean and Jacobean stock. He gets us a drink in and raises his glass. — *Urbi et orbi*, he says.

— Cheers, *similia similibus curantur*, I grin waspishly.

Cousin Dode's pupils expand like black holes sucking in everything around him. — Ah dunno that yin, whit's that yin, he goes, more than just impressed, actually pretty fucking excited.

Well, I didn't know what his one was, but I'm fucked if I'd ever admit that to a soapy cunt. — The hair of the dog, I wink. — Appropriate at the moment.

Cousin Dode twists his head to the side and regards me keenly. — You're an intelligent man, ah kin tell. It's guid tae meet somebody oan ma wavelength, he shakes his head and a pained expression moulds his coupon. — That's the thing, ah dinnae meet that many people oan ma wavelength.

— I can imagine, I say with a deadpan nod, which goes completely over his macaroon-bar-and-spearmint-chewing-gum head.

— Ah mean, yir mate Spud, a lovely fellah, but mibee no that sharp. But see, you, you've goat it up tap, he drums his own head with his index finger. — Aye, Spud wis sayin that yir intae makin fillums n that.

Strange that Murphy's deigned to give me such a favourable press.

Not porn, but films, no less. It gets me entertaining the sentimental notion that maybe I've been a bit hard on my sticky-fingered chum.
— Well, you've got tae, Dode. What's it they say: *ars longa, vita brevis*.
— Art is long, time is short, wahn o' ma favourites, he nods with a big grin which splits his face.

Eventually di fella Morphy comes in, looking a bit fucking wired as well. As the Weedgie rat-shagger heads off to the bogs, I make my intense displeasure known. — Whaire the fuck have you been? We're no runnin oan Tipperary time here. I've had tae listen tae that boring twat gaun oan and oan!

But he's looking fucking well pleased with himself. — Couldnae help it, man, ah ran intae June, likes. Hud tae help her wash up, it just hud tae be done, ken?

— Aw aye, I knowingly observe. I might have fuckin well guessed. That's Spud though, can't resist any form of temptation, although I'd have tae be desperate before I'd fucking well dae rocks wi June. Funny, but I wouldn't have thought it of her, especially with the bairns aroond, but I suppose everybody's on it now, and to be fair to her, she's goat those frazzled and worn-oot crack-hoor looks tae a tee. — So how is June? I ask, not knowing why. I mean, it's not as if I particularly care.

Spud purses his lips and blows air through them, making a vulgar farting noise which is too loud and might have occasioned some embarrassment had it been delivered in a hostelry of class. — She's lookin well rough if the truth be telt, man, he says, as this Cousin Dode character emerges from the toilet and gets up another round.

— I'll bet she is, I nod, and we all know why.

Dode raises a glass of lager and clicks Spud's. — Awright, Spud! Wur oan wahn the night! Then he repeats this stupid exercise with me, and I force a grin of superficial bonhomie.

Growing somewhat anxious for any diversion from my present company, I give the young barmaid a gentle sunny smile, of the kind that would have, in my youth, sent her involuntarily reaching up to tidy her hair. Now all I get is a coolish twist of the mouth in reciprocation.

So we trek around several bars and wind up in the town, eventually hitting the famous City Café in Blair Street, an old haunt of mine. I note the pool tables, a new addition since I was last in here. They'll have to go: encourages too many simpletons. On that note, I'm getting seriously fucked off with this Cousin Dode character's incessant droning on, to the extent that I'm actually delighted when I see Mikey Forrester come in with this obviously deranged but sexy-looking hoor in his slipstream.

I'll be Mister Popular in the City Café, I've really upped the quality of the client base. I've got in tow the biggest junky scruffbag Leith's ever produced, a Weedgie Hun and now scabby Forrester; rubbish dressed as fancy goods if ever there was. I'm thinking, what am I: a fuckin soap-free zone all of a sudden? The bar staff will need to get Rentokil in at closing time.

— It's Mikey Forrester, I indicate to Dode. — He's a partner in a couple of saunas and runs a stable of tasty wee hoors who gam for their supper. It's the age-old trick: gets them turned ontae gear and then has them working in the hole-sale department tae pey for it, if ye catch ma drift.

Dode turns and nods, giving Mikey a casual once-over of mild disapproval laced with envy.

— Aye, eh, Seeker does that n aw, Spud says, that slack-mouthed idiot leer of the troubled adolescent still sticking to his face like shite to the neck of a bottle, even after all those fucking years.

I shake my head. — Seeker just rides them but, it's the only way a mess-on-legs like him can get his Nat King, I explain. I allow myself to feel a slight bit of unease at this slag-off as I reach into my pocket to feel the bottle of GHB which Seeker himself supplied to me this affie. Another man who does have his uses, albeit within a strictly proscribed arena. I pull Spud towards me to whisper into his ear, noting that it has a blob of brown wax plugging it. My nose crinkles with distaste at the rancid, yeasty odour: — I'm going to have a word with Mikey about some business. I crush a twenty into his hand. — You keep soapboy happy.

— Excuse me a second, chaps, just going to say hello for old times' sake, I explain to Dode, and head over in the direction of Forrester. Forrester's the sort of guy that nobody really likes, but everybody seems to end up doing business with. He flashes me a smile and his teeth remind me of the Bingham district of the city;

the whole scheme substantially rebuilt since I last saw it. I'm surprised that Mikey's opted for a tasteful natural-effect capping, rather than going for gold. He's got a sunbed tan and his salt-and-pepper thinning hair has been shaved like a cue ball. The silver-blue cloth on him looks quality. Only the shoes, expensive leather, but needing a polishing, and, crucially, the white towelling socks, a bulk-buy Christmas pressy to every nutter from their mother since the early eighties, give him away as an ex-Murphy soulmate.

— Hi, Simon, how's it gaun?

I feel grateful that he's chosen to call me Simon instead of Sick Boy and respond accordingly. — Graceful, Michael, graceful. I turn, smiling to his company. — Is this the lovely young lady you were telling me about?

— One ay them, he grins, then goes: — Wanda, this is Sick . . . eh, Simon Williamson. He's the boy ah wis talking aboot, jist back up fae London.

This lassie's very tidy; slim, sleek and with dark looks so, well, *Latin*, she should come with a Cousin Dode phrase. She's in that first flush of junk hoordom, where they actually look really great, just before the big decline kicks in. Then she'll need to go on the pipe to get up and keep working and her looks will go and Mikey or some other cunt will relegate her from sauna to street, or crack den. Ah, Dame Commerce, a grand old lady who rocks in such predictable ways. — You the movie man? she asks wastedly, presenting that smackheid's lugubrious, slightly arrogant bearing which I seem to have encountered in every other social transaction since I was about sixteen years old.

— Pleased tae meet you, sweetheart, I smile, wrapping my hand round hers and planting a kiss on her cheek.

You'll dae, hen.

So Mikey and I quickly come to a casting arrangement. I like this Wanda lassie; even though she's completely reliant on Mikey and therefore totally in his power, she's still unguarded about showing her contempt for him. Which only really makes it all the more pleasurable for him to incrementally increase his hold over her. She's got pride though, although the junk will suck up the vestiges of that before it gets to her looks, a formula which spells quids in for Mikey.

So we're all set, and I head over to Spud and Dode, the latter telling the former, quite loudly, about women. — That's the only thing ye kin dae wi wummun, love thum, he drunkenly contends. — Ah'm ah right thair, Simon? Tell um!

— You could be on to something there, George, I smile.

— Love thum, n be brave enough, be strang enough tae love thum. *Fortes fortuna adjuvat* . . . fortune favours the brave. Ah'm ah right thair, Simon? Ah'm ah right!?

Spud tries to cut in, thankfully saving me the bother of attempting to mouth an enthusiastic affirmation to this fucking rat-shagging oaf. — Aye, but sometimes it's likesay . . .

Cousin Dode cuts him off with a swish of the hand, which nearly knocks another boy's full pint from him. I nod at the guy in mild apology. — Nae buts, nae sometimes. If they complain, gie thum mair love. If thir still complainin eftir that, even mair love, he proclaims stridently.

— Exactly right, George. I firmly believe that man's capacity to give love exceeds woman's capacity to receive it. That's why we rule the world, it's as simple as that, I curtly explain.

Dode looks at me open-mouthed, his eyes rolling slowly like a fruit machine being nudged towards the jackpot. — This man here, Spud, this man's a fuckin genius!

This Cousin Dode chap is one of those typical Weedgies who get drunk very quickly, pished as lords after about one or two peeves. Then, instead of doing the decent thing and passing out, they seem to maintain that state for fucking ages; lurching around, repeating the same mundane, obsessive message but with escalating stroppiness. — Thank you, George, I nod. — But I have to say that I'm getting a bit fed up with bars. You see, it's a bit of a busman's holiday for me, and it's full of gadges, I nod over towards Forrester, — that I don't particularly want to be around. Let's get a carry-out and head off somewhere.

— Aye! Dode roars, — everybody back tae mine! Ah've goat an absolutely fuckin blindin tape ah wahnt yis tae hear. A mate o' mine's goat this band . . . thir the best. The best, ah'm tellin yis!

— Fantastic, I smile, grinding my teeth. — Is it alright if I phone for some company to join us, as in the female sense of the term? I shake the red mobby.

— Is it awright? Is it awright! Whit a man! Whit a man! Dode exclaims to all the drinkers crushed in groups around us, as the hairs on the back of my neck attempt to leave the bar in embarrassment. Some people would be chuffed by this endorsement, but not me. I firmly believe that a good character reference from a witless moron is far more damaging to one's standing than condemnation from the hippest ranks of the cognoscenti.

We head for the door, me taking the lead and passing through the crowd with haste, pausing only to smile at a girl in a tight green two-piece who has a pretty face, but one that is topped with a bad Manchester perm. Then there's an involuntary stall as I work my way around two ballooning thirty-somethings who've ditched the diet for good and decided that the rest of their lives will consist of vodka, Red Bull and comfort eating. Then I swerve to avoid an oncoming posse of goldfish-mouthed shifty-eyed young men who push to the bar.

Dode's still singing my praises to Spud as we stride out into the night. I shiver. It's not the cold, it's not the drugs. It's me feeling the heights, depths and breadth of my deceit, and Cousin Dode's praise measuring out its monstrous but exquisite parameters. Fuck me, it's good to be alive.

35

Pin Money

We go back to the Dode cat's gaff wi some drinks. Sick Boy's boat a boatil ay absinthe n aw, which is a bit dodgy likes cause it's Dode wir wantin tae git wasted, no the loat ay us. Sick Boy looks aw distastefully at the Huns' picture oan the waw n ah faw oantae that big leather couch. The weight oaf the feet, right enough.

The George Cousin seems delighted at the prospect ay some sex kittens comin along, n tae be perfectly honest, man, it might no really be the worse thing in the world. Ah think Sick Boy wis jist sayin it tae make sure we goat back but, ken.

Dinnae tell the Cousin that but, cause these are not the words thon west-coast cat wants tae hear. — Whaire's they burds, Simon, are they gemme . . . ?

— As fuck, Sick Boy nods. — Excellent sports. They make stag movies, the lot, the sickest cat in the basket purrs as Dode rolls ehs eyes and puckers ehs lips. That one Sick Pup nods tae me, then puts ehs hand tae his mooth in a gabbing movement as eh starts filling the absinthe glasses.

— Eh, ah start, making a diversion, — so tell ays, Dode, how is it you git called *Cousin* Dode? as ah see Sick Boy casually spike Dode's gless wi GHB. Ah'm no really intae aw this, man. They say thit if ye pit too much in, a gadge's hert kin jist likesay stoap, man, jist like that. Sick Boy seems tae ken what eh's daein though, it's like eh's carefully measurin it wi ehs eye.

Dode's only too happy tae tell the tale and oblige ma curiousity, likes. — The story behind that wahn: this mate ay mine, through in Glesca, Boaby ehs name is, he jist calls everybody 'cousin'. Sick Boy hands him the drink. — It's jist the boey's patter, like, since we wir wee weans in the Drum, he says, taking a swallay. — Then a few punters fae the toon oan nights oot, whae wurnae in the know, kept hearin um talk aboot Cousin Dode . . . so it jist sortay stuck, eh goes, still nippin away at the gless.

Soon Dode's eyes ur gittin heavy n eh disnae even notice whin the Sick Cat takes oaf the tape ay that band ay ehs mates, n changes it for the Chemical Brothers. — Stag movies . . . eh slurs, n eh's sinkin intae that couch as ehs eyelids shut, then ehs right oot fir the count.

Me n Sick Boy are straight through the gadge's pockets, n ah thought ah'd feel a bit bad aboot this, cause Dode's awright really. But naw, man, that auld thievin gene kicks right in and ah'm buzzin, riflin the cunt for aw eh's worth, but Sick Boy goes: — Fuck off, leave it, nodding tae the wad ay cash ah've taken fae ehs poakits.

And he's right, man; ah'm jist gettin a bit greedy thaire, thinkin the boy widnae miss a few notes oaffay that healthy wad. Ah ken what Sick Boy wants but, that Clydesdale card, which we find and confiscate.

We go doonstairs tae the cashpoint at 11.57 p.m. and key in the number, neither ay us in the slightest bit surprised when it works, withdrawing £500, n daein jist the very same again at 12.01 a.m. — Weedgies, eh, Sick Boy chuckles a bit, then adds affectionately, — Doss cunts.

— Aye, and a good thing n aw but, ah tell um.

— Too right, Sick Boy says, handing ower half the wad, but stallin a bit before eh lits it go intae ma mitt. — Nae skag, mate. A nice wee present for the missus, eh.

— Aye, right, ah tell um. The cat's even telling ays how tae spend the dosh now, man, and that is just no oan. But this does feel good, like auld times, me n Sick Boy, scammin away tae fuck n it reminds me that back in the day we wir good but, man, we wir the best. Well, mibee no as good as a few boys ah kin think ay, mind you. Ah feel pure bad aboot the Cousin Dode boy now cause eh's awright really, even a sortay pal, but it's done now, ken. N eh shouldnae be sae superior, likesay, wi that Proddy supremacist stuff, man. Ye act aw high n mighty, somebody'll cut ye doon tae size. Sick Boy should mind that n aw; but hey, man, that's me soundin like Franco now!

But we're back up tae Dode's flat and wi pits the caird back intae ehs wallet n the wallet back intae ehs poakit. Sick Boy makes some black coffee and lits it cool, then makes Dode sip it. The caffeine brings him back up, n ehs legs sortay kick oot, hittin the coffee table n spillin some drinks.

— Whoa, catboy, whoa!

— You were out for the count, Dode, Sick Boy laughs as our favourite Weedgie boy, aw sort ay bemused, sits up, rubbin ehs eyes.

— Aye . . . Dode says as eh starts tae git ehs bearings. — That absinthe is mental, by the way, eh groans and looks at the clock oan the mantelpiece. — Fuck me, *tempus fugit*, right enough.

— Typical soapdodger, says *Felinus Vomitus*, which is like ma new Latin name fir yon Sick Cat, — they talk a good session, but when it comes down to it they can't stand the pace with the Leith boys!

Dode lurches up n staggers taewards the cairry-oot in pure defiance. — Yis wahnt tae see drinkin? Ah'll show yis drinkin!

Me n the Sickest Cat gie each other a quick wee scan, hoping that the Dode boy passes oot again before eh runs oot ay money.

36

Scam # 18,743

The clanking of heavy aluminium barrels on the stone floor. The loud camaraderie of the brewery delivery squad as they roll another one from the lorry, onto the mattress, then down the wooden chute, the guy at the bottom letting the cushion break its fall before catching it and stacking it. But that banging, those loud voices.

My head is very fucking sore. I remember with some terror that I agreed to go to my mother's this evening, for a family meal. I can't think what would disturb me more in my condition, her indulgent fussing or the old boy's indifference, occasionally slipping into full-blown hostility. That Christmas, years ago, when he got me in the kitchen and whispered in drunken malevolence: — Ah'm wide for your game, ya cunt, and I mind of being confused and fearful. What had I done that he'd rumbled? I realised later, of course, that it wasn't a specific, he was just projecting his own self-hatred, saying that he understood me, my nature, because he shared it. The crucial difference he missed, though, was that he's a loser and I'm not.

But my heid is nipping. That sesh last night: what a performance to go through for just five hundred bar of a Weedgie's cash. Of course, Mr Murphy is delighted with his share of our ill-gotten gains, but for me the whole thing was simply a trial run.

Spud may have done well in a devalued domestic Cup fixture, but that doesn't mean that he can be considered for the European ties. Alex?

It's horses for courses, Simon, and I'd be inclined to bring in the Renton fellow, from Europe. He's a temperamental player and he's let us down in the past, but sometimes you need to take that risk at this level. Alex Ferguson proved that with Eric Cantona. But I seriously think that the Murphy boy would be out of his depth in this one. I still like the look of this Nicola Fuller-Smith girl though.

I couldn't agree more, Alex. We both know talent when we see it.

This fuckin hangover is doing me in though; I'm shaking as the brewery boys sing cheerfully and Morag's shouting at me: — We're needin some Beck's up!

This is not the life I had planned. I struggle, shivering up the stairs with one case, then two, and start methodically stocking the bar fridges. Later, I submit to nerves, lighting up a cigarette in the office. It's easier to give up smack than fags. Still, the post arrives, bringing better news in the shape of a letter, and it's from the Chief Constable's office!

Lothian Police
Serving the Community

12 March
Your ref: SDW
Our Ref: RL/CC

Dear Mr Williamson,

Re: Leith Business Against Drugs

Many thanks for your letter dated the 4th of this month.

I have long maintained that the war against drugs can only be won with the support of the law-abiding public. As much of the dealing of drugs takes place in public houses and clubs, vigilant publicans like yourself are in the front line of this battle and I'm delighted to see someone standing up and being counted and declaring their licensed premises a drug-free zone.

Yours sincerely,

R.K. Lester
Chief Constable, Lothian Police

Still a good hour before opening time and I take the letter up the Walk to the frame shop, and get it encased in a smart, gold-rimmed number. Then I head back and stick it, in pride of place, behind the bar. Effectively, it serves as a certificate to deal drugs as no vigilant plod is going to bust me and embarrass the main man. *Now* I'll be left alone, and that's all you want, all you crave out of life: to be left alone while you get on with the business of inter-fering with others. In other words, to be a bona fide, fully certified member of the capitalist classes.

The sunbed I ordered finally arrives. I don't want milk-bottled bodies on the set. I get under for half an hour's try-out.

Fired up, literally, I go outside to a call box, from where I bell the *Evening News*, and hold my nostrils shut as I talk. — There's a boy doon in Leith, eh, at that Port Sunshine Tavern, eh, tryin tae start this Leith Business Says No Tae Drugs campaign, eh. Eh's goat a letter fae the Chief Constable backing him up, eh.

How hot they get at the mention of the Chief's name! Within the hour, they've sent some spotty, feeble-minded twat round with a photographer in tow, just as my first customers, old Ed and his mob are filing in, checking the blackboard for the dish of the day (shepherd's pie). The newsmen take some snaps and ask a few ques-tions, me sitting back and giving it the big one. I tell the boy that Mo's stovies are as famous in Leith as Betty Turpin's hotpot used to be in Weatherfield. The wee guy looks stupefied, but seems happy enough with what he's got.

It's not been too bad a start to the day, and I'm five hundred quid richer. Of course, this is still small beer for what we need to make a proper, high-production-values fuck-movie, but now I've got a bigger scam on the horizon. Pornography is the genre of film I've chosen to work in, but I won't be sticking around in it for too long. I'll show the Zionist family big beak. I triumphantly rack up a huge line of posh and it hits the spot, though I have to run for the Kleenex to shore up a surge of snotter-water.

It's weird that a drinking session with Spud Murphy and some fucking daft Weedgie Hun can be so inspiring. That charlie's top gear, it fair knocks the old hangover for six. The phone goes and Morag answers it, holding it up at the other end of the bar. Worth her substantial lard in gold, yon auld yin. Yes, I could get a fuckable young student, maybe like Nikki, for some eye and cock relief, but no way would she be able to run the place like this old boiler. — For you, she goes.

I'm expecting it to be some top fanny, even hoping it's that Nikki, but no, it's fucking Spud, wanting to go out to a club and spend poor soapy Dode's cash, as if me and him are big mates again.

— Sorry, mate, too busy at present, I swiftly inform him.

— Eh, what aboot Thursday likesay?

— Thursday's out. How about never? Is never any good for you? I ask curtly, then snap, — Excellent! at the stunned silence on the other end of the line before slamming down the phone. Then I pick it up and dial someone who can be of use, namely my old mate Skreel in Possil and ask him to check out somebody for me.

At an early age I decided that other people were objects to move around, to position, as it were, to obtain the outcome from which I'd derive the optimum satisfaction. I also found that it was better to use charm rather than threats, and that love and affection worked easier than violence. With the former, all you had to do was withdraw it, or threaten to. Of course, some people fuck up your masterplan. Usually it's friends and lovers. My best mate ran away with my money. Renton. A second person who fucked me up was my wife's old man.

I shall get both of the cunts. But right now, it's Skreel I want to speak to, *my* old Weedgie pal. Yes, it's time we caught up, now that I'm back North of the Border permanently. I give the greetings, go through the banter, then get down to business, and Skreel can't quite believe the request. — Ye wahnt me tae find you a lassie that works *whaire?*

— In the ticket office at Ibrox Stadium, I repeat, patiently. — Preferably a shy lassie, vulnerable, quite innocent, maybe who lives at home with her folks. Doesnae matter what she looks like.

The last part makes him even more suspicious. — What the fuck are you up tae, Williamson?

— Can ye dae it?

— Leave it tae me, he snaps emphatically. — Onything else?

— A specky cunt who lives with his ma . . .

— That's easy!

— . . . but who works in a central Glasgow branch of the Clydesdale Bank.

Skreel again asks me to repeat the request, and starts laughing down the blower. — Are you matchmakin?

— In a manner of speaking, I tell him. — Just call me Cupid, I quip, before signing off and digging into my pocket to feel that reassuring wrap of ching.

37

'. . . a politically correct fuck . . .'

Lauren has taken the strop with me big time and I can't find her anywhere. She may have gone back to Stirling. On the plus side, this shows she cares, yes she does. Dianne's relaxed about it, working on her project. Drumming her pencil on her teeth, she considers: — Lauren's an intense wee lassie, but she's still quite young and she'll lighten up soon.

— The day can't come quick enough, I tell her. — She makes me feel like a fucking whore . . . I get the word out and it cuts me in half: I'm thinking about what I agreed with Bobby and his mate Jimmy yesterday. About where I'm going tonight. It's different in the sauna, the extras are up to you, although it's expected that you'll perform at least handjobs, which is as far as I go – my clumsy, unskilled extensions of my poor massage technique. I need the job and I need the money, especially with the Easter break coming up. But going out, up to somebody's hotel room, it's crossing another line I said I wouldn't cross. It's just a drink and a meal, Jimmy said. *Anything you negotiate separately . . . well, that's between you two.*

I head out, done up to the nines, my red-and-black dress under my black Versace overcoat. I'm trying to get out before Dianne sees me, but she does and wolf-whistles. — Hot date, eh?

I smile as enigmatically as I can.

— Dirty, lucky cow, Dianne laughs.

I head out into the street, unused to making progress on heels, and flag down a taxi. I stop about fifty yards away from the plush New Town hotel, I don't like arriving abruptly in a place, I like to savour my arrival, take everything in. It has a grand old Georgian façade but inside it's been gutted and everything is ultra modern. The reception area has huge windows, almost down to the floor. The automatic doors swish open and a doorman in tails nods at me. I can feel my heels clicking across the marble floor as I head to the bar.

I don't want to give away that I'm looking for someone, which I am, in case they ask me who, because I don't know. What does a Basque politician look like? I can never keep cool in situations like these. The barman is this hotel has seen me before, I know it, at the sauna maybe, and he gives me a tense nod. I smile warmly back at him, feeling a flush rising in me, like I've downed a double Scotch too quickly. No, it's much worse than that, I feel totally naked, or like a hustling street-corner tart with a bum-hugging mini and a big pair of thigh-length boots. The escort thing works well though; they don't want their clients upset, the men who use this hotel. If I was just some freelance strumpet I'd be out on my ear by now, probably with a couple of cops standing around.

My client is a prominent Basque nationalist politician who is, ostensibly at any rate, over here to see how the Scottish Parliament works. I was told he would be wearing a blue suit. There are two men at the bar in blue suits, and both of them are looking at me. One has white hair and a good tan, the other dark hair and olive skin. I'm hoping it's the dark-haired, younger one, but I'm expecting that it's the other.

Then, suddenly, I feel a tap on my arm. I turn round and there is this almost stereotypical Spaniard in a blue suit, light blue, which matches his eyes. He's in his fifties, but well preserved. — You are Neekey? he asks hopefully.

— Yes, I say as he kisses my face on each side. — You must be Severiano.

— We have a mutual friend, he smiles, exposing a row of capped teeth.

— And what would his name be? I ask, feeling as if I'm on the set of a Bond movie.

— Jeem, you know Jeem . . .

— Ah yes, Jim.

I was worried that he'd try to take me upstairs there and then, but he orders drinks and says confidentially: — You are very beautiful. A beautiful Scottish girl . . .

— Actually, I'm English? I tell him.

— Oh, he says, obviously disappointed.

214

Of course, he's a Basque. I have to be a politically correct fuck now. — Although I am of Scottish and Irish descent?

— Yes, you have Celtic bones, he says approvingly. So much for Miss Argentina. We make some small talk and finish our drink then head outside into a waiting cab, travelling the short distance to the other side of the New Town, which is no more than a fifteen-minute walk, maybe twenty in my heels. I preserve a saccharine smile in face of an unbridled commentary of approbation. — Beautiful Neekey . . . so beautiful . . .

We have dinner in a restaurant which is rated the current place to go. I have a seafood platter to start, which includes squid, crab, lobster and prawn and is garnished by an imaginative herby lemon sauce. The main course is a nouvelle-cuisine-style roast lamb with spinach and assorted vegetables and for the dessert I enjoy a caramelised orange with rich ice-cream topping. This is washed down with a bottle of Dom Perignon, a fruity, but quite heavy Chardonnay, and two large brandies. Excusing myself, I vomit everything up in the toilets and then brush my teeth, swallow some Milk of Magnesia and gargle with Listerine. The food was excellent, but I never digest anything after seven. Then Severiano calls a taxi and we head back to the hotel.

I'm a bit nervous and rather tipsy with the drink when we get to the room, so I switch on the television where a news programme or documentary shows clichéd scenes of famine in Africa. Severiano takes the complimentary wine from the ice bucket and pours two glasses. He slides off his shoes and eases himself onto the bed, resting on the puffed-up pillows, and grins at me, the smile pitched halfway between endearing little boy and sleazy old pervert. In it, you can see what he's been, and what he will shortly become. — Seet beside me, Neekey, he says patting the space next to him.

For a split second I'm almost tempted to obey, but I click into business mode. — I'll give you a massage and some hand relief. That's as much as I do.

He looks at me sadly, his big Latin eyes almost seem to be welling with tears. — If thees ees how eet ees to be . . . he says and then starts to unzip. His cock bounces out like an enthusiastic puppy. And what happens to enthusiastic pups?

Well, I get started stroking alright, but then that old problem presents itself: I'm simply not very good at handjobs. I'm eating him with my eyes, loving my power over him. His burning eyes contrast with the ice in Simon's, the ice, as they say in that advert, that I'd love to melt, but I feel my wrist going tired with the repetition and it's just not stimulating enough for me. No, it fucking bores me. This transmits and he's looking frustrated, upset and even irritated. However, I like the way that fruit pops up through the implausibly long foreskin and decide that I want to feast on it. I look at him and lick my lips and tell him: — I don't normally do this, but . . .

This Basque man is delighted at the bonus on offer. — Oh, Neekey . . . Neekey, babee . . .

I quickly negotiate a very good price, capitalising on my high-bargaining power right now, and I take him in my mouth, making sure that I generate enough saliva first, to act as a barrier against any acridness. He does have a big foreskin so the chances of his cock tasting foul on the first few licks are high. However, on my initial contact he has a fresh, sharp taste, which makes me think of Spanish onions, but that could just be the ethnocentric association. I might be clumsy at handjobs but I know how to give a blow job alright: even as a child I was always an oral, suck-it-and-see type.

I can tell when he's about to blow, so I pull his reluctant prick from me and he's moaning and begs and pleads but I'm not taking his cum. He's deranged now and my body freezes in a spasm of fear as he gets a grip on me and I'm coldly thinking for a couple of seconds that I'm going to be raped and trying to work out what defensive violence I could employ. Then I realise that all he's doing is rubbing up against me like a dog, his hot breath in my ear muttering something frenzied in Spanish as he shoots his load against my dress.

It wasn't rape, but it wasn't consensual either, and it felt demeaning. I push him away in anger and he's crumbled back onto the bed, full of regret now, apologising profusely. — Oh, Neekey, I am so sorree . . . please forgive me . . . and he's rolling over to his jacket to produce the notes in order to make sure I do exactly that, while I'm heading through to the mirror-walled bathroom, and I'm finding a towel, wetting it and removing his discharge.

Afterwards he's quite charming, still full of apologies, and I calm down and we finish the wine. I'm getting a bit drunk and he asks me if he can take some Polaroids of me in my bra and knickers. I give him the poor-student routine and he produces more cash. I take off the dress and dry the wet patch with the built-in hairdryer, while he gets the camera ready.

He gets me to pose, and I'm glad I've got on the wonderbra, as he takes a couple of snaps. I notice that I look quite cruel and disapproving in the first one, so I try a cheesy smile for the second. I worry about my bony knees in the pictures, and I'm sure I'm getting the start of a pot belly. Warming to his enthusiasm and my own going-to-seed paranoia, I put on a show, demonstrating some supple gymnastics. Big mistake, because Severiano is getting amorous again, and he leaps off the bed and tries to kiss me. I'm worried now, conscious of being semi-naked and thus more vulnerable. Backing away, I raise a palm, which, accompanied by a glacial stare, seems to cool his ardour. — Forgeeve me, Neekey, he pleads, — I am a peeg . . .

I get back into the dress, put the money in my handbag and say a cool, sweet goodbye, leaving him in the room.

I go down the hall to the lifts, experiencing a crazy blend of debasement and elation, both emotions seeming to vie for supremacy. I consciously force myself to think of the money, and the ease of the work, which makes me feel better.

The lift arrrives and inside is a young porter with bad skin and a trolley full of luggage. He nods curtly, and I squeeze in, noting the rash that spreads along his jawline. It's not acne though, as it's only on one side of his face. I realise it's like he's been in a fight, or drunkenly scraped his face against the wall or the pavement. As we descend he looks at me with a guilty smile and I give him what I imagine to be a similar one back. The doors of the lift click open and I'm out, head still racing, confused. I just want to be out of the hotel, extricated from the scene of the crime.

So I'm heading out across the lobby and I can make out, through the glass door ahead, the pavement outside glistening with the street lights and the rain. Then it opens suddenly and a horrible recognition jolts me as in discomfort I see who's coming into the hotel.

It's my fucking tutor, McClymont, and he's walking right towards me, his face moulding into a grin in recognition.

Oh my God.

That face crumples up like a crushed newspaper and a look of sleazy contempt fills his eyes. — Miss Fuller-Smith . . . that voice, harsh yet soft, rasps into my consciousness.

Oh my God. I feel my heartbeat rising and the sound of my soles clicking on the floor seems deafening. An overwhelming sense takes over; it's like every eye in the hotel foyer is on McClymont and me, like we're being framed at the centre of a picture. — Hello, I . . . I try to start, but he's giving me a strange look, like he knows all the secrets of my soul. He looks me up and down and there's a steely glint in the eye of this most decidedly lecherous lecturer. — Join me for a drink, he nods over to the bar, more by way of a command than a request.

I just don't know what to say here. — I can't . . . I ehm . . .

McClymont shakes his head slowly. — I'd be very disappointed if you didn't, Nicola, he says rolling his eyes, and I get the message. Of course, I've handed in my last piece of work, but something still compels me to obey. My attendance record has been poor and he could still fail me on that. If I don't stick it, my dad will cut off my allowance and that'll be me. I make the humiliating U-turn and start to regain my composure and follow him over to the bar, the barman looking coldly at me as McClymont asks what I want to drink.

So I'm sitting at the bar with this dirty old git, and before I can establish the upper hand in asking him what he's doing here, he asks me the same question first. — I was waiting on my boyfriend, I tell him, raising a glass of malt whisky to my lips. This is Simon's doing, and McClymont obviously approves of the choice of drink. — But he called me on my mobile to say that he'd been delayed.

— Oh, how sad, McClymont says.

— What about yourself? Is this a haunt of yours? I ask.

McClymont goes a bit stiff, he obviously feels that I'm either his student, or a woman, or younger than him, or all three, and there-fore he should be the one asking the questions. — I was at a Caledonian Society meeting, he says pompously, — and on my way

home I got caught in a shower and decided to stop here for a drink.
— Do you live near here? he asks.

— No, up Tollcross, I . . . eh . . . I shudder as out of the corner
of my eye I see Severiano the Basque man coming down into the
bar, with another guy in a suit. I turn away, but the guy in the suit,
not the Basque, comes straight over to us. — Angus! he shouts, and
McClymont turns round and grins in recognition. Then he notices
me and raises his eyebrows. — And who is this lovely young lady?

— This is Miss Nicola Fuller-Smith, Rory, a student at the university. Nicola, this is Rory McMaster, MSP.

I shake hands with this mid-forties rugby-bore type.

— Why not come and join us? he says, pointing over at the
Basque, who looks across at me with a twisted grimace.

I try to protest, but McClymont's grabbed our drinks from the
bar and he's taking them across to the table. I try to flash a tense
'I'm sorry' grin at the Basque, who looks harshly at me, as if he's
being set up. I sit down in as chaste a position as this dress allows.
I feel more powerless and objectified here than I ever could fucking
some stranger in front of a DVC lens. — This is Señor Enrico De
Silva, from the Basque regional parliament in Bilbao, McMaster says.
Angus McClymont and Nicola . . . ehm, Fuller-Smith, is that right?

— Yes, I smile meekly, feeling myself shrinking into the chair.
Enrico; he told me that his name was Severiano. He glances at me
in mournful connivance. — Thees young laydee is your partner, no?
he asks McClymont, in some trepidation.

McClymont flushes a little, then lets a smile crinkle his face before
laughing: — No, no, Miss Fuller-Smith is a student of mine.

— What ees eet she is studying? Enrico, or Severiano, or 'the
Basque' asks.

I feel something rise inside me. I am fucking here, you know. I
cut in. — My major is film. But I do Scottish studies as an option.
It's very interesting, you know, I smile in pain, thinking about how
I had that man's penis in my mouth only a few minutes ago.

I excuse myself and get up to go to the toilet, aware that their
eyes are on my arse as I depart, that they'll be talking about me, but
I can't help it, I need space to think. I feel helpless and I don't know
who to call on my mobile. I almost phone Colin at his home, that's

how desperate and irrational I am, but I decide on Simon. — I'm in a bit of an embarrassing jam, Simon, I'm at the Royal Stuart Hotel in the New Town. Could you please help me?

Simon seems quite cold and tetchy, and there's silence for a while, but he eventually says: — I suppose Mo can handle things for a bit. I'll be there presently, he coughs out and hangs up.

Presently? What the fuck does that mean? I retouch my make-up and brush my hair and go back out.

When I return to the table, the three men are sitting in lecherous complicity. They've been talking about me, I know that they have. McClymont, in particular, is pretty drunk. He makes a long-winded rambling statement about something, I think it's about Scotland's prominence within the Union, finishing up with: — . . . and that's exactly what our English friends fail to take into account.

It's not so much his comment but his intense waspish gaze on me that riles. — I don't follow you. Are you making a nationalist or a Unionist point there?

— Just a general one, he says, eyes crinkling.

I reach for my glass of Scotch. — It's funny, but I always thought that 'North Britons' was a term used in irony, in sarcasm, by nationalists in Scotland. I was surprised to find out that it was coined by Unionists who wanted to be accepted as part of the UK, I look across at my Basque and the MSP. — So it was an aspirational term, as no English person has or probably ever will refer to themselves as 'South Britons'. In much the same way as 'Rule Britannia' was written by a Scotsman. It was a plea for an inclusion you can never have, I shake my head sadly.

— Exactly, the MSP says, — that's why we believe . . .

I'm still looking at McClymont as I talk over the politician. — But on the other hand, it's a bit sad that Scotland still hasn't been able to obtain its freedom from the Union. It's been a long time. I mean, look at what the Irish have achieved.

McClymont looks very angry and starts to say something but I catch Simon coming into the hotel foyer and wave in his direction. He's looking smart in his casual jacket and crew-neck top, but somehow darker than before. Yes, it's obvious that he's been on the sunbed. — Ah, Nikki, baby . . . sorry to be late, darling, he says, bending over and kissing me. — Ready to trip the light fantastic? he asks, then he looks at the other men for the first time. His expression is like a spoilt cat that's offered the leftovers, grudging but scalpel-sharp, and he briskly shakes hands with each of them. He's full of commanding bombast, completely in charge of the situation. — Simon Williamson, he spits abruptly, then, softening a little, enquires, — I trust my girlfriend's been in good hands?

The others look at the Basque and break into guilty, nervous smiles. They feel ill at ease in his presence, he's effortlessly intimidated them. But I feel horrible, humiliated and for the first time in a long time, for the first time since that first handjob, just like a whore. Simon helps me on with my coat and I'm so glad to get out of there.

We get into the car and I realise that I'm crying, but the prostituted feeling was fleeting and it's now gone. I know my tears are insincere because I want Simon to take me home, to take me to bed. I want him to think that he's preying on me, when I want him, and I want him tonight. But Simon's unimpressed with the waterworks. — What is it? he asks evenly as he eases the car up Lothian Road.

— I got myself into a situation that freaked me out a bit, I tell him.

Simon contemplates this, then says wearily: — It happens, though, by the tone of his voice, obviously not to him. We pull up outside my place and look up at the sky. It's clear and there are loads of stars. I've never seen that many, not here in the city. Colin once took me down the east coast, to a cottage near Coldingham and the whole sky was a rash of them. Simon looks upwards and says: — The starry heavens above me and the moral law within me.

— Kant . . . I say in a mixture of admiration and consternation, wondering what he's getting at with the moral-law stuff. Does he know what I've been doing? But he just turns around quickly and he looks vaguely insulted. He says nothing but there's an urging look in his eyes. — You used my favourite quote from my favourite philosopher, I explain, — Kant.

— Oh . . . it's a favourite of mine as well, he says, his face breaking into a smile.

— Did you study philosophy? Did you study Kant? I ask him.

— A little, he nods. Then he explains: — It's the old Scottish lad o'pairts tradition. One goes from Smith to Hume to Euro thinkers like Kant, you know, that old Jock Central route.

There's a smugness in his tone that makes me cringe a little as it reminds me of McClymont. I so *not want* to think of him that way, so I venture: — Come upstairs for a coffee, or we could drink some wine together.

Simon glances at his watch. — A coffee would suit best, he says.

We get up the stairs and I'm thanking him again for his intervention, hoping that he'll ask me about it, but he's making light of it. Inside the hallway my heart stops as there's a crack of light from under the door of the living room. — Dianne or Lauren must be up burning the midnight oil, I explain in a whisper, ushering him into my room. He sits down in the chair, then, seeing my CD rack stands up and goes through the collection, his face still inscrutable.

I go and make some coffee and bring two steaming mugs back to the bedroom. When I get back he's sitting on the bed, reading a book of Modern Scottish Poetry, one of the course texts for McClymont's class. I set the cups down on the carpet and sit beside him. He lowers the book and smiles at me.

I want to devour him, but there's something granite-cold in those eyes, it makes me hold off. They are looking through me, into me. Then suddenly they fill with an incredible warmth which would have been inconceivable only a second ago. The glow from them is so strong I'm mesmerised, feeling myself to be formless, of no magnitude or density. All I'm aware of from within me is my hunger for him. Then I hear him say something, a foreign phrase, before both his hands clasp softly onto the sides of my face. He stalls for a while, his abundant, ebony eyes drinking me and then he kisses me: on the forehead, then both cheeks, each kiss strong and soft, exploding with precision, sending thrilling data to the now nebulous core of me.

I'm aware of my body and mind separating, I can feel the force of it seeming to rattle in concert with the central-heating radiator by the side of us. As he strokes my back I think of the red roses, the closed petals opening up, and I fall back onto the bed. It's at this moment that a sudden force of will enters me, and I'm thinking, he's changing me, I have to alter him too, and my arm goes around his head and I'm pulling him onto me and opening my mouth. My hand's clamped around his neck and I'm kissing him so hard our teeth crash together. Then I'm kissing, licking at his eyes, his nose; tasting the salt track from nostril to top lip, then on his cheeks and his mouth again. My hands let go of his head to move to his torso and I'm pulling up his top but he's not raising his arms to assist me, he's sliding the dress off my shoulders. But I'm not moving my arms, because my nails are now digging softly into the muscular flesh of his back, so there's an impasse, he can't get the dress off me either. Then somehow through the back of the dress he's managed, like a master pickpocket, to unhook my bra strap. Moving to the front of me, he pulls the frock and bra away with a violence that makes me let go of his back, because if I don't my dress straps will tear. Then he frees my breasts and everything slows down as he strokes them, handling them with a careful awe, like a kid who's been entrusted with the care of a soft, furry pet.

Once again he's looking deep into my eyes, and with an earnest, almost sad, disappointed look on his face he says: — Looks like it has to be now.

Then he stands up and pulls off his top as I swing my legs off the bed, push up and pull my dress off, then my pants. There's such a throbbing heat between my legs that I almost expect my pubic hair to be aflame. I look up and Simon's stepped out of his trousers and white Calvin Klein underpants and for a split second I'm shocked because it's like he has no penis. It's gone! For that brief moment I almost think he's been emasculated, insanely considering that would explain his reticence in making love, he's no cock! Then I realise that he does have one, oh yes, he most certainly does, it's just that from my angle of vision his cock is pointed, like a loaded gun, straight at me. And I want it. I want it in me now. I don't want to have to say to him we can *make love* later; later I can suck you off, you can lick me, frig me, explore me any way you want, but please let's just get this out of the way, just fuck me right now, right this second, because I am on fire. But he just looks into my eyes and nods, this man fucking well nods at me, like he's read everything

223

I've thought. Then he's on me and in me, filling me, extending me, pushing right up into the centre of me. I gasp then adjust and he grows harder, but I roll us over and we're a twisting, buckling, thrashing mass and I don't know who slows it down but we're savouring it again, and then the velocity of our love pumps up like a force of its own accord and we're pummelling each other in this fucking war of one against one which feels like all against all. For a second I feel like I've defeated us both, me and him; that I want more, more than he can ever give, more than *anyone* can ever give. Then the force wells up like something inside me that seems to have escaped and is running away before it grabs and drags me along with it. I climax in explosive, angry bursts, aware only as my orgasm subsides that I've been shrieking loudly, and I'm thinking that I hope neither Lauren nor Dianne are in as it seems show-offy, ridiculously performative. Simon takes this as permission to do what he needs to do, sweeping back my hair and holding my face to his, forcing me to look into his eyes as he comes so intensely that his orgasm prolongs mine. Then he pulls me into his chest and as I briefly catch his eye I'm almost sure I see a tear. He won't let me move to check and confirm this though, his grip is hard, and anyway, I'm totally spent. We lie in the wreckage of the sweat-drenched bed and all I'm thinking, as I drift off to sleep with his sweat, scent and the musty fried-breakfast smell of our sex in my nostrils, is just how good it feels to get fucked properly.

38

Scam # 18,744

That was a pleasant surprise, as a phone call on the white mobile generally is. Of course, having sex with Nikki was excellent but it was that first-shag syndrome: no matter how good it is there's always a perfunctory element which you can't help but find distasteful. Later, when I got ready to go, she asked me if I was playing mind games. As a comment it was playful rather than heavy, or perhaps the brevitas was designed to conceal something weightier at the same time as it flagged it up. No matter, cause it's like any sport: the most gifted know you always concentrate on your own game rather than the opposition's. So I grinned enigmatically without answering. Fuck liberals wittering on about 'honesty' in relation-ships: what a colossal bore that would be. Nope, relationships are all about power and now is the time to cool it with her. She'll crack before me, I know she will, and it'll be a sweet moment. I tell her that I've changed my number and give her the one for the red phone. The best part is erasing the number from the white mobile and sticking it onto the red.

That was a strange one outside hers when she caught me looking up at the stars. I gave that quote from a Nick Cave song and I thought she called me a cunt. I didn't realise that she was referring to Kant the philosopher. I even called Renton up about it. He reckons that Cave lifted that line verbatim from a Kant book. What the fuck is the world coming to when your favourite lyricists let you down with such shoddy plagiarism?

Yes, the sex was excellent. Her level of fitness, power and supple-ness impresses and means that I'll need to watch the weight and keep those gym visits up. But the buzz I got from it is nothing like the one I get when I nip into Barr's Newsagent at the fit ay the Walk and pick an early edition of the *News*. The story is on page six, with a picture of yours truly and an insert of Chief Constable Roy Lester, a surprisingly youngish guy with a mowser who looks a bit like a Village People extra. I nip next door to Mac's Bar and have a bottle of Beck's as I read eagerly:

LEITH PUBLICAN IN ANTI-DRUGS CRUSADE
Barry Day

One Edinburgh publican has declared war on the ruthless dealers of killer drugs such as Ecstasy, speed, marijuana and heroin. Local man Simon Williamson, the newly installed proprietor of the Port Sunshine Tavern in Leith was disgusted when he caught two young men taking pills in his bar. 'I thought I'd seen everything, but I was shocked. What got me was the openness and audacity of it. This so-called drugs culture is everywhere. It has to be stopped. I've seen what it can do to wreck people's lives. What I'm proposing is more than a campaign, it's a moral crusade. It's about time we businessmen put our money where our mouth is.'

Mr Williamson recently returned to his native Leith after a spell in London. 'Yes, I feel sorry for a lot of youngsters today who haven't got any opportunities outside a life of lawlessness. After all, I'm only human. But there comes a time when you have to say that enough is enough, and take off the kid gloves. Too many people sit around in darkened rooms feeling sorry for themselves . . .'

This is excellent news for one Simon David Williamson. The picture has a grimly serious Williamson at the bar, with the sub-heading: *Drugs menace: Simon Williamson's fears for Edinburgh's youth.* But best of all is the editorial the newspaper carries:

Leith can be proud of principled local businessman, Simon Williamson, whose new initiative signals the start of a grass-roots fightback against the scourge that has infected our communities. Though such problems are international and by no means confined to Edinburgh, local people have a crucial

226

role to play in eradicating them. Mr Williamson typifies the new Leith, progressive and forward-looking but at the same time having a sense of responsibility towards his 'ain folk', particularly the young kids who are prey to the evil dealers whose sole aim is to wreck and destroy young lives. The ne'er-do-wells should remember, though, that Leith's motto is 'persevere' and Simon Williamson is doing just that. The *News* unswervingly supports his campaign.

Wonderful. I down the drink and go back to the flat and chop out a huge line to celebrate. My campaign. They love a trier. I think back to Malcolm McLaren and the Pistols. Well, Malcolm, that worn-out old manual of yours is about to be updated.

I decide to take a cab up to my mother's. When I get there, she's absolutely delighted. — Ah'ma so proud of you! Ma Simon! In-a the *Evening-a News*! After all ah went through with they-sa drugs!

— It's payback time, Ma, I explain, — I know I was far from an angel in the past, but it's time to make amends.

Casting glances of obstinate smugness at my old boy, she quotes from the paper. — All for the young-ah people! Ah knew he'd turn out alright! Ah knew it! She sings in triumph at my father, who looks completely unconvinced by her enthusiasm as he sits impassively watching the racing. He has it on all the time, although nowadays he never bets.

So I might as well just rub the auld fuck's face right in it. — There's a new girlfriend on the scene as well, Mum, and this one's a wee bit special, I tell her and she gives me another hug. — Aw, son . . . ye hear that, Davie?

— Hmmph, grumps the old scoundrel, looking sceptically up at me. A season-ticket holder at Cad Rovers can always spot a kindred face in the Bounders' Stand. Matters not though, Pater, Simon David Williamson is still in pole position. David John Williamson, on the other hand, is a fucked-up, bitter, old has-been who's achieved nothing except give a good and saintly woman a hell of a life for years.

I mind of when I was a kid, I used to really look up to him, and, to be fair, he was kind to me. Took me everywhere, even to his girl-friends' places. Used to bribe me not to tell my ma. Aye, he always treated me well back then. The other kids used to say to me, 'I wish my dad was more like yours.' Then, as soon as I hit puberty and started taking an interest in fanny, that was it. I was a competitor, to be shunned and undermined at every corner. Didn't do him much good, though, because I was on the move by then. — Pick any phantom winners then, Dad? I ask him.

— One or two, he says grudgingly, only making the effort to be civil because she's in the room. If we were alone, he'd just drop the paper, look steadily at me and ask in a low growl, 'What is it you're wantin here?' That would be the extent of the fucking welcome I'd get.

My mother's still going on about my special lady, and I suddenly realise that I'm not really sure as to who I was talking about there, only that I need one in my life. Do I mean Nikki, after last night's adventures, or Alison, who's going to come and work at the bar, or is it this wee fat Weedgie bird I'm thinking about? Probably. I can't seem to see past the scam. If this one comes off it'll be a work of genius. Whoever becomes my new woman, she's got her work cut out with Mama. — As long as she looks after ma laddie, n doesnae try tae take ma bambino away, she purrs in threat at this invisible harlot.

I don't stay long; after all, I've a bar to run. But no sooner do I get out the door when the green mobby goes off and it's Skreel, back with the information. — Ah've went n done the business for ye, he tells me.

I quickly express eternal gratitude, then, wasting no time, I bell the bar leaving Mo and our new employee, the lovely Ali, to cope, muttering something about a licensing trade conference that had slipped my mind. I head straight to Waverley and get onto the Glasgow train. I take the script with me and go over the shooting order of the scenes. We'll do the fuck scenes first, just shoot loads and loads. Start off at the orgy and work back. When I alight at Soapsville, I've an erection which is crushed instantly (and thank God) as I register Skreel waiting for me on the platform. He looks what he is, a man so ravaged by junk that he'll always have that traumatised, wild-eyed bearing. That's the big difference, the look of blighted intensity that separates the working-class ex-addicts from their middle-class counterparts. It's skag plus the culture of poverty and the total lack of experience, or expectation, of anything else. Mind you, Skreel's done better than even the most optimistic fucker could have hoped. The fatal OD of his mate Garbo on high-quality gear fair concentrated his mind. Now he's clean, well, as clean as a soapdodger can be. He asks after Renton, which distresses me, and also about that renowned old east-coast scruff. — Whit aboot Spud, how's he daein?

I shake my head in sombre judgement of a man who was once a friend but can now be described as a barely tolerated acquaintance. No, that's incorrect, he's more like a fuckin adversary. I consider that Murphy should just move here, he's nothing but a displaced Weedgie. — He's no really moved on, Skreel. Ye kin lead a horse tae water, eh. I mean, I've tried my best wi the cunt for years now, I pause, considering this deceit for a second, but, well, I suppose I did within my ability range, — we all have, I add piously.

Skreel's hair is long now, to conceal those flapping, open-taxi-door lugs. His Adam's apple bobs underneath a ratty, sparse goatee. — Shame, an awfay nice boey.

— Spud's Spud, I smile, almost savouring the idiot's demise as I think of how me and Alison . . . no, cancel that. Lesley. I get a strange gnawing feeling in my chest and I have to ask. — Lesley . . . she still kicking around?

Skreel looks at me doubtfully. — Aye, but dinnae go fuckin her about.

I'm surprised that she's still alive. I think the last time I saw her was in Edinburgh, no long after wee Dawn died. Then I heard she was in Glasgow, hanging out with Skreel and Garbo. Then I heard that she'd overdosed. I assumed that she'd gone the same way of Garbo. — She still on the gear?

— Naw, leave her alaine. She's clean, sorted oot. Merrit, wi a wean.

— I'd like to see her again, for old times' sake.

— Ah dunno where she is. Ah saw her one time in the Buchanan Centre. She's straight now, and she's sorted oot, he insists. I can tell he wants to keep me away from Lesley, but fair enough, cause there's bigger considerations.

My man has definitely come through for SDW as well. We get into the Clydesdale and the boy he points out behind the counter of the bank looks perfect: an overweight frame with a slothful bearing, dulled, almost tranquillised eyes sitting behind Elvis Costello glasses. When that hot wee bitch comes on to him the blood will flood from brain to groin and he will be at her beck and call. Aye, Nikki'll have him speaking in tongues as he gratefully cleans out her toilet with his toothbrush. Yep, he's my boy. Or rather, her boy.

She owes me one for getting her out of that mess with those three suits last night. They had that sort of look like they all wanted up her at once. She was a bit fazed then; the cool, posh, sexy wee bird. This work requires bottle, and I hope she's as game as I thought she was.

As for me, I can hardly wait to get started on the girl of my dreams. I'm feeling so Terry-Thomas-on-an-ocean-liner-deck-with-a-rich-widow, I touch under my nose to make sure that I haven't actually sprouted a large mowser. My scam, my movie, my scene.

39

'. . . a question of tits . . .'

Lauren has returned from Stirling. I'm wondering what happened at the parental home to give her such a hearty infusion of live-and-let-live spirit. She almost apologises to me for interfering, while maintaining, of course, that I'm wrong. Thankfully the phone goes and it's Terry, who invites us out for a liquid lunch. I want to go as we're engaging in filmed sex in two days' time, so it might be good to get to know him a little better. It took Lauren a bit of convincing to come out as she wanted to celebrate our new-found unity by having a joint and laughing at the TV news before heading to this affie's lecture. I insisted though, even managed to get her to put on a bit of eyeliner and lippy, and we headed downtown.

Just as I prepare to leave, the phone rings again and this time it's my dad. I'm feeling guilty about my activities the other night at the hotel as he goes on about Will, still in complete denial that a son of his could possibly be queer. What's the difference between his two children? They both suck cocks but his daughter does it for a living. I can't wait to get off the phone and out.

The Business Bar is one of those places which is somewhere between a club and a pub, with a DJ box and a set of decks in the corner. It's mobbed because word of mouth has it that N-Sign's doing a DJ-ing set in here; apparently he's an old pal of Rab's brother Billy and Juice Terry's. Terry introduces us to Billy who's pretty hunky. In fact, looking at Rab, it strikes me that Rab's like a watered-down version of his brother. Billy smiles and shakes our hands in a gesture which seems quite gentlemanly and somewhat old-fashioned without being at all contrived. He looks so fit and wholesome, I confess to an immediate hormonal reaction but he's back behind the bar, too busy to flirt with.

Terry's trying it on with Lauren who is really uncomfortable. At

231

one stage she tells him to keep his hands to himself. — Sorry, doll, Terry throws his hands skywards, — ah'm jist a tactile sort ay gadge but, eh.

She screws her face up and goes to the loo for respite. Terry turns to me and quietly says: — Huv a word wi her. Is she uptight or what? If ever a bird was in need ay a decent length but, eh. Guaranteed.

— She was actually a bit more chilled out until you started, I tease, but I find it so hard to disagree with him. If somebody was fucking Lauren, I'd be indebted to them, because it *would* chill her out. She's too much time on her hands and all she does is get frustrated, anxious, and she starts worrying about crap. Other people's crap.

— Is that no Mattias Jack at that table in the corner? Rab asks Terry.

— Aye, ah mean ya! Billy telt ays eh hud Russell Latapy and Dwight Yorke in here last week. Where there's fitba players there's fanny, Terry grins. — But what aboot this pair, ain't they visions, Rab? He has an arm round my waist now and with the other extended, as if to entice the approaching Lauren in. She's keeping her distance from him though and looks at the clock. — I'm going back up for the lecture.

Rab and I take the hint. We finish our drinks, leaving Terry quaffing happily with Billy at the bar. As we go, I smile: — See you Thursday.

— Cannae wait, Terry cheers.

— Sorry aboot aw that shite, Rab says as we head up the North Bridge passing the new Scotsman Hotel.

Although it's a bright day, there's a strong, rattling wind and it's blasting my hair all over the place. — It was fun, don't keep apologising for your friends, Rab, I know what Terry's like and I think he's brilliant, I tell him, pulling my hair down and trying to stick it behind my ears. I see Lauren, who's chomping a chunky KitKat, brace herself and screw her face up against the wind, curse and blink rapidly as some grit gets in her eye. I'm thinking about how it's the Bergman seminar next and I'm almost tempted not to go as I've made inroads into this assignment. I stick it out and feel guilty at being bored, as Rab and Lauren are totally engrossed. Afterwards, I don't feel like hanging about; Rab gets off and Lauren and I head home where Dianne's made some pasta.

The food is fine, in fact it's excellent, but I'm almost choking on it, because *she's* on the television. Britain's Olympic-medal sensation, as Sue Barker calls her, Carolyn Pavitt. And Carolyn's got the toothy smile and the dyed-blonde hair, which she's letting grow a bit. She's being all cutesy-pie but with that subtle hint of dynamism, which is bringing out the wolf in John Parrott and some guest footballer. I'm hoping Ally McCoist's team thrash the thick, titless cow, and make her look like the imbecile she is. '*A Question of Sport*'? What the fuck does she know about sport? It should be called a question of tits. Where's yours then, darling?

Then I look again. There *are* tits there. In horror I gape at her and realise: she's had them done! Britain's Olympic medallist anti-performance-enhancing titless gymnast cow, has, along with the bottle-blonde hair and the capped teeth, had a set of implants fitted in cynical preparation for a new, media career.

I fucking know the lying hypocritical cow . . .

Dianne heads out to her folks' place that evening. Lauren and I are staying in, watching more television. She's irritated by an arts show where a group of intellectuals discuss the phenomemon of Japanese girl novelists. They display a selection of author dust-jacket photographs which show pretty young girls in almost soft-porn shots. 'But can they write?' one pundit asks. A Professor of Popular Culture, completely serious, barks impatiently, 'I don't see how that's of any importance at all.'

Lauren is fairly enraged by that! We smoke some dope and get the munchies. I have another plate of pasta and Lauren opens a bottle of red wine. It's only a small second bowl I've had but I decide it's sitting too heavy in my stomach and I think of the Polaroid Severiano/Enrico took and I go to the toilet and vomit it up, brushing my teeth and swallowing some Milk of Magnesia to calm the stomach lining.

When I get back I enviously watch Lauren eat her food; she eats so much for a tiny girl. She's how they'd like to be: all these showbiz girls who claim they are not anorexic and eat like horses. We know it's lies though, but not our Lauren. She's always munching away at something. The wine soon goes and a bottle of white gets opened. It's a relaxing night and it's like old times, me and her, on our own, a girls' night in. Then the door goes and Lauren actually jumps in fright then scowls in anger. — Don't answer it, she urges. I shrug, but the knock is persistent.

I get up.

— Oh, Nikki, don't . . . Lauren pleads.

— It might be Dianne, she could have lost her keys or something. I open the door and it's not Dianne of course, it's Simon and he's grinning from ear to ear. He looks so dazzling, so edible, that I have to let him in, although I know he's messing me around. As he comes through into our front room, Lauren's face falls. — I smelt the pasta, he smiles broadly, looking at her near-empty plate. — The Eyetie in me, he beams.

— You can have some if you want? There's plenty left? I tell him as I see Lauren look away.

— Thanks, but I've already eaten, he pats his stomach as his eyes drift over to Lauren. — That's a nice top, he says to her. — Where did you get it?

She looks at him, and for a moment I think she's going to say 'What the fuck do you care', but she mumbles: — It's only from Next. She gets up and takes her plate to the kitchen, then I hear her going straight to her bedroom, and I'm wondering if that's the reaction Simon intended to provoke with his comment.

As if in confirmation, he arches his eyebrows and drops his voice. — Badly needs a makeover that lassie, he sings in soft, impatient conspiracy. — Very pretty girl though. You can see that, even under all the crap she wears. She isnae a lesbian, is she?

— I don't think so, I tell him, nearly laughing.

— Pity, he says thoughtfully, with an almost palpable sense of regret.

I do chortle then, but he stays impassive so I speculate: — I'm always reminded of the opening chapter of George Eliot's *Middlemarch* when I see Lauren.

— Refresh my memory, Simon requests, adding, — I'm quite well read, but I'm not much of a referencer.

— 'Miss Brodie had the kind of beauty which seems to be thrown into relief by poor dress, and seemed to gain the more dignity from her plain garments,' I quote.

Simon seems to consider this, then decides that he's unimpressed. I feel bad about this and hate myself for feeling that way. I should be telling him to fuck off. Why has the approval of this man of dubious character suddenly become so important to me?

— Listen, Nikki, I've a proposition for you, he says gravely.

Now my head's starting to spin. What does he mean? I keep it trifling. — I know all about those kind of propositions, I inform him. — I had a drink with Terry? At dinner time? I don't think he can wait till Thursday.

— Aye, it's a big day, he says thoughtfully, — but no, this is nothing like that. I'd like you to help me, on eh, the fund-raising side of things. It's strictly business.

Strictly business? After the other night? What is he saying here? And then he starts to tell me about this strange plan of his, which sounds so exciting, so intriguing, that I just have to agree.

Sick Boy, for sure.

I know he's trying to play games with my head, the flowers and all that, but that's exactly what I'm trying to do to him. All that intimacy, all that tenderness of the other night has gone. I'm now just a business partner, a porn star. I'm walking through a minefield and I know it but can't stop myself. Fair enough, Sick Boy, I'll play this game for as long as you want. — I met Rab's brother Billy today. He seems nice, I tell him, looking for any reaction.

Simon raises an eyebrow. — Business Birrell, he says. — Funny, I didn't know until the stag that Rab was his brother. You can see the similarity. Aye, I had a bit of a falling out with him years ago, when he'd just opened that Business Bar. I was in with Terry who was in these work overalls. We got a bit pished. I said to Business: 'Boxing, a bit of a bourgeois sport, isn't it?' I was being ironic, but I think it went over his head. Anyway, he barred us, he chuckles, seeming more disdainful than jealous of Rab's brother.

— It's a good spot he's got down there, I contend.

— Aye, but he's just the frontman for it. The Business Bar is owned by the money men behind Billy Birrell, he rasps sourly. — He's just a glorified barman. Ask Terry if you don't believe me.

Simon may not be jealous of Billy but he's certainly jealous of his bar. It has to be said that it is a bit more upmarket than the Port Sunshine.

— Listen, Nikki . . . Simon begins, — about the other night . . . I'd like to take you out properly sometime. I'm away to see my old pal Renton over in Amsterdam on Friday, to do with this fund-raising shit. We're filming Thursday so that'll be a piss-up afterwards. What are you doing tomorrow?

— Nothing, I say a bit too quickly, wanting to add 'fucking you' but refraining. I must stay cool. — Well . . . I was planning to go to the Commonwealth Pool? After I finish my shift at the sauna?

— Brilliant! I love it there, I use the fitness centre as well. We can meet there and I'll take you for a meal after. Is that okay?

It's more than okay. My heart's racing because I've got him now. He's mine, and that means, well, what does it mean? It means it's my film, my gang, my money: it means everything.

He doesn't stay long after that, and Lauren comes back in, heartily relieved at his departure. — What did he want? she asks.

— Oh, he was just giving me some details about the movie? I say, watching her face screw up.

— He really loves himself, that guy, doesn't he?

— Oh for sure. When he wants to have a wank he books into a hotel first, I tell her.

We laugh loudly together for the first time in a long time.

Well, I still don't know him *that* well, but I strongly suspect that self-esteem has never really been too much of a problem for Simon. But it's him and me now; unavoidably, inexorably.

40

Scam # 18,745

It was a cracking meal at Sweet Melindas in Marchmont. We'd met up at the Commie Pool, Nikki so devastating in a red two-piece swimsuit I thought I was going to have some kind of a seizure. Fearing loss of self-control, I threw myself into the swimming and she enthusiastically matched my sixteen lengths, which is about thirty in a normal pool. Then it was a cab round to the restaurant. She looked beyond beautiful, almost ethereal as she glowed from the exercise, it was all I could do to keep my eye on the meter. I think Nikki was a bit miffed at being taken to a neighbourhood rather than city-centre restaurant, but that soon changed when she saw the ambience, service and above all the seafood on offer. I enjoyed a fried squid with Pernod and chive mayonnaise while Nikki was wowed by the fried king scallops with sweet chilli sauce and crème fraiche. I picked a nice Chablis to wash it down, with mouthfuls of that gorgeous home-made bread.

All I can think about is getting her to my place, the image of that perfectly toned body in that red two-piece searing into my brain to the extent that it was difficult to talk, or even think of scamming. And she's not shy at coming forward. In the back seat of the taxi she has my ballot open and her hand slips inside and she eats my face with unnerving ferocity. At one stage the pain of her teeth chewing on my bottom lip is so severe that I almost squeak and push her away.

We stop and pay the cabbie and my flies are still open and as we get in the stair she's unbuckling my belt. I pull her cardigan over her head and lift up her top, whipping her bra off. We're tearing each other apart in the stair and the door opposite mine opens and this paedophile sort of guy who lives with his mother looks out from behind the door and slams it shut. I fish out my keys and open the flat door as Nikki pulls down her black brushed-velvet jeans and my strides fall to the floor as we're in the gaff, kicking the door behind us shut. I remove her jeans and pull down her lacy white pants and I'm slurping on her fanny, which tastes faintly of pool chlorine, enjoying my tongue's exploration, then sucking hard on her clit. I feel her nails digging into my neck, then the side of my face, and it's hard to breathe, but she's forcing me back and she's moving round, me not giving up on that sweet minge but her twisting round to get at my cock. Her tongue hits it with sharp, electric flicks, then she's enclosing it with her mouth. This impasse goes on for a while until we instinctively break, our eyes meet and things turn woozy and slow like a road calamity. We've got our hands all over each other's bodies, mirroring each other's patient, almost forensic, caresses. I'm feeling every muscle, tendon and sinew below her feather-soft skin and I feel her probing me sharply, like my flesh is being slowly taken off the bone.

It hots up and she pins me down with the tremendous power she has in those thighs, which appear so deceptively slight. She's got the end of my cock and she's rubbing it against her bush, then inching it into her. We fuck slowly for a bit until we both get there. Then we stagger to bed and lie on top of my duvet. I reach for the drawer and pull out a wrap of coke. She's reluctant at first but I chop two up and, rolling her over, I dry out the wet hollow of her back at the base of her vertebral column with the corner of the duvet. Almost choking at that beautiful arse in front of me, I put a line on that nook at the bottom of her spine and snort. My finger goes down between her buttocks, over her inverted pout of an arse-hole making her tense a bit, then shoots into her soaked vagina. Then, as the coke rush tears into me like the Norwich train through Hackney Downs, I'm in her again and she's back up on her knees, thrashing, pushing against me. — Snort it . . . I gasp, pointing to the line on the bedside table.

— I don't . . . do . . . that . . . shit . . . she heaves, as she twists back like a snake, skewing onto my cock with ferocious power and magnificent control.

— Get it fuckin up ye, I shout, and she looks round at me with a wrenched leer on her face and says: — Oh, Simon . . . and she's reaching for the note and snorting as I'm fucking her, slowing down to let her hoover up the line, then I'm going as hard at her as I can and my hands are round her thin waist; that arching snake has gone rigid and we're like two parts of a piston and we scream together as we come.

We shagged another couple of times in the night. When the alarm rang, I got up and made a Spanish omelette and put on some Italian coffee. After we had breakfast we fucked again. Nikki headed up town to the uni and I snorted a line, had another double espresso, put some clothes and toiletries into my bag for the Dam, slung it over my shoulder and went to work in hazy exultation.

There's nothing like going into that fucking place to bring you back down. I'm having problems, and I'm trying to work out whether they are of a staffing or plumbing nature. A bit of both, as it seems like there's an old boiler on the verge of exploding. — Amsterdam again? Yuv jist been! It's no oan, Simon, it's just no oan, Mo says, head birling tersely, refusing to meet my eye, as she polishes the bar.

— Morag, I appreciate that I've been a bit demanding of late, but you've got Alison in as extra help for you. It is a *très* crucial business meeting, I tell her, leaving the old battleaxe grumbling away to herself.

It's freezing as I get out to the airport. My flight is predictably delayed and it's early evening by the time I meet Renton round at his pad. There's a bit of an atmosphere at Chez Rents, it's very edgy between him and this Katrin bird, which I (fortunately) don't help by presenting her with some duty-free Calvin Klein perfume. It's okay for third-division fanny. — For you, Katrin, I grin, holding the gaze but meeting only Teutonic steel in her eye. That wee Kraut yin might be some fuck right enough. After a couple of beats the stare softens and she even looks a bit coy. — Why thaaaank yooo . . . she drawls.

Of course, this is all done to wind Renton up, but if he's upset, he's not giving me the satisfaction of showing it. We head out to the Café Thysen, the onanastic ging-ger clicking on his mobby to bell some pal of his whom he wants me to meet. The guy apparently works as a porn distributor across here. Yes, the bastard does have his uses. The idea we've hatched is that we'll set up two bank accounts in Zurich, different banks, one for a general film-account fund, one for production. The instruction to the first bank is that when the general account goes over £5,000, any surplus monies are transferred to the production account in bank numero duo. — The Swiss banks ask no questions, Renton explains, — and using two of them means that the money's practically untraceable. The porn punters here all use them, and some of the big club people.

— Excellent, Rents. Let's sort it out, I tell him. We crack on, but after a while he seems a bit distracted, and I know why. — The lovely Katrin not going to come over and join us for a drink, Mark? I smile as we cross a sloped canal bridge to the pub on the corner.

He mumbles something by way of a reply as we hit the bar.

It's such a beautiful bar as well, an old Dutch brown bar, with wooden floorboards and panelling and huge windows letting in the fading light. I stop to admire the view so that Renton has to get them in. Old habits die hard. — *Mak ik twee beer*, he says to the smiling barmaid.

After a bit, this friend of his turns up, a Dutch guy called Peter Muhren whom he refers to as 'Miz'. Miz is apparently a distributor of what he prefers to call 'adult erotica'. This chappie looks like the term 'sleaze' was invented with him in mind. He's thin, with short, black hair, a wizened face, keen rodent eyes and a dirty, sparse beard. I'll keep my eye on that snidey fucker. As he takes us over to the red-light district, he's blethering twenty to the dozen. — I have a small office in Neuizuids Voorburgwall. From there I distribute videos; from my own production company, friends' stuff, European and American imports to gonzo and even stag stuff if it's well made. If the pussy is hot, the image is sharp and the sex is inventive or enthusiastic enough, then I'll handle it, he says, pulling on a tab. Fucking loathsome greabo.

We head over to the red-light district, and go up a narrow stair-case to his office. There's a glass-partitioned room at the back of it with a huge video-editing suite, a couple of monitors and a console desk. A lot of Miz's work seems to go on here. He explains to me that he imports loads of American DVDs and pirate-edits them, cutting and pasting the scenes to make new films. — It's all in the editing, he says nonchalantly, — that and the packaging. I use my friend's desktop-publishing facility.

Miz's trying to pass himself off as a big shot, but I've seen all this kind of shit before in London. It's impressive enough in the dosh it brings in, but it's hardly challenging. After a while it bores me and I suggest we adjourn for another beer.

We head out, passing the red neon-bordered, glass-fronted hoors' shop windows. I'm starting to recollect things about this place now. — Mind when we first came here when we were sixteen, Rents? I turn to Miz. — We had a shot each at this dirty big hoor. We flipped a coin and Rents went in first; I waited ootside. When it was my turn she goes, 'I hope you are for lasting longer than your friend. He finished so quickly but then he asked me if he could sit here for a while, so I made him a coffee.' So when I gets out, a couple ay hours later, leaving the lassie shagged like she'd had a Japanese bullet train up her . . . I laugh as ol' ginger pubes snorts something about it being as quick as a Japanese bullet train. But I press on, over his pathetic aside. — I sais tae this wanker, 'Did you enjoy your coffee?'

We go on to a club. Rents breezes in, nodding away to everyone like his cock's at least four inches bigger than that skinny white thing which hung out of those ridiculous ginger pubes in the pictures we used to put down the back of bus shelters. Being with him again seems strange. It feels horrifically good, there's no sad-case nostalgia about it, and still not trusting each other gives the enterprise a hell of a buzz.

I have a few bops and a couple of beers, but I'm taking it easy. After a bit Rents pulls me aside, and just like in days gone by, his weakness is, for all his stoical observation of things, when he gets to a critical mass of alcohol, he just can't stop talking. He seems worse than ever, as he tells me he hardly drinks now and seldom does class As. Fortunately for him, you're usually too pished yourself to remember what he said. But not this time, Rent Boy. — It's no workin oot wi Katrin, he tells me. — I'm definitely gaunnae come back over for a bit. I like this scam, it might even work . . . he hesitates for a second. — Begbie's still inside, right?

— For a good few years yet, they tell me.

241

— On a manslaughter charge? Fuck off, Renton scoffs.

I shake my head slowly. — Franco was hardly a model prisoner. The cunt did a few people over inside. And a couple of screws. The key has been flung away, I sweep the back of my hand through the air.

— Good. I'll gie it a go then.

Good news for Simone de Bourgeois, or Simon the soon to be bourgeois here. The night picks up after that as Miz provides some coke which he's procured from these Moroccan fags, one of whom is simpering at me as if I'm interested in his slimy arse. I hit the toilet with the gear and take a line up each hooter.

After a discussion about race and drugs in which Renton accuses *me* of making a racist point, we head through and sit down beside Miz. — Don't do the anti-racist thing with me, Renton, cause I wrote the script. I huvnae got a racist bone in my body, I tell him. I note that Miz is in conversation with a girl who has an outsize nose. It seems to start in the middle of her forehead and end just on top of her chin where a pretty little mouth sits. She seems so fucking . . . I want to make love to her so *crucially*, not talk with Renton who's now gibbering something about cocaine in my ear.

And that lassie with the lovely big conk has vanished and I turn to Miz and ask her who she is, and he says just a friend and I say: — Does she have a boyfriend? Find her. Tell her I fancy her. Tell her I want to fuck her.

He looks all hurt and serious and says: — Hey, that is a good friend of mine you are talking about, man.

I make a transparently insincere apology and, having no sense of irony, he grudgingly accepts it. I get up to look for this girl at the bar but instead I find myself talking to Jill from Bristol. I don't know if she can read, write or drive a tractor, but I reckon that she can bang like an ootside-lavvy door in a gale. I'm subsequently proved correct as we spend most of the night cheerfully doing just that back at her hotel. I call Rents on his mobby and he gives me a sulky, — Where did you get tae?

I inform him that I've met a nice young lady while he can go back home to his nutty bird and enjoy the only kind of fuck he ever gets, one of the head variety. For Katrin, substitute . . . what was that screwball lassie he went out with in the bygone days? . . . Hazel. Yes, the more things change, the more they stay the same.

This Jill's a goer, a totally unpretentious lassie on holiday who does what totally unpretentious lassies on holiday do, and thank fuck. The next morning we go through the stilted motions of swapping phone numbers.

I'm a bit miffed that I don't have any time to freeload a breakfast from her hotel as I have to get to Renton's flat and pick up my holdall. When I get there I half expect to find Rents in a cosy foursome with Miz and the Moroccans, but it's Katrin who answers the door in her dressing gown and lets me in. — Si-mahnn . . . she says in her tenebrously dramatic way.

Renton is up, draped on couch in an orange towelling bathrobe, channel-hopping as usual. The carrot-visuals are overwhelming. — Mark, my mobile's down, can I borrow yours? I just need to text a message off to this hot chick.

He gets up and digs the phone out of his jacket pocket. I punch in the text:

HI DOLLFACE. CAN'T WAIT 2 GET LOOSE ON YOUR PRETTY ASS AGAIN. HOPE PRISON HASN'T SLACKENED IT 2 MUCH. IT'LL BE MINE AGAIN SOON. YOUR OLD CHUM.

I fish out my address book and punch in Franco's number. Message sent. Just call me Cupid.

I quickly say my goodbyes and head round to the station where I catch the airport train just in time. On the train I sweat just in case Renton has taken anything valuable, and check the contents of my bag. My excellent Ronald Morteson sweater's still there. More important, has he seen anything incriminating? I know his mentality, he'll have been through the lot with a fine toothcomb. No, everything still seems to be there.

I get off the flight, into a taxi and down to the pub. Rab's there with a couple of student mates and loads of equipment. Betacams, DVs, 8 mil cameras, a monitor, sound stuff and lighting. He introduces the students as Vince and Grant and I let them upstairs.

Our set is minimalist: a load of mattresses on the floor. As they set up the equipment and the talent starts to file in, the air is crackling with excitement. My heart skips as Nikki dances in, stealing up to me and purring: — How was Amsterdam?

— Excellent, more of which later, I smile, turning to wave at Melanie as she walks in. My second leading lady is a very sexy girl – in the sense of a deep-sea fish supper being *exactly* what you want on occasion – but hardly haute cuisine. She should be beautiful, but economic and social circumstances have made her handle herself differently to Nikki. When I start to think like this, I thank the Lord I've got an Italian mother.

My cast, my crew; and what a bunch they are. Apart from Mel, Gina and Nikki, there's Jayne her sauna-hoor pal, and the Swedish (or is it Norwegian) lassie Ursula, who isn't as good-looking as she sounds, but is a total fuck-machine. There's also Wanda, Mikey's hoor, who looks a bit deranged with her smacked-out eyes, sitting cross-legged in the corner. Myself, Terry and his shagger mates Ronnie and Craig are present. Rab and his student chums are looking a bit uncomfortable.

It becomes evident in rehearsal that I am going to have problems with Terry and his firm. The sex parts they're not too bad at, they get enough practice, but they don't understand the difference between shagging for the camera and making a porn flick. Moreover, the acting is atrocious. Even the most rudimentary lines, and they are very fucking rudimentary indeed, are invariably fluffed. My idea is to build their confidence by starting off with what they can do. So we'll shoot the sex scenes first, starting with the orgy, which is the end scene, but which will give them encouragement, and should help with building a sense of *esprit de corps*.

There are so many basic problems. I've cast Melanie in a teenage role, which should be roughly appropriate to her age. But I'm looking at her arms, with 'Brian' and 'Kevin' tattooed on them. — Melanie, you're supposed to be an innocent virgin. Those tattoos need to be covered up.

She raises her eyes through a fog of Embassy Regal, then has a giggle with Nikki. That Gina's looking around as if she wants to fuck, tear apart, then eat every person in the room. *Très* game. Tis a pity she's a hound.

I slap my hands together for attention. — Righto, folks. C'mon, luvvies, c'mon. Listen! Today is the start of the rest of your lives. What you've done before is stag. Now we're doing a proper adult movie. So the ability to get right into it, to stop and start is crucial. Has everybody learned their lines?

— Yeah, Nikki drawls.

— Suppose, Melanie sniggers.

Terry shrugs, in a manner that tells me that cunt has learned fuck all. I feel my eyes rolling and my head scanning the ceiling for inspiration. It's as well that we're starting with the shagging.

Melanie and Terry are raring to go. The kit comes off unselfconsciously and Rab's mates are busying themselves with the equipment. It *is* weird watching Juice Terry in the buff, as Rab shows me the shot through the Betacam's monitor. I switch on one of the digital video recorders and pull out to get them both in frame. Grant fusses a bit over the lighting, getting burn-out off the shot, and Vince tells us that we're running up on sound. — Action! C'mon, Tez, take your cleaver to that beaver, I say, no that he needs any encouragement in that direction, cause he's straight on her, working her with his fingers and his tongue. I zero in slowly, my intrusive eye on that slurping tongue and that moist gash. She's a bit stiff though, so I stop the action. — You seem a little bit tense, Melanie, love, I observe.

— Ah cannae git intae it wi everybody watching, she complains.

— It's no like back in the pub whin wir aw gaun fir it.

— Well, you'll have to. That's the porn business, darling, I tell her. I watch Nikki looking at them, wanton and animalistic, her sharp wee tongue flicking horn-salt from those slightly cruel lips, and I feel a bit of inspiration. I can read a bitch like a book, and she is hot for action. — Look, a new rule on the set. Either you take off your clothes or you fuck off downstairs, I say, unbuckling my belt.

Rab looks mortified, standing there behind the tripod. He glances at Nikki, then at Gina, who's already peeling off her top. Nikki starts to take hers off as well and I pause for a second to admire the motion of it being pulled over her head. Fuck me, that lassie's well fit. In quite a wholesome, sporty, PE-girl manner, Nikki says to the

245

crew: — C'mon, boys, as she removes her bra and exposes those tanned tits, which look as firm as rocks, sending a strong radar signal to my groin. She unbuttons the skirt and then pulls down her pants and steps out of them to expose a freshly shaved minge.

— Ni-kay . . . I say, involuntarily sounding like Ben Dover in his videos, that appreciative punctuation absolutely essential.

— Ready for action, she pouts and purrs.

Fuck me, this was the lassie I was supposed to meet years ago. We would have ruled the world. Still will.

Concentrate, Simon. I take refuge behind the lens trying to snap into technical mode.

Now Gina's big tits are bouncing around everywhere and Terry's eyes are popping out of his head. Sometimes he distresses me, this sordid appreciation for quantity versus quality.

Poor Rab is still shiteing it, but you can tell that he wants to stay. — I'm just on the creative side . . . my fiancée's having a kid . . . I don't want to do this . . . I want to be a film-maker, not a fuckin porn star!

— Well, the crew can do what they want, but I'm getting into the spirit of it, I announce, taking off my T-shirt and glancing at the wall mirror. The gut doesn't look too bad, the gym and the diet kicking in. I put it on easily, but I lose it easily. Just a fine-tuning of the regime; no fried food, spirits rather than beer, the gym three times a week rather than just once, walking rather than piling into motors, cocaine in and weed out, and yes, back on the cigarettes. The result: the pounds fairly fly off.

Wanda looks up and announces in a smacked-out drawl that the sexiest-looking guys are the ones with their clothes on, which disconcerts me, and the rest of the talent. — See? Yir big wi junky hoors, Rab, Terry says, and Wanda flips him a casual V-sign.

My tactic has worked, though, because soon Terry and Melanie are really going for it and I'm getting horny. Then Nikki comes over to me and says: — I think I'd like to sit on your knee?

I'm almost ready to respond with 'go away, I'm directing' but it comes out as: — Okay, in a low gasp as those delightful buttocks are gracefully lowered onto my thigh. I feel my cock stiffen and bend up into the hollow of her spine as we watch Terry and Mel in action. I must remain focused, remember that I'm in the director's chair. — Lie back, Terry; sit on it, Mel . . .

Discipline.

Mel's sucking on Terry's dick, flicking the end, slurping the shaft and after a bit Terry guides her across the back of the big padded chair . . . Nikki twists a little, easing further back against me . . .

Discipline will ease my hunger . . .

Mel's elbows are on the chair and Terry's slipped one in from behind. Nikki's hair flows down her back, its peachy scent dancing in my nostrils . . . threatening to drench my senses . . .

Discipline will quench my thirst . . .

Now Terry's withdrawing and I cough out some words of encouragement as my hand rests idly on Nikki's thigh, that smooth, unblemished silk-like skin . . .

Discipline will make me stronger . . .

Terry's in again and he and Mel are fucking piston-hard now, Mel setting the pace, thudding back into that dick of his like she's trying to devour it. Terry's got that complacent, dreamy look men have when they're enjoying sex, like it's no big deal. That kind of zoning-off when you're with a tidy bird to stop you from blowing your muck, or when you're with a hound, only then it's in order to keep it up. Basically, though, it's the same fucking thing.

. . . if it doesn't kill me first . . .

I decide to stop the action there. — Cut! Stop, Terry! STOP!

— What the fuck . . . Terry groans.

— Right, Mel, Terry, I want you to try the Reverse Cowgirl, the classic shot we need for a porn movie.

Terry looks over at me and moans: — Ye cannae git a good fuck that wey.

— This isnae aboot you having a good fuck, Terry, it's aboot you *looking as if* you're having a good fuck. Think hireys! Think art!

I briefly glance round to see that the others are sleazing each other up, except Rab and the crew. Gina's looking at me with a predatory smirk on her face. She asks: — When dae we go in?

— I'll tell you, I nod, fully intending, even at this point, that most of her scenes won't survive the edit.

Melanie's got a good frame for the Pope John Paul (as we in

the trade call the Reverse Cowgirl, or RC), light and lithe, but with a bit of power to her. Terry's just lying there, that fine piece of wood he packs enclosed by Melanie who's going up and down on it. His hands grip her waist as he alters the pace and digs a bit more and she starts scowling. — That's the game, Terry, earn your corn. Fuck her! Mel, try to keep your eyes on the camera. Keep looking at the camera. Fuck Terry, but love the lens. Terry's just the fucking prop, just an appendage to your pleasure. You're the star, baby, you're the star . . . Nikki's reached behind and wrapped a hand round my shaft, — . . . and you're beautiful, this is your show . . .

I push Nikki away gently, then, standing up and taking her by the hand, I shout: — Cut! Then I explain to Nikki: — I want you in there, down on Terry's cock. Terry, you're doing great. Now you lick out Mel while Nikki sucks you off.

— Bit ah want tae fuckin come! he moans as Ursula approaches him with towels and he pulls a face before heading to the toilets for a clean-up.

— C'mon, Tel, I shout at him, — don't be so fucking ungrateful. I said you're licking out Mel while Nikki's sucking you off. Aye, it's a hard life right enough.

We get that shot sorted out. Nikki down on Terry's knob makes me feel strangely weird, especially as she seems to be loving it. I'm relieved when it's over and we knock off for lunch, or at least the rest do. Rab and I go over what we've filmed on the monitor. I have to mobby the others because they're just sitting in the fucking pub. Nikki seems to have been drinking, probably needs it for Dutch courage. It's strange but I'm starting to feel that uncomfortable, proprietorial way about her. I'm not happy at the thought of her being done by Lawson on camera. And there's a lot worse to come.

Gina's still whingeing at me. — Me n Ursula n Ronnie n Craig huvnae done nowt yet.

— We introduce each person one at a time, building up to the climax, I tell again. — Patience! I get Terry and Mel back pumping away. — Try it in her arse now, Terry, I say, — c'mon, Lawson, let's see some anal action . . .

My motivating powers aren't really needed here: it's like encouraging Dracula to go for the jugular. Terry pulls Mel from him, lays her out and bends her legs right back over his shoulders. He spits ferociously, working the gob into her arsehole and then edges in slowly. I nod to Nikki and we each take one of Mel's buttocks and we're pulling them apart as Terry pushes in. I've instructed Rab to attend to the position of the cameras so we've one close up on the arse action and one on Mel's face so we can cut between them in the edit.

Melanie's grinding her teeth and grimacing (a required shot for the misogynistic power merchants who 'want to see the bitch suffer') but as she gets into it, and starts finding the space to accommodate him, goes off in that dreamy way (required shot for the lazy transgressive romantic yuppette who's had a hard day at the office and just wants to lie back and enjoy a relaxing butt-fuck). It's so important that the expressions cover all emotional bases. That's what porn is essentially, a social and emotional process. Anybody can do genital interaction . . . Nikki kisses me hard on the lips and she's going down on my cock, and I can see Rab standing by the bar and Gina still looking at him and then looking annoyed and Craig's sucking on Wanda's nipples and I'm thinking that none of them will control me, ever . . . then I realise that there's something missing. — Cut! I shout, as Nikki starts to suck my cock.

— What? Terry's still pumping away. — You're fuckin joking!

Nikki takes my dick out of her mouth and looks up at me.

— Naw, Terry, naw, c'mon. We need tae dae this in the cowgirl position. RAC, Reverse Anal Cowgirl.

— Fuck . . . eh says, but he's pulling oot.

Nikki looks at Terry, then at Mel. — How was that? she asks.

Mel seems happy enough. — It's sair at first, but then ye git intae it. Terry's really good, he always pits it straight in. Some laddies dinnae ken how tae dae it, they batter the bit ay skin, the perineum, and make it really sair n tender. Terry kens how tae pit it straight in, she says.

Terry shrugs proudly. — Experience, that's aw.

— Saughton nights, eh, Tel, I quip, and Rab Birrell laughs at that, and so does that Gina, a lassie with 'Corton Vale Bound' writ large all over her. Warming to the theme, I sing to the tune of

'Summer Nights' from *Grease*: — *But ah-ha, those Saugh-haugh-tin nah-hahts . . . tell me more . . . tell me more . . .*

The laughter rises and even Terry joins in.

Nikki now seems in a businesslike mode though, taking my lead and shedding the horn, anxious to move on. — Listen, Mel, Nikki says, — you know what I found really beautiful, what really turned me on? It was when Terry spat on your arse? And, like, worked it in? Could I do that for you?

— Aye, if ye like, Mel smiles.

Terry's not bothered, but I'm elated. Yes, Nikki's the star here. The lassie has quality. Alex McLeish?

The predators will be circling unless we get her tied down soon, Simon. Think of Agathe, Latapy . . .

I think it's got to happen, Alex. Don't worry, I'm moving on that one. There's a lot going on behind the scenes.

But right now it's back to the coaching as I remind Terry that it's a team game and we need to keep our discipline and our shape. — Mind, Terry, don't shoot your duff up Mel. It's got to be a withdrawal, then a wank off and a cum over her face. Remember the narrative of pornography, our sequential journey: blow jobs, frigging, licking oot, fucking, different positions, anal, double penetration and, finally, the cum shot. Remember that old training-ground routine.

Terry looks a bit doubtful at all of this. — Ah'm no intae shaggin a burd withoot blawin ma muck in her.

— Remember, Terry, this is not sex. This is acting, this is performance. It doesnae matter whether you're enjoying it or not . . .

— Course ah'm enjoyin it, it's the spice ay life, he says.

— . . . cause you and me, we're just cocks. That's all we are. The lassies rule.

In the background I've got Ronnie and Ursula going through a routine and Craig's fucking Wanda, who's lying like a corpse. They're just wallpaper as I'm setting up the main action to the fore.

— Ah'm ready, Terry says, finding wood, as Rab looks inscrutably on. That cunt Grant is holding things up with the light. Then we're ready to go. He nods at Rab, and Vince announces that we're running on sound.

— ACTION!

So we're rolling as Nikki gobs hard on Melanie's arsehole and works it in. Gina sucks Terry's knob and Mel, crablike above, is ready to lower herself onto it. Then just as she descends, the door goes and big Morag comes in. — Simon . . . oh . . . she gulps, her eyes popping out her heid, — . . . it's . . . eh . . . the man fae the *Sunday Mail*'s here. They've a photographer . . . she turns on her heels and heads out, slamming the door.

Sunday fuckin *Mail* . . . photographer . . . what the . . . at the back of my mind I'm thinking that I've a Leith Business Against Drugs meeting tonight, but that's a while yet . . .

Then I hear a terrible scream behind me. I turn to see that Mel's slipped, with her full weight falling on top of Terry.

— AAGGHHH! YA CAHHNNTTT! he wails in agony.

Melanie's up and she's saying: — Aw, Terry, ah'm really sorry, the door went n ah goat a fright n ah slipped . . .

It's Terry's cock; it looks like he's ruptured the fucker. It's crumpled, and it's black and blue and red. He's screaming, and Nikki's phoning an ambulance on her mobby and I'm thinking: the fuckin *Sunday Mail* . . . what the fuck are we going to do if his cock's knackered? He's my leading fucking man . . . — Rab, take charge here, get Terry to the hossy . . .

— But what . . .

— The fucking press are downstairs!

When I get down, there's a young, keen tabloid sleazebag that you can imagine doing the same job in a grubby mac in twenty years' time. — Tony Ross, he extends his hand. I'm shiteing it about the cameraman being here and looking to Mo who's making nonplussed signs back at me. — It's about the Leith Business Against Drugs. We're doing a feature.

— Ah . . . how timely. I'm just on my way to the first meeting, round at the Assembly Halls. Come with me, I urge, anxious to get them out.

— We need shots of the bar, the lensman pouts.

— You can get those any time. Come down to the Assembly Rooms and you can meet the main players, I explain to the journo as I'm heading out the door, forcing him and the flustered cameraman to follow.

But Morag's in pursuit as well, waving me back. — Simon, she hisses, — what's aw this?

— It's a first aid-thing, Mo. Terry's no well. Take charge!

As I head down Constitution Street with the newsmen in tow, I realise I'm early for the meeting but I say to the guy on the door at the Assembly Rooms: — Bummer, I thought it was seven thirty. This Tony Ross guy suggests we go back to the Port Sunshine, but I herd him into Noble's. It gives me the chance to give it the big one about the drugs project, but I'm distracted a bit, worried about Terry's cock and how it's going to hold us back. I excuse myself, slipping outside and belling Rab on the green mobby. It doesn't look good.

Then I take Ross and the photographer back to the Leith Assembly Rooms for the inaugural get-together of our Leith Business Against Drugs organisation. Paul Keramalindous is the main man to network with, a yuppie adman who pushes alcohol for the corporate drug barons trying to keep their share of the market for their products.

Paul stands out here. The others on this Leith Business Against Drugs forum are your classic concerned citizens; namely clueless fuckers who never have had and never will have any drug experience, or will even know anybody who has. There's a couple of old-school Leith shopkeepers, but most represent the incoming blue-chip businesses. There's one guy from the local council, a red-faced alcoholic who ran out of steam twenty years ago and is ploddingly attending graveyard meetings nobody else wants to go to.

Ross asks a few questions, his buddy takes some snaps, but they get bored quickly and depart, not that I can blame them for that. There *is* a fair bit of expertise round the table, but it comes from about three heads here, the rest are beyond gormless. At least they have the sense to remain silent, which ensures that the discussion progresses intelligently. We decide to apply for a wad of cash earmarked by some government department or quango for local education purposes and we're electing a committee to administer these monies and run the business of the group. I've already bonded quite a bit with my Mediterranean-origined mate Keramalindous, and second his nomination for chairman, feeling sure he'll reciprocate with my own preferred role. Yes, I'm happy to be Gordon Brown to his Tony Blair and I set myself into a fiscally prudent, dour Scot mode. — It's a thankless task, but I don't mind being treasurer, I tell the herd of tight faces around the table. Fuck me, if this lot represent the cream of Leith Business, then the port should really worry about the stability of its supposed regeneration. — I mean, I strongly feel that it should be someone in a cash-handling industry. I think it's important with public money that not only is everything above board, but that it's *seen* to be above board.

There's a lot of enthusiastic nods all round.

— Very sensible. I propose Simon for treasurer, Paul says.

It's seconded and carried. After an interminably dull meeting, I take Paul over to Noble's Bar for a drink, managing to shake off the council man, who was hanging around in the hope of being invited. The nips flow quite freely and we get a bit pissed. — That jumper, he asks, — is that a Ronald Morteson?

— It certainly is, I nod in brisk pride, — but note: Shetland lambswool, not Fair Isle.

There's a young, attractive-looking lassie behind the bar and I give her a flashbulb smile. — Not seen your face in here before.

— Nope, I just started last week, she tells me.

We engage in some banter, Paul enthusiastically joining in, without him realising I was initiating all this for his benefit. Unlike in my teen and twenties days, I usually now only make the effort to do a serious chat-up if an obvious financial as well as sexual gain seems likely.

It's closing time too quickly in Noble's so, having established that Paul both likes a bevvy and is a fanny rat, I take him back to the Port Sunshine and open up upstairs for a late drink for the both of us. — That was a smashing bird in the pub back there. I reckon you could be in there, mate.

— I'll show you something better, I tell him. Paul's eyebrow raises involuntarily, giving him away as a total sex case. Good. I nip off into the office and switch on the pub's video security system, making sure there's a blank cassette in. Then I find a tape we shot earlier today and take it through, putting it into the vid below the big bar telly.

Nikki's gorgeous arse fills the screen and we pull away to watch her sucking Terry's knob, as he's lying back licking Mel's fanny, her crouched over him. The corkscrew hair seems to merge with her pubes at one point as she leans back across him. — This is incredible . . . Paul gasps, — you do this here?

— Yeah, we're making a full-length film, I say, as the camera cuts to Nikki going down on Terry's knob in close-up, her hungry eyes devouring the viewer's soul, as surely as her mouth does his knob. She's a fucking total pro, a real star. That was a good shot. — That bird is tidy, eh?

Paul sips at his nip, his eyes bulging out like he's a papillon getting shagged by a Rottweiler. His voice goes thin and wispy. — Yeah . . . who is she? he croaks.

— Her name's Nikki. You'll meet her. She's a good friend, a nice girl, educated, like. A student at the uni, the proper uni, Edinburgh Uni, not Hairy Twat or one of the basket-weaving colleges that got made up back in the eighties.

His eyes hood and a little grin creases over his face. — Does she eh . . . is she . . . I mean, does she do other things?

— I'm sure I could talk her into something, for you.

— That *would* be appreciated, he says, an eyebrow rolling heavenwards.

I start racking out the lines of posh, just to see what this cunt says. — Ching time!

Paul looks at me in that startled, uncomfortable manner like a young bird in one of those gonzo porn movies, just at the point they suddenly realise that they're getting it up the shitter for the first time and the world is potentially watching via the digital video camera and the Internet and it wasn't *quite* what they had in mind. — Do you think we should, eh . . . it, eh, might not be what you'd call appropriate in the circumstances . . . ?

And here's me giving him the 'you love it' routine. If this cunt's not a chinger then I'm Mister Daniel Murphy's fashion consultant. — C'mon, Paul, I smile as I chop up, — dinnae start playin funny fucks. We're businessmen, educated guys. It's not like we're schemies. We know the score, we know where to draw the line, and yes, pun intended, I smile.

— Well . . . I suppose, a discreet little one, he grins, and raises a pensive eyebrow.

— Too right, Paul. As I said, we're not like the underclass, I see some of them in here, mate, I can tell you. We know when to ca' canny. It's just a wee tickle, for Christ's sake.

I snort down a beauty, then Paul shrugs and follows suit. And they are big lines, more lamb's torsos than poodle's legs. I thought the onanist would see the security camera filming him, but obviously not. — Oh . . . that's good gear . . . Paul goes, and his hands are all over the shop and he's gabbing away like fuck, — my boss at the agency, he gets his stuff off the rock. A guy flies out from Botafogo to Madrid then over here. Straight out the guy's arse in a wax seal. I've never had anything like it . . . but this is excellent . . .

It certainly is, old chum. Now, mission accomplished, I decide to draw the night to a close in almost indecent haste. — Righto then, Paul, you'll have to excuse me, buddy, I say, showing him the door. I've got certain things I need to do.

— I fancy carrying on a bit . . . I'm buzzing . . .

— Have to be on your own, Paul, I'm meeting a lady friend, I smile, and Paul nods back with a grin but he can't hide his disappointment that he's been left a bit high and dry. I escort him outside and shake his hand, this poor bastard is wired tae fuck. He waves down a taxi and heads off. I would have let Paul stay but he played his hand too soon. My old man used to habitually use that old line from a Cagney movie, 'never give a sucker an even break', and it turned out to be the best bit of advice he gave me. It's positively cruel to do so. If you let them get away with it, they won't learn. Therefore, in the future, they'll be even more comprehensively done, and by someone more ruthless. Cruel to be kind, as Shaky said. Or was it Nick Lowe?

Paul. What a fool. Introduce that to Nikki, to *my* Nikki? You have to be kidding. Minge like that comes at a premium price and it's too rich for a sad case like that.

I've been thinking about her all day. Some lassies get inside you because it's so hard to nail down exactly what it is about them that ignites you. She's like that; beautiful yes, but capable of showing you something different every time. Contacts or reading glasses. Hair loose and flowing or ponytailed or pigtailed or tied-up. Clothes vampishly designer expensive or sporty casual. Stance and body language warm, then distant. Knows *exactly* what buttons to push in men, does it without even thinking about it. Yes, she's my girl.

41

Leith Will Never Die

Saturday morning, man, n Ali's still asleep so ah heads up tae the library. Ah've been better wi the collies cause ah'm right intae this book, but it still isnae lookin that good, wi me n hur, likes. Ah'm sure somebody's been pittin poison in hur ear. Dinnae ken whether it's her sis or, mair likely, Sick Boy, wi hur workin at that pub now. That sneaky cat jist used ays tae work that scam wi Cousin Dode. Didnae want tae ken eftir that. At least ehs no blabbed tae Franco about Renton's cash but, and probably willnae now cause we've goat stuff oan each other.

At least huvin nae mates hus pure geid ays the chance tae git oan wi ma Leith book. Saturday's a bad day for temptation, wi loads ay cats n drugs around the streets, so ah gits up toon n heads tae the Edinburgh Rooms. That microfiche stuff is weird. Aw that info, aw that history, even if it's selectively written by the top cats tae tell their tales, on one roll ay film. But ah reckon thit thir's other stories thit kin be teased oot.

Leith, 1926, the General Strike. Ye read aw that n what they aw said then, n ye pure see what the Labour Party used tae believe in. Freedom for the ordinary cat. Now it's like 'get the Tories oot' or 'keep the Tories oot', which is jist a nice way ay sayin 'keep us in, man, keep us in, cause we like it here'. Ah takes tons ay notes but, n the time jist whizzes past.

When ah gits back doon the road tae the Port, something's up. Ah bounces intae the flat wi ma notes, aw fill ay cheer. Andy's goat ehs Cabs-away strip oan, and then ah look at Ali, standin thair wi a couple ay bags packed. N aye, it looks like thir playin away awright.
— Whaire ye been? she asks.
— Eh, ah wis jist up the library likes, man, this history ay Leith book, research, ken?

She looks at me like she doesnae believe me and ah want tae sit her doon n likesay pure show her the stuff, but her face is aw sortay strained n guilty. — We're gaun tae ma sister's. Things have been . . . she looks ower at Andy who's got a plastic Luke Skywalker battering a Darth Vader, n she droaps her voice — . . . you know what I'm saying, Danny. Ah wis gaunnae leave ye a note. Ah jist need a bit ay space tae think.

Aw naw, naw, naw, naw, naw. — For how long likes? How long?

— Ah dunno. A few days, she shrugs, takin a drag oan a ciggy. She usually never smokes aroond Andy. She's goat big hooped gold earrings oan n a white jaykit n she looks so good, man, jist so good.

— Ah've no been huvin nowt, ah tell her. — Thir's nowt in muh pockits, ah say, makin a show ay turning them oot. — Ah mean, ah've hud nowt fir yonks, ah'm jist intae ma book.

She just sort ay shakes her heid slowly n picks up the bag. Ah'm gittin nowt fae her, she willnae talk.

— What is it ye need tae think aboot? ah ask. Then ah goes: — It's tae think about him, eh? That's it, eh? Ah sort ay raises ma voice a bit, then ah calms doon cause ah'm no wantin a scene in front ay the wee man. Eh disnae deserve that.

— There is no *him*, Danny, whatever ye think. The problem is you n me. There isnae much you n me either, is there? Yir mates, yir group, now yir book.

It's ma turn tae say nowt now. The wee man looks up at me and ah force a smile.

— You know where I am if ye need me, she says and steps forward n kisses ays oan the cheek. Ah want tae grab her in ma airms n tell her dinnae go, tell her that ah love her n want her tae stay for ever.

But ah say nowt, cause ah jist cannae, ah jist pure cannae. Hell would freeze ower before ah could drag they words oot ay ma mooth n ah want tae say thum so much. It's like . . . it's like ah'm jist physically incapable ah daein it, man.   .

— Show me you can cope on your own, Danny, she whispers, squeezing my hand, — show me you can keep it together.

And wee Andy looks back n smiles n says: — Cheerio, Dad.

N thir away, man, pure gone.

Ah looks oot the windae n sees thum gaun doon the road towards Junction Street. Ah slumps doon in the chair. Zappa, the cat, suddenly jumps up oan the armrest, shittin ays up. Ah stroke ehs fur n ah starts greetin, in dry, tearless sobs, like ah'm huvin some kind ay fit. At one point ah kin hardly breathe. Then ah gits it thegither a bit. — Jist you n me now, gadge, ah tells the cat. — It's easier fir you, Zappa, man, youse cats dinnae git emotionally involved. It's jist yin oan the roof, n that's it, wham bam thank you mam, ah sais tae the boy, then looks intae ehs slitty green eyes. — You're well oot ay it but, man, ah goes, then ah laughs, — ah mean, sorry aboot the nuts n that, out ay order really, but it's fir yir ain good, man, ken. Ah did feel bad but whin ah took ye tae git done but.

The cat opens ehs gob n mews, so ah gits up tae see what's fir nosh. No much fir either *Homo sapiens* or feline, the cupboard's pretty bare. The auld shit tray is minging n aw, and wir oot ay cat litter. — Thanks, man, ah say tae Zappa, — you've helped ays. Instead ay sitting here feelin sorry for masel, cause ay you ah'm forced tae git oot fir cat grub n cat litter. Engage wi the world n that. Ah'll head doon the Kirkgate n mibee git some ay that catnip shit n aw for ye, man, git ye stoned.

Aye, the wee ants are pure diggin in, so ah cannae settle. Ah gits doon the road n hits the Kirkgate n does ma shoap at Kwik Save, comin oot at Queen Vic's statue at the fit ay the Walk. It's busy doon here cause it's a surprisingly mild day fir March. Wee guys hing aboot, playin hip hop oan beat boxes. Wifies and kids munch at sweeties. Loads ay they political cats huv stalls set up, urgin ye tae buy revolutionary papers n that. It's funny though, man, but they political gadges aw seem like they come fae posh hames, students n that. No thit ah'm knockin it, but ah think, it should be the likes ay us that agitate for change, but aw we dae is drugs. No like in the General Strike n that. What happened tae us?

Joey Parke's comin doon the road, n ah catches ehs attention. — Awright, Spud? How goes it? Ye gaun tae the group oan Monday?

— Aye . . . ah tell um. Ah didnae ken wi wir meetin oan Monday.

N poor Parkie gits it aw, man, ah tell um that Ali's away, shi's taken Andy tae her sister's.

— Too bad, mate. But she'll be back, eh?

— Says that it's jist fir a few days, she needs tae sort her heid oot. Wants tae see if ah kin cope oan ma ain. That put ays on a right downer, man, ken? She's working at the pub, Sick Boy's pub n aw. The thing is, man, if ah cope well oan ma ain, then she'll say, 'eh's awright', n leave ays. If ah fuck up, then she'll say, 'look at the state ay that waster', n leave ays. It's lookin pure grim, likesay.

The Parke boy's goat things tae dae so ah gits the litter up tae the Zappa felly and sorts the boy oot wi some grub and a fresh bog. Ah wraps the cat shit n pish n a newspaper n sticks it in a placky bag. Ah sorts um oot wi the catgear, watchin um scratchin that patch ay it oan the flair, then runnin roond in circles n rollin ower, n ah'm thinkin, ah could dae wi some ay thon action, man.

So ah'm oan ma ain in the hoose n totally desperate fir company. Ah starts thinkin thit mibee art kin save the day, so ah git oot the notes ah've taken oan the history book, n read through thum again. My handwritin's no really aw that hoat, ken, so it takes ays a while tae read it aw. Then the door goes n ah think it might be her, come back, thinkin, 'naw, it's silly, Danny Boy, ah cannae go through wi it, ah love ye', so ah open it up aw excited n nup, it's no Ali.

It's as far fae Ali as it's possible tae git.

It's Franco.

— Awright, Spud? Jist came roond fir a fuckin blether, eh.

Ah thoat ah wanted company, any company, but it was really, likesay, *almost* any company ah meant. Ah wis nivir really that keen oan jail tales whin ah wis inside masel. In the hoose, thir a total nightmare. So ah'm tryin, n it's hard wi Franco, tae keep the subject oan other things, like ma history ay Leith book. So ah'm tellin um aboot it. Ah sais tae um that ah should interview the likes ay him aboot Leith. But it's, likesay, ah've, ehm, said the wrong sortay thing tae Franco, cause this cat isnae happy at aw. — What the fuck dae ye mean? You tryin tae take the fuckin pish?

Whoa, whoa, whoa, feral boy. — Naw, Franco, man, naw, it's just that ah want the book tae be aboot the real Leith, ken, aboot some ay the *real* characters. Like you, man. Everybody in Leith kens you.

Franco stiffens up in the chair, but thankfully ah think that eh's deciding that eh's a bit chuffed now.

And ah'm tryin tae git ma point across, crawlin like a cat oan a hoat-tin roof. — Cause it's aw changing, man. Yuv goat the Scottish Office at one end and yuv goat the new Parliament at the other. Embourgeoisement, man, that's what the intellectual cats call it. Ten years' time, there'll be nae gadges like me n you left doon here. Look at Tommy Younger's, man, it's a café-bar now. Jayne's, they call it. Mind some ay the nights, some ay the mornins, we hud thaire!

Franco nods, n ah ken ah'm gittin oan ehs tits, but it's like ah'm nervous n whin ah git nervous ah jist pure talk, man, ah cannae stoap . . . shy ye say nowt, nervous ye jist spraff. — It's like the sabre-toothed tigers, man. They only want cats wi cash in toon, ah mean, look what they're daein tae Dumbiedykes. They want us aw oot in schemes oan the edge ay toon, Franco, ah'm tellin ye, man.

— Fuck off, ah'm gaun tae nae fuckin scheme oot ay toon, eh tells me. — Wis oot at Wester Hailes fir a bit whin me n hur goat thegither. Only one fuckin pub, ya cunt, what the fuck's gaun oan thair?

— Ah but, very soon, Franco, auld Leith will be gone. Look at Tollcross, man, it's a finance centre now. Look at the South Side: a student village. Stockbridge's been yuppiesville for donks, auld Stockeree. Us and Gorgie-Dalry'll soon be the only places left in the inner city for working-class cats, man, and that's just cause ay the fitba clubs. Thank fuck they steyed in toon.

— Ah'm no fuckin workin class, eh says pointin at ehsel, — ah'm a fuckin businessman, eh goes, raisin ehs voice.

— But, Franco, what ah'm sayin is . . .

— You fuckin goat that?

This is like, man, an auld route ah've been doon before that many times. So if thir's one thing ah've learnt it's how tae slip oantae the back fit in such situs. — Aye, sure, man, sure, ah raise they mitts in surrender.

The Beggar Boy seems a bit pacified by this, but eh's one stroppy, uptight gadge, that's fir sure. — Tell ye something else fir nowt, Leith'll nivir fuckin die, eh goes.

The cat's no gittin ma drift here but. — Mibee no Leith, man, but Leith *as we ken it* will, ah tells um, but ah'm no takin it further cause ah ken the score. He goes, 'naw it willnae', ah say, 'aye it will, man, it's dyin already, how will it no', and he'll say, 'cause ah fuckin well sais', and that'll be it.

Eh racks up two big lines ay coke n ah'm mindin ay ma promise tae Ali, but well, ah sais ah'd keep oaf the gear, n tae me that means smack, n ah said ah'd keep oaf base, but no ching, man, nae cat mentioned ching. Also it's Franco, so ye cannae really refuse.

Pure buzzin, we head doon for a beer n ah steer Begbie away fae the Port Sunshine which is easy cause eh ey drinks in Nicol's. Franco gits a text message oan his mobile. Eh stands lookin at it in disbelief. — What's up, Franco, man?

— SOME CUNT'S TRYIN TAE GIT FUCKIN WIDE! eh shrieks, n two lassies wi pushchairs passin us jist aboot shit thir thirsels.

— What's up?

— A fuckin text message . . . it doesnae say whae it wis fae . . . the cat is not amused, eh's fiddlin wi the buttons oan the phone. We get intae the pub n eh's still playin wi the phone as ah git the drinks up fae Charlie fae behind the bar. Begbie's mobile goes off again, n eh answers it, aw cagey this time. — Whae's this?

Thir's a pause n eh lightens up, thank fuck. — Right, Malky. Sound.

Eh switches it oaf n tells me: — Caird school up at Mikey Forrester's. Wi Norrie Hutton, Malky McCarron n that. Lit's git a cairry-oot.

Ah tell um thit ah'm skint, which isnae true, but a caird school wi Begbie means ye pure play until he wins aw yir money, no matter how long it takes the cat. So ah'm no intae that. — Jist come up fir a drink but, ya cunt, eh goes.

Well, ye cannae really refuse so wi hit the offie, n Begbie's still gaun oan aboot Mark Renton n how eh wants tae kill um. Ah'm no happy wi ehs mood, man, n ah'm no that keen oan the likes ay Malky n Norrie n Mikey Forrester. Thir sittin roond the table n thir's loads n loads ay ching oan the go, n boatils ay JD n cans ay beer. Ah bows oot the hand eftir losin thirty quid. — You kin keep pittin the sounds oan, Spud, Begbie goes, but ye cannae really pit oan what ye want, cause he ey pure tells ye. — Pit oan Rod Stewart, ya cunt . . . *every day ah spend ma tahmm . . . drinkin wahnn, feelin fahnnn . . .*

— Dinnae think uv goat any Rod Stewart, Mikey goes. — Used tae huv, bit when she moved oot she took loads ay ma records.

Franco looks at um. — Git thum fuckin back oaf the cunt! Cannae huv a fuckin caird school withoot Rod Stewart. That's what ye dae at a fuckin caird school: git pished, sing Rod Stewart. Ye cannae fuckin beat it, ya cunt!

—Ye see they pictures ay Rod Stewart in the inside ay that CD? Norrie goes. — Eh's done up in drag, like an auld tart in one ay thum. N thir's yin whair eh's dressed up like a poof!

Ah pure mind ay they pictures; Rod Stewart hud ehs hair slicked back, wi a moustache n a pair ay glesses. Ah'm sayin nowt but, cause ah kin see the reaction fae Franco.

— What ur ye fuckin sayin, Norrie?

— It's jist this album, this *Greatest Hits* album. Eh's dressed like a bird in one picture n done up as a poof in another yin.

Begbie's jist shakin. — Whit dae ye mean dressed like a poof! You think Rod Stewart's a fuckin poof? Rod fuckin Stewart? Is that what ye fuckin think?

— Ah dinnae ken if eh's a poof or no, Norrie laughs.

Malky sees the signs n aw. — C'moan, Frank, deal the cairds.

Mikey says: — Rod Stewart's no a poof. Eh shagged that Britt Ekland. Did ye see her in that film wi that Callan boy, the yin thit they filmed up in the Highlands?

Franco's no hearin anything but. Eh says tae Norrie: — So if ye think Rod Stewart's a poof, ye must think thit cunts thit like Rod Stewart are poofs n aw.

— Naw, ah . . . ah'm . . .

It's too late, man, ah look away bit ah hear a crash n some shouts n when ah turn roond ah cannae see Norrie's face, it's like eh's goat a black mask oan.

But it's jist a cowl ay blood cause Franco's went n broke the boatil ay Jack ower ehs heid.

— Aw, Franco, man, thir wis still some nips in that boatil, Mikey moans, as Franco stands up and heads tae the door. Malky's helpin Norrie through tae the bathroom. Ah jist follays Franco oot the door n doon the stair. — Fuckin wide cunt wi ehs snidey remarks, eh goes, starin right at me, but ah'm no lookin at um, ah'm jist thinkin, git tae Nicol's n huv a pint, chill um oot, then pure vanish hame. Ye dinnae want company that bad, man, ye nivir want it that bad.

42

'. . . ruptured his penis . . .'

Poor Terry, it was a bad one alright. We called an ambulance and
they took him straight up to the hospital where they examined
him and told him that he'd ruptured his penis. It was serious, as they
took him straight from casualty up to a ward. — If it responds well,
the doctor said, — then things should be fine. It'll be fully func-
tioning. There can be complications though, but at this stage we
shouldn't be thinking about amputation.

— What . . . Terry said, absolutely terrified, realising that they
didn't give beds away unless it was an emergency.

The doctor looked grimly at him. — That is only the worst-case
scenario, Mr Lawson. But I can't emphasise how serious this is.

— Ah ken it's serious! Ah fuckin well ken that! It's ma cock!

— So you must rest and avoid any strain. The medication we've
given you should prevent you from getting an involuntary erection
while the tissue hopefully repairs itself. This is one of the worst
ruptures I've seen.

— But we wir jist . . .

— This is far more common than you think, the doctor tells him.

Rab's mobile goes and it's Simon. Rab says he's very upset, but
it's obviously because of the problem that this presents for the film
rather than Terry. Even Rab and I are finding it hard to joke.
Eventually he turns to me and says: — I always thought that Terry's
cock would get him into trouble, everybody in the scheme used tae
say that. We never thought that *he* would get *it* into trouble though!

But we just can't find the humour in it. Gina, Ursula, Craig,
Ronnie and Melanie are stunned in disbelief and Mel feels terrible
now that the reality is setting in. — Ah couldnae help it . . .

— It was an accident, I say, rubbing her back. I kiss them all and
head home, where I'm telling Lauren and Dianne the story. Dianne

raises her hand to her mouth and Lauren's little face can barely conceal its glee. She's made some vegetarian lasagne and we sit down to eat.

— So that's put paid to your porn-film plans then, Lauren says, pouring herself a glass of white wine.

It's almost a shame to deflate her, she looks so happy. — Oh no, darling, the show must go on.

— But . . . Lauren looks really distraught at this news.

— Simon's determined, we're still shooting the movie. He'll find a replacement.

Now Lauren explodes with anger. — You're being exploited. How can you! They're using you!

Dianne puts a forkful of food into her mouth and looks at me with a strained expression. She swallows hard and shrugs evenly. — Lauren, this is nothing to do with you. Please calm down.

This is doing my head in. I have to try to make her see through her own neurosis here. — I'm fed up studying film when I've got the opportunity to make one. Why are you getting so het up about it all?

— But it's pornography, Nikki! You're being used!

I let out my breath slowly. — What do you care? I'm not stupid, it's my choice, I tell her.

She looks at me with a quiet, composed rage in her eyes. — You're my friend. I don't know what they've done to you but I'm not going to let them get away with it. What you're doing is against your own sex. You're enslaving and oppressing women everywhere! You study this, Dianne! Tell her, she urges.

Dianne grabs the wooden forks and pulls some more chopped salad onto her plate. — It's a wee bit more complex than that, Lauren. I'm finding out a lot about this as I go along. I don't think porn per se is the real issue. I think it's how we consume.

— No . . . no, it's not, because the people at the top are always men!

Dianne nods in assent as if Lauren's proved the point she wants to make. — Aye, but probably less so in the porn industry than any others. What about girl-on-girl action filmed by women for the consumption of women? Where does that fit in with your paradigm? she asks.

— It's false consciousness, Lauren bleats.

I'm too busy to debate, even if I had the notion. — You're no fun, Lauren, I tell her, rising from the table and picking up my holdall. — Leave the dishes, girls, I'll do them when I get back? I promise. I'm running a little late.

— Where are you going? Lauren asks.

— To my friend's place to practise some lines, I tell her, leaving the sad, frigid little bitch choking on her hang-ups.

She even stands up, but Dianne grabs her wrist and yanks her down, talking to her like she's the child she has evidently become. — Lauren! That's enough! Sit down and eat your food. Come on now.

I hear some noises as I leave and head downstairs and out into the cold. I take the bus to Wester Hailes and Melanie's place. It takes me ages to find her flat. When I get there she's just put her son to bed. We practise our lines, then we practise a little action as well, and I end up staying the night.

Next morning we wait for her mother to come before getting the 32 bus down to Leith. There's a spray of fine rain, which soaks us through by the time we reach the pub. The shaggers are looking somewhat upset and I realise that there's not a camera in sight. Instead a tall, lean man of about thirty-five with curly hair, sideboards and piercing eyes is sitting in a chair.

— This is Derek Connolly, Simon explains to me. — Derek is a professional actor and he's going to coach us. You might have seen him on the box as the Scottish villain in *The Bill*, *Casualty*, *Emmerdale* or *Taggart*.

— Actually, I was an advocate in *Taggart*, Derek says defensively.

We start off doing some role-play exercises, then working on the script. If he's frustrated at our attempts at acting, he doesn't show it. It has me wishing that I'd done more in the university drama groups. Nothing is wasted.

After, I head up to Simon's flat with him and tell him that I was practising with Mel. — Should have invited her up, he says.

But no, that won't do. I'm having him all to myself.

43

Scam # 18,746

Even though it's now spring it's still nippy, and it's not easy to pull myself away from Nikki. Additionally, I'm starting to dread facing Mo and Ali at the pub. I put it off, taking her breakfast, then out to the editing suite in Niddrie where I run off a few copies of the tape of Paul having his fun.

— What's all this about?

— Oh, just a wee bit extra-curricular, I tell her, belling the Leith adman on my green mobile phone. Nikki announces that she has to go to classes, and she'll call me later. I watch her getting ready to go, her arse moving elegantly in that long skirt. It's funny, but in our sickening ladette culture, very few women have the grace to wear a skirt properly these days, so you notice one that does. She pulls on her long hooded coat, zips it up and I can see her dazzling smile even under the fur-trimmed hood as she waves farewell and exits.

I tell Paul to meet me urgently at twelve noon in the Shore Bar down by the Water of Leith. We get there at exactly the same time. Paul looks flustered, but not as much as he will be. I stick an invoice, chequebook and pen in front of him. — Right, Paul, if you'll just countersign this.

— You're keen, he says, pulling on his specs, obviously long-sighted, and then studies the invoice and the chequebook. — Can't this wait . . . what . . . this is the money for the education video . . . where is it going? I haven't seen those invoices. What is this Bananazzurri Films?

I look around the high-ceilinged, solid wood-panelled bar with the huge windows. — It's my film production company. Called after the Banana flats round the corner, where I grew up and with a natty little reference to my Italian roots.

— But . . . why?

— Well, I explain, — Sean Connery called his film production company Fountainbridge Films, after where he grew up. It just seemed a pretty fucking nifty thing to do.

— But what's this got to do with the Leith Business Against Drugs video education project?

— Absolutely nothing. It's to part finance a movie called *Seven Rides for Seven Brothers*. There's some start-up costs. It's an adult entertainment, or if you like, pornographic film.

— But . . . but . . . what the fuck is this! You can't do this! No way! Paul stands up, like he's going to have a go at me. I hadn't bargained for this.

— Look, I'll put the money back once I get my other finances in place, I placatingly explain. — It's business. Sometimes you have to rob Peter to pay Paul, or the other way around, I smile, thinking of the Dutch porn man, Peter Muhren, aka Miz.

Paul gets up and starts to walk out. He stops and points at me.

— If you expect me to sign that you're crazy. And I'll tell you this right now: I'm going to the committee and to the police *and* I'm going to tell them just what a crook you are!

He's being quite loud. Fortunately the bar is still empty. — Funny, I tell him, — I thought you were a cunt that knew the fucking score. I was wrong. I pull out a copy of the video. Your boss might be interested in this, mate. Destroy it if you like, I've got copies. Not just for him; there's one for the *News*, and one for that cunt on the council. It's got you doing that line of ching, and talking about the gear your gaffer gets.

— You're joking . . . he says slowly, looking steadily at me. Then there's a shiver in his eye.

— In a word, no, I say, handing over the cassette. — Take it with you if you don't believe me. In fact, take it anyway. Now sit down.

He seems to consider this for a second or two. Then he flops in crushed obedience into his seat, as a lassie comes over with two big bowls of cappuccino. They know how to make a cappuccino down the Shore. I've a sad feeling that it may go to waste on Paul, as his mind is elsewhere, in fact it's probably already downsizing his taste-buds for prison food. This is way, way far in excess of his biggest nightmare. I don't want him moping around all destroyed though, people will notice and he'll give himself away easily. — Don't go beating yourself up about it. You're not the first cunt to act a bit flash and get stiffed, I say, thinking of Renton, — and you won't be the last. See it as a learning experience. Never trust a schemie with a wad, I wink conspiratorially, — cause it inevitably came oot ay some dippit cunt's pocket. You're the dippit cunt, I tell him, pointing the finger. — But you'll emerge stronger, I guarantee it.

— What gives you the right to do this to *me*? he pleads.

— You've just answered your own question, mate. Think about it. Now if you'd be so kind as to fuck off, I've business to attend to. I mean, have your cappuccino first, they make great cappuccinos here.

But no, he leaves it, and I think of how I'm trying to cut back on the drugs of the millennium: caffeine and cocaine. Yet as he staggers off, broken, into his car and back to suburbia, a career hanging in the balance, I take his coffee and, as I sit watching the circling, squawking gulls, I think, yes, Leith is the place to be. How could I have stood it so long in dirty, drab London?

There's been a bit of a bonus with Derek Connolly, the actor. He and his bird Samantha are into playing the part of the brother who wants straight sex and gets seduced in the B & B. So we hire a scabbo place down the Links. Rab protests about his college work but, after a bit of cajoling, I've got him down with Vince, Grant and the riggings and DV cameras. We do a quick bit of guerrilla filming of the straight-shagging sequence with the seduction part, and the results are very good. If you count the incomplete orgy, I've 'done' two brothers from the seven.

I head back to my pub to look in on the troops. It's pretty busy. I check Begbie, his face set in hunter-killer mode, and that Larry heading in through the side door, so I decide to visit Terry before I go to Glasgow with Nikki. Mo's doing her nut about being left on her ain again. Ali comes in, looking rough. I tell Morag it's just the way things are and I'm off to Glasgow to examine expansion potential. — Expansion? Glasgow? What ye talkin aboot!

— A Leith theme-pub chain. Take the Port Sunshine franchise through west, then down south. I look around at the decaying slum. — Export the brand, I laugh. — Notting Hill, Islington, Camden

270

Town, Manchester city centre, Leeds . . . they'll fall like dominoes!

— It's no oan, Simon, she says shaking her heid, but I'm trying to get offski before Begbie and his bum-chum clock me. But it's too late, he sees me and he's over.

— No steyin fir a fuckin peeve? he more or less commands.

— I'd love to, Frank, but I'm visiting a sick buddy in the hossy before catching a train through to Glasgow. Bell me on the mobby in the week and we'll hook up for a gargle.

— Aye . . . what's your fuckin number again?

I spit out the green number and Begbie punches it into his phone, obviously noting that it's not the one that the text message came from. — Is that the only mobile you've fuckin goat?

— No, I've another one for business. Why? I enquire. Actually, I've three mobiles, but the ones for chicks are nobody's business but mine.

— Ah goat a fuckin text message fae some cunt tryin tae git wide. It wis like oan an abroad number. Didnae work whin ah called it back.

— Aw aye? Abusive phone calls, eh? You'll be getting stalked next, Franco, I joke.

— What's that fuckin well supposed tae mean? Begbie glowers.

I feel my blood run cold and I'd almost forgotten the sheer depth of the man's paranoia. — It's a joke, Frank, lighten up, buddy, for fuck sakes, I quip, closing my fist and making a matey but flimsy contact with his shoulder.

There's a pause of about two seconds, which seems about ten minutes, as I see a huge black hole opening up and my life spilling into it. Then, just when I think I've taken too much licence, he seems to calm down, and he even makes a joke himself. — Nae cunt's fuckin stalkin me, every cunt's keepin oot ma fuckin road it seems. Ma so-called fuckin mates n aw, he says, now looking at me hopeful and hard.

— Like ah sais, Frank, we'll hook up in the week. I've been a bit busy recently, learning the ropes here, but I'll be in the clear soon, I tell him.

That Larry looks at me with a sly grin. — Ah've heard thit yuv been busy oan other things n aw, mate.

A cold nick tweaks my spine as I wonder who's been blabbing, but I nod enigmatically and head off, smiling at Franco and Larry. As I go, I turn to Morag. — A beer for the boys Mo, on my tab. Cheers, chaps! I sing, and when I'm out of sight I fairly skip up the Walk, legs as light as a child's, delighted to have extricated myself from the mess in the bar.

44

'. . . record-breakers . . .'

It must be the company I'm keeping, but I find myself starting to think like a local. Life is sweet; it's a warm spring day so there's a bounce in my step and I take some builders' wolf whistles with a casual, snooty contempt, feeling like a nasty, hot, arrogant bitch. I can do it wholeheartedly now that the coursework is over. I'm heading through the increasingly tourist-clogged city streets to get up to the hospital to see Terry. Poor Terry.

The air has a cold, fresh sting, but with a jumper on it's not unpleasant. I realise that I really am enjoying myself with the movie. Surprisingly, not so much the sex. I'm up for it but it's never as good as I anticipate. It's too much like work, too much like playing to the camera, and because of that it's often dull and uncomfortable. Sometimes you feel like those record-breakers, that one hundred people in a mini sort of shit, and Simon's stop-starting seems to go beyond the needs of the film, it's like a way he exercises power over us. But the main thing is being part of something, being involved, that's what makes you feel alive.

Yesterday we shot the castle scene, one of the potentially most difficult, down at Tantallon in North Berwick. Simon had a joiner friend make up a pair of false stocks. He got Ronnie with his glasses on and Ursula done up to the nines in a short white skirt and T-shirt, showing the blonde hair and sunbed tan to best effect. Early morning we filmed Ronnie getting on a tour bus, with her stalking him. Then we headed down to the bus station. The bus to North Berwick was almost empty. We filmed Ronnie inside sitting down, looking a nerd with glasses, notebook and camera. Rab was outside in the back of a van driven by Craig, shooting the exteriors.

Inside the bus we shot Ursula saying to Ronnie: — Mind if I sit here? I am from Sweden.

Ronnie's had the most benefit from the acting lessons, and Derek reckons he's a natural. — Not at all, he explained. — I'm exploring old castles.

Then we did the stocks scene, where he sees her and she explains that she's stuck. That's when he can't help but take her from behind. Thus the third brother bites the dust.

As I get up to the ward, I note that the arguments between Rab and Terry haven't stopped just because Terry's laid up. I think Rab is secretly enjoying Terry's predicament, although Terry himself seems in better spirits now. His bedside locker is piled up with fruit, which you can tell won't be eaten, and all sorts of tinned foods and take-away cartons. There's a frame around his hips which bulges out under the bedclothes to protect his damaged penis. — This fascinates me. Is it in plaster? Or a splint? Or what? I ask him.

— Naw, it's just like a bandage.

Simon breezes in looking around the hospital like it's a piece of property he's just purchased. It's warm in here and his jersey is off, not tied to his waist in the conventional sense, but around his neck like a toff cricketer. He smiles at me, then turns to the patient, — So, how are they treating you, Terry?

— Thir's some barry nurses in here, tell ye that, but it's fuckin killing ays. Whenever I get a stiffer it's agony.

— Ah thoat they gied ye some medicine tae stoap ye gitting hard, like, Rab speculates.

— That kind ay stuff might work on the likes ay you, Birrell, but thir's nae wey anything kin stoap me gittin hard. The doc's worried n aw, eh says tae me, you've goat tae stoap gittin a fuckin root oan or it's no gaunnae heal.

Simon looks glumly at him, dispatching some bad news. — We can't put back the shooting now, Terry. We'll need to find a stand-in. Sorry, mate.

— You'll never find anybody tae replace me, Terry says to us in a matter-of-fact way, beyond arrogance, just what he saw as a wholly neutral appraisal.

— Well, the shooting's going great, Simon enthuses. — Ronnie and Ursula were brilliant yesterday, and Derek and his girlfriend were great in the lift.

Terry contemplates Simon, obviously determined to deflate him.
— By the way, Sicky, what huv ye goat that jumper roond yir
shoodirs fir, like a poof?

Responding with a tetchy, icy look, Simon rubs the lambswool
between thumb and forefinger. — This is a Ronald Morteson sweater.
If you knew anything at all about clothes, then you would understand what that means and why I choose to wear it in this manner.
Anyway, he looks at me, then back to Terry. — I'm glad that you're
okay and that things are on the mend. Nikki, we have business to
attend to.

— We certainly do, I smile.

And Rab looks daggers at Simon, dying to ask where we're going
but his chance is gone as we leave together and head downtown to
the station and the Glasgow train.

On the train Simon's briefing me about our intended prey, and it
all seems exciting but at the same time strangely worrying that we're
putting all this effort into tracking this guy. As he describes him, I
can see our man. Simon, in his clipped delivery, done without irony,
makes me feel that we're MI5. — A nae-mates, stay-at-home-type, a
model-railway enthusiast, who's slightly overweight. There's a breed
whose parents try to keep them at home, either consciously or subcon-
sciously, by making them unattractive to the opposite sex by forcing
them to eat implausibly large and disgustingly frequent meals. In this
case our subject also has some rather bad skin, caused by the kind
of rampant seventies-style acne which modern diet and skin-care
products have all but eradicated. You still see one or two East European
footballers, on the telly and that, with that kind of pallor, but it's very
rare here in the West, even in Glasgow. Our boy must be a tradi-
tionalist. What we need from him is a list of customers; names, addresses
and account numbers. Just one printout, or better still on disc.

— What if he doesn't fancy me? I ask him.

— If he doesn't fancy you he's a fag, it's that simple. And if that
proves to be the case I'm on him, he says, his face breaking into a
smile. — I can do queen if I have to, he grins wholesomely, — the
flirty bit that is, his face twists in distaste, — not the sex.

— What you say is rubbish though, not every straight man fancies
me, I shake my head.

— Of course they do, or they're gay or in denial or . . .

— Or what?

His face creases in an even broader grin. I see the crow's-feet spread. But he really does look Italian, there's such character in that face. — Stop fishing.

— Or what? I urge.

— Or don't want to mix business with pleasure.

— Hasn't stopped you, I smile.

Simon pulls an exaggeratedly sad face. — That's my point. I'm powerless to resist you and he will be too, mark my words. Then he says softly: — I believe in you, Nikki.

I know what he intended with his words and they have the desired effect. I'm raring to go. And we get off the train and find the pub and I see him at the bar alone, the man of my sweaty little persecution nightmares. Simon nods, then vanishes, as I swallow my pride and make my move.

45

Easy Rider

My heid's, likesay, well fucked; basically cause ah got oot oan the Lou Reed n took a few jellies tae come doon, so ah wisnae thinkin right when Chizzie the Beast phoned ays. Never thought much ay the cat, a bad gadge really, but eh sort ay latched oantae ays in jail. Didnae ken eh wis oot. Thing wis ah wis desperate for company n Chizzie hud the name ay this hoarse which wis a tip thit came fae a mate called Marcel, whae never gies oot a loser. So Benny at Slateford takes the bet and we go back tae the cabin cruiser tae watch our boy, the 8–1 outsider, Snow Black, romp hame at Haydock in the 2.45.

Ah couldnae believe it, man. Right fae the off our boy makes the runnin. By the halfway stage eh's way oot oan ehs ain. A couple ay other gee-gees narrow it a bit ower the last furlong, but our boy's cruisin, pure cruisin. In fact, it's the maist one-sided race ah've ivir seen. No that we're moanin or nowt like that, man, we are very far fae complainin. Wir gaun: — YEEAAAHHHSSSS!!! n wir in a big hug under the telly in the bar n ah suddenly freeze fir a second, thinkin aboot whae else's been in they airms n how they must huv felt. Ah pulls away makin the excuse thit ah'm gaunnae hit the bar n git in mair drinks tae celebrate. In ma pocket, as ah'm diggin oot the notes, ah find some mair ah they jellies.

When wi git back intae the cream cookies, Benny's face is tripping him. — Hot tip, eh grumbles.

— Too true, catboy, ah smile.

— Goat tae keep yir eyes n ears open, eh, Chizzie grins. — Luck ay the draw, chavvy. Win some, lose some.

N it's the best feelin ever, man, cause ah'm oan four fuckin grand, man, and Chizzie's on eight n a half. Four grand! Ah'm gaunnae take Ali n Andy oan hoaliday, Disneyland, Gay Paree! Nice one,

Marcel, and aye, nice one, Chizzie, fir sharin it wi ays, it hus tae be said!

Wi go back tae the boozer and down a few beers tae celebrate, then decide tae hit the toon. Ah want tae dump the Chisholm felly as soon as, but the gadge's done awright by ays, n ah owe um, so it seems right tae tag along fir a bit. We're waiting on a taxi, or a bus even, but nowt's doin; Scottish man, just totally Scottish Fitba Association in the passenger-cairryin motorised road-vehicle stakes. Chizzie then disappears intae the car park ay S&N Breweries. Ah thoat eh wis jist gaun tae take a slash, but eftir a bit a blue Sierra pulls up and who should be at the wheel but the cat-beast known as Gary Chisholm.

— You carriage awaits, chavvy, Chizzie says, gold tooth glintin like a tiger's fang.

— Eh aye . . . ah go, climbin in . . . N ah suppose, man, they politician cats say it's a classless society, so it disnae really matter whose motor ye take. Everything fir everybody, ken?

— Goat tae git intae toon n git a lash oan fir the witchin hour, ya cunt, eh goes, n eh breks intae this weird high laugh which could jist sortay tear strips ay flesh oaf ay ye.

We leave the motor in Johnston Terrace and bounce round tae the Mile and hit upstairs at Deacon's. Nod tae a few faces whae've jist come fae the Court. Eftir a bit the beer's gaun for ays, ah jist cannot take it much now, ah wis eywis mair ay an other-drugs cat.

Chizzie starts talking about old acquaintances: jail boys, wideos n the like. It's no the kind ay conversation ah like, man, cause it's always, likesay, the damaged cats eh minds ay. Ah goes tae the lavvy n ah'm thinkin aboot this money in ma poakit, man, thit wi this money ah could pure git a lassie, n fir some reason ah buy a packet ay spunkbags fae the machine n poakit thum. Ah feel the jellies, burnin a hole in they troosers, man. They're gittin necked soon.

Whin ah gits back oot ah sees thit Chizzie's thinkin along the same lines as me, n that makes ays nervous. — Gantin oan a fuckin shag, eh, eh tells ays. Then eh explains: — This is a good time fir the fanny, between four n six. Ye git they fucked-up slags thit've been oan the pish aw eftirnin n dinnae ken whaire they are. Well, Chizzie's oan the prowl.

And right now, ye dinnae huv tae look very far. Thir's this lassie wi red hair in the bar. Her white leggings are aw stretched n baggy, like the elasticity's gone and they seem tae have what looks like a lump of shite in them. She is just totally pished, man, like ye widnae go near her, but fuck, Chizzie's straight ower. Eh buys her a drink, says something and she comes ower tae sit wi us. — Awright, pal? she asks ays. — Ah'm Cass, she sais. Fuckin hell, this lassie's sortay a near-jakey. She's laughing loudly, n she pills her face close up tae mine, n her hand rests briefly oan ma baws then settles intae a grip oan ma thigh. This big, rid face, aw bloated n flushed wi alcohol is right next tae mine, n ur teeth ur aw yellaw n rotten. Mind you, ma teeth ur shite, n, thinkin aboot it ma face is probably like hers wi the drink, cause Chizzie's gittin that Belisha beacon wey n aw. Ah dinnae git a rid kip whin ah drink but, cause wi me it jist sortay drains oot aw the colour n ah pure go white. She's made a bit ay an effort, cause she's goat loads ay eyeliner n lippy oan, n she's asking us what star signs we are and aw that kinday bird stuff.

But she's mingin, man; she really has shat herself.

Well, ah'm pretty like bleary-eyed because naw, ah'm no much ay an alcohol cat these days. That heavy, sludgy beer, man. Chizzie's takin control but, n ushering us oot ay the pub and we're back up tae Johnston Terrace n intae the nicked car again. Chizzie nearly reverses back intae this parked motor but sorts it oot n wir drivin doon the cobblestones tae Holyrood Park as darkness starts tae faw.

This lassie's sortay well dodgy, likes. She's been swearin fir the USSR n now she's exposing ehr ginger pubes n climbin ower us fae the back intae the front seat, sortay sittin between us. Chizzie curses cause she's oan the gearstick n eh cannae git it n wi make a racket fir a bit gaun doonhill. — Look at this then, ya cunts! Whae wants thir fuckin hole then? she roars at us. Ah mean, ah've no hud it offay Ali in yonks, but ye'd need tae be nutty tae go near this burd.

Chizzie laughs and nearly crashes the motor intae the big black gates ay Holyrood Park, but eh swerves in time n wir in. Eh pills up n wi git oot intae the park. Ah looks around at the big hill ay Arthur's Seat. Thirs load ay buildin work gaun oan behind us. Some sortay government gig, fir the votin n the Parliament n aw that, likesay. It's goat a wee bit nippy wi the sun gaun doon.

— Whaire we gaun, she slurs once in a while, as wi follay Chizzie roond tae the back ay the site. Wi git behind this big fence, away fae the road n facin the hill. Thir's naebody roond, though ye kin hear ower the waw thit thir's still builders workin overtime, but they cannae see us.

— Findin somewhaire cool tae perty, eh, Chizzie winks. It's gittin a bit dark now. Ah finds a jelly in ma poakit n neck it, pure through nerves, man, pure through nerves.

— It's time you goat the fuckin message now, hen, Chizzie laughs, n the radge jist unzips ehs flies n pills it oot, likesay ehs cock, a fat rubbery thing. Other gadges' cocks look pure ugly, man. — Hi, you, c'moan, eh says tae this lassie, wi real menace in ehs voice, — git thum roond that.

The radge lassie sort ay looks a bit puzzled; it's like she's realising for the first time what it's aw aboot. But then she shrugs aw hard n gits oan her knees and starts sucking oan Chizzie's dick. Chizzie just stands and looks bored. After a minute or so, he's gaun: — Fuckin rubbish. Dinnae even ken how tae dae it, eh sais. Then eh looks ower at me wi a grin n goes: — Ah'm gaunnae have tae teach this daft slag how tae suck cock here, Spud.

He stoaps n grabs her hair n pulls her ower tae they taped up piles ay bricks. — Awright . . . ah'm comin . . . ah'm fuckin comin, she screams, hittin ehs wrist.

Eh's right oot ay order here. — Chill oot, Chizzie! Fuck sakes, ah shout, but the jelly's kickin in n ma voice jist sortay tails away.

— Shut yir fuckihn mooth, Chizzie snaps at ehr, ignorin me, n she looks aw that petulant wey back at um. Eh forces hur back onto ehr knees by the side ay the bricks. — Stand up oan that, Spud, eh says. Ah'm pretty wasted now so ah jist climbs up ontae the bricks.

— Right, Chizzie goes, — git yir fuckihn knob oot.

— Aye, right! Git tae . . . fuu . . . ah slur as the Dynamic Earth Dome pure sortay shifts fae the side ay ma vision . . . then ah starts laughin ma heid oaf.

— Aye, yuh fuckin crappin bastard, the radge lassie shouts at ays, n her face is aw nasty, man, like it wis me thit wis pillin hur hair n ah nivir did nowt.

— Naw . . . it's no likesay that, ah goes, — ah'm jist tryin tae be pals, likesay . . .

Chizzie's laughin n shoutin: — Goan, ya cunt! Ah'm jist tryin tae fuckin well prove a point tae this fuckin hing-oot here . . .

The lassie's sort ay loast it n ah'm losin it. — Raymond sais tae me, ye'll be able tae git the bairn back, the lassie mumbles, drunk, in a world ay her ain, like me . . .

— Moan, you, ya cunt, Chizzie goes as ah look at ehs weird face n start sniggerin like a daft wee laddie as eh sortay unzips ays n takes ma dick oot. Ah cannae feel a thing but Chizzie's goat a hud ah ma knob. Chizzie! Eh looks doon at this lassie. — See, burds n blow jobs? eh says back at ays. — Nivir met one whae could dae it right. Then eh's back tae hur. — You fuckin well pey attention here because this is the best fuckin education yill ivir git, eh goes, n turns tae me again. — That's fuckin birds for ye. It's like ye eywis think birds kin cook cause ay yir ma, bit while thir awright wi simple food, ye nivir lit thum near anything that needs imagination or . . . subtlety. How is it aw the best chefs are gadges, likes oan telly n that? Same wi blow jobs. Maist ay thum jist cram it intae thir mooths and suck, gaun up n doon oan it, like thir tryin tae make a fanny oot ay thir mooth. Whin ah wis oan the beasts' wing a boy showed ays how it wis done . . . first ye run yir tongue the length ay the cock . . . n eh grabs ma cock n starts lickin it . . . disnae take ye long in Spud's case . . . huh huh huh . . .

Dynamic Earth . . . it's supposed tae be barry in thaire.

— Cheeky bastard, ah gasp as ehs cauld tongue traces lighly along ma pure sensitive penile skin . . . Chizzie's soundin like a *Blue Peter* presenter or Fanny Craddock or something . . . the place is spinnin n it's gittin dark . . .

— Dae it, slaagg! Chizzie hisses, and ah think thit eh means me fir a bit, but it's the bird, n she's started followin his lead, takin the end ay ehs cock intae her mooth.

— Better . . . better, eh goes, — then ye have a flick at the heid . . . gittin nice n firm here, chavvy . . .

Ah wis n aw, but ah felt nowt. Jist nowt . . .

N ah hear Chizzie n ah'm thinkin aboot that boy thit won the Oscar, when eh goes 'ah'm the king ay the world' aw cause eh'd made this film fir the pictures that wis sortay a bit long, ah thoat, cause ah saw it last summer n that, n ah think ay Sick Boy, n ah bet ye eh does that kind ay thing in ehs mirror, goes like 'ah'm the king ay the world' . . . n Chizzie's gaun oan . . . — . . . then ye start takin it in yir mooth, gently . . . gently does it . . . it needs fuckin subtlety . . . it's no a fuckin contest tae see how much ye kin cram intae yir mooth . . . keep the tongue workin . . . loll it roond the length ay the cock . . . better . . . beh-tur . . .

— Aw fuck, Chizzie man, ah gasp, ma stomach feeling weak, looking at Chizzie's nasty face around ma cock n if ever thir's a face thit ye dinnae want roond yir cock, ever, it's that yin n ah sortay realise fir the first time whit's gaun oan here n ah pill oot . . .

Ehs eyes glare n eh looks at ays, then doon at the jakey lassie whae's still suckin oan ehs cock. — See that! he sais aw victoriously.

— Hud the cunt gaun thaire . . . whoa . . .

— It was jist thit ah wis fawin oaf the bricks . . . the bricks . . . ah telt um.

But now ah'm lookin at everthin through a sortay thin watery porridge as Chizzie grabs her heid violently. — Now it's time tae increase the pace, now it's time tae suck . . . suck . . . SUCK, YA FUCKIN HOOR! N ehs fuckin violently at her mooth, fuckin her heid, forcin it right down into her throat n daein a ranting race commentary: — And it's Chizzie on the final furlong, eh's givin the fuckin slag a good seein tae and it's Chizzie . . . WHOOAAAAHHHH!!!!!

Eh hus her ginger mane in a vice-like grip, thrustin ehs groin intae ehr face, then eh withdraws, leaving hur gagging on his spunk and chokin, coughin n wiping ehr mooth. Eh nods ower tae her.

— Congradulations, you've just graduated fae the Chizzie School of Sex.

That wisnae right, man, naw, naw, naw, so ah sortay stagger forward n ah'm doon oan ma knees beside this lassie. — It's okay, likes, ah say, comforting her, n it's like wi baith sortay need that, man, the two ay us, ken. N she suddenly says: — The baith ay yis then, they baith ay yis ya bastards, n shi sortay starts mashin at ma groin n ah'm no gittin hard so ah start kissin her oan the mooth n ah'm gaun: — Awright . . . awright, n ah've goat her leggings and pants off. Ah pull at them tae shake loose that dry lump ay shite, sortay like a broon golfbaw, and then ah finger her fanny n ah'm gittin hard. Ah'm strugglin a bit tae git the flunky oot ay packet n oan ma cock but ah huv tae . . . huv tae . . . huv tae . . . thir's sticky, vile-smelling globules ay sortay congealed fanny-goo dripping fae her, ken, n ma knob goes in easy. Ah kin hear um, the Chizzie cat; mockin and sneerin while aw this is gaun oan n she's sortay growlin back at him n ah feel as if ah'm no really there. Ah'm sortay ridin her fir a bit, but it's crap, it's no like ah thought it would be n how am a such a mug tae even think it would be like what it is wi Ali n ah'm angry, man, angry at masel n she's screamin, sortay mockin, gaun: — C'moan, you! Fuckin harder! Is that aw yuv fuckin well goat! N ah keep thrustin till ah blaw muh muck intae the bag ah'm wrapped roond . . .

Ah rolls oaf n tries tae pill ma breeks up, wi the flunky still roond ma cock. Now Chizzie's doon at her and eh grabs her n pushes her ower ontae her front n hacks up some phelm from ehs throat and she's gaun: — What the fuck . . . ? but ehs sookin some snot doon fae the back ay ehs nose, mixin up a swirlin cocktail in ehs mooth. Then eh droaps it ontae hur shite-encrusted arsehole. Chizzie's positive, in the sortay medical sense ay the word, just but, jist in that scenario likesay, cause in sortay real life, that is one negative gadge, ken, so eh doesnae bother wi a spunkbag. Ah'm sortay assuming that eh kens or thinks she might be n aw but eh's probably jist no bothered cause eh's fuckin her hard up the erse. Yir no meant tae dae it that wey, yir meant tae start oaf slow . . . no thit me n Ali dae that or dae *anything* now . . . but she's jist groanin and greetin soft tears, lookin like a bloated beached whale or seal that jist cannae struggle intae the water.

When eh finishes, eh gits oaf hur n wipes ehs shite-covered cock oan a clean part ay hur white leggings.

She's rolls roond, her face aw rid n snotters are runnin oot her nose n she shouts: — Yuh fucken bastard! as she pills the leggings oan.

— Shut the fuck up! Chizzie snaps, punchin ehr right in the face. It makes a snappin sound n ah jist go aw tense n paralysed, even wi the jellies n the drink, like it wis me eh hit. Then she lits oot this high squeal as he gies hur a boot that nearly knocks her tit inside oot.

Ah find ma voice at that cause that's like, fucked, man. — Hi, c'moan tae fuck, Chizzie . . . ah say, — that's ootay order.

— Ah'll tell what's ootay order, chavvy, eh says pointin doon at hur, as she sits sobbing quietly, massaging hur tit, — dirty slags that need a fuckin wash! Well, here's a fuckin wash fir ye!

Then eh jist starts pishin in hur hair, likesay dirty auld stale lager urine, man. N she disnae move or nowt like that, jist sits thair greetin. She looks that pathetic, man, so wretched, no like a human bein, and ah'm sortay thinkin, is that likesay how people see me, whin ah'm like really fucked up n that? This solitary jogger, aw in whites, runs past us, looks, then turns quickly away withoot brekin ehs stride. Ah kin hear the boys fae the buildin site shoutin at each other. Chizzie's a nasty cat awright, everybody kens that. Anyone whae'd dae what he did . . . but Chizzie's done ehs time for that. Peyed ehs debt tae society n aw that. What dae they see when they look at me bein wi him but?

N it hits ays, man; it hits ays thit ah'm a nasty bastard n aw. But it's sortay like ah dinnae huv the kind ay . . . malevolence, man, the malevolence tae be sae sortay . . . contrived aboot it. Like maist people in this world, ma nastiness is like a kind ay passive nastiness, a sortay nastiness by omission, by no daein anything cause ah dinnae really care aboot anyone strongly enough tae sortay intervene, except the people ah really ken. Why kin ah no care fir everybody like ah care fir the people ah ken? Chizzie, well, eh's a dangerous radge to pal aboot with, but eh was a mate in the jail n eh phoned ehs up wi the tip n that has tae likesay count for something . . . cause ah'm takin Andy n Ali to Disneyland n everythin'll be jist hunky-dory again n it's really aw cause ay Chizzie . . .

We head off, me n Chizzie, crossin the park at the Abbeyhill exit, tae hit another pub. Wir leaving the daft lassie tae her misery and sortay degradation n ah look back at hur, cause she's whaire ah'm gaun, man, ah ken that, once Ali chucks ays that's it, end of . . . n she awready hus really, so mibee it is . . . but naw, cause ah've goat money n ah'm gittin back proper wi her n ah've goat the Leith book n wir gaun tae Disneyland, man . . .

Wir staggerin aroond fir a bit n wi gits in this pub. Ah sortay tells Chizzie thit eh wis oot ay order n eh turns tae ays n says: — Dinnae huv any sympathy wi they cunts. That's your problem, Spud, yir too nice tae cunts. Cunts like you think thit if every cunt likes aw they fuckin refugees n that, then everything pans oot awright, bit it disnae work that wey. Ken how, chavvy? Ehs face is inches fae mine, but ah kin still barely focus oan it. — Ken how? Cause they take the fuckin pish, that's how. Mark ma fuckin words.

Ah'm half-cut, oot ay ma boax n thir's a wad in ma pockit. But thir's something in Chizzie's face that annoys ays. It's no really anything tae dae wi what ehs been saying or what eh's done tae that woman or nowt like that. Ah sortay work it oot n it's the wey eh kind ay raises ehs eyebrows n stares at ye then throws ehs heid back. Ah ken that ah'm gaunnae punch the cat, a good couple ay minutes before ah do. That couple ay minutes is spent winding him up, soas that him n ah both sortay ken what's comin.

Then ah pure swing at um, n ah think ah've missed cause ah felt nowt n ma hand or airm, but ah see blood comin fae ehs nose n hear shouts roond the bar.

Chizzie's pit ehs hands ower ehs face eftir ma blow, then ehs up, oan ehs feet n eh's picked up the gless n the beer spills. Ah'm up n aw, n eh's swung at ays n missed n the barman's shouting at us. Chizzie's droaped the gless but eh's screamin: — OOTSIDE!

N ah'm heading oot but ah stoap n think; ah'm no gaun oot wi Chizzie, no way, man, so ah stoap at the door n let him go oot first. When he's oot ah shut the pub door behind um n ah snib it loaked. Chizzie's trying tae kick it in, tae git back intae ays, but the two barmen are over, n thir openin the door n shouting at um tae git the fuck away. Chizzie tries tae git in but the boy grabs um so Chizzie punches the cat. The boy n Chizzie are swedgein n the other boy grabs me and throws me oot. N it's now sortay Chizzie and me against the boys fae the pub, which is sortay easy for the pub gadges because ah'm drunk n jellied n Chizzie's drunk n besides ah cannae really fight. So we take a bit ay a doing n then they go back in, leaving us aw battered n groaning in the street.

Wir walkin apart fae each other shouting and cursing one another up the road and then wi sortay make up n try tae cairry oan drinking.

Wi dinnae git served in any pubs but, except this real rat-hole where they let any radge in, no matter how pished n battered n bloodied they are n eftir a bit ah sortay black oot, n whin ah wake up ah realise thit ah've lost Chizzie. Ah git up, go tae the door n ah'm in Abbeyhill somewhere n ah cannae dae nowt but press oan.

— ALISON! A-LI-SAWWNN . . . ah hear a shout as wee bairns playin in the street ay the Abbeyhill Colonies look at ays aw wary like, n ah slip n faw doon a few steps n haul masel up oan the banister. The shout goes up again n ah realise fir the first time thit it's comin fae me.

Ah stagger doon intae Rossie Place, passin the big red tenements oan the wey tae Easter Road n ah'm still shoutin, it's like ah've goat two brains, one's thinkin, the other's shoutin.

Two lassies in Hibs tops pass by n one goes: — Shut up, ya radge.

— Ah'm gaun tae Disneyland, ah tell thum.

— Ah think yir awready thaire, pal, one ay them says back.

46

Scam # 18,747

Nikki is a goddess. I've been watching her; she knows how to play people, how to make them feel special. For example, she doesn't ask you if you fancy a fag, she says, 'Would you like to smoke a cigarette with me?' Or, 'Shall we drink some wine together?' and it's always red, never white wine. That marks out a class bird from a bad Manchester perm from Fife or Essex with her white-wine farts. 'Shall I make some tea for us both?' or 'I'd really like to listen to some Beatles with you. Norwegian Wood. That would be grey-ayt.' Or, 'Why don't we choose some new clothes?'

In our financing scam she's doing better than me, and I'm just starting to worry about my lack of progress. At least the filming's going better, although I had the dubious honour of shooting Mikey Forrester getting a blow job from Wanda in the lifts at Martello Court last night. Brian Cullen, an old mate from Leith, is doing the security for Edinburgh's biggest tower, Martello Court that is, not Mikey's skinny cock. Still, that's the brother number four satisfied.

The scam's been worrying me, but thankfully my prayers are answered as Skreel comes through on the blower. — Awright there, ma man, he says as I stifle a sneeze to avoid expelling the big line of posh I've just snorted back. These days most of the shit seems to settle in my cavities and sinuses. When I blow my beak I get more in my hanky than my lungs. It makes me want to wash up my snot. My nose is fucked, I need the pipe.

— Skreel. I was jist thinking about ye, ma auld mucker. Just saying to this pal ay mine: Skreel, ma mate through in Glasgow, he's the boy. Never lets me down. Any news then, bud? Eh?

— What the fuck ur you oan, Sick Boey?

— Is it totally obvious? I snigger. That's ching for ye. I'm in league with Satan on a fucked-up, slow and expensive trip to hell.

— Isnae hauf. Onywey, the lassie ye wahnt is called Shirley Duncan. She's a fat wee bird, steys wi her maw doon in Govanhill. Nae boyfriends. Shy type. Her n her pals usually drink in the All Bar One on a Friday after work. She'll be there the night.

What a human being that Gleswegian is. — I'll meet you in Sammy Dow's at six.

— Done n dusted, big man.

I'm clad in Armani jacket and slacks with the lambswool Ronald Morteson sweater underneath. My shoes are Gucci. Unfortunately, I can't find a decent pair of socks in my drawer so I'm forced to put on Adidas white sports efforts with the sick towelling effect. I have to get rid of them and find a Sock Shop up the Waverley before I get on the train or I'm fucked.

I buy a pair of navy thin efforts, and think about keeping the Adidas for Skreel, but he might take it the wrong way. Just before boarding the train I'm checking the messages on my mobile. Renton tells me he's back in Scotland. The cunt is well paranoid alright. Won't even tell me where he's staying, presumably in case I spill the beans to one of François' associates. I'll find out soon enough.

I call Malmaison in Glasgow, thinking that if I book into somewhere expensive, it'll make me double-determined to pull.

Off the train and into Sammy's and Skreel's standing at the bar. I realise that it's been about four years. I try not to wince when he intros me as Sick Boy to another couple of Weedgie tinkers present. — Sick Boy here's an Embra man, Skreel laughs, — a wee bit ay a contradiction that, but there ye go.

Weedgies. If you take away their knives and teach them personal hygiene, they'd make excellent pets. Skreel's in the chair though, and he's done the business, so I'm perfectly prepared to snack on humble pie right now, and let him go through the wind-ups, in anticipation of the big meal to follow. — Anyway, whaire's this wee bird? I drop my voice, and start singing, like a cartoon I saw once, I think it was Catnip out of *Herman & Catnip*: — *I'm in de moood for luff* . . .

— Ah dinnae even wahnt tae know aboot the scam yir tryin tae pill here, ya bastirt, Skreel smiles, which means he most certainly *does* want to know. The envelope I thrust into his pocket silences him.

— One day I'll tell ye, but no quite yet, I say with a starkly cold finality.

We exit and head across George Square through the dull drizzle, into Merchant City as the Weedgies hilariously call this tarted-up part of their doss. A polisman stops a jakey for drinking and tells him to put his can away. What bullshit. If Glasgow was serious about operating a zero-tolerance-of-jakeys scheme, they might as well just put the entire city population on cattle trucks and transport them all up to the Highlands.

I tell Skreel this, and he tells me that he'd stab me if I wasn't his mate.

I tell him I expected nothing less.

It's your classic All Bar One, could be anywhere. And the lack of character in such places seems to suck any out of its customers. It's an Ikea showroom where people go to get drunk with colleagues when their office has shut down and hopefully find somebody who's pissed or desperate enough to take them home and fuck them. I spy a sea of bad Manchester perms; more than you'd get in the Arndale Centre on a Saturday.

We get up to the bar and Skreel points out Shirley Duncan to me, leaving me with a jaunty, — Good luck.

Well, hello, baby. I would have guessed that she was the one straight away. She's there with two other lassies, one of whom is awright, the other a bit of a hound. But my lassie in question, my Shirley, is more than a few pounds overweight. One thing I agree with Renton on is the repulsiveness of fat. You can't put a decent spin on it, it's a socially strangulating deformity, which hints at greed and lack of self-control, and let's face it, mental illness. In a woman, that is: in a man it can show a bit of character and a *joie de vivre*.

I'd say she's late teens or early twenties (that's another thing about fat, the more of it, the less age becomes of any import) and is dressed by a domineering mother. 'That 1950s retard's dress of cheap material I picked up in the market looks awfay nice oan ye, hen.' I stand at the bar nursing a JD and Coke and wait for her friend, the hound, to come over. I flash her a smile and she reciprocates, sweeping the fringe from her eyes, her expression plastic coy. But this starlet is fooling nobody that she's not desperate for the real column inches that count in the audition to the next stage of this great 'I'm alive, honest' game we must all now play.

— Is it always so busy through here this early on a Friday? I ask her, as Sting sings about being an Englishman in New York.

— Aw aye, that's Glesca, she says. — So where are you from?

Oh, this is such easy work. If only it was her instead of Fat Girl Gross over there. — Just Edinburgh, through on business, but I thought I'd grab a drink before heading back. You just finished work?

— Aye, just a while ago.

I introduce myself to this lassie, who is called Estelle. She offers to buy me a drink. I insist upon buying her one. She tells me she's got friends, so being a proper Edinburgh gentleman, I buy the round.

The lassie's impressed, and ain't it just obvious why. — Is that a Ronald Morteson jersey, she asks, feeling the wool quality. I just smile in ambiguous affirmation. — I thought it was! She gives me that couthie, evaluating look that you never really in see in Edinburgh or London women unless they're twice her age. *I'm a Leither in soap-dodger-land, oh, oh . . .*

As I get over with the drinks, I ascertain that they're all quite pished, even Shirley Duncan. Estelle looks at me and turns to Marilyn, the other lassie present. — She's in the mood tae snare a bear, she giggles, coughing out some of her drink.

— Did it go doon the wrong hole, I smile, catching Shirley Duncan's eye, and getting a traumatised look back. She's certainly the ugly sister of the three.

— Funny, it usually goes *up* the wrong hole wi her, Marilyn laughs and Estelle nudges her. I try to curb my natural instinct to fire into that Marilyn, and even Estelle would do in an emergency, but this is business.

Shirley looks embarrassed, yes, she's definitely the odd one out in this company. — What sort of work are you in, Simon, she asks timidly.

— Oh, PR. Advertising mainly. I moved back up to Edinburgh from London recently to set up some projects here.

— What sort of clients dae ye work with?

— Film, television, that sort of thing, I say. I keep chewing the shit and more drinks come over and I see their three faces with the blotches on them getting bigger and redder as the alcohol rapidly fires through the system, flashing them like beacons, as the hormones shoot all over the place. Aye, it's like a Vegas sign which says: COCK PLEASE.

And I just know that that fuckin Estelle; I could have her singing on her back for her supper in six months' time down in King's Cross if I gave her the full treatment. Aw aye, there's some chickies you just smell damage off-of, some you know that bad daddy or step-daddy's left some psychic scar tissue that just cannae be healed, and that while it might be dormant like a social eczema for a while, it's just waiting to erupt. It's just there in the eyes, that blighted, wounded aspect, manifesting itself in the need to give a destructive love to an evil force, and to keep giving it until it consumes them. Chicks like that, their whole life is underscored by abuse, and, make no mistake, they have been programmed to hunt their next abuser down just as relentlessly as the predator seeks them.

The night sprawls up to Klatty's and I'm peeling away from Estelle and Marilyn, all over Shirley Duncan, to their complete shock and to hers. She's fat and fresh and I feel like a stoat and a social worker combined and soon we're kissing and heading out and up towards Malmaison. She's saying: — I've only done this once before . . .

As we get into the bed I grit my teeth and think of the scam. I'm as hard as fuck and my hands are all over her heavy breasts, up and down those flabby thighs and across that lunar landscape of an arse. No sooner am I in than she's off. For control purposes, I opt not to shoot into the rubber but give a false grunt and let my body hold a rigid stretch with a spazzy pelvic thrust to simulate ejaculation.

I consider that this is the first time I've ever faked an orgasm. It felt quite satisfying.

When the morning light spills in, the extent of my sacrifice becomes apparent, causing me to feel nauseous. Then she gets out of bed saying: — I've got to go, I'm working this morning.

— What? I ask, a bit concerned. — Do you work when Rangers aren't at home?

— Oh no, I don't work at Ibrox. I finished there last week. My new job's in a travel agent's.

— You don . . .

— That was so lovely last night, Simon. I'll call you! I have to hurry, and she's out the door and I'm lying there, raped by a fat minger, thanks to that cunt Skreel's incompetence!

I have the hotel breakfast and head self-loathingly towards Queen Street, calling Skreel on his mobile. He's protesting innocence, but that soapy cunt's set me up, I know it. — Ah didnae know, big man. Never mind, hing oot wi her, n she'll be able tae tell ye if onybody else works there.

— Hmmph, I click the phone off, hoping Nikki's doing better than me.

47

'. . . the Ubiquitous Chip . . .'

I'm sore and tired. Mel and I had to do the boxing-ring scene with Craig. At least I didn't have to fuck him afterwards. The script had been changed, that was the first thing that we noticed as we met up down at a boxing club in Leith on a cold morning. Rab was setting up the camera, and he came across to me. — You shouldnae dae this, it wisnae in our script.

I don't respond to him, but I do approach Simon. — What's this in aid of? 'Jimmy pulls out an eighteen-inch dildo, which has a penis head at each end. It has ruled measurements down its length.'

— Aye, he says, as he gestures Mel over, — I felt we needed more tension between the girls before the big lesbo love scene. It was all too soft, too sisterly, too cosy. I felt it'd work best if there was an edge to the characters. They both want exclusive rights on Tam's cock, see?

I look at Mel and she strokes my arm. — It'll be alright.

But it's not an easy scene to do. Melanie and I are on all fours in the boxing ring and the dildo is between us, up us. We have to force back into each other, the one with the most of dildo enclosed when our arse cheeks touch is the winner and gets fucked by Craig. Worse is the way Simon's set this up; he's brought in people to cheer, from the pub where they watched Terry's old stag films.

It feels different. For the first time since I started this, I feel as if I'm being used, I feel dehumanised, like an object as those ugly men from the pub surround the ring, their faces contorted as they bay and scream. At one point I feel the tears rolling down my face. Simon's encouragement, — C'mon, Nikki, c'mon, baby . . . you're the best . . . soo sexy . . . is fucking irritating me, making me feel worse. I feel myself drying out and tensing up. I pray for him to just shut up. Whatever he says, I keep hearing other words in his head: *in Britain we like to see people getting fucked.* After countless retakes, Mel and I collapse into each other's arms. I feel sore, raw and diminished. — Take a break, girls. We have enough hot stuff for the edit, Simon says.

Mel as the 'winner' goes through her performance with Craig. Simon puts his arm on my shoulder. It feels like slime. — Don't touch me, I tell him, brushing it off. When Mel's done the two of us head off together, to the Botanic Gardens, where we skin up and watch men of all ages pass us by, trying to decide whether they watch pornography or not. Then we play Ys or boxer shorts, horse or hamster-hung, trying to judge the quality inside the underpants. And we become louder and stoned, more mocking and abrasive and, gaining a displaced measure of revenge, thus we heal ourselves.

Simon calls round at the flat later. — You did really well, Nikki, that was such a demanding scene.

— It hurt me, I tell him tersely, — it was sore.

Simon looks at me like he's going to burst into tears himself. — I'm sorry . . . I didn't know it would be like that . . . it was that mob that came along, those cunts from Terry's stag club . . . I collapse into his arms. — You did so well, Nikki, but I'll never put you through something like that again.

— Promise, I ask, looking up at him, loving the feeling of arms round me, feeling so small now.

— Promise, he says.

— Anyway, I tell him, — I suppose that's brother number five satisfied.

— What about the other thing? Simon asks, and I explain that it's all in hand.

Because I knew that he would call. After work, he took me out for a meal in a place called the Ubiquitous Chip. I insisted it was there, as I liked the sound of it. Simon, Terry and the others in Edinburgh seem contemptuous of Glasgow and its inhabitants, but I'd been through here a couple of times clubbing with some people from the university and, as a neutral, I find it more atmospheric, friendly and vital than Edinburgh.

The Chip was our second date. On our first, in O'Neill's, I chatted him up easily and asked him if he felt like moving on somewhere else. We went to a smaller, quieter pub and he seemed quite smitten.

At the end of the evening the poor bastard was walking on air as he accompanied me back to Queen Street to the last train. Allowing him to snog me on the platform, I could feel his erection poking against me. I was far too much of a lady to mention it.

I got on the train and waved him goodbye, as ceremoniously as I could manage. As I watched his figure recede, I started to imagine him slimmed down, with more stylish frames or even contacts and thought . . . no.

So our next date is at the Chip, where I make my pitch. Simon says to me that I should play it cool, but he doesn't know how besotted this Alan is. — All I want is a printout, of all the customers in your branch, Alan. They won't know it came from me. I want to sell it to a marketing company. Plus the account numbers.

— I . . . I . . . I'll see what I can do.

I go to the toilet and call Simon on my mobile and tell him the good news.

— No, Nikki, act coy, anticipate his objections.

— But he's mad for me! He's up for it!

— He might be up for it right now, but to pull that off, you would have to be by his side all the time, twenty-four/seven. Are you game for that?

— No, but . . .

— It's all fine now, but when he's lying alone in his bed, after having wanked himself silly about you, and the bitterness and self-loathing kicks in, he'll start getting doubts.

Simon might not know human nature extensively, but he certainly understands the frailer side of it. It made sense. But who could fail to do what their wank fantasy bids? Which man could short-circuit that?

But Simon was correct, Alan *was* having second thoughts already. When I was present, it was fine, but left alone he seemed to come to his senses quickly. When I came back he told me that he could get the names and addresses, but the account numbers, that could get him into big trouble. Why did I want the account numbers for marketing?

What could I say? — I want to sell them to a hacker who can get into the system and clean the accounts out.

— No! I couldn't!

— I am joking, I laugh at him.

He looks nervously at me, then laughs back.

— I don't know any authorisation code? Or signature? It just saves the company time on their d-base? Like if they can scan in as many details of future customers as soon as possible, that's all. I pick up a chip from my bowl. — Lovely chips, I tell him, comforted in the knowledge that the chips here are very good.

48

Whores of Amsterdam Pt 5

Edinburgh's like I remember it: cold and wet, even though we're supposedly out of the winter. I ask the taxi driver to take me to Stockbridge and my pal Gavin Temperley's flat. Temps was one of my few mates who never touched gear, so he was the one I stayed in touch with. He never had any time for the likes of Begbie.

When I get there, a girl, twenties, very good-looking, is just leaving. Temps looks coy. They've obviously been arguing. — Eh, sorry ah didnae introduce ye there, he says as we go inside. — That wis Sarah. Eh, ah'm no number one in her hit parade right now.

I was thinking to myself that I'd settle for just a fuckin chart position in it.

I put my bags down and Gav and I hit the pub, then go for a curry. This curry house is good and cheap, and it's popular with couples, but also groups of pished-up boys. There's a couple of nice curry houses in the Dam but there's not the curry culture over there. When you see the group of noisy, drunken nutters a couple of tables away from us, you think that's possibly for the best. Fortunately, I'm sitting with my back to them, so I can enjoy the brinjal bhaji and prawn madras better than Gav, who's got tae face their loud, tedious antics. After a bit we get too pished tae notice them. Until I go downstairs for a slash.

On my way out the toilet my heart stops and flies up into my mouth. A bam, fists balled, comes running down the stair straight at me. I freeze. Fuckin hell . . . it's him . . . I'll block him and smash him, coming down on his leg and . . .

No.

It's just another radge aggressively barging past me, but I've no ill-will. In fact, I want to kiss this particular sociopath just for *not* being Begbie. Thank you, you fuckin heidbanger.

— You wantin a photae? eh asks as he passes me.

— Sorry, bud, just thought ye wir somebody ah knew for a second, I explain.

The nutter mumbles something, then heads off to the bogs. For a second I think about going in after him but check it. One thing that Raymond, my shotokan karate instructor, drummed into me was that the most important thing to learn about martial arts was when *not* to use them.

After the nosh, Gav and I head back down to his and we sit up into the night, drinking, telling tales, talking about life and catching up in general. There's something in his demeanour that saddens me. I feel horrible for feeling this way about him and I'm not being superior because I really fuckin like the boy, but it's as if he's come face to face with his limitations, without learning to love what he's got. He tells me that he's on the same grade in the Department of Employment and that's as high as he'll get. He's been knocked back for promotion so many times he's stopped applying. He reckons that he's had his card marked as a peever. — Funny, when ah started there, it was compulsory to be a drinker. A reputation for hanging round the pub showed you were social, a networker. Now you're marked down as a jakey. Sarah . . . she wants me to jack it aw in and go travelling with her, India and all that stuff, he shakes his head.

— Go for it, I tell him, my voice charged with urgency.

He shoots me a look like I've suggested he take up child-bending. — It's okay for her tae suggest that, Mark, she's twenty-four, no thirty-five. There's a big difference.

— Fuck off, Gavin. You'll regret it fir the rest of your life if you don't go. If you dinnae, you'll lose her and still be in that fuckin office in twenty years' time, the shakey jakey, the sad cunt they all dinnae want tae be like. And that's as good as it gets, they might kick you into touch anyway, for the flimsiest of reasons.

Gavin's eyes hollow and glaze and I suddenly apprehend how humiliating and violating my drunken rant is to his ears. You used to be able tae talk like this, tae rip people up for shite paper about work, but they've all got so precious about it and with us being older the stakes are now higher. — Ah dunno, he says wearily, raising the glass to his mouth, — sometimes ah think that ah'm jist too set in ma weys. That this is it, he pronounces, looking round the well-decorated and furnished room. It's an excellent Victorian Edinburgh flat; bay window, big marble fireplace, sanded floors, rugs, old or replica-old furniture, colour-washed walls. Everything's immaculate, and you can tell that the mortgage on this place is the real reason he wants to stay. — I think I've maybe missed the boat, he declares, in gallows cheeriness.

— Naw, just go for it, I urge. — Ye kin rent this place oot, I tell him, — it'll still be there when ye get back.

— We'll see, he smiles, but I think we both know that he won't, the stupid fucking cunt.

Gav picks up on my contempt and says: — It's easy for you, Mark; ah'm no like you, he almost pleads.

I'm tempted to say, how the fuck is it easy for me? It's all in his head. Yet I've got to mind that he's my host, and my friend, so I content myself with saying: — It's up tae you, mate, you're the only person who can live your life and you ken what's best for you.

He looks even gloomier considering this proposition.

I decide the next day that I'll get out and about. I put on a hat to cover my distinctive red hair and I wear the glasses that I only use for football games or the movies. I'm hoping that this, plus nine years' ageing and filling out, will be an adequate disguise. In any case, I'm keeping well away from Leith, the most likely area for the Begbie associates who personally know me. I heard that Seeker was still living at the top of the Walk and I stupidly head there, to my second depressing encounter.

Seeker's bottom row of teeth is wired together in a metal brace. It makes his sinister smile worse than ever, like that Jaws guy fae the Roger Moore Bond era. Gav Temperley told me that a squad, Fife or Glaswegian, depending on who you talk to, came through and tried to extract his teeth. I'm glad that they failed, his deadly smile was a work of art. Temps said that Seeker had got grisly revenge on most of the boys involved, one by one. It might be bullshit. What is true is that he's one person I know I could be seen around with that might buy me some sort of insurance from Begbie's old crew. Perhaps.

Seeker treats me like I've never been away, immediately tries to sell me junk, and seems surprised when I decline. As we sit in his house I swiftly become astounded at my own idiocy in coming here. Seeker and I had never really been friends; it was always purely business. He had no friends, just a block of ice where his heart should be. I'm surprised, too, although he still looks big and hard, just how little physical fear Seeker inspires in me now, and I wonder if that would also be the case with Begbie. What is chilling about Seeker is his quiet, mirthless depravity. He pulls out, from under the couch, what looks like the top of a Monopoly box, turned upside down. I can't quite believe what I see on it; some used condoms, filled, but just lying there, strategically placed.

— The week's work, he grins in that slow, death's-head stare, sweeping his long hair from his face. — That wis a wee bird ah brought back fae the Pure, he coldly tells ays, pointing at one of them. They looked like dead soldiers on a battlefield, a holocaust. I widnae have liked tae have been in the room when they were fashioned.

I never really know how to respond under such circumstances. I check a David Holmes flyer from the Vaults which is on his wall. — I'll bet ye that was a good night, I remark, pointing at it.

Seeker ignores me, indicating another condom. — That wis a student bird fae Substantial. English lassie, he continues. And for a brief moment, I have a sense of them actually being women, melted and diminished into a strip of pink rubber by some laser that comes from Seeker's cock. — This yin here, he points to one, which is tinted brown, — was a bird ah met in the Windsor one night. Fucked her aw weys in every hole, he tells me, before hissing out the standard sequence: mooth, fanny, erse.

I could see Seeker on top of some daft wee lassie, him fucking her erse, her gritting her teeth in pain with the warnings of parents and mates about keeping the wrong company a ruthless soundtrack to her pain and discomfort. Maybe she might even try to snuggle up with the cunt after, in order to con herself that it was all her choice, a real collusion, not something akin to rape. Maybe she'd just get the fuck out as soon as she could.

Seeker's pish-hole-in-the-snow eyes flit over to another condom. — That wis a right dirty wee hoor thit ah fucked big time . . .

He was well known for trying to get birds to bang up. Mikey Forrester and him would give them skag and then fuck them while they were bombed. They loved getting lassies hooked then fucking them for fixes. I'm looking at Seeker and thinking how people let badness adopt them, narrow and define their possibilities for so little reward. What's he getting out of it all? A poke at a corpse.

So that's my posse now: a clapped-out junior civil servant and an old smack-dealing acquaintance that Begbie hardly had any contact with. No, I can't wait to get away. I call my ma and faither, who now live out at Dunbar, and arrange to go and see them. As I head out, Seeker goes: — Mind, if ye change yir mind n fancy a bag . . .

— Aye, I nod.

I head out and look down the Walk, Leith both tempting and repelling me. It's like being by a cliff, where you feel compelled to go to the edge, but you're terrified at the same time. I think of an egg roll and a mug of tea in the Canasta, or a pint of Guinness in the Central. Simple pleasures. But no, I turn the other way. Edinburgh's got pubs and cafés as well.

I phone Sick Boy who's still fishing for my Edinburgh abode, but there's no way I'm trusting him with it, and I don't want Gav hassled. I ask him how things are and he's high about the film and his progress with the scam. Then he gives me some distressing news about Terry Lawson. — Are ye gaunnae go up visit him this affie? I ask.

He spits tersely into my ear through the airwaves: — I'd love to but I'm playing fives up at the Jack Kane. Birrell's going, he says, and he coughs out Rab Birrell's number. I liked Rab when I met him in Amsterdam. I knew his brother vaguely, from years back, he was a good guy, a good boxer as well. I call Rab and he repeats the story of what happened to Terry. Rab's going to visit him so we meet up in the Doctor's pub, and he's with these two stunning-looking lassies, whom he introduces to me as Mel and Nikki.

I know who they are straight away, and evidently they know a bit about me too. — So you're the famous Rents whom we've heard so much about, Nikki smiles coolly, big beautiful eyes sucking me in, teeth like pearls. I feel a pull on my soul and a crackle of electric as she touches my wrist. Then she grabs her cigarettes and says: — Come and smoke a cigarette with me.

— Gave it up years ago, I tell her.

— No vices then, she teases.

I shrug as enigmatically as I can, then explain: — Well, I'm an old pal of Simon's.

Nikki sweeps her long brown hair from her face and throws back her head and laughs. Her accent is that slightly nasal suburban south of England, without the affectations of the posh or the richness of the working classes. She's such a strikingly good-looking woman, that the blandness of her voice almost offends. — Simon. Such a character. So, you're going to be working on the film?

— I'm going to try, I smile.

— Mark's going to sort out finance and distribution. He's got a lot of contacts in Amsterdam, Rab explains.

— Barry, Melanie says in a wonderful Edinburgh working-class accent that could strip the paint off walls.

I get up another round of drinks. I'm feeling envious of Sick Boy, Terry, Rab and anybody else who's in a shagging scene with those two, and I decide to get myself into this little club asap. I've absolutely no doubt that Sick Boy's shagging one or both of them.

But it's visiting time, so we get round to the hospital and head up to the ward. — Awright, Mark? Terry says warmly. — How's the Dam?

— No bad, Terry. Bummer aboot the wedding tackle, likes, I commiserate. Terry's another guy I mind of from way back, he was always a character.

— Aye . . . accidents will happen but, eh. Goat tae keep it soft, no that easy wi aw they fit nurses here.

— Well, think long-term, Terry, I urge, nodding towards the girls, who're deep in conversation, — you're going to need it.

— Too fuckin right, it's the spice ay life. A future withoot sex . . . he shakes his head in genuine fear, and it is a horrendous thought.

I'm aware that Mel and Nikki have been smirking away, conspiring about something. There's an air of mischief about them. Then they suddenly pull the blinds around Terry's bed. To my astonishment, Nikki gets her tits out and Mel follows suit, and they start kissing each other slowly and deeply, and caressing each other's breasts. I'm blown away, trying to square this with the Edinburgh I left.

— Dinnae . . . stoap . . . Terry squeals, his stitches must be splitting and his erection rising under its cage. — FUCKIN STOAP IT . . .

— What dae ye say? Mel asks.

— Please . . . ah'm no jokin . . . he whines, his hand over his eyes.

They eventually desist, laughing their heads off, leaving him spitting in agony. We keep it brief after that, with Terry longing for us to go.

— Are you coming for a drink, Mark? Mel suggests, as we make our way out the ward.

— Yeah, let's have some whisky together, Nikki purrs. I've met tons of lassies like her in clubs: flirty, oozing a forceful sexuality. It crackles around your ears for a bit and makes you feel special, before you realise that they're like that with everyone. But I don't need any encouragement to join them. I'm keen for company, although my guts are feeling a bit dodgy and peristalsis is underway. — I need tae go tae the toilet. I forgot about the curry-house and pints-of-lager culture over here.

I take my leave and find the men's WC. It's a big lavvy; latrine, a row of sinks and six aluminium partitioned shithouses. I head into the trap nearest the wall, whipping down the winners and losers and the keks before I start dropping the contents of my guts. What a relief. As I start wiping my arse, I hear somebody come into the bogs, then into the trap next door.

As they settle and I finish my hole-cleaning, I hear a curse, followed by a rap on the metal wall. The voice seems familiar. — Hi, mate, thir's nae fuckin bog paper in this trap. Gaunnae fuckin well slide ays some under?

I'm about to say, sure, and share a moan about the poor maintenance of the bog, when a face snaps into my head and my blood runs cold. But it can't be. Not here. It just fuckin well can't.

I look under the space at the bottom of the partition, a gap of about ten inches. A nice pair of black shoes. But they've got segs in them. And the socks.

The socks are white.

I instinctively pull my own trainered feet away from the edge as the voice menacingly shouts: — Git a fuckin move oan!

Shakily, I take some paper from the dispenser and slowly slide it under the door.

— Awright, the voice gruffly mumbles.

As I pull up my shreddies and trousers, I reply: — No bother, putting on as posh a voice as I can, all the time sweating in sheer terror. I quickly exit, without washing my hands.

I can see Rab, Nikki and Melanie waiting for me by the drinks machine, but I turn the other way and hop down a corridor, shaking. I have tae get a move on. I should stay cool, look out from a distance to see who comes out that door, to be sure one way or the other instead of this torture in my head, but no, ah need tae get as far away fae this fuckin hospital as ah can. That cunt is real. He lives. He is outside.

49

HOME ALONE 2

It wis that fuckin June oan the phone, sayin tae fuckin well come
roond cause Sean's fuckin hurt Michael. N ah'm thinkin tae masel
that it might teach that daft wee cunt Michael tae no be as much
ay a fuckin wee lassie. — Dinnae fuckin well bother ays the now,
ah tells her. If she wis lookin eftir the bairns right they widnae be
gittin intae fuckin bother.

Now ah've goat the other yin gaun: — What is it, Frank?

Ah pits ma hand ower the receiver. — That fuckin June. Gaun
oan aboot they bairns fightin. That's what laddies are meant tae
fuckin well dae, ah sais. Ah takes ma hand back oaf.

— Jist fuckin git roond, Frank! She's still screechin doon the
phone at ays in that high fuckin voice. — Thir's blood everywhere!

Ah slams the phone doon n flings ma jaykit oan.

— We're meant tae be gaun oot, Kate goes, lookin at me aw soor-
faced.

— Ma fuckin son's bleedin tae death, ya daft cunt! ah tells her,
stormin oot, thinkin thit she deserves a rap oan the jaw for bein
sae fuckin insensitive. Might fuckin well git yin n aw. She's startin
tae git right oan ma tits. That's birds fir ye. Aw aye, it's aw nice
at the start: the honeymoon period, nivir fuckin well lasts but, eh
no.

The van's fucked so ah'm oot intae the Walk n the first cunt ah
sees in the street's Malky, comin oot ay the bookie's. N ye ken fuckin
fine whair eh's headin if eh's comin oot ay thaire, that's intae the
fuckin boozer. Cast-iron fuckin cert. No seen the cunt since ah hud
tae boatil that wide cunt Norrie at the caird school. — Awright,
Franco! Time fir a peeve?

Ah've goat tae nash, but ah've goat a chokin thirst oan ays. — Need
tae be a quick yin but, Malky. Domestic fuckin crisis; one cunt giein

ye it in one ear oan the phone, the other one giein ays it in the hoose. Better oaf in the fuckin jail.

— Tell ays aboot it, Malky goes.

Awright cunt, Malky. Funny, thinkin aboot Norrie takes ays back tae the time whin ah smashed Malky's heid yonks ago ower an argument aboot somethin oan the telly roond at Goags Nisbet's place. What wis it again? . . . tennis. Cannae mind whae wis playin bit it wis that fuckin Wimbledon. Aye, ah broke a boatil ay sherry ower the cunt's heid. That's aw forgotten aboot now though, cause every cunt wis fuckin steamboats n they things happen. Aye, Malky's sound. Eh sets up two pints ay lager n ehs tellin ays aboot this daft cunt Saybo fae Lochend.

— That Saybo cunt hud this flick knife in ehs pocket. The radge goat intae a row wi Denny Sutherland's mob n some cunt booted at ehs knackers n missed, n hit the poakit wi the knife in it. It set oaf the knife, n it wis one ay they cunts oan this big spring, n it went right intae the cunt's baws.

Ah'm tryin tae think aboot whin ah boatiled Malky back then. Wis it aboot tennis, or wis it the squash? It wis ay they games wi fuckin rackets. He backed one cunt n ah backed the other . . . fuck knows, it wis aw a haze.

Malky's tellin ays thit Nelly's moved back up fae Manchester, n eh's goat the tattoos removed fae ehs coupon, usin that fuckin surgical technique. Nae wonder, the cunt wis a fuckin mess; desert island oan the foreheid, snake oan one cheek, anchor oan the other. Fuckin tube; makes ye a sittin duck at an ID parade. Cunt eywis fancied ehsel as the boy. Well, it'll be good tae huv the cunt back, so long as eh disnae fuckin well start thinkin ehs some cunt thit eh fuckin well isnae.

Eftir a couple ay wets ah gits roond thaire n sees her at the fit ay the stair, arguin wi some cow whae turns oan her heels and heads in when she sees me comin. — Whair you been! Ah'm waitin oan a taxi! she sais.

— Business, ah goes, lookin at Michael. The wee cunt's goat a bit ay sheet ehs hudin tae ehs chin. It's covered in blood.

Ah looks at Sean n moves towards him, n eh steps back n cringes. — What you been fuckin daein!

She butts in. — It could've severed ehs neck! Could've cut right through a bloody vein!

— What fuckin happened but?

Her eyes are poppin oot her fuckin heid like she's oan something. — Eh got a bit ay chicken wire n strung it across the door aw tight, jist at Michael's neck height. Then eh shouted the laddie through, tellin um that ET wis oan the telly, ken that phone advert when the boy's takin a penalty fir Hibs against Herts. Michael ran ben aw excited. Lucky eh didnae measure right, n eh didnae run intae it at neck height. If eh did it could've took ehs fuckin heid right oaf!

Ah'm thinkin, that's quite barry but, cause, see tae me, that fuckin well shows initiative. Me n Joe ey did that kind ay thing tae each other as bairns. At least it shows thit eh's goat the spirit tae dae things, no jist fuckin well sit playin fuckin video games aw the time like some bairns nowadays. Ah looks at Sean.

— Ah goat it oaffay *Home Alone 2*, eh sais.

Ah jist looks at that fuckin stupid cunt June, ma hands oan ma hips. — So it's your fuckin fault, ah sais tae her, — littin him watch they fuckin videos.

— How's it ma fuckin –

— Showin fuckin videos thit pit violent ideas intae bairns' heids, ah snaps at the cunt, but ah'm no gaunnae argue wi ur, no here in the fuckin street. Cause if ah do, she'll git fuckin well battered, and that wis what finished us in the first place, that fuckin cow windin ays up soas thit ah hud tae fuckin well batter her crust in. The taxi comes n wi git in. — Ah'll take um up n git it stitched, you fuck off, ah tell her. Cause ah'm no wanting seen oot wi that mess. People might think thit wir still gaun oot thegither. Ye dinnae huv the auld bones ay last week's chicken-in-a-basket whin ye kin huv a new McDonald's, that's what ah eywis say.

Aye, she's goat they fuckin crack-hoor looks awright, n see if she's fuckin well rockin up in front ay they fuckin bairns . . . but naw, she disnae even ken whit rocks are, it's jist thit she does huv they fuckin worn-oot looks.

Ah grabs Michael n takes um intae the taxi, n wi speed oaf, leavin they cunts in the street. The wee fucker's still huddin the bit ay sheet against um. It's oot ay order but, Sean daein that tae um. — Does he pick on ye a loat? ah ask.

— Aye . . . Michael sais, n ehs eyes ur aw glassy like a wee lassie's.

This wee cunt needs telt some fuckin words ay wisdom n eh needs telt thum now, or ehs gaunnae grow up wi ehs life a fuckin misery. Nowt fuckin surer. N she'll no bother, naw, no her. She'll jist wait until something goes wrong again n then fuckin shed aw they fuckin crocodile tears. — Well, dinnae start greetin aboot it, Michael. Ah wis the youngest wi yir Uncle Joe, n ah goat it jist as bad. Ye huv tae learn tae stick up fir yirsel. Jist git a fuckin basebaw bat n batter the cunt's heid in, wait till ehs asleep n ehs kip, like. That'll fuckin well sort um oot. Worked wi Joe, only wi me eh goat a half-brick ower ehs heid. That's what yuv goat tae dae. Eh might be stronger thin you but ehs no fuckin well stronger thin a half-brick acroass ehs fuckin chops.

Ye kin see the wee cunt thinkin aboot this.

— N yir lucky yuv goat me tae tell ye aw this, cause see whin ah wis your age n it wis me n yir Uncle Joe, ah nivir hud any cunt tae pit me right, ah hud tae work it aw oot fir masel. That auld cunt thit wis ma faither, he didnae gie a flyin fuck.

The wee cunt's aw squirmin in ehs seat n pillin a daft face. — What's up wi ye now? ah ask um.

— We got told not to swear at the school. Miss Blake says it's not nice.

Miss Blake sais it's no nice. Nae fuckin wonder Sean tried tae sort this wee cunt right oot. — Ah ken what that Miss Blake fuckin well needs, ah tell um. — Teachers ken fuck all, take it fae me, ah point at masel. — If ah'd listened tae any fuckin teacher, ah widnae huv goat fuckin anywhaire in life.

The boy's thinkin aboot that yin, ye kin fuckin tell. Like me, that wee cunt, a deep fuckin thinker. We get intae the hoaspital, up tae that A&E n the nurse comes n does this daft fuckin assessment. — That needs some stitches.

— Aye, ah goes, — ah ken that. Gaunnae pit thum in fir um well?

— Yes, if you just take a seat you'll be called, she goes.

Then we've goat tae wait fuckin ages. What a load ay fuckin shite. The time it takes ye tae make a fuckin assessment, ye could huv the stitches in. Ah'm runnin oot ay patience here n ah'm jist aboot tae take the wee fucker away n gie um a hame-made joab, when we gits called. Aw the fuckin questions they ask, it's like they think it's *me* thit fuckin well did it tae the wee cunt. Ah'm jist aboot tae fuckin well lose it here, but ah'm huddin oan tae make sure he doesnae grass up Sean, even by mistake.

Whin we finally finish ah whispers tae um,: — N dinnae grass Sean up at that fuckin school, either, tae yon Miss Blake, or whatever ye call the cunt, right. Tell thum ye fell, mind.

— Okay, Dad.

— Nivir mind okay, jist make sure ye mind what ah sais.

Ah tell um tae wait here while ah go tae the bog fir a fag. Cannae even git a fuckin smoke anywhere nowadays.

It takes ays fuckin ages tae find the cunts, ah end up huvin tae climb a whole fuckin flight ay stairs. Whin ah gits thaire ah'm needin a fuckin shite n aw. Ah'm sure that fuckin ching ah hud wis cut wi fuckin laxative. Aye, some cunt's gaunnae git thir fuckin jaw rapped. Ah gits intae one booth n whips doon ma keks before ah realises thit thir's nae paper in this bog. Supposed tae fuckin keep thum clean, n thir fuckin hoatbeds ay infection. Nae wonder every cunt oan the NHS is droapin like fuckin flies. Lucky thir's some other cunt daein a shite in the next fuckin trap. — Hi, mate, ah rap oan the aluminium waw, — thir's nae fuckin bog paper in this trap. Gaunnae fuckin well slide ays some under?

Thir's a silence fir a bit.

— Git a fuckin move oan, ah shouts.

Some paper comes slidin under the door. Boot fuckin time n aw.

— Awright, ah goes, n starts wipin ma erse.

— No bother, the guys sais, a sortay posh cunt. Probably one ay they doaktirs thit's pokin aroond every cunt, aw fill ay thirsels. Ah hear one door go n then the other. Dirty cunt didnae even wash ehs fuckin hands. Fuckin hoaspital n aw!

Lucky fir him the clarty bastard wisnae thaire whin ah came oot. N ah gies ma hands a good scrub cause ah'm no a filthy cunt like some. See, if it wis that cunt thit pit ma bairn's stitches in wi manky hands . . .

50

'. . . a fish casserole . . .'

That Mark is a funny guy. I'm wondering if we embarrassed him with our tit-flashing at poor Terry. We waited for him outside the toilets, but he just vanished without coming for a drink or even saying goodbye. — Mibee eh shat ehsel, Mel laughed, — hud tae go hame tae change!

So we had a couple and I went home and waited for my Glasgow caller, and cooked a fish casserole while talking to Dianne. She's been interviewing the girls from the sauna, Jayne, Freida and Natalie.

Dianne is happy with the way things are going. — I really appreciate you putting me in contact with those girls, Nikki. I've now got enough for a statistically valid group, which gives my tests some kind of scientific credibility.

She's a sharp girl and she's got the work ethic big time. Sometimes I envy her. — You'll rule the world, honey, I tell her. I head to the kitchen and fill up a watering can and put on a Polly Harvey tape. I start watering the plants, one or two of which look a bit neglected.

I can hear my mobile ringing in the front room and I shout for Dianne to pick it up. She seems to be listening to someone for a while before going: — I'm sorry, I think you've got the wrong person. I'm Dianne, Nikki's flatmate.

She passes the phone over and it's Alan. He was so pleading and desperate he couldn't even tell an English and an Edinburgh accent apart. I think about him, working up there in that bank, waiting for the gold watch.

— Nikki . . . I want to see you again . . . we need to talk, he whines, as I make my way to my room. Poor Alan. The widsom of youth married to the dynamic energy of old age. A banking combination, but not a bankable one. Not for him, anyway.

They always need to talk.

— Nikki? he pleads painfully.

— Alan, I tell him, indicating that, yes, I'm still here, but probably not for much longer unless he stops wasting my time.

— I've been thinking . . . he says urgently.

— About me? About us?

— Yes, of course. About what you said . . .

I can't remember what I said. What stupid extravagant promises I made to him. I want what he has and I want it now. — Listen, what are you wearing, boxer shorts or Y-fronts?

— What dae ye mean? he whinges. — What sort of a question is that? I'm at work!

— Don't you wear underpants at work?

— Yes, but . . .

— Do you want to know what I've got on?

There's a pause over the phone, followed by a long — Whaa . . .

I can almost feel his hot breath in my ear, the poor darling. Men, they're such . . . dogs. That's the word. They call us dogs, or bitches, but it's projection, because they know that's exactly what they are, that's their nature: salivating, excitable, undignified pack beasts. No wonder dogs are called man's best friend. — It's not sexy lingerie, it's faded, washed cotton smalls with a couple of holes in them and frayed elastic. The reason for that is that I'm a student who's skint. I'm skint because you won't give a simple printout with the names of your branch account holders with their numbers. I don't have their pin numbers, I'm not going to rip them off. I just want it to flog to this marketing company. They pay me fifty pence a name. That's five hundred quid for a thousand names.

— We've got over three thousand customers at our branch . . .

— Honey, that's fifteen hundred quid, all my debts paid off. And I'd be so keen to reward such enterprise.

— But if I get caught . . . he lets out a slow exhalation of breath. Alan's constant state of misery debunks the notion that ignorance is bliss.

— Sweetheart, you won't, I tell him, — you're far too resourceful.

— I'll meet you tomorrow at six. I'll have the lists.

— You're an angel. I must go, I've a casserole in the oven. Till tomorrow, sweetheart!

I put the phone down and head through to the kitchen and over to the cooker. Dianne looks up at from her pile of books on the table. — Men problems?

— They're no problem, the poor little darlings, I say grandly, — just no problem at all, I thrust my hips out at her and clasp my groin. — Pussy power conquers all.

— Yeah, Dianne says, drumming her teeth with her pen. — That's been the saddest thing I've found with my researches. All those girls I've spoken to, they've got all that power, all that tits, arse and fanny power, and they sell it too cheaply. They practically give it away for nothing. That's the fucking tragedy, girl, she says, almost as a warning.

The land phone rings on the answer machine and it takes a while to register who the voice belongs to. — Hi, Nikki, I got your number from Rab. Wanted to apologise for that vanishing act yesterday. It's eh, a bit embarrassing . . . Then I realise that it's Mark Renton and I pick it up.

— Oh, Mark, don't worry about that, angel, I stifle a laugh as Dianne looks quizzically at me, — we kind of guessed as much. You did mention curry? So what are you up to?

— Right now? Nothing. The guy I'm staying with's out with his girlfriend, so I'm sitting in watching telly.

— All on your lonesome?

— Aye. What are you up to? Fancy a drink?

I'm not sure if I do, and I'm not sure if I fancy Mark. — Oh, I'm not in a pub mood, but come round for a glass of wine and a smoke of grass, if you like, I tell him. No, he's not my type, but he knows a lot about Simon, who certainly is my type.

So Mark appears about an hour later, and I'm surprised, though not shocked, to find that he and Dianne know each other from way back. Edinburgh can be like that, the biggest village in Scotland. So we all sit up spliffing for a bit, me trying to steer the subject to Simon, but it becomes evident that Mark and Dianne are engrossed in each other. I feel totally redundant. He eventually suggests going down to Bennett's or the IB.

— Yeah, cool, Dianne says. This is strange; she never leaves her work like that and she'd planned another session on her dissertation tonight.

— I can't be bothered going out, I tell them. — I thought you were busy with your work, I laugh.

— It's not urgent, Dianne smiles through clenched teeth. As Mark heads through to take a quick piss, I make a face at her.

— What? she asks, with a faint smile.

I cross my arms in a shagging gesture. She rolls her eyes lackadaisically back, although there's a simper playing round her lips. He comes back and they depart.

51

Scam # 18,748

Renton still won't come anywhere near the fair port of Leith.
I can't say I blame him. He won't even tell me where he's
staying although I know that his ma and dad are now out of town
somewhere.

Nikki tells me that the sparks fair flew in the flat between
Rents and her flatmate Dianne. Apparently he was supposed to
have rode her back in the day. I don't mind of her and it's no as
if Renton's ex-shags constitute a January-Sales-on-Princes-Street
sea of faces. Mind you, he always did try to keep his birds away
from me, presumably in case I stole them. Renton was always
inclined to be surprisingly intense in relationships, even a lovesick
fool at times. But what sort of woman must she be, going out
with a ging-ger?

Skreel set me up with another bird called Tina, who was less
trouble that the first one and who gave me the season-ticket holders'
list no bother. She told me that she was a secret Celtic supporter.
That's what happens when you start an equal opportunities policy
in employment.

I'm in the pub and totally chuffed, despite eyeing the group of
young neds who're still hanging about by the jukebox. That Philip
boy's been giving it a lot of lip, I've seen him talking to Begbie a
few times. He obviously thinks he's the main man, but at least there's
a bit more respect for me in his tone of voice as he knows that
Franco and me are connected, of sorts.

Now this Philip's orchestrating a wind-up against his tall, gangly
sidekick, the dippit Curtis with the speech impediment who always
seems to be the butt of their jokes. They're showing off in front of the
wee burds that they're with, but it's pretty witless fare really. — Eh's a

fuckin poof, the guy says and another cretin's shoulders shake like he's got some nervous disease. Surely we weren't so fucking drab and uninspired at that age?

— Ah'm no! Ah'm n-n-no a p-p-poof! the poor Curtis boy howls and heads out to the toilet.

Philip sees me looking over, and he turns to the wee lassies, then back at me. — Eh might no be a poof, but eh's a virgin. Eh's no hud ehs hole. You should gie um it, Candice, he says to this glaikit wee tart.

— Fuck off, she says, looking at me all embarrassed.

— Ah, virginity, I smile, — don't knock it. Most of the real problems in life come after we've lost it, I tell them, but even the blandest throwaway lines are wasted on this crew.

I go to the bog for a slash and that Curtis laddie's in there, and yes, he is a wee bit slow. In fact, his very presence on this planet gives lie to the anarchist notion that there are no good laws; our incest legislation, for example, exists to prevent more people like him lurching around. He's a tea leaf and he's a bit pally with Spud, which isn't hard to believe. A Begbie apprentice and a Spud apprentice in the same posse, incubating under my fucking roof. That bad bastard Philip and his other mates torment this Curtis all the time it seems. Like I used to with Spud at school and down the river and the Links and the railway line. Funny, the thought makes me feel almost guilty now. The boy's daein a pish next to me, and he turns at me with an idiot's smile, looking all nervous and shy. I inadvertently lower my glance and I see it.

It.

It is the biggest prick ever; the cock, not the sad wee thing attached to it.

I finish my urination, and I contemplate my own penis, shaking it out and putting it back and zipping up. I can't bear to watch him do the same. This imbecile has a bigger fucking knob than me; a bigger fuckin knob than anybody. What a waste. Then, as I head over to the sink, I casually ask: — How's things then, mate; Curtis, is it no?

The boy turns and faces me with a nervy glance. He comes over to the sink next to mine, full of dread. — Aye . . . he replies. — No b-b-b-b-bad. His eyes are watering and blinking and his breath is

315

terrible, like he's been sucking his own unwashed cock – which for him would be entirely possible, even with a bad back – filling his gut with a spunk turned rancid by cheap drink and bad drugs. He's like one of those chemical bogs at a rave or a concert that badly needs cleaned out. But I'm thinking about this young gadge's asset. — You're a pal ay Spud's, eh, I state, then without waiting for a reply add, — Spud's a good mate ay mine. Old boyhood chums.

This Curtis boy's lookin at me to see if I'm winding him up. Not that he'd know if I was though. Then he says: — Ah l-l-like Spud, then adds bitterly, — he's the only one that disnae try n take the p-p-pish . . .

— An excellent guy . . . I nod, and I'm thinking about the boy's stutter n that line in that old anti-war song: '*The average age of the American combat soldier was ni-ni-nineteen.*'

— He kens thit ye kin git shy sometimes, the wee-big man skulks. A mate of Spud's. God, ah kin jist imagine the conversation wi they two. 'Ah git pure shy sometimes.' 'Aye, me n aw.' 'Dinnae worry aboot it, huv some jellies.' 'Aye, barry.'

I'm taking my time, nodding sympathetically while washing my hands and Christ, this minging bog needs properly cleaned right enough. Do we or do we not pay our cleaners to clean? No, life would be too straightforward, too fucking un-Scottish, if people did the jobs they were meant to do. Shy boy here, what was he meant to do? — Nowt wrong wi being shy, mate. Everybody was once, I lie. I stick my hands under the dryer. — Let me get you a drink, I smile, thrashing off the excess water.

The boy looks less than smitten by my offer. — Ah'm no steyin in here, he says pointing angrily outside, — no wi thaime takin the p-p-pish!

— Tell you what, mate, I'm going down to the Caley for a beer. I need a break. Come and join me.

— Awright, he says, and we sneak out the side door and into the street. It's fuckin cauld here, and there's spits of sleet coming down. Meant to be fucking spring! The wee guy is, as they say, all prick and ribs, it's like every morsel of nutrition that goes into his body is swallowed up by that cock. If he was with a bird he'd probably come so much that he'd badly dehydrate himself and be in intensive care for weeks. That big Adam's apple bulging away, that sallow, spotty skin . . . he's certainly no movie star. But, in the world of porn, if he can find wid on demand . . .

We get into the warm, inviting Caley, with its open fire, and I set up a couple of pints and brandies as we find a quiet corner. — So what are these mates ay yours gittin oan yir case for?

— It's cause ah'm a bit shy . . . n muh s-stammer . . .

I contemplate this problem for a while, finding it so hard to contain my indifference, before I venture: — Is it yir stammer that makes ye shy, or are ye shy cause yuv got a stammer?

This Curtis laddie shrugs. — Ah went tae see aboot it, n they said it wis jist ni-nerves . . .

— What are you so nervous about? You don't seem any different from the rest of your mates. You've no got two heids or nowt like that. Youse aw dress the same, take the same drugs . . .

The wee guy bows his heid and it's like there's nothing going on under that baseball cap. Then he says in a tormented whisper: — B-b-but . . . no when you've no di-di-done it n they aw hu-hu-hu-huv . . .

The average length of the Scottish sovied wanker was ni-ni-ni-nineteen inches . . .

I can say nothing here. I just nod as sympathetically as I can. With mounting unease, I realise that these cunts are in many cases not old enough to legally fuck, never mind drink. Thank God for Chief Constable Lester's certificate of peace above the bar.

— That Philip thinks ehs the b-b-big hard man cause ehs knockin aboot wi B-B-Begbie. Eh used tae be ma beh-beh-best mate n aw. Ah might be shy wi lassies, but ah'm no a p-p-p-poof. Danny . . . Spud, he understands that ye kin git shy in front ay bi-bi-bi-burds ye like.

— So you've never been oot wi any ay they lassies youse muck aboot wi thaire?

The wee cunt's face flushes red-raw. — Naw . . . naw . . . eh naw . . .

— Jist as well fir thaime. Ye'd split thum in two wi thon, I nod downstairs. — Couldnae help but notice, mate. Bet you wir breastfed! Any Italian blood? I ask.

— Naw . . . eh Scottish, eh. Then he looks at *me* as if *I* might be a dodgy arse-bandit.

This cunt is a total pacifist in the sex war. Just as well for the chicks, cause with a weapon like that he'd have won it single-handed by now.

— You surely must have had some opportunities, I ask.

The wee guy's really flustered now, his eyes watering as he's spluttering and stammering out a past humiliation. — Ah wis wi . . . wi . . . this lassie one time n she sais it wis too bi-bi-big, thit ah wis a f-f-freak.

Jist that poor cunt's luck that his first shagging opportunity was with a dipstick. — No way, mate. She wis the freak, the fuckin dozy cow, I shake my head, setting him right. Now, he's got stooped shoodirs, shifty, nervous eyes, breath that would make any woman rather snog his ringpiece, and a horrifically bad stammer. I'll wager, too, that it's aw because of some daft wee troll who simply did not have the sense to realise that her ship had come in. — Listen, dae ye ken Melanie?

The young chappie's eyes ignite a little. — Her that makes they stag movies wi you up the stairs?

— Fuck! Naebody's supposed tae know aboot that, I curse, pulling in a sharp intake of breath and resisting the temptation to ask him who told him about our club. — Yes, that's her, I say quietly.

— Eh, aye, ah've s-s-seen her, like.

— Dae ye like her?

The wee gadge breaks into a thoughtful smile. — Aye, everybody does . . . and the other yin, the nice-s-s-spoken yin . . . he says wistfully.

Let's just get this wee cunt walking before he can run. — Good, cause she likes you. Both of them do.

The poor wee fucker blushes.

— Naw, gen up.

— Naw . . . y-y-you're takin the pi-pi-pi . . .

There are simply not enough hours in the day to get a result with this boy. — Listen, pal, I'm half-Italian, on my mother's side. Are you a Catholic?

— Well, aye, b-b-but ah never go tae chu . . .

I silence him with a wave. — Not important. I am, and I swear on my mother's life that Melanie fancies you and would like you to have a go with her in one of the stag movies, I stand up, deadpan as I walk to the bar and order another round. Leave the cunt to think about that. When I come back, he's about to say something, but being time-conscious I cut in. — And ye get peyed. Ye get peyed tae gie Melanie the message, and other birds n aw. N no just in stag, in a proper porno flick. What dae ye say?

— You're j-j-jokin . . .

— Do ah look like ah'm jokin? My main man Terry's incapacitated and we need new blood. You're the man. Gittin peyed tae ride Mel? C'mon, mate!

— Ah jist like Candice, he sniffs defensively.

Another fuckin closet romantic. How sad. That wee hairy back in the Sunshine. — Listen, pal, ah ken they take the pish oot ay ye thaire, I point outside, — but they'll no be takin the pish when you're the porn star ridin the top-drawer fanny. Think aboot it, I wink, and drinking up, I leave the wee cunt tae do just that.

When I get back to the Sunshine, Spud's sitting in the corner being ignored by Ali. After a bit he gets up and tries to give her some money and she tells him to go. He's off his tits and he looks a fucking disgrace. It's a real speed-jakey look; unkempt hair with enough grease in it to supply every chippy in Leith, eyes so hooded that they look permanently shut, black rings like washers around them, flaming blood vessels, all housed in a fibrous skin the colour and texture of stale chapatti. Why, hello, handsome! Here comes hubby, Ali doll, wow, what a catch! I let you out my sight for a few years, n look what happens. You don't so much lower your standards as become a total fucking comedienne. But no funny-fanny from Marti Caine to French and Saunders to Caroline Aherne ever got the laughs that you did walking into a bar with that on your arm. He's raising his voice now and I sense that my presence would only inflame things, so I catch Ali's eye and I signal for her to get him out.

I see Curtis coming back in and wilfully ignoring his mates, one of whom, that Philip, is brushed off as he tries to put a friendly arm round the boy's shoulders. Instead, he goes over to Spud to help him out and down the road. My new leading man. The new Juice Terry!

Mo and Ali look to be coping to the extent that they hadn't even noticed my departure. I decide to ride my luck further and slip back out the side door and head round the corner and back upstairs to the flat. I'm about to stick on a Russ Meyer video for inspiration when I catch a look at myself in the mirror on my wall. The cheekbones strike me as more prominent. Yes, I'm losing a bit of weight okay.

Shimon, congradulations on the shuckshesh of this movie enterprishe.

Why, shank you, Sean. Pornography hash never really been my shing, but I appreeshiate a well-crafted movie, to shay nothing of a nisch piesch of ash.

Everything is coming up roses. Almost everything. I mind of Mo telling me that Francis Begbie was in again asking after me.

Sure enough I check the green mobile's messages and there's a text one from him, or 'Frank' as he signs himself:

NEED 2 C U RIGHT AWAY ABOUT
SOMEONE WHO WILL SOON SEAS 2 EXIST

I can visualise it right enough, 'Frank'. Fuckin twat. It has to be Renton. Renton will soon 'seas' to exist. There's another text message from Seeker. If ever a communication system was made for a man, it's text messages for him:

READY ANY TIME

Drugs. Good. I've only a small amount left. I produce the wrap and chop it up, taking a healthy line, which fair hits the mark. I really need a cigarette now, and I light one up, the smoke feeling so clean and fresh in my lungs with the ching.

I look in the mirror, deep into the mirror. — Listen, Franco, it's about time you and I had a wee heart-to-heart, a wee clear-the-air session. It's about this obsession you have with Renton. I mean, let's face it, it's got to be said, Franco, and I'm sure you'll appreciate my candour on this, that this goes way beyond the cash from yon time. You're like a spurned lover. Of course, that's all over Leith. Okay, let's accept that you're obviously crazy about him. All the boys in the jail, as you made love to them, did you imagine that they were him? I'm only sorry that it didn't work out for you two guys. Funny, but I used to think that it was you that gave it, and Rents who took it. Now, though, I doubt it. I can just tell that you're the crying, bleating, ginger-whipped bitch in the dress bending over with tears in your eyes while he talks dirty to you and prepares your greased arse for him, and when he gives you it, you simper and mew like the filthy little fucking lady-boy hoor that . . .

The doorbell.

I open up and he's there. Just standing there in front of me.

— Franco . . . ah wis jist thinkin aboot ye . . . come in, mate, I stammer, sounding like the young Curtis boy I've just left.

And by the reaction in his eyes it's like this bastard has read my mind. How fucking loud was I talking? . . . surely not . . . but if he had the letter box held open to spy in first . . . and he heard me from jist doon the hallway . . .

— Fuckin Renton . . . he hisses.

Aw fuck, sweet Jesus, please don't do this to me . . . — What? I manage to bark out.

Begbie's sensing something's wrong. He looks at me in that nasty, appraising way and says softly: — Renton's fuckin well back here. Eh's been spotted.

And something in my brain, as I look into that five-mile stare and freeze, some primal essence is screaming: Act, Simon, act. Act for Scotland, no, make that Italy. — Renton? Whaire? Whaire the fuck is that cunt! And I'm looking into hell, that solitary black spot behind the pupils of his mad eyes, with a hateful stare of my own which I feel is like trying to put out a blast furnace with a Woolies water pistol. I'm waiting for him to strike like a cobra, almost praying: for fuck sakes do it now, put me out my misery, cause even chinged up I can't keep this going any longer.

Begbie holds my gaze, and thankfully his voice climbs down to a low hiss. — Ah wis hopin you could fuckin well tell me.

I slap my head and turn away and start pacing, thinking back to the agony Renton caused us, caused me. I stop suddenly and point at Franco, and yes, it's in accusation, cause it was that fucker's folly that caused the bag to be nicked, he was the one that was meant to be in charge of it. — If that cunt is back here, I want my fuckin money . . . then I start to think of how Begbie would perceive me, and add, digging my forehead with my palm: — I'm trying to make a fuckin movie here, on a fucking shoestring!

An excellent pitch. Franco seems just about satisfied with that. His eyes narrow further. — You've goat ma fuckin mobile number. If Renton gets in touch wi you, you fuckin bell me straight away.

— And vice versa, Franco, I tell him, basking in the outrage now, the charlie working as one with it, feeling the power and purity of my disdain, the sheer strength of my front. — And don't fucking well touch that cunt until I've got my money, plus compensation, and then you can do what you want to with him . . . so long as I get to lend a helping hand, of course.

I must have seemed suitably tumultuous because Begbie says: — Right, then he turns and starts to exit.

Renton. I can't believe I'm protecting that cunt. Not for much longer though. The bank accounts are all set up. Once the film's in the can, we go our separate ways.

I'm following Franco out down the stairs, and he turns to me and asks: — Whaire the fuck ur you gaun?

— Eh . . . back to the pub, I just nipped out and I'm due back.

— Barry, we'll git a peeve, he says.

So the asinine specimen follows me there and I have to stand drinking at the bar with him. One bonus: he punts me a wrap of ching, which will at least tide me through until I can get up to Seeker's. Still, it's a far from ideal situ. At least Spud's gone, but not before he's upset Alison who's obviously been crying. That Paddy fleabag is now undermining my fuckin staff's morale.

Begbie's still stuck in paranoia central, going on about packages, which makes my pulse race with excitement, how Renton's a twisted poof, which is all music to my ears. Oh, I want Renton to meet him, basically just to see, for my own curiosity, how far Franco will go. Surprisingly, he asks me about the film.

— Well, I go, playing it down, — it's just a bit of fun really, Frank.

— They porn stars n that, the gadges like, is thir like . . . ah mean, huv they goat tae be a certain fuckin length?

— Not really, I mean the bigger the better, obviously, I tell him. Franco gives his crotch an orangutan-like grapple, which makes me feel queasy. — So ah'd be awright then!

— Aye, but the maist important thing is the ability tae find wid. A lot ay boys wi big dicks just cannae find wid on camera, when it comes doon tae it. The ability tae find wid is the key thing, that's why Terry was so good . . . I run down, suddenly aware that Franco's looking at me in a hateful rage. — Are you awright, Frank?

— Aye . . . it's jist whin ah think aboot that cunt Renton . . . he says, then he's throwing back the drink and he's into a rant, going on about his kids, about how June doesn't look after them properly. — The fuckin state ay her, like a fuckin Belsen horror. She looks like she's fuckin wastin away . . .

— Aye, Spud was saying she's in a bad way. The pipe does that though. Ah mean, ah dae a fair old bit ay ching, Frank, but aw ah'm sayin is that the pipe really takes it oot ay ye, I explain to him, relishing dropping Murphy right in it.

Begbie looks at me in shock, and his fingers go white on the glass. I take in a deep breath as this cunt is ready to explode. — The pipe . . . crack . . . June . . . WI MA FUCKIN BAIRNS?!

I see my chance here and move in. — Look, Spud says eh wis washin up wi her, ah'm only tellin ye this cause ye should ken, wi the kids n that . . .

— Right, he says, looking over at Alison who looks totally bedraggled. — YOUR MAN IS A CUNT! EH'S A FUCKIN USELESS JUNKY CUNT! THEY SHOULD TAKE YOUR FUCKIN BAIRN INTAE CARE!

Then Franco charges out the bar as Alison stands in disbelief for a second or two, then explodes into racking sobs, only to be comforted by Mo. — What . . . she bubbles, — what is he fucking saying . . . what hus Danny done . . . ?

I have to take the bar as they go through this lame-duck performance. I'm delighted that the simian oaf Begbie has departed, less so that he's incapacitated my fucking staff. And for my next customer on this conveyor belt of lost souls which passes as an alehouse, it's none other than poor Paul, my mate from the Leith Business Against Drugs, looking like the weight of the world's on his shoulders. I take him to the quiet end of the boozer and he's straight into a bleat about the money. — It's *my* neck, Simon!

I'm telling the cunt straight: — You'll keep it shut or your pathetic career goes, I'm telling ye! Having made the point, I then adopt a more placatory stance. — Listen, Paul, dinnae worry. You simply don't understand the economics of business. Of my industry. We'll get it back, I sing cheerfully, delighting in keeping my head when all around me are losing theirs.

What an excremental little creature.

— Now here's a man who understands economics, I smile as old Eddie shuffles into the bar, nose in the air like a Roman emperor. — Ed, how's things, auld buddy?

— No bad, Eddie moans.

— Excellent! I smile. — What will you have? On the house, Ed, I tell him.

— If it's oan the hoose, a pint ay special and a large Grouse.

Even this jakey auld cunt's blatant liberty-taking cannot knock me out my stride today. — *Certainment*, Eduardo, I smile, then shouting over at Leith's Marjory Proops: — Mo, do the honours will you, my lovely? Nodding at a destroyed Paul, I turn back to Ed. — Just putting my mucker Paul here correct on the wiles of commerce. What line ay work were you in again, Eddie?

— Ah wis a whaler, the mumpy auld shipwreck tells me.

A seafaring man. Well, hello, sailor. Or should it be, hello, whaler? — Aye, so, did ye ken Bob Marley?

The auld salt shakes his heid vigorously. — Thir wis nae Bob Marley oan the boats oot ay Granton. No when ah wis oan thum, Ed tell us in great sincerity, flinging back the Grouse.

— It's your shout, Paul, I smile beamingly, — and I'll expect you to stick another wee gold yin in there for Ed. It's a sign of a society's civilisation, how we treat the elderly, and we in Leith are several light years ahead of all the opposition in that field. Am I right or am I simply correct, eh, Ed?

Eddie just looks aggressively at Paul. — Ah'll huv a whisky, but make sure it's a Grouse, he warns the flummoxed adman, like he's doing the poor bastard a big favour.

I decide to ignore the bleating yuppie ponce and leave Mo and

Ali to enjoy the taste of bitter seamen, cause Juice Terry comes into the pub. — Tel! Discharged?

— Aye, he smiles. — Still have tae watch n keep takin the pills but, eh.

— Excellent. What are you drinking?

I'm in even higher spirits now. We'll have a full squad soon. Alex?

Of crucial importance, Simon. Unfortunately, you don't win anything with a bare first eleven these days. We need about forty in the buff, all going for it.

— Ah cannae even fuckin drink oan they pills, Terry moans, sweeping a hand through those curls. The porn-star mowser he grew for a laugh has gone.

— Crikey, Tel, what a nightmare. No shagging, no drinking, I laugh, nodding over at Ed's mates who are sitting nursing their half-pints in the corner. — Still, it'll get you prepared for the future shift, eh.

— Aye, he says ruefully, as I watch that Paul wanker, now very much aware that I can simply cold-shoulder him all night, decide to get real and head dejectedly out.

To cheer Terry up, I take him through the office and rack up a couple of poodle's legs from the gram Begbie got me. I'm telling Tezzo about about my visit from mon former colleague Monsieur François Begbee. — The words 'shoulder' and 'chip' spring to mind, I say, cutting the lines finely with my credit card and nodding to Terry to be my guest, — but not necessarily in that order. Still, it's his ching we're on, so the boy does have his uses.

Terry laughs, bending over to snort. — A chip oan ehs shoodir? That cunt's goat the whole fuckin casino, he says before firing one back.

I follow suit and start rabbiting about my plans for the movie. Terry's starting to look uncomfortable. — You okay, Tel?

— Naw . . . it's ma cock . . . it must be the charlie, but it's really nippin, really throbbin.

Poor Terry heads off, almost bent over. So sad to see a once proud man emasculated in such a way. As he's still out of commission, I worry about poor Melanie's sex life so I bell her, thinking that it might be nice if she met young Curtis.

52

CRACK HOOR

Ah'm fuckin well ragin. That cunt fuckin dies, a fuckin unfit mother. Aye, she's gittin it . . . but the bairns cannae go intae care n if muh ma disnae take thum . . . so she'll huv tae screw the fuckin nut cause me n Kate cannae fuckin well huv the cunts . . . THAT DIRTY FUCKIN HOOR!

Cause ay hur ah even gits caught in the fuckin rain, in a pishin wet shower. N thir's even water in they shoes through jumpin a fuckin puddle, like a fuckin blocked drain. Whin ah gits back ah flings ma jaykit oan right away n kicks oaf ma auld fuckin shoes n pits they new Timberland yins oan. Kate goes: — Whaire ur ye gaun, Frank?

— Roond tae see the fuckin druggy hoor thit's goat ma bairns.

Fuckin rain, does yir fuckin nut in. Every cunt's sniffin away wi the cauld, but mind you, wi half ay thum it's the Columbian flu, caused by too much fuckin sniff. Sick Boy's the worst, n ah'm no sayin nowt against a wee tickle, but no washin it up, that's a fuckin loser's game, n no in front ay ma fuckin bairns!

So ah gits roond thair n ah looks at her n shi's lookin back at ays like shi hus the fuckin cheek tae deny it n aw. Ah jist goes tae the bairns: — Git yir coats, yis ur gaun roond tae muh ma's.

Thir wis nae wey ah wis huvin thum roond at oor fuckin place. Fuck thon. Ah'm thinkin thit muh ma'll want thum, once shi kens the score, sees the danger thit thir in.

— What . . . what's wrong? June goes.

— You, ya fuckin dirty hoor, keep oot ay ma sight, ah'm fuckin tellin ye, ah jist warns the cunt. — Ah'm runnin oot ay patience n ah'll no be held fuckin responsible fir what ah might dae if ye open yir big fuckin junky mooth!

She kens me well enough tae ken thit ah'm no fuckin well jokin n hur eyes go aw wide n hur face is even fuckin whiter thin ever. Look at hur, a fuckin wreck, how did ah no see it before? Ah wonder how long shi's been at it. The bairns ur gittin ready n sayin: — Where are we gaun, Dad?

— Yir gran's. At least she kens how tae bring up bairns, ah looks at her. — N she disnae sit aboot gittin fucked up wi junkies.

— What dae ye mean? What ur you oan aboot? that fuckin sow hus the nerve tae go.

— Yir denyin it? Yir denyin thit Spud fuckin Murphy wis roond here the other week?

— Aye . . . bit nowt went oan, n anywey, she goes, a mad light in her eyes, — it's nane ay your business what ah dae.

— Washin up in front ay ma laddies? Nae ay ma fuckin business! Ah turns tae thaime. — Youse two, git. Yir ma n me's huvin a private conversation. Git oot intae the stair n wait fir me! Goan, beat it!

— Washin up . . . aye . . . but . . . she's gaun, — ah jist needed some help . . .

As the wee cunts troop oot, ah turns tae her. — Ah'll gie ye fuckin washin up! FUCKIN WASH THIS! Ah batters the cunt in the puss, n blood spurts fae hur nose. Ah grabs it by the hair, n it's that fuckin greasy ah huv tae wrap it roond ma fist tae git a good grip oan it. She's screamin as ah stick in the plug n turn oan the taps n fill the sink. Ah sticks her heid in it as it fills up. — WASH THIS, YA CUNT!

Ah pills up her heid n she's blowin water n blood ootay her nose n thrashin aroound like a fish caught oan a line. Ah hear a voice n that wee Michael's standin in the doorway n eh goes: — What ur ye daein tae Mum, Dad?

— Git back in that fuckin stair! Ah'm jist washin her cause she's goat a nosebleed! Now git! Ah'm fuckin tellin ye!

The wee cunt bolts oot, then ah plunges her heid intae the sink again. — AH'LL GIE YE FUCKIN WASHIN, YA DURTY FUCKIN CRACK HOOR, AH'LL FUCKIN WELL WASH YOU UP!

Ah pills her heid up again, but the dirty psycho hoor grabs a fuckin wee vegetable choppin knife fae the drainin board n fuckin leathers ays wi it! It's stuck right in ma fuckin ribs. Ah lits go n she hits ays wi a plate thit breaks ower ma heid. Ah fuckin batters her again n she hits the deck n starts fuckin screamin, as ah pills the knife oot ma ribs. Fuckin blood everywhere. Ah boots her n leaves her doon thaire curled intae a baw n gits oot tae the bairns but whin wir in the stairwell, thir's the auld cunt opposite standin in her doorway wi her airms roond thum. — C'mon, boys, ah tell thum, but they jist stand thaire, so ah grabs at Michael cause ah've nae time tae fuck aboot here, n then that fuckin June's oan her feet n she's oot n screamin at me, shoutin at the auld cunt: — CALL THE POLIS! EH'S TRYIN TAE TAKE MA BAIRNS!

— Ma! that sooky wee Michael cunt goes, Sean should've cut that cunt's fuckin heid oaf, probably no even mine, a fuckin wee poof like that, n ah lits him huv it wi the back ay ma hand, n she's grabbin ehs airm oan the stairs n it's like the wee cunt's caught in a tug ay war. Eh's screamin n ah jist lits go n they baith faw back oantae the stair. The auld cow's shoutin again n two polis come straight up the stair n one's gaun: — What's going on here?

— Nowt. Mind yir ain fuckin business, ah say.

— Eh's tryin tae take ma bairns away! she screeches.

— Is this right? the aulder cop asks me.

— Thir ma fuckin bairns n aw! ah goes.

The auld cunt oan the stair goes: — He battered that lassie, ah saw um! And that wee yin, the wee sowel! Shi fuckin well turns tae me n goes: — Eh's bad that yin, rotten tae the core!

— You shut yir fuckin mooth, ya auld cunt! It's fuck all tae dae wi you!

The aulder cop goes: — Sir, if you don't move out into the street, I'm going to arrest you and charge you with a breach of the peace. If this lady presses charges, you're in serious trouble!

So eftir a fuckin big shoutin match ah jist heads, cause ah'm no fuckin well wantin lifted cause ay that cunt. N they polis cunts, fuckin well lookin at me, like ah wis a fuckin nonce. Ah shouldnae huv hit Michael but, but that wis her fuckin fault, windin ays up again. Well, ah'll be oantae the fuckin social work n every cunt'll ken thit it's hur, hur thit's the fuckin dirty crack hoor takin fuckin drugs in front ay ma fuckin bairns . . .

They want tae arrest some cunt, lit thum arrest that *Home Alone 2* fucker. Ah ken eh wis jist a bairn ehsel whin eh did they films, bit ah dinnae how a cunt like that kin live wi ehsel now.

53

'. . . even flaccid it's over
a foot long . . .'

I get up to Simon's flat. It's a mess, but that doesn't worry me. I leap forward and grab a hold of him and push my lips onto his. He's tense, unbending. — Eh, we have visitors, he tells me. We go through and on the leather sofa is a young guy I dimly recognise from Simon's pub. One of those shadowy, vaguely unsavoury presences you register from the corner of your eye. Now he just seems a normal young lad: gangly, smelly, spotty, nervous. I smile at him and I can see his face turning bright red, his eyes watering, and the poor little darling turns his gaze away.

We're looking at him and I'm wondering what's going on here. Simon's saying nothing. Then there's a knock at the door and I go to answer and it's Mel and Terry. She kisses me and goes through and gives Simon a hug, then sits down beside the boy. — Awright, Curtis pal?

— Ah-ah-aye, he says.

Terry's still quite subdued. He sits in a chair in the corner.

— This is Curtis, Simon says to me. He's going to join us as an actor. As the lad forces a weak smile back I'm thinking that this is some kind of joke. Then Simon looks from Mel to me, explaining: — From this unpromising material I want you ladies to mould the hottest young stud that ever came out of Leith. Well, second hottest, he says with a mock, self-effacing swagger and bow.

— Eh's a big laddie, Mel sniggers, — if ye ken what ah mean.

— Show her, Curt, don't be shy, Simon says, as he heads to the kitchen.

Curtis's eyes water again and his face is scarlet. — C'moan, ye showed me last night, Mel grins.

I glance at her as he nervously unbuckles his trousers then unzips his flies. Then he starts to pull this thing out of his pants and it just keeps on coming. Even flaccid it's over a foot long, hanging down, almost to his knees. I'm speechless. More importantly, the width . . . I've never thought of myself as a size queen, but . . . So the young lad is in. Fourteen inches, how can he be out? A virgin (until Melanie got her hands on him last night, I'll wager), a freak almost, but he is the man for our show.

Simon instructs him to shave his pubes to make it look even bigger, like real porn stars do.

Terry says: — Look at the wee cunt's face wi the shaving. You trust him tae shave roond that asset?

— You're a fine one tae talk, Terry. Stitches still in?

I'm wondering how we're going to break him in so that he'll be able to perform, although I reckon Mel's ahead of the game there.

— Ah'll help ye shave, Mel said.

It isn't going to be a problem, that side of it. Simon bids me to come into the kitchen. — Mel took ehs cherry last night, she's sorting him out, he confirms. — We're going to have to deconstruct this kid, he says, — then reassemble in our image. We need to do an Eliza Doolittle on the fucker. Not just the shagging techniques. Any moron can fuck, and any idiot with a willing partner can work their way around the sexual positions, he sneaks a sideways glance out the door at Terry. — God, how we stupefy ourselves with our love of sex. But sort him out completely, make him into a fucking sentient being. Clothes. Look. Bearing. Manner.

I nod in agreement but first there's proper business to attend to. We tell the others to meet us in the pub, Simon handing Curtis a wrapped box as he exits. — It's a present, open it.

Curtis rips off the paper to reveal the gaudy, ghastly blonde head of a blow-up sex doll. Simon says: — Her name's Sylvie. She's for practice during those lonely nights, although I don't think there'll be many of them in the future. Welcome to *Seven Rides*!

Poor Curtis doesn't know quite what to make of Sylvie, as they head down to the Port Sunshine. Simon urges me to stall for a bit as he's keen to discuss progress on what he calls 'the scam'.

We had got the two lists, both on different discs. Rab's dad helped to reconcile them and put them in the same format. There are 182 Rangers season-ticket holders who have accounts at the Merchant City Clydesdale Bank branch. Out of that number, 137 have 1690 as their pin number. I can't think how Simon possibly knew his, and he did patiently explain it to me, as has Mark, but I still don't get it. Despite McClymont's Scottish studies programme, I've come nowhere near to understanding the Scottish mentality or culture. Of that number, eighty-six have Internet banking facilities.

The important thing is that the money in those eighty-six accounts ranges from an overdraft of £3,216 to a credit of £42,214. Simon explains that he and Mark had got into the online banking system for Clydesdale. Using the 1690 pin number, they removed a total of £62,412 from the bigger accounts, depositing them in a general account they've set up in Zurich at the Swiss Business Bank, he informs me, as he racks up two lines of coke.

— Not my tipple, I say, taking my skins, blow and tobacco from my shoulder bag.

— Oh, I know that. These are both for me. I've two nostrils, he explains, — Well, for the time being anyway. Aye, three days later the bulk of the money, except £5,000, will be transferred into a production account we've set up in Switzerland at the Banque de Zurich for Bananazzurri Films.

— So now we go down the pub to celebrate?

— Nooo . . . Simon says, — the fund-raisers are you, me and Rents. We're the only ones who know about this. Never mention it to anybody, he warns, — or we all go to jail for a long time. We keep the money in those accounts, it's way in excess of what we need to make our movie. We'll catch up with the others later. Right now, me, you and Rents are celebrating in private.

And I'm elated, excited and more than a little scared wondering just what we've got into. So we head up to meet Mark at the Café Royal restaurant, where the three of us enjoy oysters and bottles of Bollinger. Mark pours the champagne into the glasses and whispers: — You did brilliantly.

— You two did alright as well, I say, quite aghast, but now really concerned at the extent of our fraud. — This is our business, strictly between us, I nervously implore, and Mark nods in serious agreement. — That means Dianne can know nothing about it?

— Too right, Mark replies sombrely. — They throw away the key for shit like this. But listen, what about Rab? he adds in sudden concern. — He must know something as he got the info about the computer programmes from his old man.

— Rab's sound, Simon says, — but he can be a bit puritanical and he'd shit his pants if he knew the scale of the fraud. But he thinks it's just some dippo's credit card. I've squared him up for his services. Let's just not talk about it again, he smiles, then breezily sings a song: a strange ditty I've never heard before.

> On the green, grassy slopes of the Boyne
> Where the Orangemen with William did join
> And they fought for our glorious delivery
> On the green grassy slopes of the Boyne
>
> Orangemen must be loyal and steady
> For no matter what 'ere may betide
> We must still mind our war cry 'no surrender!'
> And remember that God's on our side . . .

— I love Scotland, Simon says, sipping his champagne. — There's so many fucked-up cunts who believe in total shite, it's such easy money. This whole Celtic–Rangers FC thing is the best scam ever invented. It's not just a licence to fleece morons, it's a licence to fleece their children and their children's children. The franchise goes on and on; Murray, McCann, those boys know what they're doing alright.

Mark smiles at me, then he turns to Simon. — Now that we're all rich-ish, I'm taking it that your commitment to making this picture hasn't wavered?

— Not a bit, Simon replies. — This isn't about money, Rents, I realise that now. Any fucking arsehole can make money. This is about creating something that is *going* to make money. This is about expression, about self-actualisation, about living, about showing pampered rich cunts who've had silver spoons in their gubs that we can do anything those fuckers can, and better.

— Mmm, says Mark, — I'll drink to that, raising his glass in yet another toast.

Simon's looking at me, saying nothing but pursing his mouth in pained sincerity. Then he says chidingly: — No spending sprees, Nikki, I'll keep a hold of the purse strings. If you get skint, just ask.

I don't know if I trust Simon and I don't think that he and Mark even trust each other. But I hardly care about the money or the other embellishments. I love this. I feel alive.

— Anyway, if we get done, all you have to do is roll your eyes at the judge and tell him that you were duped by a pair of evil schemies and you'll walk while Rents and I swing, right, Mark?

— Defo, he says, pouring out some more champagne.

Afterwards we head round to Rick's Bar in Hanover Street. — Isn't that Mattias Jack? Simon asserts, pointing to a guy in the corner.

— Possibly, Mark contemplates, ordering another bottle of champagne.

Simon and I go back to his place in Leith and spend the night shagging like animals. The next day I go home satisfyingly tired, sore and raw, and go through my coursework and my stint at the sauna. When I get home from my shift Mark's in the flat, talking to Dianne. He greets me briefly and leaves.

— What's all this then?

— He's an old friend. We're going out for a drink again tomorrow.

— Just for old times' sake, eh?

She smiles coyly and raises an eyebrow. There's a glow to her and I'm wondering if she's shagged him yet.

Later on, Simon, Rab and I are down at the editing suite in Niddrie, where he took me before. I didn't know places like this existed in Edinburgh, in fact I've never seen anywhere like it. The guy that runs Vid In The Nid is an old pal of Rab's from the days when he used to go to football with a hooligan gang. A lot of them now seem to be entrepreneurial types, and this guy Steve Bywaters seems more like a social worker than an ex-football thug. They seem as close-knit as the Masons when it comes to sharing skills and resources. — We've got the lot, we can do it all here, he says, looking clean-cut and born-again Christian.

As we're heading away, Rab says: — Great, eh.

Sick Boy's shaking his head. — Aye, but we can do it in the Dam. The OPA, Rab, mind?

— Right enough, Rab says, but I suspect that Simon has another agenda.

54

Scam # 18,749

The City Café is busy with pre-clubbers, as Curtis and his wee mates come in and ask me to join them. We're sitting beside some student types who are full of their dull conspiracy theories, all excited as they debate who isn't really dead: Elvis, Jim Morrison, Princess Di. Too full of their own sense of youthful immortality to believe anybody really leaves the gig. Stuck in a life-affirming, death-denying bourgeois dreamworld.

Some of the scheme kids like Philip are sneering and laughing at their foibles; they know it's all bullshit. From an early age here, they've seen enough death in the schemes and inner city through the Aids epidemic of the eighties to be robbed of such innocent notions. Funny, but I'm sure our generation used to feel the same as the suburban kids. Not any more though, and certainly not me.

— All those fuckers are as dead as they're ever going to be, I tell one student, and the sovied kids all guffaw and join in, ripping the piss out of them.

While this is going on I get Curtis's attention. — Watch your mates there, taking the pish out of those students. He dips his head slowly. — Now fast-forward fifteen years: who's going tae have the nice hoose, the job, the business, the cash, the motor and who's gaunnae be stuck in a slum on a giro?

— Right . . . Curtis nods.

— Ken how?

— Cause they've goat the education n that?

Not bad. — Yes, that's part of it. Any other reasons?

— Cause they've goat rich mas n dads who kin gie them the cash tae git started? N the contacts n that?

This boy isnae quite as dippit as I thought. — Sharp, Curt, sharp. But you put these two thegither and what dae ye get?

— Dunno.

— Expectation. They'll have those things cause they expect to have them. How could they expect anything else? The likes of you and me don't expect those things. We know we have tae graft like fuck tae earn them. Now for me, an over-educated, yet under-qualified man, there's no real point of entry into that life. Why dae you think I piss around in the black economy on the margins of society? Cause I like the amusing characters? Because bams and hoors and junkies and dealers are my kind of people? No fucking chance. I've done pimping, housebreaking, theft, credit-card fraud and drug dealing, not because I like them but because I can't break into legitimate business at a level, status and remuneration that I regard as commensurate with my knowledge and skills. I'm a tragic mess, Curt, a tragic mess. But that can and will change, I explain looking at my watch, as it's time to meet the others. — Listen, I attack my drink, — did you ever get any use out off that blow-up doll?

— Eh naw . . . he says, all embarrassed. — Ah wis jist playin wi it n it went doon on me . . .

— It went doon oan ye! Fuck me, if I kent it wis gaunnae dae that ah'd've goat one myself! I laugh at his distraught coupon.

We drink up and head into N-Sign's spot to shoot some footage of clubbers in action. Curtis is dancing with his mates and Rab's camera is on him. Then it tracks Nikki, who's been talking to Mel, heading towards him. She dances in front of him for a bit, then takes his hand and leads him into the office in the club, which Carl's emptied for us.

Then, when the club is shut down, we get into the real work and prepare to shoot one of our key scenes. Rab and his pals are setting up the equipment in the office.

— Dae ye think Melanie n Nikki r-r-really like me? Curtis asks.

— What do you mean?

— Well, ah think thir jist nice tae me cause you s-s-say so.

— Dinnae turn they puppy-dug lamps on a chick and expect her no tae cook, mate. You've got the power, I explain.

— Bit l-l-lassies dinnae f-f- . . . his face goes into a spazzy twitch — . . . f-f-fancy ays.

— The dippit wee tarts, aye. They arenae wimmin ay the world

337

but. The chick who's been past Pilrig, she learns how tae distil things doon tae brass tacks, especially if that auld pot's got a wee bit stretched. Then it's aboot the width of a circle, I smile, and I dehl-dehl, dehl-dehl-dehl-dehl-dehl . . . the opening refrain from that Bowie classic. It fails to cut much ice with Curt though. While he's away for another nervous pee, I approach Nikki. — Try and make Curt feel desired, his self-esteem is rock-bottom.

As he returns from the toilet, Nikki goes over to him and I hear her say: — Curtis, I can't wait for you to fuck me.

The slack-jawed young fool just blinks and flushes. — S-s-s-so what are ye tryin tae s-s-say?

I can't help it, I laugh my head off. — You're a comic genius, Curtis! That's going in the fuckin script! And I start scribbling like fuck on my draft of the screenplay.

After I pep-talk my stars, Rab gives me the nod and we're ready to rock.

— Right, folks, this is the key scene in the movie. This is where 'Joe' wins the bet from 'Tam'. Curtis, this is where your character 'Curt' pops his cherry for the first time in the film. So don't worry about being nervous, you're *supposed* to be nervous. I just want you both to say what you said before. So, Nikki, you lead him into the office, slam the door shut, stand behind it and say . . .

— I'd love to fuck you, Nikki drawls lecherously, looking at Curtis.

— And you say, Curt, I nod at him.

— S-s-so what ur ye tryin tae say . . .

— Brilliant. Then you get him across the desk, Nikki. Let Nikki take the lead, Curtis. Right, let's try it out.

Of course, it's nothing like as good as the spontaneous original, but after many attempts we get a couple of usable takes. We've got our six brothers shagged now, the only problem being that Terry's damaged cock still isn't strong enough for an arse-fuck. Not to worry, I've an idea.

55

Whores of Amsterdam Pt 6

I informed Martin and Nils that I needed a break from the club.
I told Katrin that I had to go home and see my folks for a bit.
But whatever I thought might have been requisite for my state of
mind, *this* is what it really was. It was all I could do to tear myself
away from her. Dianne Coulston.

We made love most of the night, in Gav's spare bed. Just wanting
her, aching for her, spent seemingly beyond exhaustion, yet soon
aroused again. Experience tells me that this is nothing to do with
love or emotion, it's just the reaction of two strange bodies in proximity to each other. That it'll wear off. But fuck experience.

This morning she's wearing my T-shirt, and that always feels good,
a girl doing that, and we're in the kitchen making ourselves some
toast and coffee. Gav comes in, ready to go to work. He sees her,
raises his eyes, and skulks out. I shout after him, as I don't want him
to feel like a stranger in his own house. — Gav! C'mere!

He sheepishly comes back in. — This is Dianne, I tell him.

Dianne smiles and extends a hand. He shakes it and he has some
tea and toast with me and, aye, with my girlfriend. But I've been
thinking about Katrin and about what to tell Dianne. It's still on
my mind as I leave her and head into town.

When the totally normal seems so strange, you know you've led
a fucked-up life. I'm in Princes Street Gardens with my sister-in-
law Sharon and my niece Marina, whom I've never met before. It's
the first time I've seen Sharon in years. I think the last time was
when I shagged her at my brother's funeral, in the toilet, when she
was pregnant with Marina.

Not only can I not emotionally connect with the person I was
then, I can't even envisage what such a person might be like. Maybe
I'm kidding myself of course, you can never be sure, but that's the

way it feels. Would I have still been that person if I had stayed here? Probably not.

Sharon's gone fat. Her body's been hardened by layers of it. The old Sharon, big-titted, voluptuous, is now wrapped in several rolls of fleshy carpet. I don't think about how I must look to her, that's her problem, I'm just being honest at my negative reaction. Once we talk I feel guilty about this skin-deep revulsion. She's a nice woman. We're sitting on the piazza having a coffee, Marina is on the merry-go-round, waving at us from a sinister-faced horse.

— Sorry tae hear it didnae work oot wi you and the boy ye were wi, I tell her.

— Naw, we split up last year, she says, lighting up a Regal, offering me one, which I decline. — He wanted kids. Ah didnae want another bairn, she explains before adding: — But, I suppose there wis mair tae it than that.

I sit there nodding slowly, feeling that disconcerted and uncomfortable way in that intimacy fest when people tell you everything about themselves straight away. — It happens, I shrug.

— What about you, ye wi anybody?

— Well, it's a bit complicated . . . I ran into somebody the other week, I explain, feeling a strange light come on in my face and a smile form on my lips when I think about her, — somebody I used to know back here. And there's somebody over in Holland, but it's a bit rocky right now. Well, no, it's finished.

— Same old Mark, eh?

I was always more into relationships than one-night stands, without particularly excelling at either. But when you meet somebody, no matter how many times you've fucked up in the past, you always think . . . yes. We're too full of hope to even consider expectation. — Listen . . . I reach into my bag and hand over the envelope, — that's for you and Marina.

— I dinnae want that, she says pushing it away.

— Ye dinnae ken what's in it.

— I can guess. It's money, isn't it?

— Aye. Take it.

— Nup.

I look at her as searchingly as I can. — Listen, I know what everybody says about me in Leith.

— Naebody talks aboot ye, she says in a way which is supposed to be comforting but is actually a bit fucking deflating tae the ego. They surely must . . .

— It's no drugs money. I promise you that. It's from my club, I explain, fighting the urge to wince at the irony of my statement. Everybody in the world who runs a dance-music club owes their money, albeit indirectly, to drugs. — I don't need it. I want tae dae something . . . for my niece. Please, I beg, then elaborate in discomfort. — My brother and me, we were like chalk and cheese. Both radges, but in different ways. Sharon smiles in response and I reciprocate in a strange affection, as I recall my brother Billy's face, see him sticking up for me, suddenly wishing I'd been easier on him now. Less bellicose, dogmatic and all that. But it's shite. You were what you were and are what you are. Fuck that regrets bullshit. — Funny, what I miss about him, it's not how we were, it's the possibility of us getting on better. I've changed in so many ways. I think he might have too.

— Maybe, she says, doubtful and cagey, and I don't know whether she means him, or me or both of us. She looks at the envelope, feels it. — There must be hundreds in here.

— Eight grand, I tell her.

Her eyes almost pop out off her head. — Eight thousand pounds! Mark! She lowers her voice and looks around like we're in a spy film. — Ye cannae walk aboot wi aw this money! Ye could git mugged or anything . . .

— Better git it tae the bank then. Look, ah'm no leavin wi it, so it stays oan that table thaire if you dinnae pick it up. She goes to say something but I talk over her. — Look, ah widnae dae it if ah couldnae afford it. Ah'm no that much ay a mug.

Sharon puts it into her bag and squeezes my hand as tears glisten in her eyes. — Ah dinnae ken what tae say . . .

This is ma cue tae get away. I tell her I'll take Marina to see *Toy Story*, while she sorts things out at the bank and has a look around the shops. As I'm walking, hand in hand with the kid, I'm wondering what Begbie would do if he ran into me now. Surely he wouldn't . . . I get all para that he'll hassle the bairn or Sharon so we pile into a taxi down to the Dominion, because I can't really see Franco in Morningside. When the film finishes I drop Marina off back at Sharon's.

Later on, I'm heading up George IV Bridge and I spy another familiar face, but it can't be, not coming out the library! I go up behind him and finger his collar like I'm polis. He nearly jumps out of his skin, before turning around and his hostile gaze alters into a beaming smile.

— Mark . . . Mark, man . . . how ye daein?

We retire to a nearby bar for a drink. Ironically, it's called Scruffy Murphy's, an old nickname everybody teased Spud with. I can't remember what it used to be. As I set up two Guinnesses, it's hard not to think that Spud looks as big a mess as ever. We sit down and he's telling me about this Leith history project he's working on, which just blows me away. Not because it sounds interesting, though it does, it's more the concept of Spud being into something like that. But he talks about it with great enthusiasm before we get round to going over old times. — How's Swaney? He cannae still be kicking aboot surely, I ask of an old pal.

— Thailand, Spud says.

— You're jokin, I reply, once again flabbergasted. Swaney always fantasised about going out there, but I can't comprehend that he actually did.

— Aye, the cat made it, Spud nods, the extent of the unlikelihood seeming to hit him as well. — On one leg n aw.

We talk about Johnny Swan for a bit, but there's one thing I really want to know, and I ask as casually as I can. — Tell me, Spud, is Begbie out of prison?

— Aye, he's been oot for yonks, Spud informs me as I experience a sinking sensation. There's a numbness in my face and a ringing in my ears. It becomes hard to focus on his words and my head starts to spin. — Since eftir New Year. The cat wis roond at mines the other day, likes. The boy's radger than ever, he says seriously. — Keep away fae um, Mark, eh disnae ken aboot the money . . .

I reply in a deadpan manner: — What money was that?

Spud beams back a big, warm open smile and he throws his arms

342

round me in an excess of enthusiasm. For a skinny guy his embrace has some strength. When he breaks off, his eyes are watering. — Thanks, Mark, he says.

— Don't know what you're talking about, I shrug, maintaining the silence. What you don't know, they can't beat out you. I don't even ask about the state of his or Ali or the kid's immune systems. Sick Boy is a compulsive liar and he's a lot less good at it or entertaining with it than he used to be. I glance at the pub clock. — . . . Listen, mate, I have to go. I'm meeting my girlfriend.

Spud looks a bit sad about this and then seems to consider something. — Look, catboy, kin ye, eh, dae ays a favour?

— Aye, sure, I reluctantly nod, trying to guess how much he'll hit me for.

— Well, Ali n me . . . we're, eh, gittin rid ay the flat. Ah'm steyin at muh mate's for a bit, but eh cannae take the cat. Could you take it for a while?

I'm thinking about what cat he means, then it dawns on me he's talking about a real one. I heartily detest the creatures. — Sorry, mate . . . ah'm no a cat person . . . n it's Gav's place I'm in.

— Aw . . . eh sais, n eh looks that fuckin pathetic that I have tae try n do something, so I phone Dianne and ask her how she fancies looking after a cat for a bit. Dianne's cool about it and tells me that Nikki and Lauren were talking about getting a cat so it would be a good trial for them, see if it actually worked out. She tells me that she'll speak to them, which she does, then she calls back immediately. — The cat's got a new temporary home, she says.

Spud's delighted with the news and we arrange for a time to bring the creature up to Tollcross. As I leave Spud to head in that direction, I'm feeling an ugly rage through my numbness, eating at the core of me. I compose myself and call my business partner on his mobile. — Simon, how goes?

— Where are you?

— Never mind that. Are you sure that Begbie's still in the jail? Somebody told me he was out.

— Whae telt ye that?

Pretentious Sick Boy's slip back intae broad Scottish is very unconvincing. — Never you mind.

— Well, it's nonsense. He's still banged up as far as I know.

Lying cunt. I switch off the phone, heading down the Grassmarket and up the West Port towards Tollcross, fevered thoughts flying through my head, horrible emotions gnawing at my gut.

56

'. . . with him draped over my shoulders . . .'

I seem to have bonded with Zappa, the cat we're looking after. I've started cat-flexing with him after seeing it done on Channel Four the other week. I raise him thirty times to position one, with him draped over my shoulders and me rising from a squatting position. I move on to position two, supporting him in the stomach with the palm of one hand, holding his chest with the other, for thirty repetitions each side.

Lauren comes in looking quite surprised: — Nikki, what are you doing to that poor cat?

— Cat-flexing, I explain, now worried that she'll think I'm into bestiality as well. — When you lead a busy life, pets tend to get neglected, so it's a way of keeping fit and socialising with your cat. It gives you exercise plus the tactile, bonding thing. You should try it, I say, laying him down.

Lauren shakes her head doubtfully, but I'm in a hurry to leave as we're doing the last porno scene with Terry and Mel, featuring Curtis as proxy shag. I head down to Leith and meet them at Simon's flat.

Curtis has a simpleton's smile on his face. The boy is coachable, in terms of shagging. He follows myself and Melanie like a sick puppy begging for food, or in this case pussy. No, that's not fair. This boy's looking for more. He wants love, belonging, acceptance. In fact, in his obvious, naked sincere way, he reminds us all of our own need. He genuinely wants us to like him. To love him even. For our part, we tease him, sometimes stopping just short of cruelty.

Why? Is it revelling in our power, or is it because, as Lauren might contend, we hate what we're doing?

No, it's as I said earlier, he's simply an undignified version of the rest of us: a sad quester who hasn't found what they're looking for.

But in his case, the little bastard has time. Maybe that affects our behaviour, our actions towards him. I fancy I can still feel it between my legs when he was inside me. I've got a small, tight fanny and I never thought I'd be able to take *that*. You can surprise yourself though.

— Do you like that? I ask, pushing my neck into his face.

— Aye, it smells barry, like.

— I'd like to teach you about perfumes, Curtis, teach you about so many things. Then when I'm old and wizened and you're still a good-looking young man breaking in virgins all over town, girls half your age, as all ageing men of substance must go for, you won't hate me. You'll remember me with a kind heart and treat me like a human being.

Mel smiles as she sips a glass of red wine, perhaps unaware of just how serious I'm being.

Curtis, for his part, is horrified at the notion. — Ah'll nivir be bad tae you! he almost squeaks.

Those young boys, so sweet and tender-hearted, how they grow into monsters. Yet they often seem to get better again as they get older; kind and gentle once more. Nobody told Sick Boy Simon that though. Curtis is as much his star pupil as he is mine. And I don't like the lessons he's giving him.

Rab and the crew come down and set up the cameras. But Curtis was sweet. He didn't want to sodomise Mel. — It's dirty, ah dinnae want tae dae that.

— Well done, Curtis, I say, while Mel stresses: — It doesnae bother me, Curtis.

Simon suddenly says: — Okay, let's just leave it for now, he looks at his watch. — C'mon, we're going to the pictures! I wonder what he's playing at as Rab starts moaning, but Simon gets us out and into a cab, up to the Filmhouse where they're showing a series of Scorsese films. It's De Niro in *Raging Bull*.

In the bar, after the showing, Curtis turns to Simon, enthralled. — That wis brilliant!

Simon's about to say something when I cut in. — There's like a reason? You took us up here? I ask him.

Now Simon ignores me and says to Curtis: — You're an actor,

Curt. De Niro's an actor. Did he want to put on loads of weight and walk around like a blob? Did he want to get battered around the ring? He glances at me. — No pun intended. No. He did it because he's an actor. Did he turn roond tae Scorsese on set and go, 'that's dirty' or 'that's sair' or 'that feels a bit cold, remote and exploitative'? No. Because he is an *actor*, he emphasises, stating: — I'm no getting at you, Mel, you're no prima donna.

I can now see that this is as much for my benefit as it is for Curt's. His manipulation sticks out like Terry's hard-on. — We're *not* actors, we're pornography performers, I tell him. — We need to set our own . . .

— No. That's middle-class bullshit. They're the only ones who haven't wakened up to the fact that porn is mainstream now. Virgin sells porn movies. Greg Dark directs Britney Spears videos. Grot mags and men's mags and women's mags are the same. Even repressed, censored British TV teases us with the hint of it. Young people as consumers don't make the distinction now between porn or adult entertainment and mainstream entertainment. In the very same way they don't between alcohol and other drugs. If you get a buzz off it, yes, if you dinnae, no. It's as simple as that.

— Don't you think it's a bit patronising to tell Curt what young people think? I say, but it feels pathetic, it lacks conviction in the face of his harsh certainties.

— I'm calling it as I see it. I'm trying to direct a movie.

— So consent means nothing to you?

— Consent is elastic, it has to be. If not, how do we grow? How do we evolve? There has to be development, a shifting of perspectives over time, there has to be an elasticity of consent.

— There's not going to be an elasticity of my arsehole, Simon. Accept that. Live with it.

— Nikki, it's not an issue. If you don't want to do anal, then fine. You have that right. But as a director of this motion picture I reserve the right to tell one of my leading actors what an unprofessional prude they're being, he smiles.

That's what he does, gets his serious points over as a joke. He thinks he's won the fucking argument, but he's not. — We're *having* sexual activity, not *faking* sexual activity. The whole point about any

347

sexual activity is consent. If there's no consent, it becomes coercion, or rape. The first question is, will I be raped to make a film? The answer is no. Maybe the other girls will. That's up to them, I say, and I can't look at Mel. I'm still staring right at Simon when I ask: — The second question is, will you become a rapist in order to make this film?

He looks at me, and his eyes open wide. — I won't make people do anything they don't want to do. That's the bottom line.

I nearly believe him until I overhear what he says to Curtis in a coke-fuelled rant in the taxi back down to Leith in between shouting at Rab on the mobile. — You fuck with your cock, but you make love with your body and soul. The cock is fuck all. In fact, I'll go further: the cock can be your worst enemy. Why? Because the cock needs a hole. That means the lassie is always in control, as long as the relationship is kept on a purely physical, i.e. shagging, basis. No matter how big your cock is or how well you use it, it's replace-able. There are thousands, millions of cocks queuing up for the berth yours is occupying and a good-looking lassie with any savvy knows that. Fortunately, most lack that awareness. No, the way to wrestle control of the relationship back from the lassie is by getting into her head.

God, I've been warned. It's not my arse I should be worried about, it's my head.

But now it's Mel's arse I'm worried about. I'm feeling as protec-tive of it as I would my own. I pull back, realising that I'm turning into Lauren. Mel's game; she's even told me that she likes it. So we're back down to the flat and the gear is set up again.

Simon's been doing more coke and I can hear him with Curt as Melanie's getting changed. — Curtis, pal, you're gittin good with that weapon ay yours. Ye respect lassies, aye, fair dos, but for this scene we need a bit mair oomph. Have you ever heard of the phrase 'make the bitch suffer'?

— Naw, but ah like Melanie . . .

Sick Simon shakes his head. — Gently tae start, but once ye get it in, crank it up, they love the pain. They can take it better than we can. They can huv bairns, for fuck sakes.

— Not out our arseholes, I cut in.

348

He realises that I've been listening to him and he slaps his head. — I'm trying to direct Curt, he spits, — will you please let me do my job, Nicola, darling?

— Make the bitch suffer, is that where you're coming from, that kind of misogynistic cack?

— Nikki, please, let me do my job. Let's finish the movie, let's have something to debate about.

Thankfully, it only needs one take in each of the arse-fucking positions: legs pinned back frontal, from behind and reverse anal cowgirl. Then we sit down with Mel. — What was that like? I ask.

— It was sair, so fuckin sair, she purses, blowing through her lips. — But good as well. Just when ye thought it wis unbearable it got good, just when you thought it wis good it goat unbearable.

— Wow, says Sick Boy, putting his arm round her. — Well done, folks, that's the final brother, Juice Terry, shagged. I'm going to get Terry and you to simulate the positions, Mel, and we'll use Curtis's cock for the penetration close-ups. We need some more stuff for the orgy scene, a few establishing shots, but that's all the brothers done. *Seven Rides*, it's a kick-in-the-arse off being a wrap!

57

Clarinet

It wis great seein Mark again n it wis barry gittin some encouragement aboot the book. Ah wis that up whin ah goat hame, thit even though ah wis a bit wrecked, ah goat ma manuscript oot n went ower that last chapter again. It's like Rents hud sort ay inspired ays, man. The last bit's aw aboot skag n Aids n that, aboot aw the boys thit wir wiped oot; the pure bams n the decent cats, gadges like Tommy.

N eftir lookin ower it ah couldnae believe it, man, cause that wis it finished. Ah mean, the spellin's no up tae much, but they kin sort aw that oot, dinnae want it too polished, cause it gies they poor cats in the publisher's nowt tae dae whin it comes tae the edit.

Ah realised that it wis nearly mornin n ah pure wanted tae git doon tae that post office n send it oaf tae they publisher's, thaim thit dae aw that Scottish history stuff. Then ah wis gaunnae see Ali n tell her aboot the money, tell hur thit wir gaunnae book up fir Disneyland, fir the bairn n that, ken. Ah tried the other day doon the Port Sunshine bit she wis busy n ah wis pished n ah couldnae talk proper. She pure wanted ays tae go. Ah thoat it's too late tae go tae bed n ah'm pure buzzin, so ah pit oan the Alabama's tape n bopped aroond tae masel fir a bit.

Then it wis doon tae the stationer's fir a big padded envelope, then straight roond tae the post office. Ah kissed that package as ah stuck it in the boax.

Ya beauty!

Ah thoat the best thing tae dae wid be tae pure git in some feather n flip then git a hud ay Ali n Andy when she goes tae pick up the wee man fae the school, tell thum aw the news aboot Disneyland! N mibee no the yin in Paris, mibee the yin in Florida! Aye, ower thair in the sun would be barry, especially wi this crap weather. Terry Lawson wis tellin ays he wis ower thair n it wis cool as.

Then ah thinks, well, ah'm entitled tae a wee celebration now, cause that's me pure done wi the book! Yes! Aw ma debts peyed oaf, money in the tail, me Ali n Andy away tae Disneyland soon. Jist a couple ah beers likesay. So ah'm thinkin, whaire tae go tae celebrate? N yuv goat tae watch Leith, man, cause Leith pure isnae Edinburgh. Thir's aw they pubs in Leith n yi'll find company, whether ye want it or no, n it might no be the right company. Yuv goat tae watch who ye celebrate wi.

Fae Junction Street ah turns oantae the Walk past Mac's Bar. Ah look acroass at the Central Bar then up the Walk n ah ken that beyond it thir's the Bridge Bar, EH6, the Crown, Dolphin Lounge, the Spey, Caledonian Bar, Morrisons, the Dalmeny, the Lorne, the Vicky, the Alhambra, the Volley, the Balfour, the Walk Inn or Jayne's as they call it now, Robbie's, the Shrub, Boundary Bar, the Brunswick, the Red Lion, the Old Salt, the Windsor, Joe Pearce's, the Elm . . . n that's jist off the toap ay ma heid n jist oan the Walk itself, no countin side streets or nowt like that. So naw, man, naw, every Walk boozer contains the prospect ay a huge sesh. Same wi Duke Street n Junction Street n even Constitution n Bernard strassers. So ah head fir the mair trendy, sedate and gentrified Shore, man, whaire a Leith man ay letters should be drinkin.

It looks different doon here, man, aw redeveloped; the docks now aw smart bars and restaurants, loads ay yuppie converted warehooses. It wis sayin in the paper thit they moved the prossies fae whaire they eywis worked cause ay the complaints fae the residents. That tae me's pure no fair, cause thuv eywis worked thair n cats ken what the place is like before they move in.

Ah gits intae this big auld bar, aw sortay wid-panelled, n orders one ay they cauld Guinnesses. Ah looks outside tae whaire the sea-gulls are swirlin, n ah kin see thit a cruise ship's come in.

Thing is, ah'm sittin thair n Curtis heads in. — Thoat ah saw ye comin in. Ah says t-t-t masel thit . . . n the perr wee gadge goes aw spazzy n the face, ehs eyes blinkin, — . . . Sp-Sp-Spud widnae come in here.

Well, man, ah made a big mistake. Wi me gittin guttered wi Rents last night, the peeve wis still in ma system n eftir a few pints ah started tae feel a bit pished. Wee Curtis is pure celebratin n aw cause eh's been in some orgy wi they lassies fir this film thit Sick Boy's makin now. Ah pure dinnae like tae think aboot Ali workin in that pub wi aw thaim roond thaire. Sometimes ah think aboot him tryin tae git hur involved, git her intae aw that, n ma blood just goes pure cauld. Cause eh kin make people dae things they pure usually widnae dae. But no Ali, man, naw, no ma Ali. N ah pure didnae want tae go roond thair tae the school tae see her n Andy aw listless n stunned, so ah take some base speed offay Curtis tae try n straighten masel oot.

Whin ah git roond tae the school, ah feel barry, bit right away Ali's eyes telt ays thit it's one ay they yins whin ye think ye feel good bit yir really wrecked. She's wearin this hooded, fur-lined jaykit ah've no seen before n a jumper n leggins n boots. She looks barry. The wee gadge is wrapped up well, skerf n hat n that.

— What do you want, Danny?

— Hiya, Dad, the wee man goes.

— Awright, sodjir? ah goes tae the boy, then tae Ali: — Barry news. Ah've come intae some dosh n ah want tae take yis tae Disneyland . . . Paris . . . or Florida if ye want! N ah've finished the book, it's posted away tae the publishin cats! N ah met Mark yesterday, Rents, like! Eh's been in Amsterdam but wi went oot n hud a few beers. Eh thinks it's a barry idea, the book n that . . .

Her face husnae changed at aw but, man. — Danny . . . what are you on about?

— Look, lit's jist go tae the café n wi kin talk aboot it, ah sais, smilin at the wee man. — A milkshake at Alfred's, eh, pal?

— Aye, eh goes, — but in McDonald's. Thaire milkshakes are better.

— Naw, man, naw, cause Alfred uses only the best ay stuff, McDonald's milkshakes are aw sugar, thir bad fir ye, man, thir evil. Globalisation n aw that, man, it's aw wrong . . . n ah sees ah'm rantin n Ali's lookin daggers at me, — . . . but wi kin go tae McDonald's if ye want, likesay . . .

— No, Ali saws coldly.

— Aw, Mum, the wee chap goes.

— No, she goes, — we're too busy. Auntie Kath's expecting us back, and I'm working tonight, she says. Then she turns tae me and goes up aw close, n fir a second ah think she's gaunnae kiss me but she whispers in ma ear: — You're oaf yir fuckin face. Keep away fae ma son when you're on drugs! Then she turns n takes Andy by the hand, n they walk away.

Eh turns n waves a couple ay times, n ah force a smile n wave back, pure hopin thit eh cannae see the tears in ma eyes.

Ah go back tae the Shore, tae another pub. It's busy n thir's a jazz band oan. Ah'm down, man, the life's been ripped ootay me. Ah'm jist thinkin what's the point in havin cash whin the people ye want tae spend it oan dinnae want tae be wi ye? What huv ah really goat wi thaim away?

Naw, man, it's aw fucked.

Ah look roond at the band, the young lassie oan the clarinet, whae's really good, makin such a beautiful sound ye could jist likesay greet, man. Then ah see the auld boy at the bar, wi a big smile oan ehs face. At that point a horrible thought hit ays; everybody in this bar, everybody here, n Ali n ma wee Andy even, they'll aw be deid soon. In ten or twenty or thirty or forty or fifty or sixty or whatever years it takes. Ah, they beautiful people, man, and aw the weird and horrible and mental yins, they willnae be here, they willnae even exist. In nae time at aw really.

Ah mean, what the fuck is aw that aboot, likes?

Ah head up fae the Shore, back hame. Ah dinnae ken what tae dae. Ah'm no long in the hoose whin Franco phones me up, tellin ays tae meet him in Nicol's the night. Says eh needs tae talk tae me aboot June. Mibee Franco's noticed that she's no lookin sae well either. Mibee the cat does care, eftir aw. Eh tells ays Second Prize is oot wi him. Be good tae see Secks, like. — Be thaire at eight bells. Ah'll fuckin well see ye.

So ah'm sortay thinkin aboot it, but ah'm no that much company the now, likes. Then thir's another call n it's Chizzie the Beast. Straight eftir Franco n aw. Must be something aboot jail time. Chizzie but, ah've been avoidin that bad cat. — Mental the other week thaire, eh. No comin oot for a wee drink, chav? eh goes.

— Nah, man, takin it easy, eh, thinkin thit ah'm no gaunnae be in *his* company again anywey.

Ehs voice goes that sortay nasal, creepy wey. — Ah saw yir missus the other night thaire, chavvy, that wis hur workin behind the bar in that Port Sunshine. She's pretty tidy. They tell ays youse huv split up but, eh?

Ah feel ma blood runnin cauld, man. Ah cannae say nowt.

— Aye, ah wis thinkin thit ah might ask ehr oot sometime. Ah bit ay winin n dinin. Ah ken how tae show a burd a good time, me, eh! Aw aye, that's one thing ah ken awright.

Ma hert's gaun pure thump thump thump, man, bit ah laugh n make light ay it n then ah say: — Eh aye, ah'll come oot fir a pint well. It'll dae me good. Mibee hit the toon again. Kin ye eh, meet ays in Nicol's pub in Junction Street? Thir's a couple ay tidy burds work behind the bar. One's meant tae be game, likesay.

Eh bites it. — Now yir talkin, Murphy. When?

— Eight a'cloak.

But ah'm no gaun, no tae that Junction Street shitehoose, ah'm gaun doon the Port Sunshine tae keep an eye oan things.

58

LUCKY BONUS

Ah've dragged that cunt Second Prize oot, n uv phoned up Spud Murphy cause ah want tae git tae the boatum ay this shite wi June. Some cunt's goat the wrong end ay the fuckin stick here, or some cunt's tryin tae fuckin well wind me up. Mates. Nae cunt's yir fuckin mate, ye see that the aulder ye git. Second Prize, oan the pool table, aw fucking edgy, tryin tae drink a fuckin tomatay juice like a fuckin poof. Ah'll gie the cunt tomatay juice. Fuckin anti-social cunt. — Aw that stuff aboot alcoholism's a load ay shite. Ye kin manage a fuckin pint, it's no gaunnae kill ye. One fuckin pint!

— Naw, ah cannae drink, Frank, the doctor's said, eh goes, ehs daft wee eyes aw that dippit sortay brainwashed wey they cunts go wi what they call the light ay they Lord in thum. Light ay the fuckin Lord ma erse.

Baws tae aw this shite. — What the fuck dae they cunts ken? They telt muh ma tae stoap smokin. She smokes sixty a day. Shi says tae ays, 'What um ah gaunnae dae, Frank, ah need a fag fir ma nerves. It's the only thing thit works, they pills ur nae good.' Ah jist turns roond n sais tae hur, 'If ye pack in the fags yi'll ken aw aboot it.' Shi'd go intae fuckin shock n that wid fuckin kill hur. Ah telt ur, 'If it isnae fuckin broke, thir's nae need tae fuckin well fix it.' So ye kin manage one fuckin pint.

— Naw, ah cannae . . .

— Look, ah'm gittin ye a fuckin pint up n that's aw thir is tae it, ah tells um n goes ower tae Charlie behind the bar, n gits up two pints ay lager. Cunt better fuckin drink it n aw; ah'm no wasting fuckin money oan bevvy fir nowt. As ah takes the pints back ah sees a cunt comin intae the bar, but it isnae fuckin Spud. Ah goes tae Second Prize tae rack up at the pool. — Right, prepare tae git fuckin slaughtered, ya cunt.

Ah'm thinkin aboot muh fuckin ma n how ah tried tae dae her a favour. No thit it makes a fuckin bit ay difference tae her. As long as she's goat hur fuckin bingo. Ah'd shut they places doon if it wis up tae me; waste ay fuckin time n money. It's no like the hoarses, it's no as if thir's any fuckin enjoyment in it.

Anywey, Second Prize's gittin it now. Ah does um one game, n wi sterts another yin, n ah'm lookin at the door. Thir's still nae sign ay Murphy. — Yuv no touched that pint, ya cunt, ah goes tae Secks.

— Aw, Franco . . . ah cannae, man . . .

— Cannae or willnae, ah goes, lookin right intae the cunt's eyes. Then, for some reason, ah looks behind ays at the boy standin thaire at the bar, readin the racin section ay the *Record*. Something aboot him. Ah kent the cunt fae inside, or kent *ay* the cunt. Eh wis a fuckin beast. Ah kent aw ay they cunts, made it ma business tae mind faces. They'd aw try n hide fae me, cause they kent ah wanted tae look thum in the fuckin eye. What wis it thit eh'd done again? Was he the yin that took the bairn, or that raped the blind lassie, or goat a hud ay the wee boy? Cannae fuckin mind. Aw thit matters here is thit this fuckin thing, this thing here, is a fuckin beast. Ah see the cunt, sittin thaire, in the same pub as me n Second Prize, jist sitting thair at the fuckin bar wi the fuckin *Record*.

Charlie at the bar, servin that cunt ehs fuckin pint, like eh wis normal, n they auld cunts, sittin in the corner, lookin at me. Aw cheery smiles n that, but thir lookin at me in the same wey as they look at yon cunt. Aw they see is some bad cunt fae the fuckin jail. Well, ah'm no like yon cunt n ah nivir fuckin well will be. This cunt, drinkin thaire, jist as eh fuckin well pleases! Walkin the fuckin streets, hingin roond the schools, waitin fir wee bairns n follyin thum hame . . .

Aye, thaire it was, grazing at its fuckin watering hole, *ma* fuckin pub. A fuckin beast. Takin the fuckin pish! — Thir's a fuckin beast through thaire, ah goes tae Second Prize whae's rackin up, — a fuckin beast oan the loose, eh, ah tell um.

Second Prize's looking at ays like eh isnae even gaunnae dae nowt. Aw that fuckin Christianity n forgiveness shite's went n turned ehs heid. Every cunt's fuckin well loast the fuckin plot back here. — Boy's jist in fir a bevvy, Frank, leave um alaine, eh. C'moan, eh goes, splittin the pack, aw quick like eh kens ah'm gaunnae go up tae the cunt.

What's fuckin wrong wi every cunt?

N ehs starin up at me n blinkin, like eh's seen the look in ma eyes n eh lowers ehs heid n goes: — You're stripes, Frank, but ah'm no really listenin cause ah'm still giein this cunt at the bar the eye.

— A beast, ah goes tae Secks, dragging out the ssss in beast, then ah goes tae take ma shot n ah gits this pain whin ah bend doon, whaire that June cunt chibbed ays. Ah grimace n fuckin well hammer a green stripe doon, imaginin thit it's that beast cunt's heid. Ah'm runnin oot ay fuckin patience here.

— Nice one, Franco, Second Prize says or somethin like that, but ah cannae hear the cunt cause ah'm lookin back up tae the fuckin bar.

— Could be oan the lookoot fir a bairn. Ma fuckin bairn mibee, eh, ah sais, n now ah'm movin up tae the bar.

Second Prize is gaun aw whingey n eh goes: — Franco . . . c'moan . . . n eh picks up the untouched pint n says: — Lit's huv that drink, but it's too late for that shite now, eh kens ah'm no listenin, n ah jist goes ower n moves up n ah'm standin right behind the nonce cunt.

— Six fuckin six fuckin six. The number ay the beast, ah whispers aw softly in the cunt's ear.

The boy turns round sharply. Eh looks wide, like ehs heard aw this before. Then ah'm starin right intae um, like um pokin aroond in ehs soul, seein aw the fuckin fear now, but seein somethin mair, the rottenness in it, the fuckin dirty rank rottenness in this cunt, but it's like eh kin see the same in me, like we're fuckin sharin somethin. So ah've goat tae act, before the rest ay the cunts see it n aw, cause ah'm no the same as that, no fuckin wey.

What kin ah see in this cunt . . .

Ehs view ay ehsel, aw forged through the brutalisin ay others; it's crashin aroond him as eh stands before ays, the boy eh vaguely kent as Begbie. Aye, eh's terrified, dizzy wi fear and pain; fuckin perversely, deliciously sick. Ehs mind and body ur playing aw sorts ay tricks oan um. N this cunt is seein the effect eh ehs power over other people by feelin the impact ay ma power oan him. Eh's feelin the absolute liberation ay surrender, ay complete and

357

total capitulation tae the will ay some other cunt. N it's fuckin well beyond violence, it's beyond even sexual; it's a kind ay love, a fuckin bizarre, vainglorious self-adoration, way past the fuckin ego even. Ah'm findin somethin . . . ah'm . . .

Naw . . . naw . . . stoap this noncey shite . . .

Bit it's what bein a hard man is aw aboot; it's a journey, a fuckin self-destructive quest tae find yir limits, cause they fuckin limits eywis come in the form ay a harder man. A big, strong, stiff-hard man whae can dae it for ye, whae can teach ye, show ye whaire ye stand, where yir fuckin parameters ur. Chizzie . . . that's the boy's name . . . Chizzie.

Naw . . . the cunt goes tae speak, n ah cannae lit um fuckin speak. Ah feel muh eyebrows raise a wee bit, jist as muh gless is risin up tae this beast's . . . what's it they call him? . . . this Chizzie cunt's neck.

The cunt fuckin well yelps n huds ehs neck n the blood's spurtin oot aw ower the bar. Must have goat a vein or an artery. Thing is, ah didnae even fuckin well mean tae dae that tae the cunt, it wis jist a fuckin lucky bonus. Lucky fir him, cause ah wanted it tae be slower. Wanted tae hear um fuckin squeal, n plead n beg, like they bairns eh beasted probably did. But the only screamin ah hear comes fae that daft cunt Second Prize as the beast's blood pumps oot, n one ay the auld cunts goes: — Jesus Christ.

Ah spins aroond n tans Secs acroass the fuckin jaw tae stoap um wailin like a fuckin daft wee lassie. — Fuckin shut it, you!

Now the beast's staggerin against the bar and fawin doon, its blood pumpin oot ower the lino flair. Second Prize is standin back by the jukeboax, recitin some daft fuckin prayer.

— Ootay order, Franco, Charlie goes, shakin ehs head, — beast or nae fuckin beast, this is ma pub.

Ah jist looks at the cunt, n points a finger. Second Prize is still sayin a fuckin prayer, the radge. — Listen, ah says tae Charlie n the two auld boys, — that cunt's a beast. Could have been your bairn or mine next, ah goes, n the cunt kicks oot n dies n it feels aw sortay peaceful, n ah feel like ah'm a fuckin saint or somethin. — So, Charlie, ah goes, — gie ays ten minutes, then phone the polis. It wis two young cunts that topped the boy, ah tells every cunt. — Any cunt grasses . . . n grasses ower a beast, well, it'll no jist be thaime thit gits it, it'll be every cunt they fuckin well ken. Goat that?

Charlie goes: — Naebody's grassin up nae cunt ower a fuckin beast, Franco. Aw ah'm sayin is thit ah'm tryin tae run a fuckin business. Mind, it's only been five or six years since that Johnny Broughton shot that boy deid in this very fuckin bar. How does that look fir me?

— Ah fuckin ken that, Charlie, bit it cannae be fuckin well helped. Ah'll see ye awright, ye ken that, ah sais, headin ower n boltin the front door shut. Dinnae want Spud or any other cunt walkin in here the now.

Ah gits a cloth fae behind the bar n wipes the edge ay the table n the cue n aw the baws. Ah empties oor pint glesses n washes thum. Ah turns back tae Second Prize. — Rab, we're oot the back. C'moan. Mind, Charlie, ten minutes, then the phone call. We wirnae here, right?

Ah gaze roond at the two auld cunts. One's Jimmy Doig, the other's Dickie Stewart. They'll no say nowt. N Charlie's miffed aboot the fuckin mess wi the polis n that, but he's nae grass. — Ah'd gie the place a good dustin, Charlie, ah goes, — ah mean, a beast's been in here, eh. Dinnae ken what's fuckin infected, ah says, turnin tae the auld boys. One ay them's cool, the other cunt's shakin. — Youse awright?

— Aye, Frank, aye, son, nae bother, the cool boy, Jimmy Doig says. Auld Dickie twitches a bit, but manages tae git oot: — Awright, Frank son.

Then we're oot the back, oot through a wee yard gaun intae a side alley, makin sure thit nae cunts ur in the street or lookin oot fae the flats above.

Gittin oot, wi head up tae Spud's n ah'm hopin thit that late cunt'll still be in the hoose. Ah tells Second Prize tae fuck off back up the toon cause eh's shakin like that Shakin Stevens, the boy thit fuckin did they bad Elvis impersonations oan *Top ay the Pops*.

Spud's oan the stairs, oan ehs wey oot, aw worried whin eh sees ays. — Eh, Franco . . . sorry ah'm late, man, ah goat stuck oan the phone wi Ali . . . tryin tae sort things oot. Ah wis jist oan ma wey doon tae Nicol's.

— Ah've no even been doon masel yit. Ah wis jist up the toon wi Second Prize, cunt didnae want tae come doon tae Leith, eh no, ah goes. — Says eh'd git involved wi the peeve again.

Eh jist looks at ays n says: — Aw. Then eh asks ays: — Ye wanted tae ken somethin . . . aboot June?

— Fuck it, it's nowt, ah goes, then sais tae um: — Listen, ah cannae come wi ye doon tae Nicol's. Ah've hud a bit ay an argument wi the bird n ah need tae go back n see hur, but ah've goat tae go roond ma brar Joe's first.

— Right . . . eh, ah'm jist gaunnae go doon the Port Sunshine fir one then, see Ali n that.

— Aye, ah goes, — fuckin burds, eh? N ah leaves um at the boatum ay the stair n heads roond tae Joe's, hopin thit that nosey hoor ay a wife ay his isnae in as a fuckin ambulance n two polis cars head screechin doon the fuckin Walk.

3

Exhibition

59

Whores of Amsterdam Pt 7

I'm back in Amsterdam, but it doesnae feel like home any more. I'm wondering if that's because I'm not with Dianne, or cause I am with that lying cunt Sick Boy. Either way, pull or push, the Dam's not the refuge it once was.

I could hardly pull myself away from her to get on that plane with him. The way her love made me fearless; even my Begbie paranoia was waning dangerously. The cunt could have been stalking me with an axe during those leafy walks along the Colinton Dell, for all I knew or cared. When I first met her she was just a hip, precocious schoolie, which is a lot more than I was. I was just a wanker. Dianne now but, she's a woman; cool and intelligent, not really the mad raver I thought she'd be, but smart, bookish and therefore sexier than ever.

Dianne.

I'm no daft enough to think that it's fate or destiny. Looking back to then, if I'm being honest, I can't distinguish her from any other lassies I went with. It's the now I'm interested in. The way she puts her glasses down her nose and looks over them when I've said something she finds doubtful. The way I call her 'owl eyes' and she refers to me as 'ginger nuts' which really is a terrible sign. Even more frightening is the fact that I quite like it. Have we been together long enough for that kind of nonsensical intimacy? Evidently.

I love her, and I think she feels the same way about me, she says she does, and I think that she's honest enough both to know her own heart and not to lie about things like that. You can't lie to your soul.

I've left messages for Katrin, asking when would be the best time to pick up some stuff. She hasn't replied. I see Martin and we go over to the flat in Brouwersgracht and I let myself in. We load up some of my personal stuff into his van, which I'll store at the office. The rest she can keep. As the last box is loaded up I feel great, like I've got away with everything.

Sick Boy, whom I left in the hotel, has been harassing me on the mobile. We get to Miz's editing suite and he's already sitting there going through the rushes with a techy guy called Jack, who's a mate of Miz's. Sick Boy is using Miz's facilities, yet being completely offhand and unpleasant to the guy. It's embarrassing. In order to salvage the situation, I take Miz out for some lunch. Sick Boy seems happy at that, yet when he arrives at an appointed Brown Bar later, his face is still tripping him.

Miz has been nothing but enthusiastic about the film and is going on about how we should give a copy to his friend Lars Lavish, the top gonzo porn operator. — Lars will be at the Cannes Adult Film Festival, he sings, — we will get together with him.

When I collar Simon at the bar, I ask him: — What have you got against Miz? Would you rather edit the video in Niddrie? Cause that's where we'll be if you don't sort your fuckin attitude oot.

— That sleazebag makes my flesh creep, he snorts. — No way is he connected with a main player like Lars Lavish . . .

— He's not bullshitting. He can help us get exhibited at top porn festivals, like Cannes.

— Aye, right, Sick Boy says under his breath. — I don't need his help to get my movie exhibited anywhere. And if he thinks he's swanning around on the Bananazzurri ticket he can wank right off now. Aye, we need the cunt at the moment, but that Dutch prick annoys me and his ching isn't very good. With my luck I'd be the first cunt to get done for smuggling a bit of percy *into* Amsterdam.

The following day I call early at his room, but he's left. Predictably, I find him at the editing suite, where he's now being overly obse-quious towards Miz. He makes it clear that my input isn't needed, so I head off to the office and start to sort out some things at the club. I reluctantly tell Martin that I'm dissolving the partnership and that he should bring in one of our other associates. He's cool about it, makes it easy for me: a fuckin brilliant man.

Later on, we meet up in a club with Miz and Sick Boy, who're now doing a nauseating best buddies routine. At least it's better than what went on before and I'm nice and relaxed. Then I suddenly see Katrin standing over me. I'm about to say something when she throws a drink in my face and lets out a stream of curses. She even tries to assault me, but she's restrained and led away by her friends.

I'm shaken, but that cunt Sick Boy has found the whole thing very amusing. — A proper sherrikin, so it wis, a proper sherrikin, he gleefully sings in a put-on nasal Weedgie accent as he slaps his thighs.

I'm looking at his mocking face, composing myself by thinking about the strange relationship we had, no less arcane through us having been apart over the years. I suppose he was a bit like me, we both knew that decadence was a bad habit for council tenants. A ridiculous habit in fact. The *raison d'être* of our class was simply to survive. Fuck that; our punk generation, not only did we thrive, we even had the audacity tae be disillusioned. From an early age Sick Boy and I were twisted soul brothers. The scorn, the sneers, the irony, the piss-taking; we had constructed our wee private world long before drink or drugs ever came along and helped us refine, and gave the permission to wholeheartedly live in it. We strutted around dripping a cynicism so deep, scornful and profound we felt that nobody got us; parents, siblings, neighbours, teachers, geeks, hard-cunts, or hipsters. But it wasn't easy to develop a repertoire of decadence in the Fort or the Banana flats. Drugs were the easiest option. Then they started to take, began to gnaw away at the dreams they once nourished, nurtured and fortified, crumbling at the life they had allowed us access to. And it all got too much like hard fuckin work, and hard work was something we both strove to avoid. Now what I fear isn't the heroin, it's not the drugs, but this weird symbiotic relationship we have with each other. I'm concerned that it has a dynamic which will draw us right back into the slaughter, now more than ever, after what Spud told me about Franco.

But Sick Boy has worked hard on the edit, no doubt about it. It gave me the chance to get a lot of my shit done with the club. — Have you a copy here I can look at? I ask him.

He grinds his teeth slowly. — Nooo . . . don't think so somehow. I'm keeping it all under wraps until I show everybody the near-as-dammit final cut.

— Aw aye? And when will that be then?

— Hopefully when we get back, the morn's morning, first thing, doon the pub in Leith.

His pub in Leith, just because the cunt doesn't think I'll be there.

— So why, I ask, sitting forward in the chair, — the big need to shroud everything in secrecy?

The cheeky cunt is still pompous to the last. — Because while you've been acting Mr Clubland and boy Birrell's been at home playing happy families, some poor doss fucker, he points at himself, — has been sitting at an editing suite until their eyes nip, putting this movie together. I'm fucked if I'm having you doing a Barry Norman on me, then showing Birrell and getting the same treatment from him, then Nikki, then Terry. No, fuck thon, I'll take all the cudgels at once, thank you.

He evidently thinks *I'll* be taking the cudgels, if I meet Begbie down in Leith. Let the cunt just try and set me up.

60

'. . . a Simon David Williamson Film . . .'

There's a blunt, drilling throb behind one of my eyes. I'm in the shower, trying to wash away another hangover, wishing somehow that the cascading jets of water could be absorbed, internalised. That instant rehydration could take place. Picking up a bottle of shower gel, squishing that gungy, synthetically herbal-flavoured detergent into the palm of my hand, working it over my body, worrying about my stomach, if it's losing its tautness. I'm thinking gym squared. Moving down to my minge, trying to be functional, businesslike. Trying not to think about Simon; his dark eyebrows, chiselled Italian face, glacier smile and the sweet words from those snake-lips. Most of all, though, the magnetic pool of those large eyes. Brown, but seeming all black, all pupil. How even in disapproval they never seem to shrink, or avert, they just lose their brilliant sheen, develop a dull tarnish so that you can no longer see your reflection in them. Like you don't exist, like you've been snuffed out.

I'm trying to concentrate on the radio, perched on the bath. A gushing, sycophantic presenter is asking a young woman about her favourite records and what these tunes mean to her. I immediately recognise those milky, insipid, slightly adenoidal tones that respond. When she mentions that record, that shit record, I know it's her before I hear the presenter say her name. — Jive Bunny and the Mastermixers, 'Swing the Mood!' Oh, I love this track! It just . . . I don't know . . . you know when you have a song when you're at an age where everything seems possible . . . well, I was fourteen and my gymnastics career was really starting to take off . . .

Carolyn Cunting Pavitt.

Carolyn Pavitt and I were once, inverted commas, best friends. It was a tag other people gave us; parents, teachers, peers, but most of all, coaches. All because little Nikki and Carolyn went to gymnastics together. But although we became bundled together through our joint participation in the sport, we never felt this great friendship ourselves. As good little girls, we were seen as kindred spirits. In reality, right from the off, we were deadly rivals.

As teenage gymnasts we seriously competed. At first I was better than gawky Carolyn, although the ugly duckling did turn into a swan when she hit the mat. The problem was that when adolescence descended on us, I got the tits and she got the trophies.

And now I realise that I've turned the shower down as cold as it'll go, and I can't hear the voice of 'Britain's Carolyn Pavitt' any more. All I can feel is the searing cold, the heaviness, the heaving in my chest and I think I'm going to pass out, but I step out of the shower, gasping. I switch off the radio and rub myself with the towel as a warm, compensatory glow spreads from my core to the extremities of my skin. Oh, you cunt, Carolyn Pavitt.

I go through to my room and get dressed, wondering which jumper to wear, the tight cashmere or the shapeless angora. I think about the need for gymwork, and opt for the latter. I wonder which one she would have picked. But nothing can get me down today for long because I'm full of excitement. Simon phoned very late last night telling me to be at the pub for nine thirty this morning because he's showing a cut of the movie! I think of Carolyn. You can stick your Commonwealth Bronze up your arse, you soon-to-be-arthritic cow!

When I get down to Leith, Simon is highly animated. It's obvious that he's been snorting cocaine. He kisses me on the mouth, winking greedily as he pulls away.

Rab's here as well and we talk about the coursework. He's done better than me, I expect. I tell him I think that I've failed because I didn't do enough work. We chat at a mundane level, but his look, slightly judging and pitying at the same time, is making me feel queasy. I sit down beside Mel, Gina, Terry and Curtis. Mark Renton comes in, looking very tense and furtive, and Simon shouts: — The Rent Boy finally makes it tae Leith! We should git the rest ay the auld crew along! A wee Leith pub crawl!

Mark ignores him, nods at me and exchanges greetings with the others. Simon's over to the bar, pouring some drinks while still going on at Mark. — I was wondering when you'd work up the bottle tae show yir face doon here. Sneak a taxi right down tae the door, eh?

— I wouldnae have missed ma auld buddy's directorial debut for the world, Mark half sneers, — especially when eh's assured me ay ma safety.

There's something going on here, but Simon just responds to Mark's obvious aggression with a pregnant smirk. — Right . . . who are we missing . . . Miguel said he'd be here . . . he turns to see Mikey Forrester entering, resplendent in an unfeasibly brilliant-white tracksuit and dripping gold, followed by Wanda. — Ah, speak of the devil! Miguel! Just in time, come and join us! Dressed for success, I see, he says sarcastically. Forrester seems not to notice, in fact seems elated, until he registers Mark Renton. There's a frozen, ugly little pause before they exchange cold, reluctant nods. The only person seemingly oblivious to the frosty atmosphere is Simon. — Here we go, folks, he roars triumphantly as he rips open a box of video cassettes and hands us one each.

Simon then racks up some lines, but everybody except Terry and Forrester refuse. — All the more for the heavyweights, he says, a mix of relief and contempt in his voice, but we're not reacting as we're scrutinising our video-box covers in disbelief.

For me the sense of disappointment and betrayal is absolutely fucking sickening. I see the cover, and get the first sniper's bullet in my heart. My face with that make-up; larger than life, gaudier, tackier with that cheap print colour used. More importantly, he'd used the picture he promised he wouldn't, the one where one tit looks smaller than the other. I look like a camp transvestite or the blow-up doll he bought Curtis; that garish, ugly picture and the big lettering: NIKKI FULLER-SMITH in *SEVEN RIDES FOR SEVEN BROTHERS*.

What really gets me, though, are the credits:

A SIMON DAVID WILLIAMSON FILM
PRODUCED BY SIMON DAVID WILLIAMSON
DIRECTED BY SIMON DAVID WILLIAMSON
WRITTEN BY SIMON DAVID WILLIAMSON WITH
NIKKI FULLER-SMITH AND RAB BIRRELL

The others evidently feel the same way as I do. — We get the picture, Rab says, shaking his head, throwing his copy of the video back in the box.

— No, he gets the picture, I fume, looking from the case of videos to Simon and back again. My lungs feel tight and my fingernails are digging into my palms.

How easy it is now to think of my Simon, my lover, as Sick Boy. The grumblings intensify but he's pretending not to hear, he's just whistling nonchalantly as he removes another video cassette from the box. — What the fuck did you have to do with the screenplay? Rab asks urgently. — Where's the high-production values in the packaging? It looks shite, he says, kicking the box.

Si . . . no, Sick Boy, is completely unapologetic. — You are very ungrateful children, he scoffs imperiously. — I could have put Terry down as co-director, and Rents as co-producer, but they want just one name to deal with, for contact purposes, to stop the business side of the operation getting unwieldy. That way it's silly cunt here, he points indignantly at himself, — who gets lumbered, and this is the fuckin thanks ah git!

— What did you have to do with the screenplay, Rab asks again in a slow, even tone, looking over at me.

— It needed some changes. As Director, Producer and Editor, I had that right.

Terry glances swiftly towards Renton, who raises his eyebrows. Terry's head moves back and his eyes scan the nicotine-yellow ceiling. I'm crumbling inside, not so much at the betrayal, but at Simon's arrogant ease with it. He's standing there in his black T-shirt, trousers and shoes, like a dark angel, arms folded, looking down at us like we're some shite off his shoe. I've given myself over to a total bastard.

We sit in a silence, now tinted with a greater sense of foreboding, as an excited, wired-up Sick Boy loads a tape into the machine. He kisses the cover of the video box. — We are in. We have product. We live, he says softly. Then he goes out to the window, looks down at the busy, bustling street below and screams out: — Youse hear that? WE LIVE!

I'm watching it, sitting next to Mel and Gina, the first edited copy we've seen of our work. It starts off as we thought, with the television scene, where Mel and I are getting it on. I can't help thinking that my body looks really good; lithe, tanned, supple. I more than hold my own with Mel, who's five years younger than me! I glance around the room to try and gauge the reactions. Terry now looks sassy and smug, losing himself in the porn. Curtis, Mel and Ronnie are anticipatory and Rab and Craig uncomfortable. Renton and Forrester are inscrutable. Gina seems awkwardly excited, almost bashful.

Then it moves into the works canteen where the 'brothers' are chatting about their trip to 'Glasburgh'. It seems like an amateurish, ham-fisted tribute to the intro scene of *Reservoir Dogs*, but it somehow works. As it progresses it's still looking okay, although Simon's muttering about 'grading' and 'proper copies'. We move into the scene where Simon and I are on the train, then fucking in what is supposedly the train toilet, but in reality is the shithouse here.

— Phoah, Terry goes. — Check that fuckin arse . . . then he turns to me and smiles, — sorry, Nik.

I wink back at him, because I'm starting to feel better. It's much as we expected, and to be fair to Simon, he has edited it quite well. The whole thing moves along at a fair pace, although the acting is poor, Curtis's stammer painfully evident on a couple of occasions, and you can tell that Rab is unimpressed with the picture quality. It does have something though, a certain energy. It's only when we get about three-quarters of the way through that I realise Mel is fucking livid. I hear her going: — Naw . . . naw . . . that's no right . . . almost to herself. I turn and see her sitting speechless as we watch her sucking on Curtis's huge cock. But she's sucking it *after* he's just fucked her up the arse. — What's this! she shrieks.

— What's what? Sick Boy says.

— They wey you've pit that thegither, it makes it look like ah've sooked ehs cock eftir it's been up muh erse, she snarls at Sick Boy.

And now it's me, getting this same edited treatment. A close-up of my face, then a cut to Curtis's cock which looks like it's going in and out of my arsehole, but it's another take of Mel's arsehole. — Nobody fucked me up the arse! What the fuck is this, Simon!

— Aye, Curtis says supportively, — you didnae want tae dae that but, eh no.

— It's just the way it's edited, Sick Boy says. — Creativity. We used out-takes of Mel getting fucked up the arse and we were able in the editing suite to colour Mel's buttock flesh to match yours.

I repeat myself, hearing my voice rising in a horrible panic. — I said nobody fucked me up the arse! Why did the scenes need to be put in that sequence? That's not me! It's Mel!

Sick Boy's shaking his head. — Look, it was an editorial decision, a creative decision. You didn't want to get fucked up the arse as an actor, and neither you did. Do you think that Ving Rhames actually got fucked up the arse by the guy that played Zed in *Pulp Fiction*?

— No, but this is a porn movie . . .

— It's a movie, Simon says. — We faked it. We did what Tarantino did with Ving Rhames, cause Ving faked it too. Did he turn round to Tarantino and go, 'Oooh, I don't want to do that scene because people might think I'm a buftie-boy'? Did he fuck!

— No, I'm screaming, — because this is different! It's a porn movie and in porn the expectation is that the performers don't fake it, they *perform* the sex acts!

— Well, Nikki, we took advice from some experienced pornographers in Holland and down in the Smoke. Mark and myself thought . . . well, you know . . .

I turn to Mark who raises his palms. — Leave me oot ay this, he says at Simon, — you're the big supremo. It says so on the cover, he picks up and brandishes a video box. Now Rab's intervening angrily on our behalf, pointing at Simon and saying: — It's no fair, Simon. We hud an agreement. You've stitched up the lassies thaire.

Mel's ready to implode, sitting there, gripping the armrests on the chair. — It makes us look like fuckin slappers. Ah dinnae ken any lassie who'd suck a boy's cock eftir jist huvin it up her erse!

Terry looks coolly at her. — There are birds that dae it, take ma word, he contends.

She seems unnerved by this. — Aye, but no oan video, Terry, no fir the world tae see!

Simon sinks his hands into the pockets of his black leather trousers, in order to stop them windmilling. — Look, people know that it doesnae work like that in the sequence ay the film. They ken that

372

once you've fucked somebody up the arse you wash your knob before you put it in her mooth, or her fanny.

— But that wisnae they wey it wis written in the fuckin script, Mel says, standing up and shouting. — You fuckin tricked us!

Sick Boy withdraws his hands from his pockets. — Naebody tricked anybody! he shouts, slapping his forehead with the palm of his hand. — Editing's a creative process, it's a craft, an art, designed to maximise the erotic experience. I was at that editing suite for four days and nights, my eyes fucking stinging, and this is the shite I get! I need creative freedom to edit the material! Youse are fascists!

Now the pair of them are screaming at each other. — Ya fuckin slimy cunt! Mel roars. Gina says: — Calm doon, but she's dripping *schadenfreude*.

— Shut it, ya fuckin prima donna, Simon's saying back at Mel and now he's looking ugly, in a way I never thought he would. Not the cool, entrepreneurial type I see him as, but a nasty, boorish ten-a-penny thug.

But Mel's not intimidated because she's become somebody else as well as she takes a step forward and screams at him: — YA SNIDEY CUNT!

They stand a few feet away from each other bawling and I can't take this, the sheer screeching volume of them both and how they are so comfortable operating at this level. It's like childhood nightmares where your parents would turn into demonic caricatures of themselves.

Gina's got a hold of Mel and Rab's placating Sick Boy, who's slapping his own head or rather headbutting the palm of his hand. Terry looks wearily at Mark. Mikey Forrester says some dumb things in support of Simon, then something to Mark about him being a beggar or going to see beggars. Mark snaps back in anger: — That's eywis been your style, ya sneaky fuckin grassin cunt . . . Mikey shouts out something to Mark about stealing from his own, and I shudder in case he means something about our 1690 fiddle. Now they're all shouting and pointing and jostling at each other. I can't handle this. I head out, and go downstairs to the bar and out into the street. I'm taking gulps of the fetid, exhaust-fume-filled spring air as I storm up Leith Walk, wanting to put as much distance between myself and them as I can. I don't even think anybody saw me leave.

I'm heading up into town, trudging through a strong, bitingly cold wind, thinking that we live in such boring times. That's our tragedy: nobody, except destructive exploiters like Sick Boy, or bland opportunists like Carolyn, has any real passion. Everybody else is just so beaten down by the crap and mediocrity around them. If the word in the eighties was 'me', and in the nineties 'it', in the millennium it's 'ish'. Everything has to be vague and qualified. Substance used to be important, then style was everything. Now it's all just faking it. I thought they were real, Simon and the rest of them.

It hits me like an iron fist in the chest that in this global communications village somehow, in some way, my father's going to see me getting a butt-fuck I didn't actually get. I hate the idea of having anal sex; as a woman it's a negation of your femininity. Most of all, I loathe being a fake. My family. The boys at the uni, some of the bitter, immature little nothings I've knocked back, all wanking off at the image in their bedsits. Others, thinking they know all about me, all about my sexuality from that image. McClymont, once his wife goes up to bed, will sit with the handset and a Scotch pulling his wire at the image of me getting it up the arse. 'Take a seat, Miss Fuller-Smith. Or perhaps you may prefer to remain standing . . . ha ha ha.' Colin will see it, maybe even come up to the flat. 'Nikki, I saw the video. I understand everything now, about you finishing with me. It was a cry for attention, which I didn't see . . . you're obviously hurt and confused . . .'

A car races past and a volley of slush batters my side; trickling, ice-cold, down my boots. When I get home I'm miserable and Lauren's in, in fact she's just getting up, still in her dressing gown. I'm carrying a copy of the video and I sit down on the couch next to her. — Give us a fag, I almost plead.

She turns, sees the tears in my eyes. — What's wrong, sweetheart?

I throw the video into her lap. The racking sobs start and I fall into her and she's hugging me. I'm crying heavily now, but it's like somebody else's doing it, all I'm doing is feeling her warmth and her fresh smells through my bubbling, snot-filled nasal cavities. — Don't, worry, Nikki, it'll be alright, she coos.

I want to be closer to the heat of her, I want to be in that heat, in the centre of that flame, protected by it, away from everything that might hurt me. I grip tighter on her, so strongly I hear a slight squawking noise involuntarily come from her. I want her to be . . . I raise my head to kiss her. She returns my kiss, a tentative fear in her eyes. I want her to be free, not the stiff way she always is, I want her to stretch and bend . . . but when my hand goes down to her flat belly and starts caressing it she stiffens and pushes me away. — Don't, Nikki, please, don't do that.

My body stiffens as much as hers. It's like we've both just done a line of strong coke. — I'm sorry, I thought it was what you wanted, I thought it was what you always wanted.

Lauren shakes her head in a look of uncomprehending shock. — You really thought that I was a dyke? That I fancied you? Why? Why can't you accept that people can really like you, even love you, without wanting to fuck you? Is your self-esteem that low?

Is it? I don't know, but I do know that I'm not taking this from her. Who does she think she is? Who the fuck do they think they are: Carolyn Pavitt on *A Question of Sport*, Sick Boy Simon, poncing around like he's a movie mogul. Now it's Lauren, moralising little Lauren, all tease until she gets what she thinks she wants then runs a fucking mile. — Lauren, you're nineteen. You've just read the wrong books and talked to the wrong people. Be nineteen. Don't be your mum. It's not appropriate.

— Don't talk to me about appropriate, not when you try to do that to me, she bats back an unbowed retort, all arrogant in her chastity.

In weak response, I can only think of a dippy thing to say. — So sex between women isn't appropriate, is that what you're saying?

— Don't be fuckin stupid. You're not a lesbian, and neither am I. Don't play stupid games, she says.

— I fancy you a bit though, I say meekly, now feeling like it's Lauren who's the big sister and me who's the silly little virgin.

— Well, I don't fancy you. Behave yourself and fuck somebody who wants to fuck you, and preferably not because there's money changing hands on either side, she scoffs, standing up and heading to the window.

Now I feel a deadening thud in my chest. — You need shagged!

I tell her, getting up and charging through towards the bedroom just as Dianne comes in the front door. She's had her hair cut: pageboy style. It suits her.

— Hello, Nikki, she smiles, struggling with the keys, her purse and some folders, her lips puckering in impish delight at what she's just obviously heard.

At that point Lauren's voice screams out after me: — Yeah, it's really done you a power of good, all those cocks!

Dianne raises her eyebrows. — Oh! Did I just miss something interesting?

I manage a weak smile in her direction as I head for my room where I collapse onto my bed. I'm not doing porn again; I'm never going to that fucking sauna again either.

61

Rejection

A h'm beyond pain, ah'm like ma whole boady's goat the toothache. Cause it was Chizzie, the boy that goat done. It said so in the paper. N ah ken whae done um n aw. N worse thin that, ah ken whae set the whole thing up: nae-mates, nae-burd, nae-nothing Murphy here. Cause ah cannae git away fae it. Mr Murphy, with Mrs Murphy and child Murphy, pure disnae exist any mair, man. It's now back tae Spud, the solitary cat, the loser.

Ali disnae want tae talk tae ays now, man, willnae even lit me see Andy. Things have gone, man, fae bad tae sortay worse. Ah went doon tae the Port Sunshine the other night tae explain things again, this time dead straight. Ah thoat she'd be pleased tae hear aboot the cash n aw ma plans fir it but aw she said wis: — Ah don't want tae go anywhaire wi you right now, Danny, n ah don't want ma son taken anywhere oan drugs money.

— It isnae drugs money . . . it's . . . n ah sees Sick Boy n Juice Terry come oot fae the back door wi a pile ay videos n head oot, — . . . it's fae work.

— Aw aye? What sort ay work? *This* is work, Danny, she sais, lookin aroond as a guy comes in at openin time n she serves him. — N ah'd appreciate it if ye didnae come in here when ah wis tryin tae git oan wi it.

So that wis me, back hame tae this lonely auld gaff again. Ah'm thinkin aboot this cat in a suit ah overheard in Bernard Street the day: 'My computer's crashed. I've lost everything.'

Ah feel like the gadge and like ehs computer, man. N the hoose is a bit ay a tip likesay, it must be said. Ye git pure depressed oan yir ain. Ah need tae git Zappa back, man, ah pure thoat ah'd jist neglect the boy, but now ah need company n ah phone Rents again but it's like ehs mobile's switched oaf.

The Port Sunshine's aboot as far as uv been since ah heard the news aboot Chizzie. Ah mean, ah thoat thir might be bother, but ah nivir kent thit nowt like that wid happen. Ah want tae git the story, but no fae Begbie, ah pure dinnae want tae see that cat again, ah want tae try n find Second Prize. But naw, man, naw, ah'm no hingin aboot Leith wi Franco aroond. Chizzie . . . what huv ah done tae Chizzie?

Bleak man, bleak as.

Then suddenly thir's a wee ray ay light n ah rush right intae it. The post comes n it's a letter, no a bill, ye kin tell right away.

It wis fae the publisher cause it hud a wee stamp wi 'Scotvar Publishing' oan it. So ah'm thinkin thit this must mean thit thir gaun tae dae it, thir gaunnae publish the History ay Leith! Whae-hey-hey! Ah cannae wait tae show Ali! That'll get her thinkin aboot Disneyland! Ah'll jist walk intae the pub n flash that letter aroond, especially whin Sick Boy's in. Oh yeah, man, oh yeah! Ah'll soon be oan the telly, talkin aboot it, likes. Ah might even git a cash advance, whoa, man, ah'm thinkin thit ah'd better open this envelope dead carefully in case thir's a cheque in thair. Ah hud it up tae the light, but it's too thick tae see anything. So ah open it up. Thir's nae cheque, but they widnae send thum thegither anywey. That fee stuff needs tae be negotiated later on but, ken?

Scotvar Publishing Ltd
13 Kailyard Grove, Edinburgh EH3 6NH
Tel: 0131 987 5674 Fax: 0131 987 3432 Website: www.scotvar.co.uk

Your ref:
Our ref: AJH/MC
1 April

Dear Mr Murphy,

Re: History of Leith

Thank you for your manuscript, which I just finished reading. Unfortunately, it's not quite what what we're looking for at the moment and, after some deliberation, we have decided against publishing.

Yours sincerely,

Alan Johnson-Hogg

Vat Registration number: 671 0987 276. Registered Directors: Alan Johnson-Hogg, Kirsty Johnson-Hogg, Conrad Donaldson QC

It's a bad one, man. Ah sit thaire jist likes, stunned; feeling aw raw n hollowed oot fae the inside. It's like whin you've been knocked back by a bird ye fancy, no thit that's happened tae me for a long time bein wi Ali likes but, like ye've been intae a lassie for ages, n ye sort go, eh, awright, what aboot, likesay, you n me, likes, eh . . . n she goes: naw. No way. Fuck off.

Rejection, man.

Then ah sortay look at it again, like. Now ah'm thinkin: but wis it a rejection? Ah mean, the boy says, it took them some time tae decide tae knock it back, 'eftir some deliberation' which means, they thought aboot takin it, man. Then, they dinnae want it 'at the moment', n that reads tae me like they might want it fir defo in a few weeks' or mibee a couple ay months' time. Once the state ay the market changes n aw that.

So ah goes tae the phone n calls the boy up. — Is there an Alan Johnson-Hogg there?

A woman's voice, no really posh, mair sort ay pit-oan posh, goes: — Who's calling?

— Eh, I'm a writer he's expressed an interest in, and I'm, eh, follayin up his correspondence . . . ken?

Well, there's a bit ay a lull n then this really posh voice comes oan n goes: — Johnson-Hogg. Can I help you?

Posh cats make ays dead nervous if ah stoap n think aboot it, but ah jist goes, naw, n ah pure fires in. — Eh hi, man, ma name's Murphy, Danny Murphy, bit ah git called Spud, ken? Ah sent ye a manuscript, likes. Ah jist wisnae sure aboot what the letter meant. Ken?

379

— Ah yes . . . eh sortay sniggers doon the phone, — the History of Leith, wasn't it?

— Aye . . . ah ken yi'll think ah'm daft, but ah wis jist, likesay, tryin tae work oot what ye meant in that letter ay yours, man.

— Well, I think it was fairly explicit.

— Ah beg tae differ likes, mate. Cause ye says thit ye dinnae want it *at the moment*. So tae me that means thit ye might want it later. So, likes, when is it thit ye think ye might want it?

Thir's a sort ay coughin noise oan the line, then the boy speaks.

— I'm sorry if I seemed ambiguous, Mr Murphy. To be more frank, it's quite an immature work, and you're not really yet up to publishable standard . . .

— What dae ye mean, man?

— Well, the grammar . . . the spelling . . .

— Aye, but are youse no meant tae sort aw that oot?

— . . . to say nothing of the subject matter being not right for us.

— But youse've published history books about Leith before . . . ah kin feel ma voice gaun aw high, cause it's no fair, it jist isnae, it isnae fair, nowt's fair . . .

— Those were serious works by disciplined writers, the boy sortay snaps, — this is a badly written celebration of yob culture and of people who haven't achieved anything noteworthy in the local community.

— Whae's tae say that . . .

— Sorry, Mr Murphy, your book is no good and I have to get on. Goodbye.

And the gadge just hangs up oan ays. Aw they weeks, aw they months, that ah wis kiddin masel ah wis daein somethin important, something big, n what the hell fir? Fir nowt, fir a pile ay useless shite, jist like me.

Ah grab ma original copy ay this rubbish, n stick it the fireplace n set it alight and watch that wee part ay ma life go up in smoke like the rest ay it. Lookin at the flames ah think aboot Chizzie . . . ah kilt Chizzie . . . a bad cat, but eh didnae deserve that, even though it wis Begbie really, it hud tae be Begbie . . . the state eh wis in whin eh came up tae mine that night . . . said eh wis comin fae toon, but ah dinnae believe that . . .

N ah'm pure sittin in here, the cash burnin a hole in ma pockit so ah goes *up* the street, cause Begbie never drinks past Pilrig, n intae the Old Salt, where ah sees Cousin Dode. The poor cat's looking as doon as me.

Eh's no as fill ay ehsel as usual, eh looks Donald Ducked. — Ah cannae understand it, Spud. Ah thoat ah hud plenty o' cash left ower for trades; ah wis plannin tae take muh daughter away. But ah wis brassic, cleaned oot. Ah cannae even afford a week at fuckin Butlins. Now *she'll* no even lit me see the wean. Ah cannae make the fuckin mortgage, cannae keep up the maintenance payments. Ah knew ah'd been tannin it a bit, but ah'm aboot a grand doon thit ah cannae account fir. It's fuckin diabolical, cannae even gie the wean hur hoalidays . . .

Poor Dode . . . a good cat likesay, eywis helped ays oot . . . it wis oot ay order tae dae that tae the boy . . . the world wid be a better place withoot useless, scruffy, junky Murphy . . . killer ay Chizzie, destroyer ay Cousin Dode . . . poor Ali . . . wee Andy even . . .

Dode tries tae protest as ah slip um three hundred quid. — Naw, Spud, naw . . .

— Take it, man, ah'm flush the now n you've eywis helped me oot, ah say tae the boy n ah cannae look um in the eye as ah head offski.

Ah hear um sayin tae this auld boy: — See that man thair, that man's a fuckin saint, so eh is . . .

N ah'm thinkin if only eh knew, man, if only eh knew n ah need tae dae one last good thing, man, jist one last good thing . . .

. . . n ah gits hame n the first thing ah sees is that book lyin thair, that *Crime n Punishment.*

62

Whores of Amsterdam Pt 8

It was strangely good to see Ali again, here, in the City Café. Strangely, because although we were in the same posse, oan the junk thegither n aw that, we never really hit it off for some reason. I think that she always saw through me, always felt that I was a hypocrite, a winner who played at being a loser. Aye, a bright, upwardly mobile cunt who would one day fuck off and leave a pile of shite behind him for everybody else to clean up. She perhaps grasped my nature before I worked it out myself.

Maybe I surprised her though, sorting out Spud like that. Never thought they'd end up together, although 'end up' isnae the right term because it's no happening just now. — Mark, she says, and embraces me with a simple warmth that makes me feel awkward.

— Hiya, Ali, this is Dianne. — Dianne, this is Simon.

Dianne greets Ali warmly and Sick Boy with more reserve and I'm thinking that my tip-off about him seems to have worked, although she makes her own mind up on such matters. It's probably more Nikki who's turned her off him. As he almost pleaded: — Come for a drink in town, Mark, Nikki's taken the strop. Won't return my calls. I thought: serves you right, you cunt. It was only when he said he'd bring Ali along that I acquiesced.

— This is cosy, Sick Boy says, — more of the old crew back together. I ought to have invited François along, he sniggers, looking sideways at me. I'm trying not to react. But I've been realising that if Begbie's still as radge as they say (and from what I've heard he's crazier than ever), then my old pal Sick Boy, my business partner, the cunt I squared up with the money, has effectively been trying tae kill me. It goes way beyond treachery, way past revenge. And now he's buzzing, obviously well coked-up. Ali pulls me aside, but I can hardly hear what she's saying as I strain to listen tae Sick Boy bending Dianne's ear. — Nikki speaks very highly of you, you know, Dianne.

— I like her a lot, Dianne says patiently, — and Lauren too.

— That, in rap parlance, is a bitch with problems, Sick Boy sniggers, his shoulders shaking, then he says: — Fancy a toot, Di? I'll slip you this wrap and you and Ali can go into the little girly-wirlies' room . . .

— No thanks, Dianne says in a calm, disengaged manner. She doesn't like Sick Boy. This is fucking great, she genuinely does not like the man one little bit! And now I can see that his powers have waned. The face is fleshier, the sparkle in the eyes less evident, the decisive movements made jerkier and less fluid through . . . age? . . . cocaine?

— Fine by me, Sick Boy grins and raises his palms.

Happy that any mind games he attempts with Dianne will be easily repelled, I can now give Ali my full attention. It's got to be said, though, that the cunt makes it difficult when I hear him say things to her like: — I don't think that you can compare a waster like Robert Burns with the great contemporary Scottish poets of today.

Dianne's shaking her head, staying cool, but reacting nonetheless. — That's rubbish. Who are the great poets of today? Name me one that's better than Burns.

Sick Boy shakes his head vigorously and waves a dismissive hand. — I'm Italian, I prefer to think in a feminine way, emotionally, rather than get into all that anal referencing thing that north European men indulge in. I can't recall the names, don't want to, but I read a book of modern Scottish poetry once and it shat on anything Burns has ever done.

But it's obvious by his raised voice and sideways glances that he wants to get me involved, so I'm trying to keep concentrating on Ali and I think she's got the same idea. — I've never seen you look so well, Mark, she says.

— Thanks, I give her hand a squeeze, — and you're looking fantastic. How's the bairn?

— Which one? Andy's fine. The other one I've just given up on, she shakes her head sadly.

— Eh's no back oan the gear again, is eh? I ask, feeling genuinely uneasy at the prospect. He seemed okay when we had that drink, well, wasted, but no skagged. Poor Spud. I'll never meet a better guy, a more strangely vulnerable but good-hearted man; but he's been so fucked up for so long it's like the essence of him is harder to find now, outside of the drugs. The good intentions will still be there, lining the route of his personal journey to Hades. He really is a form of humanity that has been rendered obsolete by the new order, but he's still a human being. Cigarettes, alcohol, heroin, cocaine, speed, poverty and media mind-fucking: capitalism's weapons of destruction are more subtle and effective than Nazism's and he's powerless against them.

— I don't know and I'm starting not to care, she says unconvincingly.

Because that's the problem with that sick fuckin puppy, you do have to care about him, and he'll just fuck up and fuck you up again. He's probably caused, in his own way, more hurt than Begbie, Sick Boy, Second Prize and me all put together ever could. And even though I've not hung out with him properly for yonks, I know this, I know that he'll always be the same. But Ali cares alright, that's why she's now crushing my hand in the two of hers and I'm seeing the lines around her brown eyes, but they're still full of fire and she still looks beautiful, yes she does, Ali's lovely and that should be enough for Murphy. — Speak tae him, Mark. You were his best pal. He's always looked up to you . . . it's always been Mark this, Mark that . . .

— Only cause I've been away, Ali. It's no been me as ah am, I've jist been a rescue fantasy. I know how he thinks.

She doesn't even try to contradict this, which is fuckin disturbing. Now I feel guilty that I'm undermining him when I should be sticking up for him. — He's worse now, Mark. I don't even think it's the gear, that's the saddest thing about it all. He's just so depressed, his self-esteem is rock-bottom.

— If he doesnae have any self-esteem wi a bird like you on his airm, then he's crazy, I say, feeling the need to keep things light.

— Exactly! Sick Boy says loudly, cutting in, then turning to her. — I'm glad you and Murphy are history, Ali.

Then, with a sudden violence of movement, he springs to his feet and bounds over to the the jukebox. To my horror he puts on Elvis Costello's 'Alison' and starts looking straight over at her. It's so fuckin embarrassing, and Dianne and I dinnae ken what the fuck tae dae.

He slides over to the bar and orders a round of brandies and we're all looking at each other, thinking about running away. Then he moves off towards the toilet, gesturing at me, and I get up and tentatively follow him down, where he's commandeered a cubicle. — Calm doon thaire, mate, I say as he racks up four lines on the cistern, — you're embarrassing Ali.

He ignores me then fires back one of the lines. — I'm Italian, I'm fucking passionate. If those cunts out there, those deadbeat Pictish pricks can't take this passion, then there are plenty pubs in Leith they can drink in. Her and me . . . he snorts another line, — ya fucker . . . her and me . . . whae-hey! . . . Her and me's a kind of fate. C'mon, Renton, c'moan, pussy-fuckin Dutch boy, stop sticking yir fuckin fingers in a dyke and git these up yir nose . . .

Without thinking, almost by the conditioning of his voice, I snort them, one up each nostril. They are fuckin road markers of lines and I feel my heart thump in my chest like a drum. That was stupid.

— . . . cause she's getting rode the night. Defo. What dae ye want tae bet that ah ride her? Anything you like. Bog Boy's no been gieing her the message, another couple ay drinks n she'll be ganting on it . . . c'mon, watch an expert in action, Rents . . . you never rode her, did ye, back in the day . . . watch this . . .

Cocaine turns men into their worst ever eighteen-year-old incarnations. I'm trying to keep it together, trying the best not to let the drug turn me into *mine*.

He heads over to the bar and I sit down with the lassies, sweating, as he comes across carrying a tray of more brandies and beers. Fuck me, I watch the terror on Dianne and Ali's coupons as he sets down the drinks. — Ah don't wanna get too sentimental, he croons and winks at her, — Spud and you is no-go, Ali. It was always you and me, he said, handing round the glasses.

Ali is angry but she's trying to keep it light. — Oh aye, so ye could put me on the game?

— When did ah ever try that wi you, Ali? Always treated ye like a lady, Sick Boy grins.

Dianne nudges me. — Did you take some cocaine?

— Just a wee line tae stop him fae being a pest, I whisper lamely through clenched teeth.

— Certainly worked, she says caustically.

In the meantime, Sick Boy's probing away at Ali, his face puppet-like. — Didn't I? Didn't I?

— Only cause ye kent ah'd tell ye tae fuck off, Ali says, raising her glass.

Then, with a tight smirk, he says: — Ah don't think you ever forgave me for gittin that Lesley up the duff.

Ali and I can scarcely believe he's saying this. Lesley's baby daughter Dawn died of cot death years back, and this is the first time we've heard him admit that the bairn was his.

He seems to realise that he's said something, and a trace of mild regret flickers across his face before it's extinguished by a cruel sneer. — Aw aye, ah hear fae Skreel that she's married a straight-peg. Aw intae suburban life. Two kids. Like our daughter, our wee Dawn, never even fucking existed, he spits in disgust.

Ali snaps at him: — What are you saying? It's the first time I've heard *you* admit that that baby existed! You treated Lesley like shit!

— She was fucking shit . . . couldnae look eftir a bairn, Sick Boy says, shaking his head.

Ali sits in open-mouthed incredulity as I struggle myself tae think ay something tae say.

Sick Boy looks at her as if ready to dispatch an important lesson. — Tell you what but, Ali, I'm no trying tae be wide, but you're the fucking same. If ye stey wi Murphy that bairn ay yours'll be taken intae care, nowt surer. That's if the poor wee cunt's no already crawling wi the vir . . .

— FUCK OFF, YA RADGE! Alison screams, throwing the brandy in his face. He blinks and wipes himself with his shirtsleeve. She stands above him for a moment or two, curling her fists into balls, and then she storms out the door, Dianne rising and following her.

A girl from behind the bar, the one who poured the brandies, comes over with a cloth to help Sick Boy. — She'll be back, he says, and there's almost sadness in his voice. Then he adds with a smile: — She works for me and she needs the money!

He knocks back the brandy. In a bizarre fear that makes me queasy, I keep looking to the door, waiting for Franco to come in. The situation is so desperate that his appearance seems almost inevitable. I was scared, not for myself, no with all this ching in me, but for Dianne. That fuckin Forrester creep and his arse-licking mooth. Just seein that cunt at the Port Sunshine set ma fuckin teeth oan edge. Odds on he'll be hunting for Begbie to blab to him about me being around. Then I'm thinking that if Sick Boy's powers have waned, Franco's might have too. In my mind's eye I see the upturned palm of my hand, rocketing into Franco's nose, pushing it up into his brain.

Dianne comes back in but without Alison. — She jumped in a taxi, she explains, adding, — I'd like to go now.

— Sure, I said, knocking back the short. As I looked at her, she appeared not so much uncomfortable or disapproving as bored, and I was impressed by that. I thought about how she didn't need this shite. I cough out my excuses and we make to leave. Sick Boy doesn't protest at our departure. — Tell Nikki to bell me, he urges, his teeth white and prominent, a grinning caricature of himself.

We get out and over to Hunter Square and into a waiting taxi. My pulse throbs uncomfortably with the gear. I'm as high as a kite and we're going nowhere. I know that I'll lie in bed next to her like a surfboard, or sit up watching crap telly all night at Gav's till the rushes run down.

Dianne's not saying anything but I realise that, for the first time, I've fucked her off. I'm not getting into that habit. After a while the silence becomes uncomfortable and I'm moved to break it. — Sorry, love, I say.

— Your mate's a cunt, she tells me.

I've never heard her use that word before, and somehow it doesn't sound right coming from her lips. Fuck me, I'm getting old. This gear used to make me feel invincible, like there was an iron rod running through me. That rod's still present, it's just that now it also

387

seems to highlight the condition of the flesh around it: old, chicken-scraggy, crumbling and, above all, mortal.

The taxi cruises past the Meadows and I see Begbie at least three times before we get to Tollcross.

63

'. . . if only you'd ease up a little . . .'

Here I am, at the sauna I said that I wouldn't go back to. And here Bobby is, hassling me again. That's the thing with them, the predators, whether old or young, handsome or ugly; they are fucking relentless or, rather, relentless about fucking. He's keeping me on because he likes me, he tells me. It's true; my massage technique is rudimentary and I still can't give a decent handjob, but most of the clients are too desperate to notice my apathy and my lack of technical ability. But now Bobby reckons that it's time I was graduating from jerking off cock to sucking it.

— The customers like you. Ye should be makin proper money, hen, he tells me.

It's too strange to try to explain that I do more than that with boyfriends and I do it occasionally with strangers in front of cameras. Why the reticence about a quick blow job behind closed doors at 'Miss Argentina'? Firstly, I don't want the areas of my life which are free from commercial sex transactions to recede any further than they already have. Everything in its place and a place for everything, as my dad says. There's other things to do and to think about doing all day besides sucking cock.

Secondly, sad but true, most of the clients are fucking dogs, and even the thought of putting their genitals in your mouth is way beyond repulsive.

Bobby, to his great credit, seems to have enough aesthetic and business sense to know that his own presence at what he calls 'the front of the house' lowers the tone. On the subject of lowered tones, I mention that I know Mikey Forrester. His countenance takes on a hostile hue and he replies: — He's a clart. A villian, a junky. He runs a knocking shop, a cesspit, no a sauna. Tars us aw wi the same brush.

— I've never seen his massage parlour.

389

— Massage parlour, ma arse! He's nae discretion, thir's no even any attempt tae gie massages. The lassies thaire widnae ken whit a massage wis! Deals drugs openly, cocaine. If ah hud ma wey scum like that wid be closed doon. Naw, they'd be jailed! Then he drops his voice in grave, confidential seriousness. — You shouldnae be hinging aboot wi that crowd, nice lassie like you. Yir askin fir bother. Thir's one thing aboot that bunch: sooner or later thi'll drag ye doon tae thair level. Tell ye that fir nowt.

I think: *they already have*, as I smile politely. Nobody seems to like Mr Forrester and I'm sure it's deserved. When I get back home, I mention this to Mark, who's in the kitchen with Dianne cooking a pasta dish. He throws his head back and laughs. — Mikey . . .

— Is this the pimp? Dianne asks.

— He runs a sauna, I say. — Not the one I work at, I add hastily.

— Could I talk to him sometime? For my dissertation? she asks.

Mark can't hide his distaste at the very thought of it. — I don't really know him, I tell her. Then I turn to Mark. — I recall that there seemed to be a bit of a clash between you two back at the pub?

— Mikey and I will never be on each other's Christmas card list, Mark grins, scooping some chopped onions, garlic and peppers into a frying pan and stirring frantically as they sizzle. He turns to Dianne and me, and, as if reading our thoughts, laughs: — If you could conceive of either of us ever having one.

I don't think Mikey, or any of my new friends for that matter, are likely to figure on Bobby's Christmas shopping list. I probably will though. With Simon now *persona non grata*, I've been spending more time at the sauna, working as many shifts as I can get, trying to get more cash together. I don't want to ask Simon, as his ostracism since the film debacle has been complete and all-embracing: in Wildean terms, he's been eating his chop alone. To show solidarity with my fellow sex workers, I've been ignoring his phone messages: strange, disturbing affairs, which indicate that he's becoming slightly unhinged. Of course, the unspoken pact between Mark and me is how we have to limit our estrangement from him. After all, we are partners in the scam.

Mark and him have such a strange relationship, friends, yet who seem to openly despise each other. While we're eating the lasagne – me, Dianne, Lauren and Mark – I can't help sounding off about him. I'm ranting about his tightness with money and his duplicitousness. Mark just says quietly, in the face of my rage: — It's always better to get even than angry.

He has a point, but I have to admit though, that for all my bluster, my hostility to Simon is waning dangerously. I miss the intrigue. Lauren, by contrast, still lets her hatred for him rage like a furnace. — He's a user, Nikki, I'm glad you're not getting back to him. He's deranged, listen to him when he leaves those strange messages on the voicemail. Don't call him, she coughs, in a terrible, rasping hack. Lauren sounds and looks, awful.

Even Dianne, who never criticises anybody or interferes in their business, is moved to remark: — I don't think that's such a bad idea, then turning to Lauren asks: — Have you got the flu?

— It's just a cough, Lauren says, then turns to me and says: — You're too good for him, Nikki.

After a bit Lauren takes some Lemsip and goes to her bed, really looking terrible, and then Mark and Dianne head off, I don't know where, probably back to Mark's for a shag. As the evening draws in I'm reading, for pleasure, rather than labouring at the sausage machine of academia. I'm so relieved to have finished those exams. As I enjoy *Captain Corelli's Mandolin*, stroking Zappa who's curled onto my lap, I'm trying not to think about Simon when I reread the passage where Corelli makes his first appearance. It's stupid, the character is nothing like him . . . it's just . . . it's been a week now.

There's a bang on the door and I start, making poor Zappa fly off me in fright. I'm nervous and elated because I know it's him. It has to be. I head down the hallway to the door, playing daft games with myself, 'if it is him we're meant to be together' games, hoping it is and it isn't at the same time.

It is. His eyes widen as I open the door, but his lips stay tight. — Nikki, I'm sorry. I've been a bit selfish. Can I come in?

It seems to me that in my sexual life of a decade or so, I've been through this a million times. — Why, I say coldly, — I suppose you just want to talk?

He stuns me with his reply. — No. I don't want to talk, he says, shaking his head emphatically. It strikes me that Simon looks good; figure quite trim, sunbed tan prominent, with that slightly crinkled look which can be acceptable in the mature man, if he's well groomed. — I've talked enough, he says, and he wears that hurt, wounded look which you know is a manipulative shield, but . . . — and it's all been bullshit, he states roundly. — I want to listen. I want to hear you talk. That's if you think I'm worth talking to, and, to be frank, I wouldn't blame you at all if you didn't.

I look back at him, saying nothing.

— Okay, he raises his hands and smiles sadly. — I just wanted to say I'm sorry for all the mess I've caused. But I genuinely believed at the time that I was doing everything for the best, he states balefully, before turning and heading back down towards the stairs.

A panic grips me in the chest and I can't control what I'm about to say. My head's buzzing, my expectations have been inverted. — Simon . . . wait . . . come in for a bit. I open the door fully and he shrugs and turns around and stands in the doorway, but he makes no attempt to come into the flat.

Instead he raises his hand like a kid at school trying to attract the teacher's attention. The thing is that it works, I can't believe it, but this fucking prick actually makes me feel like I want cuddle him and say 'there, there, sonny: come to bed, let me fuck you'. — Nikki, I'm trying to straighten myself out, he says, eyes twinkling sadly. — I'm no good to you until I do. I thought that I was further down the road to getting myself sorted than I thought, but I can tell by the look in your eyes that I've still got a long way to go.

— Simon . . . I can hear myself bleat, the sound seeming to come from somebody else, — if only you'd ease up a little? Like on the cocaine? It always brings out the worst side of you?

I think about what I've just said and it occurs to me in horror that I've never known him when he *wasn't* on the cocaine.

Now is evidently no exception. — Exactly correct, he suddenly barks. Then his eyes go big and soulful again and he says: — Nikki, I'm drowning here. You make me want to be a better person, and with your love, I know I could be that person, he says softly, as I note the beads of drug sweat on his brow.

There's that horrible-beautiful moment, that bitter-sweet impasse where you know that somebody is bullshitting you but they're doing it with such panache and conviction . . . no, it's because they say exactly what you want to hear, need to hear, at that point in time. He's standing framed by the doorway, his arm extended, with his full weight on it. He's not like Colin, not like the rest. He's not like the rest because he's fucking irresistible. — Come in, I almost whisper.

64

Just Playing

The hangover's pure kickin in n ah'm takin a walk intae toon tae clear the nut. Up past St Andrew's, whir thir buildin a new bus station. The auld one wis a dump, n the last time ah wis in it wis ages ago. In fact, it wis whin me, Rents, Sick Boy, Franco n Second Prize wir gaun doon tae London, wi aw that smack oan us. Pure paranoia, man, pure paranoia. Healthy stretch fir that yin if collared, too right!

Nae sun, man; the punters are aw wrapped up against the dull drizzle n the cauld wind, but they seem tae be comin at ye fae aw angles wi thir shoapin bags. Aye, that shopping-greed fever is pure in evidence up here the day, man.

Ah'm walkin tae think, man, tae think aboot thon Dostoevsky cat, how it wis the perfect crime. The nippy auld moneylender thit naebody liked, or missed, jist like the dirty nonce Chizzie. Pure baws that wis in the paper, ken, two young boys, Charlie at Nicol's Bar goes. Bet ye Begbie pure pit the fangs intae ehs neck, man. Naw, Chizzie'll no be missed, no a beast, jist like a junky willnae. Cause that's whair the Raskolnikov cat messed up. Eh wis still aroond, still in the basket n ready tae crack under the psychological pressure, cause eh killed somebody else. Bit ah'll no be aroond tae crack up, this crime'll no benefit me, it'll benefit the nearest n dearest.

Ah finds masel in Rose Street n ah sees um; eh's aw excited, ehs hands ur swingin aboot n ehs heid goes back in a big horsey laugh. Now eh's hudin ehs side wi one hand n the other's gaun roond this lassie's shoodir.

Been tryin tae contact the boy oan ehs mobby, git a beer, tell um thit ah need Zappa back cause ah miss the gadge. Rents' bird and that lassie Sick Boy's hinging out wey; they've got him. Aye, they're a really close foursome n aw that shite. Mind you, ah cannae see

Rents n ehs bird gaun in fir aw that swingin stuff, but ye never know. Rents mibee, aye, bit the lassie seems a bit straight fir that. Ye think: mibee aye, mibee naw. Thing is, Rents kent this wee honey back in the day, ah'm sure ay it. Now thir walkin airm in airm thegither. Rents disnae seem tae care, or believe the danger aboot the Beggar. Probably disnae even ken the rumours aboot what happened tae Chizzie.

— Spud! Awright, man, he says and gies me a big hug. — This is Dianne.

She looks at me like she's tryin tae place me, then steps forward n kisses ma cheek, n ah respond.

— Awright, doll? How's things? ah asks the lassie.

— Not bad. What about you? she asks aw breezy, n aye, this is a wee honey n aw, man. No the kind ay bird ye associate wi Rents. Eh eywis seemed tae go for the troubled type ay lassie: goth or New Agey sort ay chicks wi slash marks oan thir wrists thit ey talked aboot 'healin' n 'growth' aw the time. Eywis drawn tae the dark side, that cat.

— Well, man, still swirlin around in that auld Leith vortex, ah sort ay rap.

Rents hus sortay changed but, man. Once upon a time eh'd git intae that wi me, now it's jist an indulgent wee smile for ehs simpleton pal. — Been tae the fitba lately? eh asks.

— Aye, goat ma sister's felly's season. That Sauzee boy's excellent, ah tell the cat.

Renton looks thoughful for a while. — Aye, ah dunno if ah like the idea ay following a winnin team but. Too sheepish, too unhip, eh goes in a wey whither ye dinnae ken if eh's serious or no.

— Yeah, that's why I support Hearts, that wee Dianne laughs, looking up at him, aw sort ay indulgent. This is a cute kitten whose face changes completely in a smile.

— All that's over now, baby, those dark days have gone. Consider the Jambo albatross around your neck well and truly shot dead, Rents laughs as they pure jostle each other in the street.

— How long are ye ower here fir? ah ask him.

— Eh, it wis meant tae be a couple weeks, but ah'm sortay thinkin aboot steyin ower for a bit. Fancy a beer?

So we go intae one ay they weekender-n-tourist bars fir a few peeves. While Dianne's up at the jukey, Rents whispers: — Ah've been meanin tae gie ye a phone tae git a drink, but eh, ah dinnae want tae be, well, aroond toon wi certain parties oan the prowl, – eh screws ehs face up.

— Better watch, man, ye ken what ah mean, ah whisper.

The Rent Boy smiles like eh disnae care. Mibee eh disnae. It seems tae me thit eh disnae really realise how cracked Franco is. We depart, heading oor separate weys, them wherever, n it seems tae be a secret locale, me pure back port side n tae ma mate Begbie's. Cause now this is aw comin thegither in ma heid; the bus station, the scam, Dostoevsky, Renton n Begbie. It's funny though, man, but Renton's got what ah want. Eh's got Begbie exactly where ah want um.

So ah'm headin doonhill tae Leith, thinkin aboot how if ye come fae Leith, ye really belong tae two toons, Leith n Edinburgh, rather than just the one. The old port stretches oot before me, dank n damp as the sodium street lights kick in, floodin the broons n greys n dark blues wi white, yellay n orangey glares. Ah'm thinkin that wir jist that bit further south thin St Petersburg n mibee this is what it felt like thair tae that Raskolnikov gadgie.

Doon the Walk, passin aw the pubs, so invitin as somebody spills oot, fill ay loud chatter n music n laughter n smoke, n the odd shout. Past the chippies wi drunks n couples n groups ay wee radges ootside thum. Past the bus stoaps wi nervous auld wifies mibee gaun hame back oot tae a scheme miles away eftir a bingo session, n the auld drunks n aw, punters whae huvnae lived in Leith fir decades but ur still drawn here, still Leithers through n through.

Ah turns off intae Lorne Street, n gits up tae Begbie's stair n raps the door. Ah kin hear noises at the other side, like somebody's just ready tae leave. The door opens n it's that big Lexo cat, n eh's headin oot.

— Mind what ah sais, Begbie shouts tae um, face aw stiff, n the big Lexo boy jist nods back, pushing past me, nearly knockin ays ower.

Begbie watches him go doon the stairs then looks at me for a second, fir the first time really, n goes in, noddin at me tae dae the same. Ah follay him n shut the door behind ays.

— That cunt hud better watch ehs step. Ah'll fuckin well kill that big cunt, ah'm telling ye, Spud, eh sais, gaun intae the kitchen. Eh opens the fridge n pills oot two cans ay lager n hands ays one.

— Cheers, catboy, ah goes, lookin aroond. — Sound gaff.

Ah think ah kin smell a bairn here; thir's a whiff ay pish n powder. Then a youngish lassie, no bad-lookin, but wi quite a worried face comes through n nods tae me, but Begbie disnae introduce us. Eh lits her git an iron fae a cupboard n waits till she goes oot.

— Fuckin Lexo tryin tae pey ays oaf wi sweeties. Ah goat the cunt fuckin telt, ah goes tae um, me n you wis partners until ah heard fuckin different . . . Franco's choppin oot some lines ay ching now. — Eh jist stoaped seein ays in the jail, nivir said nowt aboot this fuckin Thai café or the partnership bein fuckin well dissolved. That means thit half ay that fuckin café's mine. Eh fuckin well turns roond tae me n starts gaun oan aboot aw the debts eh hud tae pey oaf tae set that fuckin café up, bit ah jist turns roond n says tae the cunt, wir no talkin aboot fuckin money here, wir talkin aboot fuckin mates. It's the fuckin principle ay the thing.

Ah'm lookin at a big breidknife oan a choppin board oan the worktop. It wid be perfect, man, but no here . . . no wi that lassie n her bairn in the hoose. Ah takes a line.

— That's the fuckin last ay the ching, eh goes n pills oot the mobby, — bit ah'll git some mair.

— Naw, ah've goat some up at mines, chum ays roond, will pick it up then git a beer.

— Barry, ya cunt, Franco goes, flingin oan ehs jaykit. Eh shouts through tae ehs bird: — That's me gaun oot fir a fuckin bit, right, n ah follay um n wir oot ay the door.

Eh's still gaun oan aboot Lexo. — That cunt . . . eh'd better watch ehs fuckin step or ah'll fuckin kill the big cunt.

Ah'm sortay tremblin inside, but no that feart, mibee it's the ching, so ah goes: — Aye, ye kin dae that awright, Franco. Ye did the Donnelly boy.

Franco stoaps in ehs tracks in the street n gies ays a stare thit's jist pure arctic, man. That wis ehs manslaughter sentence. It was him or Donnelly, everybody said it, n Franco hud bad injuries, plunged

twice, cause the boy tried tae dae um wi a sharpened screwdriver.
— What the fuck are you sayin?

— Nowt, Franco, c'mon, lit's git this ching then ah'll take ye for
a drink, man.

Begbie looks at ays for a second, then starts movin oaf n we head
up tae mine. We get up the stair n ah'm makin a show ay lookin
through poakits fir the ching. Ah goes intae the kitchen n lays oot
some knives. Ah'm hopin that this gadge is quick. — Come ben
here, Franco, ah shouts.

Franco comes through tae the kitchen. — Whaire's that fuckin
ching then, ya useless cunt?

— Aye, ye did that Donnelly, ah goes.

— You dinnae ken the half ay it, Spud, eh laughs, aw creepy like,
n eh snaps oan ehs mobby. — Ah'll git us some gear, ya useless
fucker, then eh's punchin numbers in.

— Chizzie the beast, ah goes. Franco snaps the phone shut. —
What're you fuckin well up tae? Begbie's startled n eh looks at me,
and eh could chill ower Hades wi that look, man. Ye see they eyes
n it's like thir's nae skin tae ye any mair, man, nae clathes, yir jist a
beatin, pumpin mass ay blood which is aboot tae lose its shape n
jist spill tae the flair.

Mibee it's the coke n the nerves bit ah'm tellin the Begbie cat
the story, the plan, and how he'd be daein me a favour. But eh's
livid, man, just pure livid, so ah decides that it's plan B. Ah nod at
the blades laid oot oan the table and ah goes: — Hey, Franco, man,
ah forgoat tae gie ye somethin . . .

— What . . .

N ah rams the nut intae ehs face, man, bit ah hit ehs mooth
instead ay ehs beak. Fir a split second, ah feel that charged-up wey
n ah almost git what the Begbie boy sees in this violence gig. Ah
stand thair, in a fightin pose, jist lookin at um. Tae ma shock, eh
disnae steam ays. Eh touches ehs lip, sees blood oan ehs finger. Then
he stands and looks at me for a bit.

— YA FUCKIN SICK CUNT! Begbie spits, then leaps forward
n smashes the heid intae ma face. Ah'm topplin back as this shard
ay pure pain like white electricity seems tae shoot right tae the
centre ay ma brain. Ah'm bein hit again n ah sortay find masel oan

the flair withoot mindin ay fawin. Ma eyes ur fill ay water n ehs boot flies intae me n ah cannae breathe n ah'm pukin up, ma boady's shakin in shock n thir's blood gaun doon the back ay ma throat. Ah dinnae want this . . . jist dae it quick . . .

— . . . dae it quick . . . ah groan.

— Ah'm no gaunnae fuckin kill you! You're no gaunnae die! IF YOU TRY TAE GIT ME TAE FUCKIN WELL KILL YE, YIR FUCKIN DEID! . . . YIR FUCKIN . . .

Begbie freezes for a minute, as ah force masel tae look up, n try tae focus oan um n it's like eh's gaunnae laugh, but eh screws up ehs face and punches the waw. — YA FUCKIN CUNT! WE DINNAE GIE UP! WE'RE FUCKIN HIBS! WE'RE FUCKIN LEITH! WE DINNAE FUCKIN DAE SHITE LIKE THAT! eh sortay pleads, n goes softly: — Littin ivray cunt doon . . . Spud . . . Then eh looks aw fuckin mental again. — Ah see yir fuckin game! AH SEE YIR GAME! TRYIN TAE FUCKIN WELL USE ME, YA CUNT!

Ah try n pill masel up oan ma elbay, try tae git it thegither. — Aye . . . ah want tae die . . . it's likes ay me that Renton gave the money tae, no you . . . eh held oot oan you. Ah spent the loat. Oan junk.

Ah cannae see um now though, ah kin jist see the kitchen strip light, but ah kin feel ehs stare. — You . . . ah ken what yir tryin tae dae . . .

— Spent the fuckin loat, man, ah smile through ma pain, — sorry, catboy . . .

Franco wheezes like ah've kicked um in the stomach n ah'm gaunnae say mair whin ah feel this blow tae the side ay ma face n thir's this awfay, awfay crack like ma jaw's broken. The pain's sickenin, but sort ay deadnin. Then ah kin hear ehs voice, n that weird sort ay plead again, man. — You've goat Alison n the bairn! How will it affect thaim if ye die, ya selfish wee cunt?

Eh's bootin me n thir jist rainin in but ah cannae feel thum, n ah'm thinkin aboot it aw . . . Alison, wee Andy . . . n ah'm mindin ay that summer, the two ay us by the Shore, the Water ay Leith, her in that summer maternity dress, me pattin her lump, feelin the wee kicks ay the bairn. Me sayin tae her, wi the tears ay joy n baith oor eyes, that that kid's gaunnae dae aw the things thit ah've nivir done.

Then it's like in that hoaspital whin ah'm huddin um fir the first time. Her smile, his first step, n ehs first word, which wis 'dad' . . . ah'm seein aw this n ah want tae live, Franco's right, man, eh's right . . . ah raise a hand n gasp: — Yir right, Franco . . . yir right, ah groan, but wi aw ma hert. — Thanks, mate . . . thanks fir sortin ays oot. Ah want tae live . . .

Ah cannae see Franco's face, it's aw jist swirlin darkness, no wi ma eyes ah cannae, but wi ma mind ah kin. N it's cauld n evil n ah hear um say: — Too late fir that now, ya cunt, ye should've fuckin well thoat aboot that before ye goat fuckin wide n tried tae fuckin yaze ays . . .

N eh sinks the boot in again . . .

And ah'm tryin tae moan oot, man, but it's like ah'm away and nothing's working n ah'm slippin . . . it's dark . . . then thir's cauld n ah'm bein slapped awake n ah'm thinkin thit it's a hoaspital but it's Franco's face. — Wakey, wakey, cunty baws, didnae want ye tae miss the fuckin fun! Cause you're gaunnae die awright, ya cunt, but it's gaunnae be fuckin slow . . .

N a fist goes intae ma face again n aw ah kin see is Alison smilin at ays, n the wee man, n ah'm thinkin aboot how ah'll miss thum n then ah hear hur Ali screamin: — DANNY! WHAT'S HAPPININ . . . WHAT UR YE DAEIN TAE UM, FRANK!

She's in the hoose wi the bairn and aw naw . . . n Begbie's roaring back at her: — HE'S FUCKIN SICK! HE'S A FUCKIN SICK CUNT! AH'M AH THE ONLY FUCKIN NORMAL CUNT IN THIS PLACE? GIT UM TELT!

Then ehs oaf, oot the door and Ali's greetin, she's doon cradling ma heid. — What happened, Danny? Was it drugs?

Ah'm spittin blood. — A misunderstanding . . . that's aw . . . Ah looks up at the bairn, eh's greetin now, aw feart. — Uncle Frank n me wir jist playin, pal . . . jist playin . . .

Ah'm tryin tae keep ma heid up, tryin tae be brave fir thaim, but the pain's everywhaire n everything is spinnin slowly n ah feel masel gaun under and blacking oot, fawin intae a whirlin dark pit . . .

65

Scam # 18,750

I'm having a drink with my old buddy and new partner in the City Café, breaking the good news. Renton, who's been looking like he's put on a bit of podge, is staring at the letter I've handed him, then at me, with undisguised awe. — I don't know how the fuck you pulled this one off, Simon.

— It's all down to the showreel I ran off and sent them, I explain. I can tell by his look he thinks it was down to that cunt Miz using his influence. Let him think what he likes.

Renton shrugs and breaks into an admiring smile. — Well, we've done it your way so far and it's no worked out too bad, he tells me, examining the letter again. — Full exhibition at the Cannes Adult Film Festival. That is a result by any standards.

Normally, flattery is the most fragrant balm to the ego, but when it's spilling from the Rent Boy's lips you're always bracing yourself for that follow-up kick in the chops. We're discussing the setting up of our film's website, www.sevenrides.com, and what we want to go onto it. My main objective, though, is to ensure that we have product to sell. That means that some mug has to sit in a warehouse in Amsterdam and stuff videos into boxes. And I only know one person who claims that they have loads to do in the Dam.

So we head off on our little jaunt but it's far from pleasant, sitting in a warehouse doing dogsbody work. The place feels horrible, claustrophobic. When I get back to Edinburgh I need a session out at Porty Baths, so I swallow hard and incur the hideous taxi cost all the way out there. Renton accompanies me as far as the city centre and grudgingly chips in a tenner.

Sitting in the tank of the aerotone baths at Portobello, enjoying the warm waters and the pummelling sensation of the jets, I'm thinking that this has been one of the main things I've missed in

London over the last decade. Ah, the aerotone baths at Porty pool. It's impossible to explain to the uninitiated the sheer trance-like, luxuriant mode one slips into here, way beyond any sauna or Turkish baths. So deliciously old school, this big Jules Verne tin tank with its dials and valves and pipes. The old mingers who come in during the day love it here.

I'm thinking that this is the frame of mind in which to spread the good news, so, reluctantly getting out and wrapping a towel round my waist, I repair to my locker and the mobby. The signal's strong for indoors. I call everyone I can think of and tell them the news about our Cannes selection. Nikki shrieks with delight, Birrell gives a grudging — Right, as if I've told him that a ten-year jail sentence he's just received has been cut by couple of months. Terry reacts characteristically. — Cannae wait. Aw that French fanny, n aw they posh birds thit'll be gantin oan it!

I head down to Leith and the pub. I'm about to sneak upstairs to my office to check the Bananazzurri messages, when Morag ambushes me on the bend in the stairs, those startled mad eyes under a newly permed mop making me stop in shock. — Mo. You've had your hair done. Suits you, I smile.

Mo is not happy, seeming now totally impervious to my charms. — Nivir mind ma hair, Simon, thir's a man been doon here fae the *Evenin News*. Askin aw sorts ay questions aboot you, n dae ah ken aboot yis makin any films upstairs n that.

— What did ye say?

— Ah telt um ah didnae ken nowt aboot it, she says, shaking her head.

Morag's no grass, of that I'm certain. — Thanks, Mo. This is fuckin harassment. If that creep comes in here again, tell me. I will have him fucking well shot and I will have his house burned down, I spit into her shocked face.

I'm about to make good my escape upstairs when the old cow moos: — Ah need help doon here, Simon. Ali's had tae go up tae the hospital, her man got hurt.

— Who, Spud?

— Aye.

— What happened?

— They dinnae ken, but eh's in a right mess by the sound ay it.

— Right, give me five . . . I say, feeling strangely concerned about Murphy. I mean, it's not as if we're bosom buddies any more, but I wouldn't actively wish harm on the fleabag. I back up the stairs, waving at that startled face below me. — Got tae check the mail . . .

— And Paula's been on fae Spain, wonderin how things are. Ah'm tellin her fine, but she's ma pal, ah cannae keep coverin up fir ye, Simon. Ah'm no gaunnae lie tae Paula.

I stop in my tracks. — What dae ye mean?

— Well, that Mr Cresswell fae the brewery, nice fellay, eh sais that eh's no been peyed for last week's delivery. Ah telt um you'd git back tae um n sort it oot.

I think about this before addressing Mo. — Cresswell's a worrier: a corporate man. Doesn't understand that business operates on credit and cash flow. No, just sits there in his fancy Fountainbridge office pretending that he understands the real business world. A day at the coalface would kill him. I'll speak to him, I rant out, getting up to the office for a quick fortifying line before attending to bar duties.

I've called a meeting this evening, in the pub. Fuck knows why, to keep them up with the state of play. More likely it's because the ching's coursing through the system and I'd much rather bend some ears up here than serve alcohol to the old and young fools downstairs. I elected to keep Forrester out of it, thinking that there would be bother if he and Renton were in the same building. Of course, Renton doesn't even do me the fucking courtesy of showing up. Rab Birrell sullenly troops in and Terry arrives and immediately asks to be weighed in. Every cunt seems to have gone money-mad all of a sudden. Who the fuck do they think I am? That's fuckin Renton; on the mobby I'll bet, putting ideas into every fucker's head. — Sorry, Tel, a distinct shortage of stocks of tinned pigeon, or, if you prefer: no can do.

— So that's it, ah git nowt for what ah did?

— You're no on a profit share, Terry, I explain. — Ye goat peyed as a shagger. Ah wis always the boy running the show.

— Fair enough, he says with a grin that makes me feel decidedly uneasy. — That's the wey it goes, eh.

Terry's enthusiasm made him a useful fellow-traveller at one point. His lack of ambition means that he'll never be a player in the industry. You do your best, you afford them the opportunity to learn and grow. The rest is up to them. But he's taking this well. Too well.

So let's see how the cunt takes this. — We have a problem, I tersely announce. — Obviously we can't all go to Cannes, cost prohibits. So it'll be me, Nikki, Mel and Curtis. The talent. Rents as well, I need him on the business side. The rest? A too-many-cooks situ.

— I cannae go anyway, Rab says, — no wi the bairn, n the course n that.

Terry abruptly stands up and walks towards the door. — Tez, I shout, trying to prevent my face from twisting gleefully.

He turns and says: — Why the fuck ask ays doon here if ah'm no gittin peyed or gaun tae Cannes? To be fair, I can think of no good reason, so am literally quite speechless as he continues: — You're wastin ma fuckin time here. Ah'm away up tae the hossy tae see Spud, he growls and exits.

— Me n aw, Rab endorses, getting up and following him. Losers or what? I'm thinking that Rab doesn't know Spud, so I take it to mean that he's leaving rather than going on visiting duties.

At this point Nikki comes in and apologises for being late. She watches in concern as they depart. I turn to her. — Fuck them right up their shite-encrusted arseholes. We don't need them, never did. You simply cannot let the tail wag the dog, and I'm tired of feeding their delusions of adequacy.

Craig looks tense and Ursula laughs and Ronnie grins. Nikki, Gina and Mel look at me as if I should be saying more. — When the sales come through, we'll work it all out between us, I explain. — Well? You can't divvy money when there's none to fucking divvy!

I give the rest of them a lecture on the economics of the industry, which goes over most of the heads present. Eventually they shoot off, only Nikki holding back. I can tell that she's not happy with the way I've treated Rab and Terry. I'm feeling a tightening inside me as I experience a gnawing contempt for her, which is horrible because I'm probably in love with the woman. Now she's sensing something, making small talk, telling me that she's thinking of jacking in the sauna. I tell her that it's not a bad idea, as these places are ran by sleazoids. I start to wonder whether she's gearing up to try and hit me for some cash. Eventually she goes to her shift and I arrange to see her later tonight.

So it seems my crew has diminished, but I can't be bothered thinking about foolhardy rascals like Terry at the moment. I go to the office and chop out and rack up a juicy line as a newspaper twat calls. — Can I speak to Simon Williamson?

— Mr Williamson's not around at the moment, I tell him. — Apparently he's playing fives up at the Jack Kane . . . or it might be Portobello.

— When are you expecting him back?

— I'm not really sure at the present. Mr Williamson has been busy of late.

— To whom am I speaking?

— I'm Mr Francis Begbie.

— Well, if you could get Mr Williamson to call me when he gets back.

— I'll leave the message, but Simon's very much a free spirit, I state to the receiver as I use a fifty-pound note to hoover up some ching.

— Well, make sure he calls me. It's important. There's some things I need to clarify, the pompous voice drones.

— You can suck my dirty jailbird cock, I tell him, slamming down the phone as the line of ching stiffens my spine. I unroll the crisp fifty, delighting in its beauty. Money gives you the luxury of not caring about it. You can affect to find it crass and vulgar, but see how crass and vulgar it is when there's none of it in your pocket.

First of all, though, the big one beckons. Let's do the Cannes-Cannes.

66

Whores of Amsterdam Pt 9

I've had enough of high-maintenance relationships. Yet, here I am back in Amsterdam, back in another one of sorts. Because Sick Boy's on one of his sulkers.

We're sitting in a cold, draughty warehouse in Leylaand, on the city outskirts, putting video cards into cases and cases into boxes. This is Miz's place and it's a shithouse, with all sorts of rubbish stacked ceiling-high on pallets. It's got the sick, blue-yellow fluorescent strip lighting which bounces off the aluminium panels that hang from the rust-red girder frames. I'm trying to think margins; 2,000 x £10 ÷ 2 = £10,000, but this is taking yonks and Sick Boy's unhappy. I'd forgotten the extent of the cunt's capacity tae complain, to moan out loud at annoyances which should be fleeting enough to keep to yourself. But even that's preferable tae this silent brooding, which makes the air as heavy as tar. It's obvious that he feels this isn't glam enough for him, but he's forgetting that once I sense that he's annoyed I can just relax and enjoy his whining and moping.

— We need staff, Renton, he says, drumming on a empty box that sits on his thigh. — Where's that Kraut bird ay yours? She definitely oot the picture now that that Dianne's gittin a length?

I keep silent, working on my old principle that Sick Boy and your romantic life should be kept apart. Nowt the cunt has done this time around has convinced me to re-evaluate that philosophy. — Piss off. Stoap fuckin whingeing and keep packing, I'm telling him, thinking all the time, where indeed; far, I'm hoping. I keep my head lowered in case he reads this in my eyes.

I can feel those big lamps burning at me. — Watch yourself getting back with that Dianne bird, he says. — In Italy we have a phrase aboot reheating auld soup. It never works oot. Reheated cabbage, mate. *Minestra riscaldata!*

I want to ram my fist into the cunt's face. Instead, I smile at him.

Then he seems to think about something, and nod in a stern kind of approval. — But at least she's the right age. I love women at that age. Never go oot wi a bird in their thirties. They're all bitter, poisonous cows with an agenda. In fact, under twenty-six if possible. But no teenagers, a bit too immature and they grate after a while. Naw, twenty to twenty-five is vintage time for lassies, he explains, then starts ranting through the jukebox of his obsessions. I get old favourites; film, music, Alex Miller, Sean Connery; and new ones: bad Manchester perms, crack hoors, Alex McLeish, Franck Sauzee, television presenters, junk movies.

He's going on and on, and I can't be bothered. I just can't be fuckin well arsed saying something like: *Solaris* shites all over *2001*, and then listening to him arguing vehemently against it. Or, alternatively, waiting for him to say it, and then being expected to argue the other viewpoint. And that way we look at each other so challengingly, as if to agree, even if we do, is a sign that we're effete poofs. I can't be bothered with it and I can't even be bothered to tell him that I can't be bothered.

I'm aware as I tuck yet another representation of Nikki's arse cheeks into a box cover that my ears are starting to close over. Nikki has a lovely arse, no doubt about that, but when you've stuck a paper representation of it into the three-hundredth box, it becomes less attractive. Maybe pornographic images are something you shouldn't view repeatedly; perhaps they do desensitise you, erode your sexuality. Sick Boy's drones increase: plans, betrayals, the lot of a sensitive man surrounded by junkies, Masons, scumbags, wasters, hoors and lassies who don't know how to dress properly.

I'm hear myself going: — Mmmm, in a steady agreement. But after a bit Sick Boy's shaking me and shouting: — Renton! Are you totally fucking Lee Van? he asks.

I'm a bit out of the Leith rhyming slang just now, so it takes me a while to register. — Naw.

— Fuckin listen then, ya rude cunt! Conversation!

— What?

— I said I want to drink tea from bone china, he tells me. He sees that he's got my attention, cause I'm fucked if I know what the cunt's oan aboot. Then he looks around, and qualifies his statement. — No, what I really want to do is to drink tea in an environment where this stands out, this porcelain shite, he holds up an Ajax mug, — and bone china fuckin well disnae, he snaps, suddenly throwing down a video-cassette box and jumping to his feet. His Adam's apple bulges in his neck like a small pig in a snake's belly.

And then he hurls the cup against the wall and I shudder as it smashes into pieces. — Fuck off, that's Miz's cup, ya cunt, I tell him.

— Sorry, Mark, he says sheepishly, — it's the nerves. Too much ching these days. Have to take it easier.

I've never really liked charlie, but a lot of people feel that way and still ram it up their hooters. Just because it's there. People consume shite that does them no good at all, often just because they can. It's naive to expect drugs tae be exempt from the laws of modern consumer capitalism. Especially when, as a product, they best help define it.

It takes us another two tense, sick hours to finish our turgid task. My hands are calloused and my thumb and wrist ache. I look at the boxed piles of videos sitting stacked up. Aye, we now have the 'product' as he loves to call it, ready for distribution after Cannes. I still can't believe that he's got us a place at the Cannes Film Festival. Not really *the* Cannes Film Festival, but the adult-movie event, which runs concurrently. When I qualify this, usually when he's chatting up a woman, which he always seems to be doing, it gets right on his nerves. — It *is* a film festival, and it *is* in Cannes. So what's the fuckin problem?

I'm happy to leave the warehouse and get back into town. We're living it up a little this time, staying at the American Hotel on the Leidseplein. I've had a drink in its bar a few times, but never, ever thought that I'd stay here. We sit at the bar, paying the mad prices. But we can afford it now and will be able to for some time. Well, some of us will.

67

FITBA OAN SKY

Ah'm waitin oan Kate comin in wi the bairn, tae make muh fuckin tea before uh goes doon the fuckin pub tae watch the fitba oan Sky. She'd better fuckin nash, cause time's tickin away. So there's me sittin watchin that big fuckin telly, it's never oaf now. Goat the fuckin boax fir Sky n aw, bit ah'm watchin the game doon the boozer the night. Better atmosphere.

Ah keep thinkin back tae Easter n that fuckin nonce animal. Thir wis a bit aboot it at the time, but jist the usual shite: did anybody see a group ay youths leavin the fuckin pub blah blah blah . . . Good time tae dae some cunt, a public hoaliday. People's goat mair tae think aboot thin a fuckin stoat. Sometimes ah fuckin think but, ah'd better see Charlie again, n they auld cunts, make sure that naebody fuckin blabs.

Cause ah've made the fuckin world a better place, cause they fuckin things deserve tae die, that's the wey thit ah fuckin well see it. Too right. The polis, if they wir bein honest, wid tell ye the same thing. Ah agree wi the paper, the *News ay the World*. Tell us whaire aw they cunts live n wi'll go roond thaire n fuckin well extermi-nate thum aw. Solve the whole fuckin problem straight away. Like that twisted cunt Murphy . . . suppose tae be a fuckin mate . . . like Renton wis . . . ah'll fuckin rip his hert oot n pish in the hole.

Then ye git worried. Worried thit yir turnin intae one ay thaime. Aw they fuckin weirdos n that, like in America. That's how they talk.

Then ye look at that fuckin book, that fuckin Bible. Plenty ay thaim in the fuckin nick. Dinnae ken how any cunt kin read that shite; doth this, begat that, it's no even in the Queen's fuckin English. But they tell ays thit the Bible says thit God made man in ehs ain image. So ah take that as meaning thit *no* tae try tae be like God wid be a fuckin big insult tae the cunt, that's the wey ah see it. So aye, ah wis playin God whin ah wasted the nonce cunt. So fuckin what?

Ah switch channels bit it's ivraywhaire oan the telly; nonces, paedophiles, stoats, the fuckin loat. Thir's some fuckin radge psychologist cunt sayin thit thuv aw been abused thirsels, that's how they dae it. Fuckin shite. Tons ay cunts ur fuckin well abused n it disnae make thum go like that. So ye could say thit ah took fuckin pity oan that cunt, cause eh's jist gaunnae git abused again, n the nick n that. Best fuckin deal aw roond.

The hoose is daein muh fuckin nut in, n fuck knows whair she's goat tae, so ah nips doon stairs fir a *News*. It's fuckin freezin oot here, so ah'm right back up again wi the paper. Thir's the usual shite, but then ah see somethin thit makes ays stoap.

CUNT.

Muh hert bangs in ma chist as ah read:

NEW LEAD IN HUNT FOR CITY KILLER

Police still searching for clues in last month's murder of a city man in a Leith public house disclosed that they had received a tip-off from an anonymous caller which yielded 'promising' information. They appealed to the caller to get back in touch.

On the Thursday before the Easter holiday, Edinburgh man Gary Chisholm (38) was found bleeding to death on the floor of a Leith pub by the owner Charles Winters (52). Mr Winters had been downstairs in his cellar changing the barrel when he heard shouts and a scream from the bar. He ran up to find Mr Chisholm lying with his throat cut on the floor of the empty pub and saw two youths aged between fifteen and twenty fleeing from the scene. He went to Mr Chisholm's aid, but it was too late.

On the new information, investigating officer DI Douglas Gillman said: 'It's true that we have received some additional information on this case which may or may not be of use to us at this point in time. We are appealing for a male caller, who phoned on Tuesday evening, to get back in touch.

Meanwhile, the victim's grieving family endorsed the police

calls for members of the public to come forward. His sister Mrs Janice Newman (34) said: 'Gary was a great guy who didn't have a bad bone in his body. I can't understand how anybody could be covering up for the monster who killed my brother.'
If anybody has any information about this case, the number to contact is 0131–989 7173.

That's fuckin shite. That's the first thing they tell ye in the nick, if the polis start daein that thir fuckin desperate, it's jist thir wey ay pittin the fuckin heat oan. Then ah starts thinkin aboot that cunt Second Prize, aboot how the fuckin cunt's no been in touch. That fuckin pish-heid mooth, gabbin shite . . . another fuckin so-called mate . . .

FUCKIN GOD . . .

No thit ah believe in that religion shite, these cunts uv caused mair bother thin fuckin nonces, ower in Ireland n that. N it's been proved thit they priest cunts ur the biggest fuckin nonces oot the loat, so the whole fuckin thing aw fits thegither when ye think aboot it. That Murphy's fuckin deid. That's the problem wi some cunts but: they nivir just fuckin take the time tae fuckin well sit doon n think aboot things. Nae fuckin brains.

Kate comes in, n eftir she's made the tea n pit the bairn doon, she starts washin her hair. Now she's blow-dryin it. Dinnae ken what she wants tae wash ur fuckin hair fir whin shi's steyin in. Mibee it's fir the morn, fir hur shift at that fuckin clathes shoap. Ah bet thir's some cunt workin thair or in some ay the other shoaps in that fuckin centre thit's goat thir eye oan hur. Some fuckin wide cunt thit thinks thir it. One ay they pretty-boy, fanny-rat types like Sick Boy, cunts wi nae fuckin conscience thit'll jist yaze a lassie.

As long as she's no goat *her* fuckin eye oan the likes ay him. That gits ays thinkin. — Mind what happened wi you n me, whin wi first goat thegither? ah goes.

She looks up at ays, clicks oaf the dryer. — What dae ye mean? she sais.

— Mind, in bed, n that?

Now she's lookin at ays like she kens whit ah'm talkin aboot. That means she thinks aboot it n aw. — That was ages ago, Frank.

Ye wir jist oot ay jail. It disnae matter, she goes, screwin up her face a bit.

— No now it disnae, bit it fuckin matters tae me what cunts ken aboot it. You've no said nowt tae nae cunt aboot that, huv ye?

She pills oot a fag n lights it up. — What . . . of course no. That's between you n me. It's naebody's business.

— Too right, ah goes. — Yuv no said nowt but, huv ye?

— Naw.

— No even tae that fuckin Evelyn? ah asks hur. Before she answers, ah goes: — Cause ah ken what happens when burds git thegither. Yis talk. Eh? Aye, yis fuckin dae.

Ye kin tell this hus goat her fuckin well thinkin. She'd better fuckin no be lyin tae me, no for her sake. — No aboot that but, Frank. That's private n aw that wis ages ago. Ah nivir even think aboot it.

Aw, so shi disnae even think aboot it. Disnae even think aboot the fact thit she spent two weeks kippin up wi a boy thit couldnae fuck her. Like fuck she disnae think aboot it. — So yis dinnae fuckin well talk then, you n that fuckin Evelyn, n that other fuckin mate ay yours, her wi the fuckin hair . . .

— Rhona, she goes, aw wary.

— Fuckin Rhona. Yir tryin tae fuckin well tell ays thit yis dinnae fuckin well talk. Aboot yir fellys, likes?

Her eyes've went aw wide, like she's feart. What's she fuckin well goat tae be feart aboot but? — Aye, wi talk, she goes, — but no aboot that sortay thing, likes . . .

— No aboot what?

— No aboot intimate stuff, stuff thit goes oan in bed n that.

Ah looks her right in the eye. — So ye dinnae talk aboot stuff thit goes oan in bed like, no tae yir mates?

— Of course no . . . what is this, Frank, what's wrong? she asks.

Ah'll tell ur what the fuck's wrong awright. — Right then, what aboot the time whin a bunch ay us wir oot, doon the Black Swan, mind ay that time? That Evelyn wis thair n her wi the hair, what's it ye call yon piece again?

— Rhona, she says, aw worried. — But, Fran . . .

Ah snap my fingers. — Rhona, that's the yin. Right, now, see that cunt ye wir wi before me, the cunt ah fuckin panelled up the toon? ah asks n hur eyes go wider. — Ah mind wi wir in the pub that time, the Black Swan, n you says thit eh wis shite in bed anywey, that's what ye fuckin well sais aboot the boy that time, mind?

— Frank, this is silly . . .

Ah points at her. — Answer the fuckin question! Did you fuckin well say that or did ye no fuckin well say it?

— Aye . . . bit ah wis jist sayin that . . . cause ah wis relieved tae be away fae him . . . ah wis relieved tae huv you!

Relieved tae fuckin well huv me. Relieved tae be away fae that cunt. — So ye wir jist fuckin sayin it fir effect. Tae impress me n yir fuckin mates.

— Aye, that's it! she nearly sings oot, like that's hur oaf the hook. Disnae fuckin realise thit she's jist fuckin catchin husel oot wi aw that crap. Jist like aw they cunts thit cannae keep thir fuckin mooths shut; jist talkin hersel intae a deeper fuckin hole. — Right. So then it wisnae true, eh wisnae fuckin shite in bed. Eh wis brilliant. Eh wis much fuckin better thin me. Is that the fuckin truth then now, is it?

Now it's like she's jist aboot fuckin greetin. — Naw, naw . . . ah mean . . . it disnae matter what eh wis like in bed, ah wis jist sayin this cause ah hated um . . . cause ah wis gled tae be rid ay um. It disnae matter what eh wis like in bed . . .

Ah gies a wee smile at that. — So, ye wir jist sayin it cause it wis fuckin ower, cause yis wir fuckin history.

— Aye!

She's talkin fuckin shite. It disnae add up. — So, what happens if *we* split up? If we're fuckin history? Ye jist start sayin they things aboot me, roond every fuckin pub in Leith? That's it then, eh?

— Naw . . . naw . . . it's no like that . . .

Ah git her fuckin well telt. — Better fuckin no be! Cause see if you ivir breathe a word ay that, thi'll be nowt fuckin well left ay ye eftir it. Thi'll be nae fuckin trace thit you ivir fuckin existed . . . right?!

She fuckin well looks through tae the bairn's room n then looks back at me. Then shi bursts intae tears. She thinks ah'm gaunnae hurt her fuckin bairn like ah'm some kind ay a nonce cunt. — Look, ah goes, — dinnae greet, Kate, c'moan . . . look, ah didnae mean it, ah says, n ah'm ower n ah've goat ma airm roond her n ahm gaun, — . . . it's jist thit thir's a loat ay people thit hate ays, ken? Some cunts've been sayin things, behind ma back n that . . . n huv been gittin stuff . . . stuff through the post . . . dinnae gie thum weapons . . . that's aw ah'm fuckin well sayin . . . dinnae gie thum weapons tae yaze against ays . . .

N she's goat ah hud ah me n she's sayin: — Naebody'll hear a bad word aboot ye fae me, Frank, cause yir nice tae me n ye dinnae hit me, but please dinnae make ays feart like that, Frank, cause he used tae dae that n ah cannae live like that, Frank . . . yir no like him, Frank . . . he wis rubbish . . .

Ah sit up straight n pill her heid intae ma chest. — S'awright, ah goes, bit ah'm thinkin: you dinnae fuckin well ken me at aw, hen. Bit ah kin feel muh heid startin tae nip n muh fuckin hert startin tae beat hard. Ah'm thinkin aboot thum aw: Second Prize wi ehs loose mooth, Lexo, that cunt Renton, n fuckin Scruffy Murphy. Aye, that cunt wis lucky eh didnae fuckin well git it good. Still fuckin well might. Tryin tae fuckin set me up! That's thinkin like a fuckin nonce. He wis fuckin lucky.

N that cunt seems tae ken aboot that Chizzie nonce n aw. Ah'll find oot whair eh kens aw that shit fae n beat it oot ay him. Thinks cause wi go back that'll save um.

Will it fuck save um.

No fuckin wey am ah gaun back inside but, that'll be the fuckin day. But ah huv tae watch ma step here. It's like every cunt kens, n even though ah ken masel it's jist ma fuckin mind playin tricks oan ays, ye jist ken thit thir aw startin tae close in. N ah'm strokin Kate's hair bit ah'm tensin up n ah need tae git the fuck oot ay here cause ah cannae be held responsible for what ah might dae. So ah sits up n tells her thit ah'm gaun oot tae watch the fitba.

— Right . . . she goes, lookin ower at the telly, as if tae say, ye kin watch jist as easy here.

Ah nods tae the screen. — It's better doon the pub wi the boys. Ye need tae git the fuckin atmosphere.

She thinks aboot this for a while, then goes: — Aye, it'll dae ye good, Frank. It's aboot time ye goat oot instead ay jist sittin in that chair.

Ah'm tryin tae think what the fuck she means by that. Mibee it does look fuckin suspicious steyin in aw the time, but ah hud that wee Philip cunt screwin a hoose in Barnton fir ays. Gave the cunt another two sovies back fir ehs trouble. Ah should git oot but. Mind you, she's awfay fuckin keen tae git ays oot. She cannae go oot cause ay the bairn, but she kin huv some cunt up though. — You jist huvin a quiet night, aye?

— Aye.

— No huvin nae cunt roond? That fuckin Rhona?

— Naw.

— No huvin that Melanie hing-oot roond? She's doon Leith aw the time.

— Naw, ah'm jist steyin in n readin ma book, she goes, showin ays this book.

Readin fuckin books. Thir aw shite, jist put ideas in cunts' heids.
— Huvin nae cunt roond at aw?

— Nup.

— Right, see ye then, ah goes, flingin oan muh jaykit n headin oot intae the cauld. Just as well thit nae cunt's comin roond. Cunts like Sick Boy, ye ken the wey his mind works. Sayin tae that fuckin Melanie, ye must huv plenty tidy wee mates whaire fuckin game tae be filmed gittin rode by . . .

FUCKIN . . .

Ah fuckin punch the waw in the stair . . .

Cunt kens what eh'd fuckin well git if eh ivir tried that.

Oan the wey doon tae the boozer uh sees that cunt June gaun along the Walk, n ah makes oot like ah'm croassin the road eftir her. Ah'll gie the cunt restrainin order; cheeky fuckin cunt, ah widnae go within twenty-five fuckin yards ay that sow. Aw ah'm daein is tryin tae fuckin tell her it wis Murphy n Sick Boy's fuckin fault, gittin aw fuckin mixed up, bit the cunt turns n runs doon the road! Ah shouts eftir her tae fuckin stoap, soas ah kin explain, bit the daft cunt's away. Fuck that dozy hoor!

Ah snap oan the fuckin mobby n remind the cunts tae git doon thaire, Nelly n Larry, cause ah ken thit Malky'll be thaire awready, hudin up the fuckin bar. Malky the fuckin alky. Sure enough, the cunt is thaire n Larry n Nelly urnae fuckin far behind. Thing is, it's the fuckin same vibe in here. Every cunt seems tae gie ye the look thit fuckin well goes 'aye, ah ken you, ya cunt'. N this is mates thit wir talkin aboot here, or so-called fuckin mates.

Wir watchin the Hibs match oan Sky. A good fuckin run thir oan now, n they nivir fuckin lose oan Sky. That Zitelli scores wi a barry overheid kick. Three–one, too fuckin easy. Everybody still seems tae be talkin aboot yon beast cunt but. N there's me jist sittin thaire, wishin thit they could talk aboot something else, but at the same time ah'm fuckin lovin it.

— Ah bet ye it wis one ay the young team, they boys drippin wi the sovies, Malky goes. — The bastard probably touched one ay thum up or something like that whin eh wis a wee laddie, eh's filled oot n grown up now, n it's bang! Take that, ya clarty beast cunt!

— Mibee, ah goes, lookin ower at Larry, whae's goat a big, daft smile oan ehs face. Fuck knows what that cunt's sae fuckin happy aboot.

Now the cunt tells everybody a fuckin joke. — This grocer in Fife is in ehs shoap n it's freezin cauld n ehs standin ower the electric-bar fire. A wifie comes in, looks at the counter n goes tae um, is that yir Ayrshire bacon? The grocer looks at her n says, naw, ah'm jist warmin ma hands.

Ah dinnae git that cunt's sense ay humour at aw. Malky's the only cunt thit laughs.

Nelly turns roond n says: — See, if ah met the cunt thit did that fuckin beast, ah'd buy the cunt a fuckin pint right now.

Funny, the wey eh says it makes ays want tae shout: git yir fuckin hand in yir poakit then, ya cunt, cause eh's right fuckin here, bit mates or nae mates, the fewer people thit ken the better. Ah keep thinkin aboot Second Prize. See, if he's gone back on the pish n started blabbin . . . Larry's still smilin away, n ah'm gittin nipped here, so ah goes ben the bog n hus a fuckin line.

Whin ah comes back ah sits masel doon, n some cunt's goat another round ay lager in. Malky points at the full gless. — That's yours thaire, Frank.

Ah nods tae the cunt, n takes a gulp, lookin ower the toap ay the pint at Larry, whae's starin at ays, wi that fuckin daft smirk oan ehs face.

— What the fuck ur you lookin at? ah asks the cunt.

Eh shrugs ehs shoodirs. — Nowt, eh goes.

Fuckin well jist sittin thair lookin at ays like eh kens everything thit's gaun oan in ma fuckin heid. Nelly's picked it up as well as ah hands um the wrap ay ching under the table. — What the fuck's up here? eh asks.

Ah nods ower at Larry. — Cunt's jist fuckin well sittin thair wi a daft fuckin look oan ehs face, starin at me like ah'm some fuckin daft cunt, ah goes.

Larry shakes ehs heid n raises ehs palms up n goes: — What? as Nelly's eyes go aw hard. Malky looks aroond, across at the bar. Sandy Rae n Tommy Faulds are drinkin up thaire, n thir's a couple ay wee cunts oan the pool table.

— So what ur ye fuckin sayin then, Larry, eh? ah asks um.

— Ah'm no sayin nowt, Franco, Larry goes, lookin aw innocent.
— Ah'm jist thinkin aboot that goal, n eh nods tae the screen behind ays as a replay comes oan.

So ah'm thinkin, awright, ah'll lit it go, but sometimes that cunt kin be too fuckin wide fir ehs ain good. — Right, well, dinnae fuckin sit lookin at ays wi that daft fuckin wee smile oan yir face, like some fuckin dippit cunt. If yuv goat anything tae say tae ays, jist fuckin well say it.

Larry shrugs n turns away, as Nelly heads fir the bogs. That's no bad ching, nowt but the best offay Sandy. For me it's nowt but the best anyway. Cunts ken better thin tae sell me gear that's cut tae fuck.

— Your mate Sick Boy's some cunt, eh, Franco? The dirty movies n that, Larry grins.

— Dinnae mention that cunt's name tae me. Cunt's goat a few wee fuckin hairies gittin rode upstairs in ehs pub n the cunt thinks eh's a fuckin big Hollywood producer. Like that fuckin Steven Spielberg cunt or whatever they call the fucker.

Nelly comes back fae the bog n Malky looks at um n goes: — Whaes fuckin shout is it?

But Nelly ignores um cause ye kin tell eh's aw that wey whin yuv been in the bogs thinkin aboot somethin n ye want tae talk tae every cunt aboot it. — Ken what gits oan ma fuckin wick, eh goes, then before any cunt kin say what, eh says: — Every cunt here's done time, n eh takes a big sup ay lager. A bit's dripped oantae ehs blue Ben Sherman, but eh disnae notice. Clarty fuckin cunt.

We're aw lookin at each other n noddin away.

— Ken whae nivir does time? You ken, eh looks at me, — ah ken, eh points at ehsel, — you ken, eh looks at Malky, — n you ken, eh sais tae Larry, whaes face breks intae that fuckin smile again.

N the thing is, ah'm thinkin aboot that big cunt Lexo, the first cunt thit came intae ma mind right away, but Nelly surprises ays by gaun: — Alec Doyle. What's he done? A year? Eighteen months? Fuck all. That cunt leads a charmed life.

Malky looks aw seriously at Nelly. — So what ur ye sayin then? Ur ye tryin tae say that Doyle's a grass?

Nelly's eyes are set aw that hard wey. — Aw ah'm sayin is thit the cunt leads a charmed life.

Larry's face goes aw serious. — Yir no wrong, Nelly, eh says softly.

— Fuckin surein ah'm no wrong, Nelly says, lookin annoyed tae fuck.

Malky turns roond tae me n asks: — What d'ye reckon then, Frank?

Ah look aroond the table at them aw, n right intae thir eyes, Nelly's n aw. — Doyle's eywis been awright in ma fuckin book. Ye dinnae jist call some cunt a grass unless ye kin back it up. N that means wi facts. Wi hard fuckin facts.

Nelly disnae like that, but the cunt's no sayin nowt. Naw, eh's no happy at aw. Yuv goat tae watch that cunt, cause eh kin jist fuckin well kick oaf like that, but ah'm fuckin well watchin um awright.

— Good point, Frank, Larry goes, nodding away aw sly, — but Nelly's goat a point n aw, eh sais, takin the wrap fae Nelly n gaun tae the bogs.

— Ah nivir called any cunt a grass, Nelly sais tae me as Larry heads oaf, — but think aboot what ah sais, eh goes, then turns n nods tae Malky.

Aye, Larry hud better think aboot things n aw. Fuckin stirrin cunt. Thir's eywis somethin gaun oan wi that cunt, n eh'd better make sure ah dinnae fuckin well find oot what it is.

Well, wir aw wired oan the fuckin ching n wi opt fir movin oan.

Wi huv one in the Vine, then a couple in Swanney's. It's still the real Leith doon here, but everything is fuckin well changin. What gits me is what they done tae the Walk Inn. Cannae believe that, ah hud some great nights in thair. We hit another couple ay boozers, then end up back where wi started.

That wee Philip cunt's hingin aboot n aw. Here, in this fuckin pub. Dinnae want that wee cunt n his mates hingin aboot a boozer ah use. — You, fuckin blow, ah tells um.

— Eh, ah'm waitin oan Curtis, eh's comin doon wi the motor, eh goes. Then eh says, aw fuckin hopeful: — Eh, ye couldnae git ays some coke, could ye?

Ah looks at the wee cunt. — Whaire ur you gittin the fuckin dosh fir ching?

— Offay Curtis.

Aye, that fuckin well figures. That fuckin crew ay Sick Boy's, they cunts eywis seem tae be in the dosh. A couple ay people huv said that Renton's been seen aboot again, up the toon n that. See, if Sick Boy's seen um n husnae fuckin telt ays . . .

But this wee Philip cunt's still hingin aboot. Ah nods ower tae Sandy Rae, whae's sittin wi Nelly at the bar. Larry n Malky are pished, playin the bandit. Sandy comes ower. Sorts the wee cunt oot wi a couple ay gram wraps. The big, gangly wee cunt wi the tadger comes in, then they go ootside intae the motor n ah hear it tearin up the road.

Nelly comes ower, n wir lookin across at Larry n Malky. — That Wylie cunt's been windin ays up aw fuckin night, Nelly sais.

— Aye, ah goes.

— Ah'll tell ye, Franco, eh's lucky eh's your fuckin mate, or ah'd've fuckin well panelled the cunt by now. Eh looks across at Larry. — Fuckin wide-erse.

— Dinnae lit that stoap ye, ah tells um.

So Nelly gits up n walks ower n smashes Larry's heid oaf the fruit machine a couple ay times. Then eh turns um roond n fuckin melts the cunt a beauty. Larry goes doon n Nelly stomps um. Malky pits ehs hand oan Nelly's shoodir n goes: — Enough.

Nelly stoaps n Larry's bein helped up by Malky, whae gits um ootside. Eh looks aroond at Nelly n sais something, raises a wasted hand n tries tae point the finger, but Malky's draggin um oot the pub.

— Fuckin wideo, Nelly says, lookin at me.

Ah'm thinkin, me n Nelly's mates, but it's gaunnae be him n me soon, that's for sure. — The cunt wis fuckin askin fir it aw night, ah nods. Malky soon comes back in. — Stuck um in a taxi wi a tenner, telt um tae git tae fuck. Nowt wrong wi um, jist a bit fuckin dazed, eh.

— Wis eh giein oot fuckin lip? Nelly asks. — Cause eh kin huv a square go any time eh wants.

— Aye, watch the cunt but, Nelly, Malky goes, — cause eh's a fuckin blade merchant n eh nivir forgets.

— Ah dinnae fuckin well forget either, Nelly goes, but ye kin see thit eh's fuckin thinkin aboot that. Then the morn whin eh wakes up it'll be 'aw fuck, ah hud too much ching n that n ah ended up daein Larry'. Cause the likes ay that cunt needs ching n a few bevvies tae dae that. That's the difference between me n him.

68

Scam # 18,751

Every time I go up to see Nikki at her place, he's always there, hanging about, sniffing around that Dianne like a lovesick fool. It's bizarre, us seeing two lassies who share the same flat. A bit like the old days. Now the Rent Boy's lying on the couch, waiting on Ms Dianne getting ready, reading a book about pornography and sex workers, whatever they are. He's found the right bird; I can imagine them sitting around intellectually discussing fucking, but never actually doing any. I offered him and his new minge a chance of some action with the real players and he says, 'I love my girl-friend. What do I want any of that shit for?' Excuse me, Mr High and Shitey.

He props that silly ginger head up on his elbow. — Listen, Si, I'm looking to get in touch with Second Prize. Have you seen him around?

I'm quite aghast at this. Second Prize is to be avoided at all costs. — Why in the name of suffering fuck would you want to see him?

Rents sits up, leans forward, then seems to consider, then decides against lying. You can see the wheels moving. — I want tae sort him oot wi the cash. From that time back in London. I've sorted every-body oot now, well, except him and you-know-who.

Renton is an idiot. Any grudging respect I once had for the man is diminishing rapidly. Me, ripped off by a mug like that? No, he was simply a desperate, foolish junky who lucked out once. — You're fuckin mad. It's a waste of cash. Just write a cheque made payable to Tennent Caledonian breweries.

Rents stands up, as Dianne and Nikki come through. — I've heard he's clean. They say he's a Bible-basher.

— I can't see it. Try the mission or the lodging houses. Or the churches. They aw gather up at Scrubber's Close, aw they religious jakeys, dae they no?

I have to admit that Dianne looks sexy, though obviously not in Nikki's league. (Well, she's going out with Renton.) — Looking gorgeous, ladies, I smile. — We must have been good little boys in a previous life to deserve them, eh, mate? I smirk at Rents.

Renton responds with a slightly pained look and goes over to Dianne and kisses her. — Right then . . . ye fit?

— Aye, she says, and as they leave, I shout: — As a butcher's knife. Use the evidence of your eyes, Renton!

I get no response. That Dianne chick does not like me at all and she's turning Rents against me. I look at Nikki. — That pair seem a real item, I observe, struggling to keep the grace in my voice.

— Oh God, she goes all dramatically, — they are just so in L-O-V-E?

I feel like telling her, watch your friend around that slimy, cold-skinned North European rattlesnake. But it seems a spiritless ploy, one must strive to be graceful in Gracemount. Nikki's been so full of herself since the Cannes news, sweeping around theatrically, like she's an old-style Hollywood star. It's been noticed. Terry's started to refer to her as Nikki Fuller-Shit.

So besotted by herself is she that she elects to change again, putting on a blue and black number I haven't seen before. It's not quite as fetching as what she just changed out of but I feign massive enthusiasm, just to prevent us being here all fucking night. She's wittering on about Cannes. — God knows who we'll meet! Me! So I nip into that Dianne's room and have a sniff around. I see this report thing she's been working on and I read a bit.

with increasing consumerism the sex industry, like all others, is now catering for specialist market needs. While it is true that there is still a link between poverty, drug abuse and on-street prostitution, this represents a very small part of what is now one of the biggest and most diverse industries in the UK. Nonetheless, our popular images of sex workers are still largely formed by the 'street-corner tart' stereotype.

What the fuck are they teaching them at the uni now? Degrees in the theory of hooring? I should get up there myself and claim my honorary doctorate.

We go out for a drink at the City Café, and I spy Terry, trying to chat up a student barmaid. It seems that he's adopted the place as his haunt. I go to signal Nikki that we should get out and over to EH1, but she hasn't noticed and now Lawson's caught our eye.

— Sicky n Nikki! he shouts, then turns to the barmaid. — Bev, whatever ma two good auld buddies want, he smiles then grabs Nikki's arse. — Solid as a fuckin rock, doll, you've been workin oot. No even a trace ay overhang.

— Actually, I've been rather lazy lately, she says, in that dozy stoner way. What's she fucking doing letting him paw her like that? Next she'll be letting him thrust his knob up her twat as he says: 'Mmm, firm vaginal walls. Been doing pelvic exercises?' I'm looking at Terry as if to say: this is my fucking bird, Lawson, you onanistic cunt.

He doesn't even see me. — Well, it disnae show on the boady, ah'll tell ye that. Ah jist want tae git doon oan ma hands n knees n worship at that arse ay yours. So if this lucky cunt here, he deigns to give me a cursory nod, — gies ye grief, ye ken whae tae call.

Nikki smiles, squeezes Terry's love handles and says: — Knowing you, Terry, you'd want to do a lot more? Than just worship?

— Too right. And on that subject, what aboot a stag night? Ah wis at the hoaspital and ah goat the complete discharge.

— In your keks? I ask. — Must have been ward 45, the clap clinic.

— So ah'm ready, willing and able, he says, ignoring me again.

— Well, Terry, we've got a wee problem. I explain about the *News* and how I want to keep a low profile until the movie comes out.

— Huv tae be ma flat then, ah suppose. Still, lit's drink tae Cannes. That'll be a cracker! Pleased for yis, he smiles in a way that chills me. Then he puts an arm on my shoulder. — Sorry ah took the strop earlier, mate. Jist a bit jealous. Still, ye cannae grudge an old buddy success.

— Couldnae have done it withoot you, Tel, I say, quite gob-smacked by his magnanimity. — Good of you to be so Graceful in Gracemount about the whole deal. It's purely down to money, mate.

423

It costs a fortune to take somebody to Cannes, even for a few days. I'll see you right when the cash comes in but.

— Nae bother. Ah've goat one or two wee things ah need tae dae roond yon time anywey. Rab's no bothered either. Talked tae um the other day. Too busy wi the bairn n ehs college n that, eh.

— How is Roberto? I ask.

— Seems fine. Couldnae be daein wi a life ay borin domesticity masel but, he waxes. — Tried it once. Nah, it wisnae fir me.

— Me neither, I concede, — I'm temperamentally unsuited for the long haul. Responsibility I can handle, in fact I thrive on it in sustained bursts, but no for the long haul.

— He's conned us all from time to time, Nikki rumbles contentedly, the drink going to her head, along with the fucking dope she's smoked all day long. A stoner, and she wonders how she never made it as a gymnast! — And we love him for it still.

— Well, sometimes, Terry says.

— Yes. Why is he like that? Why is he so manipulative? I think it's growing up in a household full of doting women. Yes, it's the Italian thing. He can bring out a dormant maternal instinct in women, she says loudly.

Nikki is starting to grate. There's no two ways about it. I don't know, this tendency to psychoanalyse wears thin after a while. My ex-wife did all that, and for a time, I used to like it. It made me feel as if she cared. Then I realised that it was just something she did to everybody, a habit. After all, she was a Hampstead Jewess whose family worked in the media, so what could you expect? So eventually it vexed me.

And now Nikki rankles too. Now I'm starting to find reasons not to be with her. I know the danger signs; when I start to look at uglier, less poised, less graceful, less intelligent birds, but with a massive horn. I'm realising that it's only a matter of time before I jettison Nikki for somebody I'll hate in five minutes. And she's not as good a fuck as she thinks, with all that gymnastics shit. She's a lazy cow, for one thing. Always fast asleep, lying in all day, a typical fucking student, while I'm up with the lark. Never was one for sleeping: two or three hours a night does me fine. I'm sick of waking up in the night with a hard-on and having to poke a warm sack of spuds.

But she looks so beautiful; why is it that I'd rather do almost anything right now than take her home and fuck her? It's only been a few months. Have I had my fill of her already? Is my threshold really that low? Surely not. If that's the case I'm fucking well doomed.

We go back to hers and she has me looking at some pictures in one of those near wankboy men's mags, the ones that have become indistinguishable from the top shelvers. This other ex-gymnast chick, that Carolyn Pavitt, she's on the cover. The one that Nikki knew, the one that she's obsessed with.

— She's ugly, I dismissively remark. — It's just cause she was in the Olympics and she's on the telly that a lot of guys want to ride her. A trophy fuck, that's all.

— You'd fuck her though. If she walked through that door now? You'd ignore me and be all over her, she says, with real bile in her voice.

I can't handle this bullshit. She's fucking jealous, accusing me of having designs on somebody I can't remember consciously seeing a fucking image of until she stuck it in my face a few seconds ago. I get up and make to leave. — Get control, I muse as I depart. She slams the door shut behind me and I can hear a quite impressive string of curses from the other side of it.

69

POLIS

That Donnelly cunt's goat a chib n eh's tearin intae me wi it n ah cannae lift muh hands up tae hit um, it's like thir weighed doon, like somebody's hudin thum or thir made ay fuckin lead, n now that beast cunt, that Chizzie's comin fir me n ah try n kick oot n eh's gaun: — Ah love ye, chavvy . . . thanks, chavvy . . .

N ah'm gaun: — GIT AWAY FAE ME, YA FUCKIN BEAST CUNT, AH'LL FUCKIN KILL YE . . . bit ah still cannae move muh fuckin airms n this cunt's comin . . . n thir's a bangin . . .

Ah'm awake in bed n her heid's oan ma airm n it's jist a fuckin dream, bit that fuckin bangin's still gaun oan, n aye, it's a knockin oan the door, n she's wakin up n ah goes: — Goan git that . . .

N she gits up, aw sleepy likes, bit whin she comes back she's aw fuckin alert n worried n she goes in a fuckin whisper: — Frank, it's the polis, fir you.

THE FUCKIN POLIS . . .

Some cunt's fuckin blabbed aboot the beast . . . Murphy . . . mibee that cunt died in the hoaspital or that fuckin Alison grassed ays up . . . Second fuckin Prize . . . they auld cunts . . .

— Right . . . ah'm jist gittin ready, you stall the cunts, ah tell ur, n she goes back oot.

Ah pills oan ma clathes as quick as ah kin. Aye, that cunt Second Prize's gabbed aboot the beast! Thou shalt not fuckin kill or some shite . . . or Murphy . . . he seemed tae fuckin ken the loat . . .

CUNT . . . CUNT . . . CUNT . . . CUNT . . .

Ah looks at the droap fae the windae, ah could git doon that drainpipe intae the back n through another stair. Bit thir might be mair ay thum in the van ootside . . . naw, if ah dae a runner ah'll be fucked . . . could still brass it oot . . . git Donaldson the fuckin lawyer . . . whaire's that fuckin mobby? . . .

Ah reaches intae muh jaykit poakit . . . the mobby's deid, ah nivir fuckin charged the cunt up . . . fuck . . .

Thir's a tap oan the door. — Mr Begbie?

It's the fuckin polis awright. — Aye, hud oan the now.

If they cunts say anything, ah'm sayin nowt, ah'm right oan the fuckin phone tae Donaldson. Ah take a deep breath and walk oot. Thir's two coppers: a guy wi ears thit stick oot under the hat, n a lassie. — Mr Begbie, the lassie goes.

— Aye.

— We're here about an incident in Lorne Street earlier this week.

Ah'm thinkin: Chizzie wisnae near Lorne Street . . .

— Your ex-wife, Ms June Taylor, made a complaint against you. You are aware that there is an interim restraining order which has been served on you until this can be dealt with in court, the polisman burd goes, aw fuckin snooty.

— Eh . . . aye . . .

Ah look at this bit ay paper she hands ays. — This is a copy of the conditions of that order. You should have been issued with one. To remind you of its contents, this polis burd now sort ay sings, — you are expressly forbidden to make any contact with Ms Taylor.

The other cop butts in. — Ms Taylor claims that you approached her in Leith Walk, shouted at her and pursued her down Lorne Street.

THANK FUCK!

It wis jist that cunt June! Ah'm fuckin that relieved here, ah jist starts laughin, n thir lookin at ays like ah'm a fuckin dipstick, then ah says: — Aye . . . sorry, officer. Ah jist ran intae her in the street n ah wanted tae apologise fir the wey ah behaved tae hur, tell hur it wis aw a misunderstandin, eh. Ah goat the wrong end ay the stick, that's how ah acted over the top. Mind you, ah sais, liftin up muh shirt n showin the wound, — she chibbed me wi a knife, n she's goat the fuckin cheek tae complain.

Kate's noddin away n she goes: — That's right! She stabbed Frank. Look at that!

— Ah nivir complained but, ah shrugs, — for the sake ay the bairns, ken.

The lassie polisman goes: — Well, if you wish to complain about your wife, you can. In the meantime, you have to comply with those terms and keep away from her.

— Dinnae worry aboot that, ah jist laughs.

The other cop wi the stickin-oot ears tries tae be aw fuckin hard, like eh's tryin tae impress the fuckin lassie polisman. — This is serious, Mr Begbie. You could be in a lot of trouble if you harass your ex-wife. Do I make myself clear?

Ah'm thinkin thit ah should jist look this fuckin dippit streak ay pish in the eye, watch thum water n him look away as ah ken eh would, but ah dinnae want thum taggin ays as a fuckin wide cunt n pittin heat oan, so ah jist smiles n goes: — Ah'll keep well away fae her, dinnae you worry aboot that, officer. Wish yis hud been here tae tell ays that ten years ago, wid've saved a loat ay soapy bubble!

They jist keep lookin aw serious at ays. Ah mean, ye try n huv a fuckin sense ay humour, but some miserable cunts jist dinnae well fuckin git it. Ah'll stey away fae that June awright, bit thir's some cunts ah'll no be keepin away fae.

70

Driving

Ali's been great man, it hus tae be said, up every day. Wi telt the wee boy that ah wis in a car crash n 'Uncle Frank' saved ays. She went roond n spoke tae Joe, Franco's brar, n telt um thir wis nae prospect ay anybody daein any grassin up aboot anything. Should go withoot sayin, but Franco's that para. Ah telt Ali tae take the money n stick it in her bank account. It's for her n the bairn, she kin spend it how she wants tae.

Ah've goat a broken jaw, it's aw wired up n ah pure cannae eat any solids, three cracked ribs, a broken nose n a fracture ay the femur. Ah've also goat severe bruisin n eighteen stitches in the heid. It *is* like ah've been in a car crash.

Ah'm gittin oot soon, n Ali's talkin aboot comin back. But ah'm pure no wantin her n Andy roond ays wi Begbie oan the warpath. Ah've goat tae sort things oot wi him first. It's a mess, a total mess, but the weird thing is, it did teach ays something, man. Ah feel mair focused now. Ah telt Ali in ma soft, daft voice: — Ah want ye back mair thin anythin, but you're right. Ah've goat tae sort masel oot, start tae learn tae cope, soas thit ah dae things aroond the hoose n cook n aw that sortay stuff whin yis come back. Ah'd like tae be able tae come roond n see the wee man n you first, likesay take ye oot oan a hot date n that.

She laughed, n kissed ma battered face. — That'd be great. Ye cannae go hame oan yir ain though, Danny, no like that.

— It's aw sortay superficial but. Eywis thoat Franco wis a bit ay a pussycat really, ah mumble through the wired Denis Law.

Ali hus tae go n git the wee man, bit whin ah git discharged muh ma, n oor Shauna n Liz ur here n they git ays hame. They make up a fire n some grub, then they git ready tae leave ays, aw sortay reluctant likesay. — This is silly, Danny, Liz says, — come n stay at oors.

— Aye, come hame wi me, son, muh ma says.

— Naw, ah'm sound, ah tell thum, — nae worries.

They head away, n as it happens it wis a pure good call, cause later oan that night, thir's a rap at the door. Nae wey ah'm ah gaunnae answer it. — You fuckin well in thaire, Murphy? the cat shouts, openin the letter boax. Even though ah'm sittin wi the lights oaf, ah kin pure feel they eyes ay evil scannin doon the passagewey. — Better fuckin no be, cause see if you are n ye urnae answerin the fuckin door . . .

Ah'm shitin it, but ah'm thinkin, that's Franco aw ower. What would happen if ah *did* open the door? Eh disnae stick around but.

Ah sleep up the chair, cause ah goat comfy, but eftir a while ah stagger through tae ma bed n ah dinnae wake up till the next mornin whin the door goes again. Ah think it's him, back again, but it isnae. — Spud . . . ur ye thair?

It's Curtis. Ah open the door, half expecting tae see Begbie standin wi a knife at the perr wee gadge's throat. — Eh, awright, Curtis man, ah'm eh, pure lyin low the now.

— It's that B-B-Begbie, eh? Ah ken cause Ph-Philip sortay hings aboot wi um.

— Naw, man, it wis some bad dudes that ah owed dosh tae. Franco wis the yin thit sorted it oot fir me, likes, ah tell um, n eh kens thit ah'm a crap liar but eh kens thit ah'm lyin tae protect him, tae keep him oot ay things. — So, ah goes, ah hear yir oaf tae that Cannes Film Festival. No bad.

— Aye, eh goes, aw enthusiastic, mind, it's no the real yin, jist the porn yin . . . eh adds, but good luck tae the boy. Curtis is a good wee cat. Ah mean, the boy wis up regular tae the hoaspital, ken. Eh's been huvin the time ay ehs life wi that knob ay his, but eh disnae forget ehs buddies n that says a loat tae me, likes. Too many people jist forget whair they come fae, like Sick Boy. Aye, eh thinks eh's a big success now, but ah'd better no say nowt aboot that, cause Curtis likes Sick Boy. Some life eh's goat now though; shaggin good-lookin lassies, n gittin peyed fir it. No a bad deal, whin ye think aboot it. Ah mean, thir's worse weys tae earn a livin, it's goat tae be said. Then eh goes: — Come oot, ah've goat a motor. C'moan for a drive. It's no choried or nowt.

430

So wir drivin doon the A1 tae Haddington n this auld car, n ah'm tellin um tae go faster, n eh does, n ah'm thinkin thit ah could jist clip oaf the seat belt n slam ma fit oan they brakes n fly through that windscreen. But wi ma luck, ah'd jist be paralysed for life or something. It widnae be fair tae Curtis, and ah pure want tae sort masel oot cause ah've goat Ali n Andy, or at least a chance ay gittin back wi thum. Dostoevsky. Insurance scams. What a load ay nonsense, likes.

Wi goes oot tae this wee country pub, only really a few miles fae Leith, but a different world aw thegither. Couldnae hack it oot here but, man. Sometimes ah think: the three ay us in a wee cottage, how peachy would that be, but then ah realise thit ah'd be bored, no wi Andy n Ali, but the lack ay general stimulus, likesay.

Ah borrow Curtis's mobile phone n ah bell Rents, arrangin tae meet um the night up in a pub in the Grassmarket. Ah cannae see Begbie in the Grassmarket, n wi both pure dinnae want tae see Begbie, ken.

71

Whores of Amsterdam Pt 10

Spud looks in a bad way. His jaw's swollen like a second head's trying tae grow out of his face and he's exhausted climbing the stairs tae Gav's. He still won't talk about who done him, just vague mutterings through a broken jaw about radges he owed money to. Sarah looks particularly shocked at the extent ay the poor cunt's injuries. If it *was* Begbie then he's no mellowed, not one bit. Gav and Sarah come out with us for a drink, then head away to the cinema.

— Everybody vanishes when ah show up, he says in a small muffled voice, — must be ma personality. Still, it's good that we're in touch again, eh, Mark, he chunters, all eager and hopeful.

I hate to burst what little bubble he has, but I lift my pint, put it down and take a deep breath. — Listen, Spud, ah'm no gaunnae be sticking aroond here much longer.

— Cause ay Begbie? he asks, life suddenly fusing into his tired eyes.

— Partly, I concede, — but no just him. I want to move away, with Dianne. She's been in Edinburgh all her life and she fancies a change.

Spud looks sadly at me. — Right then . . . ah'll need ye tae bring Zappa back tae me before ye go. Will ye dae that for ays, Mark? It's hard tae manage the cat-carrier wi they ribs aw bandaged n jist the one airm, he nods wretchedly at his sling.

— Aye, nae bother, I tell him. — But thir's somethin you kin dae fir me n aw.

— Aye? Spud says in a manner that indicates he's not used to being thought of as able to do something for anybody.

— Tell me where I can find Second Prize?

He looks at me as if I'm a fuckin radge, which I suppose I am, the shite I've let myself get mixed up in already. Then he smiles and says: — Okay.

We have a few mair scoops and I drop Spud off back at his, without getting oot the taxi. Then I head back up tae Dianne's and we go to bed. We make love and lie in the next day, doing more of the same. After a while I become aware that she's a bit tense and distracted. Eventually she says: — I have to get up and go over this dissertation. Just one more time.

I reluctantly go out and head over to Gav's to give her peace. By fuck, it's a pissing wet and cold day. Summer is round the corner my arse; conditions are still fucking alpine. My mobile vibrates inside my coat pocket. It's Sick Boy, and he's oozing suspicion when I tell him that I'm not coming out to Cannes straight away. I inform him that Miz'll be there anyway, and I need to go to the Dam first and sort out a few things at the club.

When I get to Gav's he tells me that *he* ran into Sick Boy and Nikki in town and invited them up for a meal, with me and Dianne. My face falls at the prospect and I doubt whether Dianne'll be chuffed. But when I catch up with her she's okay about it, probably because Nikki's her mate.

When we meet up Sick Boy's on his best behaviour, or as close as he gets to it. He's flirting with Sarah in such an obvious way, but Nikki doesn't seem to mind, she's just making a fuss ay Gav, who looks bemused, like he's being set up for a foursome, which, with these two, is probably the case.

After a bit, Sick Boy collars me in the kitchen. — I need you in Cannes! he wails. He's always on about trying to save money on the trip; the doss cunt can start with me. — Ah cannae just up and leave. All my stuff's in Holland and I'm taking it, I don't want Katrin getting her hands on it, which she will if ah'm no lively.

He tuts and hisses better than Deirdre in *Coronation Street*. — So when will you be out then?

— I'll be in the South of France by Thursday.

— You'd better, I've booked the fuckin room, he snaps, then his eyes go wide in appeal as he swirls his brandy around in the glass. — C'mon, Mark, this our moment, mate. All our life we've been waiting for this. Leith boys in Cannes, for fuck sake! We're quoted. What a fucking experience it'll be!

— That's why I wouldnae fuckin miss it for the world, I tell him,

433

— I've just got to sort things out with Katrin. She's pretty volatile . . . I don't want my stuff trashed. And I can't just leave Martin in the lurch like that. 'Sorry, mate, I know we've been running a club for seven years through thick and thin but now my old buddy Simon's back on the scene and he wants me to produce porn flicks with him.'

He raises his hands and lowers his head, as Sarah comes through with some dirty dishes. — Awright, awright . . .

Seizing the high ground, I add: — I've had a fucking life the last nine years, I cannae jist click it oaf like a fuckin light switch because you deem me *persona grata* again, as I watch Sarah trot out like she's walking on broken glass.

He says something back and we bitch and bicker to an impasse before catching some mischief in each other's eyes and bursting out laughing. — We cannae do this any mair, Simon, I tell him. It was awright as young boys, but now we're starting tae sound like a pair ay auld queens. Can you imagine us ten years on?

— I'd rather not, he says, looking genuinely ulcerated at the prospect. — The only thing that can redeem us is having a) lots of money, and b) young chicks in tow. In your twenties you can do it on looks, your thirties on personality, but in your forties you need cash or fame. Simple fucking mathematics. Everybody thinks I'm aspirational, but I'm not. It's a maintenance thing with me, a kind of crisis management.

It disturbs me, him opening up like this, because under the nihilistic bravado I can tell that the cunt's being absolutely honest. Can I take this scam away from him? It seems so harsh. But what would *he* have taken away from me, if Begbie had found me? Nah, Sick Boy's a cunt. It's no that he's such a bad bastard, he's just ultra fuckin selfish. When you swim with sharks you only survive by being the biggest one.

But he's strangely appreciative of my motivations, saying I was right to leave Britain. — It's clapped-out, and if you don't have wealth or money you're a third-class citizen. America's the place, he argues, — I should get over there, start my own Church and take the piss out of those naive, gullible Yanks.

Nikki comes through and says to me, eyebrows arched: — Simon

434

and kitchens? A bad combination? She regards him. — . . . You *are* behaving?

— In an exemplary manner, he says. — But c'mon, Rents, let's join the body of the kirk. We don't want to leave Temps with all the chicks.

We're back round the table and Sick Boy, Gav and I have an old-style argument about the lyrics to Roger Daltrey's 'Giving It All Away'.

— It's 'I'd know better now, giving it all away', Sick Boy opines.

— Naw, Gav shakes his head, — it's 'I know better now'.

Ah gie the cunts a dismissive wave. — Your different positions are just minor pedantic squabbles which don't change the essential meanin ay the song. If ye listen, really listen, you'll find it's '*I'm no* better now', as in *not* any better now. I'm just the same. I haven't learned anything.

— Bullshit, Sick Boy snorts, — the song's about looking back with the benefit of hindsight and maturity.

— Aye, Gav agrees, — sort ay 'if I knew then what I know now' kind ay thing.

— No. That's where you're both wrong, I argue. — Listen to Daltrey's vocal, it's a lament, there's something defeated in it; the tale ay a gadge who's finally acknowledged ehs limitations. 'I'm no better now', cause I'm the same fucked-up cunt I always was.

Sick Boy seems suddenly hostile at this, enraged like it's something important. — You dinnae ken what you're fuckin talkin aboot, Renton, he turns to Gav. — Tell him, Gav, tell him!

Our Mr Williamson seems to be taking this a little personally. The argument continues until Dianne interrupts. — How can youse get so worked up over such trivial shite? She shakes her head and turns to Nikki and Sarah. — I'd love to be able to spend just one day in their heads, just to feel what it was like to have all that crap swimming round in there, and one of her hands brushes my brow as the other falls onto my thigh.

— One hour would suit me fine, Sarah maintains.

— Aye, Sick Boy ventures, now seeing the lunacy of it all and smiling at me. — In the old days we had Begbie tae say, 'It's a load ay fuckin shite n it's gittin oan ma tits so shut the fuck up or yi'll git yir fuckin mooths burst.'

— Aye, sometimes too much democracy can be a killer, Gav laughs.

— This Begbie seems a real character? I'd like to meet him, Nikki declares.

Sick Boy shakes his head. — No, you wouldn't. I mean, he doesn't really like girls, he sniggers, and Gav and I find ourselves joining in.

— Nor boys for that matter, I add, and we're pishing ourselves now.

After a bit Nikki starts on about Cannes, which Dianne has told me is a fairly staple thing with her right now, and Sarah and Gav are getting spiky with each other. Dianne and I take this as our cue to get away, her saying something about needing to print out another copy of her thesis. Unfortunately, Nikki and Sick Boy elect to join us in the cab.

— That Sarah's fuckin tidy, Sick Boy states.

— Gosh, isn't she? Nikki rasps, her face flushed and sweaty with drink.

— I suggested a foursome but she wasn't into it, Sick Boy confirms my suspicions. — I think Temps was a bit put out as well, he adds. Then he turns to Dianne. — I haven't asked you, Di, not because I don't fancy you, but you come in a package and the thought of Rents in the buff . . .

I'd actually confessed to her that the cunt *had* already sounded me out about it. She looks witheringly at him and starts talking to Nikki who seems pretty drunk. We get up the stairs and go to our separate rooms, and I can hear Nikki and Sicky, as Terry calls him, having a drunken argument.

I start reading the latest draft of Dianne's thesis as she goes to the bathroom. I can't understand a lot of it, which I take to be a good sign, but it looks, well, academic enough; research evidence, references, footnotes, extensive bibiliographies, etc., and it reads quite well. — It seems excellent, I tell her as she comes in, — I mean, as much as I know about these things. But it reads well in lay person's terms.

— It's a pass, but probably not a great one, she says without any hint of despondency.

We start talking about what she's going to do now that it's finished and she kisses me and says: — You mentioned lay persons, and she unzips me and pulls out my stiffening cock. Holding it firmly, she rubs her tongue over her lips. — I'm going to do this, she tells me. — Loads and loads and loads more of this.

I'm thinking: we can't possibly do any more than we already are.

We sleep through and it's the cusp of the following afternoon before we wake up. I bring two mugs of tea back to bed and decide it's time to tell Dianne everything, the lot. I do. How much she knew or had figured out I'm not sure, but she doesn't seem too surprised, then again she never does. I'm getting dressed, pulling on a fleece and jeans as she sits up in bed. — So you're going to find an alcoholic friend you haven't seen in nearly ten years and give him three thousand pounds in cash?

— Aye.

— Are you sure that you've thought this through? she enquires through a yawn as she stretches. — It's not often that I agree with Sick Boy, but you might be doing the guy more harm than good giving him that sort of money all at once.

— It's his dosh. If he chooses to drink himself to death, then so be it, I tell her, but I know I'm only thinking of me, of *my* need to set the record straight.

The cold seems to settle into the fabric of the city. It's like a disease the old place just can't quite shake off, the weather forever threatening to recede back into full-blown winter in face of the cruel, icy winds from the North Sea. The Mile's looking spooky, even though darkness has barely begun to fall. I trudge along the cobblestones and find the Close. I move down the tight, narrow lane, which opens up into a small dark courtyard, surrounded by towering old tenements. A tiny vennel slopes down towards the New Town.

The courtyard is crowded with people; they're all listening to a bearded old gadge with wild, traumatised eyes, preaching from the Bible. There's a lot of jakeys here, but also plenty AA and NA rehab cases, where the need for drug ingestion is replaced by the fervoured fix of evangelical outpourings. After scanning the crowd for a bit I see him, looking thinner, clean-shaven, but like a man in recovery from something, because that's it, the frozen state of being *in recovery*, that status the temperance movement sets in stone. It's Rab McNaughton, Second Prize, and I have to give him three thousand pounds in cash.

I approach him warily. Second Prize was close to Tommy, an old pal of ours who died of Aids. He blamed me for getting Tommy on junk and even physically had a go once. The man always was endowed with quite an unequivocal nature. — Sec . . . Robert, I quickly correct myself.

He looks at me for a bit, registers me in brief contempt, then turns back to the preacher, his eyes burning, devouring every word the man says, as he mouths the appropriate 'amens'.

— How's things? I prompt.

— What dae you want? he asks, again momentarily engaging with me.

— I've got something for you, I tell him. — The money I'm owe ye . . . I put my hand into my coat pocket and feel the wad, thinking that this *is* absolutely fuckin ridiculous.

Second Prize turns to face me. — Ye ken what ye kin dae wi it. You're evil; you, Begbie, that pornographer Simon Williamson, Murphy the junky . . . you're all evil. You're killers and yis dae the work of the devil. The devil lives doon in that port of Leith, and youse are ehs workers. It's an evil place . . . he says, his eyes rolling tae the sky.

A baffled sensation between mirth and anger wells up in me and I have to fight the temptation to tell him that he's talking a load ay shite. — Look, ah want tae gie ye this, just take it and I'll see ye in the next life, I tell him, crushing the bundle of notes into his jacket pocket. A stout woman with curly hair and a thick Belfast accent comes up and says: — What's wrang? What's wrang, Raburt?

Second Prize pulls the wad from his pocket and brandishes it in front of my face. — This! This is what's wrong! Ye think ye can buy me off wi this rubbish? That ye can buy my silence, you n Begbie? Thou shall not kill! he says, eyes burning, then he screams in my face, shredding my nerves as he splatters it with slaver: — THOU SHALL NOT KILL!

He throws the money into the air and the notes swirl in the wind. The crowd suddenly realise what's happening. One dirt-encrusted man in a filthy overcoat grabs a fifty-pound note and holds it up to the light. A crustie dives onto the cobblestones and soon eveybody's in a greed frenzy, ignoring the old preacher, who, seeing the cash fluttering in the air forgets his sermon and is rummaging around with the rest of them. I back away and grab a couple ay fistfuls ay notes and stick them in ma pockets. I reason that ah gave them tae him tae do what he wanted tae do but if he opted for a pooroot, then ah wis gaunnae be right in. I head up the alley and out the Close mouth, into the Mile, reflecting that I've probably just wiped out half the jakey population of the city and smashed up the wagon of every rehab case.

I go back tae Dianne's and ah see Sick Boy's still there, all wet and wearing a towel wrapped around him. — Cannes tomorrow, he smiles.

— I can't wait to catch you up, I tell him. — It's a fuckin bummer about the Dam, but I have to do it. When's your flight?

He tells me it's at eleven o'clock, so the next day I arrange to share a cab with him and Nikki to the airport. Over breakfast he snorts cocaine, and takes another hit in the back of the cab, jabbering away about Franck Sauzee. — The man's a fucking god, Renton, an absolute fuckin god. I saw him coming out of Valvona and Crolla the other day with an expensive bottle of wine and I thought, this is what we've fuckin lacked at Easter Road for years, that sort of class, he rants, his eyes doolally and his jaw grinding. Nikki's so stoned and full of Cannes fever, she hardly seems to notice the state he's in. I see them off, telling them I'm on the twelve thirty to Amsterdam. But I'm actually going to Frankfurt, to get a connecting flight to Zurich.

Switzerland is a fucking boring place. I lost all respect for Bowie when I heard he lived there. But the banks are excellent. They really do ask no questions. So when I sign the form to transfer the funds from the Bananazzurri account into one I've set up at the Citibank, nobody bats an eyelid. Well, the rotund, suited, bespectacled bank guy queries: — Do you still want to keep this account open?

— Yes, I tell him, — it's because we need immediate access to the monies as we're going into film production. However, the funds will soon be replenished as we have investors on line for our next feature.

— We have some expertise in film financing. It might be useful to you or your partner Mr Williamson to speak to Gustave, next time you're over, Mr Renton. We can set up a film-production account from this company account, enabling you to write cheques instantly and pay off creditors.

— Hmm . . . that's interesting. It would certainly save us a lot of bother if we could do it all under one roof, so to speak, I say, looking at the clock, not wanting to arouse suspicions but anxious not to be detained. — We need to talk about this, but in the short-term I do have a flight to catch . . .

— Of course . . . forgive me . . . he says, and the transaction is hurried through.

And it was as easy as that. All I can think about is Sick Boy in Cannes as I get back to Edinburgh.

72

'. . . surging waves . . .'

We head by British Airways Business Class to the Cote d'Azur on the direct flight from Glasgow. As we approach Nice airport, there's a clear blue sky and I can see the surging waves of the Med lap against the golden sand. The seat-belt signs for landing are on, but Simon's repaired for the fourth time to the toilet and left it, as they say, flushed with excitement and intrigue. — This is it, Nikki, this is it. You want to see hustling, ducking and diving, wheeling and dealing?

— Not particularly . . . I say, gazing up from *Elle*, watching his nostrils flare. I can see bits of cocaine on the hairs.

— Those cunts won't know what's hit them. They've never met the real deal before, he sniffs, rubbing at his nose. Then he looks at me almost painfully and kisses me softly on the cheek. — You are art, hen, he says before his chameleon eyes swivel and he spots a girl with long, curled locks, who's wearing shades pasted onto her head and dressed in a Prada jacket. — Look at that, he says loudly and points, — all that effort spoiled by a bad Manchester perm. Bet she's in publicity. She should sack her hairdresser . . . no, she should shoot the cunt! he says as his jaw slides out challengingly and a couple of people tut and look away.

I smile benignly, knowing that it's useless to tell him to keep his voice down. Now he's ranting at me, telling me his life story.

— Begbie threw a glass, split a lassie's heid open . . . I used tae shoot cunts wi an air rifle . . . Renton was cruel to animals as a kid, there was something about him . . . you'd have thought he'd've grown up into a serial killer . . . Murphy stole my Coventry City Subbuteo team . . . I found it in his house and he *just happened* to have bought it after mines went missing . . . my parents weren't rich . . . that was a big purchase . . . my mother, a decent, saintly woman, she goes, 'Where's that nice new team we bought you, son?' . . . What can I say? 'It's in the scruff's hoose, Mother. Even as we fucking well speak those players are sliding across the old, battered linoleum in the hoose of a thieving scruff, being crushed underfoot by careless, drunken gyppos who stagger into bedrooms looking for children to abuse . . .' How could I say that to my mother? That hoose of Murphy's, what a fuckin midden . . .

I'm delighted to get off the plane. We pick up our bags and Simon's headed straight to the taxi rank. — Aren't we going to wait for the others coming in on easyJet? I enquire.

— Don't think so somehow . . . he says warily. — Listen, Nikki, the eh, Carlton was full, so I had to get them into the Beverly. It's still central.

— Is it less expensive?

—You could say that, he grins. — Our suite's about four hundred quid a night and their rooms are twenty-eight quid a night each.

I shake my head in mock disgust, hoping he fails to register my artifice.

— But I need a smart gaff for business . . . he protests. — It presents the wrong image to be seen in a rat-hole . . . not that the Beverly is a rat-hole, of course.

— I'll bet it is, I say. — This is very divisive, Simon, we're meant to be a team.

— We're talking Lochend and Wester Hailes here. It'll be luxury to them! I'm thinking of them, Nikki, they'd feel like fish out of water. Could you honestly see Curtis in the Carlton? Mel, with her tattoos? No, I wouldn't embarrass them or myself, he says snootily, head in the air, shades on, as we wheel our luggage trolley to the taxi rank.

— You're such a snob, Simon, I inform him, chortling loudly.

— Nonsense! I come from Leith, how can I be a snob? If anything I'm a socialist. I'm just playing the politics of the business world, that's all, he snaps, then repeats: — Renton better not fuck me about, cause it'll be a total waste of a room . . . just as well I had the foresight to cancel his at the Carlton and get him into the Beverly as well . . . that cunt's up to no good . . .

— Mark's okay. He's going out with Dianne and she's a sweetheart.

— Granted, he's as plausible as fuck when he wants. But you don't know him like I do. Mind, I grew up with Rents. I know him. He's scum. We all are.

— Such low self-esteem, Simon! I'd never have thought it.

He shakes his head like a dog coming out of the sea. — I mean that in a positive sense, he says. — But I know his nature. If that Dianne's your mate, I'd tell her to watch her purse.

We take a taxi to the Carlton, travelling down the packed coast road. — I was going to plump for the Hotel du Cap, Simon explains, — but it's too far from the centre of things and would have meant loads of taxi rides. This is right on La Croisette, he informs me as he berates the languid, Latin taxi driver in impressive French. — *Vite! Je suis très pressé! Est-ce qu'il y a un itinéraire de dégagement?*

Eventually we get there and climb out the taxi. Two porters are straight onto our bags. — Checking in, Monsieur, Mademoiselle?

— *Oui, merci*, I respond, but Simon's standing still outside, looking out to sea, watching the busy crowds milling along La Croisette and then turning back to the great, white gleaming structure of the Edwardian hotel. — Simon, you okay?

He takes off his Ray-Bans and sticks them into the top pocket of his yellow linen jacket. — Just let me have this moment, he sniffs, squeezing my hand and I see that there are tears welling up in his eyes.

We step into the hotel foyer, which exudes a breathtaking opulence, dominated by black and gold pillars. Three shades of marble are evident; grey, orange and white, all of them finished with bountiful gold-leaf mouldings. Those chandeliers of crystal hanging imperiously on huge brass chains, the marble floor, the white walls and arched gateways, they just scream wealth and class.

Up in the room, a thick pile of carpet makes you feel as if you're walking through treacle. The bed is colossal and we have a fifty-channel television. The huge bathroom is packed with all sorts of toiletries and there's a complimentary bottle of Rosé de Provence in an ice bucket, which Simon opens, pouring us a glass each and taking them to the balcony with the sea view. I'm looking out and you can see that people are well impressed by this hotel. They walk along the seafront gaping up at us. Simon, his shades back on, gives some people-watching tourists a tired wave and they start nudging each other and snapping us with their cameras! I just wonder who they think we are!

We relax on the balcony, at the centre of the world, full of contentment, drinking the rosé, the heat combining with the liberation I've had on the plane and last night's wine at Gavin's to make me feel very drowsy.

But we're here. I'm here. I'm an actress, a fucking star, here, in Cannes. — I wonder who else'll be staying here now? Tom Cruise? Leonardo DiCaprio? Brad Pitt? In the very next room to us maybe!

Simon shrugs and snaps open his mobile phone. — Whoever. They'll all have to fit in with our plans, he says idly as he punches in a number. — Mel! You're in . . . excellent. Curtis behaving himself? . . . good . . . amuse yourselves and we'll call for you at seven. After the screening there's a party on and I'll blag some invites . . . don't get too pissed . . . aye, right . . . well, go to the beach or watch some telly . . . I'll see you in your lobby at seven . . . Right, he says, clicking the phone shut. — Such an ingrate, he moans, then impersonates Mel. — Me n Curtis huvnae goat money Si-min, how kin wi shoap wi nae money?

I'm starting to feel very tired. — I'm going to get my head down for an hour, Simon, I tell him, heading through to the room.

— Aye, he says, following me through.

Simon puts on a porn film from a list that comes up on the screen under adult channels. He selects one called *Rear Entry: In Through the Out Door.* — That's wild, I never realised that that Led Zeppelin album was a reference to anal sex before. Confirms my feeling that Page was a bit of a visionary, you know, the Crowley stuff and aw that shite.

— Why are we watching this? . . . I murmur drowsily.

— One, get us horny, two, check out the opposition. Look at that!

A woman is lying on her back getting fucked. As we pull away we see that the guy has her legs pinned over his shoulders. The implication is that he's forcing her back to access her arsehole and he's fucking her up it, but it's impossible to tell at that angle whether it's going in her bum or her cunt. The thing I notice is that the woman has deep bruises on her wrists, some of them yellowing. This isn't so much disturbing as tacky, and makes me lose what vague interest I have in the film and I start to doze. The truth is, I don't really care to watch other people fucking, it bores me. This mattress is comfortable, as is the hotel gown, and I drift off . . .

I wake up slightly chilled, my dressing gown has been opened, the cord undone, and I find Sick Boy crouching over me on the bed, masturbating furiously. I urgently pull the gown to me.

— Fuck . . . you've spoiled it now, he gasps bitterly.

— What . . . you're wanking over me!

— Aye?

I sit up in bed, alarmed. — Why don't I just put on blue lipstick and play dead for you?

— Oh no, he says, — it's not a necrophilia thing, it's far more innocent. I meant it as a tribute! You never heard of *Sleeping Beauty* for fuck sakes?

— You won't make love to me, but you'll sit and wank and watch crappy porn. What kind of a fucking tribute is that, Simon?

— You don't understand . . . he grumbles and snorts, his nose streaming, then snaps, — I need some . . . some fucking perspective.

— What you need is to do less fucking coke, I shout, but half-heartedly because I *really* need to get some sleep.

And as I try to drift off, I hear his voice droning on. — Heyyy . . . you smoke too much dope and talk shit, he says, — but I love you for it. Don't ever change. Pot's a great drug for chicks, pot and E. I'm so glad that you don't do coke. It's a boy's drug, girls can't take it. I know what you're going to say, that's sexist. But no, it's an observation underpinned by an acknowledgement of the differences between men and women which is an acknowledgement of woman's autonomy, which is a feminist stance. So applaud, baby, applaud . . . he says as he leaves the room.

As I hear the door crash, I think to myself: thank fuck for that.

73

Scam # 18,752

I'm weaving through the narrow backstreets, returning to La Croisette, scrutinising everything, burning indelible prints of the layout of the town into my brain. I'm appraising the manto like a highly experienced farmer at Ingliston's Royal Highland Show does with cattle. Hear the clucking of the chicks in the sexual marketplace, a searching glance enough to form a comprehensive assessment and valuation. PRs spitting tersely through paralysed grins into mobile phones, haughty shoppers and hopeful backpackers, they're all subject to a 'casual' voracious gaze.

This producing game is a piece of piss. Why stop at porn, why not make a proper movie? Get some lottery cash and off you go. Everybody's at it. Every top gangster realises that the best criminals are ex-criminals. Capitalise and go legit as soon as it's viable. You don't need the hassle, jail's for the likes of Begbie, who, for all their posturing, are losers and victims. Getting a bit of time in, in your youth, well, six months, fair enough, a wee bit for learning experience. But if you didn't learn after being six months banged up that it wasn't you, then you were truly fucked. Nobody likes jail, but some sorry cunts just dinnae dislike it enough.

Cannes is where I want to be. It represents options. But it isn't just that it's not Leith or Hackney, it isn't the physical place, it's me. I'm not just a desperate hustler now, with nothing to trade. I'm realising that no matter how cool I'd played it in the past, I could never escape giving off that slight predictability, that edge of desperation. And I couldn't because when it came down to it, it was all a front and I had nothing to trade in the marketplace. At long last, through getting a sweaty pile of bodies together and filming the results, I have something to sell, something they value. Something I've made. Simon Williamson has a product, which isn't Sick Boy. This is business, it's nothing personal. I'm touting a Simon David Williamson film.

I go back to the hotel, intending to sunbathe and try to relax for a bit, maybe chat up some chicks. We don't have loads of time and this comedian in the hotel's pissed me off, four hundred bar a night and you still need to pay fifteen quid a day to use the private beach at the front, just like the fucking non-resident plebs who should in any case be kept off.

In the room Nikki's up but since we're pushed for time we settle for a bit of scran in the hotel. She's okay after catching me jerking off over her. I've just about managed to convince her that it was a tribute. Chicks: what else could it be? Anyway, satisfyingly full, we make our way to the scabbo hotel to pick up Mel and Curt for the screening of *Seven Rides for Seven Brothers*.

The cinema it's showing in is a small but smart pad on one of the backstreets. It's rumoured that Lars Lavish, Ben Dover, Linsey Drew and Nina Hartley (Nikki's heroine) will attend the screening, but I can't see anybody I recognise. There's a good turnout, mind you, and there's a few bodies that sneak in after the lights go down. I'm trying to scan the audience, to gauge the reaction of this half-full cinema.

I'm so hyped up I don't need any charlie but I take a hit off my card anyway. So do Mel and Curtis. I can't resist going — Phoar, when Melanie appears naked on screen for the first time. She gives me a playful dig in the ribs. It's Nikki who makes the impact though. From the moment she peels off that tight lycra top and exposes that shaved pussy and struts arrogantly across the screen, you can feel the electricity in the air. There are one or two big cheers from the crowd and I turn to catch her looking bashful and I squeeze her hand. The real smash hit, though, is Curtis, or I should say, Curtis's cock. The first sight of that pole produces a few 'wows' and I turn to see our boy's huge teeth glisten in the dark.

Outside, after the show, we're all getting our flesh pressed and cards are being produced as we're urged to go to various parties. I know the one I want though, and it's not a porno gig, it's the industry do in the big marquee on the Croisette. All the porn players want to be at that one, but I manage to blag four invites and we're in.

After a few drinks, Nikki's pished and she starts to get on my

447

tits. — Why are you talking in that ridiculous voice, Simon? she cuts in when I'm chatting to this fucking doll with long, straight, blonde hair, who's apparently something big at Fox Searchlight. — He accuses me of being mockney, then as soon as he gets off the plane he's full of that shit.

The Foxy girl raises an eyebrow and I set my face in a wheel-clamp smile. — What accent, Nicola? This is the way I talk, I say slowly.

Nikki nudges Mel and says: — Thish ish the way I talk, Nicola. The namesh Williamshon. Shimon Dafid Williamshon.

— Or Shick Boy! Mel guffaws and those fucking twisted, inappropriate jealous vixens cackle like the fucking witches in *Macbeth*, as some creepy cunt comes over and grabs Fox Searchlight's arm, leading her away.

I'm seething at their stupid pettiness. — There may be something to be gained from trying to undermine me in my efforts to network and sell this fucking film we've spent the best part of the last six fucking months of our lives making, I heave the words out in terse rage through clenched teeth, — but I'm absolutely fucked if I can see what it is.

They look at each other, silent for a split second. Then Melanie goes: — Ohhh . . . and they're off in hysterics again. Fuck this, I'm retreating into the crowd, and my searchlight's trained, looking for that Fox I've been hunting.

I hit the bog and I'm about to do some charlie when I see some guys going into a cubicle and I bundle in with them, getting a couple of lines off them. I re-emerge supercharged and I look over and see Nikki and Mel flirting outrageously with some creepy-looking arseholes. Curtis seems to have vanished. I head across to the girls. One guy who's been schmoozing with Nikki sees me approach and asks haughtily: — And you are?

I lean close into him. — I am the cunt who's gaunnae brek your fuckin nose for chatting up my bird, I say, putting an arm around Nikki. The wanker blusters a bit on the spot, then timidly exits. Unfortunately, so do Nikki and Mel, making the pretence of getting more drinks, but both singularly unimpressed with my performance.

I go back to the bog where one guy who shared his ching with me approaches hopefully. — Sorry, mate, private party, I tell him.

— That's not exactly fair . . . he complains.

— Post-democracy, mate. Now fuck off, I boom as I slam the door in his face and powder my nose.

Soon I'm back outside, swanning around, in my element, when I'm interrupted by this sing-song accent in my ear. — Si-mon! How are you, my friend?!

It's that revolting cunt Miz, and I'm about to be offhand or even rude now that he's expended his usefulness, when he says: — I want you to meet somebody, and he nods to a tall guy with a moustache beside him who looks familiar. — This is Lars Lavish.

Lars Lavish is one of Europe's premier porn actors turned producers. His ability to find wood was legend and he was known as the godfather of gonzo porn, accosting lassies in the streets of Paris, Copenhagen and Amsterdam and enticing them back to a studio to make an impromptu porno flick with him. The man's gift of the gab is renowned. All he used was charm, persuasion and cash and cock inducements. He recently signed a big deal with a major distributor and now does all his own stuff and has complete editorial control. In other words, I'm absolutely fucking star-struck. This is my hero, my mentor. I can hardly fucking well think, never mind speak.

Lars Lavish.

— Lars, I shake his hand and I don't even mind that he's now got his arm round Nikki.

— Pleased to meet you, Simon, he grins, glancing down at Nikki. — This girl is so hot. She's the hottest, man, the hottest! *Seven Rides*, man, it is so goood! I am thinking that we are going to have to be having a serious talk about the distribution of this movie. I am thinking even limited theatrical release.

I have died and gone to heaven. — Any time, Lars, any time, mate.

— This is my card. Please call me, he says, then kisses Nikki and heads off into the crowd with Miz, who looks back at me with a satisfied shake of his head.

Nikki and I are soon in a strange discussion which turns a bit narky. — Why is it all those men's mags like *Loaded*, *FHM*, *Maxim*

449

are just like porn mags like *Mayfair*, *Penthouse* and *Playboy*, scanty cover outside, nudes inside? Because men's magazines are for men who are wankers, which means all men, but who like to pretend that they're not. How can you have an imaginative space and a sexuality and not be a wanker? The shit that somebody like Renton would come out with is that he gets aroused thinking about certain things so he goes and has a nice, mature discussion with his nice, mature girlfriend and they negotiate sensibly and play out those fantasies in a loving, supportive, mutually rewarding and fulfilling way . . .

— But . . .

— WHAT A LOAD AY FUCKING PISH! No, we need tits and arse because they have got to be available to us; to be pawed, fucked, wanked over. Because we're men? No. Because we're consumers. Because those are things we like, things we intrinsically feel or have been conned into believing will give us value, release, satisfaction. We value them so we need to at least have the illusion of their availability. For tits and arse read coke, crisps, speedboats, cars, houses, computers, designer labels, replica shirts. That's why advertising and pornography are similar; they sell the illusion of availability and the non-consequence of consumption.

—Your conversation is boring me, Nikki says, and she walks away.

Fuck her. I'm cruising on a massive fucking high and everybody else, everything else, will just have to fit in with *my* fucking plans.

74

'. . . killer cystitis . . .'

L ars Lavish's trying to get into my knickers. These porn guys
are pretty thick, if brutally single-minded. It's dull, but more
interesting than Simon's company. He's being a tedious, coked-up
pain in the arse. I don't want to be too hard on him, because it
is his moment and he should enjoy it, with pride coming before
a fall and all that stuff. But he's just impossible. He wants to fuck
everything in sight, like Curtis, who actually is fucking everything
in sight. The posh girls are queuing up, morbid and squeamish
and girly-girl for a shot of *that* prick, news of which is flying
round the marquee grapevine. And his swagger tells you that the
young lad is growing into that penis at last. From burger bar to
porn star.

He vanished for a bit with a companion, and now they've re-
appeared. — How are you doing, Curt?

— Great, he says, pulling this girl along by the hand. Her eyes
are bulging out and she can hardly walk straight. — This is the best
time I've had in my life!

And I'm finding it hard to argue.

I pull him to me and whisper in his ear. — Remember what you
were saying about those guys? You were at school with? How they
teased you about being a freak? Well, who was wrong, and who was
right?

— They were wrong, ah wis right, he says. — But . . . it's a shame
that the likes ay Danny and Philip n that couldnae be here tae see
aw this. They'd love it.

Simon has heard this and cuts in. — It's like the Underground
in London, mate. They rely oan enough people tae be sheep. They
dinnae supply bins, ye see, they expect you tae carry yir rubbish
aroond wi ye. Ah don't do that, ah jist drop it anywhere. But enough

451

people do it tae make it pay for them *no* tae provide bins.

— Ah dinnae get ye . . .

— What ah'm sayin, pal, is that ye drop rubbish, ye never carry it aroond wi ye, and here, it's just excellent without the rubbish, he says snootily.

Sick Boy, God, he is that, is making a fuss of this girl called Roni, who he says is from Fox Searchlight. — Roni's invited us all to the Fox Searchlight do tomorrow, he beams.

I pull him aside. — Just take her back and fuck her now, Simon, she looks well up for it. Or is it a purely nasal romance?

— Don't be petty, Nikki, he sneers. — It's just a vehicle to get the tickets for this bash.

He's full of bullshit. The party ends and we head to a club for a bit, but it's so busy that we can barely move so we decide to go back to our suite at the hotel. — This is barry, Curtis says, impressed by the opulence of the place.

Our little party is confronted by a commissionaire who asks rather imperiously: — Are you guests at this hotel?

— No, by no stretch of the imagination could you say that, Simon replies starchily. As the uniformed official is about to turf us out, he then produces his room key. — Being a guest involves receiving some kind of hospitality, some kind of rudimentary courtesy. We do stay at the hotel, however, but no, you couldn't call us guests.

The commissionaire goes to say something, but, dismissing him with the waving motion of somebody brushing aside a noxious odour, Simon strides on ahead. I follow, with a somewhat apologetic grin, as do the others. We get up to the room and drink the bar dry, Simon irritating me with his overbearing smarm directed at Ms Fox Searchlight. The way they shovel up the cocaine together is quite frightening.

— A pornographic film . . . and Curtis here's the star? she asks, looking all bug-eyed at him. Curtis is lying on the couch as Mel shakes her head.

— Aye, well, Curtis, and Mel and Nikki too, of course, Sick Boy deigns to elucidate. — The girls always rule at porn. But Curtis has a certain asset which elevates him way beyond the standard ten-inch a penny actors! Of course, I have a part myself . . .

— Reeely . . . Ms Searchlight says, rubbing his arm as they devour each other with their eyes.

Their molten flirtation makes me feel as if I've eaten too much candyfloss. I listen to him slavering away for a bit and then I drift off to sleep on the bed. When I wake up in the night, my bladder heavy, I stagger to the toilet for a long, jagged, broken-glass pee which heralds the start of killer cystitis. The minibar is empty, Simon and Fox Searchlight have gone and Curtis and Mel are crashed out on the chaise longue in a fully-clothed embrace.

I'm sitting on the toilet seat, trying to press this toxic piss out of my bladder. I phone room service and ask them to send up some Nurofen. Fortunately I have some Cylanol in my bag and I take a powder. It's agonising though; I can't sleep, and I'm in a fevered sweat. Simon comes in and sees my discomfort. — What's up, baby?

I tell him as the room-service guy enters. Simon brings the Nurofen over. — They'll soon kick in, babes, don't worry . . . have you taken your Cylanol?

I nod weakly.

— I didn't fuck that Roni, you know, he explains hastily, — we just went for a stroll along the beach because everyone else was crashed out. I'm a one-woman man these days, baby, well, off-screen anyroads.

A stroll along the beach. It sounds so romantic that now I'm wishing he had just fucked her quickly in her hotel room. He sees Mel and Curt and goes over and shakes them awake. — It's nearly morning. Can you head back to the Beverly and give us a wee bit time alone, folks? Please?

Mel's face screws up, but she rises. — Right . . . c'mon, Curtis.

Curtis gets up and sees my tears. — What's wrong wi Nikki?

— Women's problems. She'll be fine. See you in a bit, Simon says.

Curtis doesn't accept this though, and he comes over to the bed. — Are you awright, Nikki?

I acknowledge his concern, and as he kisses me sweetly on my fevered brow, I throw my arms around his skinny waist. Then Mel comes over and I give her a hug and a kiss. — I'm okay, I think the powders are starting to work. It's just this cystitis. Too much wine and spirits. I think that corrosive champagne's bad for it as well.

When they depart Simon and I get into bed, lying with our back to each other, stiff and tense, me with my pain, him with his cocaine.

Eventually, I start to ease up and unravel in the bed. It must be mid-afternoon when I wake up, disturbed by his moving around. He comes and sits on the bed, with a room-service tray: croissants, coffee, orange juice, rolls and fresh fruit. — Feeling better? he asks, kissing me.

— Yeah, loads, and I'm looking into his eyes, the both of us in silence.

After a bit he squeezes my hand and says: — Nikki, I behaved abominably last night. It wasn't just the drink or the ching, it was the occasion. I wanted this to go so right, and I was a control freak, a fascist.

— What's new? I remark.

— I want to make it up tonight, before we all go to the Fox Searchlight party, he says, his face split with a huge grin. Then he adds: — I've got some brilliant news.

He's glowing. I have to ask. — What's that?

— We've only been shortlisted for best film at the Adult Film Festival Awards! I got the call this morning!

— Wow . . . that is so . . . like, wonderful, I hear myself say.

— Too fucking right it is, Simon gleefully observes. — And yourself, myself and Curtis have been nominated in the best newcomer categories. For actress, director and actor.

I feel such a massive surge of elation, I'm almost sticking to the ceiling.

To celebrate our nomination, Simon's taking me to dinner at what he refers to as: — One of the finest restaurants, not just in Cannes, but in France. Which, of course, means the world.

I'm wearing a sparkling pea-green Prada dress with some high-heeled Gucci shoes. I have my hair up and am adorned with a small pair of gold earrings, a necklace and some bangles. Simon, who's wearing a yellow cotton suit and a white shirt, is looking at me and shaking his head. — You are the very essence of femininity, he says, seeming almost awestruck in admiration.

I'm tempted to ask him if he said the same thing to Fox Searchlight last night, but I let it go, because I don't want to spoil the moment. We are here, and it is now, and I know that won't always be the case.

And it *is* wonderful, the sort of small Provence restaurant where cooking is raised to high art. From the *amuses-bouche* through a sublime *homard bleu, suc lie de truffe noire et basilic pilé* and chicken breast *demi-deuil* covered in an inky truffle sauce to the *pièce de résistance*, a pile of truffles that enveloped a crisp green salad. Lovely.

For dessert, I went for the coffee-chocolate *coupe glacée* with a daring cup of liquid chocolate and a *brioche* to dip in it. All this was washed down with a bottle of champagne, 'Cristal' Louis Roederer, a Clos du Bois Chardonnay and two large Remy Martin cognacs.

We're intoxicated by everything, lisping seductively at each other in pidgin French, when Simon's mobile rings, the green one. It annoys me that he can never seem to switch them off. — Hello?

— Who is it? I hiss, more than mildly irritated that our moment has been invaded.

Simon puts his hand over the receiver. He looks quite concerned for a bit, then breaks into a waspish smile. — It's François. Some wildly important news about a card school in Leith I forgot about. How remiss of me to double-book my diary. He speaks calmly into the phone. — I'm in France, Frank, at the Cannes Film Festival.

There's a sharp voice buzzing on the other end. Simon holds the phone away from him. Then he winks raffishly at me and says into the receiver, cupping the other hand over his ear: — Frank? Are you still there? Hello?

He puts his hand over the mouthpiece and giggles. — François is being rather difficult. Trust me to forget that the Cannes Film Festival and the Leith Card School clashed. I should get a helicopter to Leith straight away, he sniggers, his shoulders shaking, and now I'm laughing too. — Are you still there, Frank? Hello? he shouts into the phone. Then he scrapes the grill of the mouthpiece with his fingernail. — I can't hear you and you're breaking up. I'll phone you back later, he says, then snaps the phone shut and switches it

455

off. — He is such a prick you can't even hate him. It's beyond that, he says in stunned admiration. — The man is beyond love or hate . . . he simply . . . *is*.

Then he grabs my hand across the table. — How can somebody like him and somebody like you exist in the same world? How can planet Earth produce such a range of humanity?

And we were straight back into each other again. Simon arrogantly tossed the odd withering glance around the room, but mostly our complicit eyes ate each other, dancing and teasing in and out of each other's souls. To have enjoyed such intimacy, to fuck would actually be an anticlimax. Almost.

— Do we have time to go back to the room before we meet the others? I ask him.

— I'll make time, he says, waving the mobile.

I repair to the toilet and push my fingers down my throat, throwing up the food and gargling with mouthwash from my bag. It's lovely food, but far too rich and fattening to actually digest. Like most modern, intelligent women, I'm a Jungian, but Freud did have one thing going for him in that he hated fat people. Probably because they were happy and well adjusted and therefore didn't line his pockets like the skinny neurotics. But now, at this moment, I'm happy. I've had my cake and eaten it, then sicked it up before it could damage me.

When I go back to the restaurant, there's a row going on and, to my mounting unease, I can tell that it's over at our table.

— This card cannot be over the limit, that simply cannot be the fucking case, Simon shouts, his face florid with the drink and probably cocaine.

— But please, Monsieur . . .

— I DON'T THINK YOU'RE HEARING ME! THAT SIMPLY CANNOT BE THE FUCKING CASE!

— But, Monsieur, please . . .

Simon's voice breaks into a low hiss. — Don't fucking gies it, ya froggy cunt! You want Cruise in here? You want DiCaprio to eat in here? I'm supposed to be meeting Billy Bob Thornton here tomorrow to discuss a major fucking project . . .

— Simon! I shout. — What's going on?

— Sorry . . . okay, okay. There's been some mistake. Try this one. He hands over another card which instantly goes through. Despite the maître d's sour expression, Simon looks smug and vindicated, and not only does he refuse to leave a tip, he shouts back into the dining room in parting: — JE NE REVIENDRAI PAS!

Outside, I'm teetering between finding this whole thing annoying and amusing. As I'm still on such a massive high, I opt for the latter, bursting into a drunken, nervous fit of giggles.

Simon looks sourly at me, then shakes his head and starts laughing himself. — That was nonsense, it's the Bananazzurri company card I tried to pay with. There's loads of cash in there. All the one-six-nine-zero scam money is in there and only Rents and I are the signatories and he's in the Da . . . He stops dead for a second, and a cold panic fuses in his eyes. — If. That. Cunt.

— Don't be so paranoid, Simon, I laugh. — Mark'll be here tomorrow as planned. Let's go back, I whisper in his ear, — and make love . . .

— Make love! Make fucking love? When a ginger cunt could be taking everything I've fucking well worked for?

— Don't be stupid . . . I implore him.

Simon, as if trying to control and fortify himself, stretches his arms out in front of him. — Okay . . . okay . . . I'm probably being silly. Tell you what, you go back and give me fifteen minutes to compose myself and make a few phone calls.

I respond with a sulky frown, but he's not moving. I head away, reluctantly going back to the hotel room, where I pour myself a drink, thinking about the bastard on the beach with that Fox Searchlight bitch.

When he returns, he's calmed down and is in better spirits. — You got Mark, I take it?

— No, but I spoke to Dianne. She said he'd just called her from Amsterdam. He's calling her again later, so I told her to tell him to phone me straight away, he explains, then pleads: — Sorry, babes, I was jumpy. Too much ching . . .

I move over to him and grab his balls firmly, through the material of his trousers, feeling his cock stiffen. A big smile grows over his face. — You fuckin dirty cow, he laughs, and he's on me and in me and we make frenzied love, hotter even than our first few times.

Later, we rendezvous along with Mel and Curt and head out to the Fox Searchlight party. It's pretty dull at first but an excellent DJ livens things up and we get thrashed again. When it finishes, we get into a launch and head out to the do on the *Private* boat, an old cruise ship moored in the Med, which has been converted into a film studio. It's a porn stars' party, with banging, cheesy Eurotechno and free drinks. Simon's obviously a bag of nerves, on the mobile all the time, trying to get Mark. He attempts to make light of things. — If this music doesn't make you want butt-fucked, Nikki, nothing will.

— You're right, I tell him, — nothing will.

Myself, Mel and Curtis are going for it on the dance deck, although Curt keeps disappearing and coming back with a grin on his face and a deranged starlet in tow. Mel and I are constantly getting hit on by all manner of guys including Lars Lavish and Miz, but we're enjoying our sense of power, knocking everybody back, but flirting outrageously and prick-teasing horribly. At one stage we go into a toilet cublicle and make love, bringing each other off, only the second time we've been intimate in that way without a camera.

When we get back on deck, wired but satisfied, smirking at each other, we see Simon, still constantly trying to get signals on the mobiles. More launches arrive and the boat is filling up. I see a thin girl with long, blonde hair from the side of my vision, which isn't surprising, but the voice I can hear talking to her makes me do a quick double take. Simon even clicks off his phone in shock. — . . . aye, but people think thit ah git called Juice Terry cause ay the load ay juice that ah shoot oaf in they cum shots. Bit naw, it goes back tae the time thit ah used tae deliver the juice, or what youse Americans might call soda, bit the technical term is aerated waters, eh. Listen, doll, no fancy gaun doonstairs fir a bit, explore the ship n that? Mibee a bit mair thin the ship!

— Lawson! Simon shouts.

— Sicky! Terry roars, then he sees Mel and me. — Nikki! Whae-hae! Mel! Awright, gorgeous! He turns to his compainion. — This is Carla, she's in the business, San Fernando Valley stuff, likes. What wis your fillum again, doll?

458

— *A Butt-Fucker in Pussy City*, this blonde girl with an American accent smiles cheesily.

— Aye, Birrell's here n aw, Birrell Senior, that is. Telt ays eh wis gaun ower tae see ehs burd in Nice, so ah jist sortay invited masel along. Goat the train doon here n blagged intae the porn fillum festival tent. Telt every cunt ah wis Juice Terry fae *Seven Rides*, n goat sorted oot wi a pass, he points to an orange badge with PRIVATE ADULT FILMS, 'JUICE' TERRY LAWSON, PERFORMER emblazoned on it. — Cannae wait tae git back tae Edinburgh, hit the Slutland at the West End wi this oan.

— Delighted you could make it, Tel, Simon says curtly. — Excuse me for a second, and he heads towards the starboard, punching digits into his green mobile.

Terry grabs a handful of my arse, repeating the exercise with Mel's, and with a sly wink he vanishes with Carla, who evidently thinks – thanks to Simon's editing of *Seven Rides* – that Terry's cock is Curtis's. — She'll be disappointed, Mel laughs, — but no *that* disappointed.

This Eurotechno is so bouncy I'm almost wishing I had an E, but I'm not really a chemical sort. After a bit, an agitated Simon approaches us with another bulletin. — There's no Renton, so he must be on his way here, but that specky wee Lauren says that that Dianne's gone! Or at least that's what I think she said. The stroppy wee hoor willnae talk tae me, Nikki. You phone her, he says, now thrusting his *white* mobile at me. — Please, he urges.

I call Lauren and speak with her for a minute or two, asking about her health. Then I ask about Dianne. After, I turn to Simon. — Dianne's only staying at her mum's for a few days, that's all. She's not been too well.

—What's her mother's phone number? I need to speak to Dianne!

— Simon, will you just, like, chill out? You'll see Mark, like tomorrow? At the hotel? He wouldn't miss this for the world! I urge him, swinging back into the beat with Mel.

But Simon's shaking his head, not listening to a word I'm saying. — No . . . no . . . he moans, then smashes his fist into his palm, — that cunt Renton . . . right, you cunt, that's it! He pulls out his green mobile phone.

— Who are you calling now?

— Begbie!

Melanie looks at me in amazement. — Why does he use his green one tae call Begbie n ehs white yin tae call Lauren?

He did explain this to me once but some things are too sad to even talk about. Now Simon's listening to some sort of tirade on the phone, with mounting impatience as the red sunset falls behind his back. Eventually he snaps at the mouthpiece: — Never mind that fuckin crap. Renton's back. In Edinburgh!

Then there's a brief pause and Simon looks incredulous, he's saying: — What? Across the road? What the fuck . . . keep him there, Franco! DINNAE LET HIM GO! EH'S GOAT MY FUCKIN CASH!

He stares at the dead phone in his hand, then shakes it violently. — FUCKIN PEA-BRAINED CUNT!

Miz comes over with Lars Lavish. He touches Simon on the arm gently. — You know, Simon, we are for thinking . . .

To my horror Simon turns and headbutts him in the face at force and he's on top of poor Miz, flaying at him and screaming: — YOU DUTCH CUNTS HAVE GOT MA FUCKIN MONEY, YA DIRTY HOMOSEXUAL ORANGE CUNTS . . .

It takes all of us plus half a dozen Swedish bouncers to pull him off and restrain him. Terry arrives back on deck and he's laughing as they push Simon into a launch. — You are lucky we do not want the police on this boat, a bouncer shouts at Simon as Curtis, Mel, two girls, Terry, Carla and myself join him. As he gingerly steps onto the launch, Terry sneakily whacks the talkative Swede on the side of the face. — 'Moan then, cunt, he invites. The guy stands rooted, petulantly rubbing his jaw, looking like he's going to burst into tears as the launch pulls away from the liner. We can hear an agitated Miz screaming: — He is crazy! He is a crazy man, as we head for the shore.

Terry turns to Curtis. — That cock ay yours hus come in useful tae me, mate, he says, putting an arm round Carla. Then he contemplates Curtis, a girl on each side of him. — Mind you, it's no daein you much herm either.

I'm regarding Simon, who is sitting with his eyes tightly closed, shaking, both his arms wrapped around himself, repeating in a loud, gasping whisper: — . . . tolleranza zero . . . tolleranza zero . . . over and over again.

— Simon, what is it?

— I only hope that Francis Begbie kills Mark Renton. I pray that happens, he says as he crosses himself.

75

CAIRD SCHOOL

Eftirnin drinkin: it does ye in but ye cannae fuckin beat it. Sometimes but, ah think thit ah see thum, jist comin intae the bar. That cunt Donnelly gadge or that Chizzie beast. That's the problem: thir's fuck all tae dae n too much time tae think, especially in the hoose. That's how ah keep gaun oot, doon tae the boozer. Mind you, it's no as if ye git much fuckin conversation doon here.

Nelly goes aw silent n starts playin wi ehs pint. — What the fuck's up wi you? ah goes.

— That Larry phoned up last night. Whin ah wis oot wi youse, eh nods tae Malky. — She wis in oan her ain, wi the bairns. Eh goes, 'Ah'm comin fir yis. Aw ay yis.' Then eh tells her, 'If you've goat any sense yi'll git yirsel back doon tae Manchester or whair-ever it is ye come fae . . .'

— Your bird's Welsh, is she no? Malky goes.

— Aye, Swansea, Nelly sais, aw stroppy, — but he disnae ken that. Ah met her in Manchester. But ye ken what that sick cunt sais later, the message that eh left oan the machine?

Me n Malky ur shakin wur fuckin heids.

— Ah'll fuckin well show yis, Nelly says. — Ah'll fuckin well show ye the kind ay cunt we've been drinkin wi, eh goes, lookin aw that fuckin hurt wey tae me, like it wis me thit made the cunt drink wi Larry. Ah'm sayin fuckin nowt but, cause ah want a fuckin laugh oot ay this.

So wi goes up tae Nelly's n eh's goat the messages oan the machine. Eh plays yin back n it's Larry's voice, awright, a sortay soft, creepy whisper. — Leave toon. Leave toon, cause ah'm comin fir yi. Ah am comin fae Muirhoose tae your hoose. Ah am comin tae kiss youse aw good night.

— That cunt's been watchin too many fuckin films, Malky laughs.

Nelly looks back aw hard at um. — It's goat her shitein hersel. She's talkin aboot takin the bairns tae her ma's doon in Wales. Sayin that's what wi left Manchester fir in the first place.

Ah'm lookin at um but ah'm sayin nowt. Malky's sayin fuck all n aw.

— Ah need tae sort this oot, eh goes. — If eh keeps that shite up, eh's gaun doon a fuckin hole, ah'm tellin yis that.

Whae's he fuckin kiddin? Eh's nivir wasted any cunt in ehs life. Aw that fuckin bullshit aboot what eh's meant tae huv done doon in Manchester wi that Cheetham Hill mob. If eh wis that well quoted doon thaire, what's eh fuckin well daein back up here?

— Look, Malky goes, this is gittin oot ay hand. Franco, you gaunnae talk tae Larry, sort aw this oot?

So now it's fuckin Malky tellin ivray cunt what they should n shouldnae be daein, is that it? Wi'll fuckin well see aboot that. Bit then ah thinks, naw, play it his wey, n ah looks ower at Nelly. — If ye want.

Then Malky turns roond n sais tae um: — But you'll huv tae tell the cunt thit ye wir oot ay order n apologise fir whit ye did in the pub.

Nelly's sayin nowt fir a bit, n we're both starin at the cunt. Then eh goes: — If he fuckin apologises fir makin they fuckin sick phone calls tae ma hoose, ah'll apologise tae him fir batterin um.

— Right, ah goes. — Enough ay aw this shite. Supposed tae be fuckin mates. This needs sorted oot. The night, at the caird school at Sick Boy's.

— Will Larry show up? Malky's wonderin.

— If ah tell um eh'll fuckin show up, ah'm gaun.

So that's me daein ma good deed fir the day n bein the fuckin peacemaker as usual. They fuckin bams wid kill each other if it wisnae fir the likes ay me sortin everythin oot. Aw that shite but: it's gied ays a fuckin migraine so oan the wey hame ah stoaps oaf at the fit ay the Walk n gits some Nurofen Plus wi the paper. Ah phones Sick Boy oan ehs mobby tae remind him aboot the caird school the night.

— I'm in France, Frank, at the Cannes Film Festival, the smarmy cunt says.

Ah tipples thit the cunt isnae fuckin jokin n aw. — What aboot oor fuckin caird school? Ah telt ye wi wir huvin a fuckin caird school doon at yours!

— Frank? Are you still there? Hello?

— WHAT ABOOT OOR FUCKIN CAIRD SCHOOL! AH GOAT TELT RENTON'S BEEN SEEN! AH'M WANTIN A FUCKIN WORD WI YOU, YA CUNT!

— Are you still thair, Frank? Hello?

What's that cunt fuckin well playin at . . . ? — OOR FAHKIN CAIRD SCHOOL! AH'M GAUNNAE KILL YOU, YA CUNT!

Thir's a fuckin cracklin ay static oan the line. Then the cunt goes: — I can't hear you and you're breaking up. I'll phone you back later, n it jist goes fuckin deid!

FUCKIN RADGE!

That cunt thinks ay kin treat us like shite, swan oaf tae fuckin France wi aw ehs pals fae that dirty club, that fuckin Juice Terry n aw they other fuckin wideo fuckin nonce stoat-the-baw fuckin perverts n hing-oots . . . ah'll fuckin well show that sneaky fuckin lyin cunt . . .

So eftir muh tea ah bells Nelly n Malky n Larry n tells thum thit that cunt's let us doon n tae meet up at the Central Bar. We gits thaire n it's jist Nelly n Malky, Larry's no even fuckin well showed up but, eh. Eh bells ays oan the mobby tae say thit ehs gaunnae be a wee bit late, but eh'll definitely fuckin be thaire. Ah think it's jist tae pit a bit ay pressure oan Nelly. Ye kin see thit the cunt's lookin aw tense. Anywey, wuv goat the cairds oot in one ay the booths, n the pints ay Guinness ur gaun doon thick n fast. Ah nivir use the Central much, bit for some reason ah eywis like a pint ay Guinness whin ah'm in thaire.

Eftir a bit thir's still nae sign ay Larry.

Ah hears the tone gaun oan the mobby but it's that cunt Sick Boy. Ah'll gie um brekin up . . . ah'll fuckin well brek that cunt up . . . Ah goes ootside the pub tae git a better signal. Aye, it's fuckin Sick Boy awright. Jist as well fir that cunt thit eh phoned ays back. — Whaire the fuck ur ye? ah goes. — Ah've goat things tae fuckin well talk tae you aboot! Our fuckin caird school!

— Never mind that fuckin crap, eh goes n ah'm jist aboot tae fuckin well lose it whin eh sais: — Renton's back. In Edinburgh!

So it's fuckin true . . . ah'm tryin tae think what tae say n ah looks up, acroass the street n thair eh fuckin is! That rid-heided thievin cunt is at the cashpoint ower the fuckin road fae ays! — Eh's . . . ah'm fuckin well screamin intae the phone, — EH'S ACROASS THE FUCKIN ROAD FAE AYS!

Ah hear Sick Boy sayin stuff like 'keep a hud ay um, ah'm wantin tae see um whin ah git back . . .' bit then that cunt Renton looks right ower at ays n ah jist clicks oaf the fuckin phone.

76

Whores of Amsterdam Pt 11

Spud's fuckin cat! I remember just as I'm coming into Edinburgh. When I call him he tells me that he's given all his cash to Ali and predictably asks me if I can lend him some money, three hundred quid. What can I say but yes? He's in his hoose, feart tae go oot.

So I take a cab from the airport to Dianne's to pick up the cat. It takes me ages tae get the fuckin thing intae the carrier, they make me allergic and I'm sneezing like fuck. I lose my cool and grab the bastard and take a scratch across my arm in retaliation. — Don't hurt him, Mark, Dianne snaps, as I stuff the spitting bag ay shit into the carrier and secure the door. She's packed and I take her down to Gavin's. We arrange to meet at the airport at eight o'clock for the 9 p.m. flight, the last one to London and our connecting night-flight to San Francisco.

I know how Spud feels about being scared to go out, but here I am, in the taxi, heading down to Leith with the doss cunt's fuckin cat. My napper's buzzing and I'm thinking that this is where I came in, ripping off Sick Boy. I get out at Pilrig to the cashpoint.

The Clydesdale's fucked and there's a grey-haired guy with a Glasgow accent booting it in frustration. There are nae cunting taxis to be seen. So, with some trepidation I pull my hat down and walk, the cat carrier swinging uncomfortably against my legs, down towards the Halifax at the foot of the Walk. The cat mews treacherously, as if trying to attract the attention that I'm seeking to avoid. They do Link at this cashpoint: funny how you mind of these things after all the years. I used to feel so at home, so safe, the further down the Walk I got. Now it feels like a descent into Hades. I won't be here for long though, cause as soon as this fuckin cat's delivered, I'm offski in a fast black to meet Dianne, then it's the big white tin bird again.

My spirits soar as I see a queue at the cashpoint at the foot ay the Walk. There's a drunk trying to operate it. I approach the cunt cautiously, anxiety oozing oot ay me. I can hear some guys shouting threats at each other in Junction Street. You miss this atmosphere in Amsterdam, this atmosphere of barely repressed casual violence and aggression, this procession of paranoia. It just doesnae exist over there.

C'mon, mate. Sort it oot.

Then I hear a familiar voice and it cuts me in two, and by a wrenching effort of will I look across the road in its direction.

Begbie.

Shouting into a mobile phone.

Then he sees me and stands open-mouthed, outside the Central Bar. He's momentarily paralysed by shock. We both are.

Then he snaps the phone shut and roars:

RENNTUUUN!!!

My blood is frozen is my veins and all I can see is Frank Begbie tearing across the road towards me, face contorted with rage and it's like he'll just run right past me and do some cunt else cause he doesn't know me now and I'm nothing to do with him anymore. But I know it's me he wants and it's going to be a bad one and I should run but I can't. In those few seconds life's shredded into a million thoughts. I reflect how hopeless and ludicrous my martial arts pretensions are. All that training and practice will count for nothing, it's all shorn away by the expression on his face. I can't abstract anything, because an old childhood tape is playing relentlessly in my head: Begbie = Evil = Fear. I am in a total paralysis of will. The parts of me that envisage the simple adoption of the wado ryu stance, blocking his blow, ramming his nose into his brain with the palm of my hand, or sidestepping his lunge and elbowing his temple, yes, they are present. But they're feeble impulses, easily overwhelmed by the mortifying fear that I'm slow-dancing with.

Begbie's coming at me and I can't do anything

I can't shout.

I can't plead.

There's nothing I can do.

77

Home

Ali's sister Kath nivir really liked ays, man, n she pure disnae like Ali hingin oot wi ays again. Ali jist wants tae come hame now, wi Andy. Cause ah wis worried aboot gaun oot, but she came roond n wi went tae the pictures thegither. Ah've goat that wirin oaf the jaw, so ah'm pure back oan solids again, even though it's awfay stiff. Ali n me huv nivir necked like thon fir years, n the jaw isnae the only thing thit's stiff. Ah'm thinkin aboot sayin, come back wi ays for a bit, whin ah mind thit ah hud arranged tae meet Rents doon the hoose!

S ah tears masel away, still sair, but bouncin doon the Walk, high, but aw wary in case ah see Franco. Thir's been aw sorts ay reports, but it could be jist talk. Ye nivir really ken fir sure. Rents sais thit eh'd be doon by now n ah'm worried thit ah've missed the gadge. Whin ah gits tae the fit ay the Walk, thir's a bit ay a commotion, an ambulance n a polis car n a big crowd roond. The shivers are pillin oan me like ah wis in junk withdrawal, cause whin ye see a polis car or an ambulance in Leith, well, ah suppose thir's a few names thit crop up but thir's jist one that's oan ma mind right now. Aw ah see is HOME but ah'm thinkin, what if Begbie's got Mark?

Ma hert's banging, man.

AW FUCK, NAW . . .

Ah saw him first. Begbie. Eh's doon. *Begbie's* been done! Eh's oan the deck. Franco! Eh's fucked, cause eh's oan the groond n standin ower um ur the ambulance boys, n thir's a ginger-heided boy on toap ay um n it looks like . . . fuckin hell . . . it's the Rent Boy, n it looks like eh's awright. This is Rents n Begbie . . . and it's . . .

Naw.

Naw . . .

It's like *Rents* has done *Begbie*, and done him bad . . . then a chilly

468

spasm goes through ays again cause whaire's ma cat but, man, whaire's Zappa?

No way ... thir's no way kin ah stop n git involved in this, man. No fuckin way. Bit ah've goat tae find the cat. Ah pill ma collar up n ma basebaw cap doon n push through the mob. Then ah sees Nelly comin oot fae the crowd n eh bangs Rents a shot in the face.

Rents staggers a bit n huds ehs jaw, as Nelly shouts something n slopes back intae the crowd. A polisman goes up tae Renton but Mark's shakin ehs heid like eh's no grassin Nelly up n eh jist gits in the ambulance wi Begbie.

N then ah sees um; it's Zappa, ma poor cat, jist left thaire, left thaire in the street! So ah goes ower n picks the carrier up, wi ma good airm. This lassie thit hud been bent doon, pettin um through the wire gies ays a dirty look! — Ah ken whaes cat this is, ah tell hur, — ah'll git it back tae thum.

— That's oot ay order; ye cannae leave a cat lying in the street, the lassie goes.

— Aye, too right, ah sais, jist wantin tae git oot ay here, cause it's pure freaky, ma nerves ur jist like janglin, ken?

Then Nelly sees ays, n eh's right ower tae me. Eh points ehs finger n hisses: — Fuckin junky cunt.

Never really liked that cat n ah'm no feart ay him, even smashed up like ah ahm. Ah'm aboot tae say somethin back whin ah sees this boy, a boy ah've seen knockin aboot wi Franco, n eh comes up behind Nelly n hits um in the back, no that hard, then jist sortay dances away mergin intae the onlookers. Nelly twists roond tae scratch ehs back, like it's itchy, n sees aw this blood oan ehs hands.

Ah see the fright in ehs eyes as the other boy wades through the crowd wi a big smile oan ehs coupon. Eh gies me a wee wink, then eh vanishes. And so do ah, man. Ah'm pure away hame wi Zappa. Ah'm thinkin thit it wis bad ay Mark tae leave the cat in the road, that wis as cruel as, man, but mind you, eh wis under pressure, wi Franco n that.

Naw, bit the thing is wi me, ah've goat Zappa back, then it'll be Ali n Andy n everythin's gaunnae be better again, that's fir defo.

78

Whores of Amsterdam Pt 12

There was nothing I could do.

    I couldn't do anything. Couldn't shout, plead or nothing.

And the boys in the car didn't see him.

There was nothing I could do.

The car hit Franco at force just a few feet away from me. He was thrown right over the top of it and he crashed down onto the road. He lay there immobile, the blood trickling out of his nose.

I'm over there without consciously knowing what the fuck I'm doing. I'm down at his side, supporting his head, watching his busy eyes blaze and jive, brimming with baffled malevolence. I don't want him like this. I really don't. I want him punching me, kicking me. — Franco man, ah'm sorry . . . it's oot ay order . . . ah'm sorry, man . . .

I'm greeting. I'm holding Begbie in my arms and I'm greeting. I'm thinking of all the old times, all the good times and I'm looking into his eyes and the rancour is leaving them, like a dark curtain being drawn back, to let in a serene light as his thin lips twist into a wicked smile.

He is fucking well smiling at me. Then he tries to talk, says something like: — Ah eywis liked you, or maybe I'm just hearing what I want tae hear, maybe there's a qualification. Then eh starts coughing and a rivulet of blood trickles oot from the side of his mouth.

I try tae say something, but I'm suddenly aware of somebody standing over us. Looking up, I behold a face, which looks alien and familiar at the same time. I realise that it's Nelly Hunter, that he's had his facial tattoos removed and I'm jist gaunnae say something in acknowledgement when ehs fist lashes oot n cracks ma jaw.

My body jolts in shock and a dull throb registers in my face. Fuck me, that was a cracker. I see him spring back into the crowd of ghouls as I rise unsteadily to my feet. There's a hand on my shoulder and I turn sharply, fearing that I'm going to be battered to a pulp by Franco's mob, but it's only a green-jacketed paramedic. They get Franco onto a gurney and move him into the ambulance. I go to follow but a polisman stands in front of me and says something that I can't make out. Another cop nods at the paramedic, then the first cop. He unbars my way and I'm in the back of the ambulance as they slam the door shut and start off. I'm crouching over Franco and telling him to hold on. — It's okay, Frank, ah'm here, mate, I tell him, — ah'm here.

I rub my jaw, which is fucked from Nelly's fist, a sair one awright. Welcome tae Leith. Welcome home, right enough. But where is that now? Leith . . . naw. Amsterdam . . . naw. If home is where the heart is, right now Dianne's my home. I've got tae get tae the airport.

I'm squeezing Franco's hand, but he's unconscious now and the paramedics have put an oxygen mask on his face. — Keep talkin tae him, one of them urges.

This does not look fuckin good. The weird thing is that over the years I thought that I'd wanted this moment, had even hoped for it, fantasised it, but now I'd wish for anything other than this. The ambulance guy doesnae need tae prompt ays cause ah couldnae shut up if ah wanted tae. — Aye . . . ah meant tae git thegither wi ye, Frank, pit things right. Ah'm really sorry aboot that time in London, but Frank, ah wisnae thinkin straight, ah jist needed tae get away, tae get off the gear. Ah've been in Amsterdam but I'm back here now for the time being, Frank. Met a nice lassie . . . you'd like her. Ah think a lot aboot the laughs we used tae have, the fitba in the Links, how your ma was always good tae me when ah came roond tae yours, she eywis made ays welcome. These things sortay stick wi ye. Mind we used tae go tae the State in Junction Street on Saturday morning for the cartoon shows, or tae that scabby wee cinema at the top ay the Walk, what was it called? . . . the Salon! If we hud the money we'd go tae Easter Road in the eftirnoon, mind ye used tae be able tae git a lift ower . . . Then we got caught sprayin our names and YLT oan the back ay Leith Academy Primary and we were only eleven and nearly greetin so the polis went and let us go! Mind that? That wis me, you, Spud, Tommy and Craig Kincaid. Mind the time

471

we both shagged Karen Mackie? What aboot that time at Motherwell when you battered that big cunt and *ah* goat fuckin lifted for it!

And the strange thing is that as I'm saying all this, and remembering it, feeling it, part of my brain is thinking something else. I'm thinking that Sick Boy is a born exploiter, instinctive, a creature of his times. But his effectiveness is curtailed by the fact that he's far too into the process; the intrigue and the social side of it all. He thinks it's significant, that it actually means something. So he gets immersed in it all, and never just stops to sit back and remember to do the simple thing.

Like taking the money and running.

He won't be pleased when he sees that the money has gone and me with it. His self-hate at being done twice will probably precipitate some sort of mental breakdown. I might end up having offed both him and poor Franco. Franco . . . apart from the oxygen mask, he looks exactly the same. Then there's a ringing coming from him and I realise it's the mobile phone gaun oaf in his jacket pocket. I glance at the paramedic, who nods at me. I take it out and click it on. A shout rings in my ear. — FRANK!

It's Sick Boy's voice.

— DID YOU GET RENTON? ANSWER ME, FRANK! IT'S ME, SIMON! ME! ME! ME!

I hang up and switch the phone off. — I think that was his girlfriend trying to get through, I hear myself telling the paramedic. — I'll call her later.

We get to the hospital and I'm in a dumb haze as a skinny, nervous-looking young doctor's telling me that Franco's still unconscious, which I had already worked out, and they're taking him into intensive care. — It's just a question of trying to stabilise his condition then we'll run tests to see what kind of damage has been done, he says, so tentatively, it's almost as if he knows who they're looking after.

There's nothing more I can do, but I go up to the intensive-care ward where I catch a nurse putting an IV drip into his arm. I nod gently at her and she responds with a tight economical, professional smile. I'm thinking about how I want to be with Dianne at the airport, and how I don't particularly want to be here when Nelly

and some of Franco's mates come crashing through the door. —
Sorry, Frank, I say, before making to go, then I turn quickly and
add: — Be strong. Exiting the ward, I head off at pace along the
corridor, down the marble stair, my soles nearly slipping on the
surface, come out through two sets of swing doors and dart across
the forecourt into a waiting taxi. We're making good time out to
the airport because the traffic's light but I'm still late. Very late.

We pull up outside of Departures and I see Dianne waving to
me and I run to meet her. She stays rooted to the spot but thaws
when I get closer, her understandable chagrin evaporating as she
registers the state I'm in. — God . . . what's wrong? I thought you'd
stood me up for an old flame or something.

For a second I nearly laugh. — There was never any danger of
that, I say, shaking as I grab hold of her, breathing her in. I'm trying
to keep a grip on myself too, because I need to be on that plane,
with a greater desire than I ever wanted for any fix.

We hurry to the check-in, but they won't even book us through.
We've missed the London flight, and therefore our connection.
Missed the bastard by minutes, seconds even. But missed it.
Fortunately, we have open tickets and we book onto the earliest San
Francisco via London flight which is tomorrow lunchtime. We both
agree that we can't face the city again and we elect to check into
a nearby airport hotel, where I explain fully what happened.

Sitting on the red-and-green quilt-covered bed with Dianne, still
in shock, her hand in mine, I'm tracing the thin blue veins at the
back of it as I recount my tale. — It's crazy, but the radge bastard
would have killed ays . . . I just froze . . . I doubt I could even have
tried tae defend myself . . . The most mental thing about it though
was . . . after . . . it was like we were still mates, like ah hudnae
ripped him off or nowt like that. It's so fuckin bizarre but there's
part of me that still really likes the cunt . . . I mean, you're the
psychologist, what's that aboot?

Dianne purses her lips and opens her eyes wider in contempla-
tion. — He's part of your life, I suppose. Do you feel guilty about
your part in his accident?

A sudden, focused coldness comes over me. — No. He shouldnae
have ran across the street like that.

473

The room is centrally heated but Dianne holds the coffee cup in both hands as if to draw warmth from it, and it strikes me that she's in shock about Franco as well, though she never knew him. It's like it's transmitting from me to her.

We try to change the subject, to pick ourselves up by looking ahead. She's telling me that she doesn't think that her thesis on porn is very good, and in any case she fancies a year off. Maybe even check out a college in the States. What will we do in San Francsico? Just hang out. I might start up a club again, but probably not, it's too much hassle. Dianne and me might get into website shite, become dotcommers. We've planned and fantasised about this for long enough, but I can't think of that right now, all I can think of is Begbie, and Dianne of course. She's turned out a cool woman, but she always was. It was me who was a bit too young and immature for us to make a proper go of things at the time. This time we'll ride it out as long as the love or the cash lasts.

The next morning we're up early and have breakfast in the room. I phone the hospital for news of Franco. There's no change, he's still unconscious, but the X-rays confirm the extent of his injuries; he has a broken leg and a shattered hip bone as well as some cracked ribs, a fractured arm and skull and some internal damage. It should be a relief to have him incapacitated, but I still feel terrible about what happened to Franco. And yes, right now I do feel guilty.

We head back over to the airport, her excited about getting away, me just more anxious about the consequences of sticking around here a second longer than we have to.

79

'. . . easyJet . . .'

Simon's been phoning like crazy all morning. We're at the airport early doors to catch the easyJet back to Edinburgh, the first available flight. Terry and his American porn girl, Carla, are seeing us off, only because Terry's wanting to get the keys to our room off him which is booked for two more days and Simon won't part with them until the last minute. He keeps looking at Terry, who's now emerged from the airport shop, with unbridled suspicion. — I really appreciate you coming back with me, Nikki, he says: — cause you could stay here another couple of days with Curtis and Mel and have a ball at the awards party. You'll probably walk it as well. It's your moment, Nikki.

— We need to stick together, honey, I tell him, gripping his hand.

— Dinnae worry, Sick Boy, me n Carla here'll enjoy the suite, eh, doll? Terry says, looking at his new girl, then at me, obviously worried in case I change my mind.

— Yeah . . . it's so kind of you . . . she happily murmurs.

Simon looks wildly discomforted, and picking up on it Terry says earnestly: — Ah'll be a great ambassador fir *Seven Rides* n ah'll no take the pish oan hotel expenses.

But Simon's not hearing him. He's called the pub and he's talking to Alison and if anything he's even more deflated than ever. — You are fucking joking . . . I don't believe it . . . he turns to Terry and me. — The cunting polis and the fucking Customs and Excise are down the pub. They've confiscated the videos . . . they're closing me down . . . Ali! he snaps back into the phone, — tell nae cunt nowt, tell them I've gone to France, it's the truth. Is there any sign of Begbie or Renton?

There's a short silence then Simon barks: — WHAT! then gasps: — Hospitalised the cunt? A fuckin coma? Rents?

My heart almost jumps out of my mouth. Mark . . . — What's happened!

Simon clicks off the phone. — *Renton* has done *Begbie*! He's hospitalised the cunt. Begbie's in a coma from which they reckon he won't wake up. Spud told Ali, he saw it, at the fit ay the Walk last night!

— Thank God Mark's okay . . . I say aloud and Simon's eyes suddenly screw me in ghastly intent. — Well, Simon, I whisper, — he's got our money . . .

— What money's this then? Terry asks, his ears pricking up.

— Just some cash I lent him, Simon shakes his head. — Anyway, Terry, here's the hotel keys. He quickly produces them from his pocket, throws them to him and says bitterly: — Enjoy.

— Cheers, Terry says, grabbing Carla's waist. — Dinnae you worry aboot that, he winks. Then he considers. — Funny aboot Mark sortin oot Begbie. A dark hoarse awright. Ah ey reckoned that kung fu stuff wis shite n aw. Jist goes tae show ye but, eh. Still, he smiles, — see yis, and skips away across the forecourt with his porn star shag. I watch him shuffle off, a fly-in-shit with all his needs met, having the time of his life, while Simon, who should be the same, has a pained, ulcerated expression. Terry on his tab in Cannes for two days gives him yet something else to worry about.

During the flight, Simon's full of rancour for the world, and is still seething as we come into land at Edinburgh airport. — Now you still don't know that Mark's ripped us off, so take it easy. We had an amazing time? The film went down well? That's positive.

— Hummph, he coughs, his shades perched on top of his head, his neck craning, looking around anxiously as we pick up our luggage and head through passport control and customs.

Then he stops in his tracks, because just about fifty yards away Mark and Dianne are standing there, preparing to go through the departure gates.

Dianne goes past first and as Mark's showing his documents to the airline official, Simon screams at the top of his voice: — REHHNNNTUHNNN!

Mark looks at him, smiles faintly and waves, and then steps through the gates. Simon goes sprinting towards him and tries to run right through the gates, but the official and the security man won't let him past. — STOP THAT THIEF! he screams as Mark and Dianne's backs recede. I'm following, looking at her wondering if she'll turn around but she doesn't. — TELL THEM, NIKKI! Simon beseeches me.

I stand there in breathless shock. — What can I say?

He turns back to the official and the security guard. More of them are appearing now. — Listen, he pleads, — you have to let me through the departure gates.

— You need a valid boarding card, sir, the clerk informs him.

Simon's heaving, trying to control his breathing. — Listen, that man has stolen something that belongs to me. I have to get through that fucking gate.

— That's surely a matter for the police, sir. If I can radio the airport police . . .

Simon's grinding his teeth together and shaking his head. — Forget it. For-ge-tit! He spits and he's walking away. I follow him to the departures board. — Fuck me, they're all boarding now: London Heathrow, London City, Manchester, Frankfurt, Dublin, Amsterdam, Munich . . . where could they be going . . . RENTON AND THAT FUCKING DEVIOUS LITTLE COW! he screeches, setting aside some more of that special time he reserves to humiliate himself in public, then he crouches down in the middle of the busy concourse, his head in his hands, perfectly still.

I put my hand on his shoulder. Somebody, a woman with an orangey perms asks: — Is he alright? I smile at her in appreciation for her concern. After a bit I whisper to him: — We have to go, Simon. We're drawing too much attention.

— Are we? he says in a small, little boy's voice. — Are we? Then he stands up and strides towards the exits, clicking on the mobile phone.

We head towards the taxi queue as he clicks off the phone and looks at me with a tight smile on his lips. — Renton . . . he breaks into a spluttering sob and slaps his own face, — . . . Renton has taken my money . . . he's cleaned out the bank . . . Renton had his own masters in Amsterdam, all the finished copies in that Miz's warehouse. Who owns the masters owns the film. He has the masters

477

and the money! How did he get the information? he wails disconsolately.

I call Lauren to find that Dianne's packed her bags. We climb into an airport taxi and I say sadly: — Leith.

Simon rests his head back against the seat. — He's got our fuckin money!

It's all been the money. I have to know where he's coming from. — What about the film? I ask.

— Fuck the film, he snaps.

— But what about our mission? I hear myself ask. — What about the revolutionary role pornography has in −

— Fuck all that. It was always just a load of shite for wankers who can't get a bird to pull off tae and a way for the rest of us hitting our sell-by dates to keep firing into young, fit fanny. You've got two categories. Category one: me. Category two: the rest of the world. You can divide the others up into two sub-groups: those who do as I say, and the superfluous. It was sport, Nikki, just a bit of sport. It's the money we need. THE FUCKIN MONEY! FAHHKIN RENTUNN!

Later, we're in Simon's flat reading the *Evening News* which Rab has brought down. He tells us that they seized all the video stock and the tapes at the pub, as well as the bar accounts. The article says that both the police and HM Customs and Excise are looking for him and that charges may follow. An accompanying piece has an unflattering profile of him and his 'drugs and pornography scandal', and mentions a police investigation into his affairs.

— I'm the only fucking one they want! Me! What about youse cunts?

— Might have something to do with the credits on the box, Rab quips, and I struggle to stifle a snigger.

Simon seems a broken man as he cracks open a bottle of whisky. Rab wants to fight in court. — I'm intae sticking thegither. I'm gaunnae prepare a speech, he slurs as the drinks go down. I realise Rab's been out on the piss and he's feeling it. — What aboot you, Nikki? he asks.

— I want to see how things go? I tell them, nursing my drink. Simon snatches the paper from me and still has the pomposity to take exception to being described as a pornographer. — A pretty crass term for somebody who's made the artistic decision to work creatively within the sphere of adult erotica, he says with forced bluster. Then he looks abjectly miserable as he moans: — This is going to kill my mother.

With an expression of sheer dread, he checks the phone messages. There's one from Terry. — Some good news n some bad news, folks. Curt won best male newcomer. Eh's away oot celebratin. But some French boy goat best new director. A lassie in Carla's fillum goat best bird.

I feel a deflated sag of disappointment and Simon shoots me a tense glance that says 'I told you should have done anal'. Terry rambles on. — But it's no aw bad news, cause it wis Carla's film *A Butt-Fucker in Pussy City* that won top prize. Thir a sound crew n aw, ah'm well in thaire. Simon spits bitterly and is about to say something, but the next message silences him. It's his mother, and she's very upset, breaking down over the phone. He gets up and throws on his jacket. — I've got to square this one with my ma.

— You want me to come? I ask.

— Naw, it's better if I go alone, he says, as he heads out with Rab, who's anxious to get back to his wife and kid, following behind.

I'm relieved and I sit on the couch, my head bursting and I'm almost physically shaking as I think of what I'm about to do.

80

Scam # 18,753

I'm in shock. It's like everything good's gone, and the rest's been turned upside down. My mother's crying on the answer machine, asking how the paper could get away with telling all those horrible lies about her son. Rab calls round, obviously enjoying himself, but I'm too fucked to bother. But I call round at my mother's and manage to just about convince her that it's all jealous fabrication and is now in the hands of my solicitors.

It was some performance, my outrage requiring reserves of energy that I didn't know I had. I head away thinking about Franco, how that wanker fucked things up so badly for me and himself.

I'm heading back home to Nikki, thinking of who could have grassed me up. The list in my head keeps: Renton: SO FUCKIN OBVIOUS; Terry: THAT CUNT, CAUSE I DROPPED HIM! Paula: FAT COW HAD BEEN TIPPED OFF TO WHAT I WAS UP TO; Mo: WANTED THE PUB; Spud: JEALOUS JUNKY FUCKER; Eddie: NOSEY OLD CUNT; Phillip and his team: LITTLE BASTARDS! Begbie: 'AH'M NO A FUCKIN GRASS' METHINKS THE LADY DOTH PROTEST TOO MUCH; Birrell: THE FIRST DOWN HERE TO GLOAT; Renton again: AN EVIL PARTING SHOT FROM THAT WICKED CUNT . . .

I call Mel and Curtis in Cannes, telling them that I'll get something together again soon, I just need a bit of time to lick my wounds and pay back some scum who've fucked me over. — Then I'll be in touch. But until then, go for it and take it where ye can get it. Just watch what you sign, I warn them.

At the foot ay the Walk, I buy some flowers for Nikki and think about taking her to the Stockbridge Restaurant for a meal tonight, because she's been a rock, before we do a runner for London. She's gone when I get back, must be at the shops getting something to cook a meal. No way, fuck the polis and the customs, I want to go out, to show them all I'm not beaten. This is just a temporary setback.

I see a note on the coffee table.

Simon,

I'm off to visit Mark and Dianne. You won't find us, that I guarantee. We promise to enjoy the cash.

Love, Nikki

PS: When I said you were the best lover I ever had, I was exaggerating, but you weren't bad when you tried. Remember, we're all faking it.

PPS: As you said about the British, watching people get fucked has become our favourite sport.

I read it twice. I stare silently at myself in the mirror on the wall. Then, with all the force I can muster, I headbutt the reflection of the fool I see in it. The glass breaks and falls out of the mounting, crashing to the floor. I look down at its broken pieces and can see the blood pouring like splatters of rain onto it. — Is there a stupider cunt alive than you? I ask slowly at the bloodied face in the shattered fragments. — Now it's seven years' bad luck, I laugh.

I sit down on the couch and pick up the note again, let it tremble in my hand, then crush it and hurl it across the room.

Is there a stupider cunt alive?

Then a face comes into my head.

— François is hurt, I say cruelly to myself, imitating a treacherous Hollywood Roman senator from *Spartacus*, — I must go to him.

I wrap a bandage round my head and tie an old bandanna over it. Then I head up to the Royal Infirmary to find the intensive-care wards. Outside, I pass a hospital stationery shop and think about a card, but instead buy a big, black Magic Marker.

I'm going down a long, deserted corridor, in this Victorian part of the building, thinking about all the misery and torment which has taken place in this house of pain. There's a heaviness in my chest and the place feels cold. They've built a modern replacement out at Little France and they're running this place down. The lights seem to have dimmed badly in this section of the hospital, and as I mount the staircase, my shoes squeaking loudly on each step, I realise that I feel afraid. Things are churning around in my head and I'm terrified that he'll have come to.

When I get up to the ward, I feel easier. There only seems to be one nurse on duty on a ward that holds six people, five old boys who seem fucked, and Franco who is lying there unconscious. He looks inert and waxy, as if he's already a corpse. He's not on a respirator, but it's hard to detect any breathing with the naked eye. There's three tubes hooked up to him. Two seem to be going in, for saline and blood, one coming out for his piss.

I'm his only visitor. I take a seat close to him. — *Pauvre, pauvre, François*, I say to the dormant figure, clad in bandage and plaster. Somewhere, in all that, is Begbie.

He's fuckin well gone. I'm reading his charts. — Looks pretty bad, Frank. The nurse said, 'He's very poorly, it'll take a lot of spirit for him to pull through.' I told her, 'Frank's a fighter.'

I look at that plasma sachet going into the tube, which goes into his veins. Stupid cunt. I should piss in a milk bottle and attach it to the tube. Instead, I take the Magic Marker and write some affectionate graffiti on his stookie as I chat to him. — He did me again, Frank. I fucked up, forgot an important lesson: ye never go back. Move on. You've got tae move on or ye end up like . . . well, like you, Frank. It's good for me tae see you like this, Franco. It is good tae know that there's always some sad fucked-up cunt worse off than yourself, I smile, admiring my handiwork: *FAGGOT ASS*.

— Mind when I first met you, Frank, when you first spoke to me? I mind. I was playing fitba on the Links with Tommy and some other boys fae the flats. Then this bunch of youse came over. I think Rents and Spud were there. We were still at primary. It was the weekend after Hibs had got beaten 4–2 at Easter Road by Juventus. Altafini grabbed a poacher's hat-trick. You came up and asked me if I was a fuckin Eyetie. I telt you I was Scottish. Then Tommy, trying tae help goes, 'It's only his ma that's Italian, eh, Simon? You grabbed my hair and twisted it, said something witty like 'Scotland fuckin rules' and 'This is what we dae wi durty wee Tally bastards', as you pulled me aroond taking me on a humiliating walk, shouting in my face, 'Shat it in the fuckin war,' aw that stuff. I was trying to scream that I was Hibs, I'd been cheering them on, doing my nut when Stanton put us 2–1 in front. It was useless, I had to take it, your brutish, sensless bullying, until you became bored and picked another target. And guess who was winding you up then, encouraging you to be the bad bastard, cruelty gleaming in his eyes? Aye, Renton's grin was as wide as Victoria Dock, the cunt.

But Franco just lies there, his twisted, hateful simpleton's mouth clamped tight.

— It was all going so fuckin well, Frank. Have you ever felt that, Franco? That you were on your game, that you were rocking, and then some cunt cheats you oot ay the fuckin lot? Cause there's got tae be some fuckin rules, Franco. Even you wouldnae dae that tae one of your own. I know I wouldnae. If you're running a proper business, a real operation, ye need trust. I play games, Frank; you'll never understand this, but I'm more of a warrior than you'll ever be. I believe in the class war. I believe in the battle of the sexes. I believe in my tribe. I believe in the righteous, intelligent clued-up section of the working classes against the brain-dead moronic masses as well as the mediocre, soulless bourgeoisie. I believe in punk rock. In Northern Soul. In acid house. In mod. In rock n roll. I also believe in pre-commercial righteous, rap and hip hop. That's been my manifesto, Franco. You've seldom, if ever, fitted into that manifesto. Yes, I admire your outlaw instincts but the bruiser-psycho thing just leaves me cold. Its crass banalities offend my sense of good taste. Renton though, I thought Renton shared my vision, my punk vision. But what is he? Scruffy Murphy with a brain and even fewer morals.

I'm wondering if this cunt can hear me. No way, he's never fucking waking up again, or if he does it's as a total veg. — I'm very disappointed, Frank. You know what that cunt took from me? I'll tell you in your simple terms: sixty-odd fuckin grand. Yes, it makes your three grand seem the small fuckin beer it is. But the money means

483

nothing. He took my dreams, Frank. Do you understand that? Do you get it? Hu-low? Any cunt home? No. Thought not.

Alex McLeish?

The boy Begbie's disciplinary record is nothing short of deplorable and I can't see anybody giving him another chance now.

I'm sure that all right-thinking people would endorse those wise comments, Alex, and to be quite frank, I'd go further: I would charge Francis Begbie with bringing the game into disrepute. And on the subject of being Frank, let's hear from another well-known Frank who also plies his trade in Leith. Franck Sauzee?

Thees ees, 'ow you say, true. Monsieur Begbee ees combative, there ees no savior faire. But you cannot take ze aggression from his game, as eet would not be heem.

I'm still idly doodling on Franco's plaster cast with my Magic Marker as I pass the day with him. *I LOVE 2 SUCK COCK.*

— But I helped that Renton bastard. I kept him out of your fuckin clutches. Why? Maybe because of that time back in London when you freaked out and accused me of being in it with him. You punched me and broke my tooth. Disfigured me. I had to get it capped. Not even a fucking apology. But I was fucking well wrong to keep him from you. Never again. I shall find him, Frank, and I vow that should you manage to come out of that coma and repair your broken body, you will be the first, the absolute first, to know of his whereabouts.

I bend right over the fucking drooling vegetable stooge. — Get well soon . . . Beggar Boy. I've always wanted to call you that to your fa . . . and my heart leaps out of my chest as something fucking grabs my wrist. I look down and his hand is like a vice around it. And when I look up, his eyes have opened and those blazing coals of enmity are staring right into my lacerated, penitent inner self . . .